WHITE PASSION

❧*❧

Book 8 of the

Kestrel Harper Saga

❧*❧

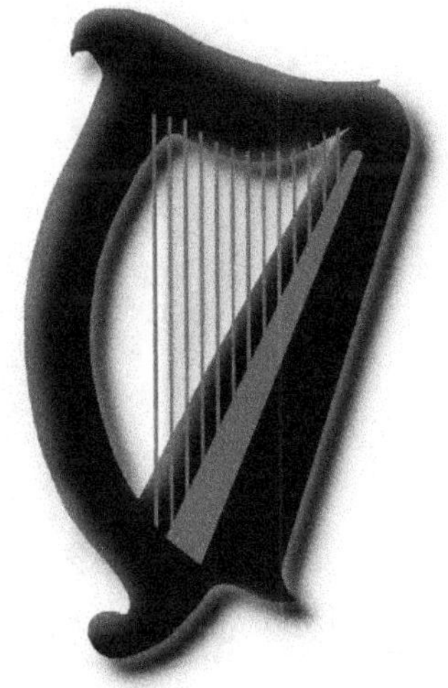

Tamara Brigham

Cover Design by: Tamara Brigham & Amanda Kazanowski

Published by:
Tamara Brigham
PO Box 151
Clearlake, CA 95422

Printed and bound in the United States of America

First Edition

ISBN # 979-8-9934615-0-2

ॐ*ॐ

For Damon & Kaya

ॐ*ॐ

❧Prologue❧

Licking her lips of the salt carried inland on the sultry sea breeze as the moon overhead announced the cusp of spring, she nodded to no one and turned from the rooftop wall, ignoring the disapproving mutterings of townsfolk collected in the street below. Every year she stood here, every year their reaction was the same. Despite their disapproval, they feared her too much to prevent the ritual forbidden for all except those who call themselves holy.

Holiness was irrelevant. A myth for those who thought themselves better than the rest.

Those like him.

She was satisfied that the breeze would not affect the moment at hand. The deck of future cards lay face down on the rutted, stained surface of the hip-high block of stone, precisely placed between the yellow tallow candles positioned on each of the four corners, undisturbed by the wind or hands of others. Beyond the table, four lean-muscled men with oiled bronze skin held the opiate-drugged buckling in its wide-legged stance. Its head lolled to the side, its tongue and jaw slack, and it offered no resistance to their handling, expressing no discomfort in its awkward position or the nearby fire's heat.

She stepped from the platform that afforded her a view of the ancient city and the rolling surf beyond the great walls that kept its force at bay, and came around the table, her bare feet silent as they carried her toward the moment she had anticipated for weeks. Kindling and logs supporting the fire shifted, its sizzle and crackle popping firefly sparks into the darkness, orange points of light joining the white of the turning season stars.

It was nearly time.

With a hand on the buckling's throat, a gesture the bowed-headed men sensed but did not see, she knelt on bare knees at its side with an ease that belied the decades she had undertaken this same ritual in the hope for the answers she sought. In her other hand, the curved bronze knife, more ancient than she, was twisted so that its inner edge faced the sky. Again, sensing but not seeing her movements, the men began a ritual chanting of words she had given them, words they did not understand, a string of sounds unintelligible to the townsfolk whose outcry began in earnest.

She paid them no heed beyond considering the fleeting question of why they were here and not at the temple for their sacrifices. Something hard struck the back of her head. She squinted as her head tipped up to study the position of the stars. A man screamed and burbled as the tip of the knife tore through the buckling's underbelly. A shrieking commotion arose in the street as the blade slashed from rib to groin in a single stroke.

Like her assailant below, the buckling spasmed and thrashed, aware of pain even in its stupor as vital organs spilled out in the dancing fire's glow upon the cool, mottled rooftop, perfuming the air with the aroma of blood and the internal scents of life. Her fingers at the buckling's throat tightened, digging deeper, cutting off the flow of air, the sounds of frantic, squeezing until the death rattle bubbled and the initial gush of life gave way to only a pumping drip as its heart forced the last of that life onto her hand and the blade it held.

Open-mouthed, she gulped the smells, tasting the blood and offal that mingled in the air with the sea salt and incense smoke. Her gaze moved from the stars to the organ display beneath the buckling that her assistants held upright so the animal would not collapse into its waste. She studied where each organ lay in relation to the rest, the twists and bends of the intestines, and the pattern made by the splattering blood. The crowd was silent now, having carried away their fallen with curses and vows of vengeance she knew they would never keep.

Soon, she mused, satisfied with what she saw, she would have the power to destroy them. Enough power to rule the petty lives of those who refused to show her the respect she deserved.

She cut the threads that attached the organs, sheathed the knife in the belt of the crimson loinwrap she wore, and then scooped the bloody collection to spread in a half-circle around the future cards. Two of her men lifted the buckling onto the pyre grate. One of the others hoisted a large pitcher of olive and nut oil perfumed with onion and garlic, and a small keg of powdered salvia, nutmeg, black pepper, anise, and poppy seed. She watched from the other side of the table, hands dripping red, as the oil and powder splashed onto the carcass so that the already burning fleece and skin began to crack and screech its protest into the bloom of smoke it birthed.

Watching the patterns, the sparks and swirls in the smoke, drinking in its fragrance as the men resumed their sing-song chant, she turned the future cards over one by one, adding fresh blood smears to their already stained surfaces as she lined them up in neat rows of three by three. Her splayed left hand covered the center card with practiced precision so that its image was not visible. The men took their positions at the cardinal points around the pyre, watching the fire devour their yearly offering, arms crossed in an X over their bare chests so that their flat palms were pressed on each side of their necks, their thumb tips touching at the hollow of their throats.

She did not witness any of it. The power in the smoke made her faint and erased all traces of the immediate surroundings from her perception. Instead, her head, her eyes, filled with visions of war, of death, of erupting fire and conquest. Her right hand reached absently for the buckling's still-warm liver, and as the smoke entwined with the stars, speaking secrets to her in voices only she could hear, she bit into the soft, sweet, earthy, flavorful thing, heedless of the juices dribbling down her chin and neck.

By the time the entire thing was consumed, the ceremonial smoke had thinned to leave only the fragrance of burning flesh, oil, and wood in its place. She blinked and looked at the upturned cards, moving her gaze from the right top card to the left in a circle around her spread hand. Each card was carefully studied, the implications of the images woven into the fabric of details she had gleaned from the sacrifice of life and smoke, and after she was satisfied with the meaning of each, she lifted her hand from the center card.

She stared at the final image as the powder's influence burned through her veins, drawing the passing minutes of the night with it. She did not blink. She did not move. She did not sense the absence of smoke or the fire's dying warmth as the last of the buckling was turned to gray ash. She did not listen to the footsteps of her minions as they scooped the ash into covered urns that were taken indoors, nor the gradual murmurs as dawn roused the sleeping city.

Nor did she notice the warming of her skin as dawn caressed her naked back nor the slight frown that tugged the corners of her lips as a thin sliver of ice passed through her. Only when the daily morning pealing of the bells from the seawall towers announced the arrival of daybreak did she lift her hand from the table and gather the cards without a sound.

Those who offered her servile adoration would see to the debris of life remaining on the table. They would clean the blood from the stone and erase the evidence of what had transpired here this night. They would ask no questions, demand no answers. They would do as they had always done in silence, as would she.

Future cards in hand, she stopped at the doorway and glanced over her shoulder at the pink and gold of the rising sun, reaching within, reaching without, to guide those who awaited her command.

The time for action had come, regardless of that sliver of trepidation. The defiler and those who gave him succor and shelter would pay for their blasphemy.

The end of centuries-long conflict was at hand. The defiler would pay.

Dhábhiyhá Coryllien would have his due.

❦Chapter 1❧

Ignoring the giddy, gleeful giggles of the young men and women clustered at the edge of the gathering that surrounded the makeshift wooden table upon which the gdhcdcdhásur of IIes á Redh Náós were accumulating donations for the needy, Kavan allowed the black kestrel harp between his knees to speak for him, bright, cheerful, tempter's notes encouraging their fawning in ways he had once been loath to encourage. To draw donations, however, from the host of early morning revelers out to enjoy the bounty the Festival of St. Mátán offered, the effort was worth every awkward moment of attention. He glanced up as dedhá Tusánt placed a hand on his shoulder, the Elyri head of the Faith in the Teren church squeezing between Kavan and the Elyri dedhá Bhídígís with an armload of sweet cakes someone had provided to further lure donors to their cause. He nodded as he set the cakes on the table and wiped his arm across his brow.

"You've grown into yourself," Tusánt teased with a light smile. "I remember when…"

Fingers not missing a note, Kavan shrugged nonchalantly. "I was a different man then," he admitted. Since his return to the Sovereignties from Dhóbhaen, since his marriage and the birth of ten-year-old Ágdhállán who sorted donated clothing at the other end of the table with the Cáner boys, Phaedr and Cáym, on either side, Kavan had settled into the roles of father, tutor, and duke in such a way that his life-expression as a harper had again become more natural to him than breathing. For the first time since aiding Prince Arlan to reclaim Enesfel's throne, he found a joy in public performance that he had, admittedly to his shame, allowed to languish. He now took advantage of every opportunity that arose to play, to sing, wherever his duties took him and he was happy for it.

He was comfortable. He was at peace.

Despite his childhood beliefs to the contrary, his life had become something he had only dreamed it could be.

Seren McCábhá, Regent Níkóá's only child, leaned across the table to offer a ragged-looking child a pair of donated shoes to replace the shabby ones he wore. She caught Kavan's eye as the youngster, perhaps a boy, perhaps a girl, gave a shriek of delight and scurried away to sit on a short burial stone to remove the old shoes and don the new. Prince Lorant, his blonde curls loose about his face despite his efforts to tie them back with a crimson ribbon, picked up the discarded shoes, brought them back to the table, and handed them to the newest Elyri novice, Ybherd McLenon. His smile at Seren, as he bent to tie the laces on the child's shoes, was warm, encouraging, and affectionate, a look that prompted his red-haired companion to shuffle in awkward, impatient frustration.

Seren smiled back, first at Lorant and then at Prince Jerit, her expression shifting to one of understanding and acquiescence that appeased the older prince's unease.

"Lord Cliáth," Lorant began after smiling at Jerit and ruffling the child's hair. "We will take leave of you now. We want a good seat when the tournament begins."

"You always have a good seat," teased another novice, the pale-haired, perpetually grinning Charlos Rion. dedhá Thrismund lightly cuffed the back of his head, muttering something about respecting royalty but Lorant only laughed and winked at the senior novice.

"Yes, well, there will be crowds to get through if we don't go now," Lorant countered with a shrug, the mischievous glint in his grey-blue eyes belying his feigned ignorance.

At that moment, as in so many others, he reminded Kavan of Prince Muir, the grandfather Lorant had never met. He wished Muir, and the boy's father, could have lived to see the man Lorant had become.

Phaedr tugged at his father's hand, pushing black hair out of his eyes as he bounced on his toes. Bhríd had brought the boys to the náós to leave their donations as the people expected of Levonne's duke, but Phaedr was not inclined to remain here, even if listening to their kinsman's music was tempting. There was an abundance of food, drink to savor, and games to play, sights to enjoy as each hour's passing thrust the festival into full swing. It would be a shame to miss any of it. The mirror image of his father, although with his mother's brown eyes, Phaedr tugged again and squealed, "You must joust, bhydhá. You must!"

"You must," mimicked his twin whose mop of pale red curls swung around his face.

"I haven't signed to enter," Bhríd protested.

"You're the chamberlain," countered Phaedr. "You can do anything you want!"

His father chuckled. "Not anything."

Cáym giggled. "You can do this."

Between the brothers, Ágdhállán, without taking his eyes off the donations he was sorting, agreed in his usual tone of quiet calm, "You can do this if you wish."

"Tell them you have my consent," grinned Lorant. "I'd like to see it."

"As would everyone else," agreed Jerit. Chamberlain Cáner did not often joust since King Arlan's death. When he did, his participation drew a hefty crowd and lined the pockets of many who placed wagers in his favor when some fool opted to bet against him.

"Let us go then," remarked Seren, kissing Kavan's cheek as she passed and taking Lorant's hand to pull him towards the open náós gate. "We expect a good show, Lord Cáner."

With a sigh of mock resignation, Bhríd fell into step with the princes, drawing his sons behind him. Ágdhállán met his father's gaze and Kavan nodded after a tilt of his head to Rhyrdan who stood protectively behind him. Once the worst of the plague had subsided, as Enesfel grew stronger year by year, Rhidam remained a place of peace and security. So long as Rhyrdan looked after Kavan's son, Ágdhállán would be safe. There was no reason, despite the odd random prickle of premonition that had plagued Kavan since waking that morning, to fear that his son was in danger.

He attributed his sense of premonition to night-time recollections of days long past, to memories of his first visit to Rhidam to play before King Farrell as the monarch sought attractive talent for his court. To memories of another time when he had shared St. Mátán's Festival with Prince Muir, Princess Diona, Prince Bertram, and Prince Wilred…and the reminder of the violence of that day and the man he had endured it with.

Wortham.

Not a day passed when he did not miss his dearest steadfast friend. Not even his intense love for the man's son, his mirror image in so many ways, could erase the longing for Wortham at his side.

A melancholy pang crept into his song. A pair of young women in the crowd wrapped their arms around each other's shoulders and stifled sniffling sobs. Kavan swallowed his sigh, swallowed those gray emotions, and turned the music once again to happier thoughts as the princes and their entourage disappeared into the bustle of Rhidam's streets, pushing past Asta and Zerio who were crossing towards the table at the náós doors.

From their perturbed expressions, Kavan wagered neither had been having a good morning. The festival had barely begun. Given the uneven, unorganized, unruly behavior of the unguided Association of late, the inquisitors' day was not likely to get easier.

Setting his harp aside in exchange for the bottle of pressed fruit nectar Zerio offered, relieved when Dhóri and Bergis decided to entertain the disappointed crowd, Kavan followed the inquisitors further up the náós steps to a place they were unlikely to be overheard. As he uncorked the bottle, Kavan asked, "That bad?" understanding that it was, but using the question as an opening for the dialogue the pair had come to have. Involvement with the Association was not Kavan's responsibility, but these two trusted him, and today, on Lorant's last day as the heir-apparent to Enesfel's throne, last day as a prince, Asta and Zerio did not want to trouble the prince with their complaints.

Nor did they want to intrude on the day's celebration.

"As little sway as I have with them," Asta sighed, tugging her braid over her shoulder as she scanned the streets beyond the náós gates, "they're not going to take direction from the Queen of Neth…even if I am a Dugan."

"And to most of them, I'm no one." Zerio sat on the step and pulled off his boot, emptying it of small stones and dust that had entered through the torn seam at the arch. He had the income to replace them, or to have them repaired, but thus far he had done neither.

Asta nodded and continued. "Without Marta, they're like rabid dogs following stray scents on the air."

"Can't blame her for wanting revenge," the slim man, his brown hair now regrown into all its Vants glory, replied before pulling his boot back on. "Inness had no right…"

"I don't blame her. But it's been ten years." Ten years since Fen's execution. Ten years since Inness Lachlan de Corrmick's disappearance. Longer still since Neth's rightful king had been overthrown. There were moments when Asta's outrage at those things, and the death of her eldest son, still burned, particularly when confronted by the damage those events had left upon Kjell. But Asta no longer lived for revenge. She only wanted the justice of Kjell's return to Neth's throne and the setting of Neth once more onto a path of peace and prosperity.

Perhaps if she knew for certain if Inness had contributed to Oska's death, she too would seek restitution the way Marta was doing.

But Inness was gone. There was no restitution to be had. Marta was hunting a fool's dream that would never be fulfilled and Asta wished she would return to Rhidam and snap the Association to heel.

The longer Marta was away, the more the Association failed as an information source for the Lachlan Inquisitor.

"Has there been…?"

Zerio's head shook. "Petty larceny and a few fights, but the day's young."

"And the alcohol has just begun to flow," added Asta with a scowl.

As if in response to their words, the shout of another physical fracas erupted a few streets away where she could not see it but it was quickly subdued by the interference of Lord High Justice Madoc Delamo's barked command. The disagreement might have been among ordinary townsfolk.

It was just as possible that the fight had involved one or more members of the Association.

A bald fellow strode past, meeting Zerio's gaze with a barely perceptible nod. Zerio side-eyed Kavan as if to affirm the bard's suspicions but he did not speak. Not all Vants had reaffirmed their hair vow after Inness' persecution and the slaughter of suspected Vants members. With no Grand Master to hold the vow, there seemed to Zerio little use in returning to the old ways.

The Vants, as far as he could tell, had collapsed. To his knowledge, only he, the Cíbhóló Tau, and a handful of others who occasionally traveled through Rhidam and Alberni, remained. Zerio was in no position to make demands of them.

He was just thankful he was not the only one alive.

"Should get back to it."

Kavan had sensed that their coming to him was as much about Association business as it was Zerio's desire to check in with the bard he had adopted as a fellow Vants tova. As he got to his feet, Kavan lightly caught Zerio's wrist, conveying the calming effect the other man was seeking, and said "Be watchful."

Zerio relaxed.

Asta's scowl turned into a frown. "Something we should know?" The Elyri bard could read most situations better than anyone else she knew. If there was a cause for his apparent anxiety, it was worth looking into.

"I don't…there's a sense of…" He reminded himself that his unsettled premonition might be no more than the product of nostalgic melancholy, but finished, "something feels off."

"A threat to the prince?"

Kavan shook his head. "I don't think so...but I cannot be certain."

"We'll be alert and spread the word," Asta promised as Zerio covered Kavan's hand with his and said, "If you learn anything..."

If the Sight spoke to him. So far today, it had not. Kavan bobbed his head. "You will know," he promised.

At the table, not having heard the conversation, Dhóri turned from the restless crowd, satisfied with his efforts to replace his father but yearning for the White Bard's return, and called, "bhydhá...will you join us?"

"Go on; Zerio and I've got work to do." It was festival day but the Association would not rest. If anything, Asta was expecting the influx of tourists and revelers into the city would make the Association twice as active.

Prince Henrik was in good hands elsewhere, enjoying the festival with a child's fervor until the noise and press of people became too much for him. Asta's concerns today lay elsewhere.

"We'll be there this evening," Zerio promised with a curious glance.

There. At the stage erected at the keep's wall, currently occupied by mimes, minstrels, mummers, and players from across the Sovereignty and beyond. A place of memory Kavan was determined to visit this year as he had done every year since returning to serve in the Rhidam court.

"I will be there," Kavan promised.

Only a catastrophe or the Sight would keep him from it.

"You worry too much," Prince Lorant, heedless of royal decorum, stripped out of his crimson half-cloak, white silk shirt, black leather belt, and polished leather boots and handed them into Jerit and Seren's care with a playful grin. More than a dozen young men of similar age, likewise bared down to their trousers, were gathered at the end of the street that stretched from Lorant's favorite bakery to the turn in the road that led back the way they had come from Hes á Redh.

Bhríd and the children, along with Rhyrdan, had gone ahead to the tournament field, not wanting to risk applying too late to participate. Prince Lorant, as usual, was sidetracked by the first physical contest he found and left the chamberlain's company to join the race. There were no royal guards with them, but so long as Prince Jerit remained at his side, few worried about his safety. Both princes were cautious, careful young men and Jerit had sworn oaths, both private and public, to keep the soon-to-be-king safe.

Unless they ran afoul of the Association, most believed both would be as safe in the city streets as they were in the royal keep.

And it seemed everyone loved Lorant as deeply as Jerit did.

"Someone has to," Jerit reminded him in a low voice, resisting an awkward shuffle that would have made his stance more comfortable and avoiding looking at his dearest friend to prevent his eyes from straying down Lorant's chest and abdomen. Younger and shorter, though not awkwardly so, Lorant had been a staunch believer in physical activity and contests from a very young age in the hopes of overcoming his early childhood weaknesses. Jerit often found himself pushed to keep up but he did not often complain. Not about that. "You'll soon be king…"

"A better reason to do this now. Do you think anyone will want to challenge the king?'

Lightly kissing his cheek as another woman and young girl, both nobly dressed, pressed through the crowd to join them, Seren murmured affectionately, "Some of them would," making a show of affection so that the scowling woman's demeanor softened. The princess was here. There was no cause to believe in impropriety.

"Papa!" The girl with waves of fawn brown hair and wide-set hazel eyes set into her round face did not hesitate to rush past Lorant to wrap her arms around Jerit's waist. "We've been looking for you! There are horses! Will there be a joust? Mother said…"

Jerit, his countenance torn between sincere affection for the daughter acquired through the marriage his father had arranged, and the annoyance he felt when confronted again with his wife's dour, accusatory glare, shifted the bundle of clothes to Seren to pick the child up. With her settled on his hip, her arms around his neck, Ida was the perfect shield to present between him and her mother.

"There will be soon," he replied, shuffling sideways as Lorant's bare arm brushed against him when he sauntered towards the race's starting line. Internally, Jerit squirmed. Externally, he did no more than focus his gaze up and down the street in search of threats.

Lorant chuckled.

"We were on our way there to…" started Seren.

Cutting off the princess without considering the impropriety of it, Gerna Buetette de Corrmick, the daughter of a Ruidoso noble forced into exile after her husband's death when the city fell to Queen Inness' forces, said, "Then we shall go together." She was five years Jerit's senior. Lovely enough, with curls the color of her daughter's framing her face, and expressive brown eyes she was unable to hide behind, she had the regal demeanor of a woman born into an entitled court. She was educated, skilled with the embroidery needle, and with managing household affairs and public duties, she could mingle her way through society with ease. Though robbed of her family's wealth with the fall of Ruidoso, her noble name and family history made her a wife that many men would be honored to claim. But Jerit was not one of them. Duty may have forced him to capitulate to his father's demands, but that was as far as Jerit was willing to concede.

As jealous as he sometimes was over the relationship with Lorant and his betrothed bride, even he would not have treated the princess with the rudeness Gerna had just shown. Gerna realized that too, as she quickly bowed her head and curtsied with a murmured, "Apologies, my lady…"

Seren nodded, as much to Jerit as to Gerna. "Accepted."

Lorant cordially greeted the young men around him, shaking their hands, accepting bows and acquiescent gestures of respect to those who recognized him, ignoring the comments and rumbling murmurs that ran through the gathered onlookers as they realized their prince had joined the race. As he often wrestled, sparred, and raced with the men of Rhidam, as he often pitted dogs and horses against theirs for contests of strength, speed, agility, and obedience, and was known to scale trees, walls, and rocky hillsides with any who would accept his challenges, his presence was not unusual. But it was, as always, unexpected. To continue to avoid Gerna's gaze when she straightened and stared at him, and to avoid staring at Lorant, it was easier for Jerit to keep his eye on the crowd.

Poised in his starting stance, prepared for the required burst of speed when the starting signal came, the fabric of his trousers stretched taut in places that created an involuntary flush on Jerit's cheeks, Lorant met his gaze across the distance that separated them and winked with a grin.

Jerit shifted Ida on his hip.

Gerna tried to maneuver closer. The press of the crowd and Seren's unmoving position between them prevented her from reaching Jerit's side.

A whistle cut the air from the other side of the street, setting the barefoot runners off in a flurry of dust and the uproar of the onlookers. Ida squealed her encouragement. Seren whistled and shouted Lorant's name as he sprinted at the front of the runners toward the finish line. Jerit, unable to force sound out of his constricted lungs, held his breath and clenched his jaw as he watched Lorant's retreating back.

It would not matter to Lorant if he won or lost. Only the exertion of the contest mattered.

But winning mattered to Jerit.

He wanted Lorant to succeed at everything.

Roaring cheers erupted at the end of the street as the onlookers closed in around the runners, blocking Lorant from view. Heart pounding, Jerit put Ida down and strode towards the gathering, chiding himself for a dereliction of duty that might result in harm to the prince. Gerna took a step after him but Seren hooked one arm around hers and took Ida's hand in the other, holding them fast where they stood.

"They'll be here soon," she soothed. If they were not, if the princes took advantage of the opportunity to escape public scrutiny, Seren would permit them that and more. They were both her friends. They had become a family of sorts since the day both men had come to live in Rhidam's keep. Unlike Gerna, Seren felt no need to intrude on the men's time together.

Elbowing his way through the cheering cluster, Jerit's breath erupted from his constricted lungs in a relieved whoosh when he saw Lorant's upraised hand holding the winner's purse...and then saw his beaming blonde face between the heads and shoulders of the men and women in front of him. By the time he reached Lorant, the coin purse had been emptied and distributed between his opponents, and the empty pouch was returned to the woman who had given it to him.

"I did it!" Lorant exclaimed as he rushed to Jerit, caught his red-stubbled face between his hands, and kissed him with an exuberance that flustered Jerit every time it happened. As Lorant was prone to such displays with everyone, no one saw it for what it was except Jerit. His tanned skin glistened with sweat, a scent Jerit found intoxicating, and his face was red with exertion. Jerit pulled back, his mien schooled to one of pride and affection to mask other emotions he felt forced to hide, and then pulled Lorant to where the women waited with the rest of his royal attire.

"I never doubted you," Jerit murmured as they walked.

"You should enter with me, next time. That would be..."

"An unfair race; you know I am no runner."

"I could offer an incentive..."

Jerit was spared the need to comment or respond to Lorant's seductive grin when Ida met them with coins of her own pressed into Lorant's hand.

"What is this?" Lorant asked, crouching to accept Ida's embrace.

"I do not have a trophy for you," Ida replied with an ear-to-ear smile. "This will have to do."

"I tell you what," Lorant said, glancing at Seren and Gerna as they reached him. "Keep this and use it to buy something for our soon-to-be queen. We will call it a prize paid."

Ida looked between the two women and asked, "May I?"

"It is the prince's command," Seren said warmly, offering Lorant's clothes to the awkwardly fumbling Jerit as Lorant got to his feet. "Why don't you and your mother…?"

"But the tournament," Ida bubbled, her tone bordering on a petulant, if obedient, whine of disappointment. "You said we could go together." Her mother hated such loud, violent displays. If Ida had any hope of watching, she had to do so with her adoptive father.

"Yes," Gerna said coolly, her gaze holding Jerit hostage as Lorant took each article of clothing and put them back on. "I did say…"

Jerit found his voice and stammered, "I can take Ida with me; there is no need for you to…"

Only Seren noticed the twitching at the corner of Jerit's eye. The solution was not ideal, but appeasing the girl Jerit adored while removing Gerna from the men's sphere was better than all of them attending the tournament together.

Hoping to diffuse the awkward situation, Seren again hooked her arm through Gerna's with a gentle, eager smile that lightened the mood without any spoken effort to do so.

"I am in search of a gown; I could use another woman's advice if you are willing…"

The corners of Gerna's mouth twitched as if she would protest. Jerit held his breath. Such a request from the soon-to-be queen was an honor, an opportunity to garner royal favor that many in the Lachlan household desired. There were twelve years between them and they had few interests in common over which they could bond, but within the keep, there were no other women Seren's age who were not servants of the court. Gerna already resided in Seren's sphere.

Not, Gerna thought with a barely perceptible sneer at the tremble in her husband's hands when he assisted Lorant in fastening the half-cloak at his throat, that Jerit had any further need of royal favor.

"I would be honored, My Lady," she finally said with another curtsey. "Ida, are you sure you would rather…?"

Ida stubbornly planted her feet as if she were about to be forcibly dragged away. "I want to see the horses."

Dressed now, his appearance dutifully regal, Lorant cocked his head at Jerit, smiled at Ida, and then put an arm around Ida's shoulders to steer her toward the tournament field. "Then the tournament it is. But remember, you have a pledge to the Queen."

"I won't forget," Ida promised, slipping a hand into Jerit's and the other into Lorant's to pull them along with her. She was happy that he never seemed to mind her bonding efforts.

Ida's actions and her husband's retreat without meeting her gaze or looking back were things Gerna very much minded. Seren's gentle steering in a different direction, however, permitted no opportunity for bitter words or complaints.

❧*❧

"So, they talked you into it?"

"I doubt it took much convincing," Ártur chuckled.

Bhríd shrugged at Syl's sisterly jab and ignored Ártur's teasing when the healer let go of Ónyká's hand so she could cling to her father's. "You know how boys can be."

"That depends on the boy." Bhríd had found his daughter, Prince Henrik, Princess Hella, and Kaedís MacLyr in the protective care of the court healers, the nursemaid Aunes, and three members of the Lachlan Guard, fawning over a crate of puppies.

Ágdhállán had joined the girls in their admiration of the yipping bundles of fur, and Phaedr, never one to be far from his father, rocked impatiently on his toes and tugged at Ágdhállán's hand muttering, "We're going to miss it," now that his father's delay with their kin had lasted longer than an exchange of niceties.

"Will you be there?" asked Cáym, putting down the puppy he carried.

Syl shook her head with a side glance at Kaedís. "I don't think so." For some reason, their healer-daughter had developed an illogical fear of horses that her parents were thus far unable to alleviate. The noise of the joust was unlikely to help. And shy, withdrawn Ónyká, a year younger than Kaedís, hated the press of large groups of people, particularly if they were uproarious and excitable.

"You can come with us if you wish, Ágdhi," offered Ártur, knowing the boy, like his father, generally preferred quieter pursuits.

Ágdhállán looked up from the puppy that was licking his hand and said, "Thank you, k'bhydhá, but I will go with Cáym and Phaedr."

"I want to go," Prince Henrik piped up, his round, pudgy face reminiscent of his father's. He typically avoided excitement-rich events like tournaments but today, perhaps out of some desire to prove himself to the Elyri boys, he decided to take the risk.

Princess Hella wiped the dust from her knees and shins as she stood up, eyed Henrik skeptically, and said, "I should like to as well."

More surprised by Henrik's decision than Hella's choice to go with him, Ártur asked, "Are you sure?" He looked at the royal guards and escorts assigned to them and wondered if they would feel obligated to split, some to follow the royal children, some to stay with the healers and the children in their care.

"I will be with them," promised Rhyrdan from over Bhríd's shoulder, the young man finding no reason to insert himself into the conversation until now. "I will watch over the Prince and Princess too."

"Not alone you won't," snorted Bhríd. He trusted Rhyrdan and believed Wortham Delamo's son capable of protecting the three boys he had started with. Adding the royal children, however, might not be enough watchful eyes to counter the additional risk.

Prince Henrik was the son of Neth's last legitimate king. Keeping him safe required additional resources.

Rhyrdan bowed, unfazed by the remark. "I welcome the help." He recognized several of the soldiers given escort duty this day. He would be honored to serve with any of them, even if he was not officially a member of the Lachlan Guard as his father had been

"I will go with them and Aunes can stay with you," offered Ártur, glancing at his wife and then at the soldiers behind her. "Take a few of them with us, we should be fine."

Syl nodded, kissed the top of Princess Hella's head, and said, "If it's acceptable to you," she looked at her brother and Rhyrdan, "we can meet you afterward…"

"We should hurry," Bhríd agreed. His sons squealed with delight.

"At the stage at sunset," Ártur promised. They had a whole day ahead and would likely find each other before then, but that stage, watching his cousin perform, was one thing he would never miss.

Rhyrdan nodded with a grin, "We'll be there." Kavan would be very disappointed if his son and Rhyrdan were not.

∾*∾

Lord Regent Níkóá McCábhá turned from his conversation with Lord High Justice Delamo at the cry that arose from the colorful array of festival attendees in their finest clothes, not expecting to hear "Father!" erupt from somewhere unseen. He had left Seren at Hes á Redh with instructions to remain there until he came for her so they could enjoy the festival together and perhaps find the gown for the upcoming marriage she persistently reminded him about. His private misgivings had prompted him to push off the inevitable, but with the royal wedding just over a week away, he could not put the duty off indefinitely.

He liked Prince Lorant, loved him as a son, but despite agreeing to the betrothal, he was not certain this marriage was the best thing for his only child. Seren was his joy. He did not want to see her unhappy. He did not want to disappoint her.

"Why are you here?" he began in a lightly scolding tone as Seren and Gerna emerged alone from the crowd. Madoc bowed and led his attending lieutenants away.

"I grew weary of waiting…you should have been there by now." She smiled and kissed both of his cheeks. "We were on our way to the tournament, the princes and I, when we met Lady de Corrmick. They went ahead; the lady has agreed to accompany me in the search for gowns. I've already seen…"

"Gowns?" he frowned, stressing the plural.

Seren giggled. "There must be one for the coronation and the banquet as well, don't you agree? It would not do for the queen to be dressed like a common…"

"Nothing common about you," Níkóá snorted with a chuckle. In his eyes, her angelic face shone with all the grace of her diluted Elyri heritage. Just how uncommon she was was evident in the gazes of every young man whose head turned as she passed. "It is not safe…"

"I am fine, Father. I promised the tailor I would return with you, to see them again, and we can look for others if…"

Hoping that the discerning eye of the older woman had tempered Seren's choices and kept the selections modest and tasteful, Níkóá sighed and nodded. "Very well. We welcome your attendance, Lady de Corrmick. We would appreciate your aid in…"

With the blatting of the contest horn, announcing the imminent start of the event, Gerna faltered as if torn between conflicting desires before finally saying, "I should join my husband…"

Seren grabbed her hand and hastily said, "You must come, my lady. How else am I to select something appropriate?"

"You have a good eye for fashion…and you have your father to accompany you. I must think of my daughter…"

"But I need your…"

Níkóá drew Seren back with a shake of his head and a cordial, "Of course, you must think of Ida. Thank you for seeing Seren safely to me."

Flustered, feeling patronized and unsure of her choice, Gerna curtsied and murmured, "Good day and health to you, Your Majesty…My Lady…"

Seren did not hide her frown as Gerna hastened away, a look Níkóá did not fail to notice. "What was that?" He was unaware of any friendship between the two women, did not see any evidence of that in this short interaction, but Seren's disappointment and determination to keep Gerna's company were unmistakable.

"It is nothing," Seren mumbled, accepting her father's offered arm. He sighed and began walking towards the street of garment sellers and tailors. Looking both ways before crossing the avenue toward a trio of street-corner mummers engaged in a high-spirited, friendly challenge and a traveling puppeteer turning some bit of Enesfel history into easily digestible fare for the masses whose reading ability was limited.

Guessing as to the undercurrent she would not reveal, he gently chided, "It is not your concern if…"

"But it is," she countered. To the outside world, the affectionate relationship between the princes appeared much different than it did to her and a handful of observant others. Most thought it was fondness between cousins, nothing more. Anything that affected the happiness of the soon-to-be king affected her, and she wanted her two closest friends to be happy.

"Are you having second thoughts?"

Noting the tremor in his voice, she squeezed his arm and lay her head against his shoulder. "No. It is my choice, Father. I have no doubts, no second thoughts."

"I know it might not be the ideal…"

"What marriage is?" Every marriage she was aware of experienced difficulties and challenges. Why should hers be different? "He loves me…"

"Yes…" Having served as Lorant's regents for a decade and watching the children grow up together, Níkóá had few doubts about Lorant's affection for Seren. He also had no doubts about his affection for the Nethite prince. "But is it enough? What will you do…?"

"My duty, of course." There was more to her decision than royal, familial duty, but that was the answer she chose to give her father. Another street was crossed, another intersection traversed, until they stopped outside of the first seamstress shop she wanted to show him. "What about you? What will you do when your service is no longer required as regent?"

He shrugged and opened the door. "I'll be his advisor, as he wishes. The difference will be that decisions will be his to make, not mine. Frankly, I will be happy to be done with it." Despite his early childhood fantasies that had come with the knowledge of his Lachlan heritage, Níkóá had never earnestly wanted to be a king. He had wanted revenge on the Corylliens that had brought him into the proximity of the Crown and he had wanted to assist in the elimination of the anti-Elyri threat, but he had not expected to end up on the Lachlan throne. Ten years of ruling was enough.

It was time to step down.

"You'll go wherever Lord Cliáth is."

He met his daughter's smile with an enigmatic one of his own. "Lord Cliáth is not going anywhere. This is his home."

"Precisely. Come, let me show you what I found. I hope you like them."

Chuckling at her playful tone and a little concerned about her selections, he replied, "I hope I will too."

❧*❧

Captain Raenár Magk stood at the end of the tournament field, balancing the screaming, cheering blonde boy on the fence rail in front of him as the big gray gelding high-stepped into position, its rider awaiting another pass across the field. Lifting the helmet visor to wink at her son, setting off another frenzy of encouraging shouts, Bhetá turned her horse and face forward to watch the man she expected to be her final opponent if she made it through every other contest ahead of her.

Bhríd Cáner would win this match. He had never, to her knowledge, lost a joust or a sword match. Both were two matches into the tournament now, with another six passes each before they might face each other. Despite seven-year-old Balint's expectations, she did not know what to expect when she met the Elyri on that field.

She hoped that watching him as he balanced his lance and braced himself in his saddle for a pass that unseated another opponent with ease, she would notice some advantage she could use against him.

To Bhetá, he did not appear to exert any effort, as though he had been born on a saddle with a lance in his hand.

"You can do this," Raenár encouraged, his voice barely heard over the cheering crowd, but it did not make her feel calmer to hear it.

The foot-stomping of the crowd drowned out Gerna's approach so that, when she sat beside her husband, catching him between her and Prince Lorant, Jerit jumped, startled and red-faced as though caught doing something he should not. With Rhyrdan and a handful of Lachlan guards seated on the bench in front of them with the royal and Elyri children sandwiched between, and Physician Mauret and the second royal tutor Pras Najar from Hatu seated on the bench behind, there was nowhere for Jerit to escape to. Though he had been the picture of propriety and royal decorum in this place where all the crowd could see him, the feeling of being caught would not leave. He was relieved when Ida, seated with the children in front of him, gave up that coveted spot to sit between her parents.

Maybe it was on his behalf, though he doubted she understood the complicated dynamics between him, her mother, and Prince Lorant. More likely, he decided as Ida curled one hand in his and one in her mother's and briefly put her head on Gerna's shoulder, her action was intended to reunite with her mother and enjoy the security of being with both parents.

That did not happen very often.

Gerna scowled at Jerit over Ida's head; he could see the look from the corner of his eye as he joined the crowd on their feet when Bhríd paraded the black and white speckled charger he had borrowed for this event in front of the stands. Phaedr leaned over the rail and pushed the customary kerchief into the winner's hand.

If Lorant noticed Gerna there, he offered no acknowledgment.

The passing of two more contenders resulted in the rearing of one horse so that it faltered, fell, and deposited its rider into the dust, causing Princess Hella to squeak and scramble from her seat onto her older brother's lap. Jerit wrapped his arms around her, murmured something into her ear that made her shoulders sag in relief, and allowed her to watch without doubts about the safety of the animals.

It was rare for a horse to be injured in a tournament. They were too valuable to risk or mistreat. Riders took care to protect them. There were sometimes exceptions and accidents, but Jerit did not believe that today's overly cautious contestants, conserving their mounts' strength for the draw order that would pit them against Daema Magk or Chamberlain Cáner, would fall prey to disaster today.

With Lorant's focus on his sister and the Daema set to ride again, Jerit yielded to further public expectation and did not flinch when Gerna took his hand. He hoped his anxious clamminess would be enough to repel her.

It was not.

Jerit sighed and kept his eyes on the jousters.

❧*❧

St. Kóráhm's courtyard was open to the comings and goings of Alberni's population, offering cut flowers and budding grape vines, meticulously hand-copied books, paintings and sculptures, and craft trinkets produced by the abbey's residents, as well as an array of foods cooked within or donated by anyone who came. An offering of any sort, monetary or material, was all that was required in exchange. Seated at one of the four long tables erected at one side of the courtyard, Kjell kept precise records of each transaction under dedhá Khwílen's friendly eye while Tau stood at the head of the table looking for any hint of threat that might filter its way inside the unmonitored gates.

Khwílen refused to leave guards at the gates today. He wanted St. Mátán's festival to be a welcoming affair, not marred by something that might frighten and drive away the vulnerable they would aid with the donations they received. Tau was not satisfied with giving anyone unmonitored access to the exiled Nethite king, but since he could not countermand the gdhededhá's order, he kept watch, swinging his attention between those who entered the courtyard, the raucous rabble gathered around the games and contests being held on the other side of the courtyard, and those who stopped at Kjell's table to exchange their donations for one of the books offered there.

Kjell did not want to be there. He wanted to be with his wife, son, and grandson. But after another year sequestered within St. Kóráhm's walls, he knew leaving this shelter for a walk through Rhidam's streets would be a foolish thing. It would take only a single person to recognize him, to send word or rumor back to Glevum, to bring ruin upon him, his family, and perhaps those in Alberni and those serving in the chellé. He might not be Inness' prisoner any longer, but he remained a prisoner all the same.

Tau nudged his arm and gestured with a head tilt towards a broad-shouldered man with waves of blonde hair, deep-set gray eyes, and a scar that ran across one cheek, across his nose, and the other cheek as well. The scar did nothing to mar his handsome face or detract from his personable smile as he shook hands with the dedhá he passed, placing coins in the palms of each before stopping at Kjell's table and depositing an additional fist full of coins into the locked, wooden donation box at Kjell's elbow.

Geiel Vagn had been to the chellé many times. Most of the residents knew his face and name.

"I'll return shortly," Kjell murmured to the pock-scarred, sightless woman at his elbow, one of many who had come to the abbey seeking solace and purpose after the Yellow Sisters passed through Alberni. With hands that moved between the books in front of her to guard against theft, and experience in recognizing the feel of coins from each of the Sovereignties and Káliel, selling books allowed her to retain her usefulness.

Dhóri had made sure the abbey assisted every blind person possible who came to St. Kóráhm's after the plague. He did not want to turn anyone away, not even those who eventually acquired enough skill and confidence to leave under their own volition.

The woman muttered something in agreement; Kjell pushed his chair back and followed Tau with slow, limping steps to a place several yards from the table where the scarred man joined them.

"What's the news?"

Geiel straightened his tunic before speaking. "Nothing vital…except the growing numbers of those who support us seeking refuge in Ruidoso. Estimates were at least three hundred…"

"Three hundred's not going to take the throne from Fraen," Kjell muttered bitterly.

Geiel nodded, his expression sympathetic, and shrugged. "There are others…across the south beyond the king's reach. There's said to be nearly a thousand around Pravek, up and down the coast, but I haven't met them. In Gorea and Glevum they are harder to count while his spies work to weed us out. Forced conscription has embedded some into his army, making them hard to count…but they're there. Appears he's up to something, planning something, but there's only rumor of what it is or where he intends to send them. Best guess," he sighed, "is Ruidoso. It's the key to the in-between."

"Vants?" Kjell asked. In the years since his escape from Glevum, the region south of Lake Curo to the mountain forests that separated Neth from Enesfel had been contested but largely left beyond either kingdom's control. The plagues and the previous conflict that had cost Enesfel King Merrek's life had devastated each Sovereignty's military might so that neither had been able to muster the strength to reestablish rule in the region. There had been periodic squabbles and clashes over resources. Gradually that situation was changing as children who had survived the Yellow Sisters were now maturing into adults capable of fighting for their kings. It was only a matter of time before one side mustered up the might, or the determination, to take the step of reclamation.

That Neth might be the first to do so as Enesfel prepared to welcome the rule of a prince come of age was no surprise to anyone.

Geiel sighed again. "Don't think there's many of us left. Maybe some of the loyalists were Vants once. After the purge…many have yet to come out of hiding."

"I'll protect them if I can. You've been good to me…good to my grandson." There was little else Kjell could do, particularly while in exile, but if he regained his freedom, he would knight every member of the Vants he could find. "Go to Pravek, learn what you can." Three hundred supporters were better than none, but a thousand hearty men hardened by the harsh weather along Neth's northern coast was better. If that rumor was true, an effort made to mobilize them might lend to the formation of a plan to take back Glevum. It was time to begin planning in earnest.

When it was his time to die, Kjell wanted to do so at home in the halls of Glevum with his family at his side instead of stuck here in the well-meaning company of the brothers and sisters of St. Kóráhm's.

"Avail yourself of the festival, take your rest…then take word of my survival to any in Pravek who prove trustworthy and willing to act." It was a long ride from Alberni into Neth, longer to reach Pravek. Even on a swift horse, Kjell expected it would be a month or more before he learned anything else he could use.

Oh, to be an Elyri who could use the Gates.

"Yes, Your Majesty. Thank you." Geiel moved away, heading to the table where food was being offered, careful as he moved in case anyone was watching him who might be a threat to Neth's king.

Tau lowered his head and muttered, "Shall we share this news with your wife? With Lord Kaas?

"Not yet." There was no need for haste in sharing news that was already weeks old and not immediately pressing. He would see Asta soon. He would share it with her then.

What Tau shared with Zcrio Kaas was beyond Kjell's control.

❧*❧

Metal-tipped lances met point to point with enough might that both wooden shafts splintered, creating a shockwave of force that reverberated through Bhetá's hand, up her arm, to wrench her shoulder and twist her sideways in the saddle. The effort to steady herself with her knees pressed into the gelding's sides failed and she slid off on the opposite side of the horse to land upon her already throbbing shoulder.

She knew that tearing pop. As the horse skittered with high, tense steps away from her, she used the hand of her good arm to raise her visor to stare unobstructed at the mid-afternoon blue sky.

Bhríd dropped his broken lance as he dismounted, took off his helmet to the cheering of the crowd, and approached his opponent. He did not need the Nelori crest emblazoned upon her chest plate to identify her. He recognized her from her riding style and the way she carried her lance.

"Are you well?" he asked with an offered hand to assist her. Many riders would object to such an offer from the one who had beaten them.

He was unconvinced his win was valid. She would not be the first rival to allow him to win. If there was anyone in the Sovereignties who could unseat his record, he believed it was the Daema.

"Shoulder's dislocated but I'll live." A visit to the MacLyrs would be enough to have her on duty within hours. She took his hand and as she got up, the crowd's cheer grew louder. Her helmet was awkwardly removed and dropped into the horse-pounded grass. An amicable contest was always, in Bhríd's opinion, better than a bitter one, and their long friendship had not suffered for the victory or the defeat.

Clasped hands raised above their heads, they turned in a circle to greet the entire crowd. From the sidelines, a high-pitched cheering shout of "Mama! You did it!" brought Balint sprinting across the field to her when Raenár let him go.

Bhetá grinned at Bhríd who nodded to her in reply. For the moment, they would give Balint the joy of believing his mother had won the day. Later, when the exultation and memory of the moment had faded, she would tell him the truth in private.

Bhríd was agreeable to that, even if Phaedr, standing on the guardrail of the raised bench area, clinging to a post with one arm while waving frantically with the other as he screamed his father's praises, was not.

❧ * ❧

The fawning of the gathered crowd, the swooning ooo's and ah's that once made his knees knock and his skin flush with awkward embarrassment, no longer troubled Kavan as he perched on the tall stool at the center of the stage and propped one foot upon the lower one in front of him. The platform was built for others, for traveling actors who came through Rhidam every year on this day, for the scores of musicians who came both to perform and to meet and impress the renowned White Bard. It was erected for mummers and mimes, for poets and orators, for anyone seeking a platform upon which to reach the masses.

But the sinking of the sun in the west, replacing the faded blue of a cloudless late spring day with the mauve, rose, lavender, and gold of evening, had cleared the stage and drawn so many revelers that there was barely room for them in the square. Shirtless men and untidy women leaned out of the Eagle's Nest windows to watch and listen. Others collected in shop doorways behind their dingy glass display windows, against the sills of those on the upper floors flung open to allow the sound inside.

The air crackled with anticipation. His skin prickled with it.

For a few moments, he hesitated in breathless silence, his eyes closed, remembering the faces who had been part of this audience in years past, picking out from the crowd the familiar auras of the ones who were with him today. Ártur, Syl and their daughter, Aunes, and the royal children. Níkóá and Seren speaking softly with Zerio as Asta and Madoc secured a one-eyed cretin in the center of the bustle and escorted him out of the crowd. Dhóri and Bergis amidst the dedhá, restless for the sweet notes to come. Rhyrdan, Ágdhállán, Lorant, and Jerit, near enough to Ártur that Ida had mixed into the group of children there with enough Lachlan guards around them that there was little danger of them wandering off or being taken.

But not Sóbhán, who was home with his family in Bhryell.

Not Wortham.

Wortham should be here. Raebhá should be here, their sons at her side.

His hands trembled.

Rhyrdan, Ágdhállán, and Dhóri were here; that was enough.

The notes began, hymn-like chords sung by brass harp strings, a song written long ago on the trail toward war that Prince Arlan had led Kavan down seventy-three years previous. Most around him now had not yet been born. Most would not know the songs brought forth tonight nor remember the events that inspired them. Few would recall the reclamation of the Lachlan throne nor the passings of kings and a queen in the years that came after. Of those who did, some bowed their heads, some closed their eyes as they relived what had been, while others shed tears for those they had lost.

Most could not remember. Those who did were enough for Kavan.

Behind his closed lids, behind the surge of nausea that abruptly knotted his stomach and forced him to open his eyes, Kavan felt something else he had not felt in a long time. A twinge of anticipation. A sense of caution. A fleeting glimpse of someone he had not seen in ten years and in many more before that, a shade of the past that was there, near the lip of the stage one moment before melting back into the crowd beyond those younger people, the needy and ailing who pressed to the front with reaching hands for proof of the bard's existence, for the miracles that touching him might provide.

But there had been few miracles of late, at least few Kavan knew of, and the awkwardness of their desire shriveled beneath the flash of warning that told Kavan one thing.

The music did not falter. Harp tunes bled into a vocal display and back without anyone aware of the thoughts behind them.

He had suspected that if he saw Eridel again, there would be another attempt on his life or the lives of those he loved. The creeping sense of finality that had blossomed all those years ago had returned.

Eridel was here.

The premonition that came with the disappearance of the blonde minstrel meant only one thing.

Destiny could not be outrun.

If he could find Eridel and prevent him from taking whatever action he had come to fulfill, perhaps Kavan could hold off destiny a little longer.

People needed him. There were works to accomplish. A son to meet.

Mournful, beseeching notes reached for the sky, for Kóráhm, for Raebhá, for anyone to hear his prayers and spare him a while longer.

Kavan did not want to die.

Not now, as St. Mátán's celebration drew to a close.

Not when he had so many hopes and dreams to live for.

Not when there was so much music to make.

Not when there were so many people he loved who would be cast adrift in the world without him there.

❧Chapter 2❧

Numerous messengers had been sent over the last two years, but each had been turned away, messages delivered but ignored, messages undelivered when the recipient refused to accept them. Olaric Fraen the Elder, now called King of Neth, was at first furious at each snub, but over time that fury waned to be replaced by an emotion he had not taken the time to identify. If the recipient had been anyone else, he would have been arrested, dragged to the throne room, condemned, and strung up in the gibbet, or worse, for refusing the demands of the king.

Others had died for lesser offenses.

But despite his grumbling rants about cowardice and failure to perform duties on behalf of Neth's throne, the self-anointed monarch understood the dire need for this duty, the need that kept the other man alive. Understood the need for setting aside past grievances to make peace with his son.

He was not getting younger.

Without a true de Corrmick to sit on the throne, as he did not want a return of rule to the de Corrmick dynasty, Olaric the Younger was the only legacy Neth's current king could leave behind.

He arose that morning with a dogged nagging in his brain that prompted him to make the trek across town and deliver this message in person.

With his cloak hood drawn up to shield him from the early morning mist and spring drizzle that blew in off the calm sea, without a collection of royal guards to mark his importance, none of the common rabble knew him. He disliked being anonymous, wanted his subjects to acknowledge, fear, and respect him, to fawn and bow and preen, to move aside so that he could pass with an air of prideful self-importance. But reaching the apothecary shop and getting inside without being turned away demanded stealth. A gaggle of followers would detract from the mission at hand.

He did not want public conflict today. He wanted to see his son.

"I will be with you shortly."

The voice that accompanied the brass door chime belonged to the pretty woman behind the counter, plump from childbirth and an adequate diet, bright-eyed and rosy-cheeked in the bloom of health that was only beginning to return to Glevum's populace as the Yellow Sisters receded into memory. He did not know her face or name, but from the deft movements of her hands as she ground herbs with a stone pestle, poured them into a leather pouch, and handed it to the stoop-shouldered, nondescript person at the counter, he assumed her to be the apothecary wife he knew his son had taken. The customer slid a few coins across the counter, barely enough to pay for the medicinal herbs requested, but the blonde woman smiled and waved her customer out the door after dropping the coins into a box beneath the counter.

Young enough, he thought, to be capable of bearing many children. That was all that mattered. A bloodline to pass his legacy to.

"May I...?"

Her words fumbled to an abrupt halt as he pulled the hood away from his face. "Your Majesty," she stammered before straightening her shoulders and dusting off her hands on the stained, faded canvas smock she wore. She did not bow as he would have preferred but her fumbling words and demeanor were respect enough for him today. "Are you...?"

"Is he here?" he asked with a haughty grunt as if she should know his business without him stating it.

"Taking supplies to storage; let me summon him." With a note of reluctance in her tone and hesitation in action he thought might be covering a lie, she tugged a length of cord that ran up the wall behind the counter, through eyebolts along the ceiling, and disappeared behind a curtained door at the back of the room.

The king heard another chime as expected and glowered as if seeking a sign of trickery. Maybe, he thought bitterly, the signal warned his son to flee instead of serving as a summons. Without taking her eyes from him, the apothecary busied her hands with cleaning spilled herbs from the counter, wiping clean the mortar and pestle and returning them to the shelf, and fidgeting absently with the items contained within her apron pocket.

Eventually, there was a creak, footsteps on loose wooden floorboards, and a gruff clearing of the throat before the woman said, "Lari...your father is here," as the door curtain was swept aside.

"Lari?" Fraen snorted again, this time with distaste as he turned to meet the cool, weathered gaze of his son. "That is not your name."

The men stared at each other, both older now, the elder bald and bearded, the younger with black hair beginning to grey. The creases of age touched both their faces. To the younger, his father bore a skeletal visage, as though his skin had shrunken to cling to the skull beneath, his piercing eyes receding into their sockets, the ends of his ears protruding slightly as if they would droop and fold down upon themselves like the ears of a hunting dog. To the elder, his son looked hardened, the soft edges of his face having gained a sharpness that Fraen had seen often on men who experienced too much war.

But his son had not fought in the battles ten years previous, a contentious matter he was loath to forgive, though his son's absence from the field had come at the behest of Queen Inness's command.

What had come in the years between, as plague ravaged Neth, Fraen did not know. He had not seen his son since leaving Glevum for battle. His son, his son's life, were unknowns. His clothes, however, expensively tailored of the finest fabrics, proved he had done well for himself during that decade, and his square shoulders and straight back proved that he was fit and healthy, strong enough in body if not in temperament, to take up the mantle of king.

"It is the name Kes and I share," Olaric said with a twitching shoulder shrug. "What do you want?"

Again, Fraen snorted. Pet names and nicknames irritated him as if such things were a disgrace to one's sense of self, but he swallowed the irritation and said, "You look well."

"I am well." From another back room, an eruption of giggles filled the air and Olaric side-eyed Kes with a tilt of his head. "See to the girls, please."

Kes bobbed her head and rushed from the room with visible relief.

Fraen watched her go, studying the young woman with new interest now that there was proof of children in his son's life. "You have no sons?"

"Those I had were taken from me," Olaric replied with a dark expression. "I have children. That is enough."

Sons that Queen-Regent Inness had taken, a wife too. Fraen was sorry for that, but not enough to apologize or offer sympathy. He pushed down his disdain, nodded, and forced as much warmth into his voice as he could muster. "Of course it is." Kes was still young enough to bear sons. There was no reason she should not be able to provide Neth with an heir to rule in the years to come.

The door chime jangled. It pushed open but the pair of women who peeped inside retreated hastily upon noticing that the king was there. The sun was higher and more people were entering the streets to start their day. Realizing that his son's shop was not an adequate place to engage in the sort of conversation he intended, Fraen straightened his posture to match his son's, realizing as he did so that his son was taller, broader, and undoubtedly stronger now that the toll of age was creeping over him.

"Please," he began, his distaste for that word dragging behind it. "Come to the keep. It has been too long. There are things you and I need to…"

Cutting his father off without care for the man's rank, Olaric muttered, "Do I have a choice?"

"If I was interested in retaliation for the times you have refused me, it would have been meted out already." They stared at one another, equal parts challenge, discomfort, and distrust, with narrowed eyes and pursed lips until Olaric relented with a single nod. Inaction before did not mean his family was safe now that his father had found them. They might only be safe if he gave in to his father's demand and heard what he had to say.

Besides, Olaric took his father's gesture of coming here as a sign. Perhaps it was time to take the next step and take action of his own.

"I have responsibilities and appointments; we are expecting a shipment. Two days…if that is agreeable," Olaric offered, internally bracing himself for the protest he expected.

Instead of demanding instant acquiescence, Fraen nodded and offered his hand. Two days might be two days longer than he wanted, but his son's willingness to come to him was worth a delay in his plans.

"Two days," Fraen agreed.

Olaric paused, stared at the offered hand, and then reluctantly clasped it in agreement. Fraen was not his king and he did not feel like the man was his father any longer, but he was a man with significant influence and a head for tactics. Those were things to respect and not take for granted.

The way he expected Fraen would take the bond of familial blood for granted so long as the relationship suited him.

Thank the stars, he thought with a slowly released breath as Fraen lifted the hood of his cloak and strode out of the shop, neither asking for an escort nor expecting one. The King was unaware of the three people sequestered in the hidden Vants chambers beneath their feet.

❧*❧

The room the Gate deposited the four into overlooked St. Kóráhm's courtyard, where the sounds of clashing swords punctured the day-to-day sounds of life in the chellé hábhai. The clatter drew Prince Henrik to the window so he could see his grandfather practicing swordsmanship with young Balint, the boy barely old enough to hold the oversized wooden practice sword he had selected. Henrik, familiar with the halls of a place he had visited many times, raced from the room without an escort. Asta rolled her eyes and feigned annoyance and followed, and Zerio, recognizing another familiar face in the courtyard, chose to join them.

"End of the day?" the bearded man asked.

"I'll be here," Kavan agreed. "If your business is finished soon, you may find me at the manor."

"Agreed."

Kavan listened to the retreating footsteps, savoring the prickle of power that reminded him of the newness of this Gate, before leaving a chamber sometimes used for residents to sequester themselves in for solitary periods of prayer. It was the first k'rylag he had attempted to construct after his return from the desert, after his confrontation with Bhás and the death of Wace Elotti. Only a few had been made aware of this Gate, even fewer were aware of the handful of others that had come after, and though he was proud of this achievement, he had never used that new knowledge to find his way back to Raebhá. There was a threat out there still. Having touched it once, he had sworn to his wife, to himself, that he would never expose her or the son he had never seen to a danger he did not know how to contain.

He paused in the doorway at the rear of the chellé and scanned the burial plot with a twinge of remorse. Ten years ago, only two men and one woman had been buried here. After the plague, that number had multiplied. He had not counted them, had not tried to learn all the names the plague had taken. The grief of knowing would be more than he wished to bear.

The grief of the loss of those first three was strong enough.

He paused at Jermyn Tythilius' burial marker, the first to rest here, the martyr who had prompted the identical naming of many children throughout Enesfel in the years after. He dropped to one knee, genuflected with a bowed head, and touched the marker with a short, murmured prayer before continuing to the next. He lay a single spring lily at the foot of Zelenka's marker, dusted dirt and debris from the stone, and whispered a good morning to her before moving on again.

He had appreciated Wortham's wife, Rhyrdan's mother, as someone who had given him devotion without asking for anything in return. Despite the years of sharing his home with her, despite the love and loyalty she had given Wortham and her children, Zelenka was a reminder of a dark period in his life that he did not like to think about. None of those memories had been her fault and he regretted that he could not disassociate them from her, regretted that he had not been here for her after Wortham's death when the plague had come. So he made it a point to honor her whenever he came here, hoping that, wherever she was, she understood and accepted his actions and forgave his failings and mistakes.

When he stopped at Wortham's grave, he wiped it clean from top to bottom with both hands and then sat with his back to the sun-warmed stone with a heavy-hearted sigh.

"Lorant will be king tomorrow," he murmured. Another Lachlan on the throne. Another generation gone, another moving on. "I do not know if I can bear it…and I think…Eridel has returned." He lay his head back and stared at the clouds.

But the voice on the wind, perhaps Wortham's, perhaps Kóráhm's, perhaps his own internal one, reminded him that he must bear it, that he must go on, just as he must see to the matters he had come to Alberni to tend to today.

If Eridel had come for him again, Kavan had to be ready.

For these short, blissful moments of stillness in communion with his dearest friend, however, those duties would wait.

⮞*⮜

"Can I try?" Prince Henrik, red-faced and sweating from his short run from the Gate to the courtyard, pushed into the sword practice group with a small wooden sword selected from the bin at one side of the practice area. For a moment, Balint frowned at the pudgy, breathless older boy, keen to voice his protest. When Kjell noted his wife and Zerio Kaas in the distance, both still several yards away, he gently prodded Henrik forward in his place and left the two boys to their practice. Balint's shoulders rose and fell with a groan of resignation, accepting an opponent he would have to coddle.

"He needs the practice; it will be good for him," Kjell began, cutting off the protests he imagined Asta was about to make. The health issues brought upon him by his childhood fall, a tale Kjell suspected Zerio had not told in full, prevented Henrik from being as active as other children.

With a level of acumen and fortitude that counteracted his physical deficiencies, Henrik reminded Kjell of Oska. He also reminded Kjell of how Inness had robbed Oska of his life and robbed Kjell of his throne.

"Still here?" Zerio asked the other man Kjell had invited to join them, he, too, endeavoring to cut short any retort Asta might make in the hopes of preventing an all too familiar argument between the exiled king and his inquisitor-wife. Kjell quirked his brow, unaware that Zerio had knew of Geiel's presence but not surprised by it. There was likely some Vants code that had announced his arrival without anyone else being aware.

Geiel shrugged and gave a sideways half-smile, reminding Asta of her father in his more playful moments. "Slept in after too much ale…and my horse threw a shoe. I'll be heading back in the morning, bound for Pravek."

"What's in Pravek?" Asta asked, both annoyed and relieved to have another disagreement with Kjell cut off. She recognized the blonde stranger from his single visit to her on the night Merrek assumed Enesfel's throne, but she did not know his name. Nor did she ask. He would tell her if he wanted her to know…or Zerio would.

Flashing a friendly smile, acknowledging the validity of her memories, Geiel replied, "Nearly a thousand men if my sources are true. Hope to reach them before more forced conscriptions yank them into Fraen's service."

With her gaze turned from his face and from Kjell's scowl to the boys and their clashing wooden swords, Asta asked, "He is planning war?"

"When isn't he planning war?" Geiel refused to call the man king. The king of Neth was the man standing in front of him. He had no use for Fraen the Elder. "Looks like he has his sights set on Ruidoso, but I've got vines into Cordash, looking for support to keep the city free. Heading back to see what I can learn there, too."

"Any word on Marta? Inness?"

Hearing the second woman's name, Henrik froze, his focus distracted by the adult voices so that he missed parrying Balint's strike. The sword was knocked from his hand, and he yelped and yanked his wrist away, covering the already-forming bruise with his other hand. Asta stepped toward him, but Kjell caught her arm with a sour expression meant to prevent her from interfering.

Henrik needed to learn to manage such moments on his own. He would never be a strong man otherwise. There was no blood that Kjell could see. The injury was likely minor.

Henrik looked between Asta and Kjell, sniffling and huffing his pain and rejection, and plopped down on the dusty, cobbled stones. Balint waited for what he expected would be a rebuke by the inquisitor or for Henrik to continue their play; when neither came, Balint dropped his practice sword into the bin and wandered away to find his father or Dhóri and Bergis in the hopes of finding another distraction.

Asta continued to frown.

"Haven't seen or heard anything about either...although I do think Lady Marta's in Glevum. Association had a shakedown not so long ago; Glevum has been less chaotic. Seems like it's getting back to the way it used to be...except for Fraen."

How it used to be before Onea Pantel and Fen Geli burned at the stake.

The plague had kept the Association down for several years and then allowed for a resurgence with no firm hand to guide them. Marta had gone to Glevum both as a spy for Asta, with the intent of restoring order to the Association, and with the hopes of avenging Fen's death.

How much of any of those things she was accomplishing was questionable. How much of the intel Asta received from Neth came from her, or from the Vants, was impossible to judge.

Geiel waited until Henrik, left to his own amusements, wandered away before he continued, "Still looking though. Don't think she's a prisoner in the castle, siding with Fraen...think it more likely she's dead...but who knows." He knew the Vants had raided the castle, a secret he kept between himself, Zerio, and a handful of others, and that Queen Inness had not been seen since. But if the Vants had taken her life or held her somewhere, Geiel would not say. Or could not.

Zerio believed he would not have revealed the truth even if he knew it.

"Want to ride north with me?" Geiel offered when he met Zerio's gaze.

Zerio shook his head. "Things to do here...gotta keep a presence in Rhidam if I can..."

"He is needed here," Asta agreed.

"Worth asking," Geiel said with a shrug. "Change your mind, you've got until morning."

"I'll consider it, but don't wait for me." Whether Asta needed him or not, he had other duties in Enesfel beyond serving as the Deputy Inquisitor. Responsibilities to Kavan and to St. Kóráhm's that he had taken upon himself without being asked.

"We need to plan, discuss options. Zerio, please bring Tau to my chamber." Without looking to see where Henrik had gone, Kjell wrapped an arm around Asta's shoulder and began to walk towards the chellé door.

It was Zerio who waved at the prince who stood quietly aside, observing the changing of the chellé guards, and beckoned him to join him. His parents would not want the prince in their business, but Zerio refused to let him feel discarded. "Help me find Tau," he said quietly...and maybe we can find Dhóri. He must have something you can help him with."

Henrik wiped his bruised arm across his face, ignoring the ugly purple mark, and sniffed, "I'd like that, Uncle."

On anyone else, that bruise would have indicated a broken bone. On Prince Henrik, who bruised far too easily, the mark was not unusual. It was, in Zerio's opinion, still disconcerting to see.

❧*❦

The distant glow of Enda's early morning lights was visible as the mass of men and pack animals descended the slope of the mountain range separating the wild lands south of the Sovereignty of Hatu. The town, unprotected by walls or battlement, had been overrun by such southern hordes more times in its history than could be counted or remembered, and the goatherds in the fields, spying the dust kicked up by innumerable feet, spread their panic back to those who were still asleep. Men and women scrambled for any tool or implement that could be used as a weapon and came together to form a formidable, but not impassable, wall between their homes and the invaders.

But the assembly, a much larger force than any the people of Enda could remember, did not invade their streets, did not attack. As the sun crept over the horizon, the stragglers joined their companions at the foot of the mountains where tents and fires were erected as though they were awaiting further instruction…or waiting for a more opportune moment to act.

Waiting would give the king's wrath time to assert itself. Waiting would bring the Hatu army to them. Waiting was a gamble.

Waiting made no sense.

Imagining their confusion, aware of a long history of incursion and futile attempts at subjugation that rarely amounted to anything but the deaths of scores of young men, Kaj Yetek remained on the slope, standing on an outcropping, watching the specks of townsfolk gather as he made certain none of his soldiers were left behind. The spy glass he had finagled off a sailor met in the last fishing village they had stopped in before beginning the climb into the dividing mountains revealed the actions of those tiny, frightened figures, and his handsome, sun-bronzed features tightened in concern.

"Do not fear them," said the woman at his side, brushing back tendrils of straight, platinum-blonde hair that had escaped the queue at the nape of her neck.

Kaj snorted, a sound that made her chuckle. "I don't fear them." For the city-dwellers to attack when they were grossly outnumbered would be suicide. But it would also mean a loss of men from his ranks and k'ílshwythnec had pressed upon him the need for so many, the importance of gathering as many as he could and making certain they reached their first destination alive. The ranks had swelled since leaving the southern sea on this march, picking up stray farmers, untethered adventurous sons, miscreants hoping for fortune, and zealots willing to go wherever she sent them. Kaj had not been the first to be swayed by the charismatic beauty and words of She Who Sees.

Having followed and obeyed her unageing beauty for these last ten years, barely more than a boy when she first found him but now a man, he trusted her implicitly.

He was not afraid…but he was concerned.

"Do not engage while I'm away. Stay here, see that the men rest. I will secure our right to passage and return to you before morning."

The corners of Yetek's mouth twitched but he did not give voice to his thoughts when she brushed her pale fingers across the side of his neck at the edge of his short black beard and began to climb down the slope alone. He did not know where she was going, how she intended to secure royal permission to march across Hatu from a king that, as far as Kaj knew, lived several days march across the kingdom. But he knew she had her ways. By dawn, they would be rested and ready to march again if that was her command. They would take advantage of a day and night's rest, so long as the people of Enda did not attack.

On the oratory steps, absently caressing the marriage mark on the hand that clutched the sunstone Audh and Iólán had given him, Kavan reached across the miles to the one who owned his heart. They could not speak, could not share thoughts, and he could only see her through memory and the occasional flashes of her face, her surroundings, her world, that the Sight allowed. Occasionally he found glimpses of her life through her eyes and glimpses of the nine-year-old boy who only knew him through such intimate contact with his mother.

They would never be truly strangers, but he could not guess if he would ever meet the boy. Not a day passed when he did not long for the moment he could embrace that child as lovingly as he did the son who had traveled with him from Dhóbhaen.

A static pop, a sense of familiar company he had not felt in too long tickled his senses and forced his distracted focus of power back to his immediate location. But the oratory was empty and there was nothing unusual about the random household sounds he could detect. There were no visitors in his home. There was no cause for alarm.

There were only the gradual heaviness of power and the shifting of the Purification Chamber curtain before Dhóri emerged from the k'rylag to greet him with an apologetic smile and an embrace after the young man made it past the hazard of the oratory steps.

Dhóri's presence was comforting and warm and similar enough to the brief flash he had experienced for Kavan to believe that it was his son's impending arrival that had caused the interruption.

"I'm sorry for intruding, bhydhá. Zerio and the others are dining with the dedhá but will be ready to return after that, if you are ready. dedhá Khwílen has invited you to join us."

"So soon? What is the hour." He had not heard the chellé bells or the bells of St. Maicel's.

"Mid-day," Dhóri replied. "I dare say some concern for Prince Henrik's arm and duty are driving the return to Rhidam." That and the never-discussed chafing that often flared when Asta and Kjell were in the same room for too long. It was an unfortunate thing to watch but a situation Kavan was unable to change. Haunted by the demons of his year-long solitary imprisonment and the toll it, and the passage of years, had taken upon his health, there were times the exiled king's company was unbearable to those who loved him best.

The friction their son generated did not help.

"What happened to Henrik's arm?"

"Healer Síraelís says it is bruised, nothing more, from sword practice with Balint…but you know how Lady Asta worries."

She had good cause to. Kavan nodded, relaxing his hand into his lap, the communion with his beloved reluctantly aborted. "I shall join them shortly." Dhóri could have taken them to Rhidam himself, but it was Kavan's company Zerio desired, and Kavan's company that soothed Prince Henrik's fears when traveling through the Gate was required. He wanted to see to the prince's condition.

And Ágdhállán was waiting for him in Rhidam.

❧*❧

Gamal Lachlan-Harcourt, uncle to the soon-to-be king of Enesfel and king in his own right, entered the sitting room where the striking blonde woman with the flawless complexion had been instructed to wait. Her pale, sea-green eyes followed him as he entered, and though she did not bow, her head dipped forward in a show of respect and she waited for him to address her. He was silent until he settled on the cushioned bench nearest her and motioned for her to sit, curious about the sort of woman who dared to approach a Hatu king.

Hatu's patriarchy was so ingrained, despite his unusual public rapport with his wife and children, that few women in Hatu dared to approach him. But this woman was not one of his subjects. Nor, from the cut of her pale cream and gold gown, its hem and neckline uneven, one sleeve longer than the other, one shoulder bare, was she from any land he knew.

"What is it you seek?" His voice trailed off, dangling two questions that made her smile faintly.

"Earé," she replied, accepting the invitation to sit. Then, using a name she rarely used, she added, "Cliáth."

Gamal's eyes lit just enough to acknowledge that he had heard it said that the White Bard had a daughter as well as sons, though few outside of Rhidam's keep had ever seen her. There was enough similarity in the shape of her face, her eyes, her serene composure and expression, to support her claim without requiring further proof. He nodded and bid her to continue.

"You know the rumors of impending war."

The king's expression darkened. "Enesfel speaks often of a war to come, your father as well. There has been no evidence…"

Earé's expression, unlike his, did not change. "I am that proof. I come with the army promised to King Merrek and ask for the right of passage through Hatu, the right to leave men at your command…"

Gamal stood as if he would pace but he stopped after the first two steps away from her. As he understood Kavan's warnings, when war came, it would be with Neth. Gamal had pledged support if he had to give it, but Neth would never reach Hatu's border. He refused to believe it was possible. "Hatu does not need…"

"When war comes, it will come for all of us." Her words were uttered in a prophetic tone that Gamal had only ever heard from Kavan's lips. It was enough to make him shudder. "We will require ships to cross the bay from Kílyn, ships to grant forces to Káliel as well if they, too, wish to withstand what is ahead. I promise there will be no violence against your lands as my people cross; they serve only Kaj and my words through him. If you decide not to retain any of these men in your service, that is your choice. But I urge you to consider the offer and to allow my people to pass.

"Your people? How many?" Gamal waited, beginning to understand the things she was not saying. Her army, whatever its size, had come from the south, from the bosom of Hatu's only reoccurring enemy. Allowing them to cross Hatu without accompaniment was a risk. Allowing them to cross at all was also important.

Refusing them passage was a bigger risk still if Kavan spoke true.

The White Bard was rarely wrong.

"Wait here."

Gamal needed no council, no advisors, no aides to make such a choice. In Hatu, the king's word was law. Like his mother before him, however, growing up with the experience of the Lachlan court and way of rule, such advisors did exist for him now and he often sought their advice.

But not this time. There was no time for debate and extended discussion. He made the decision himself.

When he returned to the chamber, he found Earé had not moved. She sat where he had left her, the position of her hands in her lap, her feet pulled back and crossed under her beneath the bench as still as a stone carving. She rose to greet him when the door closed to accept the missive he offered, as though she had known it would be provided. Such knowing made him scowl and shiver as he had when Kavan had revealed his misdeeds as a little boy, but he gave her the sealed scroll without hesitation.

"Stay true to your word and your people may pass unhindered. Word is being sent to every town between the border and Kílyn…and I will have ships waiting for you there. How many…?"

"As many as you can spare without leaving your shore exposed.

His scowl deepened but he nodded. So many ships suggested a larger army than he had seen in his lifetime. For a moment, he second-guessed his choice to permit passage, worried about any single woman's ability to control so many and hold them to obedience. His mother could have done it. If anyone else could, he mused, the White Bard's daughter seemed the best choice, particularly if she, like her father, had an array of Elyri abilities to influence them…perhaps as she had influenced him.

"I will do so," he promised, deciding he was too steadfast to be influenced or manipulated by anyone.

❧*❧

The sun was setting when Earé pushed back the flap of Kaj's tent without announcing her arrival. Though it startled him as he set aside one boot and rubbed his foot with the other hand, it did not surprise him.

❧39❧

She never announced herself to him.

He never minded when she came. He would have bid her to stay if he thought she would accept.

"Take this with you across Hatu. Show it to anyone who asks," she instructed, passing the scroll case and the writ it contained into his care. "Protect it…and do not give it to anyone else."

"We are free to cross." He set the scroll on his discarded shirt on the bedroll beside him so that he could pull off his second boot, feeling not at all self-conscious.

"To Kílyn, yes."

"I've never been to Kílyn."

Earé chuckled. "You've never been to Hatu."

"That is true," he countered with a grin. "How will I know the…"

"I will guide you."

"Then you're coming with us."

"I…" She looked mildly amused by the way he thought he had trapped her. "When I can be. You know you do not need me to…"

Kaj shrugged. "Need you? Perhaps. But your company is welcome."

"There are things that must be done, but I will be with you when I can. So long as you heed my guidance due north, you will find your way. King Gamal will have ships waiting."

Turning on his bedding to stretch his bare legs and lean with his hands behind his head against his rolled cloak pillow, Kaj asked, "What then?"

Earé bent and affectionately kissed the top of his head, casting a dreamy smile over his face that satisfied her in a melancholy way. "Then will take care of itself."

"You're not much help, you know."

"You would not be here without me."

"True; you are right about that." He opened his eyes to look at her and said, "You won't be here in the morning?"

"Leave at daybreak. You cannot waste time."

Not answering the question was answer enough.

"We will," he promised. Though he did not understand the destiny she often alluded to, he believed in it, the same as every other man in every tent around him. Whatever k'ílshwythnec demanded, they would give.

Even if it was their lives.

⟫*⟪

Not for the first time, the ground beneath him shook, rattling the walls and the glass-paned windows frosted with a thin sheen of icy mist that blew across the remote island from the churning sea that surrounded it. The movement was enough to jar him out of the sleep that he had finally caught and he groaned in frustration to have lost slumber just as he found it.

Sooner or later, he mused, as he rolled to face the window, into a position where he could see the heavy door barred from outside to prevent him from leaving, the shaking was going to pick away at the mortar that bound the stones until the structure imploded upon him. A faint sulfuric smell seeped into the room through the places where the window seals had begun to fail and he crinkled his nose in distaste while simultaneously welcoming some scent other than that of the wood fire, the uneaten portions of his meal, his own body, and the ever-present salty, fishy smell the sea provided. A small part of him wished it would happen tonight, that the walls would come down while he slept so that he did not have to face another day in this dismal gray place.

He did not know why the door was sealed to bar him inside. He could not overpower the men in the other room. He had seen the western perimeter of the island with its waves taller than houses, often thundering against the rocky coast. There was no beach. There was no dock. Only a single ship ever came here with supplies that were ferried across the open water on a rope and pulley system that he sometimes heard creaking and swaying in the wind, or whining its protest as the gears brought a delivery in.

Ten years and nothing in this place had changed. The locked door was pointless. There was nowhere to go.

When sleep refused to return to his restless mind, he swung his feet over the edge of the bed and reached for the robe hanging on the headboard post. It was threadbare but took the chill out of the air as he pulled it on and trudged to the fireplace to add more logs.

He did not know where they came from, how they came to be here, but every week enough appeared to feed the warming flames. Even when he failed to stoke it, in the dreary periods when he wished he would die so this isolation would end, his prison never suffered more than a mild chill the robe offset. Well-sealed construction…which might not outlast the shaking ground, or else his captor had placed some enchantment upon it so that he would not suffer unduly.

There came candles, food, and water each day, slid beneath the hatch on the door three times a day and left until he chose to eat it, hot, healthy food even if bland in its unending sadness. There were occasionally books delivered to add to the collection already piled on the two narrow wooden shelves the room possessed, treatises on farming, architecture, animals, sailing, but never history, never philosophy, never religious topics of any sort. His bedding was adequate, the bed, table, and chair were sturdy but simple, and a jake carried waste out to sea. Occasionally he reorganized his meager furnishings to counteract the sense of isolation intended to wear him down for a purpose he did not understand.

He only knew it had something to do with Kavan.

He ignored the click of the door locks, the scrape of the wood against metal as the cross brace was raised from the iron angles that cradled it, and the creaking of old hinges used only on one occasion.

When she came.

He refused to look at her as he squatted at the fire, making a show of warming his hands as though he had not heard her enter. For several moments, she stood there, the door open behind her, the men exiled with him to be his guards busying themselves with whatever supplies she had brought this visit. He mused over the notion that, if she had been any other woman, he could push past her, maybe overthrow the scrawny, unkempt fellows who provided his care, take her boat, and be free. But he was no sailor, could not overpower the sea, and thus there was nowhere for him to go unless he threw himself into the icy waves. And there was one truth he had learned long ago.

Bhás was no ordinary woman.

"I would like to see you try," she said wryly, a tone that mirrored the smirk he could not see.

"You don't need me. Whatever this is…you don't need me." He shifted his queue of nearly black hair over his shoulder with one hand and reached for the fire poker to stab at the flames with pent-up frustration.

Rather than contradict him or confirm his bitter claim, she said nothing until she remarked, "The room is different."

He snorted. It did not sound as if the change mattered. Hers were empty words to fill a void that had existed so long it felt comfortably familiar.

She made a sound that might have been a sigh, might have been her light footsteps as she crossed the room to stand behind him. He could feel her there, closer, within striking distance, and absently wondered if she had grown tired of this decade-long game and might be done with him at last.

Instead, she hissed, "You know your path to freedom, Myreth. You know what you must do."

Shaking his bowed head, his eyes squeezed shut as he clasped his hands in his lap in a pious posture learned as a small boy in Gorbesh. He refused to face her. "My answer is the same." It did not matter how often she asked. His answer would never change.

"You think he will come but he is too much of a coward for that."

Feeling her looming over him, her gaze bearing down upon the top of his head to the hands in his lap that fidgeted with the ancient ring once more upon his hand, he forced his fingers to be still and began to pray aloud to erase the impact of her words.

She chuckled darkly. "And if, by chance, he follows your lure, you know he will die. It is written…"

Myreth's prayers grew louder and morphed into a melodic chant as he squeezed his eyes tight. He wanted to hold his breath until she was gone, but the ingrained urge to expel evil with prayer was his only comfort.

One minute. Five minutes. Ten.

There was the eventual soft thump of something being placed on the table then the room fell quiet. She was gone. He did not hear the closing of the door or the finality of locking it. He only heard the voice in his head that screamed in opposition to the words of supplication his mouth uttered.

Kóráhm's ring, having slipped from the bard's hand into Myreth's the last time they had seen one another, was the lure that could guide Kavan to him, if he tried. He should destroy it. Throw it into the fire, smash it with the fire poker, break the window glass, and throw it into the sea.

But Kóráhm's ring was the only link Myreth had to the saint, the only link he had to Kavan. It was the only thing in his darkest moments, that spurred him back upon a monastic path and gave him hope and faith that he would be found and set free. It was the only thing, despite Bhás' hostile promises, that allowed Myreth to believe that Kavan would not die before seeing him again. That Kavan would not die because of him.

Inside, however, the tiny seed of doubt remained.

What if he was wrong?

<h1 style="text-align:center">Chapter 3</h1>

The string of royal carriages wove from the castle to the gates of Hes á Redh, passing through streets lined with Lachlan guards to keep Prince Lorant and his entourage safe. For the first time in Enesfel's history, as far as any of them knew, the king was to be crowned within the hallowed Gathering Hall of Enesfel's most prestigious náós amidst his subjects rather than in the castle hall surrounded only by lords and ladies, advisors, dignitaries, and sycophants from around the Five Sovereignties. Many had tried to talk Lorant out of his choice but he refused to be swayed.

He was a man of Faith. He wanted to be a good and pious ruler. He wanted people to trust him, to love him. He wanted them to know that, despite the small amount of Elyri in his blood, he was no different than they were. He wanted to be as much a part of them as he could be, as much a part of them as they were of him.

And so, the wagons adorned with flower garlands and crimson and amber banners rolled through the throngs of jubilant onlookers.

Kavan rode in the first carriage with Prince Jerit, Prince Henrik, and Rhyrdan, his eyes closed, his senses tuned to those in the street rather than Henrik's nervous excitement and Jerit's anxious fidgeting. Somewhere out there, Eridel was waiting. Waiting to hurt him by hurting those he loved, waiting to take his life the way Kavan had robbed him of his. Perhaps waiting to do both. After St. Mátán's evening performance, there had been no opportunity to express his concerns as he had played long into the night until his guests dispersed in search of slumber. Yesterday had been filled with a flurry of activity as the final coronation preparations were made. Kavan had been pressed, along with Master Pras, to keep the children out of the way. Since dawn this morning, there had been dressings to tend to, the carriages to adorn, and now, midmorning, they were on their way.

If Eridel were to strike, this would be the opportune day to do so.

"Was my father a good king?" Henrik asked, his sweaty hand clutching Jerit's. Though Jerit was his uncle, being raised by the same woman bound them more as brothers. But that bond was not enough to prevent the squeaking gulp behind Jerit's caught breath nor allow the full truth to come forth. Jerit had been young himself then, not so much older than Henrik. He was not sure he knew what the truth of those events was.

"I was not in Glevum when he was king," he admitted softly. "From what I've been told, yes, he was a good king." As he understood it, Oska had not had the opportunity to be either a good king or a bad one. He had become king and then he had died, with no one in Enesfel or Neth knowing for certain how.

"I think Lorant will be a good king," Henrik said, face pressed to the window to watch the people they passed. "He has you to help him."

Kavan opened his eyes long enough to see Jerit turn his gaze to the opposite window. He covered the older prince's hand and was pleased to feel much of Jerit's anxiety bleed away. The release of tension as their carriage halted in front of the náós permitted Kavan to refocus on avoiding the threat he expected to come and step down from the carriage after Daema Bhetá opened the door.

In the third carriage, Princess Hella and Lady Seren rode with their attendants and guards, with Asta, Zerio, and a half dozen men she had selected weaving on horseback between and around the carriages to deter any Association outbursts. In the center of the carriage procession, Rhyrdan and Níkóá attended to Lorant who, in his eagerness, toyed with the half-moon pendant on his chest, something he understood bound him to every Lachlan before him back to King Arlan and bound him in some way to the White Bard who had been instrumental in raising him after his parents' death, in saving his life multiple times as an infant. He wanted Kavan in the carriage with him, wanted Jerit here, but there were appearances to consider and the rule of tradition and so he accepted the company and protection of his regent and Kavan's right-hand man.

"You will stay as my advisor?" he asked in a low, nervous voice. He had not dared to ask his regent to remain as his chamberlain as he felt that would be an unwanted demotion. He had offered Níkóá a duchy of his own, a new territory to be named and governed as he chose, but the regent had declined. Lorant did not know Níkóá's intentions but he feared that, once the royal scepter passed from his hand to Lorant's, the man who had helped to rule Enesfel for the last ten years would slink away like an outcast. "You know…your experience is invaluable. If you desire anything…"

The carriage stopped. On the náós steps, Kavan, Jerit, and Henrik waited, the bard looking pensive and distracted. Níkóá frowned as the carriage door opened and Rhyrdan was the first to exit, drawing several of the Lachlan Guards to him.

"I have everything I need, Lorant. I will remain in Rhidam and assist as long as I am welcome." As long as Kavan remains, he added without saying it. "It is my home." He had properties of his own, gained through multiple marriages long lost. He had land income and inherited wealth that would sustain him far into the future. Soon, his daughter would be queen. There was nothing more he could ask for.

He stepped from the carriage and offered his hand. "I trust your decisions and will aid you as I can in making them."

The crowds gathered beyond the náós gates roared their approval and adoration when the prince emerged.

Lorant nodded at Níkóá, smiled and waved at those who hoped for their glimpse of him on this day, and followed Rhyrdan up the steps toward the recently constructed anteroom with the Lachlan Guard trailing before and aft to keep stray fanatics at bay. Jerit fell into step beside him when Lorant reached them, and Kavan, on the other side, caught Rhyrdan's hand long enough to convey the one pressing thought occupying his mind.

'Be watchful, sínréc. I believe Eridel is here.'

Rhyrdan frowned and tightened his other hand upon his sword. Guards around him, noting the action, did likewise. Lorant, with his eyes on the door ahead, did not notice the shift in tension, but Jerit, in his over-protectiveness, cast Kavan a worried, questioning look.

The bard shook his head. He was not going to fill Lorant's head with fears today. If Eridel were here, he would be a threat to Kavan foremost. So long as Kavan remained vigilant, he believed he could thwart any action Eridel might take.

His reassurance was not enough to ease Jerit's mind. Or to soothe Bhetá's. Their hands remained on their weapons until Rhyrdan reluctantly lowered his. The guards did likewise. None of them, however, reduced their watchfulness now that they were alerted to some potential, invisible threat.

The guards stopped outside of the náós door, and the others entered the gilded anteroom, a space big enough to house several dozen people or permit townsfolk to meet without entering the Gathering Hall. Soon it, too, would be filled, as were the Hall benches, with those waiting to come inside to witness this historic day. For the moment, Kavan and Jerit escorted Lorant to one side while Bhríd, who met them inside, escorted Henrik,

Hella, and Seren to their reserved boxes at the front of the náós. Níkóá entered the Gathering Hall to see that the last of the preparations met his demands, while Rhyrdan remained at the anteroom door, scanning the crowd outside for the one Kavan feared would be there.

It would not matter, Kavan thought with a sigh, if Eridel was already inside the Gathering Hall.

Jerit's hands froze where they were as he adjusted Lorant's cravat when a voice called from the inner náós door, "Oh! Good. You are here." He gritted his teeth to avoid hurling hurtful words at Gerna for the interruption, for obviously having awaited his arrival.

Of course he was here. There was nowhere else he would be. The frenzy of the cries outside broadcast Prince Lorant's arrival, thus declaring Jerit's as well. He should have realized Gerna would hear it and be waiting.

Lorant's hands on Jerit's wrists politely pushed them down. Both were red-faced but silent as Lorant stepped closer to Kavan.

Ida squeezed through the crowd and took Jerit's hand with a beaming smile. "We have reserved seats, Father. Right up front. There's so many flowers! You must sit with us and see!"

Gerna said nothing as her daughter gushed her enthusiasm, but she curled her hand around Jerit's bicep to draw him back when the familiar shadow of hesitancy settled on his face. "People expect it," she finally muttered beneath her breath but loud enough for him to hear. It was colored with a demand that made Jerit wince.

Ida's coaxing and pulling to draw Jerit inside created enough distance between the two young men that other arriving dignitaries and guests pushed between them and swept them along like the morning surf.

Kavan resumed the repair of the cravat with a gently murmured, "It is good he keeps appearances."

Lorant's cheeks flushed redder at the inference. He was not ashamed of his feelings for Jerit but despite his often-flagrant shows of affection, there had been no public declaration. While there were undoubtedly rumors, inside the castle and beyond, Lorant did not think that anyone except Seren knew the truth. Her father might, Jerit's mother might, but it had never occurred to him that the always perceptive bard would know.

In the weight of Kavan's words, Lorant realized the bard had probably known the truth longer than Lorant had.

"I know," he murmured, twisting to the side to view his reflection in the mirrored walls on the interior surfaces of the anteroom. This was the only part of Hes á Redh adorned in the fashion of many noble halls, gilded with gold and mirrors, carved statues of saints, and painted imagery on the ceiling of the popular representation of Ethenae. Inside the Gathering Hall, though its stained glass had been restored after Rhidam's devastating fire at the start of Queen Diona's reign, it remained as unadorned as it had been since Jermyn Tythilius had resurrected Rhidam's congregation.

Once Enesfel's faithful had broken from Clarys and elected their own Faith Council, the decision to acknowledge that separation with the building of this room had come with the support of both Hatu and Cordash, and their contributions had resulted in the grand spectacle in which they stood.

"You're allowed to be nervous, My Prince."

"Were they? My father? Queen Diona? King Arlan? All the rest?" he whispered.

Kavan nodded. "Of those I have known, only Diona could be said not to have been nervous on her coronation day," he chuckled. Her lack of nervousness might have come at the expense of her brother's life, but Kavan was also sure of the sort of confident woman she had been.

"Women are always stronger."

"In some ways, yes," Kavan agreed. "I have often thought so." He had Power, he had Faith, but he readily admitted that in many ways, Raebhá was the stronger of the two of them. He doubted he would be the man he was without her strength.

"It is time if you are ready, My Prince?"

Bhríd's arrival, with Jerit at his side, made Kavan wonder what his black-haired kinsman had said or done to pull Jerit away from his wife but Lorant did not care. From his relieved grin, it was clear that Jerit's company had a more calming effect on his nerves than anything Kavan had said.

The prince nodded, resisted squeezing Jerit's hand for assurance, and said, "I am ready."

"Or you will be." Jerit adjusted the crimson mantle around Lorant's shoulders and smoothed it across his back.

"Then I leave you here." Kavan beckoned Rhyrdan from the door with a thought and once the young soldier was at the prince's side, Kavan left them to play his part in the ceremony.

At the front bench, Sóbhán stood with the black kestrel harp and offered it to Kavan when he approached, revealing the unanticipated guests seated beside him. Kavan was aware of the invitation Níkóá had sent to Bhyrhán but he had been uncertain if the piper-turned-diplomat would ever return to Rhidam. He had not come since Diona's death though he had traveled to Alberni a few times to discuss matters of Faith, politics, music, and the future with the bard. Nor was Kavan surprised that dedhá Paul had returned from Clarys to celebrate this day. But it was the man and woman seated with them who were the most unexpected.

Few in the room would recognize either of them, for it was the first time in known history that both the head of the Elyri Faith and the High Mother had come out of Elyria into Enesfel.

Kavan's hands trembled as he nodded to both.

He settled on the bottom step with the kestrel harp upon his knees and began an improvised rendition of the same Lachlan coronation march he had played before, allowing for subtle changes that, for him, better suited Lorant. For each monarch, the song had been different, but he doubted most would notice. Most had not been there for those other royal coronations. Most who had been would be so focused on Lorant that they would not remember the earlier details.

But Kavan did.

With each note, he waited for the inevitable flash of Sight that each coronation seemed to produce, waited for the nausea, the possibility of fainting that came with it, as the royal procession, led by Bhríd and Jerit, came down the aisle between benches packed with people from all over Rhidam and beyond. The anteroom filled with more townsfolk as the procession moved, until Prince Lorant was trapped by the calling he had been born into. When his knees grew weak, he locked his focus on Kavan and allowed the notes of the song to bolster his resolve and pull him to the foot of destiny.

Seated on a bench behind Kavan, in front of the altar where the bard had prayed and bared his soul to k'Ádhá, Kóráhm, and his cousin so many times, dedhá Rankin waited, his thin legs no longer able to support him, his rheumy eyes barely able to see the procession until they reached the place where Kavan played. The Rite of Coronation should have fallen to Tusánt, as the head of the Teren Faith, but a decision made by Lorant and Tusánt had bestowed the right to the senior Teren gdhededhá. It was both a political maneuver, accepting the right of rule from the longest-serving Teren dedhá Rhidam had known, and a way of honoring the man himself. As he struggled to his feet, wheezing with the effort it took to remain upright between dedhá Thrismund and Novice Hebel, it was obvious to all that Rankin would not survive to see another ruler crowned.

Those gathered fell still with the silence of the singing harp strings. Kavan left the step unnoticed and sat between his sons on the front bench. He listened to the familiar coronation words, almost inaudible from

Rankin's cracking voice, and focused instead on seeking the threat he believed to be there. In the Purification Chamber to his left, behind the mostly drawn curtain, another figure watched, not the threat he sought but a man who could not publicly show his face, a man many believed to be dead. Someone had deemed it important that Kjell be present, possibly dedhá Khwílen who sat on the end of the bench nearest the chamber. Kavan could feel Kjell's scowling countenance though he could not see him, but he did not have the focus to dwell on that puzzle and keep his sense attuned for Eridel's emergence.

Perhaps Kjell's mood was no more than annoyance that his wife was not seated in the royal box where he could see her, was not there as a representative of the de Corrmick Royal House. Instead, she had taken a position at the náós doors with Zerio, Lord Justice Delamo, a score of Lachlan Guards, and many of the sheriff's men.

Perhaps it was because his son was not there either and his own family was relegated to the public benches like commoners.

Perhaps he remembered his coronation and the bitter way the crown had been stripped from him.

The scepter, the crown, and every other piece of regalia were transferred from Níkóá to Lorant. Words repeated, the relinquishing of rule, the acceptance of it. Vows made to k'Ádhá, to Enesfel, to the peace of the Sovereignties and the throne upon which he would sit. A fanfare of trumpets from the wings on top of the altar steps and Rankin's weary collapse into the chair behind him as Lorant faced the congregation of faces he now ruled.

The crowd cheered.

It was not until that moment, as Lorant caught his gaze, that Kavan realized the ceremony had passed without the Sight's intrusion and without any interruption from the threat he expected. He wondered if he was being paranoid and foolish, if someone in the St. Mátán crowd had merely reminded him enough of Eridel to have planted irrational fear in his head.

He frowned as Prince Henrik, ignoring royal protocol, raced forward to throw his arms around the new king with a rare hug. Henrik did not often embrace anyone or tolerate the touches and embraces of others. That it was the most unusual thing about the ceremony troubled Kavan almost as much as his concern for what the Sight could have shown him but had not.

The Lachlan Guard entered to form a protective barrier along both sides of the center aisle so that the king and his entourage could walk unhindered. As Jerit passed the front bench where his family was seated, Ida caught his hand long enough to smile while her mother took a step forward, intending to join her husband in the procession for the carriage ride back to the castle regardless of the demands of protocol. Seren caught her with an arm around her shoulder in a sisterly manner and whispered something in her ear with a cordial, happy smile. Gerna hesitated, watched Jerit's retreating back, and then nodded her agreement to whatever Seren had said.

Watching as the náós emptied and the bells in the tower pealed, Kavan remained where he stood until he was the last man present, with only Rhyrdan at the náós doors as if waiting for him. Even Kjell was gone, and Kavan's sons had retreated through the k'rylag to go to the keep without needing a carriage.

Not the Sight, perhaps, but he had missed the passage of time. He had missed the movement, the retreat, while something unnamed ate at his brain, devouring his thought and awareness.

Rhyrdan came down the aisle and stopped beside him, looking with an up-tipped head at the seemingly vacant spot in the choir loft where Kavan appeared to be staring. Seeing nothing, he murmured, "Shall we, m'lord? They are waiting for us."

"I don't…I…" Kavan shuddered, shaking off the unidentifiable echoes and shadows with a squaring of his shoulders. "Yes, we shall."

There were people he needed to see, to speak to.

Maybe then he would identify whatever haunted him.

☙*☙

The line of foreign men had started off before dawn and disappeared to the north without turning their attention to the people of Enda who watched them depart with trepidation. This was like no invasion the sprawling agricultural town had ever known. They wondered if they were supposed to fight, send a messenger to the king, or try to distract the host until soldiers from Natrona arrived at the command of the monarchy. Instead, they did no more than watch until the dust stirred by the final, retreating wagon and the feet of those surrounding them dissipated and settled out of the spring air.

❧Chapter 4❧

"May I add my welcome to Rhidam?" Kavan said to the woman before him, raising her hand to his lips in deference before she, chuckling warmly, pulled him into an unexpected embrace that froze the astonishment on his face.

Her predecessor would never have done such a thing.

"You are so surprised that I am here?" Phílóá asked as she released him. k'gdhededhá Ylár clasped his hand without any offense for the bard's lack of acknowledgment. The Kyne's overpowering embrace was unexpected enough to have overthrown any sense of decorum.

"No kyne has ever…"

"And I am honored to be the first," she added, still smiling. "It is time we honor our friendship with the Lachlans and," she glanced warmly at Ylár, "with the Faith, by extending our trust and generosity. If, as you say, there may be a time when our lands will be forced to rely on each other, it is time for us to express our openness to cooperation." The somber change in her voice was quickly replaced by a brighter note as she continued, "I wish to offer the handsome young king my support and friendship."

"That handsome young king," Ylár reminded her with an amused smile, "is betrothed."

Phílóá's smile widened. "That should stay an introduction?"

Approaching with three drinks in his hands, one for the kyne, the k'dedhá, and one for himself, Bhyrhán nodded at Kavan and answered the question. "Of course not, Kyne." He knew his kinswoman had little interest in Lorant and knew the difficulties that would arise if a kyne ever married, or enjoyed a romantic dalliance with, a Teren monarch. But the jovial banter between them was a pleasant change from the tedious day-to-day duties of rule she was most often engaged in.

"And you?" Kavan said to Bhyrhán. "I did not expect to see you here, though I hoped…"

Bhyrhán delayed his reply to glance around the Great Hall full of lords and ladies welcomed into the keep in celebration of Lorant's crowning. While the new king changed his attire and calmed his nerves from the day's earlier events, the tables around the Hall were filled with food and drink for the guests to share. The last time Bhyrhán had stood in this room, it had been empty of everything except a glass box that protected Diona Lachlan from hands that might wish to defile her before she was laid to rest.

At the time, he had sworn he would never return to the Rhidam castle.

For Diona's grandson, however, the change of heart had seemed worthy of her memory.

Now that he was here, he admitted it was time to step back into this world. The sting of that bittersweet memory had turned into the soft glow of loving melancholy. The sorrow had lessened.

"k'dedhá?" Kavan asked, curious about what had prompted Ylár to likewise make this visit when fear had kept his predecessors away. But the eruption of applause that grew as Lorant and Seren entered the Hall, making a rare united appearance as king and soon-to-be queen, kept Kavan from continuing and prevented Ylár from responding.

Lorant hesitated in the doorway long enough to raise one hand and call out over diminishing voices, "Thank you for coming…for your faith in me," before heading directly toward Kavan and those surrounding him instead of the empty throne at the head of the room. He had yet to sit upon it as king and Kavan knew he was nervous about doing so as it would bring the weight down upon his shoulders. Seren came with him, her arm wrapped around his, but when they stopped and Lorant offered his hand to Bhyrhán, Seren demurely let him go.

"Lord Bhíncári, it is good to see you again." Lorant had not known the bard well but he remembered his face and how important he had been to his grandmother. "I'm happy you have come. This is Lady Seren." He kissed her temple and though she smiled, she did not speak or interrupt the introductions.

Before Bhyrhán could do so either, the young king's excited energy prompted a stream of words and emotions that made him continue speaking without trying to be rude. "Who are our guests, Kavan?" he asked brightly, recognizing the man's religious robes and the expense of the woman's pale pink gown, but knew nothing else about them.

"My King…this is k'gdhededhá Ylár from Hes Dhágdhuán in Clarys…and Kyne Phílóá Bhíncári."

"Kyne! k'gdhededhá!" His exclamation prompted the turning of several heads and revealed their visitors' identities to others who likewise had not known. "You came to Rhidam for me?" He clasped the woman's hand between his and kissed her knuckles.

"It seemed appropriate to do so," she admitted. While having been kyne for more than ten years, she still felt new to the position and appreciated his nervousness and exuberance.

"I know the division in the Faith is troublesome," added Ylár, "but talks of reunification or alliance cannot progress without a willingness for us to work together. I respect that and hope we can find common ground upon which to build a solid bond between our lands."

"With Kavan's help," Lorant agreed with a grin. "I am sure we can accomplish anything we set our joint sights on."

Kavan shook his head sheepishly. "You do not need my assistance."

"Assistance, perhaps not…but your calm wisdom and guidance do make such things easier," Phílóá said.

"You will remain in Rhidam for a few days, I hope? I should like the chance to talk with you both, but this," Lorant gestured at the gaiety around them, meeting Jerit's gaze across the room long enough to flash him a giddy smile, "is not the most conducive environment for private diplomacy."

"Diplomacy can wait while you celebrate," she agreed.

"And I would like to hear Lord Cliáth play in a more unconstrained environment before Tusánt pulls me away." Ylár smiled at Kavan with an unexpected playfulness that made the bard bow his head. He had played many times at Hes Dhágdhuán and within the Kyne's household, but those had always been more formal settings than this feast was tonight.

"Yes, Kavan, please do! We lack music. I hope you will remedy that and explain that sword," he gestured at the uncustomary item on Kavan's hip before continuing, "and you as well, Bhyrhán. Play, if you would."

Bhyrhán bowed. "Alas, I did not bring my pipe…but do not let me stop you, Kavan."

Not feeling put upon, relieved Phílóá and Ylár would stay longer and that he might have the opportunity to learn why the pair chose to meet Lorant, Kavan bowed and said, "As you wish, My King."

As he left them, he heard Lorant bid the visiting dignitaries to enjoy themselves and promised them rooms in the keep if they desired.

Kavan would be surprised if either took Lorant up on his offer. With so many Gates close at hand, there was no need to stay in Rhidam while still being available to meet with the king in the morning.

The stool on the raised dais, one Kavan had occupied many times, awaited with his harp propped beside it. As soon as he sat and allowed the first notes to perfume the air with a merry, exuberant tune, Lorant pulled Seren into the night's first dance. With Rhyrdan standing behind him the way his father often had, Kavan entertained the guests alone for several hours, confining his music to the strings beneath his fingers, watching the dancers as he shed the day's earlier distraction. The court healers, old and new, Lord Pras and his wife, all free of their duties for the night, danced around him. Bhríd, restored to the position of chamberlain at Lorant's request sat near the throne alone but did not appear melancholy. Raenár, the captain having come to Rhidam that morning when Dhóri arrived for the coronation, fawned over his wife as though they were newly married.

It made Kavan happy to see it.

He watched Prince Jerit dance with his daughter multiple times, once with Seren with their heads together in conversation, and occasionally with Gerna when she threatened to make a public display. But the prince's gaze perpetually followed Lorant's movement around the room until eventually Gerna gave up her ineffectual pursuit and abandoned him, mid-dance, in the middle of the Hall.

He did not seem embarrassed by her abrupt departure. If anyone noticed, he did not appear to care what they thought as he crossed the room with long, purposeful strides. Seeing him, Lorant broke off his dialogue with one of Enesfel's many lords and joined him in front of the gilded throne that had seated every Lachlan monarch before him.

It seemed Lorant had found the courage to face that throne at last.

Kavan did not see Kjell.

He did not see Asta.

Zerio flitted from one dancing partner to another, wove into conversations around the room as it suited him, seeking information he could use or pass on to Asta, and Lord Justice Delamo stood at the Hall door monitoring the comings and goings of every guest.

There was no sign of Eridel.

It seemed the threat was illusory, and Kavan's mind was at ease.

When Lorant finally sat, gripping the armrests as if he might break them, Kavan abandoned the harp and his music into Dhóri and Sóbhán's hands to join the king there. Responding to the disappointment of the crowd, Bhyrhán joined Kavan's sons and filled the silence with their voices, thus drawing the focus away from Kavan long enough for the bard to rest.

Rhyrdan was behind him as he crossed the room.

Suppressing the nervous tremor in his hands, Kavan drew the sword from its scabbard and held it forth, dreading this day for reasons he could not put into words. This was a sword of prophecy, the sword, if his visions were correct, used by, or made for, Zythán Bhíncári. He questioned whether this sword belonged in Lorant's hands, but that question was not enough to prevent him from bestowing it.

The Lachlans already had one hereditary sword, passed from King Innis to King Arlan and every heir since.

What need did they have for another?'

"This is for you, My King."

Lorant cocked his head, took the sword, and turned it many times to admire the unusual quality of its craftsmanship and the glint of its blade in the light of the candelabras and sconced torches that filled the Hall with a daylight glow. Kavan sighed with relief as the veiled images of a sword in a man's hands dissolved into memories. Those hands in battle had not been Lorant's hands. His were too fine and young to be the ones Kavan had seen the day he freed the sword from its forgotten place and brought it home to Alberni to be stored with other relics and treasures below St. Kóráhm's.

Perhaps the hands he had seen had been Zythán's.

Perhaps they belonged to the individual who had buried it in that cavern with him.

Behind Lorant, Jerit peered over his shoulder to admire the weapon too.

"Ancient, exceptional technique," Jerit said. "Where did you…?"

"Ancient in deed, agreed Kavan, choosing not to voice the name of the presumed owner as he removed the scabbard belt from around his waist and offered it as well

"I did not think you wore this as your own," Lorant teased, not giving Kavan a chance to answer Jerit's question. Though the bard had worn the sword as if experienced and comfortable with it on his hip, Lorant had never seen him hold or practice with one. He did not believe the bard knew how to use it. "It's lighter than it looks." He slid his thumb along the blade and then sucked away the thin line of blood it drew. "And sharper."

He shifted sideways on the throne and handed the blade to Jerit. "See that this is put somewhere safe," he instructed, passing on the belt and scabbard as well.

Jerit's hand closed around the hilt.

Kavan's vision went crimson.

Not Lorant's hand…but Jerit's.

The sounds of war.

The smell of blood.

A woman's cruel laughter.

St. Kóráhm's ring on a long-missed hand.

Kavan's legs buckled. Rhyrdan caught him on one side as Ágdhállán, having appeared on the other side without warning, took his father's hand and murmured, "There are ships…"

The crimson became black and the words bled away.

❧Chapter 5❧

All of his previous visits through these wood and iron gates had been as a soldier, a captain, in the employment of the exiled king and the queen-regent who had come after. The decaying bodies of the unfortunate swung in the gibbets on either side of the gates, their flesh feeding the ravens who pecked and pulled at them through the bars, while on spikes and stakes that protruded from stone walls, the heads of others gaped their horrific warning tales to those who passed and to those who dared to enter the presence of the imposter-king.

The notices of caution did not frighten Olaric the Younger as he waited for the guards on duty to search him for weapons that might threaten the man he had been summoned to meet with. Some knew his face well enough to attempt to stave off the intrusion. Others, younger men or those from regions outside of Glevum, or who had been blessed with the fortune not to need the apothecary's care during the last four years, saw him as another merchant come to gravel at court for favors from the king.

Olaric was pleased to disappoint their misjudgments.

It was the Captain of the Guard, a fellow called Sparding who served beneath both Fraens at the time of the last war, who spared him further indignities by arriving before the interrogation turned more intimate and waved him past those soldiers enthusiastically performing their duties.

"He will see you," Sparding muttered, his tone clipped and business-like as Olaric fell into step beside him. Using the excuse of monitoring a motley host armed with a variety of polearms practicing lunges and parries on Olaric's other side, he managed to make occasional eye contact with the long-absent captain as they walked.

"This all there is?" There were barely enough men to guard the keep for a single shift, even when added to those currently on duty along the walls and parapets, at the gate, and in the towers, to defend the castle from attack. Olaric pondered the logistics of that option often. He had breached the castle before. He could do it again. But this time there were few Vants and likely no support from the Association to make it happen.

A land approach by anyone except the townsfolk might be successful. Likewise, an attack by sea might stand a chance if the navy was strong enough. An attack from below still seemed the most solid option. He had done it before; he could accomplish it again.

His father, he believed, would be a more difficult target to corner than Queen-regent Inness had been.

Captain Sparding's headshake was slight. "More elsewhere…a lot more according to Waller. Don't have the numbers, but I'm told he believes he has enough to secure Ruidoso if he gets the word. Think they intend it once the marshes at Curo dry up."

Olaric huffed. There were vast miles to march through, a host of farming villages and small towns to assault if the choice was made to cross the Kelari and target Ruidoso from the east. Approaching from the northwest, however, crossing the Poldris and Dagar after the marshiness of the spring thaw eased, would limit the loss of Neth's forces. It was a tactically strong decision that did not surprise him.

His father had always seemed to him a smart tactician.

The castle doors were opened ahead of them and Sparding nodded at the soldiers there, some sort of signal, Olaric decided, while not assuming that the gesture was either for or against him. Through twisting corridors he could have traversed blindfolded, passing three giggling, but somber-faced women in regal attire who ceased their laughter when he met their gazes, lowered their heads as though to hide their faces, and then side-eyed him curiously without speaking as he passed. Each one blonde and buxom. Each one in the prime of their child-bearing years.

"Mistresses," Sparding murmured.

He did not need to say it. Olaric already knew.

The door to the Black Room was ajar and through it, as Sparding stopped and motioned for Olaric to enter, the older man sat near the fire with an equally young, equally buxom blonde perched on his lap as he nuzzled her neck. A blank expression of moderate distress fell over her bored mien when she saw the two men stopped and one entered, and when Fraen lifted his head to the sound of boots on stone, prepared to reprimand the intruder for interrupting, she immediately lowered her head to appear demur and appease what she first presumed was his annoyance with her.

Seeing who stood in the doorway, however, Fraen's irritation dropped away. "Olaric. You came." He pushed her from his lap so that he could stand, not harshly to cause her to fall but gruffly enough to express his overall disinterest in her. Following the track of his son's gaze, he grunted, "My wife," and then, to her, added, "Leave us."

Fourth wife, Olaric thought with bland bitterness. His mother had died when he was a child during the birth of what would have been his baby sister. There had been three wives since then, three since taking Neth's throne, and not one of them had conceived.

Olaric had not heard what happened to the first two royal wives. Perhaps the Yellow Death had taken them. Maybe they were alive somewhere in the castle. Maybe he had murdered them for their failure to provide the heir he sought.

The woman curtsied and scurried past Olaric and Sparding without addressing or acknowledging them. Olaric thought she looked eager to comply with that request and he was happy to have provided her a means of temporary escape.

"Have you eaten?" Fraen gestured to the spread of fruit and cheese on the low table between four cushioned chairs and waved Sparding away. "Please, sit. Join me."

Sparding closed the door as he retreated, leaving Olaric in a room lined with shelves mostly devoid of books but filled with displays of knives, model horses, carved battle statues, and expensive trinkets his father had collected as spoils and tribute in his years here. On the window table, the curling edges of a parchment map fluttered in the breeze that pushed through the opening, but Olaric could not see its contents, could not determine what region his father might have been studying before the intrusion of first wife and then son.

"I have eaten, yes," he responded. He was here, at his father's bidding, but he was not prepared to accept the hospitality of a meal. "Kes would not permit me out of the house without doing so."

"She takes care of you then. Good. As a wife should. But do not let her command your time." He sank into his chair to pick at the fruit, his narrow gaze demanding compliance that Olaric finally submitted to. While he did not want to be here, coming had been his choice.

"You know why you're here?"

Olaric shifted on the chair to make himself comfortable. "Can't say I do. You didn't come to me for the last four years…"

"I sent messengers. You did not…"

"You should have come yourself if it was important."

Fraen scowled, formulating a retort that he allowed to die before finally admitting, "I came now."

"And I'm here," countered Olaric.

After an annoyed snort and a swallow of something odorless from a metal cup, the king started again. "You've done well for yourself."

"Trade's been good in Pravek these last ten years."

"What brought you back to…?"

"Glevum is Kes' home. She wanted to come back and take up the shop again. We had the means to do it." He shrugged and added, "It's too damn cold in Pravek in the winter."

Glevum could be bad enough when the weather off the sea turned foul and blew ice storms across the city. Whether from an east, west, or north wind, Pravek was bombarded with cold all winter. It had not been only Kes who longed to return to Glevum, however.

There were things in Glevum to do. Things it was time to do.

"Don't know how anyone bares it," Fraen agreed. As the primary trading hub with Cordash, however, it was fortunate for Neth that those hearty folks born there chose to remain.

"Being born into hardships makes one stronger."

Fraen's jaw and eye twitched as though he was trying to read something into that remark that might not be there. He had given his son everything a good father should. The Fraen name, money, and his military rank and status. What more could he have wanted?

He decided the comment was harmless.

"Would your wife have a curative to ensure conception?"

Olaric narrowed his eyes and cocked his head.

"Neither of us is getting younger." The snorted change of topic came with Fraen setting down his cup before leaning back again. "They refuse to provide a son…no matter what I offer them." He shrugged. "Maybe there's something she can give them to…"

"I do not believe she does, but I will ask." Two children long ago did not mean he was still capable of fathering children. Tempted to ask if his father had considered the problem with conception might be him and not the myriads of women he persistently tried to impregnate, Olaric took the wiser path. "You could have asked her yourself when you came…"

"You are my son. I went to see you. And as my son, my heir, this throne shall be yours when I…"

Lips pursed, Olaric shook his head. "I don't want it."

"Nor did I," Fraen snorted in an unconvincing tone. He had taken the name de Corrmick though no one used it. No one had forced him onto Neth's throne. He could have elevated anyone to take it. "But until a proper de Corrmick returns, it is our duty to…"

"Your duty. Not mine. My duty is to my family."

"I'm your family. Neth is your family. Someone needs to see to the care of the kingdom."

A clatter and crash of weapons and a whoop of finality and Captain Sparding's barked commands to stand down interrupted Fraen and announced the end of the morning's training. The suffocating silence that followed, the unexpected chill in the room that wrapped around Olaric's throat prompted him to pluck a cluster of dried grapes from the platter to break the mood. Rather than look to see if his father was watching, he focused on the color and texture of the last of the previous year's grapes.

Fraen cleared his throat. "Besides, it might be unnecessary. I am told that Prince Jerit and Prince Henrik are both in Rhidam."

"That's been a rumor since…" Olaric started with a scoffing snort.

"My sources have verified it; they've been seen in Rhidam. All that is needed is to bring one of them to Glevum as the heir….and I have a plan to see it done. In the meantime, it is right that we protect Neth from civil war should I die without appointing a successor. You are that successor."

Queen Asta was in Rhidam. The word of her serving as the Lachlan Inquisitor had circled through the ranks of the Association and Neth Guard alike. It was a reasonable assumption that Prince Jerit was with her since the two had disappeared from Glevum the same night. Prince Henrik, however, had disappeared along with his mother much later.

Only Olaric knew that the child had last been seen in the arms of Zerio Kaas. And Zerio, too, was in Rhidam.

How Fraen could know Prince Henrik's whereabouts, who his spies were, were details Olaric would have to uncover unless he wanted to risk a spy in his circle.

The only way to uncover the truth and protect the princes from his father's nefarious plans was to seemingly accept his father's offer and dig for the truth from the inside.

Getting into the castle was Olaric's key reason for returning to Glevum.

Sounding more put out than he felt, sounding hesitant and unsure, Olaric muttered and said, "I'll contemplate your wishes…and speak with Kes. I won't say yes, but I will give the matter consideration."

Fraen stood with a smile that stretched the thin skin of his face into a more pronounced death's head mask and gestured for Olaric to follow. "Come, see the keep. There have been changes since you served here…I would like you to see them. Perhaps they will help you decide."

Refusing to scowl or show curiosity, Olaric replied, "Perhaps."

࠾*࠾

"k'bhydhá? Are you well?"

Kavan was unsure if it was the proximity of the pair in the oratory next to his room that had roused him or if it was simply the passage of time that allowed him to swim to the surface of the Sight-mire he had slipped into. He did not remember being carried from the Hall, brought upstairs, and deposited in his bed, or the ghosting flurries of people coming in and out of his room during the night who left their imprint in the air but gave no clue as to who had brought him here. He presumed, since Rhyrdan had been standing beside him, that it had been Rhyrdan to bring him up, but the younger man was not with him when he woke.

It was just as well that he was alone. There would have been a barrage of questions, exactly the sort Sóbhán intimated now, when Kavan entered the oratory to find them there.

"I am," he replied with a bow to Ylár at his son's side. Rather than wait for additional questions, he asked, "You are leaving, k'dedhá?"

"We met with the king over the noon meal…at least those advisors not incapacitated by overindulgence." Kavan's look of imminent protest made Ylár shake his head with a smile. "Not you, of course. I was told," he tilted his head toward Sóbhán, "such symptoms are common with the Sight."

"They are," Kavan said with relief.

Disallowing a direction of dialogue that would make his father uncomfortable, Sóbhán drew Kavan into an embrace and said, "I am due home. I promised Chethá I would not be long. Ydrís is a handful even on her best days. You will come visit soon?"

"You know I will." Now that the people of Bhryell no longer spurned him, now that he was no longer excommunicated, his visits to what had once been his home came easier.

Thanks to Raebhá, he thought with a fleeting wash of bemusement, many things came easier.

"We'll keep your room ready." He stepped back, bowed to Ylár, and murmured, "It was my honor to meet you, k'gdhededhá. Thank you for your kind words…and for supporting my father."

"There is no need for thanks but you are welcome." Ylár did not offer his hand for fealty kisses as others before him had, but he did clasp the hand that was offered before Sóbhán entered the k'rylag and, with a spark of energy that raked across Kavan's skin, was gone.

Though curious about the nature of the dialogue between Ylár and his son, Kavan chose not to ask, assuming he would be told if it was something he needed to know. Expecting further awkward questions in the uncomfortable silence, Kavan climbed the steps and splayed his hands upon the altar to soothe himself with the give and take of power it provided and asked, "Was your time with the king profitable?"

Ylár watched his movements, noting the flow of energy in the air that continued to amaze him whenever he was in the bard's presence. "Let us say there shall be a new era between Teren and Elyri if the king holds to his word. I believe the rapport we have begun to nurture will benefit us."

"So long as war does not damn us all before then," quipped Bhyrhán from the oratory doorway as he and Phílóá entered. Kavan looked up from the altar top and met their gazes one by one.

"So cynical, aindhá," she chuckled, squeezing his arm with hers.

"And you are overly optimistic," he reminded her, the easy banter between grandchildren of Kyne Morne a heartwarming thing to witness. The responsibility of kyne was held for life and Phílóá was very young. It would be a long, potentially lonely, isolated, grim life for her without close kin, friends, and allies to support her.

"I am realistic, she countered, climbing the steps to take Kavan's hand. "War will come, as you say…"

There had not been proof of Kavan's claim in over a decade as the after-effects of plague burned away, but the undertaking of war, like so many other things, took time and planning. As populations swelled and the availability of food was replenished, she knew that the hearts of Teren men would turn toward power.

War would come again.

"So long as our alliances are strong and k'Ádhá is with us, I have faith in the future. King Lorant and I shall continue our dialogue."

"Then you will return to Rhidam?"

She leaned forward and kissed Kavan's cheeks. "I'm sure I will. In the interim, Bhyrhán will be my ambassador and spokesman and will bring our lands closer together."

"I aim to do so, Kyne," Bhyrhán mumbled with an awkward bow.

Kavan looked at the piper. "You are remaining?"

"I will return in a few days. Kyne and I will share our conversations with the k'lómesté, I will gather some things and set my affairs in order in Clarys, then I shall call Rhidam home again…or at least one of my homes."

Diona would have been pleased to hear it. Kavan did not say the words but knew Bhyrhán was thinking the same thing.

"And I will take those same words to the k'phóredhet," agreed Ylár. "They may not be as welcoming to this step, but it is necessary." After a decade of stubborn conversation between the Faith leaders in Clarys and Rhidam, there had been little progress toward reunification but the tensions had eased. Like Ylár, Kavan did not know if it would be enough.

"It is what you Saw last night…is it not?" asked Phílóá. "War?"

"Nothing specific, but hints of it, yes." Prince Jerit's hand around the sword hilt was not a glimpse he viewed as specific but the smattering of blood and smoke, screaming and weapon clatter were enough so he did not think his words were a lie. It was the first drizzle of war visions to come over him in years, despite his belief in the inevitable. He, like the three with him, assumed the same thing.

The return of premonitions meant the inevitable was closer.

Kavan followed them towards the Purification Chamber. "If I learn anything, you will, of course, know at once."

"Let us know if there is anything we can do," Phílóá said as she pulled back the curtain and stepped inside.

"You can prepare. It is all we can do," Kavan relented with a sigh.

Bhyrhán and Ylár followed her into the Gate, the k'dedhá hesitating long enough to offer Kavan a respectful bow that the bard found unsettling and unnecessary, and said, "You have been too long absent from Clarys, Kavan. It would be good of you to come."

Kavan cocked his head. "Is that an invitation or a summons?" With Ylár's always soothing voice, it was often difficult to read his intentions.

Ylár chuckled, relieving the anxious tickle that raced up and down Kavan's spine. "Whichever you wish."

Then the three of them were gone. Kavan waited until the residual trace of energy dissipated, until it was captured in the palm of his upturned hand to form a prickling ball of pale orange light, like that of the candles in sconces on either side of the Intercessor's carved feet.

He had told them the truth as he knew it, but not all of it.

Ágdhállán had said something about ships.

It was time to learn precisely what his son had Seen.

⊱ * ⊰

Despite a lifetime aboard Cordashian cogs defending merchant and fishing vessels from infrequent Neth pirates, the crew of the Vindeks had never seen a ship like the one that turned swiftly at the bidding of its oarsmen and glided through the calm spring surf like a fishing spear aiming for a whale. There were ancient myths, tales told around crew tables and in pubs back home, hints of silent, deadly ships from the misty, turbulent northern waters that swirled and snaked around the uninhabitable Togrish Islands, but no Cordashian alive, as far as the Vindeks' crew knew, had ever seen one of those ships to know what they looked like.

Let alone a dozen or more of them.

"Hold on!" shouted the captain moments before the second crash of the galley's pointed, iron-tipped snout rammed into the cog's port side. Men were thrown to the deck and slid backward as the hull cracked and split and the sea began to gush into the Vindeks' open wound. Some fell over the edge and into the sea. The oarsmen reversed direction. Flanges on the galley's snout ripped back as the ship pulled free, gutting the Vindeks as though she were a fish.

The cog groaned. Struck powder kegs erupted into flames by the sparks the iron nose threw, flames that spread quickly across the oiled surfaces and licked at the hem of the sails to send its fingers racing up the curling folds of fabric hanging slack in the whispering wind. The deck boards shook and splintered, sending more crewmen overboard as the great mast shuddered, groaned, and snapped, toppling as its footings were ripped free.

Its belly open to the icy ocean, the Vindeks gave up its crew; men screamed as they fell and scrambled for something to hold on to, flailing to avoid chunks of burning timbers that rained across the surface. Cordash's protective shore was a thin outline on the southern horizon, reachable for a strong swimmer so long as the cold did not stiffen their limbs, or the hail of bombarding arrows that followed did not hit their targets.

Screech after screech. Beneath the arrows' bites, men floundered in pain and then bobbed still, the blood staining the sea. The Vindeks began to roll, exposing its gash towards the early morning sky.

The crew on the deck of the attacking galley were silent. The others held their distant ground and waited for the short-lived battle to be over. One by one they drew anchor and started forward again. The attacking galley turned its bow east, leaving the splashing chant of the oars to wash over the bodies of the dead and the dying.

❧*❧

There were only two reasons Asta could concoct for members of the Association to risk graffiti and a public drunken brawl at the Eagle's Nest, so close to the palace gates that she and Zerio arrived in time to throw open the tavern door so that the three grappling, gray-haired men tumbled into the street without breaking through it.

Folly, she snorted as she caught one man's leg to pull him out of the altercation, or a desperate desire to get the Inquisitor's attention.

Why they would wish for that when no one in the Association's turbulent, unstable hierarchy was willing to speak to her since Marta had left Rhidam, Asta did not know.

She knew they were Association. She recognized all three faces. Older than she was, she imagined each had known her father.

If Caol had been here, he could have ended this disarray.

Zerio pulled another man away by his long gray braid. The fellow yelped and reached back with both hands to free himself, the gesture forcing him to release his hold on the third member of the brawl. No longer entangled, his weight fell back onto Zerio, resulting in lost footing and both landing in a heap. Zerio released the braid and fought to wrap both arms around the fellow's torso and neck while trying to keep away from the thick, scarred hands flailing for his throat.

There were more combatants inside, hurling bottles and platters, furniture and firewood. People shouting and screaming in fury and fear. But the pair could only do so much. The chaos would have to be managed by the barkeep and the trio of Lachlan guards who had chased after them when Asta and Zerio ran through the gate.

Some thought to escape the rough might of the guards, but their faltering exit placed them in the path of an obstacle they had not anticipated.

Lord Justice Delamo and his sheriffs.

The man's cloth shoe slipped off into Asta's hands; the abruptness of the act caused him to land face down onto the stone street, hitting with enough force to bloody his nose. The third man, now free of the other two, kicked the down man in the head. Asta threw the shoe, striking the kicker directly in the face so that the dirt carried within it sprayed into the man's eyes. He growled, swiped at the offending projectile too late to prevent it from hitting him, and as he wiped at his eyes with his other hand to remove the dust, Asta's fist followed.

The blow was enough to stun him and drop him to the street.

Deprived of oxygen, the man Zerio held slumped in his arms; Zerio dropped him as well.

"You got this?" he asked.

"We're good."

Zerio nodded. The Royal Inquisitor had been doing this longer than he had. She knew these people. He trusted her judgment. He left her there to rush into the dim din where the Justice's men weeded out the perpetrators and dragging them into the street to be bound. Asta counted eight in all, men and women who spat and sneered as they paraded past.

She frowned.

So that was the attention they desired. Not to speak, not to confront, but rather to show that they had the might of chaos on their side. She could not arrest them all and if she did, she would no longer have the Association's resources she and her father had relied on for so long.

But what good were they, she muttered curses beneath her breath as Zerio pushed the last combatant out the door…Fen Geli and Marta's oldest son…if she could no longer trust them? Of what good were alliances from which she, and they, no longer benefitted?

Perhaps it was time to end that relationship.

"What do we do with them?" asked Madoc, wiping blood from his knuckles on the front of his trousers.

"Lock them up," she snorted. It was not the entire Association, but it was a start.

"All of them?" He skeptically eyed the disheveled bunch, not seeing them as Association as she did, but as drunkards looking for trouble. "A few days in the stocks…?"

"Only if you keep them under guard and put them on the bridge crew after. I don't want to see them at this again. If I do," she stared at the man she had punched, down at the groaning man holding his head at her feet, and the one flopping beneath Zerio's boot, "my leniency will not last."

Madoc nodded and gestured to his men to round up the offenders. It would not be the first time men were conscripted into forced labor; Níkóá had standardized that practice for numerous city projects in the hopes of lessening the need to execute members of the plague-lean population. The construction of another bridge over the Tegid had just begun in the hopes of easing the congestion on the single bridge that had existed for decades. There were men in Rhidam who needed work and Rhidam needed a bridge.

If the king was content with the inquisitor's order, Madoc was too.

Zerio stopped next to Asta as the troublemakers were marched toward the structure that housed and controlled those pressed into royal labor. Noting the glance between Asta and the youngest member of the group, he asked, "Think it'll do any good?" He knew the face. He knew the history. He knew a disgruntled, bitter young man when he saw one.

"No." This was not the first encounter with Brulyn Geli. It would not be her last.

She wished Marta was here to deal with her son and fix this.

❧*☙

Faceless men in low wool hats, high scarves, and oil slickers, and women in high boots and long woolen shawls wrapped around their heads, huddled and bent over the spluttering form the sea had burped up onto their beach. They had watched the battle, watched the fire burn near the horizon. They had noted the specks of ships creeping east and had waited in terror for what they assumed would be an inevitable pirate attack. It did not happen often, as most Neth ships, even during the Sovereignty's darkest periods, had respected the need for trade. But some pirates inevitably grew bold enough to come ashore in search of goods or slaves the Cordashians could not offer.

Today the ships had passed them by.

Today the sea had brought the dead, one at a time, to the beach where they were gathered and hauled up the shore for burial.

This, it appeared, was the last.

This man, however, the sea had not claimed.

"Tell the king…" The words stuttered through chattering jaws and thick blue lips. He coughed; he choked. He spit water so that it bubbled down the side of his face, into his hair, and onto the sand beneath him. "War ships…dozens…maybe hundreds…"

A voice called over the heads of the gathering. "Get him inside to a fire. Fetch the duke…and for k'Ádhá's sake tell the king!" Matina was the last coastal defense Cordash would have before the Sovereignties were at risk.

They had to do something.

❧Chapter 6❧

Marta's swinging feet kicked repeatedly against the legs of the wooden stool upon which she sat, refusing to look at Olaric who sat across from her sifting through documents on his table in the light of the sputtering nubs of three candles. Instead, her eyes followed the movements of Kes' hands as the younger woman let out the hem of one of her daughters' dresses. The streets of Glevum were quiet at this hour, the night silence broken by the occasional barking of dogs and the infrequent clatter of armor as the King's Night Watch passed by the door.

The last set of boots had passed not long after Marta arrived, but the pair of guards paid no attention to the candles' glow in the apothecary shop. The sick did not heed the time of day and every soldier in royal employ knew that King Fraen de Corrmick's son resided there. No one would disturb them.

"You haven't told me the plan," she griped. "I've been patient."

"Yes," Olaric agreed. "My father finally made his move, so now we begin to counter him by calling up our supporters to be prepared…"

"For what? Meet in the square and protest? Lay siege?"

Her scoffing tone prompted Olaric to raise his gaze to meet hers with a scowl. "If he does what he intends, if he's about to wage war…we need to be ready. To resist from within, if we're conscripted, from without if we can. Have shelters in place for those who wish to avoid enlistment…"

"They are."

Olaric nodded. "Then maybe some of us can avoid being forced to fight if he can't find us." He did not know where those shelters and safehouses were. Coordinating them had been Marta's responsibility, her experience with Association safehouses lending itself to securing locations for men and women hoping to avoid the heel of Fraen's boot. He did, however, know of a handful of Vants properties with hidden passages and rooms for such purposes in Glevum, and had contacts who had established hiding places in the foothills and forests where men would be difficult for Fraen to find.

Avoiding recruitment was the surest way to avoid fighting for a cause and king that most did not believe in, the surest way, with stashes of weapons and armor available, to be ready to serve the true de Corrmick heir if one ever arrived.

Prince Jerit would be of age now. Prince Henrik nearly so. Olaric would lay money on the odds of one or both seeking to regain what had been taken from their fathers.

"He'll notice if so many go missing," fretted Kes.

"Not if we do this right. Traders missing on the road, a family relocating, a colony for false plague victims. Abductions, staged murders," Marta smirked. "He can focus on war or a rise in crime but not both." She looked at Olaric. "You sent word south?"

"Sparding's sent it off. Sent off the doves too…now we need the rest. We wait"

Marta slid off the stool. By her estimation, she had thirty minutes before the guards passed again; she wanted to be gone before that. They did not know her face as she had been very careful to hide her identity since coming to Glevum, but she did not want to risk being wrong.

"Whatever you're doing, whatever this is, it better work. We can't afford failure."

Olaric nodded. He did not intend to fail. He could not, however, guarantee success.

❧Chapter 7❧

"I'm sorry, my lord…I shall not be there for the king today…" Voice thin and reedy, cracked and barely audible in the commotion of servants in the corridor, Rouvyn Tallis coughed and tried to prop himself against the headboard with a strength he did not possess. Kavan held the physician's frail hand while Physician Aland Mauret adjusted his pillows to prop him into a position that eased his coughing and gently pushed him back into them, preventing him from sitting as he intended. As weak as the old man had become in recent weeks, it would have taken all his effort not to topple forward when the next coughing fit came.

"I can escort you if you wish," Aland offered, brushing his disheveled curls out of his eyes. "We were there for…"

Rouvyn shook his head. "I know my limits; I think I've reached them."

"Would you like me to stay?" began Kavan, hiding his disappointment that he had no miracle to give that would combat the passage of years and time's inevitable ravages on the body.

"And disappoint the King and Queen? I think not." Light laughter gave way to coughing and Aland pressed a cup of warm, herbal brandy to the man's stretched thin lips. "I'll be fine for a few hours."

"I will not leave you alone," Aland promised with a glance at Kavan, "unless you think…"

"Lorant will forgive you duty." Lorant was fond of Rouvyn, perhaps considering him a kindred spirit in a way that was difficult to come by in the keep. The new king might even feel tempted to postpone the day's events to accommodate the physician.

But it was too late for that. The final preparations for the much-anticipated royal wedding were underway, with many of those involved already gathering at Hes á Redh. Lorant would forgive a physician his duty in staying with a patient, but he would not forgive the harper for missing his participation in the ceremony.

He squeezed the frail hand lightly, as though afraid he would crush the delicate bones within, and pressed it to his lips. "I must take my leave, but I promise I will return if you will…"

"I will wait, my lord. I'm not going anywhere without you here."

Aland glanced at Kavan and bobbed his head, "I'll see he keeps that promise." He had been Rouvyn's apprentice for the last nine years. He was not ready to allow Rouvyn to slip away without a fight.

❧*❧

The curt rapping on her door turned Seren from the mirror and Aunes' hands as the Elyri woman tried to add the final pearled comb into her coifed and curled hair. There had been numerous callers already this morning. Yóáná and Asta, Lord and Lady MacLyr, and more, servants to bathe and perfume her, to dress and adorn her in fashions she was unaccustomed to wearing. She was a simple woman, despite bearing the often-unused title of princess; she would have preferred a simpler gown.

But as Lorant had playfully reminded her the evening before, after today, she would be the Queen. She would have to grow accustomed to a lot of new things.

Just as he would.

This gown, bordering between simple and elegant, was her compromise to that reality and suitable, she thought, for a woman about to make the same manner of compromise.

"It's me."

"Come in, Father," Seren called brightly, posing again so that Aunes could finish with her hair while a younger servant added the final blushing touches to her cheeks and another finished sinching and tying the crimson ribbons of the black bodice and adjusted the flow of the amber velvet gown. She smiled at her father through the mirror when he stepped into the room and tried not to giggle at his tight-lipped, strained expression.

"You're more nervous than I am," she teased.

The servants continued to work.

"It is not every day a father gives his only child to another," he said, clearing his throat behind his fist. "The carriages are being readied. I thought you should know…"

"I am nearly so." In unison, the servants drew away from her so that she could inspect herself from all angles in the mirror.

"If there are any doubts…"

Arms out to the side so that he could inspect her too, she asked, "Do I not appear ready?"

She knew that was not the doubts he spoke of, but she chose not to give the servants more rumors to gossip about. Enesfel needed a queen, a mother of heirs. Having observed the tension between Prince Jerit and Gerna since their wedding, Jerit's unhappiness, and Gerna's perpetual scowling frustration, Seren believed there was no one else who could give Lorant the things she could.

"You, my star, are perfection." He held her face between his hands and kissed her forehead, her nose, her cheeks. Careful not to wrinkle her gown, Seren wrapped her arms around him and welcomed his embrace in return.

"Will you send Jerit before we go?" she murmured against his chest.

Níkóá kissed the top of her head again and sighed. "You have your mother's heart." She certainly did not have his. He did not think he could settle for the future she was choosing with the same ready and willing spirit. "I will send him if you promise me something."

Tipping her head to look into his face, she asked, "What do you ask of me, Father?"

"To be happy. Happiness is all I want for you." Happiness and long life. Barring illness or some other catastrophe, what little Elyri blood she carried ought to afford her the latter. The first, she would have to find and make for herself.

"I am happy." She smiled and kissed his cheeks before letting him go. "I could not be happier.

❧*❧

He supposed Lorant's excited rambling, as he suffered the indignity of allowing the servants to dress him in the royal regalia required for this day, was understandable, even if he had not felt that way himself on the day of his marriage. Lorant and Seren had grown up together, been educated, and lived in the same home for most of their lives. They had learned the laws of rule from the same sources and had watched Níkóá pull Enesfel back from the disaster of plague to create something prosperous and healthy. They adventured the grounds, the city, the countryside together, all three of them, inseparably close, bound by royal blood and the duties put upon them. The king and princess were of similar ages and outgoing temperaments.

Jerit was eight years their senior, an outcast from his home, a prince without a throne.

Not that he wanted one. He never had. Unable to serve his brother as inquisitor as planned, he wanted no more than to serve Enesfel's king in the ways that Oska's death had denied him. He did not want marriage.

Seren had been Lorant's choice, a relationship that duty demanded.

Gerna had been Kjell's choice. Jerit had not known her, never met the woman who was six years his senior. He had been manipulated into accepting his father's wishes. He had been unable to muster a morsel of happiness that day as Lorant watched him bind himself to an outsider.

He supposed he should be happy for Lorant. But the changes looming over them, between them, hurt his soul.

All he could manage, when Lorant faced him and took Jerit's hands, was the start of a forced smile as the door opened behind him.

"My Liege. My Prince," the reversal of titles felt both awkward and natural after so many years, but thus far, Níkóá had not embarrassed himself by using incorrect titles or making demands that were no longer his to make, "Seren has asked to speak with you…and the carriages should be ready.

Lorant released Jerit's hands, unconcerned about what the gesture looked like or how Níkóá perceived it. "You will ride with her, with Rhyrdan and Lord Cáner…"

Jerit frowned. "I should be with…"

"You should keep Seren safe. I'll have Níkóá and Kavan to protect me. Nothing's going to go wrong."

The only thing that could go wrong would be the two of them alone in a carriage on the way to Lorant's wedding. Lorant was mindful enough of temptation to choose to avoid it today.

If anyone wanted to strike at Lorant, they would have done so on the day of his coronation. This was a wedding. He could not imagine anything going wrong on such a joyous day.

But Jerit recognized the note of strain in Lorant's voice and bowed his head. They wanted the same things. Lorant's decision was wise.

"Very well, but you will owe me for this."

Lorant giggled. "I think it is you who still owe me…"

Jerit forced his expression blank as he squeezed past Níkóá with a half-bow and closed the door. The current and former rulers, the groom and his soon-to-be father-in-law, had words to share that Jerit did not need to hear.

He was certain he did not want to hear whatever Seren had to say as he weaved through corridors between servants and those heading for the náos. Forcing his anxiety from the back of his throat and down into the already sour knot in his stomach, he knocked on the door once and waited with his breath caught in his chest.

One of the servants opened the door, curtseyed, and scurried past with an armload of items that might be needed to adjust Seren's gown or appearance once they reached the náos. Aunes was gathering other items after placing the beaded-patterned long shawl into Seren's hands. It was the first day of Kailar, the first day of summer, but the morning was cool; it would not do for the bride to catch a chill during the short ride across town.

"You sent for me?" He did not call her princess or queen. He did not call her by name. Today he did not know what to call her.

"I did."

She sounded nervous to him, but he had heard that many young women felt nervous on the day of their marriage. He had no experience with that, as Gerna had shown no nervousness but rather gleeful determination on their wedding day. The tremor in Seren's hand when she drew him inside so Aunes could likewise go out made Jerit assume that the story was true.

"Lorant bid me to ride with you."

"Be my protector?" She chuckled as she let go of his hand to pull on the shawl. He took it from her and wrapped it gently around her shoulders. "Thank you."

"I think he doesn't want me to see…"

"He doesn't want to risk riding off with you and giving up his throne," she interrupted warmly. "He knows how hard this day is for you, as do I. He doesn't want to make it worse." When Jerit frowned, she continued, "I will not come between you any more than duty demands; you know that, don't you? Being the king requires certain concessions if he is to…"

"I know." The gruffness in his growl made her smile and kept her from pointing out the obvious.

"Whatever I have of him, whatever he gives, it is only a little piece of what is yours. Believe me…I will not interfere with that."

Another knock and a low, "It is time, my lady," from the chamberlain cut her off. She covered Jerit's hands where they lingered at the shawl clasp and gently pried them away to fasten it herself.

"This is a change in title and duty," she murmured. "Nothing more."

Jerit nodded but only said, "Shall we go?" As far as he could see to the contrary, by the end of this day, everything would change.

He wondered now if Lorant had felt the same way on the day he watched Jerit marry Gerna.

❧*❧

❧77❧

For the second time, a week apart, the streets between the keep and the náós were lined with cheering adulation, with flower petals strewn before matching royal carriages adorned with wildflower garlands. Trumpets on the náós steps and Lachlan Guards in gleaming armor and crimson and amber tabards lined the path from the carriages to the open náós doors as they had before. There were fewer people seated within, the decision having been made to protect the sanctity of the royal union and protect Seren from threats Lorant did not want to risk. Watching Gerna impatiently waiting at the inner Gathering Hall door, her expression stern and frustrated as Jeren helped Seren from the carriage, Lorant understood how fortunate he was.

If forced into such a union, he would have torn his hair out.

Praise be, he was fortunate enough to have earned Seren's love, devotion, and trust, despite having done little to deserve it. Given who he was, he hoped he could do right by her for the sacrifices she would be presented with.

Jerit's face, when he noticed his wife and daughter waiting for him, grew more unhappy and fearful than Lorant had seen him all morning. He had tried to ease his friend's concerns but it was obvious he had failed. Or else Seren had said something to him that had undermined Lorant's efforts.

A mask of neutrality and feigned warmth fell over the red-haired prince's face, an expression useful in courtly interactions with annoying lords and petitioners. He said something to Seren then left her in Bhríd's care so that he could reluctantly join his family.

Lorant wished he had done more to help, but he had worries and concerns of his own that he had been unable to voice to Kavan within the crowded confines of the carriage…not when Níkóá would hear him and could, if he was inclined, call off his daughter's wedding before it transpired. Now that Seren stood beside him at the back of the Gathering Hall, entwining her arm around his as Kavan joined Tusánt at the alter to give his musical gift as a blessing to the young couple, it was too late to express those fears to anyone.

If he failed Seren, if he failed Enesfel, all the disappointment he was heaping onto Jerit's shoulders would be for nothing.

k'Ádhá, she was beautiful.

With Bhríd at his side and Níkóá at Seren's, they took five steps, reaching the back-most bench before their escorts fell back to protect them as they proceeded forward into their new life alone, together. With measured, regal steps, they passed the familiar faces of lords and ladies, palace staff, trusted advisors, and members of the wealthiest families from

Rhidam. They passed Jerit and Gerna, with Ida strategically between them, the prince refusing to meet Lorant's gaze. They passed dedhá Khwílen and his disguised guest on the other side of the aisle, one smiling at the couple, the other barely hiding a scowl as he stared past Lorant at his son instead. The wafting, passionate notes of glee and anticipation carried them past the front row where Princess Hella, standing in the aisle, wrapped a length of woven flowers around their joined hands and Prince Henrik, on the other side, sprinkled both with perfumed water blessed by k'dedhá Rankin who was unable to attend the service today. First Seren, then Lorant, kissed their young foreheads and, with the two men stopping there at the end of the aisle, the couple mounted the altar steps and stopped in front of Tusánt.

Henrik and Hella went with them, smiling hand in hand as they stopped on the couple's left side.

On their right, the harp in Kavan's hands fell still. He bowed his head as though to pray.

Tusánt raised one hand in blessing, but before he could speak, shouts and the clash of steel erupted in the náós yard. Asta, despite the finery she wore in deference to Seren, strode down the aisle picking up Zerio and Madoc from the congregation as she went.

Men from outside pushed to get past the Lachlan Guards at the door. Rocks and debris were hurled, most of it striking the armored soldiers, some of it clattering into the Gathering Hall and bouncing down the aisle. Some of those in attendance screamed and pushed as far from the center aisle as they could. Others shuffled anxiously and held their breaths. The other dedhá at the altar left their posts and formed a protective barrier around the king and his bride. At the head of the aisle, Bhríd and Níkóá faced the doorway, ready to charge if the instigators burst inside.

Kavan's head snapped up, the surge of panic the sudden sulfuric smell and the sound of running footsteps charging around those two men generating a knot of power in his core that begged to be released. But there was no one there, no immediate targets despite what his senses told him, and when he searched the air and the auras around them for the threat he feared, he was relieved that Eridel was not among those fighting outside nor anywhere inside the Gathering Hall. Rhyrdan lurched to his feet in response to Kavan's actions, a hand on his sword, watching the bard, the open náós door, and Bhríd and Níkóá for instruction.

He could get Lorant and Seren and the young royal children to safety if required. He knew Kavan could protect everyone else.

Jerit was likewise on his feet, pushing past Ida and Gerna to stand in the aisle, a mid-aisle deterrent if anyone dared to try to approach.

As quickly as it had begun, the sounds of combat ceased, the mass now pushed back by the Lachlan Guards and, it seemed, pulled away by others behind them. Voices raised in ire, however, indicated at least a dozen participants continuing to hurl incoherent insults and threats at the sheriff and inquisitor's intervention.

Someone pulled the interior Gathering Hall doors shut, and then the exterior ones, creating additional barriers between whatever was happening outside and those inside the náós.

"Let's do this while we can," grunted Níkóá, his attention divided as he faced the front again. Lowered weapons did not mean the end of the problem, particularly if the troublemakers brought reinforcements. There were enough Lachlan Guards, as well as the inquisitors, justice, sheriffs, and others, to put down all but the biggest riots. He did not expect it to come to that but did not want to risk the safety of the king, his daughter, and the children with them.

This time when Kavan lowered his head, the act was accompanied by a surge of power big enough to shield the royal families and the gdhededhá gathered at the altar if anyone came for them. He could have done so for every person in the Gathering Hall but did not think they were the targets. None of them were as important to Enesfel as those standing at the altar.

He did not hear the words of the ceremony as they passed, did not hear what became of the combatants outside. What he heard was a continual roar of wind, the sea crashing over rocks, a sizzling, breaking glass sound he was unfamiliar with. He felt only the fluctuation of power as if something sought to drain his away until eventually, a small hand slid into his as if to supplement his efforts to protect those at the altar. There was no nauseous turning in his belly as the Sight typically created, no dizziness, so he did not think his son heard, smelled, or felt the same things he did, but he did feel his father's distress and sought to ease it. The hand on his other one, Kaedís MacLyr, was a presence he did not expect. He was grateful to them both, as their touches broke through the deafening din in his head, bringing a dark veil over his mind's eye that shut the swirling images of orange, yellow, and black away. Their touch severed the draining power thread and, through them, he again became aware of the room, the cheering congregation greeting the royal pair who descended the altar steps together the way they had climbed them.

Rhyrdan returned to the bench and motioned for Ágdhállán and Kaedís to join him, seeming to regard their retreat to Kavan's side as a fear response to the interruptive chaos. Níkóá and Bhríd relaxed, and the gdhededhásur returned to their positions, though they were standing now as the ceremony ended. The guests were standing to greet the King and Queen.

Jerit, however, had not moved. He remained in the center of the aisle, sword in hand, as Lorant and Seren approached, stone-faced as though he would not yield the right to pass. Neither man spoke as Seren held her breath, only stared at one another as if they would come to blows. Only when the doors at the back of the Gathering Hall opened, allowing the dusty, bloody, clothes-torn Zerio to stagger through them, revealing that the exterior doors were also spread wide and that no one else stood outside, did Jerit nod once, turn, and lead the royal couple to the top of the outside steps into the glow of the mid-day sun.

The congregation applauded his protectiveness.

Kjell did not.

Kavan was not the only one to interpret that moment as something completely different.

❧*❦

It had been more than a decade since Kjell had been in a room as crowded and chaotic as the Rhidam Hall, as guests moved on and off the dance floor to the tinkling merriment of the White Bard's music or clustered around the bountiful offered feast that had likewise been absent from his life. The last time he had enjoyed an evening like this, drinking with his friends, dancing with his wife, offering toasts of well-being and prosperity, had been Jerit's eleventh birthday.

Then the world had imploded, and everything he had known was lost.

That son, the only one remaining, stiffly danced with his daughter, his wife, his daughter again, but always with his gaze shifting to the doorway through which the King and Queen were expected to arrive. Mid-dance they stopped, Gerna seeming to berate him with harsh words before storming away towards the tables, leaving Jerit standing alone in the center of the room. He was only prompted to move by Lorant and Seren's arrival, when the movement of the applauding guests turned him to face them.

Kjell could no longer see Jerit's face but he did not need to. He knew his son well enough to interpret the set of his shoulders, the shuffling of his steps, the flexing of his hands as Lorant, radiant in amber and crème, escorted Seren into the space between tables to dance in the expected, traditional manner of royal marriages.

Lorant, his blonde waves refusing to obey the confines of the ribbon they were tied in, was a radiant young man. Kjell could not deny that. He looked much like his father, grandfather, and great-grandfather before him, the mix of the best of the Lachlan, de Corrmick, Dilyn, and McHador bloodlines of those who had gone before. Men and women alike around the room were prone to swoon in his presence, and Lorant was prone to encourage such attention with a light, coquettish smile.

Jerit was not the only one smitten.

But Jerit's duty, Kjell thought bitterly, lay elsewhere.

He took a couple of steps into the crowd, forgetting he might be recognized, forgetting the discomfort of their press around him. Before he reached Jerit, before he could utter the words that prompted his steps, an arm wrapped around his waist and Asta, after encouraging Henrik and Hella to find the other children, asked, "Are you here for a dance, my lord? It has been a long time."

Briefly, he considered denying her. The year of malnutrition in the filthy dankness of Glevum's tower had robbed him of more than his crown. His legs had never regained their steadiness; his arms had never regained their strength. In the confines of St. Kóráhm's, avoiding things like dancing had become too easy. Resuming the role of husband and father had been easy enough to avoid.

Here, avoiding such things would not be simple.

He should not have come.

But watching Hella coax Henrik to the platform where Kavan played, where Ágdhállán and the Cáner children, and other children of the house were gathered, reminded Kjell of a resolution that had come during the day's earlier ceremony. He needed to be here. A dance with Asta, both welcome and feared, would offer an ideal opportunity to speak of such things before he returned to the chellé at the end of the evening.

"I take it you ended that commotion?" he asked, bowing with a flourish that prompted her to walk with him into the cluster of dancers.

She snorted. "They pick the most inopportune times to remind me they're there…like I could forget." Half of the time, the Association avoided her. The other half they seemed determined to be as visible as possible by causing as much chaos as they could. Someone needed to get them in line.

Kjell nodded with a smile of understanding and sympathy but focused on the movement of his feet to dance steps he had nearly forgotten. He was grateful Asta was not troubled by his clumsiness. Several unspeaking steps later, as one song bled into a second and a third, relishing this forgotten sensation, brought them back within sight of Jerit who, having approached Lorant only to be rebuffed by the king's quiet words, pushed through the crowd and crossed the Hall without looking back. It was a reminder of Kjell's earlier intentions, the decision he had made, and so he said, "I propose, Lorant willing, that Henrik and Hella be betrothed."

Asta stopped moving. "Be…they're children…"

"Henrik is the same age as Oska was…the same age as Rika when…"

"That was her choice," Asta reminded him. As headstrong as any Dugan, when Prince Govert came with his father to Glevum for the first time, Rika had bluntly announced to the world that she would marry the Cordashian prince and demanded that her parents make it happen. The older Govert had thought the announcement amusing and briefly discussed the idea with them in jest. Four months later, after further meetings, letters, and negotiations between both houses, the betrothal was set. At fourteen, as was customary in Neth, she was wed.

There had been no discussion of betrothal for Jerit before or during his final birthday celebration in Glevum. That was to come later. Asta had not considered the topic to be on Kjell's mind until he pressured Jerit into an unwanted marriage for the sake of the de Corrmick dynasty. She presumed that was the same rationale that prompted this decision now.

Jerit was unlikely to ever produce the male heir the Neth throne required. Ensuring Henrik did was the next logical choice.

"It is a good match; Henrik adores her and she…"

"Betrothals are different in Enesfel." She dared him to continue with the thoughts she cut short. Despite the host of problems Henrik was prone to, or perhaps because of them, Hella rarely left his side. She saw past things others viewed as deficiencies and never treated him differently than she did anyone else. Asta imagined the two would someday decide to wed on their own. She did not want to decide for them.

"Think of the alliance…"

"Look at what our alliance created," she muttered bitterly. Thanks to the alliance between Enesfel and Neth's royal families, strengthened by their marriage and the one between their son and Queen Diona's oldest daughter, Neth had imploded. It was not her fault, not Kjell's, but she had mixed feelings about what results another de-Corrmick-Lachlan marriage would have.

"I will have the throne again. We will reclaim Glevum." Kjell hoped his sincerity sounded stronger than his belief in his words. "We need this, Asta. It is already decided. As soon as I speak to the king…"

"We should discuss this with Henrik first. See if he is…"

Kjell growled and dropped his arms from where he held her close. "He will do as he's told." Unlike Jerit, Henrik, he believed, was easier to control.

Jerit had married as ordered but he had yet to produce an heir. Despite his efforts to suppress his reaction, when Lorant and Seren left the dance to take their places on the thrones where servants placed food and drink on little side tables, the way Jerit's face lit when eye contact with Lorant was made, told Kjell what he needed to know.

Unless Henrik married a suitable bride, the line of de Corrmick kings would end.

"I will not be commanded, Kjell. This isn't Glevum. Neth's ways are not Enesfel's. I will talk to Henrik; if he is willing…only if…and if Lorant and Hella agree…I'll permit this. If any are against it…"

They stared at one another, both adamant in their positions. Once it had been her willingness to challenge and defy him, to make him rethink his choices and actions, that had made him adore her enough to marry her. Denied more than a decade of control over his life, however, that defiance made him angry.

Asta did not relent. Dugan defiance was in her blood. No amount of wrath would make her give in to his demands. She would not, however, draw attention to such a challenge in this public place.

"They will agree," he grunted with stubborn certainty before barreling off in Lorant's direction. Asta counted to five, releasing slow breaths to calm herself, and then headed through the crowd in the direction she had last seen Henrik.

If she did not speak to him now, the odds of Kjell reaching him and forcing his will into place were too high.

Both Henrik and Hella were still in Kavan's orbit when she found them, seated with the other children, talking quietly amongst themselves. She considered drawing Henrik aside alone to speak to him, but there was no reason not to share this with them both at once. From Kavan's small nod, the bard looking unusually haunted and uncomfortable, she guessed he was already aware of her intent, a thought that made her shiver as she beckoned the royal children to follow. As they had been an integral part of the day's ceremonies, Hella assumed they would be asked to perform some other duty, while Henrik followed out of obedience. They went out of the Hall into the quieter corridor and stopped when she paused to look back toward the throne.

Kjell was waiting impatiently for Lorant to finish his conversation with Bhríd, a delay that frustrated Kjell but relieved Asta.

"I want to…your grandfather has decided, Henrik…if the king approves and you are both willing, you are to be betrothed…"

"Betrothed?" asked Henrik with a tilt of his head and perplexed furrows between his eyes.

"You mean married?" asked Hella with a surprise.

Her last word made Henrik blink and squeak.

They were the reactions Asta expected.

"It is like marriage…but not. Betrothal means that you will be promised to one another so that, when you are older, you will be officially wed…"

Hella sat on a corridor bench, her expression both thoughtful and serious. "And if we don't want to be?"

"Then say it now and it will not be. It is a Lachlan tradition not to arrange the marriages of their children, to allow them a choice, but in Neth, the rules are different."

"We would not be able to break it?" Hella looked at Henrik who sat beside her as she took his hand to calm his nervous fidgeting. She could almost hear his methodical counting in his head, one of the ways he stilled his racing thoughts. She did not know if he understood. Her knowledge of such details, Asta guessed, had come from servant gossip, through books, or from Master Najar during formal etiquette training. That she understood the gravity of the situation made Asta's job of explaining easier.

"It would be possible to break it," she replied, "but it would be a tedious undertaking. You do not need to decide now…you could refuse and decide to marry later if you wished. But Kjell is speaking with your brother," she met Hella's gaze, "and he will try to force a choice."

"Tonight?"

Asta nodded.

Still wide-eyed, Henrik watched his swinging feet and stuttered, "What does it…how…we wouldn't have to…you know…?"

His embarrassed tone and awkward shifting made Hella squeeze his hand. "We wouldn't be married yet, Henri. That only comes later."

"How much later?" Henrik did not like change. The longer he had to adjust to something, the easier that change would be for him.

Asta began to speak, but Hella continued explaining in a lady-like fashion, "Marriage doesn't come before fourteen, so at least three years…"

"Three…?"

Again, his brow furrowed and Asta kept quiet. Hella had learned a way of connecting with Henrik, of speaking with him instead of at him, that helped him understand emotional concepts. He excelled at languages, at numbers, at geography, which was, for him, like pieces of a puzzle, but history and reading he found tedious, and anything that held an emotional or interpersonal component was a severe challenge. If Hella understood something enough to translate it for him, Henrik eventually grew to understand as well.

"We would still be friends?"

Hella smiled playfully. "Of course. We will always be friends. Just as Lorant and Seren are friends. That won't change."

"Is it what you…?" He left the question incomplete as he glanced at Asta as if seeking her approval as well, but he just as quickly looked back at Hella to ask, "You would want to marry someone like me? I'm not…is that what you…?"

"There's nothing wrong with you, Henri," Hella assured him. "If you want…if that's what you want…" She hesitated and glanced at Asta as well. "If Henri…if my brother agrees…then I accept."

Henrik shifted closer to Hella without touching anything more than her hand. "Me too," he whispered. "I'll marry a princess."

If he had ever thought about marriage, it seemed he had never thought he would marry someone of his station. After having seen marriage forced onto his uncle to a woman beneath his class, it appeared that Henrik had assumed that the same lack of choice would befall him.

"And I will marry a prince," Hella agreed.

At least, for now, it seemed to be a future they both agreed to. At least, it was a relationship of compatibility. So long as neither changed their mind, perhaps Asta could give Henrik the happy life she had been unable to offer Oska or Jerit. If the betrothal fell through, she suspected Henrik would never get over it.

ક*ગ

"Thank k'Ádhá we're out of the chaos," Seren sighed, collapsing onto the padded bench at the end of the bed to remove her shoes from her aching feet. She knew she was not alone in feeling relief at escaping the public pretense of a happily married couple.

They were as happy as they could be given their personal situations, but she understood the reality of the affiliation they had forged.

Lorant sat in a high-backed chair near the hearth after removing his coat and doublet and began to remove his boots. He was not shy about undressing, as Seren had seen him stripped down to his braies when wrestling, running, or swimming, but he was unfamiliar with seeing a woman likewise undressed except for in the paintings and statuary exhibited in the homes of many lords.

It was not her nudity, however, that made him uncomfortable.

Changing the subject, filling the void between them, he asked, "Do you think I'm wrong to agree to Hella's betrothal?"

Unphased by the shift in topic, Seren shrugged. "I think they're children…but they're very close. She's good for him. I think Hella knows her mind…and they can change it later."

"Not if Kjell has any say."

"A lot can happen in three years…and you have a say in Hella's future…as Asta has in Henrik's." She stood up with her back to Lorant and began the process of undoing the ribbons and buttons and pins that held her hair, and her dress, in place. "It must be hard for him not to have any say in his life when he used to be king."

"That doesn't mean he should force his will onto everyone else."

Seren giggled. "That's what kings do."

She could not see his rattled scowl but she could hear it in his voice when he admitted sheepishly, "Sometimes we must…but not always. Especially with children…" He also understood, however, that it was an adult's responsibility to tell children what to do, to teach them and protect them from the outside world and themselves.

Suddenly being considered an adult, being a king, lost its allure. He was not sure he wanted either.

Now that her hair was free, she did not reply as she worked down to the chemise that had never been worn before today. Aunes had said it was a requirement for a prosperous, proper marriage, which was the only reason Seren had agreed to it. It was made of the finest Káliel silk and hung to her ankles, properly modest and, she hoped, adequate to relieve Lorant's nerves. After hanging the celebration gown over the back of a chair where the servants would tend to it in the morning, she joined him, now stripped to his trousers but no further, at the hearth where she sat on the floor between his knees, her back to him. Leaning against his leg, she watched the fire burn.

"This isn't about Hella and Henrik's betrothal, is it?"

Absently he stroked her hair, a display of affection that came easily to him and did not feel to be crossing any boundaries. When she lay her head on her arm on his thigh, he smiled faintly despite himself. "I didn't say…"

"We've known each other a long time…I know who you are. Have I ever tried to make you something different?"

He shook his head no but she could not see it.

"You love Jerit. You always have. I'm not here to get in the way of that. I'm here to provide heirs to the throne…"

"That's hardly fair…"

"Maybe not," she shrugged, "but it is what duty requires…and it's a duty I accept."

"You deserve better."

His fingers tangled in her hair so that it pulled a little when she looked up at him. He let go but she caught his hand and held it."

"I deserve the life I choose. This marriage…it allows me status and luxury…and it keeps me close to my friends without some jealous lord getting between us. With your permission, it will allow me to continue to aid the plague widows, orphans, and elderly. So long as you honor and respect me, give me what love you have left over…I will have the children I long for, for as long as we can…and so long as you love and respect and honor them too, what you do with Jerit is none of my concern."

"And if I cannot? Father children?"

She kissed his hand. "You will. Perhaps not tonight…perhaps not in a year…but you will. We will. We have time, Lorant. What the rest of the world believes does not matter."

Silently he nodded, pulled her onto his lap, and held her there with his head upon her shoulder and her cheek against his hair, staring at the fire until it sputtered weakly out, ignoring the distant strains of music and merrymaking that wafted through the keep's open doors and up to the cracked open window of the royal bed chamber.

❧Chapter 8❦

A host of Pravek men lined the beach and docks, many armed with weapons or tools that they could use as such when the fleet of unidentified galleys appeared on the horizon, approached the docks, and the men aboard them began to disembark without any seemingly violent intentions. Other townsfolk took refuge in their homes, in their basements, locking doors and dousing lights to ward off the perceived invasion. By the time Duke Haaral reached the shore, out of breath with sweat trickling down his fleshy, round face, the first of the strangers had begun to cluster together at military alert as if waiting for an order.

They were not attacking. They did not speak. They were not engaging the Nethites who berated them with nervous catcalls and demands for them to go home. Their faces were blank as if they did not understand the words. Their darker golden skin and slightly up-slanted eyes assured Haaral that they were not from Cordash, nor Hatu…but he did not know where else they could be from. From their direction of approach, he did not think they had come from anywhere at all, at least nowhere in the known world of the Five Sovereignties. Man after man until the beach was filled as the ten galleys emptied while, further out to sea, there were at least five times that number of ships easing their way east.

"What do you want?" Haaral barked, expecting that his heavy blue velvet robes, the gold chains around his neck, and the bejeweled gold rings upon every finger would identify him as a man of importance, a man to be respected and listened to. A man who should be answered.

None of the strangers replied.

"I demand to know your business! If you've come to trade or…"

"We have come," came a woman's voice from the back of the crowd, an accented voice that grew louder as the men parted to allow her to come to the front, "at King de Corrmick's request."

"You mean Fraen," Haaral snorted, looking the woman over with esteem and forced contempt. She was the only woman among them, and seemed to be in charge, or at least was the only one to speak an oddly accented, stilted form of Trade. Her exotic features, accentuated by the tight black braid that pulled her hair away from her narrow face into a queue down her back, would have stood out in a sea of beautiful women. She was dressed in the same beige trousers as the men but her embroidered mid-calf tunic and sturdy brown leather boots, in addition to the way the men moved aside and bowed their heads when she passed, elevated her to the status of someone important.

Haaral had never seen a woman lead an army anywhere. He had never heard of such a preposterous thing.

"He's not here."

"I know." She barely looked at him as she spoke but instead scanned the city behind him as if seeking its strengths and weaknesses.

"You'll have to deal with me, and I say you don't belong…"

The woman cocked her head, her mien both blank and menacing at the same time, an expression that made Haaral shiver and created a knot in his stomach that made him want to retch. Whatever he had been about to say withered before her, and without intending to do so, he stepped aside with a gesture that bid the people of Pravek to allow the foreigners to pass.

"I will tell him you're here," he stammered, his words tripping over themselves in their haste to be spoken.

"Do that," she replied, without looking at him or acknowledging him further, and when he asked her name, she continued to walk the path with her troops in a double file line towards the nearest side of Pravek with a field big enough to house them.

She did not need to give him a name.

When Fraen learned her army was here, he would know.

❧ * ❧

It did not matter that Lorant Lachlan was now a married man. It did not matter that he had, presumably, spent his first night with his wife. There were those with doubts about such things, but when Seren passed Gerna in the corridor that morning, Gerna knew the smile on the Queen's face. As a twice-married woman, she knew what it meant.

None of it mattered. Jerit had left the ceremony early, before the king and queen had, and had not come to their room. Where he went when he was not with her, she did not know, but it happened often enough to be an ongoing source of irritation.

She had met him this morning in the corridor on the way to the stairs. Dark shadows sagged beneath his eyes, evidence that he had not slept, and his clothing remained unchanged from the evening before. He fell into step wordlessly beside her, avoiding eye contact, and she thought they might, for once, share a private morning meal. But when Seren passed with a breakfast tray taken from one of the servants, and wished them a good morning before retreating into the king's chamber, Jerit looked abruptly mortified and, when Gerna reached for his hand, he jerked away and bustled off in another direction.

Away from Lorant. Away from her.

Lorant's new status did not matter because it would never change her husband's heart.

There was only one way Gerna could change that.

She doubted King Kjell was still in Rhidam, but there were enough Elyri and other messengers who could take a message to him. He would know how to resolve her dilemma.

Nothing Gerna had ever done had worked.

❧*❧

With the excitement and responsibilities of the coronation and wedding behind him, the spring plantings in Alberni complete, and no trace of the man he believed he had seen in the St. Mátán crowd, Kavan awoke that morning with an unexpected sense of purpose for the day. It had been several weeks since his studies had taken him to Gorbesh, when he, Dhóri, and Ágdhállán had visited and shared an unexpected morning meal with Earé before their different duties pulled them apart. He did not see enough of her, and whatever the fleeting nature of the dreams he could not recall upon waking, he felt compelled to see her today, to seek the reassurance or clarification that he hoped k'ílshwythnec could offer.

It also seemed, as he dressed and partook of his usual small breakfast left upon his desk before he had come into the room, a good day to introduce Tusánt and Khwílen to Valesce and the residents of the Gorbesh chellé hábhai. They were introductions he had intended to make for the last decade but had never followed through. There had always been some reason not to.

Today, with Ágdhállán secure in Rhyrdan's care as the younger man taught him and Balint how to efficiently climb trees, scale walls, and perform a host of other physical skills, as Tusánt tried not to fidget beside him as they waited for Khwílen to arrive, Kavan had run out of excuses. Or had decided to stop looking for any. His son was safe, both men were available. It was time.

"k'dedhá…Lord Cliáth…" Khwílen bustled into the room breathlessly, the damp edges of his sleeves noticeable as he dried his hands on the front of his tunic. "Apologies. I was in the kitchen with dedhá Edric…there was an incident. I should have changed but I did not wish to make you wait longer. Is it too late to be away?" His blue eyes were wide, his expression rapt with anticipation. He had heard so much about the place called Gorbesh, how it might one day become an extension of St. Kóráhm's, but he had yet to see this exotic place.

"We waited," Tusánt clucked with a teasing smile. "You'll dry."

"If you're ready?" Their easy banter, bred of years of familiarity, lightened Kavan's spirit as he motioned into the prayer alcove from which he and Tusánt had previously emerged. Though there was a Gate beneath St. Kóráhm's and one in the manor that the residents could access, Kavan had used the argument of necessity to create two k'rylag inside the chellé to practice his newly acquired skill at creating them. There were as many Teren residents in St. Kóráhm's as there were Elyri and someday, he believed, they were going to need these quick means of escape.

The new Gates also made Kavan's visits more direct.

Both men joined him in the chamber and took his hands. A short intake of breath later, the two found themselves in a chamber of yellow stone, lit only by oil lanterns hanging on the walls around them. The air was dry, the chamber cool and empty, and the only sounds they could hear were the echoes of distant movement somewhere beyond the room which grew louder as it approached the archway across from them. As neither was accustomed to the speed and ease with which Kavan moved them through the Gate, they stood, catching their breaths and steadying their legs as the bard left the Gate circle to approach the archway and the nearing footsteps.

"My lord." Valesce bowed as he entered, his movement steady despite the evidence of age finally etching lines on his face and the growing thinness of his limbs. "We were expecting you, but I was detained…"

The quaver in his firm voice stirred Kavan's curiosity, but rather than ask what he had been busy with, he clutched Valesce's hand between his as the man expected and asked, "Is she here?"

Valesce nodded. "She is in the chapel, waiting for you."

Kavan shuddered involuntarily. He had yet to bring himself to enter that room since the day he had shed so much blood there. If Earé expected him to join her in that place, there was a reason for it. A reason, he guessed, he was not going to like.

He gestured to his companions and beckoned them forward. "This is Valesce. This is k'gdhededhá Tusánt of Rhidam and gdhededhá Khwílen of St. Kóráhm's.

"I have heard tell much of you both. You are welcome here."

"We are pleased to be here at last," replied Tusánt.

"And eager to see more beyond this room," Khwílen agreed.

Though Kavan had intended to provide the tour, Earé's presence, now that he was aware of it, prodded his thoughts like a woodpecker, demanding his attention. Truthfully, Valesce could provide his companions with more history and knowledge of this place than Kavan could, so he nodded and said, "If you would indulge them, Valesce? I should not keep her waiting."

"Indeed, you should not," Valesce nodded too. "Gentlemen, if you will follow me."

"I will join you at noon for the meal if not before,"

"You better not leave us here," Tusánt warned lightly.

Khwílen laughed, "We are capable of making our way back."

For several minutes, while the echo of their departure dissipated, Kavan refused to move. Instead of facing the inevitable, he closed his eyes to absorb the power around him, to feel the comings and goings that had last passed through this room, to seek any remnants of Qol or Myreth that might still cling to these ancient walls.

But Qol had long ago passed into whatever end came after his mortality was shed; he would not be found here. Myreth, too, had been absent nearly as long, and yet there was something of him in this room, in this place, that offered a thrill of anticipation Kavan had not expected to feel.

Perhaps, he thought eagerly as his steps propelled him into the hall without his conscious decision to move, without the use of his eyes, Myreth was here. Perhaps that was why Earé waited for him.

The radiant power of the oratory, of the woman within, drew him as far as the door where he paused, hands gripping the frame on either side, to search the room for any other aura that might be there. But there was only Earé, and when he opened his eyes, it took all his will not to keep his gaze locked on hers.

Nothing had changed. The benches, the lack of décor, the altar. Every yellow stone, every cloud-puff of spiritual force that charged this room every time the residents gathered to pray and worship, every echo of a voice Kavan would never be able to forget, was exactly as it had been when he had collapsed and been carried out. The memories of rósádhá, of the healing of his mangled hands, of the journey that had brought him this far south, were like a suffocating noose at his neck that his hands involuntarily came up to pull away. His wrists and feet throbbed. His head began to pound with a piercing ache. His mouth went dry and the wordless song he had given voice to filled his soul with enough power that the pendants around his neck began to prickle and glow.

"Why," he choked on the whisper that forced its way out of his throat, "do you bring me here?"

From the front bench, from the place where Myreth once sat with him, Earé rose and came to him to gently pry his hands from his throat. "The past will never free you if you refuse to acknowledge it."

"I acknowledge it every day." Every early morning prayer of gratitude, every spiritual appeal made before every performance, involved his thanks for the restoration of his hands, his music, and the multitude of lessons learned in those bleak, terrifying months.

She nudged him forward with her hands pulling his until they reached the front bench. When he looked to judge the bench's location to sit without falling, his gaze passed over the blood-stained stones.

Once he saw them again, he could not look away.

There was a stabbing sensation in his wrists, but as Earé helped him to sit, there was, thankfully, no bloodshed.

"It is only blood."

Is it, he thought, barely able to hear her words or his own thoughts for the roaring memories in his head and the overpowering surge of fear. There had been blessings given here. Miracles shared. A world opened to those who had called this chellé home. If what he had spilled here, in Dhóbhaen, in numerous other places, to the point each time of losing consciousness, had only been blood, why did each occurrence happen the way it did?

"Who are we to question k'Ádhá? Shed the suffering, Father. It is what he…what Kóráhm…what she… wants for you. To be happy."

The wash of Orynn's memory broke the blood spell and made Kavan blink and look at his daughter with renewed familiarity. He had the sense that a great deal of time had passed in the sea of self-deprecation though he could not say how much. Sometimes when he looked at her, he saw his daughter. Sometimes he saw k'ílshwythnec. Today he saw her mother in her eyes and it brought a different emotion into his throat that prompted him to squeeze Earé's hand and blink away tears.

If not for Orynn, there would never have been Earé and Dhóri. If not for Orynn, he might never have found his way back to himself to heal. If not for Orynn, there would never have been Raebhá.

He owed her too much to allow this room and its memories to overpower him.

"Thank you," he whispered, accepting the wave of calm that swept over him for the first time since St. Mátán's festival.

Earé's smile was faint as she leaned forward to kiss his cheek. "When I tell you why I am here, you will not be so eager to thank me."

"It is not to spend time with me then?" He refused to frown at her warning but instead teased her gently as he pushed long strands of hair behind her ear.

"I wish to see you more than I do," she admitted, leaning her head against his shoulder and welcoming his embrace.

It was the action, as loving as it was, that reignited his worry. Her solitary upbringing without family, with only the Others to raise and teach her, had created a distancing effect that made her most often resistant to physical affection. That she leaned into him now like a child seeking comfort worried him.

He did not let her go or speak, waiting for her, instead, to find the words she wanted to say.

"The armies are moving," she finally whispered, feeling his breath catch beneath her ear. "Kaj Yetek leads them across Hatu, bound for ships that King Gamal has promised to have ready at Kílyn. He is a good man, a strong man. He will not fail Enesfel."

There were questions he could ask, but even as they came to mind, he knew the answers to most of them. The rest would be questions he suspected she would be unable to answer, even if she, as k'ílshwythnec, knew them.

"So…it is war."

"She moves swiftly. She has many men. But…there is time…"

She.

Bhás.

Kavan's blood ran cold as her sharp, furious features flashed through his mind. "Can she…can Enesfel…?"

Earé's shoulders hitched. "There will be enough to match her, but I do not know the outcome. Those corners are dark, hidden even from me." She sat back, smoothed her hair, and added, "Be careful of her, k'bhydhá. She has the might of the ancestor behind her…she is not so unlike you…except that she has the strength of fury and revenge…"

"I have done nothing." He could not call the outcome of his previous confrontation with Bhás a victory. It had been a stalemate, a retreating to corners so that each side could lick their wounds.

But it was not just Kavan Bhás sought revenge against.

It was Kóráhm.

How heartbroken the Heretic Saint must be.

It was the brotherly blood feud that had prompted not one, but two Elyri persecutions. A feud that spilled Elyri and Teren blood alike, that had robbed Kóráhm of his beloved, that had killed at least one king. Why it had come down to the two of them now to right ancient wrongs, to make peace between brothers, was a mystery only k'Ádhá and Dhágdhuán could solve.

The why of prophecy rarely made sense.

It was no wonder he had not shown himself to Kavan as frequently as he once had. Kavan had experienced his presence at times, in the oratories in Rhidam and Alberni, at Wortham's gravesite, when Kavan walked alone in the forests by his childhood lake to seek solace in distant memories or when he begged for the saint's company with brass harp strings. But it had been a long time since he had seen Kóráhm's face. If the saint had knowledge of what lay ahead, it was no wonder he permitted this distance between them.

"He will help you if he can, as will I, but I fear…"

Kavan nodded with a sigh. "I understand." Whatever was to come, he had trained his whole life to confront it. Prophecy had molded him for this. Whatever was to come, he would ultimately have to face Bhás on his own.

"k'bhydhá…I did not know you were here…"

In the chapel doorway, Dhóri and Bergis stood with an assorted collection of items, books, artwork, and satchels that rattled and clattered on their backs and in their arms when the two men stopped, staring sheepishly as if they had been caught in some secret.

"I…" Dhóri stammered. "I'm here to see Earé…"

Kavan knew it was not the first time that brother and sister had met in Gorbesh. He knew they met here many times since he had first brought Dhóri here. Just as Kavan often did, Dhóri came to see his sister, sometimes successfully, sometimes not, though he had never spoken of those meetings with his father. Nor had she. The siblings shared secrets between them…as it should be.

Kavan only knew about each meeting because of the unmistakable residue of her power and presence on Dhóri's skin and clothes and the overflowing of his son's innate well of power that occurred each time.

What did surprise him was the items both men carried.

"With my books?" Not books from his study but from other rooms in the house where Kavan did not often spend time.

"We want them to be safe, m'lord," stuttered Bergis., shifting his larger, bulkier load so that he would not drop them. "No one's gonna take them if they're here."

Catching Kavan's side-eyed glance, Earé shrugged without incriminating herself in sharing some foreknowledge of events with her brother that she had not shared with their father.

Or perhaps Kóráhm had done so.

The chiming of the meal bell interrupted. There was no use in scolding Dhóri for seeing to the security of the family's wealth. If the time had come to move such things from his home, then the time had come to likewise remove the wealth of knowledge out of St. Kóráhm's. That, he determined from the expression on his daughter's face, was one of the reasons she had invited her father here.

"Should we go down?" Earé asked, drawing Kavan to his feet as she rose. "Your companions will want to know of these things."

Kavan nodded.

Yes, they would. It was time for Khwílen to see to the security of St. Kóráhm's, for Tusánt to prepare the Faith for what lay ahead.

Until Kavan spoke with Lorant, however, he would swear all of them to secrecy.

There would be no rumors of war until the king knew it himself.

❧*❧

With plans to make and Earé's company to relish, Kavan, Tusánt, and Khwílen remained speaking with Valesce, walking the halls, the grounds, and a portion of the landscape outside of the chellé's walls, coordinating the influx of books, parchments, and scrolls, the relocation of the writing desks used in St. Kóráhm's for copying books, and the removal of a significant portion of St. Kóráhm's wealth. Bergis had argued the need for such measures, for surely no war could touch St. Kóráhm's, and while Kavan understood his doubt and was equally uncertain how it could happen amidst a war with Neth, he was determined to act. He knew what he had Seen. He knew the slowly growing fear for those whose lives were in his hands. He would rather move everything to Gorbesh where they would be untouchable and then discover the move had been unnecessary than by his lack of diligence, see his work, his family, and friends, be destroyed.

Not long after midnight, Dhóri and Bergis returned to St. Kóráhm's with Khwílen to begin coordinating the move. Tusánt returned to Rhidam to pray on what he had seen, what was to come, what might be expected of him and the dedhá who served under him.

Kavan, however, remained perched on the rooftop Myreth had shared with him, staring across the arid hills and valley towards the distant collection of lights he knew to be the village of Gorbesh…the place Zelenka had been born.

He should bring Rhyrdan here to see it. He should have brought him here long before today. As the wisping clouds slid past the moon, too thin to offer rain, he wondered why he had not.

"What will you do?"

He wrapped an arm around Earé's shoulders and drew her against his side. If she had an inkling of what his next actions should be, she preferred to let him decide and speak them rather than spell out his future for him.

"There are too many who need to know about this. Gamal. Piran. Clarys and Cordash. If ships are bound for Levone, Bhríd should be prepared. And Lorant should…" He shivered. "There are many preparations to make."

"For yourself?"

He shrugged. "What more can I do? Whatever is asked of me…I have prepared for some greater purpose my whole life. Without knowing what is expected, I can only wait."

"And pray?"

His wrists began to itch. The side of his ribs ached and his feet inside his shoes burned.

He sighed again.

"And pray," he agreed.

❧Chapter 9❧

The king had not come. Two days on, with the dark wood galleys still moored at Pravek's docks, he knew the messenger would have yet to reach Glevum no matter how swift his horse. Despite Duke Haaral's effort to constrain them, when the horde of foreigners pulled up their camp and began to vacate Pravek in every direction they could travel, he was unable to stop them.

With streets littered with their debris, the city's store of goods depleted, and the surrounding fields picked clean as though by locusts, Haaral was not sorry to see them go. Nor were the townsfolk. If the king had a problem with it, there was nothing Haaral could do.

Pravek could not win a fight against so many rambunctious men they could not communicate with, with unfamiliar weapons they did not have the manpower to face.

The woman leading them was not seen again. The rest of her fleet had departed. There seemed nowhere she could have realistically gone, except ahead, alone or with a guide, perhaps, in search of the king.

Good luck to her, Haaral thought with bitter relief. Maybe the only way he could prove his efforts to stop them was to set the ten galleys ablaze.

Confiscating them for himself, or the king, seemed a better idea.

He could burn them later.

❧*❧

The debate with his advisors, men Gamal was less required to listen to than the monarchs in Enesfel or Cordash, lasted most of the day. Kavan listened, his opinions unsolicited and unneeded as Hatu's king coordinated the use of the Royal Navy to patrol the Bay of Phállá and the number of additional troops he believed he should send to Enesfel's aid, and how he could best assist in protecting the islands of Káliel. It was decided to send

Gamal's message with Kavan when the bard indicated he would be traveling to the island next, but Gamal detained him for the rest of the evening with a request for music to entertain his household through dinner.

It was rare that the White Bard was in Hatu. Kavan felt obliged, in exchange for the promised assistance and a room for the night, to give Diona's son what he asked for, though he had brought no harp with him. He no longer relied on the harp to share music, however. That was another gift Orynn and his months in the southern lands had given him.

Now, with Gamal's scroll in hand, Kavan emerged from the closet Gate into Piran's empty office. As early as the hour was, with the aromas of fresh bread and boiled eggs permeating the villa, the Prime Magistrate was likely sharing breakfast with his family, and so Kavan chose to wait at the window, his hands behind his back, staring at the glistening dew on the flower petals of the back garden in full bloom as spring gave way to summer. Petals of coral and crimson, buttery yellow and amber, snow white and lavender and pale azure surrounded the bubbling fountain. It was Piran's favorite place to be if not at the docks, so he went to great expense to make it as beautiful and prosperous as he could. Barely visible through the kaleidoscope flash of colors, the grave markers of husband and wife Kavan missed so dearly could be seen from the window and it was there, as usual, that his gaze shifted to.

He should go to them. They deserved to know what lay ahead, even if neither could offer advice or comfort from the place where spirits disseminated after death.

"Kavan. I did not expect you."

With the door open behind him and his thoughts preoccupied with a wordless dialogue with the dead about how he could keep Owain and Gabrielle's grandson safe, Kavan had not heard Piran approach.

"I was not expecting to be here." Every time he came, he could see more of Owain in Piran's features and build. Today the similarities heightened his melancholy.

"Is Lorant in need? I am sorry I could not attend his coronation. The last spring storm did significant damage to the island of Jaffe and the Council's discussion about how to manage the repairs has been more involved than I had hoped."

"He understands duty; we all do," Kavan assured him. He noted Piran's limping gate when he came around the desk to sit rather than lead Kavan into the garden. "Your leg?"

Piran dismissively waved his hand. "My hip. Too much clearing the docks after the storm. I'm not as young as I was."

"Young enough."

"Not as limber then," Piran chuckled. "What news do you bring from Rhidam if not a favor for the Crown?"

"Do you recall I once spoke of future war with Neth? Vast armies…?"

"I remember." He leaned back with a frown. "I remember Lord McCábhá warning the Council of it when he met with us…and I remember Grandmother warning of the day there would be warships in our harbor."

"There will be a fleet of ships sailing to Enesfel from Hatu, reinforcements from the southern lands. Gamal's fleet will transport them. Some will be at your disposal, ships to patrol the bay. It would be wise of your council to prepare…for my son has warned of ships from the north…"

"Neth or…?"

"Perhaps." Neth did not have a significant naval force. But since no force was said to be moving into Neth through Elyriá, Enesfel, or Cordash, Bhás' force must be arriving by sea…which suggested their origination from a seafaring land. That would lend ships for Neth's usage…and present a threat to regions Neth had never threatened before. "It is best to be prepared…and I did not want you to be alarmed by the increased activity of Gamal's fleet."

"We don't want to be involved in a war." While the island kingdom had grown less isolationist since Gabrielle had become Prime Magistrate, no one on the island desired to become the epicenter of a war. Piran had seen to the construction of ships that could quickly be converted to combat-ready vessels if necessary and had fitted several decommissioned fishing and trade ships to warships that were kept in readiness in a recently constructed port on the east side of the main island, in sight of the island of Pháne, but Piran knew the Council was ill-prepared to vote in favor of war.

"Then involve yourselves in protecting Káliel and the bay. Ships will need to circumvent Elyriá, but I do not anticipate it will come to that."

Unless his suspicions were true. Or unless Fraen had stripped Neth of her wealth to build a navy.

None of that negated Gabrielle's premonition, however. Perhaps it had been paranoia and a fervent desire to open the islands to cooperation with the lands they shared the bay with. Perhaps she had foreseen Earé's army in Hatu's ships rather than an invasion force. Whatever the case, Kavan thought it best not to risk putting faith in those positive options while disregarding the possibility that war would come to Káliel. Whether now or in the future, the islands had to be prepared.

Piran, despite the distaste for war, appeared not to wish to leave his islands unprotected.

"Come with me before the Council. Speak on King Lorant's behalf, as King Gamal's messenger. Speak from your heart as you always have. My words alone may not be enough. Hearing you, believing you, will be the only way to sway the Council…to supply your ships, to prepare our own. After the storm, everything is in high demand, but between us, perhaps we can sway them. Trade for materials if Enesfel and Hatu have any to spare."

"When I speak to Bhríd…to Lorant…when I return home, I will do my best to secure everything we can spare. And I will gladly speak to the Council with you."

"After, succeed or fail, you will join me for dinner, play for us…tell the children at least one story? It has been too long…and Alyná will want to hear about her father."

"I would be honored," Kavan agreed with a bow. "Succeed or fail."

Hatu's ships would not necessarily need the brief shelter in Káliel's harbor or to restocked supplies if they were judicious with their rations, but Kavan wanted the Council's cooperation. He wanted additional alliances that might ensure Lorant's success.

And he wanted to again play the large harp that sat silent and mostly unused in the villa's dining hall. It was but one of many things that brought him back to Káliel again and again.

❧ * ❧

Despite Owain's wish to be buried in Fiara, in the first home he had felt was truly his, and Gabrielle's choice to be buried beside him despite the tradition of Káliel's magistrates being buried in the villa's garden crypt, the decision had been made, after the destruction of the Fiara manor, to relocate their bodies to prevent possible desecration by the Nethite army. In the middle of the first snowy night after the fall, when the manor lay in ruins and soldiers from both armies had ceased roaming Fiara's streets, Kavan, Tusánt, Rhyrdan, Asta, and Zerio led a small group of men to extract both corpses, bless them properly, and transport them in carefully prepared canvas-lined crates, to the place Piran had prepared for them. It was grizzly work, work that Kavan had been unable to watch once the remains were located as he could not bear to see those he loved in such a state of decay, but once covered, once on Káliel, he had been the first to place the freshly turned earth upon them and the one to set their stones in place.

"I am sorry again…for this," he murmured, gesturing at the warm night's floral buffet and the silent villa behind him. Piran had already turned in but Kavan was restless, lured by the proximity of the pair that had meant so much to him in life and a disturbing sense of presence that he tried to push away. Owain, as Enesfel's king, had brought Kavan out of Elyriá just as Arlan had. The path of his life had been directed by that one man's choices and nothing in the years afterward had been the same for the White Bard of Bhryell.

"I know what you wanted…I hope you understand."

Only the mild breeze in the branches and the ever-present sound of the sea responded.

His plea for forgiveness again went unanswered, although that prickling presence continued to needle him for his attention.

He tried to ignore it.

Having made use of Gabrielle's harp, the one she had once tried to give him, a gift he had refused largely out of fear for the awkward bond it might have created between them, the fingers he rubbed over her stone tingled so that he felt every grain of sand that marred her etched name. He had feared owing her something in return for that harp, and though he had not taken it with him, there was so much he owed her for the years of respect and devotion she had given. She belonged here.

And yet he hoped she, too, forgave him for disturbing her rest.

"Grant your people your wisdom, Gabrielle, as you once did. Show them the errors of their thoughts…protect your son and his family…and your great-grandson as well…"

Some brutal force shoved him back as though offended by his plea and he sat upon the ground shaking his head, reeling from the unexpected burst of power that came, not from Gabrielle's stone but from the forbidden island to the east. No longer content to be ignored, the presence pushed him again, and a third time, until he got to his feet with a determined growl. The presence retreated as though demanding pursuit and so Kavan gave in and took to the sky, the white kestrel pursuing something he could not hear or see but only feel from the center of power within. Pursued it until it evaporated over a collapsed pit of earth now filling with the debris left by birds and the sea storms that pummeled the islands every year.

The dust of the dead was entombed below the collapse, inaccessible, and there was nothing left of Dawid Coryllien to feel but he was not the one who had led him to this place.

Feet on the ground, he squatted, splayed his hand over the cool stone, and felt a shiver pass through him that made him slowly lift his head as if afraid of what he would see.

Suspended on the horizon, over the sea and yet right in front of him, a writhing, black, amorphous thing, like a cloud or a mist, darker than the night sky and the ocean, intangible and yet solid enough to block out the star and moonlight behind it. A mass that brought with it the faint smell of sulfur, that crackled like broken glass and hummed with power as it grew and spread before his eyes.

Astonished and afraid, rooted in place so that he was incapable of reacting or protecting himself, he felt the void of it grow closer as if it would engulf him, and he, unable to react, merely waited…

…until another, more powerful presence swirled up around his feet, wrapping him in its protection before lashing out with a strength Kavan did not expect.

The shapeless thing seemed to wail without sound and then dissipated like smoke on the breeze.

The vining shield unknotted and unthreaded around him.

Kavan collapsed onto the ground where he lay, staring at the stars, his heart thundering loud enough to drive the hum of the sea from his ears.

In the years of their acquaintance, he had never experienced an exhibition of power like that from Kóráhm. As the saint's nearness faded like mist in the sun, he doubted he would ever feel anything like it again.

The breeze across his face planted a single phrase within his head, four words Kóráhm demanded he take to heart.

'Be vigilant, átaelás mai.'

'Kóráhm…'

The saint did not reply. No longer able to feel him, unable to feel anything except the residual power Kóráhm left in his wake, Kavan doubted he could respond. He had used the last of his strength to issue that warning.

Kavan worried he might never feel his patron's presence again.

If Bhás could lure him, overpower him so easily, it would take all of Kavan's willpower to withstand her. It would take everything he had to protect his family.

k'Ádhá help him if he could not.

No longer able to feel either friend or foe, he remained where he lay, meditating on power, praying for guidance and the strength to shed pride and not give in to the fear of failure. His meandering thoughts eventually drifted back to the villa when the first hint of purple announced the rising of the sun over the open eastern sea. Some of the members of the Council, after the day spent in discussion and debate, had come to the villa to share in the meal and music the Prime Magistrate provided, and then stayed to continue that conversation for several more hours.

Kavan escaped to the garden's serenity, near enough to be summoned if they required, but far enough to be unable to hear them without effort.

Eventually, the visitors had gone and Piran retired. Soon, with this new day, he and the Council would hear final arguments from any parties who wished to make them, and then they would vote again, hoping to break the initial stalemate.

Piran could have broken the impasse by casting an overriding vote. He chose to honor the island's traditions and enable the council to settle the matter themselves if they could. If they could not, he would act.

Kavan hoped their vote would be in Enesfel's favor.

Choosing to be at the villa when Piran woke, Kavan returned to Gabrielle's gravesite and sank with his back to the stone. If, as she once feared, the Council refused to offer succor, they could only blame themselves if no one offered it to them in return. If war came to Káliel, they would be too easily overrun. He closed his eyes and tried to listen for her voice instead of seeking the echoes of Kóráhm in his heart.

Perhaps by the time Piran came for him, Gabrielle would have provided the words he would need to sway the Council.

If he were fortunate, those words would come from Kóráhm himself.

❧*❦

"Pardon, Your Majesty," Raenár bowed as he entered the morning room, aware of the tension in the air between the king, who sat at the table picking at the breakfast delivered by the servant Raenár passed in the corridor, and Prince Jerit, who stood at the window, his arms folded across his chest, watching something the captain could not see. "My Prince, I could not deliver this last evening as you were unavailable when I arrived."

"Been that way a lot," Lorant muttered. The sound of Raenár's boots on the planked floor and the shrieking of children dashing past the door meant that Jerit did not hear Lorant's comment as he crossed to the window.

"Your father asked me to bring you this." He presented the scroll and waited for Jerit to take it, ignoring the king's comment, understanding it was not directed at him.

For several moments, Jerit did not move. Lorant, thinking to ease the awkward situation, rose from his chair to take it. The creaking prompted Jerit to accept the rolled page sealed with an unmarked circle of wax from the captain's hand before Lorant intervened. Raenár did not move until the king sat again with a wordless sigh and then, taking that as his cue, he retreated from the room adding only, "If either of you need me, I will be here awhile longer."

Though Jerit broke the seal with his thumb without looking at it, he did not open the parchment but continued to stare out the window. Lorant chewed the piece of bread he had taken, now rendered tasteless by words that refused to be spoken, and after washing it down with water, asked quietly, "Are you going to…?"

The slight shaking of Jerit's head would have been barely noticeable to most. To Lorant, it was like a tidal wave. "It's the same as all the others," he muttered without attempting to mask his bitterness. His father never inquired about his welfare. He never sent messages about his own. In the ten years the man had been in Alberni, most of his communications with Jerit had been summons that invariably turned unpleasant. After Kjell's two subsequent visits to Rhidam, his first since losing Neth's crown, Jerit could not imagine this summons would be any different.

The chair behind him creaked again. This time, light footsteps crossed the room and stopped behind him. Jerit's shoulders tensed.

"Do you want me to…I'll go with you or have words with your father."

"To what end?" Lorant was king, could speak as king to king, but to Kjell, Lorant was still a boy. Lorant was still an influence on Jerit that Kjell undoubtedly wished would cease to be. Not by dying, but simply by severing ties Kjell did not approve of.

"For what support I can…"

"No."

"Jerit." Lorant hesitantly gripped his arm and turned Jerit to face him. "I am always at your side. You have but to ask."

"He will think me a coward. Besides…you are king now, as you pointed out. You have a wife and…"

"Silly." Lorant leaned closer and kissed Jerit's mouth. Body trembling beneath the hold on his arm, Jerit bit gently on Lorant's lip as if to keep him there, to prolong the kiss and never lose it, and then let him go with a sighing sidestep away from his hands.

"I know nothing has changed…but everything's changed…"

"No more than it did when you married…" Lorant interrupted.

"I do not love her."

"I…" Lorant sighed. "It is different with Seren, yes. We both love her…and there are duties…but that does not negate…"

"I thought you and I would be…first…"

Again, Lorant sighed and shifted to stand beside Jerit to stare out the window with him. "So did I…but it hasn't worked that way…for either of us." He assumed, since Gerna had never tried to annul the marriage, that Jerit had consummated it at least once. He had never asked, never wanted to talk about it.

He did not know the reasons that prevented him from accepting Jerit as his first, however. There was the legality of adulthood recently thrust upon him with the crown, and barely a week in between before taking a wife. That week had been busy but he could have made time any day of that week for the two of them. He had not done it…and now it was too late to recover the missed opportunity.

Eventually, with Lorant beside him, standing shoulder to shoulder, Lorant's shorter stature bringing out the protectiveness in Jerit that had been there since they first met, Jerit mustered the courage to peel open the parchment and read its contents. It was as expected. He could not read his father's tone between the stylized lines of script, but he did not need to.

"I should find the captain, get this over with. Will I…will you be here?"

"In the morning room?" Lorant giggled. "Probably not. But I won't be hard to find. It's not like I have anywhere to go."

"You have the whole of Enesfel. You can go wherever you wish," Jerit reminded him.

Lorant shook his head and then pressed it against Jerit's shoulder. "Not without you."

Jerit swallowed hard, stuffed the parchment into his doublet pocket, and kissed the top of Lorant's head. "As I will be with you," he promised.

No matter how hard others made that promise to keep.

❧*❧

"Father."

Jerit did not question his mother's presence in his father's chamber. The plotting to retake Neth's throne and their relationship as husband and wife…though they often seemed at odds to Jerit…gave Asta innumerable reasons to be here. He did not think it had anything to do with him; she looked as surprised to see him as Kjell looked pleased to be obeyed.

"Good. You are here. I need to speak with you…"

Asta let go of Kjell's hand and stood. "I shall leave you to…"

"There is no need," Kjell said, although there was a note in his voice that gainsaid his words. "You understand the importance of duty and can…"

"So do I," interrupted Jerit in a low, strained voice.

Asta took both remarks as permission, and necessity, to stay.

Kjell shook his head without rising to greet his son or encouraging him to come further into the room. "I don't think you do. Your wife expresses her concerns…and I must remind you who you are. Your duty is to the future of Neth and the de Corrmick…"

Jerit's jaw clenched. "Henrik is the heir, not…"

"Henrik is a child."

"…and he has no throne," Jerit spat back, defending both himself and his young nephew. "You lost it."

Wincing, his face darkening to crimson, the accusation brought Kjell to his feet despite Asta's hold on his arm. "That was not my…"

Giving her son a scolding look, Asta said, "No one is saying it is…"

"I'm the spare! And I've taken an oath…"

"Lorant is not your…"

Jerit bristled. There was no law, religious or secular, to define the rightness of his feelings for Lorant. Only the marriages now between them and the responsibility of noble duty to secure the lineage of Enesfel's throne. "He's my king and my friend!"

"Neth comes first. Family comes…"

"He is family!"

"You need an heir if Neth is to…"

"I have an heir."

"Ida is not…"

"You," he hissed, "made her my daughter. She will inherit everything I own."

"She will never sit on Glevum's…"

"No, she will not. Nor will I. Nor," he huffed with a sour expression, "will you. I don't want it. Oska was our king; I was to be his inquisitor. Now his son is the heir and I am nothing!"

"Jerit!" Asta reached for him but he was too far away. "Don't…"

It was too late. Jerit stormed from the room and Kjell knew he did not have the physical strength to drag him back to continue an argument repeated too many times. "He didn't use to be…" he snarled in frustration.

Asta, her expression both stricken and sad, interrupted with a weary, "He used to be a boy who idolized you and wanted to please you…you turned him into a man who is afraid of you."

"I did not…my son is not a coward…"

"He is a man seeking his way, as you once did with your father…"

"I am not like my father." Regardless of his parentage, he had been raised a de Corrmick and had done everything he could to break the mold of drunken, brutal, despotism that had been their bloodline as far back as their history could recall. He had never wanted to be that man and had done everything he could to not be the man his father wanted him to be.

That had been a duty to the people.

But he understood his other duty well and had provided Neth with heirs to protect the throne when he no longer could.

One of those sons was dead. Kjell, despite his oft-spoken determination to reclaim it, knew the throne would never again be his. Henrik, as Oska's only son, should be the heir, but Kjell refused to see the boy as worthy or capable of ruling.

He was Inness Lachlan's child.

Inness had destroyed Oska's, and Kjell's, life.

Jerit, despite his blood, refused to be capable either, no matter how hard Kjell fought to make him worthy.

"You have to let him be his own…"

"Neth needs a de Corrmick…"

"We may yet have one…from him or Henrik. There is time."

"If we take the throne and he is not…"

"Then it will be yours and I will be there as before," she soothed, feeling obliged to embrace him but understanding from his furious stance that he was in no mood to be comforted. "You must allow Jerit to make his choices. The harder you berate him, the more he will fight you."

"There are no choices," Kjell muttered, limping to the door and staring in the direction Jerit's stomping steps had gone. "He is a de Corrmick. He will behave like one, do his duty…or he will never sit on the throne."

Asta did not follow. Not sitting on the throne was precisely what Jerit wanted. She wished she knew how to make Kjell understand that.

❦*❧

"You are welcome to stay for dinner," Alyná said, kissing Kavan's cheeks at the door that separated him from Káliel's only Gate.

Despite his identity and proximity to King Lorant, Kavan was not permitted to attend the Council's second day of deliberation. He had considered doing so in some other guise, listening from the vantage point of a bird on a sill or some other creature, and doing what he could to influence their decision. From where he had sat in the Council courtyard beneath the shade of overhanging wild grapes, with his senses attuned to the moods of the men inside, his interference had not been necessary.

The urgency he had felt to delay departure had warred with the need for information, so now, as the day waned, he chose to reject the tempting offer of Gabrielle's kin.

"It is late..." He should make another Gate, he mused, as Piran wrapped his arm around his wife's waist and pulled her gently back. Only the clifftop shrine might make a suitable location; certainly, one less intrusive on the Prime Magistrate and his family. There would come a day when he was less intimately connected to the rulers here but might still need to continue their diplomatic alliance.

"I know," Piran said, "but it is no trouble. The children are in bed so there is no need to entertain..."

"I do not mind entertaining. But there are others I must visit, others who must prepare..."

"Who are likewise settling in for the evening. You are already here; dine with us, sleep, and depart in the morning."

Kavan's involuntary glance toward the window, into the garden, or beyond it, made Piran sigh. It was less duty that spurred the harper than it was the proximity to those he had lost. He took Kavan's hand and shook it with an understanding squeeze before letting him go. "Where will you...?"

"Levonne next. The harbor is not ready for the arrival of such a fleet. Bhríd will need as much forewarning as I can provide."

"And my father will surely be awake at this hour," Alyná chuckled. "Give him my love and ask him to visit us soon"

"And my regards," added Piran. "If we can share provisions...to aid our storm recovery and to aid the influx of ships, tell him I am open to discussing the matter."

Kavan nodded with a short bow. "I will tell him...and Alberni will provide you with whatever we can spare. When I see the king, I will extend Káliel's commitment to this endeavor. He will be relieved to hear it."

Whatever arguments Piran had made to the Council today, the effort had been successful.

"Let us hope all of this is a futile exercise…that none will need these precautions once they are in place."

"Agreed. Thank you again for your hospitality."

"You are always welcome in my mother's home…she would never forgive me if it was otherwise." His mirth prompted a melancholy smile before Kavan retreated into the office closet. Before husband and wife could take a step away, the bard was gone.

"Cousin." Bhríd stopped in surprise as he crossed the entry hall from the stairs as his house chamberlain ushered Kavan into the manor. Kavan rarely used the manor's k'rylag despite Bríd's extended offer to use it when he needed, but he understood the sense of intrusion Kavan often expressed when arriving unannounced…just as he had done now.

"I know it is late…"

"You also knew I'd be awake." Bhríd nodded to his chamberlain with his impeccably styled blonde hair and immaculate trousers and vest that matched the powdery blue of his eyes and said, "Thank you, Jemes. Please tell Leon we will continue our discussion in the morning before he takes Phaedr to the vineyards."

Jemes Osvald bowed with a crisp, "Yes, my lord," before ambling off with the stride of a man of a higher station. His neatness and demeanor matched Bhríd's enough to make them well-suited for one another.

"Phaedr is here?" The eldest of the ten-year-old twins was set to inherit the Dubuais-Cáner vineyards and continued to express an eager aptitude for the business, whereas his brother's only interest thus far, was to shadow Ágdhállán wherever he went and intervene when anyone, child or adult, was inclined to bully or berate the boy. As such, Phaedr spent more time in Levonne, following the vintner Leon Bodil and his nephew Augustus while Bhríd saw to other duties of household management, the sale of Dubuais-Cáner wine, or those responsibilities required as chamberlain to the king.

"Already asleep. He was up before daybreak in the vineyards. His energy," Bhríd chuckled, "puts mine to shame."

"I doubt that."

"Has the king sent for me?"

"No; I've not been in Rhidam for a few days." Like Bhríd, Kavan had duties as duke that often took him from Rhidam but his position as court tutor and bard, and the presence of Master Najar, gave him more flexibility to come and go than Bhríd had. As the vines were just beginning to bear fruit for the year, it had been necessary to return to see to their care, even though the Bodils had managed the vineyards for the past decade.

It was important for Phaedr to be part of every phase of the process so that on the day it became his, he understood what was required. Hence Bhríd's visit now. In another year or two, Phaedr would remain in Levonne year-round to complete his education. For now, he traveled with his father to continue to round out his instruction in Rhidam.

"Something has happened." Bhríd ushered him toward the sitting room. They passed Leon and Jemes in the corridor heading for the front door. Kavan bowed to both and they returned the gesture before the sitting room door closed.

Bhríd sat in one chair near the hearth and motioned for Kavan to take the other. "What is the news?"

Having no reason to be evasive, Kavan replied, "Earé's army is crossing Hatu towards Kílyn. They will resupply at Káliel, leave ships and crew there, and continue here. Within a month, maybe less, they will be in Levonne. Piran wishes an exchange of supplies…to shore the troops and recover from their most recent storm."

The black-haired Elyri's brow furrowed. With one hand he pulled the ribbon from his hair and let it fall free. "There will be war."

"I have not heard of it from Neth, beyond the constant rumbling of public discontent and their continuing efforts to rebuild a military…but if Earé is correct, I believe it is inevitable."

Leaning his elbows on the chair's arms and steepling his hands beneath his chin, Bhríd said, "You have always believed that…as she does…and I believe in you. What of the children? The king and…?"

"I will remain in Rhidam with the children; I will not ride into battle as I did with Arlan." Kavan had not been present for any of the battles except the final one, had not witnessed the chaos of bloodshed, but he had envisioned enough of it, experienced enough through the Sight and through his connection with Arlan, to know what it was like. Thus far he had not felt compelled to be in the thick of a conflict in which he would not fight.

Maybe, he mused, if he put every skill he possessed to use, he could end the war without bloodshed.

To do so, he realized for the first time, would mean confronting Bhás. After what had happened on Pháne, he did not think he would be of any use against her. If she could find him on the battlefield, his presence might be the damning, deciding factor that would lead Enesfel to ruin.

He would find some other way to aid Lorant.

"Cáym and Phaedr will be safe if you choose to leave them in my care."

"You worry for Alberni's safety yet think Rhidam will be safe?"

"Alberni is coastal…as is Levonne. From what I have Seen, I have no cause yet to think Rhidam will be at risk. But St. Kóráhm's…"

"The chellé is a target?"

Kavan shrugged. Only Rhyrdan and Kavan's children knew the connection between the woman called Bhás and Kavan, or knew the connection between her and Coryllien. Only they, Tusánt, and Ártur, knew the true connection between Kavan and Kóráhm. It was a complicated twist of history that Kavan was reluctant to share, and though he had set it down in writing, he had yet to speak to anyone else about that truth. Not Níkóá. Not Rhyrdan. Not even Raebhá.

"All of it, these days, the Corylliens, the Persecutions, they are interwoven. There is a thread that, if pulled, will unravel the world."

"And we must stop it." Again, Bhríd studied Kavan's pensive mien. "You were instrumental in the downfall of the Corylliens, to end the Second Persecution. Do you think you can remain free of this now?" He did not know what Kavan had done to have such credit bestowed on him, but if the late queen had proclaimed it to be so, there was a reason.

Kavan groaned and shook his head. He knew he was integral to this fight, knew he would be a part of it. He did not yet know how. "If it comes to it, the children will be safe in Gorbesh. Dhóri will make sure of it."

Bhríd had not seen Gorbesh but he had heard enough about it to know that it was far south of Hatu, far beyond any threat Neth could present. That would be safe enough.

"I will speak with Jemes in the morning, mobilize the city, and prepare. There will be much to do. You have not yet told the king?"

"Not yet. I have spoken to Gamal, to Piran, and now you. I will aid you tomorrow, then I will go to Cordash and Clarys before I speak to Lorant. I want to know who is behind us before I give him the news. He is not as brash as his father, but I do not want to risk him heading into war ill-prepared. Enesfel has lost enough kings."

"Indeed. Please; your room is ready if you wish to use it."

He expected Kavan to squirm awkwardly at the thought of sleeping in the room where he had once suffered excruciating physical, mental, emotional, and spiritual anguish. Bhríd had never allowed anyone else to use that room, as though it was a shrine, but had instead kept it ready in case his cousin ever required it again.

He never had.

The corners of Kavan's mouth twitched. There was a tick at the corner of one eye and his arms came up as though they would wrap around him to shield him from the sick feeling his expression conveyed. Bhríd expected him to refuse the offer but instead, Kavan murmured, "I shall…if I may."

"In the morning then, we shall discuss this fleet and what we can offer Káliel…what is expected of me." Be it a fight in Levonne, in Rhidam, or in the field at King Lorant's side, Bhríd knew he was destined for war once again. If it must be, he was determined to make it home to his children, k'Ádhá willing.

"You know the way."

❧*❦

There was a place atop the keep's southern tower, a place used in ancient days to look out over all Rhidam, toward the fields to the south and the city to the north and east, to observe the Tegid's sprawling flow to the north and west as it meandered toward Levonne. It had been centuries since invaders had tried to take the city by ship, centuries since the castle walls with its mighty towers had been erected to protect the newly risen Lachlan dynasty. Since the walls had been built around this tower and the rest of the keep, there had been little need for soldiers to be on the lookout here. Lorant had found his way to the tower as a boy and had been quick to share the discovery with Jerit. It had become their secret place to hide, to scheme, whenever Lorant had chosen to avoid his studies, or when tedious public responsibilities had grown too overwhelming.

They had never shared this place with anyone. Not even Seren.

It was why, when Lorant climbed the musty, narrow stairs and pushed open the creaking hatch to allow the early summer air to gush over him, he was not surprised to find Jerit there, lying upon the stones, his hands behind his head, watching the thin sheen of clouds pass over the half-moon. Lorant did not speak as he closed the hatch and lay down on the stone next to Jerit to look at the sky too, with his hand clutched around the half-moon pendant on his chest passed down by the kings before him, binding him to the White Bard in ways he did not understand.

"When you did not come for dinner, I thought I'd find you here."

Jerit grunted.

"Would've come sooner…but I thought you wanted to be alone."

"S'why I came up," Jerit admitted, "but you're always welcome.

"After before…I wasn't sure." He scooted closer so that their arms were pressed together but he made no other intimate gesture. "How did it go with your father?"

"Gerna complained."

Lorant shrugged. "Can you blame her?" He did not like sharing Jerit with his wife any more than Jerit wanted to share him with Seren. And though the world would not scorn their affections, blood and family and custom demanded differently. Enesfel held expectations over him, as Neth did over Jerit and Henrik. There was little either could do to alter those expectations. "She didn't know what she was getting."

Rather than provide a reply he did not want to make, Jerit changed the subject. "He wants me on his throne…wants an heir for Neth…"

"What do you want?"

Jerit turned his wrist where their arms touched and wound his fingers around Lorant's. The blonde smiled.

"I want Henrik to have what Oska never did. I want to serve Enesfel…you…if you'll have me."

"You already do." Lorant squeezed his hand, swallowing the lump in his throat that made his voice husky and thick. "Next time, I will speak to him. Tell me I may. I'll make him understand. I'll make him see that your place is here, with me."

Sighing, eyes closed, Jerit murmured, "You can try."

It was not going to be easy. With his father, since the night Kjell had lost his throne, nothing ever was.

❧*❧

Though he entered the bedroom far enough to close the door behind him, Kavan moved no further, choosing to confront the emotional memories from the security of the doorway in case he needed to flee from them. But he was stronger, much different than the terrified man full of self-loathing and shame over things he now knew had not been worth the grief he had inflicted upon himself. His hands tingled at his sides, remembering, too, the mutilation he had endured, all in the name of personal growth he had not been able to acknowledge he needed.

Kavan closed his eyes and held his breath, pulling in power to calm himself, humming a soft tune to spread as a salve over the sting those memories brought back. He was stronger, he was wiser, but in reminiscing moments such as this, those recollections still hurt.

So many stepping stones that had brought him to this moment.

What had it all been for?

"What is life but building upon the past to make living better for those who come after us?"

Kavan felt the saint's arrival before he spoke but he could not be certain, until he opened his eyes, whether Kóráhm would be incorporeal or tangible. It had been so long since he was seen in the flesh, and Kavan had been so uncertain since Pháne that the whole of the saint's power had been spent to protect him, that when he met Kóráhm's gaze, he sucked a breath between clenched jaws, held it for a few moments, and then released it with a slow hiss.

"Or to atone for the past so that the future may be free of it?"

Kóráhm hung his head. "I will never be free of it, átaelás mai. You are the proof that reminds me of that every moment."

"I did not mean…I meant…"

"I know what you meant." Every Elyri alive, every person within the Sovereignties and beyond, every member of Kavan's family, would only be free of Kóráhm's unrealized mistakes if Kavan forged ahead to overcome them. Kavan did not blame him for those mistakes, for he knew from experience that no one knew what consequences their actions would have.

Kavan was sure his mistakes had birthed their consequences for which someone else, someday, would have to atone and correct.

"I wasn't sure I would see you again…"

"It will take more than that to be rid of me." Kóráhm's chuckle was forced but warm. "She is powerful…but no one is invincible. Be wary of her…be on your guard. I may not be able to interfere or protect you again."

"You have never…"

"It was not her time."

"Then you know when…?

Kóráhm shook his head. "I sensed your distress; I only knew I could protect you. If you are to…I will do my part as much as I am able." He paused to look around the room. "You remember this place."

"Always. How could I not?" Pushing aside the last of the dwindling ache in his center, Kavan closed the door and sat on the edge of the bed to remove his boots, hoping that doing so would reduce the fight or flight shadows that lingered. Kóráhm rounded the end of the bed and sat beside him. "I don't know why I waited…did not return sooner…"

"Or perhaps you do."

Kavan nodded and pushed his boots aside with his foot. Perhaps he did.

"Are you here to warn me of war as well? To advise my path?"

"I came because it has been too long since I have been in your company and I knew you were worried." Kóráhm took his hand and clasped it between his scarred ones. "I have missed this."

Kavan did not know the rules that bound Kóráhm's actions. Kóráhm had never explained them. But Kavan had, throughout his life, witnessed a pattern to the times the saint chose to be with him and when he did not. Times of turmoil, times of danger, times of need. Times when Kóráhm was afraid for him.

Any or all of those might apply now.

Kavan did not need the specifics to find comfort in his company. Tonight, he would rather not know.

"I have no harp to entertain you…"

Kóráhm shook his head. "I would prefer silence tonight. I am weary and…" It seemed he thought better of what he had been about to say and so continued, "I wish to sit with you, as you sleep, if I may."

He sounded morose, his voice heavy with the unexpressed weight of things he would not, or could not say, heavy with the unspoken longing of the sort Kavan often felt when sitting beside his sons and watching them sleep while imagining what future lay in store for them. Lives he would one day lose control over; lives he would never share as they grew beyond his influence and guidance.

"I will need you always," Kavan murmured, wanting to assure Kóráhm that he would never grow beyond those needs. Kóráhm was not his father; he was a teacher, a friend, and so much more. Without him, Kavan did not believe he would be alive today.

"I will be here," Kóráhm promised, kissing Kavan's forehead. "Never fear my love and admiration, Kavan. You have proven yourself a better man than I have ever been."

"I doubt that."

Different in some ways. The same in others. But never better.

❧Chapter 10❧

Duty to Níkóá and the Lachlan Crown had sent Kavan as an emissary, often with Asta, to the Valdis Court in the Cordash Crown city of Aralt many times before. Sometimes it had been to negotiate trade agreements and aid as the Yellow Sisters' threat began to wane in both Sovereignties. Sometimes it had been to deliver gifts on special occasions or to inquire about border issues or the punishment of criminals wanted in both lands. Sometimes the visits had been solely for familial sharing between mother, daughter, and brother. As mother to Queen Rika, Asta had been the ideal negotiator, and the mythology surrounding the White Bard made him welcome in places where others might not be. Today, Kavan sat in the stateroom alone, admiring the carved table of mahogany and marble, the matching chairs and cabinets, the lace and velvet curtains, the gilded handles, and brightly colored paintings, all of which spoke of an opulence unmatched by most places throughout the Sovereignties. Only the Kyne's home outdid Cordash in its splendor, but being many centuries older and inhabited by a race that excelled in the arts, that difference was to be expected.

There had been a flurry of activity in the mid-morning courtyard upon Kavan's arrival, visible from the pale blue glass window in the corridor directly outside of the oratory that housed the palace's only Gate, a rider shouting a panicked need to speak to the king as servants rushed to catch the head of the stumbling, frothing horse. Another servant brought Kavan to the stateroom, and Kavan assumed he would need to wait some time as King Govert dealt with whatever matter had created such a commotion. He listened to the distant rise and fall of animated voices until the stateroom doors burst open and Govert, Rika, the dusty, sweaty messenger, and a handful of advisors and men in armor clamored into the room.

"Lord Cliáth," Govert said, his voice stern and demanding but not accusatory. "Tell me you know something about this? Tell me this is why you are here." He dropped into his high-backed throne-like chair at the end of the table with a heavy expulsion of breath as others likewise took seats around the table. Govert gestured to the empty chair to his left while Rika took the one to his right.

Lit by the eternal glow of gold-plated lamps that burned every hour of every day, the opulence of the Cordashian royal hall sparkled and glowed, prompting King Govert the Second to rub his bleary eyes as he sat, with his Lord Servant, who had been at his side since he was ten years old, taking his usual position behind the king's chair.

Kavan cocked his head. "My Lord?"

Govert waved to the envoi. "Tell him. Tell him what you told me."

Stammering around the cup of water he had finally been supplied, gulping it as if he had not drunk in hours, the messenger took his cap off with one hand and replied, "Troops on the border, my lord…inland from the sea…hundreds of them…"

"Neth?" asked Kavan with a frown as a cold prickle chased up and down his spine. Neth had suffered from the plague as everyone else had. It seemed unlikely they would throw hundreds of soldiers at the Cordashian border…particularly if Enesfel was their target.

The man shook his head. "Not de Corrmick's armor. Never seen anything like them. Style's all wrong. They're moving through Neth but people on the border…they say there'll be war…"

"Most likely the sea invaders." Again, Kavan cocked his head as he looked at Govert. "Galleys from west of the Togrish. A couple dozen I'm told. Maybe more. They sank one of my ships near Matina but didn't dock…they went on toward Neth. We don't know who they are…there were no flags…don't know what they want since they didn't come ashore…but if they're scattering across Neth…"

Galleys might mean hundreds of men. Kavan tensed to suppress the shudder that ran up his back.

"Maybe they're conquering Neth?" offered one of the advisors.

"Or they're allies," another suggested.

"Is this what you told my mother and me about?" Rika asked quietly, in a more level-headed voice amidst the animated volume of the men. "Does this have to do with Kjell and…?"

Though Kavan shook his head no, he shrugged one shoulder and sighed. "Not directly…but it will. The war I foresaw is here." He imagined Neth would use a mercenary army to regain the lost territory south of Lake

Curo and that a clash over the throne of Glevum would ensue, but none of those were the causes of Bhás' war. They were the by-products of it.

The time of this invading army's arrival with the movement of Earé's troops was not coincidental. Enesfel was not yet ready but the threat was already here.

"Only way they'll get the south back," Govert grunted with his arms crossed over his chest, "is to get outside help…but where in the bowels of the Togrish did they come from? Who are they? What do they want? Why are they lining my borders?"

That question he could answer for himself. Foreign troops on Cordash's border either intended invasion or were situated to prevent Cordashian troops from crossing and coming to Enesfel's aid.

A man near the other end of the table, a man with a droopy, convex nose, sharp brown eyes, and curving lips that made him appear amused even when he was serious and stern, tapped a finger on the table as though to attract attention before speaking. "Do those questions matter, Your Majesty? We need to rally the force, reinforce the outposts before…"

"We don't know if it's war they want, General," countered a shrill-voiced, hawk-nosed, fleshy fellow on the other side of the table.

"Maybe we can negotiate with them, stay out of their affairs if they leave us…"

"And abandon our alliances?" the general countered bitterly.

"Protect our own…"

Govert stared at Kavan as his advisors argued, as if expecting him to weigh in with his opinions or speak on Enesfel's behalf. The king's gaze gradually lifted the swirl of choking fear brought on by the possibility that Earé's aid would arrive too late, until at last, Kavan managed to nod and find his voice.

"I do not think this foe can be negotiated with, My King." His gaze turned briefly to Rika. "I received warning of this; I have spoken to King Gamal and Prime Magistrate Piran who are uniting to face this threat. The militia in Neth may not act yet, but when they do, it will be swift and formidable. When I leave here, it is to seek the support of Clarys as well."

"Elyriá will never…" someone snorted.

"To fail to act is to risk the downfall of the Sovereignties. I have Seen it…" Kavan started again.

"If you have Seen it…can you prevent it? Is there something you can do to subvert this threat?"

Another shiver, stronger and thus more noticeable to those around him, made Kavan want to close his eyes and rub the bridge of his nose to block out the shadow images that raced behind them. Not the Sight, but memories of past visions that replayed without prompting.

Rika covered her husband's hand and shook her head to the advisor who asked for the bard's intervention as if to say 'Lord Cliáth is only one man,' as Kavan replied, "I assure you, my lord, I am doing everything in my power to end or prevent this…or to prepare us if I fail. I do not want anyone to suffer needlessly due to inaction if I cannot find a solution."

Though Govert grunted and gently withdrew his hand from Rika's as he leaned back, he did not sound angry. To Kavan, he sounded concerned and resolved. "General Tablyn, ready the force. Shore the borders, the forts, and outposts. Send additional resources to Ruidoso before our access is cut off…send men as well if we can spare them. Conscript what you can. Lord Ingott, call the council to meet on the hour. Lord Cliáth, we bid you stay…share dinner with us…speak to my councilors, and take back what we decide to King Lorant. He will fight with us on this? He will not leave Cordash to shoulder Neth's violence alone?"

Kavan nodded. "Enesfel will not break her alliance with Cordash, I swear." Govert would not likely ride into battle, any more than Kavan expected Gamal, Piran, or Kyne Phílóá would. If he had any influence on Lorant, the young king barely a man and barely a king, would not see battle either. But a significant number of men on all sides would. "I will await your decisions and take it to him."

"And you will play for us," Rika asked hopefully. "It will soothe the nerves of many."

"I will sing, yes," Kavan agreed.

Music might soothe his nerves as well.

❧*❧

To further appease his plans and meet his father's demands, Olaric went to the castle every day since that first summit between them, following the older man, attending conferences with advisors, listening as the imposter-sovereign spoke of his lofty, hard-fisted tactics and dreams for Neth and how he intended to reach them. Today they were inspecting the gathering of fresh-faced young men in the courtyard, men barely old enough to wield the weapons they were provided when General Waller was ushered into the barracks they would call home during their three weeks of rigorous training. It was a practice once implemented by the de Corrmick kings of olde, forcibly training men with a brutality that guaranteed obedience out of fear before sending them off to serve whichever city, town, village, or fortress it was deemed important to staff.

In a land where the common person was not permitted to wield a weapon and could be put to death for using a working tool as one, the addition of trained forces to monitor them meant ongoing suppression.

It also provided many of those men training they would not otherwise be allowed.

King Kjell had abandoned those things, seeking loyalty instead of fear, freedom instead of tyranny. There had not been time, in the chaotic months of Inness' reign, for her to resume the old customs.

Olaric was unsurprised that his father, a man who first served beneath Kjell's father, had chosen to reinstate the old, familiar customs…customs that cemented his hold on the throne as it left no one to stand up to him.

Watching the struggles, the suffering, on several of the young men's faces, their stoic weariness, and their fight to stay on their feet instead of collapse in pain and exhaustion, this sort of cruelty was not a custom Olaric was interested in continuing. The military needed training, but this was not the best way to manage men. If he was forced into his father's place, it would be the first custom he abolished.

"My Liege…a word."

The messenger who arrived at a gallop had the good sense to dismount near the gate, to straighten his clothes and hair, and to wipe the sweat from his brow before striding around the fringes of the practicing troops to stop in front of the king. He did not speak until Fraen nodded to acknowledge his presence and then he bowed, pushed his unruly greying brown hair out of his face, and said, "There are ships in Pravek…foreign ships from the west…not from Cordash. Galleys with hundreds of men come ashore to camp. Duke Haaral tried to repel them but the woman who leads them…she gave him this. She said you know her…that she has permission to…"

Frowning, Fraen cut the emissary off as he took the offered scroll with a noticeably trembling hand. He recognized Haaral's unbroken seal but did not open it to learn what the duke had written.

"Tall? Black hair? Strange accent? Peculiar attire?"

"Aye, My Liege. I did not speak with her, but I heard her…and saw her disembark and speak to Lord Haaral." The messenger's gaze shifted back and forth anxiously between father and son. "You know her, My Liege? Is it true they are here on your behalf?"

Ignoring the questions, Fraen asked, "How many men did you say?" Though his sharp tone spoke of interest, his gaze returned to the training men as his brow furrowed.

"Hundreds. I did not count them, My Liege, for some ships sailed east; they were still disembarking when the duke sent..."

Fraen whistled. General Waller, in turn, whistled to the men on the field, permitting them to cease their efforts and lean on their weapons or bend forward with hands on their knees to catch their breath as Waller approached the king. About halfway there, Waller changed his mind about allowing a protracted rest, turned around, and barked an order that started the group running at a struggling pace in a circle around the ground.

Satisfied, he pulled off his helmet before he reached the king and ran a hand over his brush-cut scalp. Olaric remembered him as a handsome, if dour-faced, young officer when he, like Olaric and Captain Sparding, were recruited. Now Emil Waller's dourness was enhanced by his narrow face, chiseled with maturity and physical labor, and the short trimmed black mustache and patch of hair beneath his lower lip.

Fraen's molding had shaped him into a pointed weapon to carry out his will without question.

Olaric wished he had reached the man sooner as he had reached Earon Sparding.

"Bring me a horse," Fraen grunted. It was an order he could have given anyone, an order wasting Waller's talents, but if the command insulted him, the general did not show it. "We need more," the king continued, gesturing at the running men. "She's here."

"How many?" asked Waller with a growing feral grin and a nod. He did not ask who the 'she' was. Noting the peculiar nervousness in his father's voice, Olaric presumed Waller already knew.

"All of them."

Assuming his father meant every man in Neth capable of fighting, Olaric huffed. "You can't strip Neth of all men. We will starve!" Fraen would not care about the rest of the population but he did care about feeding his gluttony.

Waller had already bowed and marched toward the stables leaving the trainees to continue running, forced into compliance by the king's lingering presence on the sidelines.

"They will have all the food they need when the south is ours..."

"And us? Shall we starve in the meantime?"

Fraen's frown deepened, but he said, "There's wives and children and the elders, are there not?" He cleared his throat, visibly rethinking his order but not yet ready to repeal it. "You will remain in Glevum and oversee…"

"I am not king…"

"You are my son," Fraen barked, frustrated at being argued with.

"You go to meet her? These foreign troops? Who is she? Who are…?"

"I am going to make sure it is as…"

"You don't trust her?"

Choosing not to show how accurate his son's assessment was, he huffed and turned toward the castle, determined to be away before the hour drew late. "I don't trust Haaral," he muttered.

The woman had kept her word before. She had made him king, giving him the power she had promised. Now, if the dismissed messenger's report was true, she had brought him the army he needed to grind Enesfel to dust and reclaim what had been stolen.

But that did not mean he trusted her.

Olaric's fists clenched but he refused to watch his father walk away from him as though he was not there. From the palace doorway where Fraen issued sharp commands to the pair of guards stationed there as he passed, one hurried into the castle ahead of the king while the other waited until both were out of sight and replacements were in place at the door before he left his post and came to Olaric.

"You'll be in charge then?" murmured Sparding. "Is it time to…?"

"Could choose not to be…but no…not yet. He needed to know his father's plan, and he did not yet have the backing to successfully overthrow his father without killing him and taking the throne.

He wanted an heir in play before he considered any drastic action.

Refusing to take the reins of control, however briefly, was not in Neth's best interest. It was a test, a part he must play if he was going to win his father's trust. Voice low so he would not be heard over the moans and grunts of the men who continued to run past, Olaric muttered, "He is meeting a mercenary army in Pravek…an army big enough, they seem to be a threat to Enesfel. Tell Geiel or one of the others; Rhidam needs to know."

Sparding nodded.

If a rightful de Corrmick king was to have any hope of reclaiming the throne, now was the time to prepare and act.

❧*❧

Govert's conclave with advisors and generals had carried on through dinner and stretched late into the night before Cordash's king was satisfied with the barebones plan they had devised. It had been centuries since Cordash had instigated war, and Govert had no intention of being the first monarch to break that cycle. He would, however, reinforce the troops stationed along the Cordash-Neth border with as many men as he could recruit, as well as shore up every coastal town and fortification in case further ships sailed through the Togrish and decided to invade Cordash's soil. Aralt, deep in the heart of the kingdom, should be safe, but only if the borders remained so. Only if Enesfel did her part.

Cordash would send men to aid her ally too, should they make it as far as Fiara and Ruidoso. Lorant would need more men than she could raise alone. If Neth had mercenaries on her side, an army of unimaginable size would be needed to defeat them.

Govert would wait for Enesfel and follow Lorant's lead. If the choice was made to squeeze the foreigners out, that was what Cordash would do. Otherwise, they would protect their borders, harass any enemy troops stationed there, and prepare Ruidoso for war.

Ruidoso was key to retaking the southern lands. Continually hit by Glevum's fist whenever Fraen scraped up the manpower to risk doing so, her people would again become the victims if, as General Tablyn expected, the reclamation of the south was Fraen's goal.

Fraen's goals were not the cause of Kavan's fears.

It was the causes of the woman who must be, based on the army's presence, Earé's words, and the snippets of Sight that blinked on and off within Kavan's mind as he tried to sleep, that worried him.

"You should be sleeping"

Phílóá's teasing tone prompted an involuntary grin despite the heaviness of Kavan's preoccupied thoughts. Having escaped Cordash too late to meet with the Kyne in Clarys, Kavan had, instead, accepted the room her staff escorted him to where he could rest until morning. Too restless to sleep, however, he found his way to the highest point of the Kyne's palatial home, the bell tower with its ever-burning flame, and stared across the rooftops of Clarys toward the sea.

Clarys was the largest city in the Sovereignty, its streets and districts spreading from the sea cliffs to the shores of Lake Eladhán. From where Kavan stood beneath the moonless sky, he could see over the whole of it. The tower had seemed a good place to be alone, even if being here brought with it an overlay of burning rooftops and shouting in the streets.

"So should you."

Phílóá shrugged and leaned her arms against the white marble barrier that prevented anyone daring enough to come here from falling. "Once I learned you were here…"

"They should have waited to tell you until morning…it can wait."

"If it could wait, you would not have come at this hour. I presume it is no casual message? That you did not come seeking company?"

If either were true, he would have come at a more diplomatic hour.

"From your silence, your pensive brow, I assume it is important."

A shooting star streaked across their field of vision, a momentary blur of light that seemed to burn into the blackness before it reached the horizon. Taking that as an omen whether it was one or not, hearing the prompting of Raebhá's voice in every celestial event he had witnessed since the sky ribbons in Dhóbhaen and the tailed star that had heralded King Merrek and Wace Elotti's deaths, Kavan spoke without moving or looking at her.

"My daughter's army, Enesfel's reinforcements, are approaching from the south, traveling through Hatu bound for Rhidam. Likewise, another army has sailed into Neth to bolster King Fraen's numbers. They are amassing at Cordash's borders as we speak and King Govert is sending an emissary to Glevum in the hopes of buying time. I fear for that man's life."

"Fraen does not seem the sort to negotiate," Phílóá agreed.

"Particularly if his heart is set on war. We know he has been preparing, that he intends to retake the south, I believe this is bigger. The Sight confirms war, no matter what we wish." He paused before adding, "I See fire in Clarys, from your halls to the sea…I hear screaming…"

Phílóá shuddered. How terrible it must be to experience such things. "This…will be?" she whispered. "Or might be…?"

"Or might be, if precautions are not in place. The Sight is most often what will be, but sometimes…" He shrugged. "Events do not always unfold as I See them, but they do unfold."

"I do not doubt you, aindhá." The Sight ran in the Kyne's family too, although instances of it were rare. Phílóá, like her grandmother before her, did not possess it. She had faith in Kavan's reputation, however, and was unwilling to risk Elyriá by ignoring his warnings. "There is nothing to be done tonight. In the morning, I shall call the advisors and I will discuss with them what you have revealed to me while you share this news with Ylár and the gdhededhá. They will confer, as we will, and then we will jointly come together. I hope you will stay, to sway the doubters and relieve our tensions with music when they get too high."

Doubting he could sway those who did not want to be swayed, particularly many of the gdhededhá serving beneath Ylár, Kavan nodded his agreement. "I wish to return to Lorant with a promise of alliance and action as I have received from Hatu, Káliel, and Cordash. If music is the price to pay for it, I shall gladly pay it."

"Then come and rest. Tomorrow promises to be a long day."

~•*∾

Fraen's three-day forced ride through the northern duchies with the small contingent of soldiers brought from Glevum took him to an empty stretch of fields outside of Pravek strewn with the remnants of fire pits, discarded food waste, and trampled earth, evidence of a large group of people having camped there long enough to destroy any infant crops that might have grown. There were the reported galleys in the harbor, a number he did not bother to count as he marched through the early evening streets in search of Duke Haaral who was not in his home when Fraen had arrived there. By the time he found the duke and a gaggle of others arguing about what was to be done with the galleys as their presence at the docks prevented fishing and merchant boats from mooring, Fraen already knew the obvious truth.

Bhás and her soldiers were no longer in Pravek. That damned arrogant woman had sent the rest of her fleet around the horn towards Glevum and deployed foot shoulders south and west to fortify the Cordashian border against the strongest of the Sovereignties. No one could tell Fraen if she had gone with the army or sailed with the fleet. A wise course, perhaps, but the fact that she had neither asked for permission or guidance before crossing his land and had taken it upon herself to deploy her mercenaries throughout his territory without permission or instruction angered him enough that he had been tempted to push Haaral off the dock into the sea out of spite.

Instead, he tromped and stomped through the first galley, seeking clues about who these mercenaries were and whether they could be relied upon and trusted to serve him as she had promised. The long galleys, water-tight and sturdy, were stripped clean of food and valuables, leaving only the oars, sails, and a collection of fishing nets behind. The canvas sails were of an unfamiliar weave and texture and the nets were sewn of a material he was unfamiliar with, like no rope he had ever seen. The wood beneath his feet, the hull, and the solid heavy oars that would require three men each to row with, while polished smooth from construction and use, appeared to be from a stock normally knotted and gnarled, as though the source had thrived in a place where the wind and sea took a heavy toll.

He knew of no such place in Neth. He did not believe there was such a place in Cordash. He had no other answers.

Unwilling to permit Bhás free reign without someone trusted to monitor her, he divided the soldiers he brought and those from Pravek he pressed into service to follow the soldiers who had left Pravek three days prior and join them, with instructions to report every detail, every order, to him immediately. He ordered the galleys to be anchored off-shore so the docks were clear, and then rode back to Glevum with three men…without taking the opportunity of hospitality Haaral offered.

He did not care if the duke was offended. Fraen expected he knew where Bhás would go next and he intended to be there ahead of her. He would have an explanation for her decisions, even if he had to beat it out of the woman who was, technically, his ally.

⁊Chapter 11⁊

The visit with his family, his aunt, his cousins, his nephew and his wife, had been as awkward as ever, less so than before his excommunication, less so every time he returned to Bhryell, but he doubted they would ever sit as anything more than distant, barely known family with whom he shared only blood in common. Dháná offered a mid-morning meal with the air of one trying to make up for a lifetime of failures, but Kavan, instead, drifted into the workshop where Sámel, Aleski, Llucás and his wife Whíllá were stringing a newly minted full-scale harp while Sámel's sons, age fifteen and six, polished another full-scale harp brought in for repair and a smaller half-scale harp that had been recently carved. Kavan remained long enough to test his skill on both completed harps, satisfying Sámel with both instruments' conditions. With the two men he most wanted to see away until evening on business, Kavan left them when they left the shop for the house and the lunch that awaited them and stood in the pine-perfumed street listening to the sound of the náós' clanging bell.

The students, too would be adjourned for their meals. Bhryell's bhydáni and gdhededhá would be likewise occupied. They and the lómesté needed to be informed of the decisions Clarys had made. But this was not the time. He stared at the peaceful, familiar streets, nodding at those who bid him a pleasant day, searching his soul for the source of the melancholy knot in his stomach. He followed the pull, allowing it to direct him, and by the time his feet stopped moving, he knew where he needed to be.

The familiar woodland path was overrun with spring growth, proving that few came this way now that he was no longer in Bhryell often enough to make the pilgrimage. Bhen sometimes…Sóbhán others…sometimes the two men together…the lingering traces of their power having left puffs and sparks on the trees they had touched. It seemed both must have climbed this trail together after the winter thaw, seeking the tiny spring the Llaethlágárá birthed here and sent tumbling away toward the narrow river that passed on Bhryell's northeast side.

Birds twittered and hopped from branch to branch overhead, engaged in an eternal battle for seeds and berries with the squirrels that chattered at them from somewhere hidden by needles and new summer leaves. A covey of quail erupted from the brush and scurried across the trail, startled by his footsteps, disrupting a hare in the thicket on the other side. It was tempting to join them, to shed himself in favor of the White Hart form he had not enjoyed in far too long. But today, he wanted to see the path with his eyes, wanted to find the place where the water erupted from the ground, the place where Tíbhyan had sat beside him for the last time. When he found the wide trunk that had supported them as he spoke to his mentor of the Dhóbhaen, of everything he had learned and become, he leaned forward, both hands splayed on the bark, hung his head between his arms so that his hair fell around his face and said to the air, to the animals, to the energy around him and anyone else who might hear him, *'áti ibh krá,'* with an outpouring of every bit of power he could muster.

The marriage mark on his hand flashed hot. He flexed his fingers and closed his eyes to absorb whatever came next.

'áti ibh krá.'

There were no words. There was the echo of a voice that might have been Raebhá's or might have been Tíbhyan's. It was only the overwhelming reassurance that Kavan was not alone, that both were with him in an intangible, powerful way that made his knees buckle so that he sank against the tree with a soft gasp.

There was no clear vision of what path lay ahead of him, only a growing gnawing of dread, a vision of light threads that he felt vital to capture and knot together while there was time, before the shadows reached him and pulled each of those threads away.

He wanted someone, anyone, to take these feelings from him. Tíbhyan. Kóráhm. Wortham. Raebhá. Anyone. But no one could. No one came. He was alone except for the sensation of a hand on his cheek and another, smaller one, wrapped in his.

He squeezed his hand. The small one squeezed back.

He did not understand it. He did not want to understand it.

But he had to. To do anything else, he was sure, was to condemn those he loved to ruin.

꜈*꜏

Olaric watched the lead galley maneuver into port as the sun sank over the city rooftops behind him, sleek and quick, while others like her waited beyond the breakwater on the day's surprisingly placid sea. Kes' hand in his trembled, belying the calm of the water's gentle slap against the dock as the ship came to a stop and another woman, tall and dark-haired debarked with a scrawny young man following behind. Though dressed in plain trousers, an embroidered knee-length tunic slit to the hip on both sides, and a thick cloak adorned with the spray created by the ship's slippage through the surf, the stranger walked with the sort of regal confidence or arrogance indicative of her importance. Or self-importance, he mused as he met her halfway down the dock, keeping his nervous wife protectively at his side.

Kes should not be here.

It was too late to reverse that decision now.

The collection of royal guards and armed townsfolk with him awaited his command.

If the other ships came to ground, those de Corrmick guards would never be enough to hold them off.

"We do not want your warships here. Glevum has nothing for you." If the fleet intended war, he doubted this woman would have come ashore peacefully. The ships would have attacked, and Glevum would be sacked and burned. The appearance of peace and generosity might be an act meant to lure them into lowering their guard. "Go back where you come from."

The stranger's haughty, smirking gaze meandered past him across the soldiers waiting at the other end of the dock as though he was inconsequential. Without looking at him, she gestured to the youth behind her and said, "I have the right of passage," as the malnourished fellow offered something with a trembling hand.

Kes' expression softened at his meek, beaten expression, unsure if he trembled from the cold water, an illness, or fear of the woman he followed. She reflexively reached to take the leather tube he offered, hesitated when the dark-haired woman glowered at her with disdain as if to warn her away, but then took the tube despite the warning. The stranger scowled and looked about to retort, but when Olaric accepted the tube from Kes and glowered at the stranger in warning, her expression fell flat and emotionless.

"The king is not here," Olaric eventually said after scouring the document's contents. So, this was the one who had left ships in Pravek. This was the mysterious source of aid Fraen had spoken of that was meant to arrive when the time for war came. The writing appeared to be his father's, the de Corrmick seal unmistakable, but he was not convinced this was real.

"He does not need to be…"

"Glevum is not equipped to accommodate…"

"We will not be here long, I assure you. It is foretold. If you are to regain what was lost, you will permit my men…"

"Foretold? What was lost?" He scoffed and cleared his throat. Her words, her square-shouldered bearing, and the confidence with which she spoke of prophecy made him purse his lips and narrow his eyes. He was Vants. He knew prophecy. His world was built on it. But he had never come upon a prophecy that implied what this woman did.

If restoring what was lost meant the return of King Kjell or another de Corrmick to the throne, a possibility his father would never imagine, giving in to her demand until his father returned might be worth the risk.

He suspected, however, that restoring the de Corrmicks was not what she had in mind. She likely referred to the return of the southern lands his father had 'won' back to the Neth Crown, and if Olaric sent away the aid Fraen had enlisted, he would lose whatever leverage he was beginning to gain with his father.

Allowing the strangers to come ashore and wait for the elder Fraen to deal with them was better than risking an assault on Glevum by the fleet of galleys beyond the breakwater. Wherever Fraen had stationed all the men he had trained, they were not near enough to protect Glevum from this.

"You will take your men beyond the southwest edge of the city; I will have someone guide you there. You will stay there, you will not trouble anyone in Glevum, nor damage or destroy anyone's property. Once he returns, you will go if he says go. Any fighting, any theft, any trouble, anything at all…there will be consequences."

The corners of the woman's mouth twisted in a way that caused a barely concealed shudder to run up Olaric's spine. A single-handed gesture sent the youth behind her scurrying back to the ship while she sauntered past Olaric and waited at the end of the dock beyond the reach of the multitude of weapons the waiting soldiers carried. One by one, men from the docked galley began to disembark, carrying sacks and crates and bundles until everything the ship held was removed. Other ships began to round the breakwater in search of a berth, while others remained where they were.

Olaric did not move. He elected to remain where he was and count every single man who disembarked for as long as it took to do so, but he did bend low to Kes' ear and murmured, "Tell Marta to watch them…and that we need a messenger south."

If these men were a threat to Enesfel, Rhidam needed to know. Kjell needed to know.

If they were a threat to Glevum and Neth, he needed to know that too.

❧*❦

Neck and shoulders stiff from the unanticipated sleeping position, Kavan eased to his feet and stretched, trying to judge the hour by the sun's position behind the branches overhead. It appeared as if little time had passed, but the rumble in his stomach and the collection of dew on his clothes spoke of the passage of a day and night spent in this place. The echo of unspoken voices still resounded within, offering warmth and reassurance that he had not felt the day before, proving that coming to commune with Tíbhyan's memory had been a wise decision, even if he had stayed longer than intended.

By now, the lómesté would be convening for daily business and Bhílári would be overseeing the start of the day's schooling. Dháná would either be beside herself with concern for his absence or else would have taken his failure to attend dinner as proof that he had not intended to join the family or had been called away to something more pressing. That error would have to be rectified once the new day's business was addressed.

Deciding that four legs would bring him more swiftly to the forest's thin edge than two would, he gave in to the previous day's longing and allowed the hart's hooves to carry him over creeks and shrubs, through tangled brambles and thick brush, a sensation almost like flight as the nimble animal's feet barely touched the ground. Too soon he reached the end of the forest, an outcropping on the edge of Bhryell's burial ground. He glanced across the markers, locating from that distance those that belonged to Tám and others he had known, the final resting places of those he had attended as a boy, reminders that, for all their years, for all their gifts that set Elyri apart from Teren, they were still mortal beings.

That acknowledgment was set aside with the resumption of his natural form so that he could climb down from the overlook, cross the graveyard, and approach the naós without attracting unwanted attention. dedhá Mádhu, who served with Bhílári, sat at one of the wooden tables on the side of the building surrounded by Bhryell's children there learning to read and write and practice basic Elyri skills from bhydáni Aendrás seated with him. Both men, colleagues of Tíbhyan's though many decades younger, nodded at Kavan. The children chirped their greetings and waved until he retreated through the side door into the quiet Gathering Hall that had been the first place where the public had witnessed his blossoming power.

How had that been nearly one hundred years ago?

"Dháná told me you are here." Bhílári joined him at the altar, the dedhá's age beginning to show in the slowing of his movements though his face bore little hint of it beyond the creases around his mouth and eyes. Kavan had never asked his age and had always had the impression that Bhílári had been here before his birth and would be here long after he was gone. He was as much a fixture in Bhryell as Tíbhyan had been.

Now, however, Tíbhyan was gone.

Kavan looked away from the figure of Dhágdhuán on the wall above the altar, grateful there had never been bloodshed here as there had been in the oratory in the Rhidam keep, and met the man's welcoming smile. "I have been to Clarys and then…" he shrugged, "the night escaped me."

Without asking what he meant, familiar with Kavan's idiosyncrasies and unpredictable nature, Bhílári nodded. "Is there news from Clarys?"

Kavan nodded but at first said nothing. The people of Bhryell had grown more tolerant and accepting of his differences, but the Sight remained something most Elyri, like most Teren, found difficult to accept or believe. "I need to meet with you, the bhydáni, and the lómesté if it can be arranged."

His warm expression turning serious, Bhílári nodded and ushered Kavan down the center aisle to the main náós doors at the back of the room. "We can go now if you wish. Madhu and Aendrás can manage the children. What is so pressing that requires…?"

Falling into step beside him, feeling none of the awe he had once felt for men of Faith with more experience, Kavan whispered, "War."

Bhílári swallowed hard.

There had been rumors of war for a decade or more, the quiet recruitment by officials in Clarys of men willing to take up a duty that had never been held in Elyriá's history.

Now, it seemed, the time had come.

The dedhá swallowed hard again and walked without talking. There was nothing he could ask that would not be answered in time.

Kavan was grateful for his silence.

Bhryell's lómesté took the news of impending war better than Kavan expected, although few could agree about how to address the Kyne's demands and k'gdhededhá Ylár's plea for men and women to defend Elyriá against potential invasion. Just as the leadership in Clarys continued to disagree on how to expand their growing militia, the leaders of Bhryell would debate the best course of action, as would every other town and village in Elyriá, until they were forced to act.

For people who lived hundreds of years, the art of debate and philosophy was something they excelled at. They were rarely confronted with a need for expedient action.

But armies were marching from the south and west, rising in Neth, allowing no time for dalliance. Decisions had to be made, a process not up to Kavan to conduct. He could only share the High Mother's direction, the k'gdhededhá's instruction, and confide what the Sight had shared.

He could not make their decisions for them.

Weary of political and theological debates that he could influence no more than he had without manipulating the thoughts of those engaged in them, Kavan left the lómesté hall where he had first met Tíbhyan and started across town to share dinner with Dháná as promised. By the time he reached the town square fountain, now dedicated in his honor, where it had once been dedicated to other Cliáthan ancestors, he paused, distracted by lights and voices coming from the house to the right, and smiled.

His house, but now the home of his son. But they were Bhen and Dháná's voices he heard, and so he turned from the monument that would one day, he was sure, be replaced to honor someone else, and climbed the stairs to the door.

Hand on the railing. Lorant's hand. Arlan's hand. Memories tangled with snippets of Sight washed over him until they swept him off his feet to drop him at the door. He rolled to sitting just as hurried steps prompted the throwing open of the door and elicited Bhen's exclamation of surprise as he helped Kavan to his feet.

"k'aendhá, are you alright?" he cried. His shout brought others from inside hurrying to join him at the door.

"I am. It was…" Nothing would be a lie, but because he could not explain the tangle of images and sounds, memory, and Sight that had assaulted him, and embarrassed by the fuss his fall created, Kavan shrugged and asked, "Was your trip successful?"

Steadying his father from the other side, Sóbhán maneuvered him to the fireside chair kept vacant for his use whenever he came to visit, and helped him into it, despite Kavan's effort to walk there on his own. The fall had not injured or disabled him, only left him disoriented, but Sóbhán would not take that risk. What little errant healing power Sóbhán possessed flowed out of him to erase the minor aches each fresh bruise generated. Maelís promptly climbed onto Kavan's lap.

"The naós in Bhástyán now has two new Cliáthans to replace those lost in their fire. There were complaints that it took too long," grinned Bhen, "but they praised the quality and timbre to Ethenae as soon as they were heard in the new Gathering Hall.

"I think they're pleased," Sóbhán agreed with a chuckle.

"And your girls are happy to have you home," Bhen teased.

"Yours will be too."

Bhen shook his head with a smile. "Maybe, but she's not due back from Clarys until the day after tomorrow…with a cart of fabric and more orders for gowns than she will be able to easily fill."

"Don't expect me to be her apprentice…and the girls are too young," Chethá said as she accepted the empty fruit basket from Dháná and placed it on the unlit hearth. "Kavan, you must join Sóbhán and me for dinner…"

"Yes, eat with us," Maelís begged, sliding down and tugging on Kavan's hand to pull him from the chair.

Kavan looked at Dháná, reluctant to disappoint her a second time, wondering if she was here to join them. She shook her head, however, and said, "Sámel and the others are expecting me."

Making his decision easier, Bhen thrust a plate of food into Kavan's hands and began, "You met with the lómesté. Is there news?"

Dháná reluctantly kissed Kavan's cheek, kissed Maelís' forehead, and saw herself out. Upstairs, Ydrís began to cry.

"Not a topic for children," Kavan murmured as Sóbhán disappeared up the stairs to rescue his youngest daughter from her failed attempt to sleep.

Kaven expected Bhen's earlier cry had awakened her.

It was a pleasant change to spend a quiet, intimate evening with family though he regretted that Ágdhállán and Dhóri were not there and that he had been away from his youngest son for too long without an explanation. The boy was under Rhyrdan's protection and had many to care for and watch over him, and Kavan believed the boy with the Sight would understand. Yet he also knew that understanding did not negate the absence of a parent and Kavan promised himself that, after Maelís and Ydrís were settled down to sleep, he would make it up to Ágdhállán as soon as he could.

Again on the porch where he had once stood with Arlan, watching the starlight and listening to the twilight sounds from the homes around them, Kavan waited until Chethá closed the door and the four of them were alone together. He could have slept here tonight, but thoughts of Ágdhállán made him long for home. He would walk Bhen to his home, reassure himself that the house that had been Tíbhyan's was secure, and then return to Rhidam.

There was much to do.

"There are mercenaries in Neth," he began, "who have attacked a Cordashian ship. They are gathering on Cordash's borders. Earé's army is crossing Hatu for Enesfel, and Gamal and Piran are preparing their fleets. Kyne has decreed raising an army, and k'gdhededhá Ylár and his council support her…albeit reluctantly for some. I have spoken to the bhydáni; by midsummer…possibly before…"

"There will be war." Sóbhán wrapped an arm around Chethá and pulled her to his side, understanding what war meant to an Elyri healer, particularly one whose father had begun his career as an army healer for a Lachlan king.

"Will it reach Bhryell?" she whispered.

"I do not know." He had not Seen it, but there were too many outcomes, too many paths and possibilities in the present or the future for him to be certain. Neither k'Ádhá or Kóráhm were providing answers. "There will be bloodshed in Elyriá…Clarys for certain…but elsewhere, I wish I knew."

"I should go with them," Sóbhán said.

Chethá shook her head in protest as Bhen added, "As should I."

Sóbhán scowled, momentarily ignoring Chethá's reaction. That would be a discussion to have in private. "You've never held a sword in your life," he challenged Bhen.

"I can learn."

Surprised that either would volunteer for war, that either would risk the shedding of blood, possibly their own, for this unavoidable cause, Kavan struggled to find an argument that would change their minds. All he could say was, "There is time still…and if the enemy does cross the Llaethlágárá, there will be need for men here to protect Bhryell. I will let you know if I learn more, so please…" he took both men's hands in his, "think carefully about your choice."

Elyriá might only survive if men and women sacrificed for the survival of the whole. Unconsciously, he had believed those sacrifices would be the sons, daughters, friends, and families of others. He had not considered that those sacrifices might be some of his own.

"We will," Sóbhán promised. He released Kavan's hand, as did Bhen, and Kavan started down the steps.

"Tell Mother and Father I must speak with them." It was unlikely Syl would go to war, but Chethá knew her father's proclivities. Whether she could convince him otherwise, if that was her intent, remained to be seen.

"I will."

Kavan and Bhen walked silently until they reached the fountain before hearing the closing of the door behind them. Kavan frowned at the discord he had sown but it could not be helped. He could not protect everyone, regardless of his desire to do so.

"Will you go to war?" Bhen asked, pausing when Kavan did and falling into step again when Kavan resumed walking.

"I do not believe I will go with the armies; that is not my place. Lorant does not need to concern himself with my welfare if it comes to battle..."

"You mean when it comes."

Kavan nodded.

"There is something you are not saying." Bhen could feel that something was wrong, that his uncle's demeanor was more reserved and pensive than he had seen in many years, but Kavan shook his head and refused to discuss whatever was troubling him.

"I cannot speak of things of which I am uncertain, but I do wish..."

The little home in which Kavan had spent so many hours as a child, a home once filled with tomes and scrolls and folders full of assorted parchment and paper sheets that had now been relocated to St. Kóráhm's and would soon be moved to Gorbesh, looked smaller, quiet without the bhydáni puttering about, dark without Nóráh seated at the hearth with her sewing supplies in hand.

"k'aendhá?"

Kavan let out a held breath behind clenched teeth and tore his gaze away from the door to look at Bhen instead. "I wish to bequeath this house to you and Nóráh." There was little room for the growth of a family, two bedrooms and a small detached structure in the rear that could be used as such, but for a young couple starting a family, it would be a good home. It would never serve as Kavan's home; so long as he had Alberni, he had home enough. Soon, he suspected, Gorbesh would be the place he called home, if the nature of this war unfolded in the way the Sight suggested it would. How many others, he wondered, would come with him?

Bhen laughed warmly, though the offering made the hair on the back of his neck stand on end. "This is already my home. I don't need to own it for that to be true. And Nóráh stands to gain her father's home when his time comes." Nóráh, one of two daughters, was the youngest, her father's favorite. Her much older sister had married and established a family in Bhryell decades before. She had a home of her own. As much as Bhen adored his uncle and the home Kavan provided, he had visions of a large family and a sprawling room in which Nóráh could create beautiful things with as many apprentices as she could collect. "You're not planning to leave us again, are you?" he asked, the forced teasing tone barely masking the silent alarms in the back of his head.

"For Gorbesh, eventually." Perhaps, one day, when the threat of Bhás was behind him, he would return to Dhóbhaen. That was a frantic desire but one he dared not wish for until his family was safe. He had spoken of Gorbesh before. The announcement was nothing new, but the prospect of war brought the possibility nearer.

"Perhaps we will go with you if Nóráh is willing. We would like to see it. She's quite taken by the thought of mountains in the desert, somewhere without snow and cold."

At the foot of the short stairs, Kavan stopped again. "When this is over, I shall take you both so you may see it for yourself." he promised, accepting Bhen's embrace. Despite the exchange, he was not dissuaded from deeding the house to Bhen.

Tonight, it was too late to consider or act upon his options.

Ágdhállán would be in bed.

Kavan desired nothing but to be there beside him, in a land of dreams far away from the prospect of war.

❧Chapter 12☙

Empty ships remained anchored beyond the breakwater, and Marta had brought him word of three dozen men remaining in the field beyond Glevum's border. But it was her other news, the dispersal of the remainder west and south that occurred during the night that troubled Olaric. The woman who led them had come every day to stand within sight of the keep, watching with an unnerving obsessed fixation, but she never asked for entry, never sought an audience. Now she was gone, taking her host with her, before Fraen returned. It was said that the ships, too, had sailed south, likely toward Gorea; Marta had the foresight to send word to her connections there so that the seaside city might be prepared. She also sent spies to follow the foot soldiers to see where they were going.

It would not be enough. If this was an invasion, Olaric had allowed it to happen without a fight. With the legitimacy of the writ in question, without knowing why these people were here beyond the woman's claim, Olaric felt his hands were tied.

His father would be angry about the dispersion of spies without order but he would not need to know about that.

He would be angry about the ships and soldiers. That was a truth Olaric could not hide.

No matter how he handled this, his father would be angry. The only choice was to prepare the Vants to act, set up protective contingencies for his family's welfare, and prepare them to get as far away from Glevum as possible if his father chose to retaliate as Inness had done.

As the Vants had done to Inness, if it came to it, they could do the same to his father.

❧*☙

"Two weeks, Kavan! Two weeks without a word!"

As seemed often to be the case when Kavan found Lorant and Jerit together, the two were positioned as far apart in the library as possible, Jerit at the window, his face dour and annoyed, studying a rolled parchment delivered by the soldier the bard had passed in the corridor, and Lorant at the desk with a map spread out before him, held down at the corners by the inkwell and books. The smell of breakfast permeated the room from the tray left on the small carved stand near another window by the bitter-faced Gerna whom Kavan had also passed. Ágdhállán, having not eaten breakfast yet, struggled in his father's arms to get down.

Some looked at Kavan askew when he carried his ten-year-old son this way. Ágdhállán seemed not to mind most of the time. After such an absence, the affectionate bonding was welcomed by both.

Kavan released him, regretting the loss of the shield against Lorant's annoyance. He straightened his tunic as the boy went to the abundant tray. "There were duties..."

"Dhóri said you left Gorbesh for Natrona. What business was there with my uncle that...?"

Kavan cut him off. "My daughter's army is crossing Hatu, coming to Enesfel. It was necessary to inform Gamal, Piran, Bhríd, the High Mother, and King Govert. A mercenary fleet has attacked Cordash and its army is setting station along her borders."

Jerit left the window and offered the scroll he held to Kavan before Lorant could speak. "We are aware of that fleet. How many ships? How many men?"

"They made it to Pravek, and Glevum, or so Asta's sources claim," added Lorant with a pout that reminded Kavan of Arlan when he felt betrayed by duties Kavan kept from him. His anger was, however, diverted by the prospect of war. "These armies...do they mean the war you have warned of...?"

Before Kavan could reply, Ágdhállán answered, "Soon. Yes."

The three men looked at each other as the unfazed boy continued to eat. Lorant smoothed his hand over the map as if tracing a path from south to north before murmuring, "How soon?"

Ágdhállán did not reply. Jerit leaned over Lorant's shoulder to study the map. "It will take several weeks for the lady's force to reach Kílyn, to sail the bay and reach Levonne...and days after that to arrive here."

"I know it does not seem soon enough, but I trust Earé's timing." Kavan was forced to do so despite his misgivings. "I do not know how many have infiltrated Neth, or where Fraen found them. I do not know who leads them. But I do believe Enesfel has time to…"

"Daema Magk and General Declan are making preparations based on our spies' reports," Jerit said. "There is no need for us to aid Glevum if this army is an invasion, but…"

"If this could be an opportunity to restore Kjell to the throne, it is worth preparing." Lorant glanced over his shoulder at Jerit, noting his frown but also his reluctant nod, before continuing, "It is worth being prepared. I did not think this would be the war you once spoke of but…" There was no denying now that it might be.

"Shall I summon the war council? The lords, Daema, and General Declan? My mother and father if they will come?" asked Jerit, his voice soft and strained.

Lorant snorted. "We would have known sooner if you had come straight to me with this news." He swallowed additional protests when Kavan bowed his head to accept the admonition. "But it is good our allies are aware of what is coming. Will they aid us?"

"With troops? Some will sail from Hatu if there are enough ships to carry them. Cordash is focusing on her borders and coast, and intends to shore up Ruidoso, but there may be soldiers forthcoming. Káliel and Elyriá will have fights of their own. If fortune is with us, the fleets of Hatu and Káliel will prevent ships from reaching Enesfel if they attempt to…"

The king sank against the back of his chair. "You think they will."

"I have Seen war at St. Kóráhm's gates. Unless an army forces its way south through Enesfel or Elyriá…"

"They won't."

"I pray you are right, My Liege, but even so, that will mean ships."

"We shall alert all cities where invaders can come ashore, and set patrols throughout the bay. Jerit, see to the summons and messages."

The red-haired prince bowed and murmured, "At once," before leaving the room and breakfast with quick, measured steps, comfortable in the role of aide to Lorant despite his noble birth.

"And you," Lorant said, side-eyeing the boy who had been the one to tell him that his father was away on important business without revealing the nature of that business, before focusing on Kavan, "Don't make this a habit. If there is war, I need you here."

"I must prepare Alberni. I am no military…"

"Perhaps not, but you are the wisest man I know. See to Alberni and return to me. The lords respect you. I'd prefer to have you close if we need to sway any of them to back the Crown."

"If they don't choose on the side of their security and Enesfel's protection," Kavan replied, "nothing will change their minds."

Ágdhállán set down the glass he had just emptied and murmured, "They'd be foolish not to side with the king."

Both Lorant and Kavan believed that to be true.

Hearing his son speak so calmly about war made Kavan feel no better about the path ahead.

It was a rare morning waking up together with the rays of dawn in their eyes, a rare night shared in Kjell's small room after an evening's discussion about what Geiel's news meant to Glevum and the future of Neth. Mercenaries recruited on Fraen's order presented a new challenge leading both them, Geiel, and Tau to agree that what Vants recruits they knew of, even if backed by what members of the Association Marta was able to recruit and control, would not be enough to secure the throne.

Only with Enesfel's backing would that happen, and none of them believed Lorant could muster the Sovereignty's army to fight on Kjell's behalf unless he could spin it as a fight for Enesfel as well. Despite Kjell's insistence on necessary action, Asta was not the only one to believe that Enesfel would be crushed if they faced an army of the size Geiel reported.

Fingers entwined in his, Asta spoke without shifting her head on his chest to look at his face. "I will speak with Lorant when I take Henrik back this morning. I will present your ideas…"

"But you think them foolish," Kjell grunted, making no effort to pull away from her. These moments were too rare as the differences highlighted by the passage of years and the paths their lives had taken continued to pull them apart. He knew he had become a difficult man for his younger wife to tolerate, and often wondered why she remained faithful, but he was thankful every day that she did.

Even when she was angry enough at him over their views about their son's predilections to avoid him for weeks at a time.

"It doesn't matter what I think," she shrugged. "The choice isn't mine. I do think it unfair to expect Enesfel to solve our problems, but if not…"

"Then who?" From the movement against his chest, he knew she nodded. "Tau may be right…" He sighed and met her gaze when she lifted her head to look at him. "The Vants may be our only choice. Zerio got me out once…perhaps he can get me back in to do what…"

"You swore not to be like the de Corrmick kings of history…"

He snorted. "This is different." Such an action now would not be to gain the throne by killing a family member. This time it would be to take back that which had been stolen.

"You think you're…?" Asta did not finish, cutting off the reminder that he was no longer in prime physical condition. Fraen the Elder was older, but that did not mean Kjell had the capacity to best him in a fight.

"Zerio then. Zerio and Tau…and you. We can do this, the four of us. I know it." Both men had been instructed to travel north after Henrik's upcoming betrothal ceremony to contact and recruit as many Vants as possible, to issue a call to action to reclaim the de Corrmick throne. There were no orders to act yet, but Kjell intended to make them soon.

Asta sat, leaned to kiss his forehead and mouth, and then rose from the bed to dress, leaving the blinding beam of sunlight pointing at the place on his chest where her head had been. "Let me speak with Lorant. Let me learn his thoughts; I will let you know what he says.

"Mercenaries threatening Cordash must not be allowed to stand," he reminded her. "They must be routed."

"I'm sure Govert's handling it." Cordash had always been strong and she believed Govert would do everything in his power to protect Rika and his children. It was up to Enesfel to protect her own.

"You will see to Henrik's betrothal? It needs to be done."

"Two days from today. The arrangements have been made." As he did with all important rites, Lorant had arranged for the ceremony to be performed in the náós to consecrate the pact between kingdoms before the eyes of k'Ádhá and the Faith. There would be no need for a hall full of people, for crowds to gather, for the public to be aware of a ceremony that would cement the future bonds between Neth and Enesfel. Asta understood how this news of mercenaries impacted the necessity of this alliance, even if she was still uncertain about binding the hands of children.

"You will come?"

"I should, yes." Kjell had risked public exposure twice and not suffered for it. No one seemed to recognize him. There had been no negative costs. For something as vital as the continuation of the de Corrmick bloodline, he would risk it again.

"I shall see you then, if not before," she promised, kissing him once more before leaving the room in search of Henrik and someone who could take them to Rhidam.

❧ * ❧

Works of art accumulated throughout his life were absent from many of the walls and shelves that had borne them, and many of his belongings had been removed from Raebhá's room and his own, leaving only a handful of sentimental items over his hearth and his clothes to suggest that Kavan continued to consider Alberni home. By the time he changed out of clothes he had worn for the last two weeks, cleaned only when he had been in Clarys and Bhryell, and descended the stairs to visit his staff, he expected that his study, too, had been stripped bare, or nearly so, by Dhóri's persistent efforts to protect the Cliáthan wealth.

Praise be, Kóráhm's tapestry still hung in the oratory.

"My lord!" called Emeria from the dining hall door, her arms laden with freshly washed bedding. "Say it isn't so. Say you are not leaving us."

Her words made him shiver, a cold chill that settled between his eyes and made him wince. "I…will you bring Laney and the others to the dining hall? I will address the rumors with all of you."

"Aye, right away," she murmured, her eyes wide, the request increasing her fears as she bustled away to deposit the bedding and call her family and additional staff together as he bid. It took time to collect them from their scattered duties around the house and grounds, but Kavan waited patiently because he did not want to explain himself more than once. There were the inevitable questions as he explained the rumors of war they would inevitably hear, and voiced to them, for the first time, his belief that Alberni and St. Kóráhm's would fall victim to this conflict. If that came to pass, the estate would be a primary target. He offered them the same protection as was offered to the residents of the chellé, escape to Gorbesh, but Laney, Emeria, and even their cocky, often disobedient son Dewel swore they would stay where they were.

This was their home. This was their hard work on behalf of the duke, a successful estate they took pride in. They would not, despite Kavan's worry for them, abandon it to invaders without a fight.

Their devotion and determination warmed Kavan's heart and reassured him that if his estate survived, it would be on the shoulders of those seated with him, but it did not erase his worry for what was to come.

❧*❧

"Head them off at Gorea!" Fraen barked at the red-faced General Waller, taking his anger at his son out on the man who was not to blame. It had not been the General's choice to ride to Pravek with the king. It had not been his fault he was not here to stand up to the mercenaries who were, to Fraen, seeming more like invaders instead of troops intended to fight for and with him as they spread through Neth like a plague without his permission. "Take every man we have. Keep them there. Don't let them move. Stop the rest before they reach Curo and do something stupid. Find out what the rest are doing and report to me immediately."

"And if they insist on disobeying?"

Olaric had the sense that Waller was looking for an excuse for a fight. His father, whether wisely or not, replied, "You're in command, General. You have my permission to stop them by any means necessary."

Waller bowed, threw Olaric a snide, self-satisfied smirk without lifting his head, and marched from the room. Olaric remained to one side, avoiding the throne he had chosen not to sit on in his father's absence, refusing to be cowed by the old man's anger.

He had few qualms about gutting the man if he charged at him.

"She gave me this." He offered the writ he had been given. "You said you had an army; you were going to Pravek to meet them. I thought they were permitted here under your order. This is your seal…"

"You should have kept them here," Fraen growled, snatching the scroll out of his hand. "You should have awaited orders."

Olaric shrugged. "I thought they had orders, that you agreed."

"You should have known…consulted…"

Drawing his shoulders back for the first time, he met the insulting tone with self-defensive annoyance. "You weren't here. You asked me to rule in your absence but you tell me nothing of your plans to allow me to…"

"You are not king yet." It had been Fraen's mistake to entrust responsibility to his son without giving him the information and tools necessary to manage the plans the king had set in place. He could not legitimately blame Olaric for that.

But he did blame Bhás.

She was not here, however, to face the heat of his anger.

Snorting, Olaric huffed, "They were here, now they are gone…Glevum stands and you're here to deal with them. There are still a few dozen on the southwest edge of the city. Talk to them if you want answers." If he could succeed in communicating with them. "I kept Glevum from burning to the ground. I kept anyone from dying. I protected the keep. That should be good…"

"They'll die soon enough." The war with Enesfel he wanted, the war of reclamation that would solidify his hold on the throne was at hand. He wanted to lead the charge into Enesfel, obliterate her meager force with his mercenary-infused army, but he knew he could not. His health would not permit it. General Waller had been schooled and prepared for this day. He knew what needed to be done.

Fraen wanted a royal presence at the forefront of the upcoming battles. Unfortunately, he did not yet trust his son to be the face of Neth.

"Bring me Captain Sparding. We need recruits. We need more men in the ranks. I won't let her do it all for us."

"And Glevum? If we send all our men into battle…?"

"Glevum will protect itself. We always have."

❧Chapter 13❧

It was a smaller procession from the keep to the náós than it had been for either ceremony prior, two carriages that often made the weekly pilgrimage to Hes á Redh when Lorant felt compelled to attend a Gathering and duty did not prevent him from it. Henrik traveled in the front carriage with his grandmother, uncle, and Zerio, while Hella traveled in the second with her brother, Níkóá, and Rhyrdan. Troubled by featureless dreams and Sight premonitions that had spiked throughout the morning with few visual or auditory clues, Kavan rode with the eight Lachlan guards tasked with accompanying the carriages today. His horse skittered and nickered in reaction to his agitation and he could feel Rhyrdan watching him from the carriage window. Both he and Zerio interpreted the bard's choice to ride alongside rather than inside the carriages as a bad omen.

He blamed their concerns on something Ágdhállán must have said rather than his distracted, pensive mood.

If Ágdhállán suspected anything, something that had prompted them to watch his father, then something must be wrong. The soldiers around him, while watchful, were not overly so, and the people they passed in the short stretch of street between the castle and the náós paid them no more than curious glances and bows of respect and adoration. Their king passed this route often enough to make the sight of the carriages unremarkable.

There was suddenly something amiss, a familiar smell he could not identify, a sound like metal against leather, a memory of an unwitnessed death at this intersection within sight of Hes á Redh where an innocent minstrel had died for the sake of a holy relic. A hand on his shoulder made Kavan pull his horse up short. He turned his head toward the sensation. Before he could identify the sound or the scent, there was movement on the other side of the street, someone darting out of the opposite alley. Almost too late, Kavan lashed out with every bit of unprepared power he possessed in a circular direct spread around both carriages.

The first pair of horses screeched and reared, causing Prince Henrik's wagon to tip. Screams of fright. Shouts of surprise. The horse pulling the second wagon lurched and spun the carriage sideways. Retreating cries as Teren vermin scurried back into the alleys they had rushed out of, but at the head of each, seven men in shabby clothes armed with knives and sticks and iron wheel spokes, were held frozen mid-stride, their eyes expressing terror, the only sort of expression they were able to make.

He knew what he expected to find in their eyes. It was him they wanted, him they had come for.

But Eridel was not among them and their trajectory was not aimed at Kavan. Perhaps not him after all.

Then who?

Asta, the first to scramble out of the upturned carriage, shouted, "Zerio!" as she reached inside for Henrik.

"I've got him," Jerit assured her, not yet seeing what had happened but having made sure that the boy was conscious and relatively unharmed. "Take care of this."

Zerio was already clambering through the thrown-open door where Asta had gotten free. He expected Association.

Rhyrdan tumbled out of the second carriage and stared at the frozen men around them as Níkóá lifted Hella down and held tight to her hand. "Get them inside," barked Lorant as he lost his footing and slipped down the step to land in the street.

Jerit stepped forward to assist him, but Asta yanked the prince back and repeated the command. "Get them inside. We'll handle this."

Jerit frowned, and expecting Lorant to follow him to safety, scooped Hella up in one arm, grabbed Henrik's hand, and ran towards the security of Hes á Redh as fast as Henrik's shorter legs permitted.

"Zerio." Asta pointed to the alley across the street. He was already running. Níkóá followed. "Rhyrdan, with me."

He hesitated, but Asta was running too. Pursuit would leave Kavan and the king unprotected, except for the soldiers who were trying to herd the immobile captives into a manageable group. It was only then he noticed the bard's concentration on those frozen men; he nodded and did not question Kavan or Lorant's safety further.

Kavan had saved them.

He would protect Lorant too.

One by one, as the soldiers took control of those seven men, Kavan released them from his hold and slid down from his horse. Lorant watched in wonder, after making sure Jerit made it safely into the náós. Shaken but cocky, feeling secure with Kavan at his back, he punched an angry finger into the nearest captive's sternum and barked, "What did you do?"

Kavan caught Lorant's arm, his body a-hum with unspent power that had been too-long untapped, and said, "This is not the time for interrogation. We must get you…"

"I want answers!"

"You will have them. But not here. Not now. We must see to your safety…we must be sure Hella and Henrik are safe…"

Lorant scowled. The carriage drivers were working with local men to right the upturned carriage and move it to the other side of the road. He could not leave the captives in the street, but if he could not interrogate them here, there was only one other option.

"Lock them in the dungeon…separate cells. I don't want them near each other, talking to each other. If Inquisitor de Corrmick brings you more," which he assumed was her intent, if there were others to capture, "we'll take care of them all at once."

"Yes, m'lord," replied one of the soldiers who turned the dirty, scrawny fellow in front of him in the direction of his fate. Another groaned in dismay as he was forced to move as well. A third, bare knees knocking so that he could barely walk, side-eyed Kavan with fear and moved as far away from him as the guard's hold on his arms permitted.

Kavan sighed. It had been a long time since anyone had shown fear of him. It had been a long time since there had been a public display of power, beyond purported miracles that he could not disprove, for people to fear.

More cautious now, guiding his horse by the slack lead in his hand, maintaining a bubble of power around them so that no person or projectile could get through, Kavan crossed the intersection, staying as close to Lorant as he could. He continued to expect Eridel in the shadow of every building, behind the tallest burial markers as they entered the churchyard, behind Hes á Redh's closed door, but leaving the horse to munch on the spring grass in the burial yard, Kavan got Lorant inside, closed and locked the doors to keep anyone else out, without incident.

"What in k'Ádhá's name…?" exclaimed Kjell as he stormed down the aisle toward them, leaving Jerit flustered at the altar steps where dedhá Thrismund sat with the children, offering Henrik and Hella cups of water and gentle words to soothe their fright.

Jerit shrugged at Kavan and Lorant without speaking. He had been unable to satisfy his father's demand for answers, having no idea what had just happened despite being a part of it.

"We were ambushed," Lorant replied, pushing aside his apprehension to meet Kjell king to king.

"By who? Who did this? What do they…?"

"Those we apprehended have been taken to the keep. Asta and Zerio are pursuing the rest."

"Were they after you?"

Kavan sidestepped between them to break up the tirade of blame and argument he felt building, knowing that Kjell's challenge came out of fear for his family and the reminder, with both Lorant and Jerit in the same room though not near each other, of a relationship he did not care to acknowledge.

"We do not know, My Liege. They might have been after me…"

"There's been no Elyri persecution in years," he huffed.

Ignoring the interruption, Kavan continued, "…it could have been any of us. It could have been a crime of opportunity…"

"We'll know when we make them talk," Lorant growled.

"I think it safe to say," said Thrismund approaching them in the aisle now that novice Charlos had joined the children, "there will be no ceremony today." With Hella white-faced and silent and Henrik visibly shaking beside her, he did not think this was the time to continue. "They should be taken home, Lord Cliáth."

"And you should return to St. Kóráhm's," Lorant said, his cool voice sympathetic enough not to prompt a protest from Kjell. The ambush could have been intended to get access to him as well.

Jerit did not look at his father, trusting from experience that Lorant's interference and suggestion would be blamed on him in some way. Kjell always found a way.

"You will let me know what is…"

"Asta will be sure of it," Lorant promised.

Muttering in a haughty but still suspicious tone, Kjell said, "We postpone for now, but do not think you will undo our agreement."

"I have no intention of doing so," Lorant countered. "This is about what is best, not about what we want."

"What we want is what is best for them." Kjell relented to the pressure of Thrismund's firm grip on his arm and followed him toward where dedhá Bhídígís waited in front of the Purification Chamber.

"I wish to join the…" began Jerit.

"You're as likely a target as I am," Lorant snorted, throttled emotion making his voice quaver. "Kavan will take us all home…and we will send men out to aid in the search. Kavan…?"

"Aye," the bard agreed, helping the children to their feet with a nod of gratitude at Thrismund and Charlos. Jerit and Lorant might not be able to join the hunt, but Kavan intended to. Using the smells, sounds, and impressions he had felt before the attack, if anyone could aid in finding the guilty, Kavan was confident he could.

❧*❧

Lorant stormed out of the oratory as soon as they arrived, leaving Kavan and the children in his wake, shouting for Bhetá and Lord Justice Delamo as he stomped away, his rare outburst of anger pushing the prince and princess close to Kavan as they cowered away from the blast. Wrapping his arms around them, Kavan looked at Jerit, the younger man flexing his fists, his jaw twitching, his eyes narrowed as he stared at the still-open oratory door. Kavan did not need to read him to know the prince's thoughts.

"Take care if you go out," he warned gently. Trained by his mother in the ways of the Association, as his mother had been trained by her father, Jerit was stealthy enough, strong and skilled. He could protect himself. But he was still King Kjell's only surviving son, and if he was the target, stealth, strength, and ability might not be enough to protect his life.

He had yet to be truly tested. He had yet to prove himself to anyone except himself and his mother.

"When Madoc comes, if you must, go with him and be watchful."

Surprised that Kavan would countermand Lorant's wishes for Jerit to remain in the castle, Jerit nodded, kissed Henrik and Hella's heads, and left them in the bard's care.

After what he had witnessed today, there was no one better to protect them. Likely no one better to protect any of them.

Hella wiggled out of Kavan's embrace and shuffled around to Henrik's other side, sandwiching the boy between her and their Elyri tutor. She held Henrik's pudgy hand, ignoring the nervous clamminess she was used to, and looked at Kavan with eyes still wide. "Why was someone trying to kill us?" she whispered. "We didn't do…"

"Wasn't you," Henrik stammered. "Had to be me and Jerit…"

Kavan shook his head and drew them down onto the altar steps with him. There would be bedlam in the keep for hours as the would-be assassins were found and arrested, as lords and ladies reacted with alarm and concern for their safety. Keeping the royal children out of the way, as well as removing them from unavoidable gossip, seemed the wisest thing to do.

He reached within himself, reached without, and sought Ágdhállán's thoughts with a gentle summons. The company of other children ought to help alleviate the pair's fears.

"We do not know who they were targeting. It might not have been anyone. It might have been me…"

"Why would anyone want to kill you?" Henrik asked skeptically.

"I am Elyri."

"Only Nethites…"

Hella shook her head. "Not just Nethites. Remember what Master Najar told us about the persecutions? Bad people…scared people…were afraid of Elyri too…all over the Sovereignties…"

Kavan smoothed her hair. "They might not have intended to kill anyone. They might have meant to rob us. Your grandmother will do her job, find all of those involved, and we'll learn the truth."

Henrik finally lifted his dazed stare and murmured, "They were all frozen. Did you do that? How…?"

"Because k'bhydhá can do anything." Ágdhállán bounded into the oratory with a grin, bringing Phaedr, Cáym, Kaedís, and Ónyká with him. He immediately embraced Henrik, who typically did not like to be touched, in a way that made the prince relax and sag against him. Ónyká squeezed in to sit beside Hella and the other boys sat on the floor in front of them.

Kavan shivered at Ágdhállán's words, at the burden to live up to his son's expectations, even if the words were only meant to give Henrik peace of mind. Perhaps, if he had made skin contact with the prince, Henrik would have calmed sooner. Or perhaps it was his friendship with Ágdhállán and the acceptance of the Cáner children that made him feel safe.

"Are you okay?" Cáym asked as Phaedr pulled out the bag of wooden dice Henrik enjoyed playing with. Jerit had taught him how to play and Henrik was good with numbers. Kavan was proud of whichever boy thought to bring them as a distraction.

"I…I'm okay." He relinquished his hold around Kavan's waist so the bard could get up and then focused on the dice when Phaedr dumped them on the floor. Trusting they would be safe in the oratory, Kavan left them and joined the three women who entered behind the children, meeting them halfway down the aisle.

"Is it true?" Seren begged. "Did someone try to kill Lorant?"

The twisting of fabricated truths in the absence of details made Kavan sigh. "We won't know the motive until the Inquisitor completes her inquest. Seven are in custody; if there are more, she will have them soon and then we will learn what has happened."

"The princess…they do not appear injured," Aunes murmured breathlessly, wringing her hands. She had served as the princess' nursemaid since shortly after her birth, making sure she did not stop breathing in her sleep and failed to start again. Hella had grown out of that phase, thankfully, but Lorant, having suffered ill health in his childhood, took no chances with his sister's welfare. Aunes had remained with Hella as her attendant ever since, a duty the Elyri woman was well-suited for.

"Bruised and frightened only."

Yóáná shivered. "That's enough. I would like to see to their care."

Surprised that Ártur had not come to do the same, Kavan nodded. It was a wise precaution, particularly with Prince Henrik who was prone to accidents and infrequent seizures and was monitored closely when he fell or struck his head. "Will you stay with them? The king requires my council, and I may be able to aid in the manhunt."

"Of course." Aunes and Yóáná were already joining the children but Seren hesitated, took Kavan's hands, and leaned close to murmur, "There is nothing you are hiding, my lord? Lorant will not tell me…"

"There is little to tell, My Queen. Brigands ambushed us near the náós. Whatever they intended, they failed. No one was seriously hurt. You will have to accept that answer until we know more."

Accepting the bard's words as truth as he had never lied to her, Seren released him and bobbed her head. "Thank you. With the rumors of war and…it is bad enough to consider he may go and not return."

"I do not believe that will be the case. I saw a long life for him at his birth; I do not believe war will take him as it did his father. I will return when I can and see how the children are faring.

The Sight did not show him everything and a long life was relative in the eternity of history. Nor did a long life mean that Enesfel would stand

Kavan chose to believe, however, that it was true.

❧Chapter 14❧

Despite the woman's effort to hide her disbelief, General Waller saw it in the flash of her eyes as she disembarked the ship at Gorea's dock and approached alone with long, deliberate steps.

"Leave them and walk with me," he grunted. He had seen this woman before, during the campaign to retake Ruidoso and the southern lands. He had seen her in the castle, before Queen-Regent Inness' fall. Both Fraen's and Inness' respect for this stranger left Waller inclined to comport himself likewise, but he was not afraid of her. He would cower to no woman, no matter how many ships and men she had at her call.

Three galleys that bobbed further out to sea awaiting the woman's command did not frighten him the way it did some. Waller had that many men behind him, conscripted in his hasty push from Glevum, most trained enough that he felt cautiously optimistic about their chances against men who had undoubtedly spent at least a month at sea to sail this far.

Gorea was the farthest south in Neth that could be reached by sea. Anywhere else she and her men intended to go would have to be reached on foot. They would have to get past Waller first.

"You are not the king."

He ignored the disdain in her stating-the-obvious tone and began walking toward the sea wall that kept the waves and the always anticipated but never materialized threat of Elyri from the faint cliffs on the distant horizon across from them, from breaching Gorea.

"He's seeing to business." It did not matter to Waller what that business was or why he had sent the general instead of coming himself. "You have not received…"

"We have an arrangement."

Waller shrugged. "Maybe, but I don't think invasion was part of that."

The woman chuckled. "If I intended invasion, we would not be having this conversation."

Trying to place an accent that made her words difficult to understand, Waller countered, "Troops marching across Neth without the king's…"

Her face darkened. "We have an…" she began to repeat.

"…knowledge," finished Waller, cutting her off with a word she had not expected, "could be considered an act of invasion and war."

As quickly as her face flushed red with indignation, it now fell neutral and flat as she shrugged. "I have no interest in Neth."

Waller nodded. "Enesfel then."

She did not reply. Waller did not care about her motives so long as she remained an ally to accomplish the king's goal of the reunification of Neth.

"Those men," he pointed to the incoming galleys, "are under my command the moment they set foot on Neth's soil. My captains have been dispatched to take command of those traveling elsewhere. They will follow my orders, the king's orders, or they, and you, will not be welcome here."

Her smirk made him frown. "They will do whatever I say," she assured him. "They will obey whomever I choose."

"And you?"

"I obey no man," she replied in a low, cool voice, "but you have my word that, so long as our goals align, our alliance will hold."

"When they don't?"

"That day will not come."

She spoke with certainty, enough that Waller was prompted to nod once and say, "Bring them ashore. We have camp prepared; you and I will discuss strategy at sunset."

He did not trust that, should the time come when this woman felt their interests no longer converged, her army would either turn on Neth or abandon their allegiance to the king in favor of this woman's commands.

In war, that was expected. Allegiances were fragile things. That was as it should be. Waller would do his utmost to abide by whatever arrangement the king had made, though he did not yet know what that was, but he would not allow this woman, or her men, out of his sight. They might be allies, but he did not trust her.

Even if the king did.

❧ * ☙

Kavan sensed their arrivals during the sleepless night, restless day, and second uneasy night as captives were found, brought into the keep, one by one or in pairs, frightened men dragged in by the inquisitor and lord justice, by Rhyrdan, Zerio, Níkóá and Prince Jerit as Lorant glowered and fumed about Jerit's disobedience.

Twenty-one men who attacked, or intended to attack, the carriages.

With threads of power and his bond with Rhyrdan, Kavan had flown over the city directing those in royal employ to where some of those men were found. Eventually, however, Lorant's frustration at being unable to find him brought Kavan back to the keep, only to wait in the oratory, in prayer, for the king to summon him. With the waning of the day, the women had seen the children to bed, and again the night passed. Come dawn, he was aware of voices that rose and fell in the Grand Hall as the interrogations began, echoes he could feel within him more than hear with his ears, questions targeting purpose and intent that Kavan chose not to ascertain from the altar steps. By the time he was summoned to the Grand Hall, Justice Madoc was returning with the last fellow in custody.

With the twenty-one men under royal guard, Rhyrdan left them to stand at Kavan's side, his face red and sweaty from the exertion but refusing to acknowledge that. He was more concerned about the uneasy expression on Kavan's face as Lorant waved him forward and gestured at the man held in Asta's grasp. The man made repeated attempts to be free of her only to have Zerio, on his other side, poke him in the ribs with the dagger he held there.

It was a painful enough reminder that escape was not possible in a room full of soldiers, but not painful enough to prevent him from trying again.

"That one, Lord Harper. Read him. I want the truth."

Kavan scowled and eyed Bhríd and Ártur whose troubled expressions revealed they had already performed that duty throughout the long hours of interrogation. He could not tell which men had been read, which had been judged and found guilty.

"They have been tried, My Liege?" Except for perhaps the last man, they might all have received judgment already.

"Read him," Lorant repeated.

Bhríd nodded. Uncertain what the nod was meant to convey, Kavan approached his target. The man struggled again, hissing curses under his breath. Zerio's dagger drew blood, penetrating deep enough to strike bone but not deep enough to kill him.

The man stopped moving.

Kavan touched the side of his face, cleared his mind of expectations, and opened it to the tumbling thoughts behind the man's wide brown eyes.

Despite the easing of anti-Elyri sentiment, the beliefs about the pain they could inflict by ripping thoughts out of someone's head persisted.

Faces. Voices in the shadows. Messages and conclaves and secret directions provided to each of those here…and a few more who were not. Spying, seeking, awaiting an opportunity.

"Not Association," he mumbled without breaking the mental connection, expecting that revelation would be a relief for the inquisitors. Nor was the man from Neth, not even the old southern Neth region. Not a merchant, not a spy, but a soldier…soldiers for hire. Not a man with a vendetta, not a man with allegiances to any single cause or person. A man…men…whose only loyalty was to the money someone paid.

"I do not…I cannot see…" Kavan shook his head. Without holding the coins they had been paid, without touching the written message the fellow had received, there was no accurate way to follow the trail of evidence back beyond the hooded, faceless figure who delivered both. There was a faint smell about the stranger, a blend of acrid pepper spice and coltweed smoke that made Kavan shudder and nearly retch with the power of the knot it created in his stomach.

He knew those aromas but could not recall from where.

He only knew them as scents of a threat. Eridel was not part of it.

"Not you, My Liege…but rather…the princes…"

As Kjell had suspected.

"Not the princess?" Lorant pressed in a whisper stretched thin by outrage. He looked from the back of Kavan's head to stare at Jerit.

Jerit's lips were pursed, his eyes narrowed.

"No. Not Hella. Jerit…Henrik…"

"Then it is Neth's throne they hope to…"

"Would Fraen dare such a thing?" asked Bhetá, cutting the general off.

Jerit looked at his mother. "Why now? Why not sooner? We haven't been hiding."

"But rarely are there occasions when you are in public together," Asta reminded him. Jerit was often outside the castle, an easier target for someone to take advantage of. Henrik, on the other hand, was rarely beyond the keep unless he was in St. Kóráhm's. If someone had gotten wind of the betrothal ceremony, that the two princes would attend together, it would have been deemed the perfect opportunity to be rid of them both.

Or not to kill him, Jerit mused. Not to kill the de Corrmick willing to give up everything for Enesfel's king. But rather…to kill King Oska's only heir before he could seek the throne of Neth. To kill him before a betrothal would be a step closer to ensuring the end of the de Corrmick succession.

Most in the Hall came to the same conclusion. No one had to say the words out loud.

"Lord Cáner, Daema…erect the scaffold." Lorant might not have been the target, and his sister was safe. Lorant might not have been the one marked for death this time, but eventually, he would be. This was not treason against the Lachlan House, but it was a threat to royal blood and there had been Lachlans in those carriages that could have been killed. They were reasons enough to order the executions of all twenty-one men. He would prove his loyalty to Kjell by doing what the exiled king could not. It might win him the favor and respect that his love for Jerit had kept at bay.

"Midday tomorrow, I will have your heads." He swept his gaze across each face. "Assassination is not tolerated. Treason is not tolerated."

"I demand to speak to Novice Franc," croaked one of the captives.

"What has he…?" Lorant began, rising from the throne with narrow-eyed suspicion.

Lowering his hands with Lorant's proclamation, not surprised with the execution order as he had been when it had been issued by some of the previous Lachlans, Kavan said, "It is right they should be allowed the rite of Purification if they wish it." It would not erase their crime, but it might ease the guilt upon their souls. Like the king, however, Kavan was concerned about any connection between these would-be assassins and the youngest dedhá in Rhidam, who would have known about the day's ceremony and could have alerted someone…intentionally or accidentally.

Perhaps there was no connection. Kavan would have the truth when dedhá Franc came to the keep.

Lorant released a hissing breath and reluctantly nodded. "Mr. Kaas, summon Novice Franc…and bring him and k'dedhá Tusánt to the stateroom. General, take these men," he glared at the guilty without looking at Jerit or Asta, before saying, "out of my sight. No water. No food. No visitors."

"Yes, Sire," the general nodded. Asta followed, shoving her hostage after the others while Zerio wiped the man's blood from his dagger and sheathed it before heading for the náos.

"Lord Cliáth…with me."

The king did not dismiss the others but the room emptied as Kavan, meeting Ártur's gaze with a shrug, followed Lorant out of the Hall. Soon only Jerit remained.

"This cannot happen again," Lorant snapped as Kavan closed the stateroom door. "With the Association…Neth…"

"This was not Association," began Kavan.

"But it could have been…they're out of hand as it is. War is looming, and if this is Fraen's effort to frighten us, prevent us from acting…"

"I do not think he can know your intentions yet." Kavan had spoken to a select few about Earé's encroaching army. Lorant's war council had yet to convene. Only if Bhás possessed the Sight or some gifts like Earé's could she know that Enesfel was preparing for the war she intended to wage.

Lorant snorted and perched on the edge of the table, refusing, as many Lachlans had done, to seek solace in the liquor cabinet at the far side of the room. "I will hear k'dedhá Tusánt's endorsements and employ one of the dedhá here, in the keep; there will be no further forays to Hes á Redh until this war is behind us. The betrothal ceremony will be conducted in the first-floor oratory in two days…as soon as the bodies are disposed of and the scaffold is removed. All further Faith ceremonies and weekly Gatherings will be conducted here for us. I will not risk this happening again. Not until I can guarantee everyone's safety. You and k'dedhá Tusánt will make the arrangements and elect someone to go with the troops when I leave…"

"There has been no…" Kavan began to protest.

"You know we will go. The men need Faith to go with them. I need Faith. Unless," he paused for effect, "you will travel with us."

Kavan shook his head. "You know I cannot; my place is here."

"Where it should be." Lorant did not sound convinced, but rather resigned and marginally hopeful that he might change the bard's mind or at least convince him not to disappear from Rhidam for weeks without a word. "You will select someone to join me in your place, with k'dedhá's approval…and you will beseech Ethenae to keep us safe."

"As you wish, My King." Kavan bowed. As if he were not already praying to each of those holy entities, and more, every time he got the chance for a moment's peace.

∿*∿

By noon the following day, twenty-two headless corpses, the twenty-one original criminals, and an additional fellow Lord Justice Madoc and Zerio had tracked down during the night, were disposed of, leaving their heads on spikes around the gradually disassembled scaffold until the sun set and the last board were removed. Lorant had been there all day, with Jerit and Asta at his side, providing unity between Lachlan and de Corrmicks he believed the world needed to see as the rumors of war, carried on the breath of Lachlan servants and the convergence of nobles from across the land, began to spread throughout Rhidam.

This time, Enesfel would not be fighting the de Corrmicks.

This time, they were fighting with and for them.

Kavan had not been present but he had watched the prince and king from Rouvyn Talis' window as the weak man wheezed and rattled his way through a restless, troubled sleep. Rouvyn's request for his company had been the excuse Kavan needed to avoid the killing, an excuse none would hold against him.

He had seen enough death.

But he could still hear it.

It had been up to Master Najar to collect the children around the altar in the upper oratory and read to them as Kavan attended the dying man. From there, they would not be able to hear death the way Kavan could.

Not wanting death to overshadow the solemn joy of betrothal, it was mid-afternoon on that second day, with the dead removed and the scaffold taken away, before the royal house collected in the first-floor oratory, along with Kjell, to further bind Lachlan to de Corrmick. Novice Charlos Rion, elected to serve the Lachlan house as dedhá as soon as he passed his ordination ceremony, now pushed from three months out to one, was given the duty and honor of performing the betrothal ceremony to further his attachment to the Lachlan House. One of the first-floor billeting chambers was assigned to him and this oratory would become his sanctuary.

The oratory on the third floor remained Kavan's.

He was grateful for that.

He was also grateful, as Jerit attempted to present a familial front with Ida and Gerna beside him, Kjell casting critical glances at his son now and then and Ágdhállán's uncharacteristic fidgeting on the bench next to him, that this time the ceremony was uninterrupted except for the lingering smell of pepper and coltweed Kavan could not dispel.

Rhidam needed normalcy.

War would strip that away soon enough.

❧Chapter 15❧

In Durham's largest náós where he had once discussed the Faith with Prince Arlan on the altar steps, where rain had trapped them for days and the spiritual entities who often visited Kavan when he prayed had driven a wedge into their friendship that never fully healed…where Caol Dugan had been welcomed into the prince's company and begun to build a lasting relationship with the Lachlans, Kavan hesitated long enough to run his fingers across the top of the altar as if to refresh the memories this place contained. The Gathering Hall was empty, the dedhá out on errands, so there was no one to question the small group of people behind him.

It had seemed a peculiar request to accompany the women and Zerio to Durham when Syl could have delivered them herself. At the náós door, Asta glanced at Zerio as if to say, 'You know what to do,' and then fell into step beside Syl as Zerio headed into the heart of the town alone. Determining that this was Association business, unsure which direction he was being asked to take, Kavan decided that joining the women was his path.

If anyone might need his help, it would be Asta in dealing with her brother's wife. Wilred had avoided the Association after his earliest experiences with them. Asta had not. It was rare that Bianca welcomed her sister-in-law into her home.

Several of Bianca's six children, however, had made different choices, some with their parents' knowledge, some without. If reaching out to them and others in the Durham Association was Asta's plan, Zerio could do so without raising suspicion or Bianca's ire. He might not, however, have enough sway to succeed.

Kavan did not know what Asta hoped to accomplish with Bianca.

"Momma." Bianca descended the stairs of the wide, two-story structure that the Dugans called home, with a slowness in her steps that had not been there the last time Kavan had seen her more than a year before. Downstairs was for business, where trade goods from outside the city were housed and exchanged for others Durham produced. Durham was the only city in Rhidam with a central trading hub, with a constant flow of goods moving into and out of Cordash and the Cíbhóló from there, a business founded by Wilred and managed by other family members.

Some did not trust the business because of the family's Association ties. But the Association was powerful in Durham and Wilred had gone out of his way to limit connection or interaction with them. Doing so resulted in an overall increase in city wealth, which was enough to prompt the Association to leave them alone.

Kavan hoped the business would continue to thrive when Bianca was no longer there to manage it.

"Lord Cliáth, this is a surprise." She embraced Syl, embraced Kaedís as a sister despite the girl being young enough to be a grandchild, but she only smiled at the bard and coolly clasped Asta's hand, acknowledging her, accepting her visit, despite the awkwardness between them.

"It has been too long. I come," he cleared his throat, hoping his excuse would not disturb Syl, "as an emissary from the king to…"

"The war council. I know." She gestured to the stairs and led them up. "I regret I am unable to…"

The title of duke had passed to her eldest son Horis, but the plague had taken him without leaving any male child to replace him. Kavan did not know if Níkóá had chosen a successor or if the family had selected another in Wilred's place.

"You don't need to be there," Asta assured her as she accepted one of the offered chairs, her side glance at Kavan expressing gratitude for his picking up on the excuse she had intended to use for being in Durham. Kaedís scampered off toward the sounds of children in a distant room. "The king understands."

"The boys are too young," Bianca continued, cutting off the words she believed would come next. "I will not rob them of their…"

"Doing nothing means to rob them, all of us, of Enesfel's future," Syl began tenderly, sympathizing as a mother with Bianca's desire to protect her family. If she had a son in Enesfel old enough to face war, she would worry for him too…as she worried for Llucás in Bhryell.

"What about Warde?" Asta asked offhandedly.

Bianca's expression turned dark and bitter, but the retort she intended to make was cut short by Syl's hand on Asta's knee and a warm, "How are the boys?"

"And girl now…Melana has finally given me a granddaughter." The relief at the change of topic was evident in her voice and she ignored Asta's scowl as the inquisitor sat back and curled her hands around the arms of the chair. "And Annet is expecting…"

"Already? She was not due until…"

"She wished to come early…two weeks ago now." It was no one's fault that Syl had missed the birth, that the child had chosen to arrive during the upheaval of crowning, wedding, and betrothal in Rhidam.

"Annet is due after the turn of the year."

"I will not miss another one," Syl promised, her regret obvious.

"Come, meet her. All of you. We will talk of war later."

Asta was both surprised and not surprised to be included and walked ahead of Kavan after he gestured to her. Odds were, as she exchanged a glance with the bard, her brother's wife did not trust Asta alone in any part of her house.

❧*❧

The Goose Feather Tavern looked to Zerio like any other, with a raucous crowd already bustling around the fire pit and tables, with men engaged in dice and others hunched in conversation. The room smelled of sweat and smoke, bread and salted mutton, alcohol, and an assortment of burning herb pots meant to overpower the less pleasant smells. He scanned faces and the backs of heads hoping to bypass some of the steps he expected he would have to take, but there were no Dugan redheads in the room and no one stood out as Association or Vants.

He wondered if the Vants had spread as far as Durham.

Surely, with Durham an Association stronghold, with ties between the organizations, they must have.

He approached the counter, set a pair of coins upon it, along with a token Asta had provided, and slid them toward the white-bearded barkeep with missing front teeth and a scar from his ear, across his cheek, to his nose, a man Asta had instructed him to look for. The man looked twice as old as Asta, possibly older, and did not appear prone to conversation.

"Mead, if you've got it."

The man scooped up the coins, glanced at the token before pocketing it, and then filled a tin cup from one of the kegs behind the counter. He set the drink in front of Zerio without a word, only a scowl and a clipped, gruff hissing sound at two loudly swearing, arm-wrestling men seated at a table nearby. The distraction was enough to cause the one with sparse curly hair to lose focus and lose the contest. The loser slid a coin across the table, finished his drink, and then the pair slunk out of the tavern taking their unruly expletives elsewhere.

"Looking for a Dugan," Zerio started, deciding to be the first to speak when the barkeep did not.

"Sure that's what you're looking for?" The flick of the man's gaze seemed to indicate the queue of hair hanging down Zerio's back.

Zerio scowled to hide the excitement of recognition and picked up his drink. "Don't think there's many like me, so yeah, I'm sure."

"Know your way around town?"

"First time."

The barkeep grunted, filled three steins with ale, and waited until the serving girl took them away. "Can't help you, but if you find the ram's skull, you'll find what you want. Might not like what you find though."

"Long as there's…"

"Might not like you," the older man clarified.

Zerio chuckled. "Doesn't have to…told to give a message…"

"Not a messenger. Do it yourself."

Though frustrated by the man's demeanor, Zerio finished his drink and left the cup where it was, making no effort to push it closer. He understood such secretive doings; the Vants had been full of such coded and evasive speech. He had not expected Asta's request and instructions to be easily filled but he had hoped the copper token she had provided, with its four raised diamonds on one side that formed a diamond themselves, and a line figure that reminded him of a walking man on the other, would be proof that he was trustworthy.

The sense he had of being observed, of being followed as he left the tavern and began a methodical search for anything resembling a ram's skull told him otherwise. He found dancing sheep on another tavern sign, three sheep of varying colors carved and painted on a swinging sign above a tailor's shop, and a sheep and ram's head embossed above a money exchange door, before returning to his point of origin, back to the náós appropriately called Hes Pheldór…Lamb's Heart in Standard Elyri. He turned from the sign and looked in the direction Asta and the others had gone debating seeking her out, but then his eyes narrowed as a dilapidated, dirty structure with boarded windows and a chained-closed door just beyond the corner of the náós yard caught his eye.

Its end-of-the-block, adjacent to the burial yard position suggested it might once have housed a grave-keeper, groundskeeper, or even an executioner or the gdhededhá themselves. He had not paid attention to the building before, but the location of the door and those on the structures adjacent to it siding the edge of the burial yard with only narrow alleys between them, most with doors on the other side, was peculiar enough to warrant investigation. There were rickety wooden walkways between the upper floors, collapsing and unused, and the entire row, he noted now that the day was waning and the sun's position made the alleys darker, showed no signs of occupancy.

But something else that caught his eye as he drew closer. A scratched-in rune that would have gone unnoticed by most. A narrow V crowned by a wider V that stretched to both sides as though the horns of a narrow head…

Shadows emerged from the nearest alley but Zerio did not turn to face them, allowing them to think he was oblivious to their company. He reached to trace the mark with his fingers but fell short of doing so when two sets of arms grabbed him and dragged him into the narrow dimness from whence they had come.

"You wanted me?"

Another figure dropped ahead of him from the unstable catwalk above, making the wood shudder and clatter enough for Zerio to hear it and stop walking despite his captors' efforts to propel him forward. The sounds were not loud enough, however, to be noticed by anyone in the daylit streets beyond and might have been unnoticed as anything other than night noises when Durham slept.

"Not me," Zerio countered, shrugging off the hands that held him and glancing side to side to see the faces of the pair of arm wrestlers from the tavern. "Asta wants a word." He rubbed his biceps to ease the ache where fingers had dug into his flesh, but he refused to show annoyance or offence. Neither would be conducive to a successful negotiation.

He referred to Asta not as queen, not inquisitor, not seeking an audience in any official capacity. The desire to keep a meeting personal, unofficial, was one of the reasons she had not sought this young man herself; she was just a woman wanting to talk to a man. Just a Dugan looking for her kin.

The man lowered his hood so that his red hair caught in the light filtering between cracks in decaying wooden slats. "So why isn't she here? Who are you?"

"Business with your mother." He shrugged, as he did not know the nature of that business, and answered, "Zerio Kaas."

"Heard of you."

Zerio nodded. Of course he had. As the Lachlans' secondary inquisitor, as he aided Asta in trying to control the Association's influence in Rhidam, it was inevitable that Zerio's name had spread. He never expected notoriety. He had never expected anyone would pay much attention to him at all.

Queen-Regent Inness had changed that.

"She wants a word…to discuss Rhidam."

"Not interested."

Zerio shrugged. "Think you will be; hear her out. If you're still not interested, tell her that yourself."

"Not going to the house."

"Of course not." That would be a less-than-neutral meeting ground if what Asta said about his mother was true. "Tell me where. She'll be there."

The younger man stared at him for a few moments as if considering his options before replying, "Tenth bell tonight. She'll know where."

"Give her time. She'll be there."

"I'll wait…but not long."

Only when he blended into the shadows did Zerio notice the two men behind him were gone. He waited, listening to see if they were nearby, and then backed quietly out of the alley.

Now, he mused with a glance at the sun's position, he had to get a message to Asta.

❧*❧

Most often since the king's resurrection and exile, Geiel Vagn delivered messages from Glevum directly to the man called Tau, with or without the king present in the chellé Hábhai known as St. Kóráhm's in the city of Alberni. He was the only messenger, sworn to secrecy on the penalty of death, permitted to do so, the only one who had seen the exiled king face to face. Occasionally, however, his instructions were different. Sometimes messages were delivered within Neth, sometimes into Cordash, and sometimes, like this day as he dismounted the mottled gray horse he had swapped at his last exchange point, he was sent directly to the Lachlan palace in Rhidam. He liked it here, liked the sturdiness of the façade, the sense of security he felt when he passed through the gates to be met by retainers, soldiers, and stable hands, some of whom recognized his face after ten years of these sporadic visits.

He thought the exiled king would be better protected here, but he supposed Rhidam came with a higher risk of recognition by any of the lords and nobles who came to call, a risk that Kjell could not afford. As far as Geiel knew, Fraen the Elder did not know that Kjell was alive.

It was better it remained that way until it was time to act.

"Mr. Vagn. It is good to see you."

The man who had been the regent ruler offered a hand and swept his unruly, wind-tousled red hair away from his face with the other. He had left the guard quarters and dialogue with General Declan and the Daema in time to see Geiel's arrival and crossed the courtyard to greet him.

"I wish the circumstances were better, m'lord," Geiel said, accepting the offered hand instead of offering a Nethite bow. "Is Queen Asta here?"

"She is away on business. We do not expect her back until tomorrow. You are welcome to wait if you wish."

Geiel looked disappointed, like a spurned suitor, but replied without the weight of that dissatisfaction in his voice. "No, there is no time for that. There are mercenary ships in…"

Disrupted by a quarrel between three soldiers and Bhetá's barked demand that made the three move sheepishly apart, Níkóá asked before Geiel finished. "We heard a fleet had arrived in Pravek?"

"They were in Glevum when I left, and dispersing ships to Gorea. I saw them, hundreds of men, led by a woman…"

Níkóá scowled. "Inness?"

"A foreigner. Some say from Hatu, but her accent's not the same."

A woman from Hatu would never lead an army. Nor would Gamal have forged an alliance with Fraen against Enesfel. If he had sent ships to the north, someone would have reported it. And the news from Pravek and Cordash claimed the ships had sailed from the west. A fleet from Hatu would never have made that journey.

"If they are preparing for war to reclaim the south, their dispersal makes no sense…unless they intend to attack from both east and west of Curo. Our sources say General Waller was sent with Glevum's force to join the fleet in Gorea, and spies are following their progress inland. We recommend that Enesfel act now if you intend to…"

"Sources?"

"Myself and…others allied with us," Corrected Geiel, refusing to name his sources. Olaric had, thus far, kept his ongoing participation with the Vants clandestine. For four years he had kept his return to Glevum a secret from most, although now that he had begun to interact with his father, his location was no longer secret. It would not be long before the dispersed

Vants and those outside of Neth knew the younger Fraen was alive. He did not think it would take Enesfel's Vants long to ascertain the truth.

Níkóá nodded. "The king has called his war council; a decision will be imminent, but I cannot say how long. If you wish…?"

"It is enough that Enesfel intends to act; it is what we need to know. It will give hope to those others…knowing that Neth may not be hostage to this mercenary force indefinitely. We can work with that. Knowing we have allies will spur others to action."

"Nothing foolish, I hope.

Geiel offered a one-shouldered shrug as if to say that what was foolish depended on one's point of view.

Níkóá chose not to inquire about the actions the Nethites were considering. "Stay as long as you wish, sir; rest, eat, rest your horse. Take food with you and my words to your contacts. Speak to me before you leave; if there's a decision from the king or a message from Asta, I will be sure you get it.

"It will be good to be off a horse for a few hours," Geiel agreed. Good, but it would not last. Olaric needed to know that help would soon arrive.

He hoped it would be soon enough to make a difference.

❧ * ❦

Browsing the collection of crates, barrels, and bundles awaiting redistribution out of, or within, the town, Zerio listened to the pregnant woman and a man he assumed was her husband as they planned with a client for the next delivery and debated where they would put it if the next outgoing delivery was not picked up as scheduled. They were not responsible for shipping or delivery. The large room only served as a secure, guarded storage facility for a fee, so that goods could be distributed efficiently.

Both eyed him as they recorded the client's name, contact information, and the amount he was expected to pay when he brought his first wool harvest and then how much would be charged for any extra days it remained on site. When the client was satisfied, the young woman, her pale red-blonde hair tucked into a braided knot on the back of her head, stuffed a slip of paper beneath the blue fabric at her breast. As her husband accompanied the client out of the building, she turned her attention to Zerio.

"May I help you, sir?"

"Kaas," he said, offering his hand. "The Dugans live here, do they not?" He glanced around in confusion, as there was no visible sign of residence and no noticeable way to access the second floor.

"Aye, they do," she smiled, concluding from his tidy, regal manner of dress and the trace of a Nethite accent, that he was not Association.

She did not appear to recognize his name as the men in the tavern had. "I am returning to Eleva with a missive for Duke Marin when I saw Queen de Corrmick this morning."

"You know my aunt?"

"And uncle," he assured her as if knowing the King of Neth made him important. "I was once employed by both before…" He sighed, knowing she would know what he meant. The overthrow of King Kjell was no secret. "I was detained then and could not speak with her but I should like to inquire about her health, perhaps meet with her if she is still here."

"She is, sir. Shall I fetch her?"

He bowed and murmured, "I do not wish to trouble you, or her."

"We'll let her decide. Wait for me. I'll take your message."

"You are gracious, m'lady." He bowed again and watched her retreat through a door at the back of the structure. He continued to browse as he waited, her husband glanced at him but did not question his continued presence as though he assumed his wife was taking care of his needs. He went about the business of closing the warehouse for the evening and allowed Zerio to silently wait alone. There were armed men positioned outside the building. Zerio would not get away with any crime he might be inclined to commit. Minutes later, when the door opened, the young woman returned with Asta in tow, followed by the sweet notes of brass harp strings. The door remained open, the music continuing, as Asta crossed the room. Despite her feigned surprise and delight at seeing a lost acquaintance, Zerio could read the scolding flash in her eyes.

"It has been too long," she said warmly, offering a hand for a kiss to her ring as would be expected. "Would you care to come up and…?"

The younger woman, satisfied with the reunion, joined her husband in his work. She was not near enough to interpret the warning in Asta's eyes nor to hear that invitation.

"No, I may not. My caravan departs soon, but I wanted to see you again. I could not allow this unexpected crossing of paths to pass. "Is that…?" he gestured toward the door. "Is the White Bard with you?"

It was a reasonable assumption, as both were known to reside in Rhidam, but the question was primarily meant to provide the appearance of small talk for anyone watching them.

"He is," she replied.

"It has been years since I heard him, since Glevum.

"Indeed," she agreed.

Deciding to get to the point, Zerio adjusted his tunic and said, "I have recently spoken to Mr. Feld. Do you remember him?"

"It has been some time."

"Likewise. We spoke across the way; I inquired about his business and if he was open to a new negotiation. We are to meet tonight at the usual place at the tenth, to discuss the imposter king. He is skeptical about you being here, but if you wish to join us, I am sure he would be interested in seeing you again, to hear how he can help."

Asta nodded once. The nuances of tone told her as much as the words did. Her nephew would meet but he was skeptical about the purpose. Years of practiced stealth ought to enable her to get out of the house without Bianca's knowledge, but getting back in would be more difficult. As would winning her case with Warde.

She had to try.

"I will be there," she promised. "You will be there too?"

"Of course," he agreed. It might take both to convince her nephew of the responsibility she hoped he would assume. She wanted someone with her in case she failed.

᠀*᠀

Bianca had fallen asleep to the dulcet notes of Kavan's harp in a sitting room chair, an impediment intended, Asta believed to prevent her from sneaking out to do precisely what she planned to do. Why Bianca would suspect her when she had not once spoken of the Association or made any reference to a family member who was part of it, except one inquiry about Warde, Asta could only guess. It might have been the discussion of war; it might have been the arrival of the messenger or something else that made Bianca suspect her of some underhanded motive.

Perhaps she knew Asta too well.

Still in the chair when the náós bells chimed the ninth hour of the night, Asta retreated to her room where she stood with her hand on the knob, considering her options. The room she had been given had a single narrow window, too small to serve as an exit or entry, without sufficient footholds outside to make an exit possible even if she could squeeze through it.

The door opened behind her.

"Come."

Her initial scowl turned into a look of bemusement as she followed the summons and entered Kavan's room. As an honored guest, the bard had been offered the best room available, one with a wide, double window already unlatched and open to allow the cool evening air to come in. Below the window, the stable roof was visible, an easy leap for a well-trained Dugan. Durham stretched to the forested horizon beyond that, the skyline of single and double-story houses and shops broken only by the single square tower of the náós.

"You knew." It had always been hard to keep her choices, her actions, hidden from him, though she continued to try during the years of training and guidance her father had given. She could fool many, hide objects, motives, thoughts, and feelings from them, and sneak silently in or out of a room or the castle, but Kavan had always known. Her father said it was because he was Elyri. Asta believed it was something else.

"I suspected," he corrected with a wry grin. "Zerio can be persuasive, but your kin…you would wish to be the one to do the talking." His voice was low, barely heard, and so she came closer to his side at the window to gauge a path out and back in.

"I don't know if this will work, but I don't know how else to control them without taking the role myself. Father would have…"

"Caol would have done the same thing you are, I suspect."

"Even if it put him at odds with the king?"

"You think this will do that?"

She shrugged but did not speak.

"He put himself at odds with Arlan at least once…"

This time, Asta nodded. She had not been born but she knew the story from Wilred, Diona, and Muir. Until Wilred's abduction, Arlan had not known about Caol's Association affiliation. Her father's choices to save his son and Prince Bertram had created friction with the king, but in the end, Arlan had been open to using the Association's resources to aid the Crown when necessary. That reliance had gradually dulled after Caol's death until Marta's disappearance.

Asta still had a few viable, reliable contacts, but it was not enough, and the Association, without leadership, was quickly becoming a liability the

Crown could not tolerate. If she did not somehow manage them, she knew she would lose the few connections she had.

Lorant never asked the source of her intel and did not seem to realize how connected the Crown and Association were in some ways. He might not approve of her choices to solve the surge in crime when he did learn of it, but she had no other choice, she believed, but to try.

"I'll be awake when you return," he added. "I'll be here."

"Sure you won't follow?" she teased.

He picked up the harp from the dressing table and shrugged. "I am of more use here. She will never know you are gone."

He often used music to lull children to sleep. He had used it at times to ease the restless spirits of adults, allowing them to sleep as well. She did not know how he did it, but if it worked on Bianca, she was not going to ask questions.

As he settled cross-legged on the bed and began to play another gentle tune that carried on the breeze both outside and through the crack around the partially ajar bedroom door to the room where Bianca slept, Asta swung one leg over the ledge, pulled the other up behind her, and then slid silently down to the stable roof. The wood clattered, and the horses nickered, but no one in the house stirred. She crabbed carefully sideways, looked left and right and back toward Kavan's dark window, then dropped to the ground.

She waited for the unsettled horses to grow calm and then followed the shadows of the house to the city streets.

She was not as familiar with Durham as she was with Rhidam. Caol had brought her here to visit Wilred as a child, and after his death, when she became a mother herself, she had made those visits without him until her duties as Neth's queen interfered. Each time she studied the layout a little more, each time she learned an Association point of interest, taverns where they safely conducted business, and local landmarks that could be used as covert meeting places.

None of those were the landmarks Warde had instructed her to tonight. She knew where he would be.

The streets were empty as she wove toward the náós but the murmured voices behind closed doors, the lusty crooning from an alley as a drunkard fawned over the prostitute he had paid, and the dwindling raucous cheerfulness within the taverns she passed reminded her that Durham did not yet sleep. That would not come for another few hours, when all but those prostitutes and their clientele, certain members of the Association out on more nefarious deeds, and a few members of the City Watch hopeful to catch them in the act, would be the only ones slinking through the streets.

She saw not another soul as she opened the náós gate and picked her way through the markers erected in a haphazard pattern as the bells finished their count until she reached the one site she most often avoided when she came to Durham.

Just as she avoided her parents' markers in the Rhidam keep.

She did not like reminders of those she had lost. She wondered, as she ran her fingers over the top of the stone with her brother's name, if she would be able to face Oska's resting place if she ever returned to Glevum.

"Didn't think you'd come."

Asta shivered at the voice, enough like her father's to generate an additional ache that she had to swallow and shake her head to ignore. "Some things are worth a little discomfort." She looked at the man who stopped beside her but just as quickly looked away. Taller than Caol. Broader shoulders. Hair a little blonder. But his moonlit profile was similar enough that she choked on those same emotions again.

"You can tell them all to stand down." She cocked her head in a sweeping fashion toward the shadows of those she could sense but not see. "I'm not here to arrest anyone. Not here for trouble."

"I'm sure Mother believes otherwise."

"Of course. With war on our heels, there'll be nothing but trouble."

"Rumors are true then?"

"Not sure what rumors you've heard, but Neth's stirring trouble; the king's preparing for the worst."

"I'm not a soldier."

"Not asking you to be one. Think there's a better way for you to serve…if you're interested."

"What your man said." Warde squatted and traced his father's name on the stone. "No promises…but I'm listening."

Knowing he was not the sort to want to serve anyone, but at least was willing to listen, she began, "You know there's a power vacuum in Rhidam. Association's out of control. I'm looking for someone I can trust to fill it."

"You mean someone you can control."

"Not even my father controlled them. I certainly don't, and don't want to. I let them be as much as I can in exchange for information. What happens between them and the Justice is out of my hands, so long as it doesn't involve the Crown. Once Marta left, there's been no one to manage them."

She knew why Marta had left and understood the compulsion of revenge. For a time, the communication had flowed between them. Then it had stopped. There were messengers Asta believed Marta had sent but she could not prove it, and did not know if those messages she sent north were ever received. For all she knew, Marta was dead.

"You think I can tame them? Who am I to…?"

"You're a Dugan. More than I am to them, at least." She had been a Dugan in the Association's eyes until she married Neth's king. Until Onea Pantel's death. After that, more of the Association had shied away from her.

"Who do you think will manage Durham?"

"I don't know. Whoever's running it now." She did not know the names in Durham's hierarchy, but despite how much sway Warde carried here, she knew he was not the person at the top, where his ambition wanted him to be. "Right now, I don't care. You'll find someone." She knelt beside him and covered his hand on the stone. "Your father didn't like what I do…what you do…but he knew we're good at it. Just as good as your grandfather. You're a Dugan by blood and birth. They all know it."

She touched the name on the stone as well, acknowledging in doing so the absence of her brother and the fact that she was, despite her marriage to Kjell, the Dugan matriarch, the oldest living Dugan in Enesfel. Among those Association members who respected her, she knew she could order Warde to take the Rhidam post if she wanted to.

She did not want to. She would rather he accept the charge on his own.

"You'd have control. You'd have the freedom to organize your way. I'll do my best to see you have the protection of the Crown…within reason," she added with a chuckle. "All I ask in return is information when needed…and some restoration to peace."

Warde weighed her words against whatever measures he deemed important. Eventually, when voices shouted commands to someone else to stop, orders followed by a crash and another shout, he looked up from the marker and asked, "When do you want an answer?"

"I'm returning in the morning. Sooner's better." Though she knew morning was too soon for a decision, she said. "You could come with us."

"Don't think that would be wise."

"Me either," she agreed, but the offer needed to be made. "With a war council in the offing, with the tumult it will generate, the Association will use it to their advantage. I need to control…"

"I will think about it." He stood and helped her to her feet. "No promises…and if I do accept, there are things I need to address here.

Whatever I decide, you'll have your answer within a week…two at most. If I do this…I'll expect you to honor your word…"

"I will," she promised, offering her hand. "Dugan's word."

He looked at it, paused, and then accepted the gesture. "Dugan's word," he said, sealing the pact.

For Asta, the gesture was as good as his agreement.

❧Chapter 16❧

Kavan emerged from the Purification Chamber into an unexpected atmosphere of choking dismay. Syl and Kaedís had remained in Durham and Asta had been taken to St. Kóráhm's to speak with Kjell, so it was only Zerio, who emerged from the chamber behind him, who caught his elbow when he stumbled and aided him onto the frontmost bench before he collapsed.

"What is it?" Zerio murmured. He did not yet know how Asta's negotiations had gone with her nephew, as he had met them inside the náós just after daybreak, but he did not think this near-faint had anything to do with the Association. Rather, he believed it had something to do with the melancholy on Rhyrdan's face.

"It is…" Unsure how to finish, not wanting to believe what his senses told him, Kavan clutched Rhyrdan's arm.

"Aland needs you," Rhyrdan choked. "Physician Talis needs you."

While Kavan's white skin could not lose color, Zerio saw the same sort of change come over him. "What has…?" he began, asking the question Kavan could not ask.

"Last night, during your absence…he began retching blood. They're doing what they can to sustain him, as he swears he will not pass until you return…but he does not have much time."

Kavan groaned and nodded. This day had been creeping up on them for months without any miracle to stave off the inevitable. "Take me to him." He looked at Zerio as he stood on shaky legs and nodded. Zerio nodded back. Asta had given him duties to oversee, none of which involved a man he did not know well. He would address those before returning to Kavan. Perhaps, by then, something would be different.

Knowing that age was the inevitable, gradual equalizer of Teren and Elyri, an opponent no miracle could defeat, Kavan entered the room after Rhyrdan opened the bed chamber door. The young man remained in the corridor to stand watch over those within, the way his father had been prone to do. Physician Aland washed his hands in a bowl as Ártur collected blood-stained towels and kerchiefs into a bundle and Yóáná, leaning over the bed, wiped water from Rouvyn's chin that he had failed to swallow. Propped against the headboard with pillows in a position that lessened his coughing, the old man looked thinner, his cheeks hollow, his eyes sunken into dark pools, his chest distended so that his ribs showed through the linen of the sleep shirt he wore.

Yóáná looked at Kavan, nodded, and stepped away after adjusting the blankets. Kavan did not see the exchange of expressions behind him, faces hoping for a miracle Kavan did not expect, but one by one the healers and physician left the room, Aland with the bowl of pink-tainted water, Ártur with the soiled linens, and Yóáná with the barely touched breakfast tray. From the wheezing rattle that came every time Rouvyn's chest inflated and the long, shallow hiss that followed as it emptied again, no one expected breakfast to be of any use to the dying man.

"I am here."

Kavan set his harp where the tray had been and sat on the edge of the mattress. Rouvyn weakly reached for Kavan's hand; the bard closed both of his around the seeking one.

"Knew you'd come." His voice was so airy, so faint, that Kavan had to lean closer to hear him.

"Would you like me to play?"

Rouvyn shook his head. "I want the quiet…to know how Wace…"

The bounty hunter's death was not something Kavan felt they should discuss in Rouvyn's waning hour, but he respected the man's right to choose his end. "I did not see it, but Rhyrdan said it was an honorable end…protecting both of us." What Kavan had seen had been gleaned from Rhyrdan's memory when they secured the waji in the chasm below St. Kóráhm's: the fight up until the thrown waji shattered his ribs, Rhyrdan's removal of the sword that prevented Wace from bleeding out or drowning in blood. Before, Rouvyn had not wanted those details and preferred the mythos that Wace wished to leave behind, the story that he had disappeared into the desert rather than met his end there. Despite guessing the truth, Rouvyn had preferred to hold onto the slim hope that someday, the Cíbhóló hunter would return, that they would see each other again.

Now he was ready to join him.

"He wasn't as bad as most people…he had his faults but…"

"As do we all," Kavan agreed. It had been a peculiar friendship between bard and bounty hunter, but Kavan had called the man a friend.

"As do we all. You will stay with me?"

Kavan kissed the man's fragile hand. "Until he greets you." He did not know if Wace would be waiting beyond death's curtain, but he chose to give Rouvyn that last moment of hope since he could not give him his life.

Hand in hand, he sat with Rouvyn as the sun's position outside of the south-facing window shifted with the passage of day. When Rouvyn was awake, they spoke of Wace, of their first meeting, of the days they had traveled together to find Prince Bertram, and of all the days that had come between. When Rouvyn coughed, or when he slept, Kavan sang soft prayers of forgiveness and redemption set to music that filled the room with an ever-increasing number of spirits that replaced the waning day's warmth with their balmy glow. Sometimes Ártur returned to feel Rouvyn's forehead with a touch meant to ease his physical discomfort. Sometimes Yóáná came to do the same. Sometimes Aland came to wipe away the tears and spittle that leaked down the side of his face and kiss his mentor's forehead.

Once Lorant and Rhyrdan likewise came, but they did no more than touch Rouvyn's hands, meet Kavan's gaze, and then leave again.

Mostly, however, Kavan was the one who remained, reliving events he tried not to dwell on, remembering the contributions and friendships of others who had come and gone. Their last exchange was about such things, about what constituted a good life, and then, reassured that his life met those criteria, Rouvyn's eyes closed one more time. They did not open again, nor flutter with the movement that suggested dreams. When the last shallow wavering intake of breath gave way to a too-long wheezing rattle that ended in silence, Kavan held his breath, squeezed the man's hand, and waited.

Rouvyn's breathing did not return.

Another link to Arlan, to a past that had been, to the person Kavan had been before, was gone. He let out a long, morose sigh of regret and hesitant relief. No more pain. At last, Rouvyn had found peace.

Wishing he could find the same, Kavan remained seated beside him, in the darkness, alone.

❧*❧

They did not see her arrive. They never did. As she passed amidst the sleeping camp on the shore of Lake Curo, ignored by those on watch as if she was not there, she took stock of those around her, the ignorant, the unwitting, the obedient, and the fanatical. None of her recruits had been lost at sea, none had grown disheartened, none had needed punishment for willful disobedience. Whether here because they had chosen her cause or because she had twisted their wills to match her own, she was confident there were men enough for what was to be done. Fraen would rally what he could, his vanity unwilling to accept a mercenary army larger than his own. There would be more than the ones General Waller had already added. Together, both armies would push south to claim the only prize the man sought, draw Enesfel north, and crush them in their greater number.

But the defeat of Enesfel was not her goal. Only the distraction it created for the one she hunted mattered. She did not care about any other conquest. It was a means to an end.

He would come to her and he would die. The blood oath would be fulfilled, the debt paid, the feud settled.

"Ilshaj…"

She bristled.

"A word…"

By the time the speaker reached where she stood, she was gone.

There was no burial in the Lachlan plot, despite Rouvyn's decades-long dedication to the royal family. Only Lachlans were interred in the garden. Instead, the small procession of healers, Kavan, Rhyrdan, and Ágdhállán, and a handful of others who had known him best, led by Novice Rion, trekked through Rhidam to the burial plot at Hes á Redh that had already been prepared. Tusánt was waiting, and there they honored the loyal deceased with the sort of generous words they all felt should have come from the Lachlans.

After the attack on the carriage, Lorant was not willing to risk another trip to the náós. Not even for his cherished Rouvyn.

Choked with emotion and the fleeting shadows of Sight that roused him from the chair at Rouvyn's bedside, Kavan could not speak either. Rouvyn had not been as dear to him as some, but he had been a friend.

Praise k'Ádhá Rouvyn would be spared what was to come. Praise k'Ádhá that Ártur was there to speak for Kavan when he could not.

Afterward, when the body was covered in dark, moist earth and the marker Kavan provided was set in place, after Rhyrdan escorted the collection of healers back to the castle, Kavan remained silent at the graveside with his son's hand in his, staring at the name on the stone and the unsettled earth.

Death was all around him. Too many sick and injured, hopeless and aged. What he would not give to see some of those faces again. What he would not give to walk once more with some of them at his side, with Wortham's hand in his, to ease his distress.

"We should go to Dhóri," Ágdhállán murmured.

Kavan squeezed his hand affectionately but did not otherwise move. Go to Dhóri. Go to Wortham. His son tried, in his way, to put his father's mind at ease. He could not remove his father's unvoiced burden, but family, the boy hoped, would ease it.

"Yes…today we will see Dhóri." There was something Kavan suddenly felt compelled to do, something vital his other son needed to see, to know. "And tomorrow, you and I will spend the day together."

"Can we fly?" Ágdhállán bubbled, rocking up on his toes in giddy excitement.

The idea filled Kavan with a flush of unexpected warmth. It had been too long since he had expended power that way. Too long since he had been allowed any significant use of power except for the day of the carriage attack. Perhaps that unspent energy was why he felt so anxious and out of sorts during the past few weeks. Perhaps that untapped power had fed into an internal loop that prompted episodes he believed were the Sight but might have been something different.

He pushed the boy's red hair out of his eyes, seeing Raebhá in their mismatched hues, and smiled, "I would like that. That's a good idea."

"I know it is…I thought of it," the child teased as he tugged Kavan's hand to pull him away from Rouvyn's grave toward the náós doors and the k'rylag inside.

Dhóri was occupied with Faith business when they arrived, an accounting of financial intake and expenditures for the previous month that needed to be handled promptly so that the agreed-upon percentage could be sent to Clarys for distribution to the needy while the remainder was set aside for St. Kóráhm's upkeep and the care of those in Alberni. But Balint was there and, bored with the company of adults who did not have time for him, he latched onto Ágdhállán and dragged him off to practice swords and play with the litter of pups one of the stable dogs had delivered. Ágdhállán had little interest in swords, but the puppies were a welcome distraction that allowed Kavan to address his own spiritual needs at Wortham's grave.

Someone, he noted, had recently tended the plot, as Wortham's, Zelenka's, and Jermyn's were free of weeds, dirt, and debris. They were adorned with handwoven wreaths of spring flowers and burned-down candles in cups that now contained only pools of solidified wax. He hoped, as he sat with his back to Wortham's stone, imagining he was leaning back-to-back with the man himself, that Kóráhm would come, would sit with him, would bring Wortham's words or address him with a few of his own. Instead, he was addressed only by the voices of songbirds in the trees as he watched the ebb and flow of the ball of light in his open palms, gold and silver sparking and popping as his internal energy fed into it.

"I know you hear me, sínréc; I know you are there," he whispered, ignoring the passage of time, ignoring the distant noises within the chellé and the courtyard beyond. "War is coming…and if you keep your children…keep all of us…safe…"

They had not talked about it, and Rhyrdan had not mentioned the proposition, but with men to fight in Enesfel's defense so limited, it seemed likely that Rhyrdan would be called up to war the same as other men his age. Madoc would be spared by the needs of his position, the need to keep Rhidam safe when so many were absent who could do likewise. Being without Rhyrdan, unable to protect him or be protected by him in return should someone make either of them a target, frightened Kavan the most and ignited a cold knot in his belly that distracted him from the ball of sunlight. It sputtered into nothingness in his hands.

"Did I do that?"

Squashing the warring, fearful sentiments within, opening his eyes to meet Dhóri's apologetic expression, Kavan got to his feet. Dhóri could not have seen the glow but he would have felt the power and heat of it. "No, I am distracted."

"Ágdhi told me about Physician Talis. I know you were friends. I am sorry he is gone."

"Thank you. I'm surprised he did not commandeer you to…"

"He and Balint are occupied with the puppies. I believe he has already picked the one he wants."

Kavan chuckled. Perhaps when war was past, there would be a time for puppies. Ágdhállán had been begging for a dog since he turned five years old. Five years was a long time for a child to wait.

"Has there been news? Lady Asta did not speak of any when I saw her."

"The mercenary vessels in Neth made land in Glevum and were bound for Gorea…or so Lorant said this morning." Kavan had not spoken to the king upon his return from Durham; until this morning, when Lorant had come to Rouvyn's room to pay his respects, he and Kavan had not spoken at all. The activities of the force in Neth made him wonder about the progress of Earé's promised men. Had they reached Kílyn? Were they crossing the Bay? How soon would they reach Levonne? He did not know. He could not give Lorant an answer.

Both felt as though they would not arrive soon enough to be of any use.

"I want to show you something…if you are free."

Curious about what sounded like a secret to him, about whether it was connected to the impending conflict or some private matter of the Alberni estate, Dhóri nodded eagerly. Anything Kavan deemed worthy for him to know was worth the time spent. He still felt on occasion that he owed his father for the disrespect he had shown to him and to the woman Kavan had taken as his wife. "We have finished the books. Bergis is with the boys. I'm here for you, k'bhydhá."

"Remember the path I show you." Kavan led him into the hábhai to the hidden door that only Khwílen also knew about. "Remember the locking patterns I teach. You will practice each until it is mastered. There is a Gate you may use as necessary…but it will be difficult for most to access…and you must never show another the path…or what is at the end."

"I know these passages." The underground tunnel that linked the manor and the chellé was not often used, and had been designated a path of emergency that could take residents of St. Kóráhm's to the manor Gate, or take those from the manor into the chellé for safety if those in the house were hunted. After Kavan constructed a k'rylag inside of the chellé, the need for that passage lessened, but with what he feared lay ahead, Kavan thought it best to encourage the tunnel's use.

"Indeed…and you may need it…but there is another path, the one you were forbidden to…"

Shivering at the warning he perceived in his father's words, Dhóri whispered, "I remember."

"Lead me to that path…then I will take you the rest of the way."

Although he could not see Dhóri in the black passage, Kavan sensed his bobbing head and allowed his son to pass and lead. Dhóri was unaffected by the darkness and so moved without hesitation as far as he dared with a surety that told Kavan how often his son used this path to and from the manor. He stopped when Dhóri stopped, took his hand, placed it upon the wall, and directed him to a small symbol carved into the stone.

"Kóráhm's mark?" The martyr's pyre. A simple mark. Easy to miss but easy to identify if one knew what they were seeking.

"Follow it. It will take you forward, but for now, count your steps, remember the turns. If you go too far, if you veer, you will fall to your death. Stay behind me. Follow my voice."

Voice trembling, Dhóri murmured, "Yes, k'bhydhá."

He counted each step that Kavan counted out loud, found each symbol on the wall that coincided with three steps taken, and shivered at the increasing power that emanated from somewhere ahead. There were no tripping impediments, and the stone beneath him felt to have been worn smooth by what must have been a host of feet. The decline took them deeper below St. Kóráhm's, but curiously, it was not yet too deep to block out the voices from above.

When Kavan eventually stopped again, Dhóri stopped too.

"Can you feel it?"

"The power is strong," Dhóri whispered.

"It is ancient, a natural source as far as I can tell, enhanced by those who made this place what it is. I have seen veins of power in the stone…a sight you would not believe."

"Perhaps I will see it without my eyes."

"Perhaps."

"Do you know who built this way?"

"No," Kavan admitted. "I wish I did." Elyri, Dhóbhaen, phae k'kairá, or someone else. He had no proof to guess who had generated the tunnels and the cubicles at their end. "Now…follow close, do not stray to the side. For those with eyes, this part of the path cannot be seen, so if there comes a day that you choose to bring Ágdhállán, or anyone else, to this place, you must assure them of the path. Follow the power, the pull of the k'rylag before us, and you will be safe.

Dhóri's hand on his arm trembled and Kavan could feel the hesitation in his steps. Having made this crossing many times, Kavan's steps were steady, but by the time they reached the other side of the narrow chasm that protected the treasures stored here, Dhóri's nervousness had dwindled.

"There are items here, books and…more…that must be protected from the world. The power surrounding us guards them from detection so that no one else can ever remove them. I have warded them as well, as a precaution. The Coryllien daggers…the Books of Kóráhm…his cloak…"

"It is here then? I heard rumors during your absence…that it had been found and brought here…but I was unaware it was here."

"Khwílen held it in safe-keeping until my return. It, and so much more…when you leave this place for Gorbesh…take it all with you. Valesce and Earé will direct you where it must be kept. You may bring Zerio and Tau to assist you…Khwílen of course…but no one else."

Dhóri jumped back with a start when he grabbed the grate that shielded the items in their niches behind it. Rubbing his palm as if burned, he croaked, "You did this?"

"As I said," Kavan took Dhóri's hand and rubbed his soothing fingers over his palm before placing it back on the grate, his covering it. "I have warded them well."

"A lot of effort for things already hidden."

"There is always a chance that someone could find their way here." Having heard Bhás' laughter in this place, a memory that made him shudder, he suspected that, if anyone found their way here, it would be her. "I found it, after all. Additional protection seemed prudent at the time."

"There's a chance someone could get past this?" His tone, however, was dubious.

"There is," Kavan admitted. Another ágdháni, perhaps, or someone particularly adept at the sort of bindings he had taught himself to create. No protection was foolproof unless k'Ádhá wanted it so. "But it will not be easy. Now follow…learn…"

"I will never be able to…"

"You will learn to open it." Kavan believed he could burn the instructions into his son's memory if he had to. "When the day comes to remove these things……there will be no need to reset the bindings." Once they retreated to Gorbesh, there might never be a need to return here. If it needed to be done, Kavan would do it himself.

Through the mental link their physical touch allowed, showing Dhóri the fullness of the bindings he had built, he instructed him how to untangle the interwoven threads of power each step of the way. He worked through the process slowly several times, reset them, and then repeated the process until he was satisfied that Dhóri could open the reliquary on his own, albeit slowly. Then Kavan pulled the grated door open and approached the wall of cut-out recesses where the objects of power, bloodshed, and history collected over the years were kept. He did not speak as Dhóri explored up and down, left and right, finding each full space, learning which were empty, reverently touching some, avoiding others with trepidation.

"I didn't know these were…" He knew his father collected books, knew his father was well-versed in the Articles of St. Kóráhm, but this collection of artifacts and relics was more than he had imagined.

"There was never a need for anyone else to know."

"Does Khwílen…?"

"He knows there are items kept here but I have never brought him behind the grate. I expect you to do so in the days ahead."

"Me?" His skepticism was obvious.

"Kóráhm will aid you if I cannot." The saint had not said it, but Kavan was placing that onus on him and expecting him to follow through. "I trust you with this because you are my son. Sóbhán is not here and Ágdhállán is too young. There is no one I trust more. As these events unfold, as Enesfel prepares for war, I may not have the opportunity to come here again. I want you to lead them, those I said, and remove all of this to safety."

Dhóri bowed his head and swallowed hard. "I will make sure of it, 'k'bhydhá." He had disappointed his father's trust before.

He did not intend to do it again.

Sliding to the floor with his back to the wall of relics, Kavan pulled Dhóri down beside him and clenched his hand. "I know I have taxed you thus far, but there is one more skill I wish to teach you if you are willing." He should have taught these things to his son sooner, but he had never thought, even after the first glimpse of an assault on St. Kóráhm's, that Dhóri might have a use for it, that he might be able to learn things Kavan had learned on Dhóbhaen and had been practicing ever since.

"Show me what you want me to know."

"There are means of projecting a shadow of yourself…using it for protection, using it to confuse others…using it as an attack. The shadows are formless, man-shaped, and yet not…"

He shivered, wondering then if that was what he had seen on Pháne, how close Bhás might have been…or how far such a shadow could be projected. "You can strike with it…you can kill…"

"I have no intention of…" Dhóri said in gasping protest.

"I pray you never have to. But if you choose to remain in defense of St. Kóráhm's, you may not have a choice. Defense will only benefit you for so long. You sense only me and yourself in this place, yes?"

"There is no one else here," Dhóri concurred.

"See it through me. Sense it. I will teach you how, and you will practice here, with me, until you have no more power to spend."

It took time, something that could not be calculated in the dark cavern, for Dhóri to draw enough power to focus on his first featureless shadow and project it in the air. There were boundless shadows here from which to crawl a form, and akin to his father's ability to create forms from sun and moonlight, the darkness, too, could take shape. The figure did not last long and, in his initial excitement, he was unable to direct it to do anything, but he could feel it there, like another person in the room, and the unexpected achievement spurred him to try again, to repeat the effort, even after his father let go of his hand.

Satisfied with his son's progress, relieved that his knowledge of this place had provided Dhóri with enough additional external power to continue his focused practice longer than he would have normally, Kavan shifted his attention toward trying to make that external power endure longer. Hand on the stone wall beside him, calling upon the power of the crystals and pendants he wore and Kóráhm's strength that he could feel trickling down from the Saint's protected cloak above Kavan's head, he poured as much as he could gather from the air, the earth, and forced it, in turn, into the rock until the veins ran with green, blue, and white gradient iridescence. The circulating flow fed into Dhóri, without his conscious realization, enabling him to practice longer than he ever had before.

But his body, unaccustomed to so much power flowing through it, weakened and grew tired, creating noticeable delays in his reaction time and focus until Kavan reluctantly removed his hand from the stone and instead took hold of his son's once more.

Kavan believed he could have continued that exchange for several hours, expending power, feeding upon it so that his internal well felt to increase in capacity each time. But his vision blurred beneath the assault of the pulsating light shimmers and his hips were stiff and sore from the cold stone, forcing him to admit that he, too, was not an external power source. He was as mortal as his son and just as prone to exhaustion. He sat still and quiet, recentering his equilibrium, watching the light in the stone veins gradually fade, waiting as Dhóri regained his senses before eventually asking, "How do you feel?"

"Tired," Dhóri admitted. Unaware of what his father had been doing, assuming that he had been watching his progress, he asked, "How did I do?"

"For your first time, very well. I suggest you continue practicing when you can…where others are not watching you…or if you believe Bergis can be trusted, you may ask him to observe your progress. The longer you can hold your shadow to your will, the more you will be able to do with it."

"Can you do the same with the light you capture?"

Cocking his head, realizing he had never tried to control light in the same way he had learned to control shadow, Kavan stood up and answered, "I have never tried."

It was something, now that the possibility had been suggested, he would be sure to practice.

"Thank you, Dhóri." He pulled his son up by his outstretched hand, moved him onto the space of stone where the k'rylag was constructed, closed the gate, and bound it again with threads of power exactly the way it had been so that Dhóri could unknot it next time.

"For what? I should thank you."

"For reminding me there is still much to learn. I'm sure Ágdhállán wants dinner."

"As do I," chuckled Dhóri.

"Will you join us if Emeria has enough prepared?"

In the darkness, Kavan could feel Dhóri's grin as though it was the light of the power veins itself.

They did not often share meals as a family anymore. Despite spending so many hours in his father's solitary company, Dhóri would not miss this additional opportunity to share a little more.

"I'd like that, k'bhydhá."

<h2 style="text-align:center">❧Chapter 17❧</h2>

nable to sleep after Dhóri's return to St. Kóráhm's, emotionally drained from the meal shared with two of his sons and those in the household who were available, and restlessly full of the power he had fed upon in the presence of so many relics, Kavan spent the night in the chapel of his Alberni home, praying, seeking guidance to something he did not yet have the questions to ask. There had been no unnerving laughter in that place, no sense of her nearness, but still, after leaving the vault, he had been troubled by the sound of footsteps when there was no one there, the sensation of breath on his neck as he dined, and felt certain that a blanket of hostility hovered above him, waiting until he retired to drop and smother him in his sleep. The realization that she could manipulate shadow as he could, the premonition that he would be unable to surprise her, that she would know his every action and intention before he did, would not leave him alone. He was certain he would remain at a perpetual disadvantage as his private war loomed larger and he had no way to counter it.

One error, one moment with his guard down, would mean death.

His death, he believed, would result in Enesfel's fall to Neth and the crumbling of the foundation on which most of the Sovereignties were built.

This had not been his plan for his life, but it was, he sensed, the reason for it, the purpose for which he was born, the reason he was blessed, or cursed, with such potent raw power. To fight a battle he did not want. A fight he doubted he could win. A conflict of retribution and revenge, a righting of old wrongs that neither she, nor Kavan, had been part of.

Where was the justice in that?

What if he chose not to fight?

Would the results be any different than dying?

The promise of a day in flight made Ágdhállán more cooperative than usual when it was time to sleep, but it resulted in him bounding into the chapel before daybreak, eager to begin the day's adventure. Carrying a satchel of food collected before finding Kavan at the altar, bringing two slabs of bread smeared with fruit paste, he sat on the step and restlessly tried to wait until his father finished his prayers. His nervously bouncing leg, however, proved enough of a distraction that Kavan ended his prayers with a promise to Ethenae that he would return to them at a later hour.

"Where will we go?" Ágdhállán asked, giving Kavan the other piece of bread and the satchel, and then fidgeting while he ate until he saw his chance to pull his father by the hand to the back garden. Laney, Emeria, and the rest of the staff were beginning to stir or had been up for an hour or more already, but none of them would see father and son here unless they walked around the flowering bushes to come to this spot. No one would witness the transformations, a skill they knew nothing about. "Can we go to the lake?"

The lake had been Kavan's first choice, as it was a place both loved, but something else was poking at the back of his thoughts, a pestering memory of a place he had not returned to in several lifetimes, a place that had, as far as he knew, no cause to be the lure it was proving to be. Chewing the last morsel as they came down the stairs and left the house through the kitchen, he asked, "Would you like to see the place where Arlan and I began our journey together?"

Always curious to explore new places, Ágdhállán asked, "I thought that was the lake?"

"That was our first meeting." Not including the day of Arlan's birth, a detail Kavan had explained to his son before. "This is another place...the place where he decided to become king."

"Where is it?"

Hooking the satchel over his shoulder, Kavan replied, "It is near the lake, not so far from it. We can go to the lake after."

That agreement and the lure of something new made the boy bounce on his toes and exclaim, "Yes. We will go to both places."

It was a long flight for a child, but Ágdhállán, like his father at his age, had a taste, an aptitude, and a preference for shape changing. His favorite small swallow form was off into the air before the final word was complete. Pleased by his excitement, by the joy of having someone to fly with, the white kestrel was not far behind.

Together they circled, they dove, they climbed, with Ágdhállán always trying to steer his father towards the lake while Kavan strove to redirect him toward the cabin he intended to visit. After so many decades, he expected it to no longer stand or to find it claimed by someone else as their home or hunting cabin, someone who would have mixed feelings about allowing the

White Bard into their home merely so he could reminisce in search of something he could not name. The pair stopped twice so the boy could rest, drink, and eat a portion of the abundant food Emeria provided. Ágdhállán could fly the distance but lacked the stamina and the control of his power to make long forays possible in one step.

Stamina would come in time. He had the best bhydáni in the world, the boy often said, to guide him in such things.

When they flew the third time, despite Kavan's urging, Ágdhállán's flight path veered away from his father's destination and away from the lake, following a tickle of something Kavan sensed but did not recognize. His focus was not that of a playful boy eager for a swim but rather someone who had Seen something that needed to be explored and understood.

Kavan had seen that focus before, in instances where Ágdhállán experienced a premonition exclusive to him. Sometimes those moments made Kavan insecure in his gifts, but he understood that, just as he had gifts his son lacked, Ágdhállán was his own person. He was not an extension of his father. His individuality had to be nurtured and respected for what it was, not condemned the way people had shunned Kavan as a boy.

Kavan elected to follow him. Like his prayers, the cabin would wait.

When Ágdhállán dove through the trees, Kavan followed. Before they touched the ground, Kavan knew where they were. He had not returned to this place in years either.

"What is this?" Ágdhállán asked as he resumed his ten-year-old form in a tumbling roll and came back to sitting with twigs and leaves caught in his red curls. The crumbling remains of rock walls spread around them, trees and bushes now grown in places where once homes and fields had been. Moss and vines and the elements continued to eat away at the mortar, to cover what walls had not yet collapsed, so that, in another handful of generations, nothing of this place would exist. Nothing except the Gate with its faintly emanating power that would likewise disappear one day when there were no Elyri to use it.

"An ancient village," Kavan murmured, pushing through the tall weeds and grasses towards the Gate. He had never taken the time to investigate it. "No one knows its name any longer…or what happened here. When I found your mother…when she was injured, I brought her here from the lake and took her home to be treated."

The only other time he had been here had been one snowy night when he had rushed Prince Arlan and Guthrie McHador to safety.

It might have been the traces of his mother that had coaxed the boy here as it drew him to the lake and occasionally caused him to sleep in the bed that she had used when the Sight caused him restless nights and bad dreams.

Kavan could feel her here too.

"Is this a good place to eat and rest? Is it safe to explore?"

Reaching around them, Kavan felt no trace of another soul except for forest creatures that gave the Elyri a wide birth now that their voices echoed and bounced between the trees. "It is safe," he agreed, setting the satchel down and settling cross-legged in the circle of the Gate he could feel beneath him. Maybe if he channeled power into it, the Gate would outlast the collapse of the village by millennia instead of decades or centuries. "Eat first…and do not go far."

Ágdhállán obediently sat across from him and devoured his remaining portion of roast pork as quickly as he could so he could begin his climb over, under, through, and around the shambles of the remaining village walls. Kavan was content to lay back on the ground, hands behind his head, staring at the patches of blue overhead as his senses followed his son's adventures.

He wondered what Raebhá and Arlan would have thought of one another if they had met. He wondered what Arlan would have thought to know that Kavan had married and fathered four children. He wondered what Arlan would have thought of the predicament Enesfel faced now.

The warmth of the summer day brought its memories of so many summers past, so many lives intertwined that had contributed to the man he had become. He missed those faces, those voices, and wished they were with him, but he had no desire to go back to what had been and negate every lesson he had learned along the way. He only wanted his friends.

"k'bhydhá…what is this?" When his father did not immediately respond, Ágdhállán came bounding back to tug on Kavan's arm. "Come…come see what I found!" Sighing for those moments of reminiscing lost, leaving the satchel, Kavan followed over a portion of a broken wall, around brambles, across a bubbling pool where water emerged from the ground, and the traces of animal trails around it. Ágdhállán brought him to a section of wall that might once have contained a hearth, where the moss of the north-facing façade had been stripped back to reveal the stone beneath. Likely by deer wandering to and from the pool, he guessed, noting what looked like the fresh scratches of hooves on the ground and lower portions of the stone.

He had never explored the ruins to guess what this structure might have been, but he recognized an etched symbol on the stone that he had never encountered anywhere in Enesfel.

He had seen it in religious texts. He had seen it in historical manuscripts. He had seen it on a door in the village of Bhórdh.

But never Enesfel.

The stylized flame-eye that denoted the cult of Zythán.

"k'bhydhá?" Ágdhállán whispered at his father's sharp breath.

Kavan outlined the mark with his fingertips, but there was no trace of its history any longer, no trace of those who had carved it, why or when. No spark of power, no faces, no indication why the village had been abandoned except for the echo of screams in his head that could have meant anything. Only that impossible symbol, a tear-shaped mark with a raised dot in the center, crowned by three up-arcing leftward hooking sweeps, like lashes over an eye or wisps of smoke rising from a flame. No one had been able to explain the symbol, or how it was related to the one called Zythán, and he was certain no one in Enesfel could tell him why it was here.

He suspected few in Enesfel would recognize it.

The knotted stone in his stomach and the faint sense in the air of Kóráhm's presence assured him that finding this was no coincidence. Kóráhm had led Ágdhállán here. Ágdhállán had led Kavan. There was something about this place he was meant to know.

"Is it the k'kairá?"

Realizing his labored breathing was coming in short, rapid bursts, that he was in danger of fainting if he did not slow his tumbling thoughts, Kavan removed his hand from the symbol and stepped away, wishing he had the means to remove that stone to take it to St. Kóráhm's with him to be studied, preserved, and understood.

"No…it is…I have only seen this in one other place…in Elyriá…" As he spoke those words, he knew he was meant to go back there again and see for himself what he had not investigated before. He had tried to avoid the lure to Bhórdh, a lure that had given him a sword. This time, what Bhórdh had to give was knowledge. Someone there would know the connection.

Maybe there was a connection to Bhás and Coryllien and Kóráhm as well, even if the saint had never revealed one.

"We must return home."

Ágdhállán's shoulders slumped. "We just got here…"

"We have been here for nearly an hour," Kavan countered, judging by the position of the sun. "It will take more than four to return unless we use the Gate. It has been a long day for you…"

"And you want to study this." Ágdhállán sighed. He could not blame his father for this. He had been the one to initiate the impromptu detour, a detour that had led to a significant find. It had to be significant; his father's interest proved it so. Being the one to find it made Ágdhállán feel proud of himself, even while being disappointed that they did not reach the lake. "The Gate will be better," he sighed. Though he did not want to admit it, he was already wearied. If he could not swim, all he wanted now was to go home, perhaps help his father in the study, or perhaps collapse in his bed and relieve the ache of over-exertion in his limbs.

"I am sorry, Ágdhállán." There were no words to add to his apology that would help. Ágdhállán nodded, stretched up on his toes to touch the carving too, but he felt nothing to explain his father's reaction to it. Then, holding Kavan's hand, he led the way back to the discarded satchel, lifted it from the ground as Kavan lifted him, and then embraced his neck with the satchel between them as they took the unused Gate home.

Once again, Kavan had the feeling that he would need to make up for lost moments with his son as soon as this mystery was solved, as soon as what he was meant to know had been revealed.

❧Chapter 18❧

The halls of St. Kóráhm's were silent, the residents asleep, allowing Kavan and Zerio to peruse the scriptorium shelves uninterrupted. Little was found in Rhidam's limited library and with many of the histories and memoirs, philosophical treatises and discussions of Faith, deemed more vital than works of poetry and mythology, among the first to be taken to Gorbesh, the selection in the chellé was limited. Still, Kavan studiously poured through manuscript after manuscript, even after Zerio gave in to exhaustion and fell asleep with his head against the edge of the open window without reacting to the hourly claxon of chellé hábhai bells. Another page of bulleted notes was collected, snippets of bad weather reports, men rumored to devour and sacrifice other men…both details that later cropped up in Zythánite folklore, stories about ghosts in the forest seeking the dead and the damned in relics of an empty village abandoned to the weeds and waste of passing time.

Those details confirmed occupancy but little else.

There was not a whisper of the Vants among them.

When dawn began to warm his skin and the first dedhá arrived to open the library doors and windows, to light the lanterns and candles throughout the room in preparation for the first shift of scribes who were not preparing items for relocation, Zerio lurched awake with a start and rubbed his neck with a sheepish glance around him. Kavan sat exactly where he had been, closed books at one elbow, rolled scrolls in their tubes on the other side, and a map unfurled on the table in front of him. Beneath his hand, the sketch of the symbol he had found in the ruins, the same as that seen in Bhórdh, with its side-by-side comparison to the nearly identical symbol Zerio had provided, was partially hidden from view.

Kavan had never seen the symbol of the Vants before but the symbol with its missing dot in the tear-shaped portion and its two lash sweeps instead of three, was unmistakably the same. As he had previously surmised from conversations with Zerio, there was a connection between the Vants and the Elyri. The Vants considered themselves Keepers of the Truth and Kavan had deduced a linguistic link between the name Vants and the High Elyri word bháns which meant truth. Though nothing in St. Kóráhm's produced support for his theory, Kavan continued to cling to the belief that it was true…that there was also a connection between the Vants and the Cult of Zythán.

"I apologize, ágdháni…I did not mean to…"

"I am used to nights such as this…you are not…"

"I've had my share of study nights," Zerio assured him with embarrassed defiance, "when Grandmaster Vissaer pressed the tova to learn and recite the mysteries."

"I am certain you had an advantage in that," Kavan said wryly.

"I did…but my memory was as much a curse as a boon…as I was expected to learn and recall much more than others. I used to believe I was being groomed to be grandmaster one day, but instead, I…"

"Did what you were forced to do. Our parts in history are not always those we envisioned them to be."

Having heard some of Kavan's history and exploits from those in Rhidam and from Kavan himself, Zerio knew the bard understood how he felt. He might have been content to remain a minstrel, to become a bhydáni in Bhryell, or a man of Faith in a place such as St. Kóráhm's.

He had not expected to become entangled in the history of Enesfel and the Lachlan Royal House any more than Zerio had envisioned he would be called upon to execute the grandmaster.

"Did you find anything?" He gestured at the map and slid away from the window.

Kavan indicated three spots on the map. "This is Chantel. This is approximately where the ruins are. This is Bhórdh. I've found no answers in the documents here, and see nothing on the map to suggest a connection. No similarities between them. I think, perhaps, I will have to go to Bhórdh and see what I can uncover, what the people there can tell me."

It had been nearly ten years since he had been to the mining village. During the times when he had been there, he had never seen a single living soul, had never spoken to anyone. Instead, he had moved about and over the village like an unseen wraith, always on his way to a different set of ruins that had likewise been the conception of questions without answers, the birthplace of mysteries left unsatisfied.

"I should like to see it if you will take me. Perhaps a new perspective from another set of eyes will help. Perhaps I will see something that has been overlooked, that you did not recognize."

"You might," Kavan agreed. Zerio's Vants experience might reveal details that Kavan had unknowingly overlooked. "Let us put these back."

It was early enough that they might pass through the Gate and Bhórdh unseen, as he thought it best, to start at the ancient stone temple and garner Zerio's opinion of it. Other answers had come to him there, answers given by the great stones, the stains that marred their surfaces, through the grotto beneath, and through the tidbits Kóráhm had offered when he visited there. The Eye of Zythán, as he now called it, was engraved into the central stone four times, once on each side, facing the cardinal directions.

Another perusal of them, with Zerio's eyes, before asking questions of Bhórdh's residents, felt like an appropriate place to begin.

Escaping St. Kóráhm's before Dhóri found him, hesitant to address questions he could not answer, Kavan led Zerio to the first floor Purification Chamber and the Gate it housed. Zerio gave his hands without trepidation as he had the night before and within minutes, they emerged from a narrow room of unspecific purpose into the main room of a building Kavan had never entered. The windowless structure was long, with six oil sconces along both walls, unlit at this early hour. The room reminded him in vague ways of some of the buildings constructed by the dhóbhaen.

They passed a stone podium that provided no trace of power as Kavan was accustomed to, and rows of backless pine benches worn smooth from years of use. Guessing the room was used by the local lómesté, a communal facility where the villagers could gather and discuss important matters, Kavan was surprised that the Gate had brought him here rather than to a náós where most were typically created. He paused to listen to the softly stirring sounds of the waking village, the distant tumble of water, and the creak and splash of wet wood as the Relzá propelled the water wheel in continual motion at the head of the river, and when he was confident they could pass through the village unnoticed, said, "Come. We must hurry."

He would speak to the lómesté or dedhá later. He wanted to return to the grove shrine first.

The single lantern post outside of the building was also unlit, there being less need in the summer for its perpetual glow, and the single-level gray stone structures with rooftops sloped to shed rain and snow were just beginning to rumble and mutter and spark with morning lamps and cookfires and the morning greetings of families. Kavan pointed at the engraving scored into the door that he closed behind them so that Zerio could see it for himself.

Zerio nodded, traced the mark with reverent fingers, and followed Kavan down the steps. By the time the first village door opened, the two men had passed through the broad pastures of wooly cattle and shaggy goats and disappeared into the cover of the towering, tightly packed conifer forest where the morning's temperature was noticeably cooler. Neither dared to speak and even Zerio was forced to admit, without the benefit of Elyri power, that the sensation of being on a holy path was a powerful one.

Claes-Arne had taught him when to be still and when to speak. Breaking the silence, interrupting Kavan's reverence and concentration on something Zerio could not see or hear would be a violation of everything the Vants stood for.

He wished the grandmaster walked this path with him.

Eyes closed, Kavan followed the familiar slow build of power as it brought him nearer to the epicenter of memory and the history he sought. It had never been summer when he had been here and he had never seen the clearing adorned with snow-white and warm saffron blooms that poked through the cracks between the stones, a floral frame like a crown encircling the blood-stained altar and the center pillar beside it. He could imagine wild, orgiastic events here, celebrations of spring, of life, ceremonies as far removed as possible from the horrific death sacrifices and eventual slaughter of Zythán's followers that this place had become synonymous with. When Zerio stopped beside him, his eyes were wide as he beheld the mountainous boulders positioned so near to one another that it was difficult to pass between them in some places. Some lay on their sides, toppled by erosion and other acts of nature, with earth mounded around them where it had given way when the stones fell or where the passage of windy time had blown it into place.

"This place is still in use," Zerio murmured, indicating the trampled grass and dirt path that continued ahead of them.

"Yes," Kavan replied. The stones of this outer circle were unmarked, the passage ungated; nothing prevented them from passing through the western entrance arch or the inner circle created by four equidistant pillars denoting the cardinal directions. The stones fed power into the air as if there had been recent activity here. Wondering the nature of that gathering, the evolution of practices that had continued from Zythán's time through the rising dominance of the Faith as the world now knew it, Kavan walked forward to stand within the inner circle without yet daring to approach or touch the altar.

There was no trace of fresh blood. That was a relief.

Whatever the villagers of Bhórdh celebrated in this place, it did not involve sacrifice.

Emboldened by Kavan's reverential comfort, Zerio mounted the circle of three steps to reach the tallest rock pillar, a smooth-edged obelisk that marked the march of minutes and hours as the shadow it cast blocked the arc of the sun. He inspected the carved symbols that were eye height when he stood on the ground, throat height when he climbed the first step, and heart height when he reached the top. Words, he assumed, though he could not read them. He could not recall any of these symbols in the Vants tomes he had studied as a boy, nor did they look like any language he had seen as he continued to learn. When he turned to find Kavan reaching for the sun-bleached altar top, he noted for the first time a place where the outer stone wall met a mound of earth as if shoring up a collapsing hill or preventing the earth from encroaching on the shrine. A jungle-tangle of vines and branches covered the front, spreading on both sides to embrace the bases of the nearest two stones, but they did not completely mask the black mouth that stretched into the mound behind them.

"What's that?"

Kavan paused before touching the altar, knowing what Zerio meant without looking. "The burial place of Zythán."

"He was no myth then? Is he…?"

"He asks why you are here."

The accent of the man at the western arch where Kavan and Zerio had entered the grove reminded Kavan more of those from Dhóbhaen than of anyone else in Elyriá and he shivered to hear it. Memories of Raebhá and his time there flooded over him and then receded as though a surging surf that would suck the earth from beneath his feet. Having been so engrossed in the power around him, in searching for answers, in remembering past discoveries, he had not been aware of being followed.

Or perhaps this stranger, dressed in russet brown trousers and a pine-beige tunic, his blonde hair braided and pulled away from his face, carrying a woodsman's axe, had been in this forest too, and they had failed to notice.

"Who asks?" Kavan countered with a slight hand gesture that bid Zerio to relax his grip on the dagger on his hip.

"You have questions. I cannot give answers here, but if you will follow, what you seek may be revealed."

Zerio snorted, "You don't know what we seek. You haven't asked."

The man's passive expression did not change but he sounded amused when he gestured to the path they had followed and said, "He knows. Come. Soon you will know too."

"He? Zythán?" The possibility that Zythán might communicate with this man, or others, the way Kóráhm did with him was chilling. Or maybe the stranger referred to the leader of the lómesté. There was only one way Kavan was going to discover what the stranger meant.

"I will follow," he agreed. He had come for answers. He would do what he needed to do to obtain them.

"Not going anywhere without me," huffed Zerio, less trusting of the axe-wielding stranger than Kavan was. He knew the rumors about the White Bard. He had seen the náós assassins held fast when they had attacked the carriage. But he was not prepared to rely on that experience or rumored tales to protect the Elyri duke.

No one would forgive him if he allowed something to happen to Kavan. After losing Claes-Arne, Zerio would not forgive himself.

Their guide did not speak again as they passed through the forest, back across the pastures and fields of grain, to the village streets. Occasionally, the bird-like sounds he emitted were answered by others hidden in the trees, but Kavan did not see or sense anyone near enough to be a threat. In Bhórdh, faces peeped through windows, men and women in the fields or collecting water from the river stopped talking and paused their work to stare, prompting Zerio to move closer to Kavan. Though Elyri were typically non-violent, he felt a sense of unwelcome that he believed could erupt into action at any provocation.

Kavan remained calm, bobbing his head at those they passed, his steps even and sure as if he was strolling through the halls of St. Kóráhm's. His eyes, however, took in every detail, and his senses made note of every stimulus that entered his periphery. He was particularly aware of their guide's mannerisms as they climbed the steps to the lómesté hall where the door was now open as though awaiting their arrival.

He glanced at Zerio who shook his head. They had not been gone long. They had closed that door. Someone had known they were here.

The bard agreed with Zerio's unspoken thoughts. Mounting the steps and passing through the doors felt as if they were acquiescing to an inquisition. But as the answers he wanted were here, if they were anywhere, and the people he had seen thus far seemed non-threatening, he chose to believe that the eight men and women gathered around the podium, dressed the same as those in the street except for the Zythán eye pendants, would be inclined to mercy or, if necessary, willing to provide answers for a fee.

Their guide approached the eight and whispered words that Kavan and Zerio could not hear, words that made the eight nod, purse their lips, and then stare at the pair with judgmental gazes.

Bowing as he had always done to Bhryell's bhydáni, hoping to appease their misgivings and express his integrity, Kavan murmured, "Thank you for seeing us. I am…"

"We know who you are." The woman who spoke without introducing herself, as ancient, he believed, as Tíbhyan had been at the time of his fading, lowered her gaze to the exposed pendants at his breast. Those on either side of her stared as well.

Ignoring the nervous flutter in his stomach, Kavan bowed again. Stories about him were widespread in most of the Sovereignties but he had never performed in Elyriá outside of his hometown, and in Hes Dhágdhuán and the Kyne's palace in Clarys. He had not considered how far the mythos of the White Bard might have traveled.

"We wondered when you would speak to us." She stepped apart from the others, and stopped about half the distance between them as Kavan blinked in surprise, wondering if one of them had the Sight, if the one who spoke with their guide had given them prophecy, or if they had been aware of Kavan's past visits though they had never encountered one another. "You bear the kestrel heart. You seek answers about Phekóntudhurág."

Old Elyri. The dialect of the dhóbhaen. He who brings the rain. Kavan locked his knees to remain upright. It seemed impossible that the oldest known form of Elyri, a form that he had begun to teach Khwílen, Dhóri, and Ágdhállán, could exist in Elyriá without anyone else's knowledge, but perhaps, over time, nothing more of the language remained beyond a title that others might not be able to translate.

But they recognized Gaed's pendant around his neck. That seemed just as unlikely.

"I have found a sword." He lowered his gaze, thinking now that they might be angry for his pilfering of the dead. "I have seen that symbol," he pointed at the pendant she and the others wore, "on ruins in Enesfel. It is," he tilted his head towards Zerio, "the mark of the Vants." He paused, lowered his arm, and swallowed hard before continuing. "I have seen his sacred place. I have seen blood on the altar. I have witnessed conflict with the Faith I do not understand. I have seen his birthplace, walked the paths of our ancestors, and yet I cannot reconcile what I have seen with what I have been taught. The leaders of the Faith do not have the answers I seek. They do not want to know. I hope you have answers. I want to know."

Glances passed between the eight, who studied Zerio as closely as they studied him, and after several almost imperceptible head bobs, another spoke, a fellow with a sweet, boyish voice and a smooth complexion that made him appear younger than the others. Carrying a squat ceramic flask in his hand, he stepped down beside the woman and offered it to the man who had been their escort back to the village.

"You seek the truth, the answers, to the path that lies ahead," he remarked as he returned to the group.

"To which path do you refer?"

Kavan's question remained unanswered.

"Do you know the history of Bhórdh?" he began again. "Do you know of the Vants? Why this symbol is…?"

The woman spoke again as she pressed an unseen object, protected by an age-worn leather pouch, into the escort's hand. "Márllís will take you to your answers, Cliáth. Only you may…"

Zerio crossed his arms and scowled. "You're not taking him…"

"It is not your journey to make," she interrupted with a stern, even expression. "You will remain with us or you may…"

"I'm not going to sit and wait…"

The youngest elder shook his head. "It is not your journey," he repeated warmly. "The answers you seek, Mr. Kaas, may be found in the Book of the Ancestors…if you dare to pursue them."

Zerio's scowl was softened by the possibility that Vants answers might exist, that he might be the only Teren to ever access them, but the glance he gave Kavan expressed his trepidation. These people knew his name without it being spoken. Kavan had a degree of celebrity throughout the Sovereignties; Zerio was no one. They intended to separate them for purposes that might not be what they claimed. He was not comfortable…but he was curious.

"Seek your answers," Kavan encouraged, trusting they would be safe. "I will see you again and we will compare what we learn."

"If you need me…"

"I will be well. As will you. No harm will come to us."

Zerio muttered, "You don't know that…" but he decided to trust Kavan's perception.

"Follow them; do as they ask. I will return."

The other six elders turned sideways and motioned to a door at the rear of the room behind the podium. Zerio threw one more skeptical glance at Kavan and reluctantly followed where their procession led.

The woman led Kavan and the man Márllís to the entrance and opened the door to the scatter of villagers gathered to hear what was happening inside. They moved guiltily away, parting so that Márllís could descend the stairs after accepting the press of the woman's hands upon his head, and Kavan followed, though he stopped at the bottom to look back at her.

He recognized the blessing of hands. Having seen no dedhá here, not expecting any given the village's history though he continued to look for a naós, he guessed that the lómesté also served as the gdhededhá, a peculiar state that contributed to Bhórdh's fringe status. "Where shall I…?"

"Follow Márllís," she repeated. "He will give you what is needed."

Swallowing the unfulfilled sigh that tried to choke him, Kavan bowed again and murmured, "Thank you, dhábhyne." He was uncertain that what Márllís would give, would reveal, would provide the answers he sought, but he chose to trust that any revelations received would be the ones he needed.

Want and need were not the same things.

They wove through Bhórdh to the head of the valley where the Relzá's icy roar grew out of the spring runoff from the heights of the Llaethlágárá and beneath the waterwheel that allowed for mining, milling, and the villagers' other needs. Their hike beyond that point was gradual at first, following footpaths worn smooth by centuries of miners, hunters, and pack animals, past first one intrusion into the rockface and then another, deep caverns that echoed with the pick and hammer sounds of mining that Kavan was unfamiliar with. A rope line upon which swung wooden pails, anchored to the waterwheel far behind, stretched up the mountain, always straight, always tight, always accessible to the wooden mining platforms and walkways constructed at the mouth of each shaft. There were other tunnels barricaded by milled boards or large boulders, other abandoned lines to the left and right. But instead of entering one of those, or one of the mines where the villagers toiled, Márllís continued upward along the gradually more perilous incline. Off the path over ancient rockslides, through patches of snow shielded from the sun by peaks or boulders, was a trail that only those familiar with the mountain could follow.

There were reasons the Llaethlágárá were considered impassible by the Teren who lived on the other side, reasons the north-south range of jagged peaks served as a protective border between Elyri and Teren. Few on the western side wished to make this dangerous climb. Only a handful of mountain passes, even fewer ports, and the Gates, allowed trade between them. Most Teren were content with the belief that the mountains protected them. Most Elyri appreciated that belief and did little to disavow it.

Kavan wondered, as he climbed, how Zythán or anyone else had found their way from the western side of the range to Bhórdh. It could not have been an easy journey.

There were traces of power left by whoever had passed this way last. There were sharp stone faces, the cooling, thinning air, and the call of ravens and eagles that circled overhead. Some of the rock was wet and slippery from melting runoff. Sometimes they were forced to take less direct paths as small rivulets and falls tumbled and splashed past. His muscles screamed in protest at this unfamiliar abuse; his nails were torn on the ends of bruised fingers created by his effort to hold on to jagged precipices to hoist himself up. He believed he had a hole in his boot and was thankful, despite the growing chill, that he had not worn a cloak that would have impeded his climb.

The sun was higher, not yet to its zenith but high enough for Kavan to know they had climbed for nearly three hours before Márllís stopped on an unsteady mine platform, brittle from continual moisture and frequent freezes, and pulled off the boards that protected the cavern behind it from the worst winter weather. In the light of Márllís handlight when he finished, traces of snow were visible upon the smooth floor as far back as Kavan could see, and at the very edge of the light, a limp rope, attached to the wall by an iron pinion and loop, descended into the darkness.

Kavan's heart sank as he suspected he would need to follow that rope into the dark.

He was mildly heartened, however, by the stronger hint of long-unused power the cavern contained.

"This was the first, founded during the crossing of the Llaethlágárá. It is here that he found our valley. It is here he made us home. It is a sacred place, Cliáth. Only those who seek the truth are permitted here. Some come…but few emerge wiser for it. What you glean will be up to you."

Kavan spread his hand on the wall, noting flecks of gold, threads of silver, and clusters of ghlághylá, that rare white, sometimes opaque, sometimes translucent stone found only in the mines of Bhórdh and Bhryell. It was prized for its sharpness, its hardness, and its rarity, as well as for the pools of color the translucent variety could produce when light passed through it. Hoping to find some ancient trace of the man Márllís alluded to, he felt nothing but the cold stone.

The cave reminded him of another, where he and Raebhá had waited out the worst of a winter storm, and mused absently if Zythán, if this same man, had been exiled from Dhóbhaen, if he had ever been held captive in the same prison where Gaed had lost his life.

Here it seemed more likely that this Zythán and the one the dhóbhaen spoke of were the same.

"Sit. Here." Márllís squatted to brush the dusting of snow away from a partially protected nook in the wall and patted the ground for Kavan to claim. From his hip, he drew the ceramic flask he had been given, surprisingly unscathed by their slippery sojourn, and unsealed the cork. From a pouch, he produced a small bit of green, the epicalyx of some unidentified flower which he dropped into the bottle. After shaking it and then swirling the contents a few times, he offered the flask.

"Drink."

Kavan frowned but took the bottle.

"It will not harm you, but," Márllís admitted with an unreadable expression, "it may not be pleasant. It depends."

"On?"

"What you seek."

Holding the bottle beneath his nose, he sniffed at the contents and grimaced. The mild smell, like fresh tallow soap, was laced with something pungent, sour berries and bitter almond, the latter of which he knew could be toxic and even fatal to Teren. It was not alcohol, however, and he chose to believe that the contents would not kill him.

If his life's purpose was not yet fulfilled, he did not think it likely Kóráhm would permit him to die here.

"All of it?"

"Yes."

Again, Kavan sighed but did as instructed. The tart berry flavor made his lips pucker and his tongue rolled side to side to remove the waxy texture from his teeth. He could not taste the bitterness he smelled, but by the time the flask was empty and set on the floor by his knee, his stomach was churning and the room began to sway and spin. He pressed his palms flat against the floor, noting the immediate spread of power veins that shot through the stone in every direction. He lifted his heavy head, tried to focus on Márllís, but he could only see the veins, could only feel a clattering in his skull reminiscent of the sounds of picks striking stone.

"Kóráhm…" he mumbled, a muted plea to undo this foolish thing he had done, and then the cavern and his vision went dark.

☙Chapter 19❧

It had been months since Kaj had seen the sea, since he had listened to the rhythmic thrum of the surf and breathed the scents of salt, sand, and fish. Standing on a hillock covered with short, three-leafed plants, their pinkish-white flowers and the tall grasses swaying in the wind, he listened to his forces setting camp around him. He did not recognize the shrine or the copse of unfamiliar trees around the base of the hillock but they were less his focus than the breathtaking vision before him of the sun setting over the glassy smooth dark azure that curled up at the edges with lacy lips of seafoam white. The sea he was accustomed to was darker, greener, often bordered with angry, swirling waves, but it was still the sea, and gazing out upon it made the weeks of overland marching worth the effort.

There were ships positioned where the water met the shore, the docks longer than those he was familiar with, as Earé had promised there would be, ships meant to take him and most of his men on the next leg of their journey. After so many months of walking, so many months of reds and browns, ambers and pale green, he looked forward to a dozen or so days where the blue of the ocean was all that could be seen in every direction.

"You Captain Yetek?"

The smartly dressed fellow in the armor he had grown to recognize as he moved through Hatu was of indeterminate age, smooth-faced but gray-haired and gray-skinned, with thick, calloused hands and limbs that looked too long and thin to support him or be of use in combat. His accent, too, was familiar now, and deciding he was an emissary of some sort, Kaj faced him and replied, "tama Yetek, yes, I am." He was grateful k'ílshwythnec had taught him this unfamiliar language.

There had been little need to interact with the people they passed. The citizens of Hatu had given them a wide berth, and though Hatuish soldiers were sporadically spotted as if sent to monitor the foreigners or be of use in combat against them, if necessary, no one had tried to stop them or inquire about their needs or destination. Before today, k'ílshwythnec had always been present whenever negotiations were required.

Kaj had not seen the woman in days.

Some thought she had abandoned them. He had more faith in her visions than that, even if he would have preferred her to be here now.

"Lord Dervis…Fleet Management," the gray man said. "We've got the ships you asked for; you got the manpower and knowledge to sail them?" He sounded dubious, as few in Hatu had traveled south of the Enda Mountains, and those who had spoken of endless parched land where little grew. It did not sound like the sort of territory to spawn sailors. Not many were aware of the thriving coastline or the need for fishermen and sea traders that existed in a reportedly harsh land teeming with violent barbarians who periodically spilled into Hatu with a fervor for expansion.

"Three balo and myself," Kaj replied.

"Tsk, tsk." Lord Dervis looked across the sea of men making fires on this sacred stretch of land, assuming the term balo referred to men with sailing skill, but not someone with the experience to captain a ship. "That will never do. There's so many…and you're leaving some here, I'm told?"

"If the king wishes. The Lady indicated some would be needed to protect the shore. balo Ruy will lead them, at your king's discretion. I was also told…"

"Well, yes…we have ship captains…called them up when we brought the fleet together, but we thought…well, never mind that. We'll get everyone across, send some with you, get you to Káliel, and then to Levonne. Got a few more ships coming, if the currents cooperate, so you've got another day or two of rest before we can sail."

"The men will appreciate that." Cocking his head toward the water, Kaj asked, "Do you have a messenger we can send ahead? A horseman or fleet runner…or a falcon so we may prepare the others for our arrival?"

His was the only horse in the company and he already anticipated the need to leave it behind when they sailed if there was no room for it on board. The animal had served him admirably, but he did not think it would hold up to a forced sprint over land to deliver a rider and message to the king they were sent to serve.

"Yes, I will see to it that Duke Cáner knows you are coming. King Lorant and Prime Magistrate de Corrmick likewise. Might I meet this balo Ruy, introduce him to the Captain of the Guard, and show him the headquarters of our guardsmen? It would be fitting if he and some of your men are to integrate into our militia. They do know they will work with us…not command us?" he asked with wringing hands.

"They know the contracts of war. They know that to rebel brings penalty. They serve k'ílshwythnec and will not disobey her commands."

Not knowing who or what k'ílshwythnec was, the gray man only nodded in the hopes of masking his ignorance.

"Good. Take me to him and I'll take you and your captain to the harbor. We'll talk and get you everything you need and I will let King Gamal know you have arrived. In the meantime, your men may rest here…but please, do not desecrate the shrine."

"We will do everything in our power to protect it; you have my word." Even if, Kaj thought as he left that shrine behind, they had no idea of its significance.

Earé had said to protect it.

Protect it they would.

❧*☙

From the north bank of the Kelari River, General Waller could see the abandoned remains of the outpost Enesfel had once maintained. The Yellow Sisters and Fraen's brutality had led to the death of every man inside, a slaughter Waller had participated in and which had, unfortunately, infected a great portion of Neth's force, resulting in additional unnecessary deaths as his army had pushed southeast towards Ruidoso.

When the signal came, Waller, his men, and the unusually obliging mercenary host would follow that same path, this time without the threat of plague and the high probability of encountering Enesfel's troops. The messengers who had come from Lake Curo spoke of the preparation of boats to cross the lake, and to his knowledge, the soldiers moving into position on the west side of Curo would likewise hold in place until the king instructed them to move.

Every action taken thus far was within Neth's boundaries, although the building of troops along the Cordashian border was dubious in intent. So long as those troops did not act, Cordash would remain in an alert stand-down posture. If they did not cross the Kelari, land boats on Curo's southern shore or approach Ruidoso, Enesfel, too, would remain at bay. With so many men behind Waller now, including conscripted recruits collected along the way, when the order was given, Enesfel's small, unprepared groups of men posted in the south would drown in their deterrent masses. Or else they would flee and avoid a conflict they could not win.

He was confident of their success.

The arrogant, black-haired woman beside him was equally confident. As always when she appeared, he found her habit of giving orders contrary to what King Fraen had given him irritating as well.

"Tomorrow," she said quietly, "we cross the river."

"We're to establish our outpost here," Waller began.

"And you shall. This'll be the best place from which to invade Elriá."

Waller's frown deepened and he stared at her as if she had lost whatever sanity she possessed. "Invading Elriá is…"

"…necessary…"

"…suicide…"

Her shoulders hitched. She did not speak of Elriá again, but instead continued, "We have the numbers to create outposts in the south, to shore up the southern forest between Fiara and Ruidoso, to take Ruidoso as…"

"By the time we reach Ruidoso, even if we're fortunate enough to meet no resistance, we will have shed the majority of…"

"There will be more. The initiative of reclamation will bring honor, bring men to our side, and offer recompense to the man who achieves it."

He rubbed his chin without replying, needing to shave, but having not remained in one place long enough for him to take the time. As he recalled, Fraen once discussed a similar promise made to him against the specific requests of the Queen-regent, when his choices had, to their surprise, secured him Neth's throne. A simple man of lowly birth, Waller's goals were not so lofty. He would happily settle for a title, some land, and the opportunity to build some wealth to his name.

But she was right. There would be more men to collect along their way. Men from Ruidoso. Soldiers from the western path, the mercenaries crossing the lake. Recruits, forced or voluntary, from reclaimed towns. Mostly undefended, there was no reason to believe he could not force them, and Ruidoso, to submit to Fraen's rule.

He gambled that her assessment of the situation was correct.

But he was not stupid enough to risk war with Elriá.

The Elyri could do things.

They could destroy Neth without trying.

"South," he agreed with a huff.

He did not expect her to be with him when the early morning march of capitulation began.

❧ * ❦

A ship plunging fore and aft, side to side, buffeted by a howling gale and the heaving sea that smashed against the hull and threw itself over the deck. A Dhóbhaen ship, where men and women shouted to be heard over the storm with words swallowed by the sucking, thrusting wind as below the deck, children screamed and cried. His hands sought the nearest solid hold but came up empty, passing through what he could see as though he, or it, were a phantom mist in the spray of the sea.

He had been on a ship like this once, though his recall of it was vague, muted by the water in his lungs and the throbbing between his ears created by nearly drowning. He had seen such a ship in a harbor south of Hatu and on paintings in Clarys, a vessel lost to Elyri memory or expressly purged from it, older than any other he had seen.

But the frightened voices echoing around him, displaced by the squall, belonged to faces he did not know, twisted faces drenched by the crests of the inky open sea as they fought to keep their ship afloat and pointed in the direction they intended to sail.

The pitching sensation, the deafening roar, threatening to overpower him as his twisting stomach clenched again against the impulse to disgorge its contents, felt to last for endless hours, the passage of time lost, until gradually his squeezed-shut eyes registered a brightening sky and his stance, while wobble-kneed and weak, felt steadier than before. The buzzing ring in his ears was swept away as his hand pushed his dripping hair from his face.

"Thank the stars you warned us…if not for securing the supplies, lashing the little ones…"

"Tell that to them," said a second voice, something like a dream that felt more familiar than the first. He turned toward the speaker he could see in profile, a broad-faced fellow whose still wet hair was the pale yellow of faded sunlight, whose blue eyes were so blue as to be nearly white. The speaker gestured to a dozen or so similar vessels bobbing on the now serene sea where small figures worked quickly to secure lines and rails and items set loose by the storm.

"Zythán…are you doing this?"

Kavan turned again, nearly tripping and collapsing onto the dry earth plowed for planting, to face the two approaching from the other side of the field, their faces grim with disappointment. The broad-faced blonde who surprisingly stood beside him stopped walking and those Kavan realized were gathered around him did likewise. His reluctant turn to respond to those who called after him allowed a clearer view of his face.

"They think I've caused this…"

"Knowing the weather is not controlling it." The second speaker, the one Kavan had heard moments before the waning storm deposited him here, bent to pick something up from the ground and held it in his outstretched hand so that the dusty soil could sift between his fingers and drift away on the arid breeze. He was a short man, thin and almost fragile, with an air of power that prickled across Kavan's skin like the brush of insect wings. His tied-back hair was golden blonde, radiant like burnished gold, and braided into a long queue that hung nearly to his waist.

The third, dressed in yellow with straight, thinning, strawberry blonde hair trimmed closer to his scalp, grasped Zythán's hand, a touch that felt to close around Kavan's hand instead and relayed the power of a healer through the sparks that passed through the contact. "Without you, we would not have made it here…"

Choosing not to debate their protests nor take credit for observations that had kept them alive, Zythán murmured, "The land here cannot support us all. Some of us must seek fertile ground elsewhere so that all may thrive and grow. You should not stay here, Llyr…there is no life for any of us…"

There was something left unsaid, a secret threat that underpinned the men's desire to keep Zythán with them and yet made his departure inevitable. A secret, it seemed, that those around him did not know.

A secret that burdened him with immense sadness.

Kavan blinked. He knew the sense of wanting to belong, the sense of seeking, the frustration and hope that surged and waned in the people around him as the steady march of footsteps along a dusty trail pulled them always north. He knew these lands, these places, stretches of summer-parched plains that gave way to eroded, ancient mountains. He knew the lands on the other side, where now a town stood sentry against invaders from the south.

He did not recognize the smattering of villages, miniature Teren settlements that would one day grow into the southernmost Sovereignty. But he knew the naked hillock and its summer-clear vista of the Bay of Phalla, a hillock now steeped in the prayers of the faithful who sought St. Kóráhm's guidance.

He also knew the bitter taste of rejection that compelled the unwanted to move onward, always seeking something that could not be found. He knew Zythán's compulsion to press on even when those around him begged to make due with one place or another. Zythán would not settle.

His soul sought something more.

Kavan likewise knew the eastern shoreline, the banks of the Tegid, and the nascent town on the other side where a tribal warlord established his roots before reaching outward to build the second Sovereignty. He knew the hostility of those afraid of differences, afraid of a man who could heal with a touch and warned of changes of weather with unerring accuracy. He understood the challenges of violence by the self-appointed kin in response to advice that could save the crops and protect the budding settlement.

He knew Zythán's sigh of defeat and the miserable sighs of those prompted to move on one more time.

Kavan knew the stretch of forest he had flown over many times, broader in vision than in memory, and the scent drew him toward a place that, in his soul, had belonged to him since he had been a very small boy. He knew the bitter cold of winter and the swirling sting of snow. He was familiar with the sense of relief when, amid the worst bite of winter, they sought and found shelter and relief in a small village of mudbrick and wood buildings in a clearing within the trees.

Kavan's soul knew this place too, though he had not seen it thus before.

He welcomed camaraderie. He welcomed the joy of a community building homes together, growing crops, and seeking commodities that the forested land around them could offer to strengthen the now doubled-in-size village. In an eye blink the passage of seasons and years, in a Sight-blur parade of images of places and things, faces, times, and events that raced through his mind too quickly to catch hold of and examine. He felt the compulsion to keep moving which again prompted Zythán to leave behind those who had followed him.

Destiny drew him somewhere else.

An agonizing, treacherous climb up and then down, over and through the Llaethlágárá's perilous passes that brought with it the discovery of a cavern and a glistening white stone unlike anything he had ever seen. More astonishing still was the settlement at the mountain's base, where people like himself, dhóbhaen and yet not, had clustered to mine these stones and the other precious metal from the riches the mountains offered.

A home. A sense of belonging. Zythán did not know where he was, but he believed he had found what he was looking for.

Years ticked like heartbeats. Gates found or constructed to satisfy his unending wanderlust. Clarys and Aralt and Glevum. The vast middle desert and scores of places Kavan had never seen. The walls of Gorbesh beheld from afar where he listened to wise, aging voices he had known and younger voices he did not, from the men he did not dare to see again.

This was not his place. Despite the ache of what had been left behind, these were no longer his people.

It was time to return to those left behind. The people he called his own.

Kavan's heart was heavy with mixed joy and dismay when the passage of time brought him back to the village in the grove, larger now, filled with Teren and the once-Dhóbhaen who embraced his return with ears eager to hear his tales of exploration. The village founders, however, were not as welcoming. The slipping of shorter Teren generations and the slower births of his long-lived followers had left his people in the minority. The integration he had expected had resulted in segregation, distrust, and fear. Whispers and rumors had replaced amity, and the warnings Zythán brought of a great winter storm to come only heightened those fears.

He felt it coming, the end of the dream for this place. Some heeded his advice, his warnings, and sought shelter through the Gate in a land behind the jagged eastern peaks. Some, reluctant to relinquish this life they had built, would not leave it.

Then, the inevitable.

Fire licking toward the tops of the surrounding trees. Lightning forks striking foliage and houses alike. Shrieks and cries and shouts of indignant fury. Death screams. Terror. The panicked retreat of those under Zythán's care through the Gate he had built.

A presence. Two. A ball of startled power Zythán instinctively fought to control. His turning from the Gate where others gathered amid swirling smoke and blue-centered flames. The walls of the room they were in crumbled beneath the fire's assault. A tongue of lightning shooting to the ground, throwing one of the two and clumps of mud and collapsed bricks in every direction. Kavan watched in horror as the other, a child no older than his son, crumpled where he stood.

Judging by Zythán's wide-eyed expression, it was an accidental horror they shared. But there was no time to offer aid, no amount of healing he could offer to undo what had been done. He hurried those around him to safety behind the Llaethlágárá and left the rest to fate.

The fire continued to burn.

The homes built next became Bhórdh…sorrow.

In time, that meaning was buried and forgotten.

A sword on a forge, healing hands compelled to create something meant to protect should those they had left behind seek vengeance. Crafting, molding, carving. Heat and arid desert scents reminded Kavan of the bounty hunter Wace. Whispered claims of divinity, of greatness beyond

Dhágdhuán's grace that Kavan had heard too often, interwoven with moments of foreign rites of bloodshed and orgiastic adoration that fed Zythán's depression, dismay, and a growing longing for peace and escape. Digging, digging…the desire for the earth to swallow him as the other longings threatened to do.

Cold earth and stone at his back.

An extended sigh of relief.

Darkness.

Out of that darkness, the same sensations of cold earth and stone behind his head, beneath his legs, dragged Kavan's consciousness out of the haze of vision that made his head throb more mercilessly than the Sight had ever done. Under the press of one hand, tri-colored power veins raced from his fingertips through the floor and walls and back, filling the cavern with the tinted ambiance of the sky during a lightning storm. His other hand was curled around something he could not see, but when he first tried to shift, to lift his arm and sit up straighter, the world spun and made him want to retch. He was forced to close his eyes and focus on balancing his equilibrium and the too-abundant power that had collected inside of him.

As he listened for Márllís' presence, for the sounds of man or beast or the wind outside, he considered the flood of images and the moments of action that were slow to congeal within his memory. Morsels of history lost to time, unexplained or unwritten, or else hallucinations meant to obscure the veracity of memory. But Kavan trusted what he had been Shown. He felt no reason to doubt it. He had not seen what had come after, the threads of history that had frayed and grown distorted by people of influence who needed to weave a darker narrative to replace the inconvenient truth. He did not doubt that someday the same would happen to his legacy, that the man he was would disappear into the wash of myth and twisted distortions.

He could already see it happening…just as Zythán had.

If only, he sighed, he could have lived the life of any normal man.

If only the path behind and ahead, and each breath swallowed and exhaled, did not rest on his shoulders with their inescapable weight.

A raven's caw was answered by another somewhere beyond the mouth of the cavern. His stomach churned in a way that suggested he had not eaten in several days and his tongue stuck, swollen and dry, to the roof of his mouth. He rolled his shoulders and his neck so that his hair caught and pulled against the stone behind his head, until finally the vertigo subsided and he could open his eyes without nausea overtaking him.

He was alone.

Near his clenched hand, a wrapped bundle and a waterskin, not the flask he had drank from before, waited for his inspection, prompting a murmured prayer as he realized that his previous folly had not killed him but had instead immersed him in visions of history he might not otherwise have discovered. Deciding to quench his thirst and appease his hunger, he uncurled his palm to take the water and was startled by the clatter of something falling out of his palm. He leaned forward, groaning with the abuse of too-long stationary muscles, and picked up what he had dropped.

Carved from the ghlághylá mined from this cavern or another like it, the rod-like item was no bigger around than many of the quills and writing styluses on Kavan's desk. As long as his palm was across, it had a small, nib-like bulb on one end with a silvery metal band behind it, another band at the other end, and a flat-nubbed cap with a drilled hole wide enough for a cord or chain to thread. The center length flared behind the first band and tapered again towards the second, creating an aesthetically pleasing tool of a sort Kavan did not recognize. Power sparked and popped faintly within it, stronger when his other hand was on the floor than when he lifted that hand to turn the tool over in his palm…an ancient power as old as the earth itself.

He had not seen this item in his visions and assumed Márllís must have left it with him when he left the food and water. He wondered, as he pulled off the black cord that held the shard of Muir's crystal and began to pick at the knot to untie it, what the stylus-like tool was for. Why it had been given to him. What it meant.

He threaded the cord through the hole, knotted it again, and hung it around his neck before inspecting what else he had been left. Bread and water, simple but effective enough to appease his parched throat and his grumbling belly but not enough, he eventually discovered when he struggled to his feet and to the mouth of the cavern, to keep him strong and steady. His condition would make the descent to Bhórdh hazardous, but the continuing wax and wane of unstable power within made flight an impossible option unless he chose to wait on the disintegrating platform for an indeterminate amount of time to feel like himself again.

The sun was rising. Zerio would be waiting. His children, family, and friends as well. And only someone in Bhórdh would be able to tell him about the object he had been given. Uncertain how long he had been away, he did not believe he could waste another delay.

Zythán had made the climb down from this cave.

Kavan could do it too.

❧Chapter 20❧

Too many times his feet slipped on the spray-damp stones. Too many times, his knees struck the rocks, his ankles twisted, or his hands lost their hold on sharp ledges and precipices that enabled his descent as the sun brought the fullness of a new day. He paused at each mining platform he reached, to rest, to drink from the water skin, to plot his course, and test his power to gauge if flight was available. But the energy within felt too unstable to control so he was forced to continue on foot. There were threads stretched taut back up the mountain to their source, power dragging him back to the mystery he could not afford to dwell on until he was on flat ground and he believed that, if control returned and flight was permitted, he would return to the cavern instead of to Bhórdh where he should go.

It was better this way.

The three-hour climb up grew to five on his way down, his limbs aching more and more so that by the time he reached the base of the mountain and stood on the banks of the Relzá, he was forced to relent to an uncustomary need for mid-day sleep beneath the towering pines that cast their shadows across the river.

The visions came back to him there, moments meant to fill in the gaps of what he had witnessed before or that unveil the course of history that had come to color the man's good name. When again the croaking of a raven in the branches brought him awake, the sun had disappeared beneath the mountain tops behind him. He glanced at the moon and scowled.

If any of the miners, if anyone coming to the waterwheel had seen him, he had not sensed them and they had not disturbed him. He ate what remained of the bread and drank his fill of water from the river, and then returned to Bhórdh.

The village was quiet, doors and windows closed for the night to lock the light of life behind them. Soft, familial voices and the cordial laughter of friends punctuated by the warm clatter of dining and the aromas of lamb and local dishes brought with it wove through the streets, leaving but a single man out alone, a man who paced feverishly from one side of the lómesté steps to the other with a perturbed frown and an occasional pause to pat the leather satchel resting on the top step. He looked up when the crunch of boots on the gravel path alerted him to someone's arrival and barely refrained from prostrating himself at the bard's feet or throwing himself into an embrace that would have embarrassed them both.

"I feared for your life," he croaked, picking up the satchel and clutching it to his chest to contain the impulse to wrap his arms around Kavan instead.

Rather than admit he had, for a few brief moments, feared the same, Kavan asked, "Have you been waiting long?"

"They kicked me out of their…" he began with a grousing grumble and shrug. "It wasn't a library…it wasn't a book…it was…" He coughed and shrugged again. "I'd seen what I asked to see but no more; they said you would come and then locked me out and I…there was nowhere else to go."

To leave Zerio in the street without the hospitality of food or shelter made Kavan frown, but he did not want to misjudge the locals based on what little information he had. Though less weary and more centered in power, the recent exertion of the climb that made his muscles ache and the visions that made his head throb prompted Kavan to sit on the steps and ask, "How long?"

"Three days…and today…so four." Zerio sat beside him. "Did you find what you sought?"

"Some, yes." He knew the connection between the village and Bhórdh and knew Zythán's history with the Dhóbhaen, Llyr and Drebhoti. He had an inkling of how the man had come to be vilified by the Faith…and how he had come to be buried with a sword he had never wielded in a place those here regarded as sacred. Why any of this had been brought to his attention now, what it had to do with the shadow of war, was an unanswered mystery.

"Do you recognize this?" From beneath his shirt, he pulled the white stone object he had found…or been given…and presented it for Zerio's inspection. Zerio leaned closer and held it in his hand, but in the growing twilight, there were no distinguishing details that might explain what it was or where it had come from.

"Perhaps an ancient stylus…a little like the Grandmaster used…but it is not long enough for that…and there appears to be no trace of ink or a receptacle for it."

"My thoughts as well," Kavan agreed with a sigh as he tucked it back inside his shirt. "Are the bhydáni…?"

"They went that way after…when they expelled me from…" He pointed in the direction of the grove with a petulant scowl. "I have not seen them since."

"You waited here rather than…?"

"Didn't seem prudent to intrude. I didn't think I should risk their anger, risk doing something you or I would regret."

Kavan bobbed his head, closed his eyes, and listened to the building at his back, hoping for a trace of the ancient ones but hearing nothing except the gradual replacement of domestic sounds of summer insects and nightbirds. Eventually, he stretched his hand to Zerio, his palm up, and murmured, "Will you show me what you saw? What you learned? What they told you?"

Though his expression remained pensive, Zerio did not hesitate to put his hand on top of the bard's. Turning his thoughts to well-practiced Vants meditations allowed his mind to go blank enough for Kavan to have easy access to his thoughts. To trace the recent memories to the large sphere of white stone positioned on an oiled pine pedestal carved with intricate patterns resembling both High Elyri text, ancient dhóbhaen, and a smattering of symbols ascribed to the phae k'kairá. With his hands splayed across the sides of the sphere, Zerio's head had been bombarded with more information than his Teren mind was equipped to absorb all at once, an experience Kavan was often confronted with when the Sight chose to blast too many details in too short a time. Given enough time, Kavan would be able to sort those details out in the same way he did other visions or the way he would eventually make sense of Zythán's story out of what was presented to him. Even with Zerio's eidetic memory, however, absorbing and making sense of what he had been shown would likely take him years, perhaps decades, to sort out.

It was no wonder he was agitated and fumbled with his words.

"When we are home, record everything you remember, everything you were shown, as it comes back to you," he said gently, using his free hand to smooth Zerio's brown hair from his face. "It will take time, and I will help you, but once it is done, you will have more knowledge of the Vants…and beyond…than any man alive. You will be their recordkeeper. You will be their voice."

An involuntary shiver ran through Zerio's body. "And you?"

Kavan nodded and pulled Zerio to his feet. "I will do the same," he agreed. He must. It was the only way anyone would ever learn the truth, the only way he would discover why these things were revealed to him now…unless Kóráhm saw fit to come and explain it all first.

∿∙*∿∙

"k'Ádhá's blessing and safe journey," Gamal said, unsure if he should offer a hand to the man before him or if there was some other gesture he should make. This was the first time in history, as far as he knew, that a Hatu king and a leader of the southern armies had cooperated. He did not expect the situation to outlast the war ahead, but he liked this serene, cordial fellow who could, in appearance, be from anywhere in Hatu.

Though not a religious man, Kaj had heard the term k'Ádhá often enough to identify it with the divine, and out of respect he bowed his head and accepted the well wishes the King of Hatu bestowed. Most of his force, minus those he was leaving behind, led by Ruy Gaddo, the youngest of his balo and a man well-versed in combat with pirates on both land and sea, had already boarded the ships. The current was said to be favorable, swift and strong, prompting the decision to set sail under the cover of darkness to take advantage of it. A few days north to the gatekeeping islands of Káliel, then they would be on their way to the destination Earé directed them to.

Kaj did not know what to expect in those lands…except for inevitable bloodshed for a cause the k'ílshwythnec deemed important.

"May our joint venture benefit us all," Kaj replied, offering a half-bow that seemed a fitting gesture of respect after witnessing others do the same. "balo Ruy will serve you well if it comes to a fight."

"Don't know why it would," grunted Gamal, "but if Lord Cliáth is right, we can be sure of it." It had been decades since Hatu had been at war on her own soil, though they had sent troops to aid Enesfel against Neth in the past. He hoped his people had not forgotten their heritage. He hoped they were up to the challenges ahead.

Kaj inclined his head and took his leave, boarding the flagship with cautious, confident steps, and with the clanging of the harbor bell, motioned for the fleet to be underway. From further down the dock, balo Ruy gave a waving salute.

Kaj wondered if he would see his youngest balo again.

∿∙*∿∙

The empty, spacious room the pair stepped into appeared no more occupied or used than it had the first time Zerio had brought Kavan here more than eight years ago. From the arched windows of colored glass, dark beneath the cloudy Glevum sky, and the featureless carved statues that lined the east and west walls, Kavan was confident the structure had once been a náós, although, to his knowledge, Neth had not allowed a functioning, legal religious establishment in centuries. It had served as an Association haven, with the organization respecting the inherent wealth present in those works of art, and then had stood empty for nearly a century until at last some wealthy member of the Vants purchased the building from the Crown to serve as a training center for architects and civil engineers, trades the de Corrmick kings had encouraged in their efforts to make Neth ever-stronger.

Such kings had not known the existence of the Vants and had been unaware of the royal funds funneled to those who manipulated the Crown from the shadows. They had allowed the Vants to work unhindered…until Queen-Regent Inness purged the land of many suspected Vants.

It was uncertain if anyone had noticed the absence of students and masters here…or if those absences were attributed to the Yellow Sisters.

If any Vants beyond Geiel remained in Glevum, they had not yet reclaimed this place. It had been the ideal location for a Gate to be constructed outside of the Glevum castle. Infiltrating the castle with Fraen as the king had not seemed wise, despite Kjell's oft-discussed wish to do just that and assassinate Fraen from the inside.

He had not been healthy enough to resume his throne, his son and grandson not prepared for the responsibility, and with the Yellow Death continuing to move through the Sovereignties, it was deemed wisest to let the plagues run their course and perhaps do an assassin's work for them.

It had not.

"Two days?" asked Zerio, as eager to record the thoughts in his head as Kavan had asked as he was to find proof of a thriving Vants community and find Marta. Geiel could not be the only Vants…and finding Marta to return peace to Rhidam, without any more than a slim chance that Warde Dugan would fulfill his aunt's wishes, had to be done so that the king could focus on the fight against Neth.

"Midnight, two days," Kavan agreed. Still weary from his ordeal in Bhórdh, he had not expected to return to St. Kóráhm's and be met with the request to deliver Zerio for a reconnaissance survey. Kjell had attempted to send Tau but the Cíbhóló Vants had refused to leave him. After Asta needled him with pleading desperation, Kavan agreed to deliver Zerio and bring him back so that his absence in Rhidam would barely be noted. With Zerio's agreement to the mission, the exiled king allowed him to go alone.

They delayed long enough for Zerio to change of clothes; now they were here. "Right here." He looked at the moonbeams that had broken through the clouds and stretched through the windows onto the floor in front of him. "If there will be a delay, if you need time or assistance, leave a message where we came…I will find it and respond accordingly."

"If I'm not here in two days, if there isn't any word, it'll be because I can't be. Are you sure you can't find them? I could use your help."

Kavan sighed and nodded, hoping the results of Zerio's efforts did not come to that. "I have other duties, and you know Glevum better than I."

"I know…but a man can hope." He nodded again and said, "Two days." There were things in this lead-up to war that only a Vants could do. As before, in the rescue of King Kjell, this was his duty. Whatever the result.

❧ * ☙

The gray-cloaked woman stared from the shoreline, hands at her side with fingers twisting and flexing as though weaving a spell to control the summer breeze and lazy lake current upon which the mass of small fishing boats, rafts, and merchant traders bobbed, waiting to ferry Nethite troops and assisting mercenaries to Lake Curo's southern shore. Her focus should have been on the boats.

Instead, it sought the one she had been unable to feel for several days, as if a veil had fallen between them for the first time. Confident she would know if he had died, confident of her path and her success, she had followed a sliver…him but not him…hoping to pierce that shield until he returned, unmasked by whatever had come between them, re-emerging into power as if emerging from a womb.

He was changed in ways she could not name, stronger but more vulnerable.

It was time to take advantage of those vulnerabilities. The portents had revealed it to be time.

The portents never lied.

❧Chapter 21❦

For nearly an hour, sleepless and determined to make sense of things he had Seen, Kavan sat at Ágdhállán's bedside, listening to the boy's breathing as he slept, hastily writing everything he could remember of the mine cavern visions. He knew it would take him weeks to set it all to paper, particularly since he was repeatedly distracted by the sound of footsteps at the bedroom door, the rustling of fabric, and repeated knockings where no one proved to be each time he checked. Come morning, regardless of how much he wrote, he knew that when Lorant, Rhyrdan, and his son realized he had returned, duties would be set upon him that would rob him of what little free time he had.

The sparking energy beneath his shirt each time the stylus-like object touched the other charms he wore was a constant reminder that he needed to solve that mystery too. If it had belonged to Zythán, a holy artifact somehow related to the staff and cup the man's companions had made, if it not only connected him to Llyr and Drebhoti but also the Dhóbhaen, then Gorbesh was likely the best place to seek answers. But if he waited until morning, his opportunity to go would be lost.

After kissing Ágdhállán's forehead, leaving his writing book on the bedside table to reassure his son that he had been there and would return, he took the time to ward the room, the windows and door, to prevent that peculiar source of footsteps from entering; he left Rhidam before dawn, escaping Lorant's requests, Rhyrdan's barrage of updates and his affectionate desire for company, or Ártur's curious worried questions. He emerged from the Gorbesh community's only Gate, listened to the distant sounds of the community beginning to stir, and started through the oil lamp-lit hall towards the room where he expected to find answers.

He did not sense his daughter. The gifts and training of She Who Sees, however, could hide her from him until she wished to be found. She, too, might have answers, but seeing her was not the reason he was here.

❧ 229 ❦

"Lord Cliáth…we were not expecting you."

Kavan paused at the corridor intersection to meet the man at the other end, surprised to see him there when he had not sensed his proximity either. Valesce, stoop-shouldered and shuffling, looked older and more tired than when Kavan had been here a few short weeks ago, or maybe, he mused as he waited for the Elder to approach, it was merely the hour and the glow of the lamplight that made him appear that way.

"Is Earé here?" Asking gave Kavan a reason for being here, although, with the movement of St. Kóráhm's books and treasures to these halls, he no longer needed an excuse.

Valesce shook his head. "I have not seen her since you were last here. May I be of assistance?"

"Perhaps." Valesce had been Qol's right hand, exposed to decades of knowledge that few others had access to. He had been the one to retrieve the staff and cup from the vaults and put them into Kavan's hands. He knew the history of those relics as surely as Qol had known them. He pulled the cord over his head, shook his hair free of it, and offered the stone stylus to the other man.

"Do you know what this is?"

Valesce did not accept the offering but he gingerly turned it between his fingers, held it up to the light of the nearest oil lamp, and tested its slight weight in his palm. "I do not," he murmured without offering an opinion or guess as to what it could be. "But there is power in it."

Though Valesce was not Elyri, Kavan knew that some Teren learned to sense power when they lived their lives exposed to it. Sometimes that exposure affected them in unexpected ways. It explained how he might have lived so long. "I found…retrieved…I have cause to believe it belonged to Zythán. When Valesce released the stylus with a scowl, Kavan scowled too. "You know that name."

As if the name made him uncomfortable, as if it meant something he did not want to admit, Valesce shook his head no but said, "Only legends of one who controlled the air…the rain…one who killed without touch…one who served as trio with Llyr and Drebhoti until he did not…"

sídysá. It was the only way of killing without a touch that Kavan knew, a gift…a curse…that he possessed himself. That much of Kavan's assessment from the vision was confirmed and he shuddered to find he had something else in common with another heretic. Though he did not think Valesce would answer, he asked, "Why was he expelled? What happened?"

Despite the reluctance to see him leave that both Llyr and Drebhoti had expressed, despite Zythán's words that made it sound as if the choice to leave his friends had been his, Kavan was certain that departing for the unknown north had not been entirely up to him. Banished, encouraged to leave, or simply made to feel so unwelcome that departure was the only bearable choice, they were all the same.

Perhaps, as Kavan knew too intimately, his departure had come down to fear. Enduring Teren fear was one thing. Facing the fear of one's people, family, friends, and community, was something else.

"It is not known." Valesce avoided eye contact and tried to still the uncharacteristic shuffling of his feet.

"Is there anyone who would? Are there books or…"

A fleeting shadow of offense flitted over the older man's normally serene face before he released a soft hiss through his teeth and replied. "It is not in our history."

Kavan bowed his head. "Apologies, Valesce. I mean no offense…but surely there are myths or…?"

"No." Adamant in his denial, Valesce wiped his hands on the front of his robe, closing the discussion with a frown. "Will you join us for…?"

Shaking his head, choosing not to push further for answers, Kavan tucked the stylus back inside his shirt. "I came for Earé…for answers…but if there are none, I must return to Rhidam and my son. I will leave this in the vault and…"

"It may not stay here."

It was Kavan's turn to frown. "Then you do know…"

Again in an aberrantly stern tone, Valesce said, "It does not belong here. It will contaminate…"

"There is no evil in it. I would feel it if there was. If Zythán did nothing to warrant…your protests mean…"

That there might be answers in the vault after all. But forcing entry might result in the loss of the welcome the residents of St. Kóráhm's had been granted. Kavan did not want to foster ill will with these people who had been kind and patient since the first day of his arrival.

Valesce shook his head and laid his hand on Kavan's at the bard's breast, pressing the stylus against the broken crystal, Kóráhm's cross, and the half-moon that once bound him to the Lachlan House. Power audibly popped and crackled, creating a burning across his skin that prompted him to yank his hand away…but he could not. Valesce held him fast.

"There are some things that must not rest there…until their purpose is fulfilled. Qol forbid it, as did those who came before him."

Shaking, trying to will the pain away, Kavan choked, "If I do not know what it is, how do I discover its purpose? How do you know…?"

"I know." He dropped his hand, took two steps back, and bowed, his expression sheepish and defiant. When Kavan's hand dropped, the searing sensation faded; he wiped the tears from his eyes with his other hand.

He wondered if there would be a burn there when he examined it later.

Valesce bowed again. "I must go, my lord. I regret I cannot assist you. When k'ílshwythnec comes again, I will send her to you; perhaps she will have answers. Or perhaps Kóráhm will hear your supplications and provide what you require. I, unfortunately, cannot. Good day, my lord."

Clenching his good hand at his side, channeling his annoyance there and away from his throbbing other hand, Kavan watched the old man hurry away with short, quick steps and wondered if what he had Seen in the Bhórdh cavern had been an accurate account at all.

❧*❦

Zerio moved from one Glevum tavern to another, seeking the assortment of contacts Asta provided, men and women of the Association who had operated under Onea Pantel until her fiery execution alongside Fen Geli and two others. Expecting them to be the sources of the smattering of useful information Asta received, he tracked down more than one of the names on her list. They accepted the tokens he presented as proof that he spoke on Asta's authority, but if any knew where Marta was, they refused to impart those details.

He had thought the women were friends. The thirst for revenge or retaliation, however, seemed to have created division between them. He had seen that sort of division grow between Kjell and Asta as each year of exile passed and Kjell's focus on revenge grew.

There was nothing Zerio could do to heal either rift.

All he could do was the duty he had been given, continue to seek Marta, and reach out to every Vants contact he could locate. Spread the word. War was coming and if Association and Vants, Nethites and Enesfelians, banded together, perhaps some alive today would see a rightful de Corrmick king upon Neth's throne.

His path eventually brought him to an alley across from a door he had not visited in a decade, a building whose windows had been dark with abandon the last time he had come, whose door had been chained shut, where dust and mud and the debris of careless passersby had blown and accumulated against the cracked walls and corners and across the unswept landing. He did not know why it had been abandoned, what had become of Claes-Arne's apprentice in the days after Inness' disappearance. He did not know if she had been killed, if the Yellow Sisters had taken her, or if she had sought refuge far away from Glevum and the rise of Fraen the Elder.

He hoped it was the latter. She had seemed a nice girl. Cheerful and friendly, sympathetic and empathetic. She had certainly been loyal to Claes-Arne and served him better than Zerio ultimately had.

This morning, while he watched from the alley as Glevum's early risers stirred within the nearby structures and trickle into the streets, the apothecary shop was noticeably different. The debris that had disgraced the outer baseboards and the grime that had marred the window and door were cleaned away and the old sign above the door was given a fresh coat of paint. An apothecary shop once more, he breathed with a sigh colored with both relief and regret that someone had dared to make use of the former Vants meeting house.

Eventually, the glow of a candle moved back and forth behind the curtained windows, the shadow carrying it too distant to identify, and the morning titter and chatter of children followed as the shop lamps were lit. Hands pulled back the curtains and then a woman's face, round and smiling, rimmed with blonde hair tucked beneath a cap that allowed stray tendrils to hang free, glanced up and down the street as though expecting to see something she did not want to see.

Kes.

Zerio's heart soared to see she had survived and had, by the sounds within, built a family to fill the hole left by Claes-Arne's death.

Without thinking about his actions, compelled only by the sight of someone he was sure had worshiped the Grandmaster as much as he had, Zerio stepped into the street just as the shop door opened. He opened his mouth to greet her, but the sight of the man who emerged onto the planked landing strangled the sound before it was made. His dark hair had receded from his forehead but had not turned gray, and the crags and valleys of a troubled life had grown deeper around his eyes and mouth, but there was no mistaking Olaric the Younger for anyone else. They had been colleagues once…friends, but after ten years, Zerio could not say if they were either of those things now.

They stared at one another for several moments as a man with a goat-drawn cart swerved to pass around Zerio, neither speaking, neither moving, neither revealing anything more on their faces except the surprise of seeing one another again.

The man at the door beckoned him in.

Zerio, steps leaden and slow, obeyed.

Before either spoke, before the door closed to offer them privacy, the woman bustling between the fire and a small kettle heating on a portable iron firepot on the counter, turned, smiled with wide-eyed delight, and hurried across the room to embrace him in wonder and welcome.

"Mr. Kaas! How wonderful to see you! We thought the Sisters had taken you when we did not hear from you!" she bubbled, kissing his cheeks, reminding him again why Claes-Arne had been fond of her.

"I feared the same of you," he choked, looking over her shoulder as Olaric herded the three girls, all under ten and looking more like Kes, except for their dark hair, then they looked like the man he assumed was their father, back up the stairs to their room. He had never been aware of a connection between Olaric and the much younger Kes, but with those dangerous last days in Glevum and the passage of ten years, she was not so young, and a lot, undoubtedly, had transpired and changed for them.

As it had with him.

Pink-cheeked and smiling still, blue eyes sparkling as she smudged her thumbs over his cheeks, Kes pulled back to stare at him and tugged lightly on the tail of brown hair tied away from his face with a leather cord, acknowledging who he had been, who he was still. "Where have you been? Not here in Glevum? We could not find you before we left for Pravek."

Again, Zerio eyed Olaric, uncertain how much of that night in Glevum Kes knew about, whether she knew about the Vants or the relationship the two men had shared.

"In Enesfel," he began. Pravek was as far in the other direction from Glevum as Olaric could have fled. Escaping his father's much different opinions had been the wisest choice Olaric could have made.

But there were questions.

Olaric cleared his throat, sharing similar thoughts, and looked from Zerio to Kes with a small nod. "We need to talk."

Taking her cue, Kes pulled her shawl from a peg on the wall and said, "I must see the butcher. This calls for something special. You will share breakfast with us, won't you, Zerio?"

Uncertain of his welcome or how long a conversation with Olaric might last, he replied, "I would like to…if I may…"

"He isn't…"

"He is here and there is much to catch up on," Kes scolded lightly, kissing her husband's mouth before hustling outside. For a moment, Olaric stared at the closed door as Zerio stared at him, but then he gestured again and led Zerio to the right-hand side of the room. Claes-Arne's bed had been here once, and a desk covered with dozens of ancient books and an armoire filled with many more. Now the bed was gone, moved upstairs perhaps, to make room for a growing family.

Zerio had never known the Grandmaster to go upstairs. He wondered now if Claes-Arne had ever used it.

The desk remained, along with many of the books, but the bed had been replaced by a settee and two stuffed chairs of matching faded pink and crimson, the room now a parlor instead of an overcrowded sleeping chamber. Zerio accepted the stuffed chair Olaric pointed to and sat with his hands on his lap, revealing anxiety despite his desire to appear calm.

"So…Pravek…? When did you return to Glevum?"

Olaric sat in the matching chair and leaned forward with his elbows on his knees. "Shortly after Greah was born, when it seemed it was time."

Not knowing which of the girls was Greah, Zerio leaned back as if putting distance between them and forced his hands to unclasp and settle on the padded arms of the chair. Still uncomfortable, his fingertips curled into the fabric but his expression revealed none of the tension his body displayed. "How did you determine that?"

Olaric shrugged as he toyed with the sleeve of his faded, deep blue woolen dressing robe. When he did speak, he avoided the question by asking one of his own. "You know it's dangerous to be here? I doubt my father has forgotten your face…or your proximity to…"

"I'm not afraid of your father."

"He thinks I am in his good graces…but you…you should be afraid." When Zerio narrowed his eyes, Olaric shrugged again. "No better way for me to get information than being inside."

They stared at one another for several minutes until Zerio nodded. Being inside the castle was precisely how he had gained the queen-regent's trust. He did not believe Olaric would turn him over to the acting king, but after a decade apart, after what he had done to Claes-Arne and then the events of their last crossing, a lot of things might have changed.

"Rumor is he captured Inness and forced her to marry him to make himself king…holds her in the tower where she held Kjell…"

The corners of Olaric's eyes twitched. "And you?"

"Think she'd sooner be dead than allow that. Half suspect you invented that rumor."

Again, Olaric's eye twitched and Zerio's lips curled into a lop-sided smile. "Thought you were dead. Kes looked for you…but I knew with the prince in your care…" He gave a one-shouldered shrug. "Know you're the resourceful sort, but I wasn't sure you made it out until word came that both princes are alive in Enesfel."

"Took him to his grandmother. Safest place for him to be."

A logical decision, even though Olaric had toyed with the notion that Zerio had taken Henrik into hiding to raise him until he could take the throne, the same way it was said the famed General McHador of Enesfel had spirited Prince Arlan out of Rhidam until it was safe for him to return. "How is Prince Henrik? Prince Jerit?"

"Jerit's a strapping fine young man, good with a sword, good with his fists when he must be…trained to survive in the Association by his mother if it comes to that. He's got his father's head for leadership…" If not, Zerio admitted without saying it, the heart for it. "Henrik…he's got his problems, after the head injury, but he is very much Oska's son. He is too young to say what sort of king he could be, but he is interested in learning and has a fair-minded heart. Either would make a fine king."

"And the king? Did he…?"

"He lives." It was the most he was willing to say until he knew if he could trust Olaric again. The princes were safe. He was less certain Kjell was. He avoided the question's deeper meaning by sweeping his gaze and hand across the books and asking, "What have you done with the rest?"

Unsurprised by Zerio's hesitancy to expose Kjell's location., a Vants loyal to the oaths to protect the king after freeing him from captivity, Olaric accepted the change in topic and replied, "Moved them below with the Secrets. Doing my best to pull together those who remain, to rebuild the Vants. I would have reached out to you if I'd known you were alive, but by the time Geiel brought the news…"

"You know him." Olaric nodded. Zerio shifted in his chair, relaxing more now that the conversation had shifted to a more comfortable topic. "There are some in Rhidam; I've found a few scattered elsewhere. Some have migrated to the chellé hábhai in Alberni. We've created a network, but without Claes-Arne or the masters…"

"We build again. Took the role of grandmaster to organize those who remain in Neth…"

"You're grandmaster?" While it galled him to have a man he had once called a friend outrank him, and while he found it difficult to think of anyone else in that position, he decided the title suited Olaric. If the Vants were to begin again, someone had to guide them.

Zerio did not want the job.

"I made Lord Cliáth an honorary master; we have been studying the Secrets together, uncovering the origins of the Order. I am writing what I know…but am not yet ready to share what I have learned. His knowledge of most things surpasses my own and I would not know what I do if not for him. Grandmaster would have liked him."

It was Olaric's turn to purse his lips, but he eventually nodded. The roots of the Vants were as obscure as they were ancient. If the abundant rumors of the White Bard's abilities and wisdom were true, if he possessed knowledge of the Order they could benefit from, bringing him into the ranks made sense…even if he would be, to Olaric's knowledge, the only Elyri member the Vants had ever had. Olaric did not know the bard, but he suspected that someday the man could fill the role of Grandmaster perfectly. "If the prophecy concerns him… however this plays…he is welcome," he agreed with Zerio. Claes-Arne would have done the same.

Relieved to hear it, Zerio bowed his head. "Thank you. With so few of us… initiating another…"

"We need as many as we can muster. You know there will be war."

"I do not doubt it. Measures are underway; Geiel, and others, bring us news when you or the Association…the Queen is determined to learn everything we can on the king's behalf. Do you…" He paused for a breath before asking, "Do know an Association woman named Marta? She came to Glevum in Ms. Pantel's stead after…"

Olaric's shifting gaze, caught out of the corner of Zerio's eyes when he looked uncomfortably away under the weight of the distant memories of torture and execution he had been unable to prevent, convinced Zerio that Olaric knew more about Marta than he was willing to share. Unwilling to force information out of him, Zerio risked another question that he also suspected would remain unanswered, a question that had persisted since the last time they had seen each other.

"Did you kill her?"

Olaric frowned. "Why would I…?"

"Not Marta," Zerio corrected, accepting by the man's expression that he knew the head of Glevum's Association conclave. "Inness."

Olaric rose, pulled a pale amber bottle of something pungent from a drawer, and took a long drink before closing the stopper without offering it to Zerio. "The less you know about that night, the better."

Zerio had known Olaric's intent. He knew what the Vants had intended the night they had infiltrated the castle as Zerio hustled Prince Henrik to safety. He had not asked questions then.

He let the matter rest as Kes came through the door with bread, salt ham, and a small basket of eggs. She smiled understanding that she might have interrupted an important conversation, and directed her attention to the other side of the room and the meal preparations.

Olaric pursed his lips tighter and nodded to Zerio as if to say they would continue their discussion later. Forced to be on two sides of the upcoming conflict by the nature of where they lived, but both silently agreeing that, as Vants, they fought for the same cause, it was important to set egos and past disagreements aside and try to rebuild the trust they once shared.

Zerio nodded too. He had two days to make this work. Two days to forge an alliance and find Marta. The urgency of war made them fraternas again. Their oaths and the cause of peace mattered more than anything that had gone before.

❧*❧

Gating to the holy vault beneath St. Kóráhm's to expose the stylus to the relics, thinking to deposit it there to avoid the continual chafing of energy against his skin, Kavan was met with a blinding flare of veins of blue and green and white sparking through every surface around him and a backlash of power that knocked him off his feet. Gasping for the air the force sucked from his lungs, trying to ignore the pounding in his head as he waited for the discomfort to subside, he blinked and wrapped one hand around the collection of pendants in the hope that it would be enough to cancel the power connection between them and the room. The interference of his hand instead felt as if it reversed the flow, pulling power from within and forcing it outward so that the metal grate protecting the relics rattled and creaked. The room trembled. He tried to open his hand to drop it to the floor so that he could push to his feet, but his hand refused to unclench as though it was locked into place.

The bud of frustration and upset that attempted to bloom was eased by the sensation of a hand around his. He jerked and shook as if slapped, the glow of the veins went abruptly dark, and the rattling, the trembling, the rumbling in the room, ceased.

Shaken, gasping in the dark, he was grateful not to be alone with this debilitating fear. The warmth of the beloved presence remained until his heart stopped hammering, until his breathing came normally, and he could summon enough pale blue-white light in his palm to illuminate the room. The power in the Gate felt dim, its dimensions pulled from the normally larger circle into the area where he sat, and the aura of the room felt unusually faded.

He could not tell where the power had gone, whether he had done this or if there was some other cause.

"Do not leave it here, átaelás mai," said the man seated beside him, solid enough that their knees and shoulders pressed together and the saint's hands continued to cover his. It was the only time Kavan had ever seen Kóráhm look uncomfortable touching him, but he did not pull away. "You would be wise to keep it with you."

Kóráhm's voice was strained, as if the act of breaking the power loop which had left Kavan weak and disoriented had taken all the Saint's strength and energy.

"Do you know what it is? Do you know about Zythán and…?" Kavan mumbled, choking on his words as if his mouth was stuffed with cloth. His grip at last loosened on the pendants and his hand fell to his lap, stinging as if burned. He did not look to see if it was.

"No more than you know, but like you, I know ancient power when I feel it. Its purpose, like all things, will be revealed in time, I suspect…and if…" his gaze dropped from Kavan's face to the stain that now discolored the front of the bard's tunic where the pendants hung, "it may prove useful in what is ahead, it might be wisest not to be rid of it too soon."

"What is ahead?" Kavan whispered, the weight in Kóráhm's words making him shiver. He had Seen and felt shadows and continued to suspect that something nefarious awaited him when he faced Bhás, but none of it was clear. He hoped, since Kóráhm had come to him, the Saint would ease his anxiety and fear.

Instead, Kóráhm shook his head before hanging it in shame, embarrassment, and remorse. "If only I had been able to save her…if only I had not loved…"

"You are not to blame for your brother's choices, for the things he did and the retaliation he seeks." While Kavan often wondered why he was called upon to right those wrongs, he did not consider any of this to be Kóráhm's fault.

"Aren't I? My mistakes are the basis for much death…"

Kavan swallowed and looked away, his breath again sucked out of him, this time by words that sounded like an acknowledgment of fears he continued to try to ignore. "Mine included."

Their gazes met but the contact did not hold. "Perhaps not," the saint whispered. He lay his hands over the hidden pendants, and with a rush of heat, Kavan felt his internal well of power overflow its normal level as though he had not expended any of it in weeks. The sensation made his skin crawl, his hands itch, his teeth chatter, and his jaws clench to contain it. The Gate expanded again, flared with unusual intensity, and Kavan was certain that, if he tried, he would be able to seek solace and security in Raebhá's arms before night fell.

If he was going to die, was it not better to spare any of them seeing his fate? Was it not better to shield her from that if he could?

He was certain that traveling to Dhóbhaen would lead Bhás directly to those he wanted most to protect.

"I think," Kóráhm said sympathetically as though trying to lift the melancholy he had laid on Kavan's shoulders, "there may yet be a chance. Keep this with you, Kavan. It may save your life."

Hope.

It was a rare glimmer of something Kavan had felt too little of in the weeks since sensing Eridel's return to Rhidam. Just because he could not find the other harper did not mean he was not there. If Bhás wanted him, Eridel would find him soon enough.

Kóráhm's words, however, brought the possibility that this odd stylus and the power it contained and conducted would do nothing or might work to his detriment. Perhaps finding it had been a trap.

To anchor himself in this place and stave off the urge to flee to Dhóbhaen, he wrapped his hand around Kóráhm's.

"Will you sit with me…until it's safe?" Kóráhm would keep him here. Kóráhm would temper the impulses that were, in every way, against his better judgment.

Kóráhm squeezed his hand. "As long as you need, átaelás mai."

He owed Kavan that much.

❧ * ❧

Neither thought it safe for Zerio to remain in the apothecary shop overnight, even if he had taken refuge in the hidden chamber beneath, where the Secrets were kept and the Vants of Glevum had once met. Nor had they thought it wise for Olaric to know where Zerio intended to spend his night when he slunk away after the sun set and Kes escorted their charming daughters off to bed.

If Fraen the Elder learned that Zerio was in Glevum, it was best that he never suspected a connection between them beyond the fact that they had once served Queen-Regent Inness together.

After a sleepless night spent in hushed conversation with Kes, speaking of secrets hidden from everyone during the past decade but keeping a few to himself, Olaric bid her to be careful and watchful, to protect the children at all cost, to hold fast to ignorance and innocence, he made the trek to the castle gate with a plan weaving tighter in his head. He had never been confident this day would come, that there would be a time or a need to implement the next phase of an idea he had spawned long ago.

But Zerio's report of amassing armies and the ongoing effort to garner support for the return of a de Corrmick king convinced Olaric that, if there would ever be a time to act, it was now. He and his supporters had gotten into the castle unseen once.

They could do it again.

"Good morning, m'lord," called Captain Sparding in greeting, stepping out of his conversation with a handful of guards as he saw Olaric arrive. "The king is in a foul mood today. This might not be the best time to…"

"It's the only time, Earon." He could not afford delay. Foul mood or not, he did not think his father would deny the request he had come to make. "I can't let him think I'm afraid of him."

"Aye, that would be counterproductive," the bearded man with the golden-brown hair nodded. "Think he got news he didn't want to hear."

Olaric frowned. "What news?"

Sparding shrugged. "Dunno. Didn't hear it. They were in the throne room; only heard the envoy say 'general' before the door shut."

Curious but undeterred about asking his father for information, Olaric said, "Need a favor, if you're up for it."

"Anything, m'lord." He could not call Olaric grandmaster in public, but the newly christened tova had gained enough respect from the younger Fraen to willingly undertake whatever was asked.

"I must travel for a few days…two weeks at the most if the weather holds…I want you to watch over my wife and daughters, see that they are safe and have everything they need…that my father does not get to them."

Sparding bobbed his head, his expression grave. "They'll be as secure as if you're here with them."

"I appreciate that." It did not eliminate all the risk to his family, but he hoped that, between Sparding's vigilance and Kes' wisdom, the family would remain safe. "Wish me good fortune…"

The captain nodded. "You're going to need it."

❧Chapter 22❧

From the prow of the lead ship, with the sun setting at his back, Kaj locked eyes with the unassuming, smartly-dressed fellow with an entourage who looked to be elders and advisors rather than guards. King Gamal had told him that the Prime Magistrate was expecting them, and undoubtedly the fleet's appearance on the horizon had given the island's ruler time to gather his greeting party, but Kaj was still surprised to see such a gathering waiting. Other ships at port had pulled their moorings and drifted out to cautiously approach the arrivals, but he did not think they would attack.

As low as the local ships sat in the water, he guessed they were trade ships or supply vessels intended to support the fleet as they continued north.

They held position without making contact, awaiting an order from the man on the dock who clasped Kaj's hand as soon as he stepped off the ship.

Kaj was grateful he did not suffer sea legs as several behind him did.

"Prime Magistrate." Kaj hoped he did not address the man wrongly. He would have preferred if Earé was here to do this.

"Welcome." Piran looked the golden-skinned man over, recognizing a shared ancestry between him and the people of Hatu, though his accent was unfamiliar. "You are here at Lord Cliáth's behest, I am told."

"I have not met the man, but his daughter speaks highly of him." The more he heard about the one called Cliáth, the more regard he witnessed for the bardic duke, the more eager Kaj was to meet him. "We travel to Levonne, and then on to Rhidam to aid King Lachlan or so I am told. King Gamal presents this." He withdrew a sealed tube of hard, boiled leather from his cloak and offered it to Piran. "We offer men and ships from Hatu as protection in exchange for fresh water to supply the rest of our journey."

Piran chuckled, a sound that irritated some of the robed men behind him. "I do not need Gamal's request to aid Enesfel…but his ships and men are welcome." His efforts to build a sufficient navy had yet to bear fruit.

Despite his council's belief, he thought the islands too vulnerable to protect themselves. Assuming most of the men on those ships congregating in the deeper seas surrounding the docks belonged to Hatu, any men Gamal could spare were welcome. Lorant would think so too.

"Come. There is room in the inn for some of the men while we dine and the Council and discuss what is to be done against Neth."

When Kaj cocked one brow, tilted his head, and said, "My men will bed with the ships so long as they may relieve their legs and visit your island…if you will allow," Piran reconsidered his first perception of how many foreign soldiers they were talking about.

"Of course," he said cordially, clearing his throat, offering his hand again, and ignoring the less-than-subtle muttered cues and protests from the men at his back. "Tell your fleet to moor and they will be supplied as we talk. I should like to hear more about the land you come from."

Kaj bowed. "A meal is welcome. I look forward to a joint sharing of our cultures."

Further out to sea, beyond the line of sight from any point on the islands, on the eastern horizon where the Bay of Phalla met the open ocean, the fleet of galleys waited, tiny specks observing the armada's approach to the island before the rise of the hills blocked them from view. The ships off the southern coast would be spreading thinner as Bhás predicted, but their naval spreading would never be enough to protect the northern coast or the island where the dead lord rested.

The man at the helm, graying black hair swept away from his tanned-leather face, was itching for the promised fight, the promised glory, that was to be his when these strange lands fell. But it was not yet time to act. No matter how beneficial the signs seemed, how certain he was that he could destroy the meager fleet of ships if he threw his galleys into battle now, her word had not yet been given.

To act without command was to suffer certain death, either at her hand or at the mutinous hands of his crew. They trusted the shi cali.

He did too.

He would wait for the order to come…and he would watch.

❧ * ❧

Having returned home long enough to retrieve his stocky dappled brown horse, an animal he was always reluctant to take to the castle in case his father took a liking to it and decided to confiscate it, Olaric kissed his daughters goodbye. Again, he warned Kes to be cautious, to trust only Sparding or Marta if she needed anything, and to hide herself and the girls if she felt threatened, then he turned the horse along the northern road at the center of town and began his journey at a casual, unsuspicious pace. Though his gaze remained pointed on the road before him, he kept his senses focused on the alleys, side streets, and doorways. His father, after a lengthy argument about duty, secrecy, and trust, reluctantly agreed to permit him to attend business in Pravek, but there had been something in the man's eyes that Olaric did not like.

His father might have brought him into his sphere of influence, might be working to persuade him to take up the role of Heir to the Throne, but there were trust issues that would never be resolved. His father had disapproved of most of what he had said and done as a younger man and was only marginally more accommodating now. Olaric would always be suspicious, no matter how much feigned generosity he presented.

Olaric paused his horse at Glevum's edge to allow him to drink at the last water trough they would see for many hours, stretching and rolling his head from side to side as if to ease some stiffness while using the action as an excuse to look around. He felt it then, for the first time, eyes watching from the shadows, but as the windows of the Fox Tail Inn, an establishment known by many to be frequented by the Association, were open to allow the end-of-day breeze inside, there were numerous sets of eyes watching travelers move in and out of the city. The coctor stood on the steps of a side door, beating a pot to dislodge its burned content onto the ground to feed the congregation of stray dogs that surrounded him, and in another alley, there was the shifting of feet and soft mutterings of men engaged in some covert sale or illegal transaction. Possibly deciding if this solo rider looked to be an easy target. Turning so the sword on his hip was visible made the mutterings grow fainter and Olaric smiled. None of those lookers-on concerned him, but identifying non-threats did not ease the suspicions that continued to nag.

He rode for another hour. Two. Past farmhouses and outbuildings, past a well-house at the edge of the road that some past de Corrmick king had commissioned to service travelers, and past a rustic, gradually decaying structure that provided shade for twin cows who munched at the overgrown grass in the field. The air of suspicion had failed to ease and so he turned off the road, worked two boards of the drooping fence so his horse could enter the pasture, and took shelter in the dilapidated building to wait out the darkness and the unseen threat he believed to be there.

The cattle lowed and shuffled as the sky grew darker until finally settling far enough from him that Olaric could not hear them. The thrum and chirp of grasshoppers and night insects replaced their gentle sounds, joined occasionally by the call of distant owls and the songs of nocturnal birds. His horse picked at the brittle straw scattered about the floor, but its ears were pricked towards noises and details Olaric could not detect.

He trusted the horse's senses more than his own.

There were no horses' hooves on the packed-earth northern road. There were no creaking wagon wheels or sounds of banter between merchants daring to travel at night nor the herding calls of shepherds or the barking dogs that aided them. But when the horse lifted its head to stare into the dark beyond the stable door that hung lopsided on breaking hinges, Olaric sensed it too.

He did not draw his sword. The sound would give his position, his wariness, away. Suspecting that the spy, if that was who had followed him at his father's order, thought he had stopped here to sleep for the night, Olaric waited for the shadowy shape to step through the opening before rushing at him; his full, colliding weight driving the stranger to the straw-covered dirt floor with a muffled cry.

They wrestled for several moments, rolling through the dust, seeking a subduing hold that would give either an upper hand. The horse snorted its displeasure with the commotion and tried to pull free of its tether. Olaric did not think the fellow's instructions were to kill him, only to report back to Fraen the where's and why's of this journey, but he would not take the chance of being found out…or that he was wrong and his father had decided he was a liability.

When he finally grappled the man's head between his hands, he slammed it three times into the dirt, each more violent than the last as the man's ability to fight waned. When the body went limp, Olaric released him and rolled away with a wheezing, painful breath. He gauged the condition of his ribs with one hand, guessing they were cracked from the blows of the man's fists, and felt the side of the man's neck with his other.

The pulse was weak, his breath shallow. Alive, but he guessed not for long. Olaric tugged the horse's reins free and left the spy where he had fallen, scooping up the pouch of coins dislodged from his belt in the tussle.

If the fellow lived, he would not likely report this failure to the king. Like the de Corrmicks of olde, Fraen was likely to execute a man for his failure rather than pardon him to try again. If he died, if he had been expected to follow Olaric to the end of his journey and back again, Fraen would not know of his death for many more days.

If this was an assassination attempt, possible, judging by the heft of the coin purse, Fraen would never expect to see the killer again.

Either way, Olaric had time.

Once on the road, Olaric kicked his horse into a gallop to put as much distance between him and the soon-to-be-dead man as possible.

⇛*⇛

Most of the residents of St. Kóráhm's slept, except for those whose chanting voices faintly rose and fell in a soothing, sing-song hum from the náós. Kjell scowled and drummed his fingers on the courtyard table where he and Asta awaited Zerio's midnight return beneath the cloudless sky. Tau was not with them, allowing husband and wife a too-rare moment of privacy in the hopes they would continue to seek ways to repair their strained relationship. Zerio's face, when Kavan followed him to the table, did not reveal either success or failure and the king, unable to interpret his expression, assumed the worst.

"You're late."

"Had no control over the palace watch," Zerio retorted from the other side of the table as Kavan sat too, the last to do so. "Kavan was there when he was supposed to be, but I was not interested in being followed, in risking Fraen's recognition. He didn't like me before…he wouldn't like me now."

"Did you find Marta?"

"Given the structuring of the Association…" Zerio began, shaking his head to Asta's question. "I did not see her…no one speaks her name…but I'm certain she knows I was looking for her. Olaric knows she's there, has contact with her…"

"She is working with the king?" Kjell growled.

"The Younger…not the Elder," corrected Zerio.

Kjell huffed, remembering now the two men with the same name. When Asta tried to cover his hand to soothe him, he jerked away, refusing to be patronized as forgetful.

"We served together under Inness…he was there to help me get Prince Henrik out the night she…" Zerio shrugged. Disappeared. Died. Olaric had not confirmed either end. Whichever it had been, it did not matter. "And he's Vants. He's been funneling information to Geiel…I think she has too. Now he's got his foot inside the…"

Gesturing as if to brush away Kjell's protest, he continued. "He's Fraen's only child…he wants someone to take the throne after him. Olaric's not interested, wants the de Corrmicks back, but feigned interest in appeasing his father has its advantages."

"It could," Kjell reluctantly agreed.

Zerio nodded. "Not many men in Glevum now…the old, the young, some fishermen, Association…some exempted from duty out of the necessity of their services…what men at arms Fraen's compelled to retain to keep order and guard the castle. Doesn't look like he'll be going into war himself…he was serving as regent when this mercenary fleet…and the woman who led it, came to Glevum…"

Beside him, Kavan shuddered. Asta noted it and asked, "You know these people? The one who leads them?"

"I have seen her," Kavan replied, leaving the statement vague enough that those who knew him might assume that her face had come to him in the Sight or he might have seen it through Zerio's eyes. "I do not know her people, where she is from, how or from where she collected an army…but I know she is more dangerous to the Sovereignties than Inness. She may have influenced Inness as well."

"Hard to believe that," Kjell snorted. "She cost me my son…my throne…untold death in…"

"As I said, I have reason to believe she had her hand in those events." Bhás might not have been responsible for Oska's death, or Inness' prompting Oska to action to imprison Kjell and take the throne, but he knew about Bhás' visit to Inness, her promise of an army when Neth needed it. That offer, it seemed, had extended to Fraen after Inness lost the throne.

"Is it Marta? She isn't the one to…?"

"No, it is not Marta," Kavan assured her. "But it is…"

Kjell cut him off. "Is the Association working with her?"

Kavan shook his head. It was possible, but he had no reason to think it was true.

"It is what?" Asta asked over her husband's interruption.

"She was in Rhidam when your father died." He did not know how she could have survived that structural collapse in the aftermath of the showdown between Caol and Halstatt Tarmajien, but Kavan knew she had been there, just as she had been at Wace's death.

Asta forced a frown to mask the quivering at the corners of her lips. "That was…is she Elyri? Is her army…?"

"They are not Elyri." Kavan had no reason to think they were or could be. The Kyne would be aware of any collection of individuals gathering into an army, and if these people had traveled by sea from Dhóbhaen, they would have likely come to Neth from the east, not from the west. It seemed unlikely that any mercenary army would be Dhóbhaen. If they were, Bhás knew that land already.

Raebhá and their child might already be dead. Kavan's efforts to stay away, to hide and protect them from Bhás, might have been useless.

But there were Teren west of Dhóbhaen, in the land where they first met Dhágdhuán. While the possibility did not explain their arrival from the west, nor exclude the possibility that the Dhóbhaen were at risk from Bhás, it seemed the most likely explanation for their origin.

"She is…there is Elyri in her blood. What she is beyond that…" His voice trailed off. Teren, like her ancestor, possibly k'kairá, possibly something more, the way Earé carried blood from her mother that made her something different than anyone else Kavan knew except Dhóri.

Bhás was older than he was, though he did not know how much older. There was very little he knew about her except one detail he could not share.

She was a descendent of Coryllien.

"Fraen's army is on the move," Zerio interrupted, bringing the conversation back to the topic at hand, to refocus Kjell and distract Asta from the memories of her father's death. "They're intending to infiltrate the south shore of Curo."

"Conquer it, not infiltrate," snorted Kjell. The unmastered, ungoverned land between Curo and the southern forest consisted primarily of farmland and small villages with no means of raising an adequate army in self-defense. The outposts Enesfel had built there were understaffed, some barely operational; there was nothing to prevent Fraen from reclaiming everything as far as the forest's edge. Whether he chose to push through the trees and mountains to Fiara, past there into Enesfel, was a matter of timing…dependent upon when Enesfel's army coalesced to stop them.

Zerio agreed. "Olaric confirms they're fortifying the border to prevent Cordash's interference…but he doesn't think they've got the manpower, even with the mercenary army, for war on two fronts."

"Unless there are more to come. You did say Elyriá…that Káliel and…" Asta's voice trailed off as she waited for Kavan to speak.

"I do not think Cordash is their target." That did not mean that war would not spill into Cordash more than it had already. Bhás would target anyone she believed might be a way to get to him.

"We cannot protect all fronts," Kjell huffed. "Cordash will have to protect their shores if it comes to it. There is only so much…"

"We must take this to the king," started Asta, pushing away from the table. "He will decide what to…"

Kjell bristled at having his authority overstepped by the boy-king.

Zerio cleared his throat. "One more thing. Fraen believes you are dead…" he glanced at Kjell, "and believes Prince Henrik is to be king. He publicly swears fealty to the de Corrmick name…but he ordered the assassination of the prince…"

"Of course he did," Kjell growled.

"Why now?" Asta asked. They suspected the order, if not from the Association, had come from Neth. "He's not yet old enough to be a threat."

"He's a threat if the citizens of Neth have someone to rally behind. Gossip in the streets is rife. They want a de Corrmick…"

"Not that Fraen's different from most de Corrmicks," Kjell snorted.

"Those who live only remember you. Those who came before are memories. They want the return of prosperity…and Fraen wants war to keep it from happening."

"He has to be stopped." Asta stood up and smoothed her tunic. "The King needs to know…"

"It is too late for that tonight," Kavan sighed, satisfied that he would not face Lorant's complaints about his absence again but disappointed by the time away from his son and Rhyrdan.

Not to be put off, Asta shook her head. "In the morning then. At daybreak. We will take this news to…"

"Dawn then," Kavan agreed, rising from the table so that Zerio could do likewise. There was barely enough time to sleep, but sleep was not what Kavan needed.

He needed prayer and music.

He needed to commune with Raebhá, to reassure her, to reassure himself, that the danger he feared had not already found her and their son.

He would have to trust the Dhóbhaen to protect themselves until he found a way to stop Bhás.

❧*❧

Rhyrdan's presence in the oratory was less of a surprise than it should have been when Kavan escorted Asta and Zerio out of the Gate. He had been there when Kavan had taken Asta to St. Kóráhm's and would have expected his return when the Inquisitor was prepared to come back without knowing of his foray to Glevum. He might have waited here for Kavan, his night spent in prayer, but that would preclude seeing to Ágdhállán's care, and Kavan assumed he returned at dawn, before the boy awakened, in the hopes of catching Kavan there. There were dark circles beneath his eyes and remorseful deep lines at the corners of his mouth that spoke of some weighty matter he wished to discuss.

The black kestrel harp upon the altar meant something as well.

"My lord…a word."

Asta cocked her head towards the door, "Come, Zerio. The king will be at breakfast. We will meet him in the morning room."

"Can't escape us there," Zerio mused with forced humor. "M'lord, we shall speak later?"

"Of course." Kavan waited until the oratory door was closed to speak again, but Rhyrdan beat him to it.

"k'gdhededhá needs you at the náos. dedhá Rankin is dying…or may be…they want you to play for him…to bring the záryph…" His voice trailed off into a tremor of emotion. However long he had been in the oratory, awaiting Kavan's arrival, it was long enough to cast doubt on whether Rankin still lived.

The harp on the altar took on a new meaning.

"Does Lorant…?"

"Not yet. dedhá Rankin does not want a fuss, but he does want you."

Kavan kissed Rhyrdan's palms in gratitude for the message and to provide comfort and apology that he had been forced to share this burden alone. There was nothing to see in that contact beyond dedhá Bhídígís bringing Tusánt's message to Rhyrdan. Rhyrdan had not gone to see the old man. No one from the keep had, except for Ártur whose healing had been requested under the guise of dedhá Thrismund suffering a stomach ailment. Not a lie, but a truth rooted in grief for a dying mentor and friend instead of sickness.

Ártur was there. He would have been the one to declare the inevitable if the man's failing condition was beyond healing. Kavan was surprised Ártur had not reached out to give him the news sooner. But dying could take hours. It could take weeks. Perhaps Ártur had not summoned him because he believed there was still time. Perhaps he had stayed with the dedhá and had not summoned Kavan because it was already too late.

"Thank you. Tell Ágdhállán where I am; I will return when I am able."

"I'm sure he already knows." Rhyrdan tried to chuckle but could not force the sound out of his throat. "If you need me…anything…"

"You will know."

Moments later, Kavan stepped out of the Purification Chamber into a náós full of scattered mourners led in prayer by dedhá Bhídígís and Dhon. The king might not yet know of Rankin's failing health, but enough of Rhidam's Faithful did that they had come together to pray for the beloved man's repose and honor him with remembrances while he still lived. Soon, dedhá Charlos would know and Lorant would follow regardless of his previous decision to avoid assassins by avoiding Hes á Redh. Kavan paused to genuflect, to lend his prayers to the congregations', and though faces turned to watch him, expecting the White Bard with the harp beneath his arm to offer worshipful music to accompany Rankin on his final journey, he continued across the náós to the side door and disappeared through it.

He had been here countless times. He knew these halls, the rooms of each dedhá, the rooms shared by the novices and the men and women who served the Faith, the room where they dined that connected the náós to the reconstructed orphan's home. He knew the scents of candle tallow and lamp oil, ink and parchment, the musty scents of old books and lingering aromas of incense, some used in celebration, some for pleading or meditation, and some, like what he smelled today, for remembrance and the dying.

Or the dead.

He followed the comforting traces in the air of the healer who had passed through these halls and the incomprehensible faint rise and fall of Ártur's voice mixed with Tusánt's and Thrismund's…and the stubborn defiance of Rankin who refused to be treated as though he was already gone.

A relieved breath escaped Kavan's lungs. Not gone yet. He was not too late. He composed his face, controlled his emotions, and then knocked once on the door before pushing it open and peering inside.

He met Ártur's gaze first. The healer nodded. Kavan nodded in return and set the harp on the table beside the door.

Nearing the bed, passing between Thrismund and Tusánt, who stepped aside to allow him through, Kavan took the frail man's hand and said, "Apologies for the delay, gdhededhá; I just returned from St. Kóráhm's."

"Where you should be," Rankin rasped.

"You asked for him," began Thrismund, draping the damp cloth he held over the lip of the water bowl at the bedside.

"World doesn't stop for me." Rankin stretched his empty hand to the door, the movement of his skeletal limb slow and weak, as though every gesture pained him despite any relief Ártur gave. There was a familiar death rattle in his barely rising chest, a sound Kavan had heard too many times, and the sunken skin of the man's cheeks was already bleeding into the waxy gray of death.

It was the invisible presence of others, those no one in the room except Kavan, and perhaps Rankin, could sense, that told Kavan what he needed to know. Rhidam's premier Teren gdhededhá might have had the strength to cling to life long enough for Kavan to arrive, but he could not win that fight much longer.

"It has stopped for you now." Kavan took the other hand in his, wrapping his white hands around the frail ones as though providing the alms he sought. "I have nowhere else to be, gdhededhá. I am here for you."

Rankin's chin bobbed. "The rest of you go."

"Rankin…" Tusánt stammered. Their friendship, the mutual support they had given each other from their earliest days of service, had gotten Tusánt through some of the darkest years of his life. He was no stranger to death, but this was one of several he did not want to face. He did not feel right about leaving him when Rankin needed his friends the most.

Thrismund wrapped an arm around Tusánt's shoulders. "Let us join the others." If there was nothing they could do here, they could pray for him in the company of those who loved him and observe his passing with them.

Ártur put a hand on Kavan's shoulder but looked at Rankin as he said, "I'll be outside if you need anything."

Kavan nodded, accepted the harp from his cousin, and then sat on the bedside chair. Neither he nor Rankin spoke until the door was closed; when Kavan played a series of tuning notes, Rankin stayed him with the clearing of his throat.

"In the desk…in the drawer…there is a bottle."

Expecting alcohol, though he had never known Rankin to drink, or a flask of blessed water sometimes used for anointing the ailing to prepare them for death…something Kavan was sure Tusánt had already done, what Kavan found was a small vial of smoky brown fluid, sealed to prevent seepage, lying on its side amidst the expected array of parchments, quills, and wax ingots for writing and sealing missives. "This one?" he asked, bringing it to the bed so Rankin could see it.

Again, Rankin nodded. "Open it."

Breaking the seal and pulling the stopper free released the fragrant perfume of cinnamon and myrrh, thyme, and rare olive oil. He sucked in his breath, impulsively relishing the mixed aromas, and looked at Rankin awaiting his next instruction.

One shaky hand lifted from the bed. "A little…on my fingers."

Pouring from the delicate opening over his shaking fingers caused a dribble to fall upon the sheets but Rankin shook his head, unconcerned about staining. "Your wrists."

"dedhá…" Kavan began to protest when the oil was smudged on first one wrist and then the other, front and back, in places where the rósádhá had been known to form.

"You'll need this," Rankin said. "In time, you will thank me. More."

One instinct told him to resist. The other, stronger one, told him that Rankin had struggled to remain alive for this moment, told him it would be wrong to refuse.

Kavan shakily obeyed.

"Your side…"

He knew where. The process was repeated with his feet, and finally his ears, his lips, his eyes, and the space between them, and finally what remained was poured upon the top of his head. There was no burning, no unpleasant sensation, but the taste on his lips was bitter enough that he was tempted to wipe it off. Trusting the dedhá's words without understanding the reasons, choosing not to press for answers he did not believe Rankin had, he bowed his head and pushed the stopper into the now empty vial."

"Wash it…keep it safe." He coughed once and continued. "I do not know what awaits you…but when I kneel before k'Ádhá and Dhágdhuán, they will hear my prayers for you."

"Kóráhm instructed this…didn't he?"

Rankin did not reply as he relaxed into the pillows with a long, shallow, wheezing sigh. "I don't ask for music. I don't need talk or prayer. I just need you to sit…be silent…and listen. To them." His eyes rolled as though looking around the room and then returned to Kavan, seeking affirmation of what his senses, both failing and heightened, recognized.

"They hear us as I hear them," Kavan assured him, grimacing again at the taste on his lips. "We will stay with you."

"Until he comes."

Kavan nodded. Whether it was Kóráhm that Rankin expected, Jermyn or one of the other saints, or Dhágdhuán himself, Kavan would stay until Rankin's soul was no longer bound to his body and the man was free of the pains of life.

Free, Kavan mused as he watched Rankin drift into a restless, shallow slumber, of the impending fears of war and whatever future Kavan was being prepared for.

꙰*꙰

Ruidoso had walls built by paranoid de Corrmick kings to keep the armies of Enesfel and Cordash out.

When it came to a fight, the residents of the south's largest city had fought with Enesfel instead of against her, choosing to be annexed with a king who would allow the people freedom from fear and paranoia and perpetual domination. Under Enesfel's rule, the city had thrived, and had opened the trade of lumber and cattle with Curo's north shore, allowing for a building boom in the north that Neth had not experienced in centuries.

King Kjell had helped that happen.

The Yellow Sisters and the destruction at Inness' hand that followed in the wake of the last war had changed everything.

Weakened by plague and Fraen's continual picking at the south's healing scabs, despite Cordash's effort to rebuild homes and fortifications, Ruidoso had not yet recovered as some smaller urban centers had. It was there that Fraen focused his attention. Ruidoso had no standing army and limited manpower with which to defend those ancient walls, and so, when General Emil Waller arrived at the head of the combined Nethite and mercenary armies, the council of Ruidoso resisted only long enough to prepare those inside the wall for the inevitable occupation.

They could not make a stand, but they refused to allow themselves to be destroyed. Waller, puffed with pride that he had succeeded in taking the city as Fraen had done, declared himself their duke and the ruler of the south in the name of King Fraen de Corrmick. The undamaged walls would be further fortified, the city strengthened, and when Enesfel or Cordash came for them, as they inevitably would, Waller, who stood on that wall listening to the efforts of some residents to assert themselves against the invading force, was certain they would not stand a chance.

❧*❧

The lights of Hes á Redh were dark. Out of respect for the departed, they would remain that way until the day after the diligent, respected gdhededhá was laid to rest, when a High Gathering would be held in remembrance for the blessed repose of his soul in k'Ádhá's hands. Those who came when the public announcement was made gathered to offer their grief and support and remained in stunned, mournful silence. Their prayers were now quiet, the warm summer air bathing them as it pushed from one open door to another, carrying the soul of gdhededhá Rankin with it. Those who had served with him were gathered in his bed-chamber, offering muted prayers and tributes, chanted songs and soft tears.

Kavan was not among them.

He had offered a burial plot in St. Kóráhm's where Rankin could rest beside k'gdhededhá Tythilius, but those who served with him in Hes á Redh agreed with Tusánt. Rankin should be buried here, where those he had served could continue to pay homage, where his spirit could continue to bless and look over the faithful he had been committed to in life.

Jermyn had not been there at the end to see him across, nor any of the other familiar faces Kavan had grown used to seeing when each Lachlan passed. But Rankin was no Lachlan. There had been only the záryph and Kóráhm, who stared at Kavan with a melancholy expression before taking Rankin's hand and pulling him towards whatever rest Ethenae offered.

Kóráhm had seen the invisible stains of christening oil.

Kóráhm knew.

As he took to the night sky to shed his grief in flight, spotting Lorant and Jerit lying side by side atop a castle tower to stare at the summer stars, Kavan wished he knew the truth, too.

⮾Chapter 23⮾

Despite Lorant's desire for the royal household to attend the High Gathering in Rankin's honor, to pay respect with their attendance, he was unwilling to risk another attack, particularly after Zerio's confirmation that King Fraen had ordered Prince Henrik's death that had resulted in the mercenaries' failed attempt. In compromise, he gave any staff who wished to attend permission to do so. The royal healers, among those who had known the gdhededhá the longest, crossed Rhidam with Rhyrdan and Níkóá for protection while Asta, Zerio, and Lord High Justice Madoc circled the náós looking for trouble before joining the massive congregation. Lorant, Seren, and Jerit traveled with Kavan through the Gate early enough that few were likely to note their means of travel. They were forced to stay too long afterward, unable to sneak away as the mourners filed past the donation box erected in Rankin's honor and then passed single-file by his burial marker to offer flowers, kisses, and short prayers to the spirit of the departed.

By the time Kavan returned them to the keep, the dinner hour was at hand, a meager meal of cold meats and breads and bottles of wine that many imbibed in too freely to dull the mourning ache. Kavan offered music to soothe and settle them, a selection of holy prayers he long ago set to music, but before the mid-summer sun had set, many in the Hall had drifted away to mourn in private. Rhyrdan, Níkóá, and Zerio sat to one side of the room, drinks in hand, murmuring together as Ágdhállán sat at his father's side with his head on the bard's shoulder, sometimes singing, sometimes humming melodies he knew by heart.

The Cáner children had not been in Rhidam for several days and Balint had been in St. Kóráhm's with his father. Henrik and Hella were escorted upstairs before the drinking began in earnest but Ágdhállán remained. Kavan had not had the heart to send him away.

"A messenger, my lord," said a fresh-faced guard with whisps of brown poking out beneath his helm who opened the door at the far end of the Hall and ushered a thin man dressed in a Harcourt tabard who clutched his turban in his hands and looked flushed from too much exposure to the summer sun.

"I'll find the king," Níkóá said, his words slurred as he wobbled.

"My message is for Lord Cliáth," the herald apologized with a bow before wiping beads of sweat from his forehead.

Kavan gave his harp to his son and crossed the room to meet the messenger at the door. The boy followed, sleepy and sad, and did not stray from his father's side. The three men on the other side of the room likewise shuffled over to join him.

"You may speak freely." There were other lords and ladies, other guests scattered about the room, but most were in no condition to care about the messenger or to make note of his appearance. With the four clustered around him, he did not need to speak loudly to be heard, thus the nature of the message was kept between them.

"I have come from Kílyn to announce the imminent arrival of those k'ílshwythnec has sent." His pronunciation of the word was stilted and awkward. "They were set to sail for Levonne the morning I departed, stopping at Káliel on the way…and should soon be on Enesfel's soil.

"Earé's force?" Níkóá asked.

Kavan nodded grimly.

"How many?" Zerio yawned.

"I did not count. Two dozen, perhaps…they were gathering as I left."

Rhyrdan whistled low. "That's a lot of men."

"Let us pray it is enough." Kavan kissed the top of Ágdhállán's head. "I must go to Levonne, prepare Bhríd." The sun had already set but in the business of the vineyard, his kinsman was likely still awake, attending to it and his children.

"I want to visit Cáym…" mumbled Ágdhállán, as Níkóá said, "I should alert the king…"

"I will inquire about bringing them back with me," Kavan promised his son. "This has been a long day. You need to sleep. As for…the news can wait until morning. There is nothing the king can do tonight…but Garran and Bhetá, they should be told to prepare."

"I'll tell them," Níkóá said, already staggering towards the door in the direction the general and Daema had gone earlier.

"I shall tell Asta…and see to our guest," Zerio said with a nodding smile at the envoy who looked pleased to be off his horse and worried that he would be immediately sent away. "Come, sir. Would you care for a meal and a bed?"

The envoy nodded eagerly.

"What shall I…?" started Rhyrdan, already picking up the pouting boy to take him upstairs. Fortunately, he was not drunk enough to endanger either of them on their way.

"I should not be gone long. See to Ágdhállán and wait for me."

Opting this time for the manor Gate, the house seemed empty when Kavan arrived, with only the voices of the servants in the kitchen and upstairs, people bustling about preparing for the night. Expecting to find Bhríd in one of the vineyards, he left the manor, paused to listen to the peculiar late-night commotion emanating from the direction of the sea, and followed the sounds to the significant crowd collected at the head of the docks. Between them and the horizon, the specks of ships grew slowly larger, ships that Duke Cáner with his sons and daughter at his side, were there to greet, sword at his hip and spyglass in one hand as he kept Levonne's citizens back.

He did not ask Kavan to retreat when the bard stopped at his side.

"Impeccable timing," he said with a light chuckle as Ónyká wrapped her arms around Kavan's waist and Cáym gook his hand. Phaedr, on Bhríd's other side, only glanced at Kavan with a smile before again watching the ships with eager excitement.

"Hatu?"

"Yes. You knew they were…?"

"Their envoy just reached Rhidam; I came to prepare you for their arrival."

"Little late for that," Bhríd laughed. "Watchers spotted them about two hours ago. I'd say, given the wind, there's another three before they make landfall. Anything I need to know?"

"Are they going to attack us?" squeaked Ónyká.

"Are they here for the war?" asked Phaedr.

"They are not going to attack," Kavan assured the girl as he lifted her so that she might see better from the security of an adult's arms. "They're coming to help King Lorant."

"They're not our enemy," said Bhríd.

"Whatever provisions they bring, they will need a place to shelter, food and drink…"

Bhríd nodded, raised the glass to his eye to look at the ships again, and then offered it to Cáym so that he could look too. "The Bodils are securing my fallow fields and Mr. Osveld is collecting what Levonne has to feed them." Fortunately, last year's harvests had been bountiful and the flocks were abundant. "Is the king...?"

"He will know in the morning." Kavan hesitated, watching the ships as Bhríd did and then looking through the glass when Cáym thrust it into his hand. "We bid farewell to gdhededhá Rankin."

"Syl told me; I regret I could not be there." There had been a day between his death and his burial, another before the High Gathering. The responsibilities of his vineyards had kept him from attending but unlike many in Rhidam, he had not been particularly close to Rankin.

Kavan gave the glass to Ónyká who held it up to her eye to look.

"Do you think...?" Bhríd's voice trailed off as the blatting of a horn announced the fleet's arrival, evidence that they arrived in peace rather than attempting to arrive in secrecy. The sound of it, returned by the men on watch in the lamp tower, was enough to reassure some of the onlookers and send them home. Others, less trusting or awaiting some command from their duke, stayed where they were. Mr. Osveld arrived, spoke softly into Bhríd's ear, and then herded the children to the house despite their adamant protests that they wanted to stay until the fleet arrived.

Once they were gone, Bhríd dared to finish the question he had been about to ask before. "Is Enesfel prepared for this?"

Kavan closed his eyes, seeking an affirmative answer, but he felt nothing except uncertainty and trepidation. "We must be," he finally said. "Neth is moving south of Lake Curo. Whether they brave the forest for war or resort to raiding parties as has been their way, they will strike."

Bhás would have it no other way. Using war to draw Kavan out seemed an elaborate ploy, the harbinger of unnecessary death meant to hurt him. If Kavan had the slightest inkling of where she was, how to find her, how he could draw her to him, he would have put an end to this threat already.

Maybe he should return to Pháne.

Earé had said it would come. He would find Bhás when it was time and history would take care of itself. How many people had to die before that?

He and Bhríd waited, feeling the approaching dawn before the sun brightened the horizon. They could see the scramble of tiny figures on some of the ships as the sails were adjusted to hold most of them back and permit another to approach the docks alone. The Elyri dukes met the ship at the head of the longest quay and watched the mooring process until a single man of about thirty-five, with long dark hair trimmed neatly around his ears and a closely shorn dark beard, came down the lowered plank to meet them. There was no hesitation in his steps, no evidence that the sea had taken a toll on his balance, but when he stopped in front of Kavan and met his gaze, there was a nervous pause and fidgeting step as if he was trying to decide whether to bow, to offer a hand, or retreat.

"Lord Cliáth."

Assuming Earé had spoken of him, if she had selected this man to lead her force in her stead, a soldier when he assumed she was not, Kavan inclined his head in affirmation. "My daughter has sent you."

"She has spoken of you, but I did not expect…she has your eyes, your features…"

Whether she had mentioned his appearance or not, there were enough rumors and stories about the White Bard to have given this stranger an inkling of what to expect. His response to the bard's appearance was a common one, but thankfully, he refrained from the fawning awe so many others displayed.

"This is Duke Bhríd Cáner of Levonne." Bhríd offered his hand and Kaj, familiar with the gesture now, accepted it.

"Kaj Yetek, tama of these men…your men." He shrugged, unsure how to refer to them, then asked, "Your king?"

"In Rhidam," Bhríd replied. "We were not expecting you so soon. You are welcome in Levonne until your men have their legs, then I will accompany you to meet him."

"And will you, my lord? Travel with us? I presume k'ílshwythnec will not be here…but I should like the opportunity to know you." To Kaj's knowledge, the lineage of k'ílshwythnec, one who was, is, and always will be, was never known. There were no legends of fathers or mothers, siblings or family, no indicators of mortality. Knowing those things as he did, he was eager to reconcile her reported immortality with a mortal father.

And he wanted to know if the White Bard of whom so many spoke with the same adoration and adulation as k'ílshwythnec, was the marvel they claimed him to be.

"If I may. I must return to Rhidam to prepare the king, but if I can do so, I will return and ride with you to Rhidam," Kavan agreed.

Satisfied, Kaj smiled and waved another man out of the ship. Dark-skinned and bald, with a graying beard and a broad nose that made him appear more a descendent of the Cíbhóló than of those of the south, the man towered over each of the three by nearly two hands.

"balo Eytor, Duke Cáner and Duke Cliáth." He offered his hand as Kaj continued. "He will get the men settled wherever you direct them to. At King Gamal's command, five of the ships, and the men to sail them, will remain at your disposal to employ when the rest of us join the king. The others are ordered to patrol the bay and protect Hatu's coast."

Bhríd deferred to Kavan with a sideways glance. He did not see how any Nethite ships would be a threat to Levonne but Kavan had suggested such a possibility. Alberni was threatened, and not so far from Levonne. If there was a chance that ships might invade the Tegid and sail toward Rhidam, having additional protection was a worthwhile precaution.

Particularly if Bhríd was not here to protect his duchy.

Jemes Osveld was a smart man, a learned and diplomatic man. A man of book knowledge. But he was no soldier. Judging by the scars on balo Eytor's face, hands, and sea-damp bare arms, Bhríd believed the towering man had seen his share of combat.

"They will be appreciated," Kavan accepted with a bow and nod.

Bhríd waved to balo Eytor. "I will have someone escort you to where you may set camp. tama, if you wish a tour of my vineyard while we speak of what is to come..."

"I will see to the security of my men and rest...and meet you later in the day if I may. We have much to discuss."

"Yes," Bhríd replied as Kavan nodded. "We do."

In the cold northern waters, nearly six hours off the coast of Pravek, the tiny island with the protected southern cove had been a haven for fishermen since the day Pravek's earliest inhabitants took to the sea. Some past lord or duke or enterprising man of wealth had built a tower upon it, a structure to serve both as a layover for weary fishermen as well as a beacon to warn passing ships that the island was there, after numerous vessels ran aground and sank on her craggy shore. Some said it had been a náós once, a stronghold where Elyri fleeing Teren persecution and Faithful fleeing de Corrmick oppression had sought refuge, but any trace of either case had vanished long ago.

Beaten by the storms, the tower had crumbled and collapsed, taking the beacon with it, but the first two stories of the narrow structure remained in use by anyone who needed it until the day the Vants claimed ownership. A second beacon building was erected on the peak of the island nearly one hundred yards behind the main building and was maintained by the island's owners, but overnight fishermen were no longer allowed.

They could anchor in the cove, but they were forbidden from entering the structures. Those who resided there would not permit it.

People were curious.

There were rumors that the de Corrmick kings used it as a prison. There were claims that great treasures were kept there.

No one had dared to find out. No one wanted to risk the wrath of a vengeful king, whether he was a de Corrmick by blood or not. If anyone had done so, they had drowned in the cold sea's unforgiving current.

It was said that the five who resided there now, three men and two women, were a coven of witches given royal dispensation to remain as caretakers and lamplighters. Some said they were there with more nefarious intent and two of the men had gained a reputation in Pravek for being frightening brutes capable of downing a man with one fist.

Their presence, too, kept the curious at bay.

Inness Lachlan de Corrmick did not know these things. She never saw them. The angle of her window, too small for an adult to enter through, only allowed an awkward glimpse of the dock where she sometimes saw the same little boat go to and fro, bringing goods that kept her alive in this spacious room she had been forced to call home.

She did not know where she was. She did not know the skyline of Pravek or the sound of the northern sea. The boat bore no banner or name and the accents of the men who sailed her were little different from any other Nethite she had known. A bit rougher and gruffer, perhaps, as though they spent too much time working around thick smoke and heavy dampness, but still Nethite at its core.

The women were the same, the pair who brought food twice a day, who brought water for bathing, who combed her hair, changed her bedding, and cleaned the few articles of clothing she was permitted to keep.

A nightgown and a robe, a set of tall, woolen stockings, and the two plain, coarse dresses of no longer distinguishable color.

She believed they had once been red. She did not have a name for the color they had become.

Sometimes the women spoke to her in that same thick accent as they washed and brushed her hair and adorned it with short strips of leather cord. Never a comb, never hair pins, never clips…as though they thought she might hurt herself, or someone else, with them.

She supposed that was the reason for so few clothes and the narrow window. There was no means to climb down if she could get through it without falling into the sea and onto the cliff's rocky base. But they did not need to fear that, she snorted every time the thought crossed her mind. She had learned the ways of the sword as a child, but she had never learned to swim, despite their Elyri tutor's urging.

What lurked in the water she could not see frightened her. The sharp stones frightened her.

Inness did not like to be afraid.

There were books on the shelves along one wall, books rotated at the urging of someone she never saw, never met. She had read them all during the decade of her entombment, read the new and the old, knew when the materials were recycled, knew the ages of the books by the feel of the pages and the texture of the bound leather covers. She did not know the name of the checkerboard game with the colored pieces of stone, but she had fashioned a game of those pieces and played it many times a day, challenging herself with ever more complicated moves.

She sang to herself. She mended her clothing when it needed mending, and she counted the fishing boats that crossed between her vantage point and the coastal city. She had seen the fleet that passed many days…or was it months…earlier. She recited lessons from her childhood, numbers and letters, poems and family genealogies the bard had taught her. She practiced swordsmanship with an invisible, weightless sword, waiting for the day when she would be able to overtake her captors and be free of this place.

In her more melancholy moments, she prayed…though she had never had much use for Faith and had no reason to believe in a god now. None had come forward to save her. None replied when she cried out. Only one voice ever responded…and it was not the voice of a god.

She had no clear idea who her captors were. Having heard her keepers talk that Olaric Fraen the Elder, the general she had trusted at the head of her army, now sat on her throne, she was convinced he was responsible for her being here. She had been warned that there was one close to her that she could not trust. She had believed from the start that one was Fraen.

There was no other to blame except herself for the mistakes in judgment that had granted their exchange in fortune.

The jangle of keys and the click of the lock at the door indicated an unexpected arrival. It was not yet mealtime and the bedding and clothing had been changed the day before. Not expecting anyone, she sat motionless at the game table, her hand hovering over the colored stones, and stared narrow-eyed at the door as it cracked open on gradually rusting hinges.

She recognized the man who entered though his face was more cragged with time than she recalled. He had served her diligently until something she did not recall prompted the death of his family.

"Hello, My Queen." Olaric forced his tone to convey surprise at finding her here, remorse for seeing what the years of isolation had done to her, and a measure of dutiful respect uncolored by the memories of betrayal that had cost him his first family. "I had heard…but I did not think…"

Her black hair was peppered with grey, as was his, but it was combed smooth, styled in a stately fashion with the few adornments she was permitted, and in the comfortable warmth of the room, her skin bore the flush of health. She had not grown thin or frail as Kjell had during his captivity, nor, he could tell by the glittering spark in her eyes when she recognized him, had she grown dull-minded.

He had come many times in his years in Pravek but he had never come into this room to see her. It had been crucial to the plan he was drawing together now.

"I should have known you did this." She put both hands in her lap beneath the game table and continued to stare.

"Me?" He bowed again, closed the door, and crossed the room to sit at the table across from her as though they were long-lost friends.

"You put me here," she hissed.

He shook his head, his expression mortified and earnest. "Not me, My Queen. The last time I saw you was when my family…" His voice trailed off and he looked away, expressing honest pain while controlling the fury the memory brought with it. "I left Glevum after that; I had no part in what my father has done." He sighed and looked at her again. "I heard rumors; people talk. Some say he forced you to marry him…"

"Betray Oska?" she spat. "I would rather die."

"Aye, I know. Your loyalty to our king would never have allowed it. I kept digging, searching, refusing to believe you were in Glevum's tower or that you were dead…until rumors led me here." He gestured to the room and turned in his chair to study the room. "This is not so bad; I expected worse; but it is no place for a queen."

Eyes narrowed, satisfied that his words supported her long-held belief about the cause of her captivity, she asked "Did he send you?"

"He doesn't know I'm here. I make it my purpose to avoid him now as I did when we both served the Crown."

She recalled the animosity between father and son though she had never learned its cause. Resentment and bitterness between parent and child were common enough. She knew that from personal experience. She had used their feud against them when she could, taking advantage of it from one side or the other in whatever way benefitted the Crown.

"He'll kill you if he finds you here." She cocked her head towards the bed where a cloth doll swaddled in a fading blanket lay against the pillows and murmured, "Henrik must be fed," before crossing the room and picking up the bundle with a gentle shushing sound.

Olaric watched her stroke the cloth doll's cheek, shift one sleeve on her dress, and press the tiny face to her exposed breast. He swallowed, shrugged, and lowered his gaze to the colored stones on the table. "He can try…but he doesn't know I'm here. They…" he cocked his head toward the door and the staircase beyond it, "think I'm here on his behalf. When I heard, I had to come, to see for myself. I had to let you know."

The act of imaginary breastfeeding did not last long. Inness had already laid the doll in the same place it had been, adjusted her dress for modesty, and returned to the table with a blank expression as though she had not heard what he said. Without sitting, she hesitated, head cocked as though listening to the sea or for voices outside or something he could not hear before murmuring, "He says you're not needed here. You've seen me, now you may tell him I'm…"

Not sure who the first 'he' was, but believing the second to be his father, Olaric rose to match her, wanting to avoid the strike he anticipated would come when he blurted, "He tried to assassinate Prince Henrik!"

"Henrik's right here," she exclaimed, pointing at the bed. "No one can reach him. No one can…"

"He's with Mr. Kaas…as you left him."

"Mr. Kaas." For a moment, the mention of that name soothed her agitation as if it brought back a moment of memory she had forgotten.

"I can help you. We can protect him; I can free you from this place but I need your help."

The morsel of memory was swept aside with a past she fought not to recall, preferring to live in the moment as she rushed to the bed again, scooped up the doll, and held it tight to her chest with a glare that challenged him to threaten her son again.

"Get out! You can't have him! I will not let you hurt him!"

At the onset of the command, he backstepped to the door, exhibiting no fear but an expression he hoped was interpreted as respect and obedience.

"I will return as soon as I can, My Queen. Think about my offer, your freedom, a chance to save your son, securing his place on Neth's throne."

"I'll not hear any more. Oska will never permit it. He's not…"

The door closed. A handful of colored stones, swept off the game table, clattered on the wooden panel between them. Olaric stood still, listening, reconsidering his options if Inness chose not to participate. He had not known what to expect from her when they saw each other, but apparent madness had not been part of it.

He might have to develop a new plan, a contingency, if he could not convince the Queen-regent to act with him to save her son.

He could give her a day, maybe two, to think about what he was trying to offer. He could wait to act no longer than that.

❧Chapter 24❧

General Waller inspected the bulwark constructed of tree branches, leaves, grass, and the damp earth of the forest floor to provide camouflaged cover for the men assigned to it. All were Nethites, some recruited during the forced march south, some recruited by the king before that, others forced into servitude in Ruidoso. There were mutterings that such forced recruits could not be trusted to do the king's bidding, but they were Nethites, Waller argued, and he trusted every one of them more than he did the mercenary host who followed and obeyed with unnerving, silent blindness as though waiting for some opportunity to rise against him. He needed these recruits. He dared not risk leaving the king's trained troops and depleting those at his back if the mercenaries did rebel.

The blind would hold. Near enough to one of a multitude of forest roads used to travel between Enesfel and Neth, near enough to strike at travelers or troops that passed, it was far enough from the road that it would not easily be noticed by those same travelers. Other roads, less usable, narrower, less passable, he left unguarded. An army would never travel such roads. It would be impractical.

Some would be a waste of time, as he doubted an army would diverge and use each road, but at least one of them would fulfill its purpose. Then survivors would alert the others and the men left would rejoin the main army. Not enough men posted at any of them to stop Enesfel, but enough to be an inconvenience, to slow their progress, to prune their numbers in the hopes of weakening them before the primary battles.

Thinning Enesfel's army was the best Waller could plan for.

❧*❧

Henrik is alive, Inness. You know he is.

Rocking the doll furiously, her eyes squeezed shut as if it would eliminate Oska's dissenting voice, Inness hissed, "He's right here."

Feel his chest. Does he breathe? Does his heart beat? Does he suckle as a child should? Test him. Tell me what you feel.

The rocking slowed enough that Inness could unwrap the swaddling and lay her hand flat upon the fabric body. As Oska asserted, there were no signs of life and when she rubbed her fingers over the fabric and then over the back of her other clutching hand, she was met with a difference in texture she could not deny. With a soft gasp, she let the form fall, an act between a drop and a throw, and waited for what she expected to hear.

A cry. A gasp. A squawk.

There was nothing.

In the silence of his lying there, she was given back a memory, another fall that caused injury to the babe's skull so that she had thought she would lose him. As she leaped from the bed to frantically scoop the doll up and feel the back of its head, she remembered other things too. The doctor. Zerio Kaas again. The tiny hole made in Henrik's skull to relieve the pressure. His miraculous survival.

Other memories came after, of her last night in Glevum. Thrusting Henrik into Mr. Kaas' arms and demanding that he protect Henrik as the castle halls filled with shouts and crying and the sounds of combat that should not have been there. Sounds that echoed the night Oska had taken his due from his father. The night all of this had begun.

What had come next? Killing a man. Another. A blow to the head. Blackness. Nothing for hours…maybe days…and then this place. Wherever this place was.

Her head slowly lifted and she stared at the window where the first traces of an early summer morning were stretching into her chamber. How long ago had that been? She stood, allowing the doll to tumble to the floor, forgotten as she pulled the leather envelope of pages out of her desk and began to shuffle through details she had written. Some important, some not. Philosophical musings and disjointed ramblings. Though she had not written anything in far too long, the pages she wanted were still there, pages where she had ticked off the passage of days as best she could.

Eight years? Nine? Maybe more. Maybe less.

He is old enough to sit on the throne with guidance. Old enough if you are with him.

"Henrik is…" She choked on the words and shook her head, allowing the pages to slip out of her hand. Mr. Kaas had sworn to protect her son but she had feared that both, by now, were dead. Fraen would never have permitted them to live.

He said it. Our son's alive. Henrik needs your help.

"There's nothing I can do from…he's better off without…"

You're a fine mother. He needs you. He needs us. You can help him. You can help them both. You can protect Henrik. Only you, Inness. Find him. Do not let Fraen succeed where I failed. Do not let him kill our son.

Inness stood at the desk until the black outside the window morphed into a powdery shade of cloudless blue. Until the warmth of it fell across her hand and the unfocused pages, until the soft clacking of a serving woman's hard-soled shoes brought with it the rattle of the key in the door.

She did not wait for the door to open. "Bring him back! I want him back! Tell the Captain I demand his attendance. I want him here now!"

Against her ear there was a chuckle, the brush of lips that ruffled her hair as the smell of sea salt wafted through the room.

Thank you, Inness.

Inness smiled.

❧*❧

"How is Gerna?"

Lorant caught up with Jerit as he passed in the corridor on the way to the stairs, his hand brushing over the back of Jerit's before they began their descent. They had been seated across from one another in an isolated alcove after leaving Rankin's Remembrance, not talking about something that hurt them both but rather silently staring through the tall arched window with their knees pressed together when Ártur bustled past with Ida's hand in his, claiming that Gerna was unwell and he was on his way to tend her. Although Jerit had no compulsion or need to be with his wife during her illness, for his daughter, who had snagged his hand and pulled him along, Jerit had relented.

Only for Ida would he be there to see how Gerna fared.

The periodic shifting glow of the lamplight hid the flush on Jerit's cheeks. "Healer MacLyr says it is something she ate, perhaps a touch of melancholia stemming from dedhá's passing…nothing more. He gave her something to soothe her stomach and help her sleep."

"You stayed with her."

Truthfully, he had stayed with Ida, who had fallen asleep on his lap at Gerna's bedside. Instead of arguing, he snorted, "You slept with Seren."

"That's different."

"Is it?" Jerit did not see how Lorant's duty as king were different than his as a husband. The only difference was that, after that first consummation of their marriage, Jerit had never spent another night in his wife's bed.

Neither spoke again until they entered the open-doored stateroom to find Kavan sharing breakfast with a host of palace children, including the Cáners who had not been in Rhidam the night before. The bard also looked as though he had passed a sleepless night. It was unusual to find children in this room, but the table was long enough for them to share breakfast together, and Kavan's expression, when he looked at Lorant, suggested he was here waiting for the king and had not wanted to be alone.

"Good morning, Lord Cliáth," both said at once. Lorant sat next to him in the chair Kaedís MacLyr vacated in favor of the bard's lap, and Jerit took one across the table to put distance between them.

"Is Lord Cáner here?" Lorant picked up a pear from the breakfast tray and savored his first bite.

Kavan shook his head. "Earé's people," he chose the word so as not to upset the children, "arrived in Levonne last night. I brought the children…"

"There are soldiers," boasted Phaedr. "Ships and ships from Hatu! I've never seen so many…!"

Kaedís' arms tightened around Kavan's neck and Prince Henrik's already pale complexion turned white. Kavan sighed. His scolding glance made Phaedr lower his eyes and offer an apology to his sister who sat beside him with wide, distressed eyes.

"So, it is war then," Jerit sighed, wrapping one arm around Ida on one side and around Princess Hella on the other.

Lorant's excitement mirrored Phaedr's but for much different reasons. "They are coming here? When will they arrive?"

"I am certain. They require rest, need to regain their legs after so much time at sea before a march is possible. And they will need to be stocked and equipped. It will be soon. Within the week, I think. Perhaps two. Rhidam needs to prepare. I will return to them in a few days and inquire…will ride with them at their general's request, if you approve."

"There's no better emissary," Lorant agreed. Bhríd was his chamberlain, loved and trusted, one of the most consular and noble men Lorant knew. But when it came to interfacing in matters of diplomacy, where it was necessary to read a room of strangers and soothe anxious nerves, to talk reason and sense and empathy into those disinclined to it, there was no one better suited than the White Bard.

"We must summon General Declan and the Daema…"

"The news was delivered last night." Kavan bowed his head apologetically and added, "I did not want to trouble you while you slept."

Lorant looked about to protest the delay but Jerit took an egg from the tray and spoke before he could do so. "They will know what we wish to discuss. It will wait until after breakfast."

"We should…"

"The day will be a busy one." Jerit held Lorant's gaze as he passed the basket of bread to him and waited for him to take it. "It is best we eat while we can. We may not have the chance to do so until evening."

Again, Lorant looked as if he would protest but accepted the bread with a sighing groan and began to hurriedly eat instead, settling for replying to Phaedr's queries about soldiers and ships and what the king's intents were when the men arrived. He would have preferred a peaceful meal alone with Jerit but the distraction of the children kept the otherwise awkward situation from being any more so.

❧*❧

"He's here."

Scowling at the interruption as Zerio bounded into the sunroom where Asta and Yóáná shared breakfast with the healer's children, continuing the ongoing effort to strengthen a mother-daughter bond they had failed to build during the younger woman's childhood as a healer-in-training, Asta set her glass down with a pointed expression and waited for him to explain. Instead of speaking about the cause of his interruption, he thrust a tattered scrap of thinly tanned hide into her hand. The material itself was old, possibly reused many times as the coloration of the leather was stained an odd, dark shade. But the new ink of the writing made the message new enough.

It could have been a forgery. She turned the hide front to back in search of clues. It could have been an older message with some entirely different meaning. But the mark in the corner, a Dugan earmark shared only within the family, looked legitimate.

"Who brought this?"

"Gate staff didn't get her name…only told me to give it to you."

"Did they read it?"

"Think they'd have any idea what it means?" he countered. He had not asked, only assumed in his haste to look it over and bring it to Asta that they had not. The abbreviated message was written in Association shorthand, unreadable to anyone not trained to decipher it. Asta had taught the script to both Jerit and Zerio, for the day when one or both graduated to Lachlan

Inquisitor, but to the palace guards, the strange figures and symbols would mean nothing.

"Get rid of it," she said as she thrust the scrap back at him. On the off chance there was someone else in the keep who could decipher it, she wanted no evidence of this matter to fall into the wrong hands.

He would never contact her directly. No one outside the Association must ever know they were kin. She had done what she could to lure him to Rhidam, now it was her obligation to protect him while they jointly worked to bring the Association and her inquisitor contacts back under control.

She was confident now that it would be done…for Warde Dugan was in Rhidam.

❧*❧

Furious with his delayed response to her demands, Inness shrieked and hurled the unwrapped doll at Olaric as he stepped through the door. "You said you would return!"

"I have," he replied after ducking out of the way of the doll and picking it up off the floor. His cloak was damp from the morning's unexpected rain that began at sunup and stopped by the time Inness had finished her breakfast and had taken advantage of her daily allotment of bath water.

"I told them to send you at once…two days ago!"

As casually as he could, he crossed the room and tried to hand the doll to her. She slapped it from his hand so that it sprawled face down on the bed, its limbs splayed like a discarded rag.

"I've been away. I can't stay in one place too long, nor stay here if I want to avoid my father. We'd be at risk if he knew I was here."

Inness crossed her arms over her chest and huffed. "You said you have a plan to save Henrik. What is it?"

"I'm working on it. The first step is to get you back to Glevum."

Back to Glevum. Inness' eyes widened and her mouth made an unexpected O as the impact of those words struck her. "Is he there? Is Henrik in Glevum?"

It confirmed she was not, but it did not tell her where she was.

"I'm no idiot…nor is Mr. Kaas. We'd never bring him anywhere within my father's reach. He's safe where he is for now, under guard…but once you and I have dealt with my father…"

"I want his head!"

Olaric smirked, his expression almost feral. "Perhaps you shall have it…perhaps even the throne if we…"

The gleam in her eyes was unmistakable.

He left that thought unfinished and continued, "He's not old enough to sit without a regent. My father wants me to rule after him, but Neth's throne is not my place. You are a Princess of Enesfel, King Oska's Queen, the Queen Regent. You should be so again until Prince Henrik is ready to rule."

Her eyes narrowed as she scrutinized his words, his tone, his expression. Her jaw went slack and then clenched again. Her hands flexed, and then she cocked her head as though hearing something Olaric could not.

"The prince needs you," he began again when she did not speak. "Glevum and Neth need you…before my father takes us down a path that will destroy Neth. You are the only one who can stop him, Your Majesty. There is no one else."

"Kjell? Jerit?" she whispered, her voice and breathing strained.

"We need you," Olaric repeated firmly. Kjell would be a better king, the monarch Neth needed, but the return of power into the rightful de Corrmick's hands could not come to pass until Fraen the Elder was erased from memory. If it meant that Neth needed a Queen-Regent to make that happen, Olaric would see it done.

She pulled her night robe from the bedpost. "Then let us be away."

Olaric shook his head. "Not today." She frowned. "I need to arrange a boat. I need a way past your watchers. I need to plan the journey to Glevum to keep you safe. I need to reach out to our allies to see it done. You will need to grant me time…"

"How long?" she hissed impatiently.

After a moment of apparent thought, he offered, "Three days."

"Tomorrow."

He frowned. "This cannot be rushed…"

"Tomorrow…or be rid of your father yourself." If, as Olaric claimed, Henrik was somewhere safe, she trusted he would continue to be so until the imposter king was removed. If Olaric was sincere in his desire to oust his father, he would either capitulate or he would be forced to create a plan without her in it. He might even be forced to temporarily accept the throne himself until Henrik was old enough to rule without assistance.

The notion of anyone else acting as regent for Henrik, however, made her shiver and swallow the surge of bile in her throat that made her cough. It also forced her to negotiate with him when he retorted, "Two days," as a compromise.

She nodded curtly. She was not accustomed to compromising, but this time, she had no choice. Henrik had no choice.

Henrik needed his mother.

"Next time you see me," Olaric said, backing away from her, "it will be time. If you don't see me…"

"Two days," she reminded him, as if the force of such a promise would be enough to keep Fraen from finding, and killing, his son.

If that happened, Inness knew she would be next.

No one would be able to protect Henrik then.

❧Chapter 25❧

Inness ignored the concerns of her female caretakers when she refused her second meal that day. When they came to her, they found her curled beneath her blankets, staring at the wall, but she only remained in that position long enough for them to depart, leaving her meal on the desk in the hopes that she would eat, stoking her fire to make the room warmer and closing the window against drafts in case the woman was ill. Once the click of the door lock indicated they were gone and the retreating sound of their shoes moved beyond the range of her hearing, Inness scrambled out of bed to throw the window open again and resume watching the movement of the boats between her and the mainland, looking for the one she expected to take her to freedom.

It would not look different than any other, but it would be different in every way. She believed she would recognize it when she saw it.

Hours ticked past. The light of day faded. The sea was calm, the air still, yet no boat approached the inlet, no unfamiliar boat waited at the dock.

Betrayed, she continued to watch, clinging to hope that something would move within the perimeter of the beacon's glow. It offered little illumination to the inlet and nothing stirred upon the water except for seabirds seeking their next meals of those fish who dared come to the surface once daylight was gone.

"My lady…may I enter?"

Inness scrambled into the bed but did not have time to turn toward the wall before the older of the two women poked her head inside. It had been four hours and the dinner plate remained untouched.

"You should eat, my lady. Such fasting is not…"

"Not hungry."

Sighing, concerned at the weakness she thought she heard in the woman's voice, the servant picked up the tray but left the partial loaf of bread on the table so that Inness could eat during the night if she wished without waking anyone. She paused at the door and murmured, "Goodnight then…perhaps tomorrow you will feel like eating."

By tomorrow, Inness did not plan on being in this room. She did not plan on being in this place ever again. She would either be free or she would be dead.

Alone again, she returned to the window. No one was there. She growled curses beneath her breath, climbed into bed, and ignored Oska's soft reminders that things would be okay, that soon she would see Henrik and Fraen the Elder would pay for everything he had taken from her.

If Olaric did not arrive before midnight, before the end of the second day as he promised, he was going to pay as well.

Eventually, there came the muffled sounds of a struggle, the crash of breaking pottery, the slamming of doors, the sounds lurching her awake from the slumber that had claimed her. She scrambled out of bed, remembering those sounds from her last night of freedom, and though she looked for something she could wield in self-defense, there was no sword to be had…not even a bread knife or heavy object she could wield as a club. She tugged at the bedpost in the hopes of breaking it free but failed to accomplish the act before the door was forced open by a sturdy kick.

Fury and fright were not eased by recognition when the man lowered his cloak hood with one hand and offered another in his other.

"You're late!"

Olaric's voice was low and rough as though afraid of being overheard and he beckoned her to follow. "Are you coming?"

She hesitated as if considering her options, noted the blood on his hands and boots but accepted the cloak and pulled it on.

"Cover your head and face and follow me. Stay silent behind me."

More inclined to give orders than accept them, she began to protest.

Listen to him, Inness. Be wise.

She growled, adjusted the hood around her face, and followed Olaric down the stairs.

Most of the lanterns were dark, their oil dripping on the ground. The remnants of a late-night meal, or perhaps left from earlier in the evening, were scattered across the floor, the dishes and cups smashed so that they crunched beneath Olaric's boots and forced Inness to pick her way gingerly through the mess so as not to cut her feet. The serving women both lay in awkward heaps near the doorway to what Inness assumed was the kitchen, shards of what they had carried broken around them. One of the three men lay at the bottom of the stairs, facing away from her, stains of red glistening on the banister and beneath his face as if he had struck his head in a fall. Another sprawled face down on the table with no visible injuries while the last lay half inside the room and half outside, his arm bent beneath him, his unblinking eyes focused on a point across the room.

Both surprised and impressed that Olaric had managed this feat with so little harm to himself, she wondered what the man's last moments had been.

"Come," Olaric whispered. "Hurry."

The five who had held her, served her, lay dead. She wondered why Olaric was whispering.

She followed.

Down a wooden plankway she had not been able to see from her room, where deliveries must have been brought in. The surface was slick from the spray of the incoming tide and when she slipped in her cloth shoes, Olaric was there to catch her. She clutched his arm, wishing for sturdier footwear, that she had stopped to steal the shoes from one of the servants, and tried to walk more cautiously. She had no interest in an undignified fall. Moored at the nearest dock, a nondescript fishing boat, the same as any others she had seen, bobbed on the calm sea, held to the dock by a second cloaked individual, while on the boat, a third man adjusted the sails.

Her grip on Olaric's arm tightened but he did not pat it in reassurance expecting she would read such an act as condescending.

On the rise behind the house, the beacon continued to glow, casting its light across the water.

"You can trust them." He would not have brought either of them if they were untrustworthy.

"I have not…" She shook her head in momentary refusal, recalling the times she had been offered passage on a ship to visit Káliel or to sail south to Hatu to visit the land of her father. She preferred to take the frightening Gates with Kavan or one of the other Elyri rather than risk drowning. She had never been on a boat before. She had undoubtedly been brought here on one, but since she did not recall it, she did not think that counted.

"You can board or you can swim…or you can stay and wait for my father to find you." Staying would mean fending for herself without servants and would mean hoping she could convince any fishermen who visited to supply her with food, firewood, and lamp oil.

Go to Henrik.

"I don't need your threats," she hissed with a toss of her head that knocked the hood of the cloak away from her face. In case the others would recognize her, in case they did not already know who she was, she hurriedly pulled it back into place and tried to step into the boat. She stumbled and the man rigging the sails caught her arm before she hit the deck.

"You will be more secure below…" Olaric said as he boarded behind her. "Warmer and dryer…"

"What of…he will know…"

"He'll never know I've been here…and should he come, he'll believe you've died too."

Doubting his claim but accepting his confidence at face value, she steadied herself with a hand on the rail and accepted his escort into the fishing vessel's cabin. The ropes stretched and hummed against their positions. The sails popped and billowed as they caught the new breeze and began to ease the boat away from the dock. The water slapped against the hull and the vessel rocked from side to side. Inness' expression turned a pale shade of uncomfortable green.

"Sleep. We have many miles to go. There is nothing you can do."

"You harm me…I'll have your head."

If he harmed her here, if they threw her body into the sea, no one was ever going to know. When he smiled and murmured, "Of course you will," that was precisely the fate she expected she would meet now that he had her here alone.

❧ * ❧

Screams swallowed by the sea.
Shattering pottery. Breaking glass.
Footsteps running on stairs.
Copper and salt upon his tongue.
Pungent fear, sweat, and bile at the back of his throat.
A cloth doll dropped at the top of an unlit staircase.
A hand clasped in another as they fled across a swaying dock.
Looking back. Blood.
Laughter, harsh and cruel and blood-curdling.
His father's pained, frightened cry.

Ágdhállán bolted upright in his bed, his heart hammering at the inundation of flashing, swirling sensations, sights, and sounds of places he did not know, glimpses of unfamiliar faces.

But his father's terror, his father's pain, were things that thrust the boy out of bed and, without bothering to pull on his slippers or a robe, ran to the room next door.

He was sure that shriek had been real, not part of the Sight but something that had drilled into his ears, into his unconscious mind to wake him out of the vision. But no one else came running, if they had heard it, and when he stumbled to his father's bedside, it was to find him staring, wide-eyed, at the ceiling, his body as rigid as the strongest tree, his hands clenched at his side.

"k'bhydhá?" Ágdhállán shook him by the shoulders. In that touch, he knew that his father had seen the same vision he had.

And he had seen something more.

Ágdhállán was not skilled enough to pry into his father's well-protected thoughts, to glean anything more than surface images. Having never seen his father in this state, not understanding what it might mean, the boy could think of only one thing to do.

With every ounce of limited power he contained, he thrust his thoughts out with all his might in a silent, desperate plea.

'aendhá Ártur!'

❧Chapter 26☙

"There is no use waiting any longer," Bhríd said to the man at his side as he adjusted his riding gloves and Kaj shift himself in the saddle. While the tama did not appear comfortable on the large, borrowed horse, he did appear, as he claimed, to be familiar with riding. They intended to begin their trip at daybreak, but delayed their departure in the hope that Kavan would join them as he had hoped. Bhríd had considered going by Gate to Rhidam to summon his kinsman, but there had been too many last-minute preparations around the estate to permit him the spare moments to do so.

If Enesfel was to be at war, this might be the last time he saw Levonne. It was necessary to be certain that Leon and his nephew Augustus, Jemes Osveld, and the rest of his staff knew how to manage the vineyards and the estate until his children were old enough to take possession of it.

He had kept his promise to Madeline thus far, had done his best to guarantee that the Dubuais estate would remain in good hands, even when he was no longer able to care for it himself.

If Kavan was not here, there was an honest reason for it, be it his family, the Faith, or some duty to the king. Bhríd was more troubled with what that reason might be than with the bard's absence itself.

"I will see to matters here," balo Eytor bobbed his head once and stepped back from Kaj's horse after patting the mud-brown beast's flank. Most of Hatu's fleet had sailed for home days ago and the men who remained had been assigned housing with the estate or elsewhere in town; they already patrolled the docks and around Levonne's perimeter seeking disturbances. They did not know what they were looking for, but Kaj had assured them they would recognize it when they saw it. Any attack or attempted infiltration ought to be easy to spot.

"Winds be with you, Eytor," Kaj said, clasping the big man's shoulder. He had known the towering man most of his life. Of all the balo he trusted, his thoughts would dwell on the older man the most until they saw one another again.

"And you, tama. She will spare your life if the wind wills it."

Kaj nodded. "Likewise, friend." He straightened in the saddle with a grim expression that suggested he was determined to endure the upcoming discomfort of extended riding on an unfamiliar saddle as he had endured the previous days at sea.

His resolution, as he followed Bhríd's horse and led the long trail of troops, wagons, and support personnel away from Levonne, reassured Bhríd of the possibility of success that he had, until today, been reluctant to hope for.

❧ * ❧

Assured that nothing was physically wrong with his father and hoping to spare the other children his concerns for what could be psychically wrong, Ágdhállán threw himself into the day's lessons with Master Najar and drew the other children with him. He pressed for swordsmanship lessons with anyone who had the time to offer them, lessons he typically avoided, and spent hours teaching his friends songs, reading to them, playing games, offering any form of comfort he could devise, to soothe himself as well.

His diligence failed to distract the bearded man who sat at the bard's bedside night and day from the moment Ágdhállán discovered Kavan's condition, nor did it reassure the healer who checked on his cousin every few hours during the next three days. Ártur had closed Kavan's eyes to avoid that unsettling, unseeing stare, but he could not unclench Kavan's hands or force his mouth open to feed him.

The only reassurance Ártur could offer when Dhóri and Sóbhán were brought to him in the hopes that the familiar presence of his sons would coax him out of his stupor, was that he had seen Kavan in similar states before. It was a response to some psychic trauma or power event, an attempt by Kavan's mind to reestablish equilibrium with his body.

He believed Kavan would wake on his own when he was ready, but he could not guess when that would be.

Standing at the window, watching the children in the courtyard following Master Najar in a game of directions, it was the creaking of the bed to his left that announced a change. Kavan's limbs had lost their rigidity, his hands were uncurled, and his head was turned toward Rhyrdan so that he could stare at the bearded young man with bloodshot eyes.

"My lord." Rhyrdan sat on the edge of the bed and pulled Kavan's hand into his. The bard shifted onto his side, his movements slow as if he was in pain, and rested his free hand on Rhyrdan's thigh.

"That was some vision," He brushed Kavan's hair out of his face. "Ágdhállán said he shared it with you…but yours was different…"

"Inness." Voice coarse and parched, he relinquished physical contact so that he could sit up and drink the water Rhyrdan offered.

"Is that who he saw? Is she…?"

"Alive. But it wasn't…that's…"

Diona's daughter was one of only two children still alive. In that revelation, he felt no danger or threat and no sense of harm to Enesfel, Kjell, Prince Henrik, or anyone else. But there was something…a bitter laugh he had learned to recognize and an attempt, it had felt to him at the time, by a pair of clawed hands to drive him into the mattress, pull him across a field of broken shards, to choke him with smoke and fire and the toxic smell of sulfur, an effort to incapacitate him by force and by fear that had taken all his internal strength to fight and come back from.

Bhás had found him. Bhás had struck at him and had, he believed, nearly defeated him in that place of dream and vision. He did not know how she had not succeeded, whether Kóráhm had intervened or whether it had been something else, but he was reminded again that he would have to be more diligent. He would have to be stronger.

He would have to find her before she found him again.

He would have to hide this battle, and his certainty about what the final moments of revelation meant, from those he loved. He could not frighten them the way he had been frightened.

He shook his head in response to Rhyrdan's unspoken prompting. "I don't know what the rest means…only that they are portents."

"Of war?"

Kavan nodded. There was no lie in leaving that answer to stand. Everything to do with Bhás was a portent of war. "How long?" he was hungry and thirsty, his body stiff. His eyes burned and the well of power within felt agonizingly depleted. He would need a meal, a decent sleep, and a few hours of meditative music and prayer at the altar or in the solitude of nature before he felt like himself again.

He did not think anyone in the royal house would permit those things once they learned he was awake, and he did not have the strength to fly to seek them out.

He did not think he had enough to Gate to Alberni, to St. Kóráhm's, to find solitude there either.

"Three days and the night Ágdhi found you like this."

"Has…is Bhríd here?"

"Not yet. The king is anxious for their arrival. There have been spies from the north, reports about the movement of troops in Neth…it is said Ruidoso has fallen. The army has gathered, and he is prepared to march, but the advisors have persuaded him to await the arrival of the support troops. It may only be your condition that prevents him from leaving, but others are eager for you to dissuade him from hasty action."

"I will go…"

Rhyrdan pushed him down into the mattress. "You will rest. Ártur will return to see to your health, and I will bring you something to eat. When you are strong, that will be enough…and if the king tries to act in haste before then, I will drag him here so you may talk sense into him."

With a reluctant, petulant sigh, Kavan accepted the command he knew was in his best interest. There was sound logic in taking rest where he could find it, before the Royal House pressed in with their needs, wishes, desires, and duties. He needed rest before Bhás sought him out again. He slid down into his pillow after giving the water glass back to Rhyrdan then added, "I will only see my children." And Ártur went without saying. He could feel the boys in his room, that all three had been here willing him to wake, and he was eager to reassure them he was well.

Under the weight of the lingering nightmarish images, he wanted to be certain his children were safe too. He would have to wait, however, to see Earé.

"Thank you for staying, for being watchful."

Touched by the note of something that suggested Kavan felt he had been vulnerable in that previous state, Rhyrdan kissed his forehead and said, "I would be nowhere else. I will bring them as soon as you awake." Like his father before him, there was nowhere he would rather be so long as Kavan needed him.

☙ * ❧

"Seventh in two days," Zerio muttered as he circled the dismembered torso with the Association mark branded across his bare chest and back. The victim had been dead less than six hours by his judgment, not long enough to emit the stink of decomposition but long enough to attract the attention of the early morning flies and the crows that retreated to the nearby rooftops when people began to gather. Without a head, identification would be difficult, unless an Elyri was brought in for a reading, but like Asta, Zerio felt no need for that.

This display, left at the end of an alley adjacent to one of the Association's many safe houses, was not meant for the inquisitor or the Crown. It, and each of the other public corpse displays left across the city, were intended as a warning to other members of the Association, a notice that there was a new power who would not tolerate the sort of unchecked lawlessness that had grown steadily over the last decade. Judging by the anxious hand-wringing of the person who had summoned Asta, new leadership was beginning to be noticed. Change was taking root.

"King's not going to tolerate this," Madoc scowled as he kept his distance and allowed the inquisitors to do their job. He assumed the quaking man nearby had informed the pair so that their arrival on the site coincided with the arrival of the sheriff and his men.

"No need to distract him with this. He's got other matters to…"

"No need?" squawked the justice. "Rhidam has not seen such a spree since the Persecution."

"This isn't that; you know it." Asta poked at the pallid, bloodless corpse with the point of her dagger as if looking for something, and then gestured to the pair of men flanking Madoc to cut it down. "Someone's trying to get them in order. Flexing their clout. The victims have been Association…and since the first one, we've noticed a decline in…"

She had not recognized the previous victims, and without a head, this one was unidentifiable too. But from the brandings, she knew enough.

"I'd as soon have them gone," Madoc cut her off, "before they turn to…"

"If it comes to that, by all means deal with them as you see fit." It was the same arrangement she had with Marta, that her father had shared with the Association during his years as Inquisitor. Crime was always a factor in any urban center, but in those areas where the Association held control, they were self-regulating. She would rather have that regulation than the chaos Rhidam had been experiencing.

"We can manage this…and we can hope that once this is over, there won't be another assault on your patrols or the royal family.

"It isn't their job to…"

"Better they manage themselves and keep things controlled," snorted Zerio, noting the meticulous single strike that had detached the missing limbs as he helped lower the body onto the cart the sheriff had brought, "then us chasing the winds without leads."

He glanced at the windows and doorways around them and wondered where the limbs and head would show up. At the man's former residence, he guessed, or on the doorsteps of his known accomplices.

Looking offended, Madoc huffed, "We caught the last…"

"Those weren't Association," Asta reminded him. "We stopped some of them, you and I…but just as many continue to elude us. When you find the rest of him…or anyone else…let me know." She looked at the messenger who had brought her here with a steely gaze as if to drive her point home. There would be cooperation with the Inquisitor, there would be order within the Association, or else there would be more death. Members in Rhidam would either capitulate to their new leadership or they would suffer the same fate.

The man bobbed his head eagerly. Asta nodded once. They understood each other. Soon, the rest would too.

❞*❝

Sick to her stomach after nearly four days of following Neth's shore over the choppy coastal current, smelling like sticky sea salt and too many days without a bath, complaining about the torture Captain Fraen had thrust upon her though refusing to beg for an overland alternative that would have meant risking identification, Inness was relieved to at last see Glevum's familiar skyline, the coastal tanneries, the royal tower. Four days it had been, hiding her face during the day, avoiding fishing vessels and merchant ships carrying food, supplies, and men to Glevum to be used in Fraen's imminent war.

The captain had explained it to her as succinctly as he could, how his father was determined, with the help of a mercenary army, to reclaim the south as he had failed to accomplish under her leadership.

An admirable goal but not, if the captain's stories were true, when there were so few Nethites for the fight. Not when they were outnumbered by mercenary forces he thought likely to turn on them when they came to the end of their aid.

She wondered, as they moored in the predawn hours within easy reach of the castle, if his intent all along had been to turn her over to his father. She wondered if her rescue had been a show for her benefit and if she was destined for a public execution to rally Neth's meager forces to battle.

She wondered where the mercenary army had come from.

One of the other two men in the boat jumped out, tied the vessel to a tall wooden stanchion, and then moved ahead to scout for threats. Olaric disembarked and offered his hand, but although Inness made it out of the boat on her own, her legs gave out, unable to manage the awkwardness of the stationary dock. Olaric, barely resisting rolling his eyes at her stubbornness, wrapped an arm around her to support her weight, the most intimate contact she had experienced with anyone, other than the serving women who had helped bathe her, in a decade, and waited for her to adjust her cloak to hide her face. When she was ready, she grunted and they began to walk, Olaric doing his best to keep her from stumbling or falling.

His effort did not seem that of a man intending betrayal.

The third man followed close, one hand on a curved knife at his hip whose eyes darted back and forth as they walked. Unaccustomed to displaying weakness or relying on others, Inness braced herself for what she expected would be that curved blade in her back.

They turned away from the castle, away from the empty, cobbled area where she had once burned captives alive, erected gallows for hanging, and had a man beheaded for high treason. Those memories made her unexpectedly shudder and prompted her to look elsewhere, to focus instead on the unfamiliar streets they were taking toward the north edge of the city. Though the sun had not yet topped the horizon, she could see in the graying light of dawn how vacant and rundown Glevum had become…or had it always been this way? With the Yellow Sisters having depleted the population and the king forcing many who survived into military servitude, there were few to restore the homes and trades that had inevitably fallen into disrepair.

It was too early for most to be out. Those she saw were hunched, wrapped in cloaks and robes against the morning's misty fog, gray forms in the gray air as drained of color and life as her city had become.

Had she done this? Was this her fault? Had the choice for war weakened Glevum enough that she had fallen to this? Or was the downfall of Glevum blamed solely on Fraen the Elder.

The sprawling, three-tiered structure they finally entered, while showing similar decline on its exterior, showed little of that decay within. The surfaces were dusty, some of the windows cracked or broken, and the chairs and tables around the wide room were tipped onto their sides; the structure looked abandoned but it was in useable condition if someone wanted to live here or turn it into a business.

Inness vaguely recalled this place serving as a school for builders and engineers in the early years of Kjell's reign, where royal monuments had been planned but never built, where the breakwaters had been redesigned and their rebuilding had been directed from. What had become of the owners, the artisans and apprentices who had resided here, one of Glevum's oldest buildings appeared to be no longer in use.

What a shame, she mused as the door closed. The Crown could have used this grand building. Those who had studied here could be put to work resurrecting Glevum's crumbling homes, businesses, and infrastructure.

"Someone's been here," muttered the man in the front, a man with dark skin and a tight braid of curly hair that she believed indicated Cíbhóló heritage. There were not many Cíbhóló in Neth. If he hailed from Glevum, she believed she would have seen him before. Perhaps he had come during her absence. Or, as she had not been one to mingle with the common people, she would not have known him at all. He pointed at the footprints in the dust that traveled to and from an entryway, indicating that at least two individuals had been there.

Brushing off the concern, knowing that Zerio had been here recently, Olaric muttered, "We're safe." They circumvented the middle of the room with measured, cautious steps that belied his certainty about their safety and then started up the stone staircase that curved both right and left from its central position. He helped Inness to the level, she clinging to the carved wooden handrail to maintain her balance, and then aided her up an even narrower set of stairs that brought them to a cramped, windowless room with only a slatted vent for air and light, bed, a desk and chair, and a wooden pail sealed with pitch in the corner of the room.

Everything in the room was covered in a thin sheen of dust, unused for some time, as though it had been intended for use but ultimately abandoned. Or as if the last occupant had tidied the room and never returned. Inness wrinkled her nose in distaste and began, "I will not…"

"I apologize for the accommodations, but it is the best I could arrange on short notice." He let the words linger between them, as if to suggest that her rush to be rescued meant that these shabby lodgings were somehow her fault. "You'll not be here long if I can help it, a few weeks at most while other arrangements are made and our plans finalized. When I am ready to…"

"I want Fraen's head now!" she jerked away but her stubborn, unsteady legs gave out and she dropped to the floor despite Olaric's effort to catch her.

He offered his hand to help her, but instead, she crawled to the nearby chair and pulled herself up as he continued, "You're in no shape for that. You must rest, regain your strength and your legs, and I need to prepare. We cannot storm the castle and demand his head without losing ours."

As much as it frustrated her to hear him say it, Inness was forced to admit it was true. She sat breathless in the chair and tried to wipe the dust from her already dusty hands.

Olaric continued. "Someone will bring you clean clothes, bring your meals and water each day, and I will keep you appraised of our progress. When it is time, we will do what needs to be done. You'll have your revenge and your throne. Henrik will be safe."

"That's all that matters," she huffed, swallowing her seasick belly's efforts to expel the churning acids its emptiness produced, channeling that bitterness into her words. Henrik safe. Henrik on Neth's throne. A de Corrmick in Glevum once again. She would not admit her private interest in regaining that throne to anyone.

Oska knew.

No one else needed to.

❧*❧

Kavan's mind continued to race instead of rest as he met Ártur's examination and questions with vague answers and waited for the meal Rhyrdan had promised. Ágdhállán was the one to bring it, however, and after setting the tray on the bedside table, he tightly embraced his father with his face buried against the man's chest. So often Ágdhállán behaved wise beyond his years, as serene, cooperative, and agreeable as Kavan had been at his age. It was easy for many to forget at times, when he spoke of visions of the past, present, and future, that he was a child who needed his father's love and guidance, who was afraid of losing him and being alone as Kavan had felt about Ártur during those same formative years.

Kavan had no desire for Ágdhállán to suffer loneliness and abandonment the way he had. Praise be for the Cáner children, his cousins, and the others who resided in Rhidam.

Eventually, the boy surrendered his hold to allow his father to eat and rest after Ártur returned one more time to see to his patient's welfare before retiring for the night. Rhyrdan also returned, bringing greetings from Zerio and Níkóá and a pleading message for attention from the king, but Kavan had no energy to face Lorant tonight. He wanted only the sleep that had eluded him all day and found it as soon as his belly was full and his head was settled into the pillows Dhóri and Sóbhán adjusted for him.

The vibrant images of arrows raining from the sky over Clarys, the churning sway of boats on the sea at the base of Clarys' cliffs, and the shouts of unfamiliar Elyri voices, the smell of blood and the striking of blade against blade in a nondescript forest that smelled of pine and cedar and oak…scents that reminded him of Bhryell…jarred him out of that too brief slumber to find his hands clenched tight around sheets he had kicked onto the floor in a thrashing fit.

The room was dark. The castle was still, without even the sound of early-rising staff to bring whispers to his ears. Squeezing his eyes tight, hoping to sleep again, brought only the ongoing echoes of the Sight crowding into every crevice in his head and so he gave up on sleep to stand at the window and stare at the starlit sky.

The position of the moon, the barely discernable glow in the east told him that dawn was not far off, that the palace staff would begin to stir, and that soon, Lorant would seek him out. There was something else in the air, the faintness of thunder, the scent of horses, details felt more than heard or smelled, that made him tremble and sigh.

Further premonitions of war had brought with them the arrival of the force Enesfel was waiting for.

He had not ridden with them as intended but he could meet with them now and ride with them into Rhidam to reassure people that there was no need to be afraid.

This army was not there to harm them.

They were here for Enesfel's protection.

The wish to be the first to greet them prompted flight that Kavan had been too weak to consider the day before, and although he successfully made the change to kestrel feathers and then back again just beyond the line of sight of the dozen or so mounted men and the host marching behind them, the change had not been as easy as it normally was and the expenditure of energy took an unexpected toll. By the time the lead riders made note of the man in the road ahead, Kavan's knees had stopped shaking, the flush on his face had subsided, and he had regained a steady breath and even heartbeat.

He did not want anyone to worry.

"My lord, it is good to see you." Bhríd's question was barely masked by the diplomacy of his words.

"There were matters to tend to," Kavan murmured, bowing first to him and then to tama Yetek with a contrite expression. "It is good to see you as well. I hope my absence was not troublesome."

The corners of Bhríd's mouth drooped as he read something in Kavan's tone, in his posture, that the bard was valiantly trying to hide.

"Everything is in order," replied Kaj with obvious relief, "though I admit concern for your welfare in these troubling times."

"I am well. The king is eager to meet you. He will update you both on the state of things; I am afraid I know little of his plans and preparations."

He knew more than he wanted to, more than he was supposed to, but most of that had come from the Sight and not from the king. He did not want to share those things and believed it was not his place to speak on Lorant's behalf.

He did not want to talk about war.

Bhríd offered his hand. "Come up and ride with us."

The offer was accepted with a nod and an awkward aversion of his gaze. He did not have the strength to fly back…and Bhríd knew it.

Nor did he have the will just yet to tell Bhríd of the portents he had recently seen. Portents the chamberlain needed to know.

❧*❧

It was too early for breakfast but Olaric found Kes seated at their table, a cup of tea clutched between her hands, when he unlocked and opened the door of their home. She looked up from the candle flame she had been staring at and met his gaze with both relief and concern.

He wondered what was on her mind, why she was awake at this hour, if she had been waiting for him.

"Is everything…?" he began.

Simultaneously, she asked, "She is here?"

He hung his cloak on the door, poured a cup of tea from the kettle, and sat across from her before saying, "It is done." Not the entirety of his plan, but this first phase of it. "She will need food, clothes…"

"Do you want me to…?"

He shook his head. "Not today…but perhaps next time. The less involved you are, the better. I will take it to her if you will prepare…"

"I have things set aside." She cocked her head towards the bedroom-turned-sitting room.

"Have things been…?" She seemed troubled, but maybe it was no more than her worry for him. "Are the girls…?"

"We are fine." She had seen no soldiers, had not seen Sparding. If any who had come for medical attention were spies for the king, she had not been able to tell. "What comes next?"

Olaric shrugged as he turned his hand to hold hers. She accepted the gesture with a sighing smile.

"I must see him, let him know I am back." He half expected his father would be disappointed to see him, if he had been the one to send the assassin, but Olaric had to return to the keep. The less suspicious he behaved, the easier his next steps would be.

"But first, I hope to share breakfast with my wife and daughters."

"I can make that happen," Kes said warmly. "Just tell me we are safe."

"Long as he doesn't find out, we are safe. I'll protect you and the girls. I swear it."

Olaric had lost his first family to one out-of-control monarch.

He did not intend to lose the second the same way.

❧*❧

The swath of land outside of Rhidam on the south side of the city, meadowlands used for grazing sheep and cattle, had been emptied on order of the king in preparation for the army said to be arriving from Levonne. The herds and their caretakers had been moved elsewhere so that tents could be pitched and cook fires built, a raucous process that Kaj decided he should oversee when more than a dozen of his followers fell into a brawl that others joined and still others broke up. His attention to the tension of his men would delay the meeting with Lorant, but rather than wait with him, Kavan and Bhríd traveled ahead to alert the king of their arrival before the news reached him through some other channel.

They left the foreign voices behind to ride in silence, not speaking until they turned onto the street that would take them directly to the palace, content to remain immersed in their own thoughts. Finally, unable to delay the inevitable if he wanted answers, Bhríd said, "Something troubles you. You hide it…but I know." He glanced over his shoulder at the man seated behind him, who had yet to meet his gaze. "Is the king…?"

"Lorant is in high spirits. He is too eager…he does not appreciate the gravity of war."

Bhríd snorted. "Neither did Arlan at his age."

Arlan, too, had decided upon war at a young age, but by the time Arlan faced his first battle, he had been four years older than Enesfel's current king, Arlan's great-great grandson. Lorant might be better prepared for it by the nature of his upbringing, his training, physical strengths, and prowess, but that did not mean he was ready for war.

Kavan was not ready for him to face it.

"I will protect him with my life. You know I…"

"I do not think…it's not only Lorant and Enesfel…what I have Seen…"

"Am I to die?"

Kavan shook his head but he did not speak for several moments. "I have not Seen it, but I have seen Elyriá at war. Clarys…somewhere near Bhryell and the pass…gdhededhá Bhílári…" The other name he dared not say, the name that scared him most. "They are not prepared. I do not believe I can sway the Kyne to offer soldiers to protect Bhryell…our kin…when there will be just as many others in need."

The castle came into view, its gates open as the expected early morning foot traffic of merchants and petitioners passed in and out across the lowered drawbridge. Bhríd pulled the horse up short and paused, watching the movement, with Kavan peeping over his shoulder to determine what Bhríd was looking at.

Eventually, the chamberlain said in a low voice, "Are you asking me to defend Bhryell?" Kavan's family was his family too. If an invading army crossed the Llaethlágárá and pierced Elyriá as far as Bhryell, there was no guessing how much of the pacific sovereignty would be destroyed.

Kavan sighed. "One man will not be enough."

Bhríd nudged the horse into action. "Perhaps not," he replied gravely, "but one is a start."

"He's back?"

The apothecary shop was one of the few places in Glevum, other than backrooms, taverns, and merchant businesses the Association controlled, where Marta felt comfortable, where she felt safe. After her arrival in Glevum, seeking the one who had murdered both her secret husband and the head of Neth's branch of the Association, the apothecary and the man who frequently visited there had become two of her most trusted allies. She had protected the shop when Kes and Olaric fled Glevum, moving another, less reputable physician, barber, and apothecary into it, and had been there to greet the couple when they returned with three girls in tow. They often discussed the actions of the interim king, the need for a de Corrmick on the throne, the future of both the Association and the Vants.

Olaric had said he was working on a plan before he left for Pravek, but he had not revealed what that plan was.

Marta did not blame him for that. She rarely told him her plans either. There was only one plan he knew for certain.

Seek revenge in every quarter of Glevum for the death of Fen Geli.

The man at the counter slid coins and a basket of carrots toward Kes in exchange for the medicine he had come for. After bidding him a good day and telling him to stay out of the sun for the rest of the day, she waited until he went out before speaking. The shop was empty except for the girls she could hear upstairs with the tutor Olaric had insisted on hiring.

"She's secured," Kes replied as she cleaned the counter of the herbs that had spilled there. "He's gone to let his father…"

"Secured? Who?"

"The queen, of course. Who else…?"

Kes' mouth snapped shut as Marta's look of confusion quickly switched to one of horror and outrage before asking, "Where is she?"

The blonde woman shook her head, contrite and flustered for speaking out of turn. "I don't know…he didn't…I thought you knew." She was not privy to all conversations between Olaric and Marta, but as one of his strongest allies, both working toward the goal of ousting Fraen from the throne, Kes had thought he would have told Marta his plan.

She realized too late that if Olaric had told Marta that Inness was alive, Marta would not have spent the last decade looking for her husband's killer.

"I'm sorry…I didn't mean to…I thought you…"

The fury bled from Marta's face and she smiled, forced but sincere, as she picked up a vial of bath oil and placed a handful of coins on the counter, the amount more than the value of the vial and its contents.

"It's alright. I forgot why he was gone…or maybe he did not mention it. It isn't…I don't blame you." She tucked the vial into her belt pouch and added, "You'll tell him I am looking for him?"

Kes nodded, counted the coins, and then stammered, "This is too much," as she pushed the extra coins back.

"For the cause," Marta shrugged with a wink before leaving Kes to count the coins again and deposit them into the box beneath the counter.

Kes swallowed hard.

Olaric was going to be furious.

ŠChapter 27Š

"You've Seen it? Are you sure?" Lorant cast a side glance at Bhetá as if to ask her opinion of the peculiar confession. They knew that, like his father, Ágdhállán had a gift for foretelling future events, but sometimes it was difficult to take the words of a child seriously.

With the announcement having come that the mercenary army was setting up camp at the southern edge of Rhidam, having sent Kavan and Bhríd with General Declan to escort their leader to the keep to share in the evening meal and sit for a preliminary meeting with him and his military leaders, Lorant presumed that Ágdhállán had overheard the growing rumors of rapidly approaching war.

His claim might be nothing more than a nightmare.

Ágdhállán sucked in a breath, trying to determine if the king believed him or was humoring him, but before he could answer the question, the partially open stateroom door opened the rest of the way, allowing his father and three others to enter. Lorant rose, as did Bhetá, the boy's premonitions set aside for the tangible evidence of a mercenary army that might be enough to win a war against Neth.

As Kavan held a hand out to his son, beckoning him to his side without asking why he was there, Bhríd bowed and said, "Your Majesty, Daema, this is Kaj Yetek, called tama by his people."

As Kavan wanted no more part in this war than he was forced to play, as he would rather avoid bloodshed if he could, it had been agreed that the chamberlain would make the introductions.

What Kavan wanted required finding Bhás.

"tama?" asked Lorant as he approached and offered his hand.

"According to King Gamal, that would be general in your tongue," Kaj replied, clasping the younger man's hand but not kissing it or bowing as many dignitaries would. His lack of reverent gesture made Lorant scowl but the expression was fleeting. He had thought a mercenary general would be older, grayer, someone with years of experience akin to General Declan, someone who knew Enesfel's customs. Instead, he guessed the black-haired man was nearer in age to the Daema, perhaps as young as Jerit, and as new to war as he was.

He bitterly assumed, without expressing his fears, that if older, more experienced men had turned down leading this mission, they had viewed this war as an act of folly.

He felt less certain of Enesfel's success.

Finding the man's accent thick and unusual but not difficult to understand, not that of the Hatu emissaries he was familiar with, he focused on Kaj's polite smile rather than his misgivings and said, "Welcome to Enesfel. We appreciate the difficulties it must have cost to travel so far."

The greeting prompted a bow of respect before Kaj's gaze strayed from the king, barely older than a boy, to the tall woman at his side and then back again as he replied, "k'ílshwythnec bid us go; now we are here and at your disposal. It is our honor to serve her…and you."

Lorant did not know the word but assumed it to be a title, perhaps referring to Kavan's daughter who had promised Enesfel an army. Noting the glance at Bhetá, he gestured, "This is Daema Magk…also general."

The tama's surprise was expected.

"My Lady." He offered her the same bow he had offered Lorant, assuming she was his mother, sister, or queen, and that it was customary here for women to ride into battle, even though he had seen no other female soldiers in the castle grounds teeming with lords and soldiers as he passed through. Perhaps leading men into war was the duty of royalty here.

Bhetá smiled despite her intent to remain stoic and neutral during war talks with the foreign soldiers they were being blessed with. She had not seen them.

Lorant continued, "You will join us for dinner? Meet my advisors, the dukes and lords…join our council tomorrow afternoon. A room will be prepared for you if you wish."

Kaj politely shook his head. "I appreciate the offer, but I prefer to share the accommodations of my men, to share with them as they do to encourage their camaraderie. I will gratefully accept the offered meal, if I may, and look forward to tomorrow to learn more about what is before us. I do not know your terrain or weather or anything about the land into which we will travel. I do not know your customs, nor those of the kingdom we face. The more I can prepare my people, the more efficiently we can serve."

Satisfied with his response, his politeness, and his loyalty to the men following him, Lorant gestured to the door. "Lord Cliáth, will you summon Lord Bhíncári to join us tomorrow, if he is able? He should be here for this summit, don't you think?"

After his visions of war in Elyriá, inviting Bhyrhán to meet with the king and tama to create a strategy to oppose Neth was essential.

"Of course, My Lord. "Shall I go to him now or…"

"Later…or in the morning. Will you play while we dine? I do not believe tama Yetek has had the pleasure." Lorant grinned as though tempting him.

Ágdhállán's earlier words and his presence in the room had been forgotten by everyone except the man who continued to hold his hand.

Kavan bowed. "I shall if you wish it."

Offering music would afford him a vantage point to observe the room and those in it. A position at the side of the room would remove him from the thick of the gathering and make it simpler to read everything around him. He would not be part of tomorrow's summit unless Lorant ordered it. Nor did he want to be there. He would learn what he could tonight and leave tomorrow to itself.

Feeling his son's frustration through his small hand, Kavan retreated from the room. He might not want to be involved in the decision making but he worried about what plans would be set forth without his guidance to temper the anticipated outcome.

❧*❦

"Let it go, Marta," Olaric hissed against her ear, his arm around her neck and the other pinning her arms to her sides, holding her motionless only because she was too surprised by being caught to react. He did not consider himself on parr with any member of the Association, particularly not in stealth; he had only out-maneuvered her after an intense struggle that resulted in a swollen eye he was sure would be black and blue by morning and a nose that dripped blood over his lips, because he was stronger and because, after Kes' confession, he had expected Marta to follow him to the place where her nemesis was housed to complete the mission she had long ago set for herself.

"Could you?" she hissed, twisting sideways to free herself. She succeeded because he let her go, and then glowered indignantly, torn between this confrontation and finishing what she had come to do. "If it was your family? Your wife?"

❧299❦

His eyes narrowed as he wiped the blood from his face. "It was my wife, my children," he reminded her bitterly. He had told her that before. Right now, he knew she was only thinking of herself and her own loss. "I know what she deserves. But this is bigger than you and me…"

A short apologetic flash crossed her face but she continued to appear betrayed and angry at his choices. "You've kept her alive all this time? Where? Why? How could you…?"

"This," he gestured at the knife in her hand that she had surprisingly not used against him. "This is why I did not tell you…did not tell anyone. We need her. We can use her. Doesn't matter where she was. It was necessary; she's a bargaining chip I intend to use to save Neth from itself. If I'm going to remove my father from the throne, put a de Corrmick…"

"She's no de Corrmick…"

"Her son is! I need her…"

"You don't need her for…"

"I've given this a lot of thought. I've had ten years. I know what I'm doing. I'm not hiring one of your assassins for this…and I'm not doing it. He's my father." As much as he despised the man and wanted him out of his life, off Neth's throne, he did not have it in him to do the deed himself. For Neth's sake, for the sake of history, he needed an opening to let the one Fraen had wronged the most to restore order for her son. "We can't count on Enesfel, on Cordash, on anyone…"

"That's no excuse…"

"I know you have cause…and I won't deny you when this is over…but until then, promise me. Promise you'll leave her to me. You can help with this or you can stay out of my way. We don't need to be adversaries. Let me use her, then she's yours."

The echoes of their whispered argument bled into the dark to be replaced by the rattle of passing wagon wheels before drawing tight around them, suffocating in the open expanse of the room. He did not think their hushed disagreement would carry into the street or up the two flights of stairs to the tiny room where the subject of their debate waited for the sack of clothing and food Kes had prepared. Olaric had been angry about Kes' confession but there had been no time to argue. Swift action had been needed to get here and stop Marta before she could undo everything he hoped to accomplish.

She did not know the place where Inness was hidden, but she could follow Olaric to it. He could have led her away instead of leading her to lie in wait. He hoped that the revelation was enough to show his trust and respect for her. He hoped his choice had not been foolish and misguided,

The moonlight shining through the years of dust and grime on the chamber's many windows was the only reason he could see her frustration. He did not blame her for her feelings of betrayal but he hoped she was wise enough to give him the chance to prove himself.

"How long?" she grunted.

"I don't..."

"How long?"

Exasperated at her impatience, he said, "We must ensure we can get Prince Henrik on the throne...or Prince Jerit...find an opening to do that. We can't trade one tyrant for another...and I won't fill in temporarily until that happens. As soon as we can be certain that will happen...then I'll know. I'll tell you everything. You'll know what you can do...and I'll stand aside and let you do it."

He had no love for Inness after his years of seeing to her welfare. Once another de Corrmick was on the throne, he would not need her...and he did not want to allow her to weasel back onto the throne the way she had before. Whether there be a public execution, or he allowed Marta to have her way, did not matter to him.

"Is it a deal?"

The red-haired woman, her face haggard by grief and years of responsibility for Glevum's Association, her children, and spying for Enesfel's inquisitor, shoved her knife into its sheath without replying. She pushed past him, made it nearly to the still-open door, and then paused to speak over her shoulder without looking back.

"Don't take too long...and you'd better keep me informed. Cut me out...back out of your promise...and we'll have a problem, whether we secure the throne or not."

Olaric nodded. She did not see it.

The structure shook as the door slammed closed.

❧*❧

"You are the king," Jerit muttered, knowing Lorant did not need the reminder. "You're needed here. It is a dangerous thing to go into battle."

"You've never been." Lorant's chuckle was undercut by the clatter of bone dice that spilled out of his hand onto the table between them. tama Yetek had gone for the evening and despite the press of several lords to meet and discuss a potentially untrustworthy alliance with people who had caused Hatu so much trouble in decades past, Lorant shooed them away and barricaded himself behind the library door. His pair of squires and two soldiers stood outside the room to shield him from anyone looking for him, bearing instructions that only Kavan, Níkóá, General Declan, or Daema Magk could interrupt if necessary.

So far, none of them had.

"Your father was…"

Lorant's amusement turned into a frown. He refused to meet Jerit's gaze and instead gestured at the dice to prompt Jerit to take his turn without immediately answering.

As Jerit scooped up the dice, Lorant said, "While you are there, I'll…"

Jerit stared at the dice in his palm. "I will not go into battle."

Lorant blinked in surprise. "Not…but I thought…it is your duty."

"Will you demand it?"

His mouth snapped shut with a huff.

The dice tumbled from Jerit's hand. "Killing my people…other Nethites…it does not feel right. If there must be…I don't think you should go…and I think I should be here to protect…"

"The tama's marching into battle with his men…"

"He is a general, not a king. You have no heir. If something happens…"

"Níkóá can…"

"He was a beloved regent but he was no king. There is no other Lachlan beside you, unless you give Enesfel to Gamal…or Henrik."

"There's Seren…"

"Lachlan by marriage, by blood; do you think she wants…"

Irritated by arguments he could not easily refute, Lorant countered, "I thought you didn't want me to father children," as he pushed from the table and stood up, the game overlooked as frustration overcame him.

Jerit's face turned red, and he snatched up the dice again to rattle them nervously in his hand. "This isn't about what I want. This is about Enesfel…the throne…this is about…I don't want you to die."

Though the words and their tone felt like a punch to his stomach, Lorant muttered, "You don't trust me, don't think I can…" to avoid concession.

"I know your skill with a sword…but that is not real combat. Why take the risk when you can stay here with me?"

"Because I am the king." He stressed the last word as he stomped to the door, needing to retreat to clear his head before he said something hurtful he would regret. "I thought you believed in me?"

"I believe in you…but I do not believe in the future…in what war will bring us. You cannot know…"

"I know enough."

"I cannot endure without you."

Lorant snorted as he opened the door, and without looking back snorted, "You'll have to."

The dice fell, skittered, and scattered across the table and onto the floor.

The ball of regret in Jerit's chest burned.

❧*❦

Inness's face looked haggard, wan, and sickly, and she had not moved from her seat on the bed except to remove her shoes and damp clothes to huddle beneath the layers of blankets Olaric previously provided. She did not rise to greet him but did pull the blankets around her neck and shoulders, hiding her nudity. She watched him set the sack on the table and empty it of bread, fruit, a robe, and a clean pair of cloth shoes, but she showed little interest in any of it.

"I heard voices…"

"Someone seeking shelter," he muttered, hoping she bought the lie and had not heard any of his dialogue with Marta. "I sent them away."

"What if they come back?"

"They won't." He emptied a small sack of coal into a cast iron warming pan that sat beside the room's chamber pot and after lighting it, brought it closer to the bed. The night was balmy, without a breeze blowing in from the sea, but if she was cold after having been damp for so long, he intended to make her comfortable and keep her healthy.

"When can I see Henrik?"

"I can't bring him here. We would be followed. If my father learns he is…he will kill him. So, not yet, but soon. As soon as I can safely do so."

"Soon." Inness rolled to face the wall and muttered nothing more as he moved about the room, bringing the robe and food within her reach, laying out the clothes upon the stand so that she could easily get them, lit the lantern he had brought, and tested the door and its lock to be certain she could not break free.

She was no fool. Until he brought Henrik to her, Inness had nowhere to go. That did not mean she would not try.

❧*❦

"Jerit thinks I'm going to die…like my father." Lorant kicked his boots aside and sat on the edge of his bed, staring past Seren at the unlit hearth, aware of the movement of her fingers across whatever needlepoint project she was undertaking. With no interest in such mundane activities, he had not bothered to ask what she was making. He had been too preoccupied over the last several days to speak with her beyond morning and evening platitudes and greetings.

"He loves you," she murmured, watching her fingers instead of looking at him. "I love you. Of course we don't want you to die."

"No one says I'm going to die." When she did not contradict or agree, he snorted again. "I have to think of morale…the people…the troops."

"You have to think of the throne, of Enesfel."

"That's what he said." He huffed and tugged the bed covers aside. "I'm not my father. I'm not going to be so foolish as to…"

"If you ask them…Kjell and Daema Magk and Tau…they do not call him foolish. Even the wise and valiant can die in war." The valiant, she mused, were more prone to it.

"Ágdhállán says I won't." When Seren looked at him at last, absently setting her sewing project on the round table at her elbow, he shrugged and continued in an apologetic tone, "Well, not exactly those words. He said I must be there."

"Needing to be there does not mean you won't die."

"Nor does it mean I will. If I must, if I'm supposed to be…and if I'm supposed to…I can't just ignore the Sight."

"What has Kavan said?"

Shrugging sheepishly, Lorant was quiet for several moments before replying, "I haven't asked him. He'll probably tell me to stay in Rhidam, to avoid the battlefield."

"You won't know what he'll say until you ask." Kavan would try to discourage him, she knew, because he wanted desperately not to believe in war or lose another Lachlan, but he would not lie to Lorant about the Sight. As far as she knew, father and son often Saw the same things. Whatever Ágdhállán believed, only Kavan could confirm it.

"I must go." He stared at the window. "I should go." Finally, he shrugged, sighed, and looked at her. "I don't…Jerit says he's not going. I will not force him…he has Neth's throne to think about." The corners of his mouth drooped and he sagged into the pillows with his hands clasped behind his head. "I didn't think he wanted to be king."

"Perhaps he feels it is his duty, like you feel going into battle is yours." She curled up on the bed beside him, pleased that he seemed a little more comfortable with her there whenever he chose to join her. "I would be lying if I said I am pleased with you going…but I do understand duty."

Wrapping his arm around her shoulders to hold her there, with her head against his neck, he sighed again, a different sound than he had made before, an apologetic sound that made his whole body groan. "I know you do, Seren. You're a better person than I am."

"Not better. I don't have your responsibilities, but I do understand them." She kissed his jaw and settled her head once again. "Stay in Rhidam for me…for Jerit…for yourself…or obey duty if you think you must. Just don't die, Lorant. Enesfel needs you."

"No intention of dying," he assured her, his voice heavy with the realization that dreams of glory in battle, in the hour of Enesfel's greatest need, might need to be relinquished to someone else.

He did not want to be like his father, or his grandfather, dying too soon. But after Ágdhállán's stern proclamation, he was haunted by the thought that dying in battle so that Enesfel could win this war might be his fate…and that if that was true, hiding away in Rhidam would be an unforgivable act of cowardice.

He had never been called a coward.

He would not be called that now.

❧*❦

Pretending not to notice Ágdhállán's determined effort to avoid being touched once they were out of the stateroom, Kavan relinquished the act of adjusting the bedding around his torso to the boy's smaller hands. It was an act to avoid being read, to hide something he did not want his father to know, to See, even though Kavan had not picked up on anything unusual in the stateroom. Once Ágdhállán was old enough to demand the privacy of his thoughts, Kavan had done his best to respect his rights to them, to never read his thoughts through any contact they shared. As a result, Ágdhállán trusted him enough to be open about the things he Saw, about things that troubled him.

That he resisted now told Kavan that something was troubling his son. With as many visions as they had shared, with the plethora of fears Kavan carried because of those visions, Ágdhállán's disquiet did not surprise him.

He did not know how to draw those things out of his son. He wished he did.

When Kavan stood and blew out the candle, when the boy's face was obscured by the shadows of the room, he whispered, "Will they ever take me seriously…like they do you?"

Kavan paused. "They?"

"Everyone."

The emotion that came out with that question was one Kavan knew more intimately than he cared to. "They don't always take what I See seriously either…even in Elyriá. When I was your age, in Bhryell…it is hard for adults to accept the gifts of a child…especially if they're like you and me. They think they know the world. They fear things that do not fit into what they know. I cannot say they will ever accept…or fully believe you. They will do what they think best, no matter what we recommend. But give it time, Ágdhi. It will get better…easier."

"Do you?" The shy question was nearly inaudible. "You believe me?"

Tempted to push the red curls out of the boy's eyes, Kavan kept his hands at his sides and countered, "Have I ever not?"

Ágdhállán's eyes squinted as he searched his brief memories and then shook his head. "No…I guess not." Hesitantly, he reached for his father's hand and relaxed when he recognized that there were no probing tendrils of energy seeking to burrow into his thoughts.

"There's going to be war."

Kavan nodded. "Yes…but it will not involve you."

"But it will involve you…and King Lorant and Prince Jerit and…"

Kavan shivered, confirming his belief in his own place in upcoming events, even if he did not yet know what that place would be. "Kings are frequently involved when…"

"In battle?"

Swallowing hard, wondering what the boy had Seen that he had not, Kavan nodded again. "Sometimes."

"Princes too?"

"Sometimes, yes."

"And you?"

"I will not go into battle with the armies." It was the only assurance he could offer.

"But you will fight."

When a chill passed through Kavan so that he trembled, Ágdhállán squeezed his hand. "I don't…"

Ágdhállán squeezed tighter and then let him go. "It is okay, k'bhydhá. It is going to be okay."

Wishing now that he had Seen what his son had Seen, knowing that he had not, Kavan bent down and kissed the boy's forehead and murmured, "Thank you, Ágdhi. Sleep well…and if you need me…"

"I know."

Still quaking, Kavan retreated to the tranquil peace of the oratory. He wanted to believe his son was right, that everything would be okay. He did not want to be guilty of the disbelief Ágdhállán experienced from so many others. With a sense of what the path was ahead of him, however, he found it hard to accept that everything would be well. The peace of mind he sought remained elusive as the hours of night passed.

Shortly after dawn, Lorant would announce to Rhidam that the army at their heels had come to help, that soon they would be at war with Neth.

Kavan did not intend to be there to hear the words spoken.

Summoning Bhyrhán from Clarys offered an excuse not to be.

If he did not hear Lorant's words, perhaps they would not be true.

❧Chapter 28↩

Jerit's discontent and barely disguised outrage were obvious as he followed his mother from St. Kóráhm's Gate to take the news of Kaj Yetek and his army's arrival to Kjell. Including his father in the coordination of an assault on Neth was necessary, but it was a duty Asta could have undertaken alone; Kavan did not blame Jerit for interpreting Lorant's command as an effort to remove his influence with the war council that was to begin at noon. Both men's behavior suggested a rift, one that Kavan hoped he could heal as he escorted the children to the courtyard.

Kavan understood Jerit's pain. He had endured such rifts with Wortham, but thankfully those rifts had always healed. Thus far, there had been no such tearing asunder with Rhyrdan, but he feared the day it came. In the face of what he sensed ahead, that sort of parting felt imminent.

If Lorant and Jerit could find their way back to one another, Kavan would have hope for such steadfastness with Rhyrdan too.

Deciding it was best not to have the children in the way of the war council, best not to have them where they might overhear discussions they should not need to worry about at their tender ages, the entire gaggle had been brought to St. Kóráhm's. Upon arrival, Cáym and Phaedr grabbed Ágdhállán's hands and ran ahead while Hella, Ónyká, Kaedís, Ida, and Prince Henrik clustered around Rhyrdan discussing their plans for the day. Only Yóáná had kept her children in Rhidam.

"k'bhydhá, I assumed you were here when Ágdhi raced past." Dhóri fell into step beside him as Bergis followed, already assuming the role of caretaker over the visiting children and sharing his animated excitement over a rainbow the morning's misty rain had brought. Hella and Ida begged to see it so she and the others followed the kindly, gentle man in the direction the three boys had gone.

"I thought it best they not be…" Kavan watched the children follow Bergis, with Rhyrdan protectively behind, and continued, "Earé's force has arrived; the council is debating war. They do not need to be part of that."

Lips pursed thoughtfully, Dhóri nodded. "We can watch them if you have duties…"

"I will not be part of the council." The bard's words were clipped, his decision set. "I'm here for the children."

Frowning at the heavy note in his father's voice, Dhóri asked, "Have you seen her? Has she said something?" He knew his father was concerned about the upcoming conflict, knew he sought an alternative to it despite Earé's predictions. It was because of those predictions and the mercenary army they brought, that Dhóri could see no other outcome except for war.

It was the cause for the current relocation of St. Kóráhm's contents to Gorbesh. Kavan was not the only one praying war could be averted.

"She is not with them." Her duties as She Who Sees had drawn her elsewhere, he assumed, or else she chose to avoid him so as not to burden him further with knowledge of what was to come or frustrate him with her refusal to share what she knew.

Not knowing was a burden growing heavier every day.

At the chellé's door, Kavan paused to study those around him, brothers and sisters, dedhá and townsfolk going about the daily duties of providing the chellé's needs, providing for the Faithful, and preparing defenses and stocking supplies in case Duke Cliáth's vision of an attack came to pass. People nodded and Dhóri nudged his father aside to allow some of them to go in and out of the Gathering Hall.

"It's made by water in the air," Bergis was explaining as he pointed at the rainbow above them. Kaedís and Ónyká had turned their attention to nearby puddles, soaking their shoes and the hems of their dresses, giggling as they challenged each other to bigger splashes.

Further away, Phaedr had already convinced Tau to provide the practice swords so Rhyrdan could offer a parrying lesson. When Ágdhállán resisted picking up a sword, the weight of war pressing heavily upon him, and Balint shoved his shoulder with a belittling retort, Prince Henrik, who had wandered away from the study of rainbows, pushed him back. Cáym stepped between Balint and the others, his glowering expression daring Balint to try again. Surprised that Henrik had stood up to him, indignant that the boy he most often bullied dared to push him, Balint raised the practice sword as if to strike but Rhyrdan grabbed the wooden weapon and yanked it from Balint's hands.

"That is not an honorable use of your weapon," he scolded, meeting Kavan's gaze across the courtyard with a nod of assurance that he had the boys under control. Balint, it seemed, was nothing like his namesake. He needed more constant exposure to other children, less to men who treated him like a little soldier, and the opportunity to learn empathy and kindness that residing in the chellé had, for some reason, failed to teach.

Phaedr clapped Henrik on the back with a proud grin that made Henrik grin too, although he moved uneasily away from the contact, as Rhyrdan coaxed them into a line and began the day's lesson.

Returning to Kavan's side, taking his hand and pulling him to the bench where Hella sat, Ida asked, "Did you know water makes rainbows? Can you make rainbows too? Like you make the moon and the sun?"

Cocking his head, exchanging a glance with Dhóri who waved Bergis away from the children to their interrupted duties, Kavan followed where Ida led and sat on the empty space Kaedís reserved for him. "I've never tried," he replied, choosing not to correct her about making the sun and moon. Strange that, in so many decades of life, the idea to capture the light of a rainbow, regenerate it in his hands, had never occurred to him.

"Make a rainbow!" Hella exclaimed.

"It will take practice, but I will try." To Kaedís he said, "Maybe you can do it too."

"Oh yes! Teach me!"

"And me," begged Ónyká. Like her mixed-blood brothers, she was not overly gifted with power, but she had a knack for handlights and for pushing objects away or dragging them toward her that she found creative uses for at every opportunity. Phaedr was a reader, judging others and their thoughts with a touch, while Cáym had inherited his father's combat skills, heightened senses and strength, and an uncommonly early mastery of the Gates that his father forbade him to use.

"Show us how it's done," added Ida. "I want to see."

"Then sit and be still…and we shall see if it can be done."

It gave him something more pleasant to focus on than the rise and fall of angry voices coming from one of the windows above them.

"I will not…"

Hand on Jerit's arm, surprised by how fast tempers flared after announcing the mercenary army's arrival, Asta stared at Kjell and said, "There's no need for him to…the king needs someone in Rhidam to…"

"Lorant has others to do the job. Lord McCábhá can manage Rhidam. Even his father…"

"He is not his father any more than I am you," Jerit snapped.

"Someone must carry the de Corrmick banner to Glevum. You can't expect Henrik…"

"Then you do it! I'm not going to sacrifice my life for the throne you lost! Oska died for it! I refuse to…"

"You're a coward!"

"I'm not the one who let King Merrek die!"

Kjell swung but Jerit was already beyond his reach, storming out of the room the way he had the last time they had provoked one another, the way that had become too common between them. Kjell lurched up to pursue, but his knees gave out and he stumbled. He would have fallen if not for Asta. Embarrassed and bitter, he shoved her away with enough force to propel himself back into the chair.

She refused to assist him again when he caught the edge of the chair, causing it to slide sideways so that he fell to the floor. He glowered at her. She did not react except to remind him, "You did not kill Merrek. That had nothing to do with…"

"Should have listened to Tau," he grunted, barely noticing her effort to shift his fury off their son. "Should have left when he…"

"You did what you thought was right. You couldn't have known."

"I should have." He struggled up from the floor and into the chair, rubbing his aching hip as he stared at the still-open door.

Asta sighed. "Sending Jerit to war isn't going to undo…"

"It's the right thing."

"For him? Or you?"

"Glevum needs to see the banner…"

She shook her head with an adamant scowl. "The banner. Not Jerit. Anyone can carry it. I've lost one son. I'll not have another's blood spilled on Glevum's soil…"

"He's a de Corrmick. He will do as I…"

"And he's a Dugan. A Lachlan. He's my son as much as yours, his own man. Unless Lorant demands it, he does not need to fill your shoes."

"He would go where Lorant demands but not obey me?" He paused but Asta did not deign to respond to his belligerence. "Someone must go. It is his duty. The throne demands…"

"I will do it." She swallowed a breath, glowering at him before adding, "I will take the banner; I will go and…"

Kjell scoffed, "You're no soldier. Lorant won't allow it. I need you…"

"You don't need me. You don't listen to anyone but Tau," she spat back. "You heed only your own council. If you insist on a de Corrmick carrying the banner, it will be me."

"You cannot…"

Asta was already gone.

He climbed to his feet with an angry shout and staggered to the window where he could see the boys lunging and parrying in the midday sun under Rhyrdan's guidance, focusing on Henrik with barely disguised disapproval.

But Henrik, while slower than the others, hampered by his weight and the head injury suffered as an infant, was meticulous in his swordsmanship, executing each move, following each instruction, without error. When Balint struck too hard at the Cliáth boy, it was Henrik who intervened a second time and when Balint tried to lash out at him, the other boys rallied to Henrik's defense. Despite his peculiarities, he had their respect and friendship and was now primed to provide Neth an heir when his betrothal was consummated. Like Oska, he enjoyed history and philosophy, political study, and law. He liked numbers and solving puzzles, and when set to a troubling task, he was prone to focus and not give up until it was solved or someone interrupted and distracted him. He was the boy Oska had been, a boy still alive and trained to carry the burden of Neth's throne.

He was Oska's son.

There was no reason he should not be Kjell's heir.

Henrik would never ride into battle, but there was no reason he could not sit on Neth's throne.

Kjell believed, staring at the chair that had betrayed him and then at the door through which his wife and son had fled, that he would never again be fit enough to do it.

But he could help Henrik be the king Oska should have been, if not for Inness, if Jerit refused to comply.

Praise k'Ádhá that Princess Hella was nothing like Inness.

❧Chapter 29❧

After dining with the residents of St. Kóráhm's and attending the evening Gathering, as well as taking time to watch an unexpected star shower he worried was a portent of things to come, Kavan and Rhyrdan herded the children, Asta, and a sullen, grim-faced Jerit back to Rhidam in time for the children to be in bed. Kavan sensed the prince wanted to speak privately, but finding both Ártur and Syl on the frontmost Gathering bench, Jerit sighed and shuffled out after the others, avoiding his mother's efforts to console him, avoiding anything more than terse words with any of the children who tried to speak to him.

Only Henrik seemed to breech his mood by begging him to share a story before sleeping, something the young prince requested every night before bed from anyone available. Sing-song storytelling soothed his racing mind and allowed him to sleep.

So did Kavan's music.

"Is there news?" Kavan asked when he was alone with the healers, weary of the emotional strain the day had taken, raw and numb and in search of solitude and music on the altar steps.

Those things would have to wait.

Ártur glanced at his wife, who nodded and squeezed his hand. Nervously, he shifted on the bench, then shifted again, before clearing his throat and saying, "Syl and I have talked. With Lorant intending to ride with the troops, we think it best if we join them."

Kavan scowled and sat on the altar steps. "It will be dangerous…"

"We have done this before," Syl said tenderly.

"That was a long time ago." More than seventy years and yet, to Kavan, it felt as if barely any time had passed.

"You don't forget something like that."

Ártur released Syl's hand and leaned forward with his elbows on his knees. "He will need us. Yóáná and Aland can maintain here."

"She has never been to war," Syl pointed out. "Neither of them has. We have the experience."

"What of Kaedís?"

"She will stay with Yóáná to continue her education," replied Ártur. "We have not talked to her, but we will."

"We're going to Bhryell in the morning, will take her with us…we want to share our choice with Llucás and Chethá, recruit other healers if we can."

As two Elyri healers serving Arlan's army, they had failed to keep up with the multitude of injured men the uprising had created. Too many had died. While he doubted they could recruit enough healers to make a significant difference in what was likely to be war on a larger scale, they hoped that, from all the healers they and Chethá knew in and around Bhryell, at least a few would be willing to take the risk. On Enesfel's behalf, it was worth asking.

"I don't suppose I can talk you out of this?" Kavan murmured.

"No more than we can talk you out of going…" began Ártur.

Noting Kavan's faltering expression, Syl asked, "You are riding with Lorant as you did for Arlan, aren't you?"

Kavan shook his head. He had been there for Arlan's first foray into war but he had not been at his side in the thick of battle. Nor had he been there when Arlan chose to stand against Neth when Guthrie McHador had died. He had not been in battle with Merrek. Each time he had more important matters to see to than lingering in a war he would not fight. This time would be no exception.

"I'm no fighter, no healer…"

Ártur snorted. "You could probably decimate Neth's entire army."

The taste in the back of Kavan's throat was bitter. "I have no desire to kill anyone, not even Fraen." He could Gate into Glevum's keep, do the deed, and be gone without anyone's knowledge or take someone else to do so. But the future of Teren-Elyri relations and the future of his soul made the thought more repulsive to him than the thought of riding into battle. "I am needed here. I must see to the children and to St. Kóráhm's. I will not leave them defenseless."

"Nor should you," Syl agreed. "You will look to Kaedís? We discussed taking her to Bhryell, but Bhríd said there would be war there…"

"I do not know where…but near enough, yes." He was familiar with those forests. He believed what the Sight told him. "You will warn Sóbhán? The rest of the family? Prepare them to be safe?"

"Where would you expect them to go? bhyne is too stubborn to leave home and Sámel will never abandon the shop." Ártur sighed and leaned back, rubbing his eyes with both hands. "But I will tell them."

"Thank you." Warning his family to take care was the most Kavan could do for them. "I beg you to reconsider the risk, but if you must go with the king, I will pray for you both." Normally, in confrontations between Sovereignties, Elyri healers were safe, their skills too valuable to waste. They might be captured and forced into servitude, but they were rarely killed. Kavan did not expect them to die. But they would be traveling in Neth. All precedent and prayer did not mean they would live in a land where fear of Elyri was rampant.

"And you should reconsider coming with us, sínréc," Ártur countered as he got to his feet. "If you are there, everything will be fine. Kóráhm, Dhágdhuán, and k'Ádhá will protect us.

Kavan could only wish that would be true.

It would be an easier path to believe, to follow, than the one that lay ahead of him.

That was a path Ártur could never know about.

❧*❧

"Jerit, you missed the council."

Gerna was the last person he wanted to encounter upon leaving his brother's room, having offered his storytelling skills until his nephew, exhausted from the day's weapons practice, fell asleep. At this hour, his wife was normally settled into her chamber but, as she seemed to have come from putting Ida to bed, he knew he should not be surprised that she had sought him out.

He wished she had not.

"I was seeing to duties for the king," he grunted without saying what those duties had been or where he had gone despite her expectant expression that demanded more details.

"You will be joining him? You will reclaim your throne?" She tried to take his hand but he evaded her before contact was made.

"It has never been my throne." He ignored the confirmation that Lorant was riding into battle.

"Henrik's a child," she snorted. "He's not fit to…"

"He is the king's son and every bit as fit as my brother," he growled, the sound low in his chest and muted by the echo of their footsteps on the stone floor. She tried to steer him toward the room they were meant to share, but Jerit stopped at the stairwell as if he intended to go down.

In truth, he did not know where he wanted to go.

"Serving your father, your king," she spat the last word derisively but stopped short of rolling her eyes, "is the honorable thing to do. You cannot disgrace Ida and me by disobeying…"

"There are no orders to disobey." He did not own land or rule peasants, and thus he had no troops to offer the Crown. He had only his life with which to protect Lorant and he suspected it was the sort of sacrifice Gerna wanted from him. Had she prompted her first husband into war to claim his title and inheritance…only to lose it when Fraen captured Ruidoso? Or had she done it to be rid of him?

Jerit had even less he could offer, either in life or death, but at least in death she would be free of their awkward marriage.

"If not for me, do it for Ida. Do not disgrace…"

"Ida would prefer me to live."

"Ida's a child. In time she will put away those childish notions. We all prefer the king to be protected and live. Don't you?"

There was a sharp, double edge to that question that Jerit avoided by starting down the stairs, leaving Gerna at the top with a sour but triumphant expression. Lorant was his weakness. The thought of Lorant's death, dying in battle without being at his side to bid him farewell, added to the unsettled mood that again put him at odds with his father. The discord between him and Lorant did not help, and the inner conflict between his moral, societal, and familial obligations, as well as the desires of his heart, placed him in a position of being unable to think, unable to choose.

He made it halfway down the level, paused on the stairs, and then started up again. He did not need to see anyone, did not need to talk. He needed to be alone to think, to feel, to hope the answer could be found in the winking of night sky stars.

Only one person could find him there.

He secretly hoped he would.

❧*❧

The blood dripping from the wooden figure, coloring the air with its coppery tang, mirrored the blood in the images behind his eyes where an unrecognizable visage stared at him, blistered and scarred, unmoving, hidden mostly in the writhing shadows created by the dancing glare of a distant fire's light. He smelled sulfur and sweat, smoke and salty surf, but it was the figure's blood and the mirroring ache it produced in his wrists, ankles, and side that warred with his desperate efforts to push the Sight closer to the fallen form.

It had been decades since Dhágdhuán had bled.

The bells of Hes á Redh tolled midnight but Kavan remained. He had no harp as he had not taken the time to retrieve it from his adjoining room, and so he hummed, producing wordless songs meant to appease k'Ádhá and persuade him to provide a sign. When it came, he begged the murmuring company of záryph and the barely detectable presence of Kóráhm to tell him what the rósádhá and visions meant, what they wanted him to know or do. But no answer came and when eventually the blood flow ceased and his wrists had been made raw by his efforts to dispel the pain with his rubbing thumbs, Kavan uttered a heavy-hearted sigh of relief and disappointment that no answers had been given.

The oratory door opened. Footsteps lingered as if waiting for acknowledgment, and when Kavan lifted his head without looking back, the visitor dared to approach.

Lorant.

Kavan knew the cadence of his steps as he had known those of every Lachlan before him back to Arlan.

"Was someone here?" Lorant whispered, eyeing the Gate as he sat on the steps, choosing the place beside Kavan instead of sitting on the benches as Arlan had most often done after becoming king.

"záryph and Kóráhm…but they are gone. You are not intruding."

Wiping the corners of Kavan's damp eyes with a kerchief from his pocket and then handing it to the bard, Lorant asked, "They did that?"

The white cloth was stained with crimson smudges, prompting Kavan to scowl and rub his eyes and face to wipe away any other blood.

It had been a long time since that had happened as well.

"Did what, My King."

"You don't need to call me that. I hope we're friends before monarch and subject…

"Or teacher and student?

Lorant chuckled softly. "Or that." He believed there was so much more the Elyri could teach him but no longer on such a formal level. "The blood…on Dhágdhuán."

"You can see it?" Kavan had thought it an effect of the Sight, not a physical manifestation.

"It's gotta be on the floor now…his toes are dripping." He was curious to see it but not curious enough to approach the divine display. "Do they do it…or do you?"

Kavan shook his head. "I do not know." Such signs had happened to him for so long without explanation that he no longer asked who caused such things to happen. They just did. "I think k'Ádhá wills it…but I do not know why or how…or when it will happen."

"I heard stories, but I did not think…" The only miracles he was aware of were the handful of tales circulating about the bard saving his life multiple times during infancy. Lorant had been too young to remember those events himself.

Rather than dwell on miracles he could not explain or control and preferring not to talk about them, Kavan shifted off his knees and asked, "Can't sleep?"

"There's a lot to think about," Lorant admitted. "Jerit won't join me when we leave…won't fight with me…and I'm wondering if he's right, if I should stay…if he knows something I don't. Maybe I'm less the swordsman than I think."

"You don't need to ride into battle. That is your choice." He would go, Kavan knew. He had known it years ago, before Lorant was born, and had confirmed it when he had been barely more than a toddler. Despite never having proof to the contrary, Kavan continued to cling to the hope that the Sight's promises could be circumvented if he was given some clue as to where he could find Bhás and end this war before it began.

"Ágdhállán thinks I must. He's seen me in battle." Lorant shrugged at Kavan's expression. "I didn't have the chance to ask for details…and I've not dared to seek them. I don't think I want to know. I believe I'm meant to be there, that I am needed at the front…that my father and those before me want this. I would feel less afraid if you or Jerit were coming with me…but I am more afraid of him dying than dying without him."

"Have you told him that?"

"He'll laugh at me."

In all the years the two had known each other, how strong and mature Lorant had become, there endured a shadow of the little boy who sought to impress Jerit, to prove himself and show that he possessed the traits he saw in the older prince. Jerit's teasing laughter had once spurred Lorant to be better. This time it made him feel like he was not good enough to deserve the older man's approval, respect, and love.

"I doubt that. I think he's as afraid of your death as you are of his."

"I know…he said it." Lorant shrugged and looked thoughtfully up at the pyre figure. "Can I not persuade you to come? Ártur will be there, and Syl…they would appreciate your company…and any miracles you can provide us."

"I cannot produce them at will," Kavan reminded him. "And I do not need to be there for them to manifest." Steering the conversation away from miracles and his part in them, he asked, "You will leave Níkóá as regent?"

"There is no one better." He would have asked Kavan to assume the duty if he had believed the bard would accept.

Nodding, Kavan said, "My place is not in battle; I have little I can offer there. But I can aid Níkóá and watch over Hella, Henrik, and the others. When the enemy comes…"

"To Rhidam?"

"To Alberni." Kavan had not seen anything to convince him that enemy soldiers would set foot in Rhidam. "They will need me. I do not think you need me with you."

"Maybe not…but I want you there. I've seen what you can do…at least some of it. I'd feel better if you were close."

"I would be a distraction."

"Only if I let you be." He got up and approached the altar, hesitating to circle it, before kneeling at the place where blood stained the floor, where all Kavan could see was his feet and the lower hem of his trousers. Several minutes later, when he returned to Kavan, his palms and fingers were stained with the viscous crimson fluid.

Again, visions of blood flashed behind Kavan's lids. Again, his breath caught, his nostrils filled with the burn of sulfur, and his ears filled with the clash of steel, shouts of men, and crackling roar of fire. He squeezed his eyes shut, forced his breath and pulse to be calm, and when he opened them, Lorant had pressed his palm to his bare chest, leaving a bloody print over his heart. When the half-moon pendant he wore, as had every Lachlan since Arlan, moved across the stain, the half-moon Kavan wore sparked with a flash of power that made the bard involuntarily close his hand around it.

Lorant did not appear to notice his response. "Do you think I should stay in Rhidam, or do you believe I should go with the troops?"

After squeezing the pendant, and the others scooped into his hand with it, hard enough that they bit into his palm, debating the wisdom of revealing what he knew and believed, Kavan gave a silent prayer for strength to the suddenly more acute presence that had now entered the room and pressed its hand upon his shoulder and murmured, "As much as I…I believe your destiny is in Glevum."

"My death?" whispered Lorant.

"Or your glory. I cannot see beyond that…but you are meant to facilitate victory. My soul is certain of that."

Lorant nodded and swallowed hard. Kavan's belief was good enough. "I hope I can convince Jerit of that." He clasped Kavan's shoulder, where the unseen hand still rested, and said, "Pray for me, Kavan. Maybe k'Ádhá will listen to you. Instead of being there with me, maybe that's the battle you need to undertake to help us win."

Kavan had not considered his part in the war that way. He bowed his head and murmured, "I will fight for you in every way I can."

Arlan, Owain, Muir, and all the others would never forgive him if he did anything else.

❧*❧

Rather than lay down beside Jerit to stare at the stars as they often did, not certain his company was wanted, Lorant sat on the lip of the parapet and stared at the bare-chested older man with his shirt folded into a pillow behind his head, unable to tear his eyes away.

Or able to do so but unwilling to. No one had ever looked as beautiful to him as Jerit did.

"Thought I'd find you here. How did the conversation go with…?"

"You know how it went. He expects me to carry the de Corrmick banner into war."

"He certainly isn't fit to do it." Lorant expected a backlash for the comment. He doubted Kjell could stay on a horse long enough to leave Rhidam, let alone ride into battle at the head of the armies. "But it shouldn't be on you to…"

"There is no one else."

Lorant did look away then, hearing his own words echoed back at him. "I can carry it."

"You're not Neth's king."

"Nor are you. There's no reason I cannot fly both banners…with Kjell's blessing, of course."

"He'd never agree." Tilting his head to look Lorant in the eye, he asked, "You're going then?"

Lorant's sigh was heavier. "I must. Something Ágdhállán saw…Kavan too. He tried to dissuade me, but even he says my destiny is in Glevum."

"He saw you die?" Jerit's body tensed and he propped himself up on one elbow with a frown. He noticed the bloody handprint on Lorant's chest and his frown deepened.

Self-consciously, Lorant closed his robe. The act covered the blood on his chest but not the blood on his hand. "Destiny doesn't mean death."

"Sounds like it does to me."

"It doesn't to me. It sounds like duty. I will be okay, Jerit. You do not need to be there. I'm not asking you to be there. Stay with Kavan, with Níkóá. Keep Rhidam safe."

"I'd rather be certain you're safe."

"You'll have to trust me. You'll have to trust Kavan. I can do this…and I promise I will come back to you."

"You can't make that promise."

Lorant gave a lopsided grin to ease the mood. "I just did."

Jerit's scowl did not change. "I promised I'd always be beside you…protect you…"

Leaving the parapet, Lorant sat next to Jerit. "I treasure your loyalty, your love…" He hesitated to see if Jerit would deny the use of that word but instead, the prince sheepishly lowered his gaze. "But maybe it is time I protect myself. I can do it, you know. You've trained me well. I'm not a child anymore."

"No," Jerit agreed roughly, "you're not. I don't doubt your skill…but this won't be a contest, a joust, a wager. This'll be different. You need someone at your back.

"General Declan will be there; Daema too. And I believe this fellow Yetek to be trustworthy and skilled. Lord and Lady MacLyr will be there, plus any healers they can recruit. And if you're here…I won't have to risk seeing you die."

"You think I'm going to…has Lord Cliáth said…?"

"No one's said anything. They don't have to. I'll miss you if you're not with me, but knowing you are safe…"

"It won't be any different than me worrying when you're a kingdom away where I cannot protect you." He lay back again with his hands behind his head and snorted. "We're quite a pair, aren't we?"

"We've lost people we love to bloodshed. We know what it's like. Makes sense not to want to go through it again. But I can't stay…and you can't go…"

"I can." The words were a whisper, strained and troubled but sincere and resolute in their thick emotion. "There are many reasons not to go…and I don't want to…but I can…I must…if you ask me to."

Lorant shook his head. "I can't ask you to die for me."

"Then ask me to live for you. For us both. Ask me and I swear I will bring us both home. Ask me and I will be there for both of us."

Instead of speaking, Lorant lay on the stone beside him as they always had, close enough that he could thread his fingers through Jerit's but far enough apart not to touch in any other way. The blood on his hand did not smudge off on Jerit's skin. The stars overhead continued their eternal parade until the náós bells marked the second hour of the new day, and the reality of what the coming dawn would bring made Lorant sigh in frustration.

"Be there for me, Jerit," he choked, "and I'll be there for you"

Jerit's breath gushed out as if he had been holding it all that time. "Always, Lorant. Always, until I have no breath to give and beyond."

"Always," Lorant promised.

It was the most each could give. It was everything each of them wanted.

❧Chapter 30❧

Jerit fell into step beside Ártur as the healer left the morning room where he had treated the irritable king for a bout of stomach nerves that he could not allow to derail the day's barrage of meetings and planning activities. Jerit wanted to be with him, as he had promised, but there was one thing he needed to do first, before he lost his nerve and changed his mind.

He answered the healer's question with a shrug. "I do not think he slept well…or at all. He was in the oratory well after the second hour. I would ask him to take me, but I think it polite to let him rest." Since Kavan had not been in the oratory when Jerit looked for him, he assumed the duke had finally retreated to his bed to sleep, or else had gone to Alberni or any number of other places to further the preparations for war.

"It's going around," Ártur huffed. The tensions of impending war were affecting everyone. Syl was tending to the queen who had also suffered an uneasy stomach during the night and Yóáná had spent the night with Aunes and the royal children when their sleep, too, was interrupted by nightmares and vague images of what they imagined war to be like. Master Najar had relieved the women and collected the children in the dayroom to begin their lessons early in the hopes of distracting them while Aunes slept and Yóáná joined Aland to tend a smattering of injuries that resulted from a restless brawl between a half dozen nervous men in the guard house.

With his plan to go to Bhryell temporarily set aside, Ártur considered whether he should see to his cousin's welfare. Kavan had seemed in reasonable spirits the night before when he left him in the oratory but he knew how adept Kavan was at hiding his fears and concerns. Any number of things might have happened during his hours in prayer.

If Kavan needed him, he decided, he would know, and if there was cause for the prince to meet with his father during this time of preparation., the few minutes it would take to deposit Jerit in St. Kóráhm's would not detract from the other requirements of the morning. There would still be time for breakfast before visiting his family in Bhryell.

"Will your mother join us? Will you need me to wait for you?" He pushed open the oratory door and shivered at the unmistakable air of holy power in the room. His first inclination was 'miracle', but if something had occurred when Kavan was alone, he did not expect to know what it was.

"She has other duties. I will have Dhóri or Captain Magk bring me back when I am ready. I appreciate your assistance, Lord Healer."

Moments later, with Ártur returned to Rhidam, Jerit stood in St. Kóráhm's listening to voices chanting in early morning prayer. With the chellé residents in the Gathering Hall, no one would see him but he imagined, as he made his way to his father's suite, they would soon know he was here by the rise of angry voices he expected would follow. He stopped outside of the room, hesitated before knocking and swallowing his trepidation, and repeated in his head the words he wanted to say. Before he could knock, Tau opened the door with one hand, the man carrying a dirty bowl of shaving water in the other.

Tau looked him over, noted he was alone, and nodded once.

"Good morning, my prince," the dark-skinned man said without bowing, hoping to avoid spilling the bowl's contents on the prince's shoes. He opened the door wider to allow Jerit to pass and then said into the candlelit room behind him, "Your son is here."

Jerit saw no need for candles at this hour, with the sun streaming in through the east and south-facing windows, but he knew his father's vision was weakening, even if the older man refused to admit it.

"I did not send…" Kjell began to protest, his stool creaking as he leaned closer to the mirror without looking over his shoulder. He could see Jerit reflected in the glass. His hands stopped moving as he stared.

Jerit had already entered the room as Tau went out. Ignoring the bitter burn within, he was tempted to ask if he was only welcome here when summoned or if his mother brought him, but he chose not to ignite the fuse of animosity so early. He had not come for that.

"Good morning to you too, Father." He tried to sound pleasant and neutral, to keep his smile sincere, but he suspected his father could see past his efforts. They had been close once; Kjell had said he was proud of him, had said he would make a good king one day.

So much had changed since that last birth day feast in Glevum.

He wondered how different things would be if Inness had not prodded Oska into an unimaginable chain of unfortunate actions that had sealed not only his brother's fate but the fate of everyone else. He wondered if the wizened man before him would still be king.

"Where's your mother?" Kjell bristled and reached for the nearby set of scissors to make a show of trimming stray hairs on the graying beard Tau had already helped trim.

Again, Jerit bit his tongue, thinking the scissors were meant to be a defensive gesture, as if Kjell thought his son intended him harm. They were accustomed to only seeing one another with Asta as their intermediary. Jerit shook his head, the multitude of ways he had considered starting this conversation having been sucked from his thoughts with the opening of the door, and decided that the straightforward approach was the shortest, cleanest way to dull the tension between them.

"Seeing to duties, I presume. I have not seen her this morning. You can put down the scissors. I will not be here long and come unarmed. I have come to tell you…"

The pealing of the náós bells interrupted, the six chimes that marked the beginning of the work day, waking those in town who continued to sleep, and making Kjell frown and wince as though the sound hurt his head. Jerit and his father stared at each other until the reverberations ceased, until the voices of worshippers began to filter into the daylight to be about their business. Jerit squared his shoulders and began again before Kjell could spew the blustering tirade Jerit could read blossoming behind his eyes.

"I will carry the de Corrmick banner into battle, not for you…not because you demand it. I don't owe you anything." He owed his father life, perhaps, but Oska's death and the loss of the throne had stripped away any affection or favoritism he had felt for his youngest son.

"I will do it for Oska…and for Henrik. I will fight with King Lorant and carry the banner and I will retake Glevum, if I can, in Oska's honor, to give his son the throne that was taken. Not for you. I will accept any tributes the war may give…not for your prestige but for my own. When it is won, I will not mention your name. And I hope," he swallowed the growing lump in his throat and balled his trembling hands, "I hope when it is done that you will have lived to regret my decision."

Kjell's face grew redder with each phrase, each perceived indictment, but he kept silent until the word regret passed Jerit's lips. He regretted many things, but his son accepting the duty of his birthright was not one of them. "There is no regret or shame in…"

"We shall see. You have your regrets, and I pray, one way or another, that you bear mine as well. If I die," he again swallowed hard at the thought, expecting his father to see those expressions as signs of weakness, "my blood will be on your hands."

Footsteps behind prompted Jerit to retreat before his father could speak. Maybe he would be a celebrated champion and outshine his father's deeds so that Kjell would live in the shame of Jerit's shadow. Maybe he would die a hero's death so that Kjell would regret the loss of his son and the wedge between him and Asta his fateful demands would certainly create.

Whatever Jerit's fate, his decision was made and his father would have to face the consequences, good or bad.

He hoped his mother would forgive him.

❧*❦

The crackle of shattered, dwindling power ripped across his skin, pulling his drowsy consciousness to waking beneath the barrage of images, sights, and scents that accompanied it, as well as to the undeniable sense of someone standing over him. Splintering wood and pitch-tipped arrows of fire. Faceless forms in gdhededhá robes falling prone surrounded by screams and fleeing feet. Dhóri's shouts, directing people to the safety of the Gate. Khwílen's angelic face, with his pale blonde hair pulling loose of its tie, spattered with blood as he pulled one of the fallen to his feet and propelled him into the flight path of the others.

Always the smell of smoke and blood. Always the underlying stain of Bhás' discordant laughter and the heavy sensation that he was powerless to stop her.

The laughter and sense of not being alone forced his eyes open. Power lashed out to drive the intruder away, but no one was there.

There had to be something he could do. He had to make certain St. Kóráhm's defenses held.

There would be a siege. There would be fire and death, but he could do his best to make certain that no one broke open the Gates, that no one could ransack the chellé hábhai and slaughter those who resided within.

The sliver of her laughter was carried away on the breeze wafting through one window and out through the other.

Kavan rubbed his eyes and swung out of bed, brushing aside the uncharacteristic dizziness, attributing it to the Sight and to the Power spent, rather than to any physical ailment or lack of sleep. He had just finished pulling on his black trousers and was reaching for his shirt when a knock sounded on his door.

Not Ártur or Rhyrdan. The sound was too hesitant.

He was grateful for the interruption.

"Enter."

Bhetá pushed open his door, looked around the room as though uncomfortable being there, and said, "Good morning, my lord. I apologize for waking you. Will you be available to take me to the chellé today? I must take the king's decree to Raenár and make plans for our son."

"You did not wake me. I intend to go there myself. When do you…?"

"As soon as I may? The king has given me leave…so long as I return to accompany Garran and tama Kaj to survey our forces."

"I will meet you in the oratory in fifteen minutes."

She bowed, awkwardly feeling she was rushing his morning rising but unable to take that back now. "Thank you, my lord."

Once dressed, his face clean, his morning meal left on the tray at his bedside, Kavan met her in the oratory and took her to St. Kóráhm's as agreed. They walked together as far as the first courtyard bench where he settled, his hands splayed palms open on his lap while she strode toward the barracks. From the chants and prayers Kavan could hear inside, words of a High Gathering that Kavan had not realized would be celebrated, he believed he would have the time to strengthen the chellé's defenses without interruption. Whether he was here to protect his son or not, he would make certain those who resided here would be safe.

Her pensive frown lingered despite her efforts to cast it off as she strode to where she knew her husband would be. Gone were the smaller items of art and décor that had adorned St. Kóráhm's corridors. Many larger items were likewise missing. She was aware of the belief that St. Kóráhm's would be attacked, but as far from Neth as Alberni was, she could not see how it could happen. Unless an attack came from within or was undertaken by agents residing in Alberni, an attack here did not seem plausible.

Raenár stood after pulling on his boots as she opened his door and held out his hand to welcome her inside. Seeing her expression, he asked, "What is it?" She accepted the gesture and sat across from him but refused the breakfast offering he made.

"The chellé is being emptied?"

"Lord Cliáth insists."

"You cannot think an army will…"

"Someone will. How or why…" He shrugged. "I trust Lord Cliáth when he says this war will touch us here."

"But where…?" She had not witnessed an influx of treasures into Rhidam, and if the fortified chellé was at risk, it seemed likely the Alberni manor would be as well. "Elyriá?"

"The land south of Hatu…a chellé near the village of Gorbesh. It is far enough away that no army will follow and find us."

South of Hatu implied the land from which Kaj Yetek came. Her frown deepened. "You will go?" He said us. While they did not reside together as husband and wife, their relationship being more transactional, in much the way her parents' marriage had been, she was fond of him and could not imagine him leaving her.

"There are Gates. Nothing is so far away so long as there are Gates. But my place is to remain here to protect St. Kóráhm's with any others who choose to do likewise. I've heard the army marches soon?"

"Within the week. As soon as the king is ready." Odd that she felt stung by the thought of him being far from her when the distance of war pressed on her seemed trivial. "I came to tell you…to ask…"

Raenár covered her hand on the table, his touch light and affectionate. "Balint will be safe. Whether in Alberni or Rhidam or elsewhere, we will make provisions for him, whatever happens to us."

It was possible neither of them would remain to raise their son. There were those in Rhidam who could complete his education, prepare him for his duty as duke. Chamberlain William Uphrey in the Nelori estate was an ideal candidate to see to Balint's care, better, perhaps, as he could teach the responsibilities of managing the duchy that thus far Balint lacked. Raenár would prefer that he or Bhetá be the one to instruct Balint in such things, but neither could say what the outcome of war would be.

"And when it is over? Will all of this be returned?" She was accustomed to the familiar halls of St. Kóráhm's, the routine she and Raenár shared. Duty kept them apart, Raenár in Alberni and she in Rhidam and Nelori, but they saw each other enough to suit them both.

Or so she had believed.

"I do not think the duke believes us to be permanently displaced, but I cannot speak to his intentions."

"But his duties to Alberni? The Crown?"

"As I said, I do not know his plan. With the Gates, he can travel anywhere. We all can." He rose a second time and pulled her up. "Come, give me your thoughts on our defenses and tell me the king's plans."

He accepted advice from very few. Under the duke's guidance, he, Tau, and others were doing their best to make the chellé as impenetrable as the royal keep. But he valued his wife's experience, her knowledge. If St. Kóráhm's was lacking, it would not be because he failed to take the Daema's advice.

Once satisfied that St. Kóráhm's power defense could not be made any stronger, that it would take someone more adept and powerful than he to undo the bindings woven in place around the exterior walls of the vast complex and the main gates and door that allowed visitors and residents to come and go, once the bells of St. Maicel's announced the morning's seventh hour, Kavan's unspoken thoughts summoned his son to the courtyard bench. Enmeshed in power, however, examining his work for the fourth time, seeking flaws or changes he could correct to make it stronger, he did not realize Dhóri and another had joined him until his son's hand clasped his. His vision cleared as he lifted his head to find not Bergis with him but Prince Jerit.

"My Prince…"

"I hope I am not intruding. I asked Dhóri to escort me to Rhidam, then he told me you are here…"

Dhóri smiled warmly. "I was counting donations when you summoned and…if you are occupied, I can take him…"

"I did not mean to interrupt you," Kavan apologized. He looked up at Jerit, noting the fading flush of outrage, embarrassment, and some other unidentified strong emotion, and assumed he had been to see his father. "I have business in the manor but…are you due in Rhidam for the summit?"

"Eventually. I'm sure he is waiting, but he knows why I am here. He will forgive me a few more hours." He preferred to return to Lorant with a clear head, unwavering purpose, and with as little observable reservation for his choice as he could manage.

"Or I can…" began Dhóri.

"It should not take me so long, if you would care to accompany me, My Prince…and you," Kavan kissed Dhóri's cheek, "I will speak to you later. I have something to show you."

"If it has anything to do with this power…" Dhóri could feel it around them, even if he did not know what had generated it or what it was for. "Or did you See something?"

"More of the same." His reply was not a lie but it did not reveal the details. What he had Seen was the result of a breach in St. Kóráhm's defenses, a breach now corrected. There was no need to share the horrors that came with it. "I only ask that you keep Khwílen safe, that you and he be away from here when war comes."

"You have Seen our deaths?"

There was no fear in Dhóri's voice, no tremor in his touch, but the set of his mouth and creases at the corners of his unseeing eyes belied his feelings.

"I Saw death, but not yours, or his. But I beg you…"

"You know we will be cautious. Our lives are in Dhágdhuán's hands, and k'Ádhá's. We will be safe."

Kavan wanted to believe that so he nodded and forced his trepidation into the pit of his stomach to ferment with the other worries tangled there. "I pray it is so."

"You know it is. Now, Bergis is waiting; he worries nearly as much as you do." Tilting his head to Jerit as he started away, he said, "Take good care of him. Like I said, He worries too much."

Flushing, Jerit murmured, "Yes." He did not think Kavan required his care, but he would do his best to ease the duke's worries.

Watching Dhóri move around people and obstacles as he retreated into the chellé, proud of his victory over sightlessness that might have destroyed another man, Kavan stood and inclined his head towards the chellé door. "Will you accompany me to the manor?"

"I would like to see it." Despite his years of acquaintance with the duke, Jerit had only interacted with him in St. Kóráhm's or Rhidam. There had never been an opportunity or need to see the rest of Alberni, or the home Kavan called his. Instead of walking through the city streets to reach the manor, however, Kavan led him through the chellé into a small room lined with now-vacant shelves, through a locked door he needed no key to open, and down a set of stairs into a subterranean corridor lit only by an orange glow in the duke's hand.

"I do not know when this was built," he admitted to Jerit's unspoken question. "I think it may have been built during the First Persecution…or before." He had never felt the need to explore its age or creation but accepted that the structures above had been built to protect and take advantage of what lay hidden beneath. Walking with silent, confident steps, they passed a branch that would have taken them deeper into the earth, that connected to the tunnel that led toward the treasures stored there. They climbed another flight of stone steps, paused at the closed door at the top, and after opening it, emerged into the larder of his home.

"To get Elyri to safety through St. Kóráhm's Gates?"

"Perhaps." It was the most plausible explanation…other than the possibility that it had been built by the k'kairá or someone more ancient to protect the reliquary.

"My lord…we did not expect you…" Emeria, hearing voices in the larder where there should be none, bustled into the room drying her hands on her apron, her face red with a sheen of sweat from her early morning work in the already hot kitchen.

"I've come to see how preparations are advancing, to see that you will be safe." He had created protections around the external gates, the windows, and doors of his home as he had St. Kóráhm's, but those would only work if his staff was inside the manor. On the grounds, in the orchards and fields with the flocks and herds, in the stables, he was less certain of their survival. He wanted to reexamine those defenses and see what else he could do. "I also came to give Prince Jerit a tour…"

"Your Majesty," she hastily curtseyed to cover her surprise, never having seen the prince before.

"This is Rhyrdan and Madoc's sister, Emeria. My home would not function without her."

Jerit bowed his head respectfully. "An honor, my lady."

Her chuckle was soft and embarrassed. "While I am sure you would find another to serve you as well if I wasn't here, I thank you for saying so."

"Your father would never forgive me if I made you feel unwelcome," he assured her fondly. Having known her since her birth, it was reassuring to have Wortham's presence alive in his home through her company. "I would never forgive myself."

She smiled and curtsied again. "Laney's taking care of everything. We've harvested what we can to prepare…culling the flocks and herds now…and we're rationing what we have in case we are besieged."

"I pray you will not need it. The prince will accompany me…"

"Will you dine with us this evening?"

"The king is expecting us before then."

"At noon then? There is broth and the bread is baking."

"We shall see how long our business takes," he promised, thinking it would be nice for Jerit to get to know Rhyrdan's kin.

"As you wish." She gestured them through the larder curtain, closed the floor hatch, and then pulled the curtain closed behind them with another curtsey to the prince before returning to the day's cooking.

As Kavan led the way through one room after another, explaining details he deemed important, Jerit studied everything with interest, happy to have something to dwell on that did not include his father, the prospect of war, and Lorant riding into it. He memorized the layout of the kitchen, the shape of the dining room and the long table that would seat many more than Kavan, his children, and grandchildren. He memorized corridors devoid of art and rooms stripped to the furnishings and the expensive Hatu carpets that warmed the stone floors. Outside, they walked the fields of crops Kavan curated from the stock of Dhóbhaen seeds, the orchards plucked of ripe fruit but still heavy with more, the pastures of animals that provided wool and meat, eggs, milk, and cheese to the manor residents or to the townsfolk in exchange for commodities they needed.

He asked questions about the crops Kavan had brought from that mysterious distant land. They discussed husbandry, the beautiful pair of riding horses set apart from the plow and wagon animals by their slender form and sleek, small heads. And they discussed as much of the manor's history as Kavan knew, how it had belonged to Guthrie McHador's family before being gifted to the Crown after the great general's death.

They discussed that man too, how he might have guided Enesfel through this impending war that Jerit tried not to think about. He was eager for anything that would ease his fears, but by the time they settled in Kavan's study so he could examine the estate's ledgers and assess what resources could be reallocated for more protections, more men, to ensure the manor's survival, the shift of topic to General McHador brought those fears surging to the surface again.

"I told my father I would take the crest into battle," Jerit swallowed hard as he sat across from Kavan's desk. By now it was noon and Emeria, having monitored their progress around the estate, brought a tray of mutton broth, bread baked that morning, and brine eggs her children favored.

Kavan, having just opened the ledger, looked up with a raised brow, bidding Jerit to continue.

"I don't want to be there…to see war…to…die…" Jerit sighed and put down the egg he had picked up, feeling abruptly less hungry. "I bid Lorant not to go, but he believes he must…"

"He confessed as much to me, despite my beseeching him to do otherwise," Kavan admitted.

Hearing a warning in those words that might not have been there, Jerit rested his elbows on the edge of the desk. "Is he in danger?"

"All in war are in danger…but I have not seen his death…or yours. If you do not wish to…"

"If he goes, I must. I will never forgive myself if something happens and I'm not there." He hesitated, forced himself to eat a polite portion of what was provided, and added, "I did not tell my father that." Both understood that, despite Jerit's silence, Kjell already knew the truth. "He only considers familial honor…his pride."

"He pushes you to do what he cannot, seeks to live through you the life he was denied. It is not easy to trade one prison for another."

"He's not imprisoned…"

"Circumstances prevent him from hunting, from seeing the world, from leaving St. Kóráhm's. He possesses every luxury we can provide…it may not be the tower, but it is a prison nonctheless."

Not having considered it that way, Jerit muttered, "It does not give him the right to criticize who I love and…"

"No, it does not. Being a parent is not easy under the best conditions. Trapped in the shadow of war, we do the best we can. Your father is no different." He gave Jerit several minutes to eat and consider his words, enough time to scan the newest ledger entries, assess the numbers, and imprint them in his memory, before closing the tome and pushing it aside.

"I Saw you in battle with Lorant…many years ago," he murmured. "I did not know it was him, or you, until recently. A glimpse, nothing clear, and though it frightened me to see that future, I did not have the sense, then or now, that either of you was in mortal danger."

Jerit sighed. "So, I must go."

"I do not know. What I've Seen…it could be this conflict; it could be another to come. I can only advise according to what I See. He is lucky to have you…your loyalty and love."

The way he had been lucky to have Wortham and to have Rhyrdan now. The way he was lucky to have Raebhá in his life. Such personal devotion, such connections to others, was all that mattered.

"Sometimes I think he does not see it or…feel the same."

Kavan smiled softly. "He has always loved and been devoted to you. Do not fear that." No matter what royal duty demanded of Lorant, that was one truth Kavan believed would always stand.

Jerit flushed and turned to eating to hide his unease. When he had consumed his fill, he glanced at the near-empty shelves where other ledgers waited and asked, "I thought there would be more. Where are they?" Kavan always had books around him. Books and his harp.

"In Gorbesh."

"The town where the residents of St. Kóráhm will take shelter?"

"Yes. Dhóri will go with them. Ágdhállán too. Perhaps, in time, I will as well. It is the safest place for them."

Jerit sighed. "I will miss you." Outside of Lorant, he felt there was no one else who understood him the way Kavan did.

"You will have him."

"It will not be the same."

"Nothing ever is." Sometimes it drove him mad to consider how much his world had changed over the years and how much it would continue to change, whether he was in Rhidam, Bhryell, Alberni, Gorbesh, Dhóbhaen, or elsewhere.

"We should return to Rhidam. Lorant will be anxiously longing for your return."

Unsurprisingly, that notion made Jerit smile.

❧Chapter 31❧

"It would not be right to lie to him," Ágdhállán said, his tone nearer to a whine than Kavan had heard since he had been a fussy, teething toddler. Now that Ártur and Syl were in Bhryell and the palace staff had settled into a routine, if extraordinarily frantic, pattern of war preparations, the oratory steps had seemed the most private place to have this conversation with his son, but the boy resisted contrition, as if what he had done had been for the best.

"It is not lying to withhold information. Sometimes…"

"He is going to war. He needed to know it was the right thing…that I Saw him there…"

"What did you See?" Lorant had not given him the details of what Ágdhállán said and, until now, Kavan had not had the chance to ask.

Picking nervously at his sleeve, an uncharacteristic gesture, he mumbled, "He was on a horse, in a forest. Men came out of the trees. There was a woman…"

Kavan shivered. "Describe her."

Ágdhállán shook his head. "I didn't see her; I heard her laugh, but you know her. She wasn't…you've seen…heard…when you wouldn't wake…"

Bhás.

Kavan's expression darkened and the boy grabbed his hand, looking as though his father's abrupt change of demeanor was somehow his fault. "I'm sorry, k'bhy…"

Kavan put his finger to his lips to silence him, his head suddenly cocked toward the oratory door. He heard them again, those footsteps that came without motion, the presence that came without form he had heard more often of late. His nostrils flared, reacting to the pungent scent of coltweed that Ágdhállán did not seem to smell. Nor did the boy appear to hear whatever Kavan heard. There were only his mismatched eyes wide with fear that he might have said or done something to anger his father.

❧337❧

As abruptly as it was there, the sound, the smell, the presence was gone. The air was still. The flicker of distant power had faded. Only then did Kavan's shoulder slump as he relaxed and exhaled with relief.

"I won't do it again, k'bhydhá. I will talk to you first when I See something, make sure others should know…" Ágdhállán whispered.

Kavan pulled him onto his lap and held him, as much to comfort them both as it was to shield him from a danger he was not certain had passed. "It isn't that, Ágdhi. We must be cautious with what we know but…"

"She scares you. Who is she?" When Kavan did not speak, Ágdhállán eventually said, "She scares me too. I know everything will be okay…I feel it here." He pressed one fist over his heart. "I know you'll see my little brother soon…that everything will be okay…but sometimes when I hear her, I'm scared too."

"You have heard her before?" he asked, ignoring the sudden hammering of his heart that came with the promise of meeting his other child at last. Seeing Raebhá again.

"When I dream," Ágdhállán replied. "Sometimes, when I'm not dreaming, when I'm awake. Like she is close, in another room."

Distressed by his son's admission, the proximity Bhás seemed to have to them both, the unexpected sparking of energy behind the Purification curtain was startling enough to prompt Kavan to throw up mental shields of energy around them as though he expected the woman they spoke of to emerge through it.

Instead, by the time Ártur, Kaedís, and three strangers, followed by Syl and four others, all exuding the same soothing healing power, Kavan was able to rein in his fear, set Ágdhállán on his feet, and stand to greet them.

"sínréc…we were not expecting you to be here…"

Syl chuckled as she reached to her husband's side. "If you expect him anywhere, it should be here," she teased Ártur.

"Well…yes…" Ártur began.

"You have found recruits." A few were faces Kavan recognized. Healer Ylltán, a scowling-faced bald man, thicker and heavier of build than most Elyri, had lived in Bhryell all of Kavan's life. His skill with knives, axes, and bows put him on the outcast fringe. He had turned his healing focus to horses and other animals, making himself indispensable to the town, and when the plagues had arrived, people had been more than willing to accept his care for their children. Kavan did not know him well but he had always felt an affinity for Bhryell's other social pariah. Kólmárá Tyrnás, a younger man with red hair cropped short around his ears but fuller on top, was a contemporary of Chethá's, someone she had trained with when she had moved to Bhryell to be near Sóbhán before they married. Healer Pháraeís Dunne, who had taught both, had once been Ártur's mentor as well.

The three youngest faces, however, were unfamiliar.

"Lord Cliáth." Healer Pháraeís approached and offered his hand. "My daughters Syróá and Tisá…and Syróá's betrothed Bhárás Mulóy. We've come to lend your cousin and king a hand."

"We are here to heal," grunted Ylltán, the edge to his voice suggesting that he would not be averse to killing if necessary either, regardless of his Healer's Oath.

"We weren't expecting so many," Ártur said sheepishly. He had thought to recruit one or two at the most.

"dedhá Bhílári was very persuasive," said Kólmárá with a grin.

"As were you." Bhárás bobbed his head to Ártur.

Syl beamed at her husband and added, "There may yet be more to meet us enroute."

"The king will be pleased to have each of you." Having eight Elyri healers would certainly be a boon to Enesfel's army.

"Would you care to join us for introductions?" Ártur asked.

"I would, yes." Through his son's hand in his, Kavan made it known that they would continue their conversation later, that he wanted the boy to be diligent for Bhás' presence and to be told whenever it occurred. Ágdhállán nodded as he let go of Kavan's hand and followed the group as far as the oratory door, when he went one way and Kavan and the healers turned toward the stairs.

He was eager to learn more about those his cousin had recruited, what they offered, what sort of people they were. So long as they were up to facing the dangers ahead, they would be to Enesfel's benefit.

But even eight healers might not be enough to win the war.

❧*❧

Over the next two days, life felt more normal in the keep than it had in weeks. Kavan allowed himself to be consumed by the furious recording of Zythán's tale and tutoring lessons that kept the children out of the way of those thrown into the flurry of travel preparations. As men arrived from other duchies and towns, some seasoned with combat skills, others inexperienced yet eager, the ranks of soldiers passing through Rhidam kept the inquisitors, justice, and all his men focused on deflating high-tempered skirmishes and petty conflicts between the Association and the foreigners who made easy targets. The periodic Association deaths continued, but no one except the inquisitors had time to investigate.

Asta and Zerio, however, were content to allow the Association to police itself.

Lorant, bound in ongoing meetings with the three lead generals that permitted no time for privacy or solitude, barely noticed. Daily trips were made to the staging field while his advisors wove and untangled the threads of finances, supplies, and arrangements necessary to leave in place when the king and his army left Rhidam.

He was eager to be away.

Jerit was less so. He wanted only stolen moments with Lorant that he was unable to find.

Only when the lull of evening set in, when the evening feasting with the White Bard's music purring in their ears was over, satisfying bellies that would soon know the meagerness of field rations and hearts that would know anxiety and fear, enjoyed soothing peace, did restless or exhausted sleep settle in.

Only then did Kavan allow himself a few moments of privacy to seek some way to protect himself and Ágdhállán from Bhás…some way to find her as it seemed she could too easily find him.

He was not in the oratory, however, as the recruited healers and others who wished to join them had come together in both to pray and hear words of encouragement they would need to move forward. As the hour of departure grew closer, both oratories and Hes á Redh were perpetually filled with men and women facing the possibility of impending death.

Kavan left them to it, preferring to fly as he had not done in many days, to float above the field of soldiers, to circle Rhidam's streets, to enjoy the shedding of bottled-up power and the fluttering caress of hot summer air over white-feathered wings.

He was tempted to invite Ágdhállán to join him.

He did not. After days filled with the constant needs of others, those moments of solitude were much needed.

On his final circle of the night, when he felt spent enough to sleep, he spotted Zerio huddled with a cloaked figure not far from Hes á Redh before both turned and skulked away in opposite directions, one into the shadows, one back toward the keep. He could not hear the discussion and there was little unusual about a covert meeting with one of many spies and informants. Feeling that Zerio's company would be a welcome relief, a conversation with someone other than children or perhaps a deeper discussion of what they had each learned in Bhórdh, Kavan followed him and resumed his shape out of sight of everyone else. By the time he avoided guards and servants, circumvented Níkóá and Seren's late-night conversation in a third-floor alcove, and reached Asta's chamber, the door was already closed, shutting him out.

Asta's raised voice, however, made the contents of their conversation audible to anyone who passed, to anyone in the rooms on either side, and to the boy who stood in the corridor looking as if he had frozen in place with his hand poised to knock in the hopes of warding off whatever nightmare had left him teary-eyed at her door.

"My mother…is alive?" Henrik choked, looking up at the bard, his eyes wide on a face blanched white with shock.

He had no memories of the woman but he knew how much his grandparents hated her. He knew many blamed her for the downfall of the de Corrmicks and the war before them. No one had been able to shield him from the rumors that she may have killed his father, from the knowledge that she had held his grandfather in a tower prison, that she might somehow be responsible for the things that others considered to be defects in his body and personality.

"Does that make me…?"

Kavan scooped the boy into his arms, one of the few Henrik allowed to touch him without asking first, and said, "It does not make you anything, my prince. You are still you. You are Neth's heir…"

He took a quick step back as footsteps approached and Asta threw the door open with enough force that it would have collided with the wall if Zerio had not caught it with one hand. She stopped, surprised to see Kavan but barely noticing Henrik before barking, "Take me to Kjell."

"The hour is…"

"I want to go," sobbed Henrik.

Asta ignored him. "Now, Lord Cliáth, or I'll find someone who will."

Zerio shrugged apologetically, guessing that both bard and prince had heard enough of the exchange to know its content, and motioned for Henrik to come to him. As usual, Henrik stiffened and held his breath when Zerio took him from Kavan's arms, a panic-like reaction only corrected when Zerio put him down.

"Come, Henrik…"

The boy shuffled after the man he viewed as an uncle, looking at his grandmother over his shoulder until Zerio shut the door. With the door closed, Kavan let out the breath he, too, had been holding and followed the woman already marching toward the oratory.

"This does not mean…" Kavan began as they reached the Gate.

"It changes everything." Zerio's informant had not provided details, only that there was proof now that Oska's killer was alive in Glevum. Asta believed Zerio when he said he did not know the woman's whereabouts, did not know how she had survived, but she wanted to look Tau in the eye and know that he knew nothing too.

She also wanted Kjell to know the truth. To know his safety was at risk, to know that the one who had stolen his throne had survived just as he had.

She wanted Kjell to know she was going to kill Inness with her own hands as soon as she found her, even if she had to spend the rest of her life searching, just as Marta was doing.

Kavan's concern, as he took her to the chellé for a dialogue he would not be privy to, was how Inness' survival would impact the war.

By midmorning, everyone in the keep would be thinking the same thing and asking the same questions.

⮞ * ⮜

"Then perhaps the rumors are true." Roused from his bed and his vain attempt to sleep by the unexpected pounding on his door, which undoubtedly woke others in the rooms around him, Kjell's face was as red as Asta's, his jaw tense, his hand flexing impotently as her words sank deeper. What had become of Inness after she gave up her son to Zerio, no one had known. Zerio believed she had been killed by those who had stormed the castle that night, but he had not been certain. The most persistent but dubious claim had been that Fraen had forced her to marry him so he could rule as king.

If she was alive, that claim had to be true. Where else could she have been for the last ten years?

It was plausible that Fraen intended to use one Lachlan to dissuade another from attack.

"Does Lorant know?"

"He will by morning."

"You must not allow this to dissuade Enesfel from action."

"It won't. Her life does not legitimize Fraen's claim to the throne." Inness had only manipulated her way into power because she carried King Oska's child and had been, therefore, the one best positioned to be his regent until he was old enough to no longer need a woman's care.

"Does she know Henrik's alive? That Fraen tried to kill him?"

"It doesn't matter. Even if she wants Fraen dead, it doesn't make her an ally. She will never be..."

Kjell caught Asta's hand when she passed in her furious pacing and pulled her to sit next to him. "No ally...but we might be able to use her against Fraen if she loves her son..."

"It's been ten years..." But the woman had ensured her son's safety, the most decent thing she had done, accomplished at the risk to her own life. The woman Asta had known would never stand for a threat against her child. She had gone to war against Kjell because of a perceived threat to Oska. She would not hesitate to go to war against Fraen...married or not...if she knew he had sent assassins after her son.

"We should crown Henrik the official heir and king."

"He's a child..."

Yet Asta understood Kjell's rationale. If Kjell emerged from hiding and announced Henrik to be the king of Neth, it was unlikely that Inness would stand against her son and Enesfel's army. She would likely think twice about supporting Fraen in a war that would threaten Henrik.

"You would disinherit Jerit." Her eyes narrowed suspiciously but her tone was unsurprised, even relieved. Jerit had resisted the notion of claiming Neth's throne his whole life, having first planned to serve his brother as inquisitor and then, after learning of Oska's death, and Oska being a father, he stood firm in the opinion that the son of his brother the king was, in fact, the heir to Neth's throne. Despite Kjell's efforts to push Jerit into the position as heir, Henrik was the successor. Only Kjell's command could change the appointment.

His demand to betroth Henrik to the Lachlan princess had made it seem that he was tipping his hand toward the boy, but until today, he had never admitted it.

He had never been willing to accept defeat to Jerit's stubbornness.

He had never been willing to admit that he no longer felt capable of resuming the throne.

Ignoring the implications of his decision on Jerit, on Henrik, and on himself, Kjell continued, "Henrik is Oska's son. Oska was the king. His claim should be known before Enesfel's troops cross into Neth. They should know that I am alive. There should be no question, when Glevum is reclaimed, about who will sit on her throne. He will need a regent, but he will be..."

"That regent should be you." They stared at one another until Kjell's hard gaze softened. "Whatever you believe you lack, your mind is sharp. We cannot go back to before, but we can go forward as a united family."

United, except for perhaps Jerit. That would be a matter she would have to address later.

"And if we find her?" he inquired, avoiding a discussion about his qualifications and the weaknesses he refused to verbally acknowledge.

Asta's tone sharpened again. "She will pay for the grief she caused, for her treason, for Oska's death."

Some might say that wherever Inness had been for the last decade, she had suffered enough.

For Asta, that ten years would never be enough.

Kjell nodded, inclined to agree.

⮞*⮜

Despite his efforts to lull Henrik to sleep on his mother's bed, not knowing when Asta would return or what her mood would be, Zerio was forced to sit helplessly at the bedside listening to the prince mumble to himself, counting as his fingers twitched to the sound of his voice and the occasional sobbing squeak.

He considered fetching Princess Hella as the girl was usually able to calm or distract Henrik, but at this hour, she was asleep like everyone else.

Everyone except the two in this room, Kavan, Asta, and Kjell.

"What was she like?"

Zerio lifted his head and opened his eyes, his attempt to doze causing an ache in his neck that he would regret in the morning. "My prince?"

"You knew her…my mother. What was she like?"

"You should ask your grandmother…"

Henrik shook his head. "She won't tell me. She'll get mad. Was she so…bad?"

Zerio shifted to sit on the edge of the bed instead of the chair; Henrik sat up and leaned against his shoulder, their backs to the headboard, his fingers still drumming without making a sound.

"She made some unfortunate choices…but we've all made our share of those." He did not want to go into details that he believed the boy was not ready to hear. "But she loved you…loved your father."

"Then why did she send me away."

"The castle was breached. She thought she would die and wanted you to be safe."

⮞344⮜

"But she didn't. Die. She's still alive?"

Zerio nodded. "It seems that way."

"So, she sent me here because she did not want me?"

"No, that's not it at all. I don't know how she survived, where she has been, but I'm sure it was somewhere she could not keep you safe. That night…I heard the fighting, heard the screams. Maybe she hid…maybe she was captured and imprisoned somewhere. She was smart. She was strong. She wanted you to be protected."

Inness had been many other things as well. Stubborn. Impulsive. Cold and calculating. Vindictive. Manipulative. Hungry for control. Smart, but not very wise.

Zerio did not speak those faults out loud. It was not his place.

"Is it true? Did she kill my father?" The more he spoke, the more his fidgeting fingers began to still.

"I do not know. I was not there. I heard it was an accident, that he fell into despair when he thought his family was dead. I've seen despair kill a man or make him careless. But I do know she loved him."

Whatever else Inness had done, Zerio believed that to be true.

Henrik put his hands on his thighs, his fingers spread, and stared at the empty spaces between them, his eyes darting as if counting each space repeatedly. "You don't think she'd kill me? That she sent those…?"

"No…I don't believe that. She would never hurt you." He was less certain about that after things he had witnessed before, but ten years was a long time. People changed. Whatever Inness had endured, she undoubtedly had. She regretted the injury she had caused her son, even if she could not express it.

"I'm not like her? I'm not…bad?"

"You're nothing like her. I've heard from the prince, from your mother, that you're like your father. He was a good man, a good king."

He scrunched his face together and asked, "But he married her…"

"Love is not always logical. It makes us do things we might not normally do." Zerio did not know that from personal experience but he had seen it often enough.

"I hope I'm never in love." Henrik slid into the pillow behind him, pulled the sheets up with one hand, and stared at the empty hearth across the room. Nightbirds sang in the back garden beneath the open window and he seemed to focus on that as his lids began to droop and his breathing evened out.

"I don't think I like her," he eventually slurred without opening his eyes. "Is that bad?"

"It is your right," Zerio assured him.

There were many reasons Zerio did not like her either, despite the sympathy he had felt during their last evening together.

❮*❯

The tavern was empty except for the two of them and the man at the bar who exchanged periodic glances with the woman in front of him, glances that convinced Captain Earon Sparding that he was Association too.

The woman with him certainly was.

The establishment was only open because Marta Geli demanded it. As head of Glevum's branch of the Association, she had the influence to make such things happen.

As Vants, Earon's presence here was barely suspect.

This was not the first time they had shared drinks, a harmless activity between a man and woman that served as adequate cover for the periodic exchange of information between Vants and the Association harking back to the time when Olaric first returned to Glevum and set about reestablishing the Vants. The men, who had known each other as soldiers more than ten years before, could sometimes exchange messages more directly when their paths crossed in the keep, but those contacts had to be kept to a minimum to avoid the king's suspicion.

A soldier and a common lady, particularly one he had been seen with before, were overlooked.

This was the first time, however, that her hand covered his on the table and she gifted him with a disarming smile.

Olaric had warned him. But it was hard to be unaffected by her charm.

"It's been eleven years," she said with a shrug. "I mourn him, I miss him; my heart is loyal. But I'm not dead. A woman has needs as does any man. If you'd wanted a wife…if I'd wanted a husband, we'd have found new ones by now. Or perhaps," she sipped from her glass without removing her hand from his and studied him demurely, "we've been simply waiting for the right time…the right person."

Though Earon shook his head no, he could not refute her words. His wife's death at the tail end of the plague and the loss of three of his children to illness and accident had left his house emptier than it should be. There was only his twelve-year-old son to fill the rooms, but the boy was most often in the care of Earon's sister as his duty to the Crown kept him away from home. There he was tutored and learned the craft of pottery, both of which Earon hoped provided a better future than a life of war could.

Earon had no interest in whores but he was, as Marta said, tired of being alone. And she was no whore.

He looked at her fingers drawing patterns on the back of his hand and shivered. She would try to get to him, Olaric had said. Now that he had something she wanted, she would try to find ways to sway him.

He shook his head and gave a smile of interest to match hers.

"I will be on duty in a few hours and I must see to my son." He was required at the keep at daybreak and he would, as he had done for his son nearly every day since they had been left alone together, share the morning meal with him. As tempting as Marta's offer was, despite the tightening in his trousers and the tingling of his hand, he would not give in to her.

At least not tonight.

"Another time then." She sounded sufficiently disappointed that he felt guilty for denying her. "You sent my message to Rhidam?"

"They should have it by now," he replied with a nod.

"Good." She placed coins on the table and stood. He did likewise. "Tomorrow night then?"

Earon hesitated, shrugged internally, and then agreed to a repeated rendezvous. He enjoyed her company and the tales of adventure she spun and she seemed to enjoy the stories of the peculiar goings-on inside the castle and its luscious gossip.

There was no time tonight to share those.

Such sharing, however, did not mean he would betray the queen regent's location or give Marta access to her as she desired.

Not until Olaric gave the word.

❧*❧

Prayer at Wortham's grave, a focus on remembrance rather than speculation about the unexpected news of Inness' reemergence after so long, brought the sun's warmth on his back and an ache in his heart that he had difficulty dispelling. He wondered if, in the relocation of treasures to Gorbesh, he should consider moving Wortham and Zelenka as well, if they would want that, to remain near those who loved them, be interred in Alberni's charnel house when St. Kóráhm's cemetery grew too full, or if they would prefer to remain undisturbed where they were, where their graves might be desecrated by the expected assailants. He reached no practical decision and was relieved when Asta found him, remaining reverently quiet until he lifted his head. She appeared less agitated, less furious, and contrite about her earlier demand to be brought here.

"Kjell is to anoint Henrik the heir. dedhá Khwílen has gone to Rhidam to retrieve him and Zerio…so that the three of you and the dedhá can be witness to the succession of Neth's monarchy until word can spread that Kjell is alive and has passed the throne to Henrik."

It was wise to publicly place Henrik on the throne he did not yet own, if it garnered support from the Nethites they were due to confront. Whether Kjell exposing himself would likewise be wise remained to be seen.

"You should talk to Henrik. He was disturbed to learn she lives."

"He heard?" It was not until that moment that she remembered him in Kavan's arms when she barged out of her chamber. Her expression fell.

"It was difficult not to. By now, most in the keep will know."

Asta frowned but nodded. She could blame no one for her raised voice, for not taking Henrik's feelings into account, except herself. "He deserves to know everything, but I do not believe I can be the one to tell him. She might have saved his life, but there were many other lives she did not save, many deaths she caused."

"I understand…but he will not."

"I know." She held out her hand. "Will you forgive my insolence and join us?"

He accepted the hand and got to his feet. "I am honored to do so."

It was a brief ceremony conducted in the Gathering Hall of St. Kóráhm's, a proclamation made by a former king recorded in writing by Zerio to be delivered to all corners of Neth ahead of the army's departure from Enesfel. There was a prayer and an anointing of blessed oil and water provided by gdhededhá Khwílen, questions put forth to the boy who was abruptly thrust into a political world he had thus far only skirted the fringes of, followed by a prayer song and the laying on of hands by the White Bard. The scroll was sealed and would be protected until the day Glevum fell.

There would be no question then about Henrik's legitimate claim.

By the time the legalities were over and both grandparents had taken Henrik to a room where they could discuss the ramifications of what had been done, Kavan decided it was time to return to Rhidam. Khwílen or Dhóri would return Asta and Henrik in the morning. There had been no trace of Kóráhm, no gathering of záryph, no hint that this was the right path to take. No reassurances of the future, only a trace of something that Kavan could not grasp that suggested this was the closing of a chapter for his beloved chellé that could not be undone.

He did not know what the feeling meant and he wanted the distraction of his son and the other children to banish the Sight-ghosts haunting him.

"Is it true?" Rhyrdan was in the oratory to greet him when Kavan emerged from the Gate, his bearded face both animated and thoughtful. "Is Lady Inness…?"

"It appears so." Kavan cocked his head as the curtain swung closed behind him, wondering how many times he would have to answer that question. "I know no more about it. If it is something Asta wishes to share with the king, she will." Asta and Henrik would undoubtedly tell Jerit and Jerit, in turn, would tell Lorant, whether Asta did or not.

"You're not here just to ask me that, are you?"

Rhyrdan accepted the teasing tone and expression and fell into step beside Kavan as they left the oratory. He had been known to wait for Kavan for less important reasons, often just to see the man's face after his absence or to assure himself of the bard's welfare. But when his grin drooped into a more serious expression, Kavan knew his first instinct was correct. Something was amiss.

"Is Ágdhállán…?"

"With Master Najar and Aunes in the back garden discussing birds when I left them, when Prince Henrik was summoned. I do not believe the Cáner boys and Balint were much interested in the lesson and the girls were sitting with the queen practicing needlework."

"The king then?"

"Preparations continue. I am told they will ride north in two days."

Kavan's expression grew immediately grave and alarmed. "Have you decided to…?"

"Leave you unprotected?" Rhyrdan scoffed. "Father would never forgive me. I will do as he would have, and stay with you and Ágdhállán. I suspect the king knows that; no one has asked me to ride with the troops."

Kavan exhaled with relief and felt dizzy at the sudden loss of air. Two days were not much time to prepare, to say what words he should to Lorant, Jerit, Ártur, and others. The intent to resume normalcy was again thwarted by reality.

"Thank you, Rhyrdan."

At the bottom of the stairs, where Kavan turned toward the garden, the younger man grabbed his arm and held him back, what he intended to say having not yet been spoken. "A messenger arrived for you earlier with a summons to the Eagle's Nest."

"A summons? From who?" He could think of no one who would seek to meet him there. Wace Elotti was the last person he had shared a drink with in that establishment. There was no one else unless it was a passing minstrel who did not dare to approach him in the keep. The possibility of sharing music with another bard made Kavan feel surprisingly light-hearted and eager for the first time in days.

"The messenger would not say or did not know their names. An older man with white hair and a dark-skinned man…possibly from Hatu he said. I sent him back with word that you were not here but were expected to return by the end of the day."

"Then we should not keep them waiting."

Rhyrdan scowled. "Two men who will not give names? I suspect trouble." Not enough trouble to prevent him from delivering the message, but enough to go with Kavan if the bard chose to answer the summons.

"You often do." Now that the expectation of meeting another bard, or a pair of bards, had burrowed into his head, Kavan was the one to smile and gesture toward the keep door. "Would it relieve your fears to join me and see who they are?"

"You'll have to order me to stay here to prevent it," Rhyrdan challenged in a stubborn tone that made Kavan chuckle.

Intrigued by this new distraction and lured by the chance to share his primary passion with someone who understood it, Kavan, with Rhyrdan at his side, walked briskly across the crowded, bustling courtyard where saddles were being rubbed with oils, weapons were being sharpened to combat-readiness, where segregated groups of men sparred or engaged in archery contests, where Garran, Bhetá, and Kaj huddled over a makeshift table with several lower-ranking officers gesturing to locations on a crude map drawn onto a plank of wood and moving bits of stone and glass into place to represent the strategies they planned to implement. The guards at the gate bowed as the Elyri passed through and wove through the line of mules, horses, and wagons that delivered the supplies the king requested.

The hour was early enough that the midday guests had not collected around the doors of the Eagle's Nest. Some merchants and lesser nobles had found rooms there when it was learned there were no more billeting rooms available, but most had departed their rooms early to conduct their business with the king, the chamberlain, and chancellor, or anyone else in the keep they had come to see.

Rhyrdan was the first to enter, scanning the ground floor of the tavern and the stairs for potential threats. There were less than a dozen people, a man speaking to a woman bent over the staircase rail to stroke his cheek, a young woman delivering drinks filled by the man behind the counter, and another distributing the last of the morning's repast to those who requested it. The rest sat in small groups or alone. To Rhyrdan, only a dark-skinned man at the table nearest the door, possibly Cíbhóló, looked out of place, and matched the description the messenger had provided. Not seeing him as a threat, Rhyrdan allowed Kavan to enter but remained protectively in front of him when, almost as one, heads turned when the White Bard entered.

The dark-skinned man spoke to the white-haired gentleman across from him who also turned in his chair to face the pair who entered.

Kavan met his gaze.

His heart stopped.

❧Chapter 32❧

"Eridel."

Rhyrdan did not recognize the white-bearded face of the man who rose slowly from the worn, wooden bench. It had been a decade since he had seen him, and that had been but a momentary glimpse before he was cut down by a blade meant to kill Kavan with its poison. But he remembered the name, recognized Kavan's apprehension, and so pulled the bard back and stepped in front of him with a growl and the drawing of his sword. The tavern owner went rigid, expecting bloodshed as the man on the other side of the table also stood and reached to pull Eridel back.

Too stunned to speak, the recent fear of Eridel coming to kill him or his family overwhelming his senses, Kavan could only stare and marvel at how much older Eridel looked. Numbers collided in his head as he fought to find his voice. Sixty-four. Eridel had to be sixty-four.

How had so much time passed between them?

Did he honestly have a reason to feel threatened by a man of such an age when he could crush him in an instant if he chose?

Would he have summoned Kavan to this place if murder was his intent?

"Rhyrdan…" His voice small as it squeezed out of his constricted throat, Kavan urged Rhyrdan to lower his sword by pushing his arm down. As the sword lowered, the dark-skinned man with long waves of thick, black hair let go of Eridel and relaxed his broad shoulders.

Kavan did not ask Rhyrdan to put the sword away. He was not yet comfortable in Eridel's presence. He was not convinced he was safe.

"His reaction is understandable," Eridel finally said with a tremulous sigh. "As is yours. After what I did…the way I left…"

"I offered a truce," Kavan stammered. "Begged forgiveness for my abysmal behavior…"

"And I rejected it, refused to give it. I was ashamed of my rage. But it was either flee or risk Bhás following me to you." When Kavan involuntarily shuddered and the movement of his eyes suggested a hasty assessment of the room, Eridel nodded. "You know her."

"We've met."

"I'm surprised she let you live…so you know why I did not dare. I've spent years roaming, hiding…until I found somewhere she could not go…and was then sent back to you. I was afraid to come back, that you would not see me…that she would find me before I found you. But it is important I'm here. Please…sit with me. This," he indicated his companion, "is Sunna. I would not be here if not for him. Sunna, this is Lord Cliáth."

Less dark than the Cíbhóló but darker than most from Hatu and the lands to the south, the bearded man's unwaveringly passive expression studied Kavan as if he was a marvel. But he did not speak, even when introduced. The most remarkable thing about him to Kavan was the bubbling of untamed power beneath his stoic demeanor that seemed to spark and pop in Kavan's proximity.

hwonághk.

It had been a long time since Kavan had encountered such a person. The last time he had, he had been with the Dhóbhaen. He could not determine his ancestry by holding his gaze, however and chose not to breech his trust by the physical contact of a handshake.

"You take a risk in coming here." No one else was likely to recognize Eridel, but it was still a risk. "Where did you go?"

"Anywhere I could where she might not find me. I don't think I outran her…I think she stopped pursuing me. I was no longer worth her time, I guess…not even for revenge for failing her…or else she knew I'd come back to you someday. She never explained why she seeks your suffering…but she made sure to feed and nurture my outrage until…" He hung his head. "I am sorry."

"As am I."

The serving girl came and took their requests, bringing back platters of beans flavored with pork fat and boiled turnips, three mugs of ale, and one of water. Having not eaten since the previous evening, Kavan was very hungry and the visiting men ate as though they had not eaten in even longer. Rhyrdan picked at the food while watching the man who had nearly killed him, who would have killed Kavan if Rhyrdan had not intervened.

Kavan wondered if they had spent every coin they had on their room and wondered why, if he was able, Eridel had not performed for a decent meal sooner.

"I hesitated coming, knowing what reception I might have, but I was told to warn you, to tell you…"

"I know what she wants." She wanted him to suffer, wanted him dead.

Eridel nodded. "There may a way to stop her. I cannot lead you to her; I dare not even if I could…but there is someone else. He says he has what you need to face her. He would not give it to me but summoned me to bring you to him…"

"You think he would follow you anywhere after what you…?" began Rhyrdan in a low, hissing voice.

"I swear on my soul I am no longer a threat. I've had ten years to consider our last words, your efforts for atonement, my behavior. I don't want to see anyone dead except her. Bhás is the threat…and I believe with all my heart that you are the only one who can bring an end to her reign of cruelty…the war she wages on behalf of whatever devil she honors. shi cali are dangerous, but one equal to her in strength could stop her."

"And if I'm not?"

The quaver in the bard's voice made Rhyrdan frown.

"He says you can. I don't question him anymore."

The unknown 'he' could be Kóráhm, some other gdhededhá, prophet or charlatan sent by Bhás to lure both him and Eridel to their deaths. Kavan sensed no deception in Eridel but that did not mean that Bhás had not deceived him too.

"What does your source have? How do I know…?"

"I've not seen it but I believe it is a relic of great power. He says it is. I believe him. To counter her, what else could it be?"

Rhyrdan snorted and crossed his arms over his chest. "How do we trust you or this unnamed source? How do we know this isn't a trap?"

Ignoring Rhyrdan's questions because he had no answers, Eridel instead said, "It is kept hidden; where it is she cannot go."

Kavan knew of such places, where artifacts of power could be hidden from everyone except those who were attuned to such things. The vault beneath St. Kóráhm's was such a place, but even there he had heard her belittling laughter. As strong as he believed her to be, infiltrating his thoughts and dreams with her presence, commanding armies and individuals to punish Kavan for crimes he had never committed, he fretted that there was no such place for artifacts to be kept from her. Perhaps she had not gone there because there had not yet been a reason to. It might only take Kavan leading her there to change everything.

But if she was unaware of this rumored relic, if in her cockiness she believed herself untouchable, then perhaps that was why she could not find or reach it. Perhaps she already knew of it, where it was, and believed it to be insignificant. Perhaps she believed that luring Kavan to it, to her, was worth the risk of the object falling into Kavan's hands.

"I was sent to bring you back with me…"

"You could have brought it…" began Rhyrdan.

"Risk losing it? Risk her taking it? He wouldn't allow it."

Even Kavan was not sure he would have taken that risk, the one Eridel asked him to take now. Men had died to get Kóráhm's cloak into Kavan's possession. Why subject others to a similar risk?"

"Where is it? Where must I…?"

"Many weeks from here…"

Frowning, knowing without looking at him that Rhyrdan was scowling too, Kavan shook his head. "I have responsibilities. War will be upon us soon and I must…"

"Between her people and yours. I know. That's why I rode hard to reach you in time. So long as she lives, there will always be those willing to obey her. She will never stop hunting you, destroying those around you to get to you. This war will be the least of her crimes. Decimation is what she does. Ruin follows in her wake. There can be no end to this cycle until she is stopped. It must be you."

Closing his eyes at the repeated press of invisible hands on his shoulders, Kavan fought the wash of fear, anger, and resignation that he did not want to feel.

He was only one man. How could he be expected to stop a war?

Rhyrdan began to stand, his face red with indignation and irritation, but Kavan's hand upon his on the table prevented it. Kavan had been seeking a way to find Bhás before war ensued. It would take several weeks before Enesfel's army passed beyond Fiara's boundaries and engaged Neth's army. If following Eridel took him to Bhás, trap or not, and he could stop her then, it was worth the risk.

"I will consider your proposition, but such a journey…it cannot be taken in haste. Such an absence cannot be decided on a whim." Not even if Kóráhm's touch prompted him to accept the offer and depart at once.

If he was going to face death, he was not going to charge into it like a jouster in a tournament.

"You shouldn't…" began Rhyrdan.

Kavan interrupted by looking back and forth between Eridel and the still-silent Sunna and saying, "Remain here; I will see to the cost of your room and have meals provided. The army is set to march in two days, and if I accept your offer, I will need time to prepare. I will send my decision. Do not leave this place, for your safety, and if she comes, if you see her…"

Though Eridel did not seem satisfied with such a delay, after traveling for so long, he nodded and muttered, "If she comes, you will know. She won't bother with me. She will come seeking you."

Refusing to be swayed despite his unrevealed trepidation and his annoyance at the risks Kavan was considering, Rhyrdan muttered, "Let her. We faced her once…"

Surprised to hear that, unaware that Rhyrdan had confronted her with Kavan before, Eridel stared. Rhyrdan's focus had been on combat with the man who ultimately killed Wace, but he had been there. He had seen their conflict. He had seen the outcome, Kavan's suffering. The memory of that suffering was etched into Rhyrdan's face more deeply than it was Kavan's, or else Kavan merely hid it better. With a skeptical expression, Eridel shook his head. "Your sword will be useless. I think the claim that only a waji can destroy her is a myth. It's folly. No weapon can touch her. If you survived before, it was because she allowed it. You do not want her here."

Kavan did not want her anywhere near his children, his grandchildren, his friends. If his destiny was to face her, it would be somewhere far away from Rhidam, Alberni, or Elyriá.

If he found her in time, before the first blood was shed in war, perhaps there would be no need for combat. Perhaps he could end this war.

"Stay here," Kavan repeated. "I will bring you my decision soon."

"We will wait," Eridel promised. This time he would not run. Even if Bhás came for him.

Outside of the inn, where patrons were beginning to straggle in seeking midday libation, Rhyrdan continued to scowl as they started toward the castle. "You should not do this…my father would say the same thing."

Kavan nodded. Wortham would have decried such risks, but ultimately, he would have accepted Kavan taking them, whether he approved or not. Kavan hoped Rhyrdan would likewise accept the inevitable, even if Kavan had not yet verbalized a decision, he, too, was reluctant to make. "I think I must. Until this is over, as long as she hunts me, I can never return Ágdhállán to Raebhá, can never see her again." He choked on the words but his steps did not falter, his shoulders did not sag. Raebhá would want him to do this. She would understand.

Bhás had birthed a Second Elyri Persecution, prompted a war, and caused Wace's death. He feared she had killed Myreth as well. "No more can die for me."

No more can die on Kóráhm's behalf, he thought silently.

The sense of Kóráhm's presence that had lingered like a blanket around his shoulders as they left the Eagle's Nest flashed with remorse and faded away. Kavan sighed with regret.

"Then allow me to…"

"This is not your fight…this is not a fight. This is to retrieve something that might help me with mine. I need you to stay with Ágdhállán. I need to be certain he is safe." If he was following Eridel to his demise, or even if he was able to return after a few days, a few weeks, or a month, he could only do this if the man he trusted most kept his sons safe.

Rhyrdan's terse expression did not waiver as they entered the keep. They spotted Bhríd through the open doors of the Grand Hall and when Kavan gestured to him to wait, the chamberlain paused.

"Promise me."

Still frowning, Rhyrdan began, "But weeks, Kavan…while we are at war? We cannot be expected to…"

"Promise me."

Hissing through his teeth, forced into a corner where he did not want to be, Rhyrdan relented. He could not refuse the bard's request any more than his father could have, regardless of his wishes. He could not disappoint Kavan. He would never forgive himself if he did.

"I swear to his safety with my life," he finally said.

"I pray it does not come to that." Kavan caught his head between his hands and kissed Rhyrdan's forehead tenderly. "I know you wish differently, but this time, you will have to trust me."

"I do trust you. It's him I do not trust." And her.

"He won't hurt me." He was not yet certain of that but he did feel it less likely than he had during the Festival of St. Mátán and the days immediately after. "See to Ágdhállán and I will come for you this evening."

He watched Rhyrdan stalk stiffly away and then joined Bhríd at the center of the hall. Bhríd did not ask about the tension between them except to say, "He is as displeased as the rest of us with this war."

"None of us are pleased," Kavan agreed. "Do you have time to draw up legal documents for me?"

"I can make time. What documents do you require?"

Kavan led him to the library. "Transferring property to Gorbesh…the heaviness of this war…have led me to consider the future dispensation of my properties."

"You're not riding into battle," Bhríd began. By Elyri standards, Kavan was still a young man. There was little reason for him to fear death, and decisions made now might not hold in the aftermath. "Have you Seen…?"

"No…but with the Sight showing me nothing certain…when war comes to Alberni…I want to be prepared. If Dhóri and I choose Gorbesh, if I return to Dhóbhaen, I wish Prince Jerit to have control of Alberni, duke in my stead if he will have it, and I intend Zerio to have control of St. Kóráhm's as a haven for the Vants…or whatever purpose he deems suitable. If they will not accept, both will be held in my name in case Dhóri or Ágdhállán wish to claim them someday."

"It is possible…or I will make it so," Bhríd promised, jotting down the details Kavan relayed to him. "And in Bhryell?"

He could not shake the feeling that Kavan was hiding something, but as the bard was not the first person to come to him with the desire to set their affairs in order as war hung heavier around their necks, Kavan's concerns were not unreasonable. Most of the remaining preparations were in the hands of others. Bhríd's had consisted primarily of arranging with Lorant and Níkóá the array of legal documents and decrees that would ensure the smooth ruling of Enesfel in the weeks ahead.

He had already settled his affairs in Levonne.

"Sóbhán and Bhen will, of course, have the right to remain where they are. That will not change."

"Good. We must think of our families."

"What about your children?"

"They will remain in Rhidam for the duration of the war…unless it is no longer safe for them. Should that happen, will you see to…?"

"I can take them to Gorbesh if you wish. Ágdhállán and Kaedís will go there at the first hint of trouble in Rhidam. There is plenty of room for your children. They will be safe there."

"Whatever you think best." He chuckled, a grim sound that made the room seem darker than the midday hour should have caused. "Phaedr wants to come with me, but I've already told him, told all of them, that war is no place for children. Cáym's content to be bodyguard to Ágdhállán and Ónyká wants to go wherever he goes. The disposition of the vineyards, the title, have been made in case…"

After his voice trailed off, Kavan shook his head. "I have no visions for you, Bhríd, beyond what I shared. I cannot make predictions and k'Ádhá has not seen fit to provide answers."

"No man knows his fate, except," his expression darkened, "you."

Kavan avoided the fishing-for-answers attempt and asked, "When will you have these ready?"

"By evening, barring interruptions. Bhyrhán and I are expected in Clarys tonight, or in the morning if the king needs me first."

"Then I will leave you to it; if you need me, I shall be here."

"I will let you read each when they are complete. They will be done before I leave."

He had not realized Bhríd would depart so soon. "Thank you." As he got to his feet he asked, "Have you seen Zerio?"

"Discussing the ramifications of Inness' resurrection with Asta and the king in the stateroom the last I knew."

He had heard the king's voice in the barracks upon his return so perhaps the inquisitors were in the stateroom alone. "I will seek him there first. Thank you, Bhríd."

But the stateroom was empty and enough responsibilities and interruptions arose throughout the rest of the day to allow Kavan to push his fears down so deep that he did not think about them again until darkness returned and his harp became his dearest friend as he sat alone on the oratory steps. He bid Bhríd a reluctant farewell as he and Bhyrhán departed through the Gate and was then forced to endure Ártur's pestering questions until Kaedís' demands took her father out of the oratory.

Now, Kavan was alone. He did not expect to remain that way.

He understood his cousin's fears, both of war and of never seeing Kavan again. It made the healer cling a little too tightly to his cousin, loiter a little too long, but each was set in their decisions. Kavan did not expect anything to change those now.

His fingers had just begun to seek refuge in the strings when the door opened again and, expecting Ártur had returned with some forgotten question, he muttered, "What is it, sínréc," with barely hidden irritation and without looking back.

"You've never called me that," Zerio chuckled.

Kavan looked at the lanky man with a self-conscious flush and bowed his head. "I thought you were…my thoughts were…I'm sorry."

"Don't be. I'm flattered." Whether the bard had meant the endearment or not, Zerio was happy to hear the word directed at him just once. "Chamberlain Cáner said you were looking for me? Association matters been keeping me busy."

"Another execution?"

Zerio sank onto the steps, stretched his long legs, and shrugged. "They're coming less now; things are settling. But it's gonna take time. Surprised this one was in broad daylight. Thankfully wasn't bad enough to ruin my appetite." He patted his stomach, reminding Kavan that he had missed dinner. "Rhyrdan said you have a visitor. Someone I should watch."

"That's not necessary. It does not concern you." He set the harp on the step. "I have made provisions, in case the days ahead take an unexpected turn…if the dedhá decide to stay in Gorbesh…or I do…if I'm unable to return to it, for St. Kóráhm's to be transferred to you."

Blinking rapidly, staring slack-jawed, Zerio shook his head and squeaked, "You're not going to…"

"None of us know what is to come. When the chellé is besieged, anything could happen."

"You said it will stand."

Kavan nodded. "I believe it will…but in what condition, I cannot promise. There will be funds for repairs. I have set it aside for the Crown to dispense to you for repairs or reconstruction if it is needed."

"I'm no dedhá. I'm no scribe. What am I to…?

"You're a man of learning, of history. You may maintain the library, refill it if you choose. I will make certain you receive copies of everything that was there before. Or fill it with Vants and turn it into a center of education. How you utilize it will be up to you, if that day comes. I only ask that you honor the graves, Wortham, Zelenka, and k'gdhededhá Tythilius…all the others but especially theirs. Protect them, cherish them, and the rights to the chellé will be yours."

Zerio studied the bard's face, his expression dark. "Have you seen your death, ágdháni? Yours or…?"

"I have yet to see specific death." There was a memory of a prone figure that lingered from the last vision he had Seen while in Dhóbhaen, a vision that had announced war with Neth long before that possibility had taken shape. But he did not know who that individual was or if they lived, and so he clung to the notion that no one he loved was going to die. Except, perhaps, himself.

"But one never knows in war." They were the sort of words Claes-Arne would have said and there was a prophecy waiting to be fulfilled. A prophecy that promised war and death.

It could happen to any one of them.

"If the day comes, I will see to all of them as though they're my own family. They'll be safe with me.

That promise was, for Kavan, good enough.

❧Chapter 33❧

The predawn sky was tinted gray and gold with the promise of a midsummer's rain as the courtyard filled with those about to ride to war as soon as the king gave the command. Kavan, again plagued by intangible sounds and scents without Sight to support or explain them, had stood in the center of it since the náós bells struck the first hour of the day, waiting with a heavy heart for the inevitable.

The accompanying musings about Eridel and the unidentified relic he spoke of were there too, but his thoughts were chased away when the first stablehands brought horses and wagons into the yard to await their riders and passengers.

k'gdhededhá Tusánt, dedhá Thrismund, and novices Hebel and Ybherd were the first to arrive, leaving their horses with an attendant and meeting dedhá Charlos at the door to speak in hushed tones together. It had been decided that the king and his men would benefit from the spiritual guidance and reassurance of the Faith and Thrismund was the only dedhá, other than Tusánt, to know the horrors of war, the only one to have wielded a sword in combat. Novice Ybherd was a restless youth with some medical experience, having spent his earliest years with his midwife mother on his uncle's farm tending to the medical care of goats and sheep and cattle. Hebel, the youngest and least experienced novice, had come into the Faith under Thrismund's guidance and it had been agreed that riding with the soldiers, tending to their spiritual needs, would give the youngster worldly experience that he currently lacked.

Whatever they discussed with Charlos, Kavan chose not to eavesdrop. It was none of his concern.

Bhetá, Raenár, and Balint were the first to emerge from the keep, the Daema showing her son how she stored her armor on her horse, how the weapons were secured, the health of the dark bay mare that she would rely on every day and the security of the tack and saddle, reassuring him that she would be safe and intended to return as soon as she could. Zerio came next, following Madoc through the palace gate looking for Asta; he nodded at Kavan and the bard nodded back. When Jerit and Gerna emerged, the prince holding Henrik and Ida's hands in his effort to keep distance from his wife, and Asta and Yóáná followed, Bhetá left her husband and son to speak with Zerio and Asta and Balint left them both to stand with the two who were closest to him in age.

He might often bully and belittle Neth's prince, but he understood that at this moment, they had more in common with each other than with anyone else in the courtyard. Princess Hella, escorted by Aunes, the host of Elyri healers and Kaedís MacLyr, joined them, though Ártur left them to speak with Kavan, his dragging steps and sagging shoulders making him look weary and troubled.

"You sure you won't come?" he asked without meeting Kavan's gaze, instead watching Lorant, Seren, and Níkóá who were the last to emerge into the mist that began to form. The three stopped long enough for Lorant to grace his queen with an affectionate embrace and lingering kiss upon her mouth, murmuring something that made her nod before he left her to take the reins of his favorite mottled brown and gray gelding from a groom.

Jerit looked at Lorant when he came out but quickly turned his attention to admonishing his older half-sister to take care of their mother and nephew in his absence. Though his head did not turn, he tracked Lorant's movements across the yard, refusing to exhibit jealousy, undue attention, or disappointment when Lorant did not look at him in return.

They would have time without familial incumbrance. This was not the moment to demand attention. Gerna, clutching his hand as she wept forced tears for his departure, threw her arms around Jerit when Lorant strode by and turned his body so that he was facing away from the king as Lorant picked up Hella and carried her, leading his horse to where Níkóá now spoke with Zerio and Asta at the edge of the group. Ida followed. Jerit extracted himself from Gerna's embrace and squatted down to Henrik's level to share departing brotherly advice.

He would do everything he could so that one day Henrik would sit upon the throne he was promised.

Henrik did not want to let him go.

Kavan noted each interaction, and the lack of them, tucking each face, each moment, each barely heard discussion into his memory. "If you are having a change of heart, it's not too late to say so."

Ártur shook his head. "They need me. As they do you. Your presence would be good for morale."

"Theirs or yours?"

"Everyone's, but especially mine." Their closeness had ebbed and flowed over the years as life and its responsibilities shifted and demanded their diverging attention, particularly after Kavan had become a father in addition to bard, scholar, tutor, duke, and royal advisor. Sometimes Ártur wished he could return to the days of Kavan's youth when they had been closest. But that perceived closeness had come at the cost of Kavan's emotional isolation from those who should have been there for him, Ártur included. Now that Kavan seemed balanced, centered, and usually content, wishing for anything different made the healer feel guilty and selfish.

"I can't shake this feeling," he shivered. "What if we never see each other again?"

Masking his mirrored thoughts, glad he had not told Ártur that Eridel was in Rhidam, and had said nothing to him of Bhás since the prospect of war had emerged, Kavan gave a scoffing huff. "Where am I going to go?"

"Might not be you. Might be me."

Kavan frowned. "You're not the only healer, and you will be protected. You will live to see your children again, sínréc."

"Are you sure?"

"I have faith."

For Kavan to have faith in anything was reassuring enough for Ártur. His shoulders relaxed as he bent to scoop up Kaedís who had left Syl when Yóáná had come to her side. Kavan was grateful Ártur did not suggest that seeing his children again was not the same as seeing Kavan again. The healer merely took the two outcomes as the same fact.

Kavan doubted he would see any of these faces again if Bhás was at the end of the journey he and Eridel were going to make.

"You'll keep them alive, won't you, k'bhydhá," the girl asked with her head on her father's shoulder. Her eyes were teary but she did not yet cry.

"That is why your mother and I are going. You'll stay with Kavan and do everything he, Yóáná, and Aunes tell you, right?"

"I will," she agreed softly.

"A word, Kavan." Lorant's interruption forced Ártur to step aside and return to his wife as the king, with his hand on the bard's elbow, drew Kavan further aside. Kavan expected Lorant to likewise plead with him to reconsider joining the caravan north, but instead, he lowered his head and asked, "Anything new? Have you Seen or…am I doing the right thing?"

As level-headed and diligent as Lorant had seemed over the last several days as war preparations consumed his time and attention, it had been too easy for many to forget that he was little more than a boy. At fourteen, Lorant should not be riding into battle. He had many with greater experience around him, however, and Kavan reminded himself that riding with the troops did not necessarily mean joining in combat.

But he would. Kavan had Seen it. There was nothing he could do to prevent the inevitable except lock Lorant away from the world, make him ill or incapacitate him in some way…or find Bhás. The first option would produce fear and unrest and was not open to serious consideration. He had to let the young man go and pray the fates of his father and grandfather were not to be his as well.

Or he had to face Bhás before the battle was met.

Refusing to be embarrassed, Kavan embraced Lorant as he often had when the king was a child. "I have faith in you. Your father will be with you, your grandfather…and all the Lachlans before them. I will bid Kóráhm and Dhágdhuán and k'Ádhá each morning and night to watch over you and those with you, to bring you home safely. It is the most I can do. I believe they have heard my pleas. I believe they will shield you and be on our side."

"I pray you are right. I will continue to pray too…and hope they hear me as they do you. You will aid Níkóá? Keep Enesfel safe?"

I will do everything I can." The strangled words came from a heavy heart, a morose sound that Lorant interpreted as Kavan's grief for watching another Lachlan head into war.

By now, every soldier who would ride out of Rhidam's keep sat on their horses, waiting for their king's order. More would join the troops waiting at the northern edge of the city under General Declan's command while tama Kaj collected those from the south to join them there. Once the king arrived, the entire force would ride north. The wagon containing the healers had finished loading and Jerit gently pushed Gerna away a second time with barely disguised exasperation; he passed Kavan to take the reins of his horse from the stable hand holding them and brushed his hand over the bard's bare wrist to bid him a silent, heartfelt farewell. It was the first time Lorant looked at Jerit and after a nod, the two men mounted their horses and turned their noses toward the drawbridge.

"May k'Ádhá sweep the road of your enemies," called Tusánt with his hands raised, his palms facing the group. "May the Intercessor ride beside you and shield your ranks, and may Saint Kóráhm," he paused to look at Kavan, "see you safely home."

"May the záryph shower you with peace, comfort, and blessings, and grant your souls bravery and rest," added Charlos, his expression less jovial than usual.

From his grizzled brown horse, Thrismund adjusted the hood of his traveling cloak as the mist of the promised summer storm turned to drizzle, and ended the blessing with, "May the hosts of Ethenae, the souls of those who have gone before, and the spirits who move among us grant us compassion, keep those we cherish in the bosom of their mercy, and protect us with their love as we seek to do the same."

Every voice around Kavan responded, "Let it be so," as he held tight to those prayers, closed his eyes, and cast them out again so that the power he put behind them would broadcast them ever louder to every divine entity who might be listening. The clatter of hooves on the courtyard stones and the creak of wagon wheels made him lift his head, open his eyes, and watch every member of the group depart through the gates and across the drawbridge as he had once watched Owain depart from Rhidam. He remained there still and silent, long after the quietness of absence settled over the courtyard along with the falling rain.

A hand in his broke his vacant contemplation, the boy who had not been here earlier beaming up at him with a warm serene expression that unexpectedly dispelled the darkness from Kavan's soul.

"Let's take Dhóri to Bhryell," Ágdhállán said. "I want to see my brothers."

Kavan squeezed his hand and nodded. Such a distraction was precisely what he needed.

Eridel would wait a little longer.

❧Chapter 34❧

"I wish you wouldn't do that," General Waller snapped at the woman who appeared without warning in the bedroom doorway of the lavish Ruidoso home he had felt it his right to claim after reclaiming the city for Neth. He had returned here a mere three hours earlier from his tour of some of the forest ambush sites, having spent long enough to appease his empty belly, quench his thirst for spirits other than stale ale, and change out of his sweat-stained travel clothes before falling into immediate sleep as soon as he hit the bed.

There were no traces of sunlight through the east-facing window, so he assumed no more than an hour had passed. He was unshaven, unwashed, naked to the waist, and his eyes were bleary with interrupted sleep.

Bhás, on the other hand, looked as though she had been awake long enough to greet a new day with unnerving strength and confidence.

Those details annoyed Waller nearly as much as the intrusion did. He had not seen her in weeks. He had hoped she had retreated to whatever hole she had crawled out of.

"They are coming," she said evenly, her typically bored, aloof tone colored this time by a glimmer of feral anticipation.

"Who?" Rolling over to force himself to sit, he refused to look at her again. He had no interest in guessing games.

Ignoring his bitterness and bile as she appraised his sturdy, battle-scarred chest and shoulders, she said, "Prepare yourself. Ready your men."

His feet hit the floor. "Speak plainly or let me sleep."

She smiled, a bemused, sinister, seductive expression that made him purse his lips and press his legs together as if to avoid temptation. "Do not disappoint your king, General. Do not disappoint me. When we see each other next, I expect the head of Enesfel's king in your hands." She looked him up and down again and then backed out of the room, closing the door without laying a hand on it.

Waller's frown deepened.

The death of the young king would be a blow to her foe. He would be easier to reach than any of the bard's family. Lorant's demise would incapacitate Kavan long enough for her to strike when his guard was down. Beyond that single use, she had no interest in the Lachlan king, Enesfel, or anyone else. War was a diversion, an amusement, but it would have its uses.

What Fraen and Waller did with the gifts of territory and resources she offered was none of her concern.

❧ * ❧

"bhydáni Tíbhyan passed here," Kavan explained as he sank against the tree in the place where the ancient bhydáni had expelled his last breath, leaving Kavan to face the world without his steadfast guidance. His sons sat with him, Sóbhán swirling a short, fallen branch in the bubbling spring while Dhóri sat against the tree on his other side, his face tipped into the dappled sunlight. Ágdhállán sat at his feet where he could see the others, his small hand pressed into the fallen leaves and needles as though to read invisible details in the earth. They had talked as they wove through the forest, Dhóri describing Gorbesh to Sóbhán and Sóbhán discussing his daughters and whether he should serve Bhríd as a soldier.

It was said a larger than normal contingent of men was to be stationed in the fortress at the head of the Rísóri Pass. Though Kavan had never been there, he was aware that the foliage, the landscape, fit within the parameters of what he had Seen. It was not so far from Bhryell, though difficult to reach, and thus the most likely place where an army invading from Neth could try to breach Elyriá's interior. It was the nearest passage from the Llaethlágárá into Neth. It was the place a tactician such as Bhríd would choose to make a stand.

Ágdhállán had not spoken the entire walk; he seemed engrossed in collecting seeds, leaves, and stones, examining the flora and insects of this unexplored forest which was much different than he was familiar with in Alberni or Rhidam.

The familial sharing, something Kavan had missed out on as a child, made him grateful that Ágdhállán had asked for this time together. After so many farewells that morning, Kavan had not realized how much he needed to reconnect with his children. His decision had been made. He had until morning to depart with Eridel. He would enjoy his family, share dinner with his sons, Bhen, and his wife, and then return to Enesfel to spend time with Rhyrdan too.

He wished Earé was here to share it with them.

"When I came to Elyriá?" Ágdhállán asked, speaking for the first time as he stuffed his collected riches into the cloth pouch at his waist.

"Yes. You stayed with Sóbhán while I…"

"Did you see it?" interrupted Dhóri, tipping his face beneath the sun's rays. It was not raining here as it had been in Rhidam.

"No, I think I dozed…or perhaps it was a trance. When I opened my eyes, became aware, he was gone."

Ágdhállán looked up from the caterpillar he had found that was crawling across his hand. "You buried him here?"

"No. He was gone. Body and spirit and.,." Curiously, Kavan leaned forward and pressed his hand to the ground next to Ágdhállán's. A surge of power, as strong as any ancient relic or holy symbol, rushed up his arm and filled his core, making the pendants against his chest throb and vibrate in a harmonic hum. He understood the question.

He could feel Tíbhyan there too, as though the sage had never left this place or had left enough of himself here to be identified by anyone who cared to seek him or notice.

Kavan's heart ached to think that perhaps Tíbhyan had waited here for the last ten years for communion with his favorite student. He wondered why he had not noticed it the last time he was here. He wondered why he had not come back sooner.

"You can reach him from here. You should…before…" The boy's voice trailed off. Sóbhán and Dhóri faced each other as though to study their faces, even though Dhóri could not see him.

"Reach him?" Kavan asked.

"Our brother."

Scowling, considering the viability and wisdom of attempting it, aware of the eyes upon him as he curled his fingers into the leaves before withdrawing his hand, Kavan eventually shook his head and leaned back against the tree. Ágdhállán spoke often of the brother he had never met, the son Kavan had never seen. This was no revelation. Nor was it a mystery why Kavan had not tried to go back to Dhóbhaen. Whoever the enemy was that he refused to lead to his wife and youngest child, they agreed with their father's protective decision.

"You do not need to be afraid for us, k'bhydhá. We understand."

Assuming the boy with the Sight was referring to their father's inevitable choice to return to Dhóbhaen, Sóbhán nodded and murmured, "Of course we do."

Kavan believed his talented son meant something much different. The little redhead, however, changed the subject by getting to his feet and saying, "I'm hungry. Should we go back now?"

With the promise of a family meal waiting, they had not brought a midday repast with them. Kavan had not eaten since the day before. He did not feel like he would ever eat again.

"So am I," agreed Sóbhán, ruffling the boy's hair as he too stood up and dropped his stick next to the water.

Tempted to tell them to go without him, desiring a longer communion with the shade of his bhydáni now that he knew he could experience that comfort again, Kavan reluctantly got to his feet and pulled Dhóri up with him. "Nóráh will appreciate our help," he agreed. Even if that help was limited to keeping Maelís and Ydrís out of the way until Bhen got home.

❧*☙

Unwilling to sit a minute longer, Lorant made a circuit with his generals and tama Kaj through part of the camp, stretching his legs and back, only to return to the campfire some of the men had built for him when the smell of food drew him back. He groaned as he sank next to Jerit and tried to get comfortable, but every position he tried made his buttocks and thighs scream in protest.

"I can ease your pain," Ártur offered, having left his campfire and the company of the other healers when the limping young man returned from his rounds.

"Didn't think riding could be…" Lorant began in protest, waving the healer away.

"You've never ridden all day?" Kaj asked sympathetically.

Despite years of physical activity and challenges of strength, speed, and endurance, rather than admit to a failure he had not anticipated, Lorant accepted the ladle of stew into the bowl he had rummaged out of his pack and slid awkwardly to his side, his torso propped on his bag so that he could hold the bowl in one hand and eat with the other.

He did not think he had ever tasted anything so savory.

"There will be others who need your attention more," he groused, surprised that Jerit did not likewise appear to be suffering. But Jerit had made multiple journeys between Rhidam and Alberni with Gerna and Ida, riding beside the carriage rather than enduring the woman's company inside as she wished.

Jerit gave a small understanding smile and pressed his water skin to Lorant's lips. "You'll get used to it. It will take a few days…and those days will be miserable…but you'll adjust."

"Before or after we get to Tarsee?" he groaned.

"Before…hopefully," Jerit assured him.

Ártur smiled sympathetically, clasped Lorant's shoulder, and said, "Summon me if you change your mind," while conducting enough healing energy through the touch, without being noticed, to cause Lorant a sigh of relief that he attributed to the stretching of his legs and the press of his foot against Jerit's thigh.

"I'll be fine," Lorant insisted.

"And if not, I'll hold you down so he can help," Jerit teased.

Lorant made a face and continued to eat. Jerit patted his ankle and chuckled.

❧*❧

Rhyrdan was on the front oratory bench, leaning with his hands clasped between his knees, staring at the carved figure behind the altar when Kavan and Ágdhállán returned from Bhryell. He did not speak to Kavan's nod as the bard escorted his son to his room, did not follow, only waited until Kavan returned to pray as he assumed he would.

The king and his army were gone. There was no obstacle to accepting Eridel's proposed journey to discover an object that might not even work against the woman troubling them. Rhyrdan had made a promise, but the possibility that the white-bearded man might be leading Kavan into a trap would not leave his thoughts. He should be going with him. He should not allow Kavan to face his fears alone.

He should be with him the way his father had always been.

"I know you want to come." When Kavan sat on the altar steps facing him, his harp tucked beneath his arm, Rhyrdan left the bench to sit with him, his back against the altar, eager for a closeness he knew he was going to miss during the weeks he expected the bard to be gone.

Rather than engage in an argument he could not win and ruin the time they had together, Rhyrdan grunted and asked, "Have you told Lord McCábhá and Lord Kaas your plan?"

"Not yet." He intended to do so in the morning, before going to the Eagle's Nest, or perhaps tonight if either or both found him here. They had been told of his day trip to Bhryell to see his sons. They had no reason to expect to see him until morning.

"Don't imagine they'll be any happier about it."

"Perhaps not…but they will understand the desire to seek an early end to the war to limit the loss of lives." Thankfully, serving as regent was a familiar experience for Níkóá. Kavan would not consider leaving him unsupported if he was not confident in Farrell Lachlan's son. He would have Asta, Zerio, Madoc, and the rest of the royal advisors to assist him. He would have Rhyrdan. Níkóá would manage Rhidam and Enesfel as judiciously and wisely as he had ever done.

"Ágdhállán knows?"

"He does." Kavan turned so the harp could rest on his knees and began to pluck softly, his fingers in search of a melody befitting his restless, troubled spirit. "He told me not to be afraid."

"Are you?"

"Of Eridel? Of this journey? No. Of meeting her again…" He sighed and allowed the black kestrel harp to express his fears, finding ease in Rhyrdan's company while wishing for someone else's.

He lost track of time, of the sense of everything except music, of the brush of wings against his skin, and of the shift in Rhyrdan's breathing as the younger man drifted into slumber, shifting, sagging until he lay prone next to Kavan. He wondered if he should wake him, encourage him to sleep in his more comfortable bed, but having him there was reassuring and so Kavan let him sleep…until another presence entered the room.

His fingers stopped moving. He hung his head to avoid knowing if Kóráhm was with him in the flesh or spirit only. Either was welcome, but tonight, he worried that looking into the saint's eyes might confirm his deepest fears.

"Will you go with him? Eridel?" The saint's voice was fully audible, not an echo inside Kavan's head, and he shivered.

"Do you think I should not?" Kóráhm did not reply, waiting instead for Kavan to answer the query he had posed first. "I think I must. If I don't, if there is something that will help end this without…"

The words dying stuck in his throat. Kóráhm's hand covered his upon the harp.

"I did not think of it sooner…but in earnest, I did not think it existed any longer."

Kavan raised his head. "What? What is it?"

The saint shook his head. "What it could be…I may not speak its name lest she hear me, but you will know it when you see it. Even in my day, there were rumors, tales…I did not think…"

He stopped speaking and lifted his scarred hand from Kavan's to stroke the head of the carved black kestrel.

Kóráhm's belief in the power Eridel offered was promising but it did not purge Kavan's fears of leaving Enesfel for so long. "Can you promise Ágdhállán will be safe until it is over? That Dhóri and Sóbhán…Earé and Raebhá and…" He shuddered. "I accept the shadow of death but…"

"You fear you will die while…"

"Can you assure me I will not?"

When Kóráhm did not reply, Kavan nodded. They had both known his fate was sealed long before this night. Long before he had been born. Such an assurance from Kóráhm would have been a lie.

But it would have made Kavan feel better long enough to leave his family behind.

"With her out there, with war…if I'm to leave for an untold number of weeks, I would like to know that those I love will be safe until it is done."

"Who said it will take weeks to…?"

"Eridel said…"

"He traveled for weeks, but he is not like us. He is not you. He directs…but you lead."

As abruptly as he had arrived, Kóráhm was gone. Rhyrdan had not stirred during the exchange. Perplexed by the saint's words, Kavan gazed at the pyre figure, studying the Intercessor's injuries as he pondered what Kóráhm meant, ignoring the throbbing in his wrists and ankles and trying, unsuccessfully, to ignore the trickle of warming power that passed through his head, through his heart, and into his hands. It was a different sort of gathering power, the power of miracles, a sensation he had not experienced in a long time, but gradually, the pull of it, revealed what it meant.

He could construct a Gate.

Wherever Eridel wanted to take him, he could get as close as possible through the generation of a Gate and make it to his destination and back again, taking little longer, he hoped, than it would take to recover from the creation process.

Did he trust Eridel to protect him that long? If this was a trap, he would be at the mercy not only of Eridel and his companion but possibly the one who wished him dead.

Choosing to believe that Kóráhm would not have suggested it if he thought Kavan would emerge from a Gate into a trap, Kavan set his harp beside Rhyrdan, kissed his dark, unruly curls with a whispered, "I am sorry, sínréc; this cannot wait," and went to Ágdhállán's room to kiss his forehead as well, to stroke his cheek and clenched hand with unspoken promises he prayed he would be able to keep. The boy, too, did not wake, though his fist did unclench as the power collecting in Kavan's touch bled into him. His breathing softened, Kavan kissed him again, and then he was left to rest.

The power strengthened through that touch. He clasped the door frame and let the spark he carried go. It did not diminish then either, but Kavan believed, as he closed the door, that so long as his son was in this room, Bhás would not be able to touch him.

No one passed in the corridor as he retrieved the pack Rhyrdan had made from the dresser in his room. The night was quiet, the pall left by the departed king and his retainers sucking the sounds of the night from every corner, creating a more stifling sense than the summer's heat did alone.

He was grateful he had left his bedroom window open.

He peered inside the pack again, assessing its contents, considering if anything was missing, if there was anything he had forgotten to request. There was food and coins, a knife, clothes, and a small collection of jewels and objects of value, should he need them to trade for something he did not have. They might not be necessary, as he could trade music for anything required, and the food might not be needed either, but better to have it than not. It was not worth taking the time to unpack and leave them behind.

He only needed one other thing.

Pack on his back, wooden case beneath his arm, he chose not to leave the keep through the doors or through the Gates where someone might be able to report his departure. He had not yet spoken to Zerio or Níkóá. Rhyrdan would have to do that for him.

"I am sorry, Rhyrdan," he said to the air before taking to the sky with the much-needed energy release the kestrel's wings provided. Rhyrdan would find the open window. He would know where Kavan had gone. How he explained Kavan's absence would be up to him.

Unable to enjoy flight as he wanted, he circled the Eagle's Nest to locate Eridel's room and reached out with tendrils of power to wake the man once he was found. It was Sunna, rather than Eridel who rose from his cot on the floor, pushed open the window further, and peered outside. When he saw nothing of note, he turned back toward his bed, only to jump, startled, when the white kestrel flew into the room and landed on the floor just beyond his reach. He snatched up the waji from the floor as Kavan resumed his form and stood tense and wary with it pointed at the bard's chest while he stared with disbelief.

The only other waji Kavan had seen belonged to Wace. Rhyrdan kept that curved blade protected and always polished and sharp. This was not the same blade, however, for there were large pearls, the diameter of an Elyri bhelt, on either side and end of the hilt. Its creator had been a man of wealth.

Or Sunna was.

"Apologies. It was…" Not necessary, as he could have entered the inn like anyone else, knocked on their door, or summoned them downstairs, but each step felt to be a delay he did not want to endure. Having made up his mind to act, trying to keep the miraculously given power at bay he believed was meant to propel him to wherever a new Gate would take him, he did not want to allow himself the chance to change his mind.

Sunna's abrupt movement, the hiss of the drawn sword, and Kavan's voice brought Eridel awake, backed into the corner with his sheet drawn up to his chin as though it would shield him from an attacker's blade. It took his sleep-addled brain longer than normal to identify that there was no threat, but that initial fearful shock was replaced by amazement of another sort as he recognized who stood in the room with them.

The door was closed, the window open.

Had he climbed through the open window?

Kavan gave Eridel an apologetic nod and said, "If you wish to take me to this individual you speak of, I will go with you, but it must be tonight."

"It's dark…there's thieves and…" muttered Eridel. He did not know the time, but traveling on foot in the darkest hour of night seemed a foolish risk, regardless of the many rumors about how Kavan might keep them safe.

"There will be no need for them. If you would permit…if either of you can conjure the remembrance of this place we must go, or somewhere near to it, I can take us there tonight."

"Tonight?" Eridel slid out of bed, grabbed his trousers from the chair, and tucked his shirt, the only item he wore, into them. "That's impossible."

"Do you trust me?"

Given how abysmally he had once treated Eridel, there was little reason the other man should. After Eridel's attempt on his life, after nearly killing Rhyrdan and then fleeing the bard's effort to win his forgiveness rather than subject him to King Merrek's punishment, there was little reason for Eridel to trust that Kavan would not somehow seek revenge.

Only the sincerity of the voice behind the question and his belief in why he had come for Kavan to begin with made him nod reluctantly as he shoved his feet into his worn, hard-soled shoes."

He nodded with a glance that prompted Sunna to sheath the waji and gather up two packs that were significantly bigger than Kavan's.

It was only then that Kavan noticed Sunna was already dressed.

"It's taken a long time to…but yes, I trust you," Eridel stammered.

"Perhaps this will help." Kavan offered the wooden case. Dressed now, his expression flustered, Eridel took it without opening it.

"You keep offering…it keeps coming back to me…"

"It's yours. I have no right to it." The first time he had kept the red kestrel harp as a reminder. The second time he had kept it safe in the belief that Eridel would return for it someday.

That day had come.

From his pouch, he left additional payment on the nightstand, a supplementary amount offered as apology for the abrupt departure of the guests. The upper floors were quiet except for the sounds of snoring and sleep mutterings, and no one was in the tavern downstairs except for a brutish fellow the innkeeper had retained to protect the premises and the guests. He looked at the three departing men with marginal interest, less concerned with them leaving so long as they took nothing with them, than he was about someone coming in the middle of the night. He noted the White Bard among them and let them leave without a word. Kavan paused long enough to listen to the street sounds, to gauge if there was anyone near enough to cause trouble, and to stare briefly at the walls of the keep.

The night was crisp and clear. The previous day's light rain had ended and the puddles left behind had nearly dried. The guards at the castle gates could not see them, would not have recognized them or paid them any interest when they headed toward Hes á Redh.

Unaffected by Kavan's confidence as they walked, Eridel shuffled as close to Sunna as he could without tripping over the bigger man's feet. Sunna strode with his hand on the waji hilt, his brow furrowed as though concentrating on the dark streets, doorways and alleys or in ponderance of Kavan's entrance into their room and the things he said and suggested about travel. Having only seen the exterior of their destination when they had traveled through Rhidam earlier, Eridel for a second time, both men stared in awe at the náos interior lit with candles at prayer stations and by oil lamps that glowed above the altar and cast slithering, writhing shadows toward the door where they entered, the doors to the right that led to the gdhededhá chambers and offices, and to the left where the curtains of the Purification Chamber hung open to indicate there was no one hidden there.

There were no dedhá in prayer at this hour. If anyone was awake, they were in their rooms seeking solitary communion with the divine.

"This way."

Both expressed anxiety in their rapid breathing and the hesitation of their steps when Kavan entered the Purification Chamber and offered each of them his hands. With the thickness of their packs and Sunna's great size, the three barely fit, but they did reluctantly join him though without taking his hands.

"Can either of you show me where we must go, where the one we are to see resides? Where the relic is located?" he asked, his hands still open.

Eridel shook his head no, not understanding what Kavan was asking or what he intended to do. What he did know was that Elyri could read thoughts through a touch, and he was afraid of what the bard might see in his head. "No one must…it must be protected. He must be kept safe…"

"Somewhere nearby then, somewhere private and secure where we will not be seen or interrupted or cause fright by our arrival. Do you have an item that will guide me?" The additional power he contained that bubbled and sizzled in his hands reacted with the power of the Gate, causing it to flare and wrap around his legs like fast-creeping vines. Sunna felt it too; his eyes were wide, and he stared at his shuffling feet seeking what he felt.

There was nothing there.

Eridel tugged on Sunna's sleeve. "Your home? It is empty…it is safe…a few days away on foot…"

A few days' walk was better than weeks. Kavan looked at Sunna.

Sunna scowled and met Kavan's gaze with narrowed, searching eyes. Hearing the man's broadcasted thoughts, unfiltered and directed at him as if he had no control over them or had stopped trying to hide them, Kavan nodded. "It will be safe. There will be no harm to either of you or your home." There would be an unavoidable trace of power remaining, a new Gate where one may not have been before, but if they were lucky, Bhás would not be able to detect it without knowing where Sunna called home.

After sweeping his curls from his face with both hands and adjusting the pair of packs on his shoulders, Sunna removed a carved pearl from around his neck and placed it in Kavan's hand, shuddering with the unexpected flash of power that passed between them when their fingers made contact. "Your hand, please." Sunna again hesitated but decided the bard seemed safe enough. He covered the pearl in Kavan's hand with his own and closed his eyes as though the darkness behind his lids made focusing on the memories of home easier. Eridel's hesitation was a little longer, but eventually, with a constricted whistle of air between his teeth, he accepted first Sunna's empty hand and then Kavan's.

With the circle complete, the power of the Gate beneath their feet flared, warping the air around them, creating a dizzying ocean wave effect that Kavan recognized from his previous efforts to create new Gates. In his mind, with the pearl serving as his portal point, he followed Sunna's thoughts through the maze of a small, arid home until he located the most plausible location to travel to…what appeared to be an open-aired courtyard full of flowers and vines and fragrant herbs, and then focused all his power there as though digging down into the earth. The pendants on his chest grew hot against his skin, threads of power wove back and forth between where he stood and where he needed to be, and when at last he believed that a stable connection had been generated, the miracle power erupted forth, spilling light from the Purification Chamber into the náós, generating an audible insect hum that chirped, pulsed, and then was gone, taking the light and misty waves of Gate power with it.

Moments later, his breath ripped from his lungs and every bit of power he contained burned out of him, Kavan's feet regained purchase on solid ground amidst a violent gale and pelting rain. The pearl clattered out of his hand and across the stony ground and the world went dark.

❧ 381 ❧

Part 2

&Chapter 35&

Jarred out of her open-eyed meditation by a wrenching of power that felt like a punch in her stomach, like the first powerful twisting of birth, Bhás spun from her cross-legged position to face the direction the sensation originated from. South. Shiirjaj.

She pinched the bridge of her nose and squeezed her eyes shut. She could not pinpoint him, did not know where in the labyrinth of a coastal city he might be, but she knew he was there. She expected him to find her eventually, and Shiighrjaj was a start…but not yet. She was not ready.

Too far away to feel her, however, and for the moment her sense of him felt scattered, a disarray of fractured, incoherent power. She remembered that perception of him from their previous confrontation. Something to do with travel, a weakness in utilizing Gates that made him vulnerable.

Not knowing why he was in Shiirjaj, what could have drawn him into her world, she pondered going to him, finishing what she had started. There would be no need for armies then, no need for a foreign war meant as a distraction, a thorn in his side. She could leave those inconsequential lives to decide their fates and keep the promise she had made to the ancestor.

The recent expenditure, however, hands-on directions given and his jarring outflow of power, left her disoriented and weakened too. It would take time to rebalance herself, just as it would him. Time, she had, judging by the traces of him that blew to her on the wind.

Whatever he sought, he was not going anywhere yet. She had time.

&*&

It made no sense to the Cordashian captain commanding the kingdom's northmost border fortress, perched atop a hillock clearing that permitted them a fortuitous line of sight across the tops of the thinning mountain forest towards the plains of Neth. The shouts and pealing of alarm bells that roused him brought with them the spilling of hundreds of men out of the forest towards their walls in the darkness of pre-dawn. There was enough time for the host in the fortress, those already at stations, to charge out to meet them, time for others to take their places on the walls and in the parapets with longbows and swords, time for the gates to be fortified to prevent infiltration of their shelter and possible loss of the region's border defense.

There had been clashes between scouting parties for weeks, the murders of many sent to determine where the enemy was camped, how many men were there, what sort of threat they posed. From their incomprehensible chatter, it was obvious that most were not Nethites.

Perhaps that was why they foolishly charged the tall walls of a structure that provided Cordash the high ground and protected the border road that enabled monitored travel between the kingdoms.

The high-ground advantage was a match for the mass of foreigners with swinging swords and stabbing tridents who, despite their frenzy, succeeded in remaining beyond the range of the Cordashian archers. A few men took their shots. Sometimes arrows found their targets. Other times they fell their comrades, until the order was given to ceasefire and leave combat to the men already caught outside of the closed fortress doors and the men preparing to join them.

By the time the sun broke the horizon, where its summer brightness hindered the Cordashian army, bodies littered the hillside and the foreign force, despite the advantage of numbers and rising sun, retreated into the cover of the forest. Those still alive limped between the dead, the dying, the injured, killing the enemy, pulling their own toward the fort where others dared to come forth to retrieve those in need of medical care. The captain watched them come in, counting, judging, and when he dared to go out amongst his fallen, he counted them too, with his young squire taking notes on a piece of parchment stretched taut over a thin slab of wood.

Their losses were heavy. They would need to beseech King Govert for more men. But the enemy had suffered considerable losses of their own and Cordash had, for now, prevented a Nethite incursion.

A distraction, he wondered, or harassment. He picked up one of the short, curved swords, split-tipped with both sides of the prongs sharpened to deadly points, and barbed on the outer edges, the sort of weapon, he surmised by the injuries he saw, meant to thrust and twist to maximize internal damage and pull organs out of the body when withdrawn. There were also shorter curved blades, thick near the hilt, perhaps as long as the sole of his boot, not seeming adequate for combat but used effectively against those unfamiliar with them.

"Collect everything that looks like a weapon," he grunted to a nearby trio. "Bring them inside. Collect the dead…and watch your backs.

The foreigners would not have forges to replace lost or damaged weapons. Keeping every weapon they found out of the invaders' hands seemed like a prudent course of action.

As for tending the dead, that might have to wait. He did not know how long they might have before the next attack came.

❧*❧

"Lady Earé, we were not expecting you."

The march to Tarsee had been accompanied by hot weather once the rain in Rhidam was left behind, and Lorant had, by the third day, accepted Ártur's offer of relief to make the day-to-day journey on horseback tolerable. By the time they reached the outskirts of Enesfel's northernmost uncontested city, he barely noticed the discomfort any longer.

He had become too engrossed in unconstrained banter with Jerit, without wives or children or the thoughts of war ahead of them, to dwell on the persisting pain.

Men from the western reaches of Enesfel, from Durham, Erleta, and the communities between, as well as from Bryn and the villages along the river and lakeshore to the north, had amassed at Tarsee to await the king's arrival before sunset eleven days after leaving Rhidam, a great number of men that bolstered Lorant's confidence as he got down from his horse to greet the ethereal woman who stood at the edge of the field as if also expecting their arrival.

He looked to see if her father was with her.

She was alone.

Kaj was the first off his horse and was already on one knee before her, clasping her hand between his and pressing it to his bowed forehead with murmured words Lorant had not heard. When a nearby eruption of loud laughter among men who were glad to stop riding for the day caused Lorant's horse to skitter and he caught his foot in the stirrup, Jerit caught the animal's head and kept it steady as Lorant, too, glanced around in the hope of seeing the White Bard here.

There was no reason he should be, but as the healers disembarked from the wagon, and Ártur saw Earé, he too bustled over with stiff-legged steps, expecting good news and the company of his cousin.

"I had not anticipated being here," she admitted warmly, laying a hand on Kaj's head, prompting him to rise with the hand he clutched. "I have…you will not object to my company as you continue north?"

"You are welcome to join us," Lorant agreed with a smile, offering his hand without expecting a kiss of respect on the royal ring. "You will be safe with us, and I'm sure Lord MacLyr," he glanced at the healer who stopped beside him, "welcomes your company as well."

Kaj snorted and chuckled. "I have seen the lady with a sword, Your Majesty. She will not need our protection. Our opponents would be wise to stay out of her way."

Lorant's smile faltered. "You do not expect to…?" He trusted Bhetá on the battlefield, but having women in combat was not normal. If anything happened to Earé, Kavan would never forgive him.

"Does this mean Kavan…" began Ártur with concern.

Earé shook her head, selecting her words judiciously. "He will not join us. This is not his place, but his prayers are with all of us. Do not fear, My Lord, I can defend myself. I would not be here if I expected to be a burden."

"You have brought us more men." Jerit gestured to the men camped around them, where Garran and Bhetá had already found the officers and lords in charge.

"I had no hand in that, but it is good they are here. I have arranged for the replenishment of food and other commodities we need before crossing the forest. We will need to be cautious; there will be traps." She looked smug, pleased with herself for taking away Bhás' element of surprise and Lorant smiled, deciding to set aside his reluctance to put Kavan's daughter in harm's way.

He would deal with that when it became necessary.

"I would expect as much, but thank you for the confirmation."

"Will you join me?" asked Kaj with an offered hand and friendly smile. "It will do the men good to see you."

"I will come to you after I share dinner with aendhá Ártur."

The address made the healer grin unexpectedly but it also creased the corners of his eyes with worry. She had never called him that before, and during the times she had come to Rhidam, she had spent her spare moments with her father and brothers. Seeking the company of kin made Ártur feel appreciated and momentarily relieved some of his concern about Kavan.

But he also worried, as he steered her toward the cookfire Healer Ylltán was building while Syróa and Tisá prepared vegetables and bits of salt pork in the pot being readied for the fire, that her desire for his company spoke of some foreboding path ahead.

Lorant feared that too as he reached for her arm as she passed. Jerit's hand on his shoulder kept him from reaching her, and Kaj's serene acceptance of her choice kept him from pursuing questions she did not seem inclined to answer.

"I'm hungry," Jerit said, swinging down from his horse. "Let us see to the tents while we have daylight and hear what the generals have to tell us. We need a count. We need to see to the distribution of forces. I'm sure the lady will join us when she can."

"I assure you, she will," promised Kaj. Everything k'ílshwythnec did was on her terms. The woman would not be rushed. If there was something she wanted him, or Lorant, to know, she would tell them when it was time.

❧*❧

"Good, you're here." Fraen waved his son into the Black Room where an unfamiliar soldier with a lieutenant's insignia on his tabard and a likewise unfamiliar captain were seated at the table with equal expressions of grim obedience and eager determination. Olaric had put off the summons as long as he dared as there had seemed no urgency to the message he received, but seeing the three gathered now, he wished he had come sooner.

The king did not seem angry at his tardiness, but rather appeared smug and self-congratulatory in his posture. Olaric took the empty seat at the far end of the table without speaking, but he did nod respectfully and rest his forearms on the table wondering what he had missed.

"We've dealt a harsh blow to that wandought Govert; they'll think twice about interfering again," Fraen said with a triumphant snort. "They shall be so occupied defending their borders they will not have the opportunity to come to Enesfel's defense."

"It has begun then? Enesfel is…?"

"On their way, I'm sure. General Waller's messenger says as much." He waved offhandedly at the smooth-faced almost too young captain who nodded in agreement. "But we will need more soldiers…"

Not knowing how Emil could have proof of Enesfel's movement without spies of his own, when Olaric's Vants and Association spies had not reported that news to him, Olaric frowned. "We're already overrun with mercenaries. Our army is strong. We have conscripted nearly every fighting man in the land. Who else is there? If we enlist those who are left…"

"It must be done, for the good of Neth. The order's already given."

"What order?"

Fraen brushed aside the inquiry with the same dismissive hand gesture and resumed his dialogue with the pair of officers, promising additional men, discussing the needs of those already deployed, offering direction on how and where the troops should be located and how they should be utilized, details hastily recorded by the steward bent over the wooden podium behind and to the left of the king. The sheepish man never looked up from his task, despite Olaric's efforts to catch his gaze, to seek answers in the meek man's eyes.

He would need to find his answers elsewhere.

When the king finally dismissed his visitors and left the Black room in search of a late evening meal, an indulgent practice Olaric despised, ignoring his son as if he had forgotten he was there, Olaric waited in the room long enough to be confident his father would not return before leaving the table. He should waylay the steward and demand a copy of the man's notes, but that might tip his father to his intent. But he remembered the important points well enough to convey them to a spy, a messenger, someone who could get the king's plans into Enesfel's hands.

There was one more thing he needed.

Further proof of the increased military might his father intended to engage. If Waller had ransacked the southern villages and farms and pressed the able-bodied men into service, as Olaric expected, Enesfel needed to know they could trust no one south of Lake Curo. Not even the women and children left behind.

"Good day, m'lord," Captain Sparding said with a nodded greeting as he passed from the castle gate on his way to deposit his horse with the waiting stablehand.

"Been away?" Olaric accepted the reins and gave them to the boy who offered a mumbling bow and hurried away with the horse.

"Around the inlet. Posting the king's decree, getting word out."

"What decree is that?"

Earon's awkward mien did not change. "He did not tell you?"

"He doesn't tell me much." Sometimes Fraen spoke and behaved as if he trusted his son to know everything. Other times he treated him as though he did not trust him at all.

"He's recruiting…"

Olaric nodded. "I told him there are no more men to spare…"

"Not men." Sparding's voice dropped to a whisper. "Boys, anyone over ten…so long as they are not the only son in the family." He nodded at

Olaric's stricken expression and was about to continue when another soldier across the courtyard called out to him and waved for him to join him.

"Inzigaen?" The Child Army had not been called up in more than a century, since the people's rebellion had deemed the practice a horrific tragedy. He could not believe his father would bring the practice back. Then again, he could believe his father was capable of anything. "I'll let Geiel know if he doesn't…"

"Maybe not yet, but he will soon. I must…"

A pair of soldiers passed, there was no suspicion in their gazes as it was known to all that Captain Sparding and Olaric the Younger had known each other for nearly two decades. But Olaric could feel the prick of another set of eyes on the back of his skull; he did not look to see if the sensation was real. Instead, he offered a gentlemanly handshake and a smile. "Good day to you, Captain," he said before continuing on his way.

Kes would be waiting with dinner and he had to check on the queen-regent to see how she was faring. More importantly, he had to find Geiel to deliver much-needed details to Enesfel. There was no need to write down the details of the king's conversation.

Geiel could remember it all.

☙*❧

The discomfort of the sultry air that clung to his skin was lessened by a cooler sea breeze that blew from his right, from the direction of the rhythmic pulse of surf breaking against stone. The smell of salt, the burden of fish and beached plant life, confirmed it was a sea and not a lake, unless it was a very large one, but Kavan was reluctant to open his heavy lids to gaze into the morning sun he could feel upon the left side of his face. His stiff body ached and the power within ebbed and flowed in time with the surf, reminding him of where he had been, how he had gotten here, of the newly created Gate and the men who had traveled with him.

He was alone now. Wherever he was.

The gentle swaying cloth cupped around him suggested a hammock as if he was on a ship at sea, but he was surrounded by an array of unfamiliar floral smells, the scents of damp stone and earth, unknown spices and herbs, complementing the breath of the not-so-distant sea, aromas that spoke of being on land rather than on a boat. Voices chattered in the distance, strange words in a singsong modulation unlike anything Kavan was familiar with. When the throaty claxon clatter of a bell somewhere near the sea split the air and echoed loud enough to make his head pound, Kavan abandoned his slow waking effort to open his eyes with a groaning sigh.

Above him stretched a striped canvas-like fabric of blue and white, supported on each end by a poled contraption meant to adjust the covering for maximum shading at any hour of the day. Curious to study the mechanism more closely, he sat up, put his bare feet on the floor, and discovered that he wore a loose, flowing, gauzy robe much like those he had seen Cíbhóló nomads wear.

He remembered the howling, stormy gale that had assaulted him as the new Gate deposited him in this place. His clothes would have needed to dry, and respecting his privacy by not rummaging through his pack, someone had provided these unfamiliar garments to provide him decency while lying on the rooftop of what he assumed was Sunna's home.

The flaring power of the Gate sizzled at the edges of his perceptions, near enough to verify that he had not been taken far from it, near enough to support his perceived location.

How long?"

On a short table nearby, woven of wicker reeds, a platter beneath a wooden cover provided garlic cheese, olives and apples, strips of savory goat, and an unfamiliar tea laced with honey. Realizing how hungry he was, he devoured it gratefully as he listened to the voices, trying in vain to identify the words or the accent, and stared at the mountains visible to his left. The sun was rising there, meaning this sea was in the west. There were portions of Elyriá, Hatu, and Cordash where the sea bordered a western coast, and much of the Káliel islands were the same, but the details he noticed as he finished eating and moved with slow, aching steps to lean against the low wall boxing the rooftop terrace, told him that this land was none of those.

The pestering question of 'how long' switched to 'where' as he looked away from the mountains towards the tall wall separating the western edge of the city from the sea. Between the mountains and the sea spread a swath of single and double-story structures, most with the same rooftop terrace, most with short-walled garden courtyards. Many were butted together to share the same upper terrace. There were a few taller, bigger buildings, palaces or places of administration or worship, perhaps, that he could not study from where he stood, and he guessed, from the direction of the loudest collection of voices, that a centralized market was somewhere to the south.

Curious to explore, hoping to find either of his escorts in the rooms beneath his feet though he did not sense them, Kavan replaced the lid on the platter, opened the reed-covered hatch that exposed a wooden ladder into the home's interior, and climbed down in the hopes of finding his clothes. As comfortable as the robe was, as familiar as the movement of fabric was, it was an uncomfortable reminder of the white robes he had long ago left behind.

Sunna had worn trousers and a tunic. Kavan hoped he would not break any local taboos by dressing in his own clothes.

The house was empty. The lower level consisted of raised bed mats divided between two rooms, a narrow table that also functioned as a counter for food preparation, four wooden chairs weathered and worn with age, and an array of barrels and crates, hanging herbs and flowers, and a wood and wicker chest upon which his pack sat against the wall, unopened, protected from the elements that might come in through the open windows and doors, each covered with sun-bleached fabric that flapped and fluttered in the breeze. Touching his pack, Kavan determined that no one had been in this room in days, but may have come and gone from the courtyard to the terrace on the stone staircase he had seen outside. He had been in this room long enough for the storm to pass, long enough to leave his imprint of power in the air, but then he had been taken to the terrace and left there.

He might have been alone for days, but the freshness of his meal suggested it had been there no more than an hour or two.

Again, he wondered where and how long.

When he was dressed in his own black trousers and white shirt, frowning at the way the humidity made the thicker fabric stick to his skin, he went into the courtyard and stood upon the Gate to assure himself that he could go home this way when the time came.

Rhidam was there, in the pinpoints of lights behind his lids. Bhryell and St. Kóráhm's too. All the familiar destinations he expected to find were touched one by one…including, he realized with a start, the Gate that would take him to Raebhá if he chose to use it, somewhere to the west…not to the east as he expected.

He frowned, cocked his head, and opened his eyes, trying to push the swirl of longing out of his head by rubbing the marriage mark on his hand and focusing on the floral vines that climbed the crevices of the stone walls and wrapped around the pillars that supported another stretch of striped fabric in front of the door. They grew from pots and boxes along the walls and in every corner. A long cistern glistened with recently collected rainwater. Yet his thoughts would not remain focused on his immediate surroundings, demanding answers instead that did not wish to wait for

Eridel or Sunna's return. There was only one way he was going to learn what he wanted to know.

This city at mid-morning awaited him.

Unsteady on his feet, the weakness of an undetermined number of days in the hammock creating slow, stumbling steps, Kavan moved cautiously beneath the narrow stone arch where a trickle of water ran and followed the pull of voices into what he thought would be the heart of the city. Buildings of yellow stone with open lattice shutters that allowed the sea breeze inside and expelled the aromas of cooking, of onions and garlic, bread and fragrant meats, to swirl. The streets seemed designed to take advantage of the ground's natural slope to provide drainage towards the sea wall or east toward the mountains. Short bridges crossed the stone-lined ditches and ponds to provide building access. Fountain cisterns dotted every available corner or nook. Unlike Sunna's home, in most places as many as six structures shared a central courtyard and water sources so that the cityscape was dotted with circular clusters of homes. Many of the courtyards contained open aired carts, tables, or tents where goods were being sold, most often jewelry, cloth shoes and sandals, wide cloth or straw woven hats, scarves and shawls, and protective eye coverings of wood or bone with narrow slits to reduce the glare of the sun's reflection off the water. Sleeping mats, hammocks, and fishing nets were offered, as well as an array of basic tools required for everyday survival, few of them designed as Kavan was familiar with.

Some were reminiscent of goods he had seen in the lands south of Hatu, in places like Pa'aliaka and Gorbesh. Others were like goods provided to the Sovereignties by the Cíbhóló. But this was neither of those places. He listened to the speech of those he passed, swarthy, dark-eyed men and women with black or dark brown hair who mostly moved away from him and eyed him with fear and gestures he interpreted as protective measures to ward off evil. He sought any commonality in the language to build a translation on but without resorting to the use of power to touch someone and open a communication link, he did not understand anyone.

He was used to people finding his white skin unsettling. So long as they did not turn on him with violence, their evasion was better than any manner of religious fawning and fervor. He could live with being an outcast. He did not want to live with being considered a divine manifestation.

There was little power here. Muted flashes here and there, sources he sensed in passing but could not identify. These Teren, with their curly, wavy hair and black powder that adorned their lids and encircled their eyes, with their long-sleeved, close-fitting knee-length coats with stand-up collars that buttoned on the side or long, loose-fitting dresses and robes that flowed softly around their ankles, bore much in common physically with both the desert dwellers and the people south of Hatu. But Kavan did not think they were either one. They were their own stock, or else a combination of the two who had developed centuries ago just as the dhóbhaen had done.

But it did not explain where he was.

In no hurry, with only curiosity and the eventual need to find Eridel and Sunna to guide him, Kavan stepped into an oval-shaped plaza filled with farmers' wagons full of grains and fruits, and pens with sheep, goats, and pigs. The chatter of transactions assaulted his ears, a pleasant, hearty sound that carried the undertones of the Festival of St. Mátán and others attended over the years. Those memories brought with them the desire to play, to win over this avoidant crowd and find welcome in this place, but he had no harp to do so and he worried that his androgynous timbre would be as unsettling to them as his appearance proved to be.

Laughter, derisive and sinister, an increasingly familiar sound that carried with it a warning, echoed in his ears, his head, close enough that he was certain the source was within striking distance. The air turned cold around him as he spun toward the sound, scanning the crowd for the woman he expected to see as his heart hammered with the certainty that coming here was a trap. For a moment he saw her, a misty, indistinct form with a bitter, haughty expression, but the crowd's movement swallowed the vision before it could materialize. Someone pushed past, causing him to stumble as the imagery of a curved dagger dripping with blood seared into his brain, making him dizzy and nauseous and causing his skin to itch and burn as though blistered in a fire.

His knees never hit the ground.

Grasping at hands that caught his arms and kept him on his feet, he looked at his savior as he steadied himself and choked on his breath, the act creating an aching pressure in his chest. Her hair was slightly longer than the others, her skin more golden than swarthy, her belly heavy with a late-stage pregnancy. But it was the healing power in her touch and the deep amethyst of her eyes that demanded his attention.

k'kairá?

The word echoed in his head as did a concurrent series of images…a birth, a death…power in the desert…blood and rebirth. Before he could ask the questions aloud, her name, who she was, he heard someone call to him.

He turned toward the voice.

Eridel.

Her hands fell away.

When he looked toward her again, she was gone.

"You shouldn't be alone," Eridel said as he reached Kavan and, with a hand on his arm, steered the bard in the direction of Sunna's home. "Hair and skin and eyes such as yours…they are taboo here…seen as a curse…"

"Did you see her? Who was she?" The consideration of his appearance being a curse went unobserved.

"Who?"

"The woman who…with eyes like amethysts…the k'kairá?"

"k'kairá?"

Kavan sighed and shook his head. It was impossible to describe or explain a mythological people few had ever seen, that no one had ever proved existed. With so many people around them, Eridel might not have seen the one who had come to Kavan's aid, and depending on where he had spent his childhood, he might not be familiar with the mythos of the phae k'kairá. After Bhás' laughter and the flashes of Sight…the dagger and blistering heat, it was possible the other woman had not been present but was also a manifestation of the Sight.

He did not know what any of it meant.

"One of us should have stayed with you," Eridel muttered, thinking the bard delirious.

"I'm not…how long was I…?"

"Six days. We feared you were harmed, that something was wrong."

"I should have warned you. The creation of a Gate takes its' toll," he explained with a headshake. Typically, he was incapacitated for nearly two weeks. He could only attribute the shortened duration to the miraculous power k'Ádhá had seen fit to bestow beforehand.

Eridel shivered. "It was…never before have I…do you do it often?"

"Create them? No. Travel through them. Yes. Travel is less demanding than creation."

"Creation is often difficult," Eridel agreed. "You are recovered?"

"I will be." His legs were still shaky, made more so by the unexpected encounters in the plaza, and the brief city excursion had made him weary, but he expected he would be well enough to travel as soon as Eridel said it was time. "I…where are we? I do not recognize these people…their language…this place," he said, changing the subject to avoid talking about himself. Their location seemed more pressing.

Only Bhás proximity was more important. Because he did not feel her any longer, he did not believe she had ever been there, had only been a vision in his mind's eye.

"They call themselves Shiigh, this land Shiighr…"

"Like shi cali?" he murmured, taking that connection as the first step towards building a language.

Eridel nodded and steered him around a street corner; Sunna's home was now in sight. "I have heard the Cíbhóló use that term. Yes, we are west of the desert."

West of the desert.

It had long been said there was trade to be had if one crossed the desert or made the dangerous trip by sea through the volcanic islands along the north coast of Cordash. Few dared to try. Those who did never returned. But perhaps, he mused, ships from Pa'aliaka could make a southerly journey to reach this place. Perhaps that was the reason for the similarities.

"How did you find your way here?"

"Bhás."

Kavan's expression darkened. Eridel shrugged.

"This is not her place; she is not welcome here. But in my wandering, in my efforts to satisfy her requests, I traveled through Shiirjaj, "He gestured at the city around them, "many times. She would not come here…as if there is something that repels her."

"The relic?"

"Maybe."

"Will you take me to it?"

"This evening, when Sunna returns. The day is hot; early evening will bring rain. When it stops, we can leave. It will take the better part of a week, less if Sunna charters a boat and we follow it upriver as far as we can."

"You said hours…"

Having believed the journey on foot would be a matter of hours instead of days, he muttered, "Less is good." He did not want to spend any more time than necessary on this task. Each day he spent here was one in which Bhás might catch up to them and make their efforts futile.

If she had not found him already.

Eridel nodded as if agreeing with the urgency of Kavan's unspoken thoughts. "There will be hours on foot, in the forest, and up the mountain, but it can be done. You will have what you need."

Hearing Bhás' laughter in his head again, feeling the cold foreboding he had felt before, Kavan nodded, and prayed that Eridel's words were true.

<h1 style="text-align:center">❧Chapter 36❦</h1>

"**Y**ou promised!"

Olaric dodged the empty ceramic bottle and refused to flinch when it shattered against the closed door behind him. Inness slunk back as he set the basket of food on the table as though she expected him to attack, holding her hands out as though wielding a sword to strike.

He shook his head with a sigh.

"I will keep that promise…"

"You said you'd bring my son! You said he will have the throne!"

"He will. You will. We are coordinating safe transport for him. We want him protected, want him close so that as soon as Fraen's removed, Prince Henrik can be installed on the throne. You will have to be patient until he arrives."

"You'll bring him to me, right here, to me."

"Or I'll take you to him, whichever location is safest for him. These things take time. You don't want him ambushed by ruffians or killed by the king's spies, do you?"

"He's not the king," she spat. Several emotions played across her face, frustration, fear, fury…and finally, reluctant determination. "Soon." She lowered her hands as if lowering her sword, and her shoulders sagged. "His father wants him safe. I do too."

As it was not the first time she had spoken of King Oska as if his words and wishes still applied, Olaric did not question her. If the late king had been here, he would, indeed, want his son safe. In whatever afterlife he watched from, he undoubtedly wanted the same thing now.

❧*❦

Driven to intoxication by the king's most recent proclamation and the consequences he foresaw for so many of Neth's boys, it was too easy for

Marta to lure Earon into the alley nearest the tavern, where whores serviced other men in the flickering of the establishment's lamplight, and allow her to seek satisfaction in ale-kisses and his broad hand that he pushed under her skirts between her legs. With his back pressed against the wall, despite his slurred protests as she slid her hands and mouth down his body, despite his attempts to push her back without hurting her as she unfastened his trousers, he did not have the will to deny the satisfaction she offered that would help him forget. Whether it was the alcohol, her skill, or his long pent-up longing for her, the interlude was over too soon, and once she straightened her skirts and fastened his trousers, he was left alone, slumped there, weak-kneed and breathless. He would have given her anything she desired if she had turned around and come back to him.

꘎*꘎

Driven by a pole against the rushing current, Sunna maneuvered the flat, narrow barge along the black, white-capped river after an exchange of coins with a man at the edge of the city. The fellow eyed Eridel and Kavan with a suspicious scowl but made the exchange after Sunna's unspoken promises. Eridel's white hair and beard were excused by age, but they had taken care to cover Kavan completely so as not to invoke superstitious curses. Once beyond the city where they could no longer be seen, he lowered the hood of the cloak he wore so that he was no longer stifled by the damp night air.

They skirted the border between miles of farmland and a forest of trees Kavan could not identify. There were few in the fields at this hour but those they saw, men ferrying felled logs down the river toward the city passed near enough to see him and repeat the familiar protective gesture and hastened to put distance between them.

No one spoke.

They took turns steering the boat while the others rested or slept, shortening their travel time by the hours they would have otherwise lost in setting up camp or finding shelter on the shore. By the morning of the third day, the river turned into the forest, and when they at last reached a broad waterfall that tumbled out of the hills and sharp mountain peaks beyond, they were forced to tie the boat to a tree on shore and begin the rest of the journey on foot.

No one would touch the boat, Eridel promised, pointing to a small metal placard upon the surface that indicated the boat's owner. It would be there when they returned.

Unfamiliar pines, broad-trunked trees bearing fluffy white seedlings like cotton, twisted trunked scrub like the cedars in the forests between Tarsee and Fiara, thinned over the next six hours until they were left with only the sparse mountain pines on the near-barren mountain face. There was a path, narrow and worn, steep enough to suggest that it was not often traveled by any except the hardiest or most determined souls.

As he followed Sunna, with Eridel coming behind him, Kavan became aware of the sort of power that sprang from an ancient, natural source, something born in the earth or perhaps created there centuries ago as he had found in the snow-covered mountains in Dhóbhaen. It gave him something to focus on other than the ache in his legs and back, something to serve as a beacon to encourage him forward when he wanted to sit down and never move again. When Sunna eventually tapped his arm and pointed to a structure built into the face of the mountain, like the Gorbesh shrine only much smaller, Kavan assessed it to be a hermit's hovel or the refuge of a religious recluse like Qol or an Elyri acolyte. Or perhaps Kóráhm awaited them there. He paused to look across the land below, seeing only the sea of green boughs lit by the dawn's light creeping over the mountaintops. He could not tell how high they had climbed or how far they had traveled. He could not see the river or the distant walled city and the sea. Wearily, when Sunna began to climb again, Kavan did likewise, wanting no more than to sit in that place of power and seclusion and send musical prayers to Ethenae for keeping them safe as they climbed.

When they finally reached the weather-stained wooden door, Sunna knocked once, the sound like a hollow echo into an empty void, and then entered without waiting for a response, ushering the others in as he held the door open. When they were inside, he closed the door and dropped his travel pack from his shoulder.

The room they were in appeared to be a kitchen, with an iron pot and empty spit over a fire that provided the only light in the room, perfuming the air with a slab of meat that dripped its roasting juices into the pot of spiced beans. A tray of mixed seeds and nuts, its warm contents steaming the room, sat upon a small, three-chaired table, and by the door behind them, canvas and leather sacks hung on pegs. A broad spade with a splintery handle, a straw broom, and fire tongs rested in the corner nearby.

There was no one in the room, but the sound of dripping water with the hissing of wind beneath it echoed from someplace unseen. The room smelled pleasantly of cooking, of the presence of Teren bodies, of past consumed alcohol, and recently dried clothing.

"Cloak," Eridel instructed, removing his to hang it as Sunna had done. By the time he took Kavan's from him and added it to the others, a faint set of shuffling steps was heard beyond the mouth of one of the two tunnel openings on the opposite side of the room, bringing with it the bobbing of a portable light.

There were no interior doors that he could see.

"Sunna! Eridel! You have returned."

The stooped woman who set her lamp on the table and embraced the much bigger man, with her gray hair and pale brown skin of mixed heritage, looked withered, weathered, and not in a condition to have climbed the mountain to get here. Her kaftan and apron were faded and stained, not often cleaned, and her cheeks were ruddy with the relative haste she had taken to greet them. She spoke with breathy relief and affection and kissed his cheeks when Sunna bent down to her, as a mother might welcome a son, and then gave Eridel the same embrace without the greeting kisses.

"Is this the one? Is this the man he sent for…wants to see?"

Eridel gestured Kavan forward. "Yes, Dola. This is Kavan Cliáth." He did not call him the White Bard. Kavan appreciated the courtesy.

Dola looked Kavan over with silent scrutiny, showing none of the fear and mistrust others had offered. She took one of his hands, turned it front to back and front again while Eridel and Sunna moved their packs to the floor beneath the hooks. "There are tales of ones such as you," she clucked with a smile. "I never thought to see you with my own eyes."

"I doubt there are many like me," Kavan admitted, weary from the climb and trying not to eye the chairs in the hopes of sitting. There was no power in her touch, but her fingers bore the stains of years of medicinal preparations, the way the hands of so many Teren physicians and apothecaries were stained.

"How is he?" Eridel asked quietly.

"Sleeping. He's been anxious for your return; too many restless nights. Last night was the worst; maybe he knew you were near. Sometimes," she looked at Kavan, "he knows things…as I'm told you do. He's had so much lavender tea I sometimes fear he will sleep without waking."

"If he's asleep, we should leave him to it. We've traveled long to get here. I'm sure Lord Cliáth will appreciate a place to rest." He grinned. "I know I would."

"As would you," Dola chided, hooking her arm through Sunna's and steering them to the split tunnel. "Sunna, see him but do not wake him. You two, come with me. This evening, when he wakes, you can visit him.

Sunna nodded but did not move as Dola led Kavan and Eridel down the other corridor.

❧*❧

He was there…and then he wasn't.

The cards spread on the table, the scatter of knuckle bones and teeth, the curling of incense smoke that she stared at until her eyes burned red and teary, told her that her senses were accurate. She had thought he would come to her, follow the thread she had laid down in the market plaza, but instead, he had fled east and then…nothing.

Her fist closed around the silver blade until the blood dripped out between her fingers onto the blank parchment, splattering, seeping into the porous surface to spread into a pattern she could read, her last immediate option to locate her prey.

He was not there.

He was not dead, she knew that. He was too much of a coward to avoid her by taking his own life. But he had gone somewhere, performed some ritual magic, that had taken him beyond where she could feel him…

…just as he had before.

Growling in frustration, she chose to play a card she had not intended to use yet.

He would know. He would feel it. And he would come.

❧Chapter 37❧

"**L**ord Cliáth, come."

Kavan rubbed his eyes, roused by the knock on the door of the room he had been given, a room barely wide enough for the narrow cot and bedside stand it contained. He was provided with a candle in a sconce which had burned long enough for him to settle in the stale-smelling bedding. Without a window, with the door closed and the heavy silence created by the stone walls, he had endured a restless, disconcerted sleep and felt barely rested as he pulled on his boots and followed Dola's bobbing lantern to the main room and into the other passage.

The nature of the room and the more than a dozen similar closed doors they passed in each corridor supported his suspicion that this had been a religious retreat, but there were no clues on the stone walls or dusty wooden doors about who had resided here, when they had done so, or why they had chosen this place and then abandoned it.

He did not see Eridel, did not see Sunna. He presumed both were asleep, though he did not know what hour it was or how much time had passed. His internal clock suggested six hours, but without the external validation of sun or moonlight, he could not be sure.

Dola did not speak as though she was afraid to break the silence, as though the walls demanded they be still. When they reached the end of the corridor where the last door was slightly ajar, she knocked again, and a feeble, cracked voice beyond bid them enter. She pushed the door with her free hand, gave Kavan the lantern, and gestured for him to enter a room he could already tell was larger than his. The interior was steamy, fragrant with mint and unfamiliar pungent aromas, none of which were able to mask the smells of a body reaching the end of its life.

The sagging, wrinkled face with its halo of sparse hair nearly colorless in its whiteness, turned toward the footsteps and the glow of the lantern, but Kavan knew immediately that the elderly man did not see its glow.

His breath caught in his chest and he nearly dropped the lantern. "gdhededhá Urian?"

The fleshy man smiled. "You remember." He was heavier than when Kavan had last seen him, his legs and feet puffy and purple, his stomach distended from something other than overeating. He held out one hand, coughed, and pressed his other fist against the center of his chest as if the dry fit pained him. When he spoke, it was obvious his throat hurt too, but that discomfort did not stop him from smiling. "I feared you would never come, that Eridel had failed to find you."

After setting the lantern on the nightstand, Kavan clasped the puffy hand between his; his heart leaped within his chest to have that physical verification that this was no figment of his imagination." "But you were..."

After the ambush by the Corylliens on the road between Levonne and Rhidam, Wortham had followed a blood trail into the underbrush at the side of the road where it appeared the blind monk had crawled or been dragged. The dedhá had not been there. It was assumed the hunting dogs that were part of the attack had dragged him away or that the Corylliens had a hidden accomplice who had not entered the fight, someone who could have taken the portly man while Wortham was preoccupied with Kavan's injuries.

"Dead? Yes, well, I thought so too...until she came." He suppressed another cough and squeezed Kavan's hand as though seeking and finding comfort in the White Bard's touch.

"She?" Kavan's eyes narrowed and his lips pursed, expecting that the man's next words would confirm that this was a trap the dedhá had been forced into participating in or had been unwittingly manipulated into. Bhás had saved Eridel for her purposes after all. It was easy to believe she had done the same with Urian. The dedhá, however, continued to smile without any expression of duress.

"Lady Orynn, who else?"

Again, Kavan's jaw dropped in amazement, and he struggled to breathe against the increased pressure within his chest.

"Or..." She had been there? Though unconscious, he wanted to believe he would have felt her if she had been with them.

"She bent over me, her hand against my face...that voice..." His own trailed off wistfully until he choked on another cough and gestured for water from the cup at the bedside. Kavan helped him drink, and returned it to its place beside the steaming bowl in which leaves, seeds, petals, and a glob of pasty white substance floated. Urian coughed again and shifted his weight on the lumpy mattress before continuing.

"She brought me here, brought Dola to tend my wounds…insisted I remain hidden, safe, for my own sake…for yours." He moved against the thin pillow behind his back and nodded gratefully when Kavan adjusted it. "I didn't mind. I'm a simple man of Faith. With you, I'd had enough traveling. I'd seen enough, done enough. I didn't expect to be here so long. But Dola has been good to me; we've been a peculiar family, she, the boy, and I…I would have gone mad without them and my devotions."

He gestured to the shelves on the opposite wall with their bundles of scrolls housed in wooden tubes tied together with a cord of dried, braided vines, brittle when Kavan got up to touch them, seeking any impression that had been left upon them, expecting what he had been sent here for to be among them. He Saw Dola's hands, Sunna's, and on two of the loose tubes, Eridel's, the author, the recorder, of every story Urian had shared. There was a faded, fragile bound copy of St. Kóráhm's first volume, a book of prayers he knew Urian had carried though he could not read the words, and on the shelf below, a leather-wrapped collection of whittling tools and a multitude of carved figures, one left incomplete on the day he had become too weak and unsteady to continue the work.

How devastating that day must have been, and every day after it.

"Is she…did you ever see her again?"

With his back to the bed, Kavan murmured, "I did not. She…she died giving birth to a son…and a daughter…"

"Yours?"

Relieved by the lack of judgment or shock in Urian's voice, Kavan replied, "Our daughter is k'ílshwythnec in her place…our son serves in St. Kóráhm's chellé hábhai in Enesfel."

"You must be a good father."

"I try to be. I made mistakes, but I do my best."

"We all do," Urian said tenderly. "The captain? Zelenka?"

The timing of his question coincided with the location of Wortham's likeness among the crafted figures, an armored soldier with his sword in his hands, the tip of the blade touching the ground between his feet in a posture Wortham had often taken when protecting him. His hand closed around the figure, and he returned to the bedside chair with a groan. "Both gone now…but their children remain, his gift to me."

"Children are k'Ádhá's blessing. I am grateful there was Sunna." He covered Kavan's curled hand and said, "Keep it. He would have wanted you to have it in remembrance…I want you to have it."

Unable to let the carved figure go now that he had picked it up, Kavan pressed his closed fist to his heart and asked, "Is he your…?" There were no physical similarities between Urian and Sunna, and none between the big silent man and Dola. Nor did he think Urian would have broken his vows. But the passing decades and his isolation here might have changed Urian just as the passage of years had changed Kavan.

"A foundling, a cast-off. Dola was there the night he was born; his mother left him in a basket in a cistern to be drowned in the rain." He frowned at the memory and coughed, the sound rough, dry, and painful as it brought trickles of blood to the corners of his mouth. Kavan wiped them away with a cloth from the nightstand. "She brought him here and he stayed with us until it was his time to go into the world…when he brought Eridel back to me. They've been good to an old blind man, better than I deserve. It was hard to send them away…they were gone so long looking for you."

"I have always been in the same places…"

"In Rhidam, yes; that is why I sent them there. But that was a long time ago…and I know he feared seeing you again." Urian fumbled for Kavan's hand and clutched it tight. "She left something for you the last time she came, something I was told to give to you when it was time. After everything I have seen, after all that she had done…the miracles…who was I to refuse k'Ádhá's bidding?"

"Time for what? How did you know? How can you be sure?"

"Eridel came. The záryph spoke in my prayers and sent him to me…then bid me to bring you here. I needed no more signs than that. I don't…" As he spoke, his face began to turn gray, his voice thin as he struggled for breath before his raspy voice gave way to a fit of harsh coughing that brought Dola immediately into the room as though she had been waiting outside the door.

"Leave us now; let me tend him."

"I must know…" Kavan stammered, alarmed that he had found Urian only to watch him die, to be directed here for something he did not yet possess and might never obtain if the ailing man died first.

"He needs rest. Send Sunna. He knows what I need."

Kavan backed out of the room, holding his breath, grimacing with every cough Urian made, praying as he retreated in the dark that he had not arrived too late.

❧*❧

"What do you think it means?" Lorant whispered to Jerit on the horse beside his, following behind the generals and Lady Earé as Enesfel's troops entered the forest that once served as the Neth-Enesfel border. The healers' wagon and others laden with supplies followed, the rattle and clatter of the wheels drowning out some of the droning thunder of footsteps that came behind. Lorant had not seen much of the enigmatic woman who spent her days walking amongst the men in camp, speaking to them, smiling, leaving peaceful expressions in her wake, like a záryph amongst mortals...

...the way Kavan and his music would do if he were with them.

Earé's effect on his forces, the boost to morale, and the reassurance she offered were much needed and welcome, but Lorant worried, as the darkness of thick trees consumed their column, that the effect and her purpose for traveling with them were meant to mask an unfortunate truth the Seeress was unwilling to voice.

That would explain the occasional pensive narrowing of her eyes, pursing of her lips, and the tension in her jaw when he noted her staring west. He had thought she was waiting for something or that some threat would emerge from Tarsee, but the glances continued as the sun climbed higher and they left the city behind and nothing else had changed. Whatever she was seeking never emerged, but it had not deterred her from continuing to look for it.

Now the sun was no longer visible, except for scattered white and orange fingers that clawed between the boughs, taking the stifling heat of the fourth day of Eltail with it as Lorant tentatively clung to calm.

"I think it means she is loyal to those who follow her," Jerit replied warmly, patting the king's shoulder, hoping to lighten his mood. Most often, Lorant was the jovial one, the one eager and optimistic and open to adventures. Every day of their journey north, however, darkened that confidence, replacing it with a growing understanding of the path he had chosen. Jerit did his best to bolster Lorant's spirit and would have done much more to distract him if not for the keenly felt eyes of the royal force, watching not with judgment but with the hope that their king was making the right choices for the survival of Enesfel.

They expected Lorant to be wise despite his youth. They expected him to be strong.

It was not an easy burden for a young man of Lorant's age to bear. Jerit would have taken it from him if he could.

"Do you think she'll fight as Kaj says?"

Jerit nodded, finally withdrawing his lingering hand to steer his horse around a fallen tree that partially blocked the worn north road. "If it comes to that, we all will. Maybe, like her father, she does not need to use the sword she carries. We'll see. We've got days to go before that should…"

"The border…?"

"At last report, Fiara stands. Four days, then we'll learn the state of things further north. We can plan, send spies, gather gossip, but there's little use in worrying about what we do not know."

"You sound like Kavan," Lorant snorted.

"I sound like my father used to sound." Jerit snorted too, his gaze distracted now as he turned his pensive face away. "And Oska." He hated sounding like his father and wished again that the man he had idolized as a boy had not been sullied by so many unfortunate events.

Enesfel would not now be riding into war.

"They need to see our…your…confidence," he continued in a gentler voice, tipping his head toward the trail of soldiers, wagons, and hangers-on behind them. "If this is a fool's errand, Lord Cliáth would have said so."

"He did try to discourage me."

"And me…but that was more out of love and the fear of the unknown, I believe, than disbelief in our cause. He said he saw us together in battle. I want to believe that means we will survive and win this fight."

Startled by a covey of quail that burst from the brush at the side of the road, both fell silent, focusing on calming their horses and absorbed in private thoughts about the destiny ahead of them until Lorant sighed.

"If anything happens to you…"

In response to the quavering tone, Jerit steered his horse near enough that his leg pressed against Lorant's. Lorant shivered, glanced at their knees, and then turned his gaze back to the road.

"Nothing will happen. We'll do this together. I am your shield…"

"And my strength," Lorant whispered with a nod, some of his uneasiness bleeding away. He had to be the strength of the men who followed him.

He was grateful Jerit was there to be his.

"That may be the last of them for a while."

"Last of who?" Níkóá asked as he entered the dayroom where the two inquisitors stood at the open window taking advantage of the breeze that cut through the mid-morning heat. The arid room was perfumed with floral arrangements the staff had prepared, but there lingered a faint stench of sweat and dust left by the messenger he had passed in the corridor before entering the room.

Asta rolled a page between her hands as she debated lighting a fire to destroy the delivered message. The day was too hot for a fire, however, and would grow hotter as the sun climbed higher. Instead, she handed the parchment to the regent so he could read it too.

"Three more Association victims…their own, not innocents," she corrected with a shrug as she heard Níkóá unroll the page and peruse it silently. The culling had slowed, more faces Asta had known, and with each death the Association's fight against her decreased as their cooperation increased. She could not thank Warde without exposing their relationship except by funneling messages through Zerio, on whom she had been forced to rely as the unraveling of the Association continued. Things were changing, their roles with it; she did not know what the eventual outcome would be

This change was a good thing. If k'Ádhá saw fit to restore the de Corrmicks to Neth's throne, she would be needed in Glevum to temper Kjell's effect on the delicate, vulnerable Henrik. She would not permit such a rift as had developed between Kjell and Oska to rise again, nor permit fate to take Henrik from her as it had Oska.

Enesfel would need an inquisitor if that day came.

Despite Jerit's childhood dreams, she did not intend for him to take her place as Enesfel's inquisitor. She wanted a different life for him. Zerio would be an adequate fit for the position if she continued to groom him.

Making little sense of the coded phrasing and terminology the Association used, Níkóá frowned and held the scroll back to Asta. Zerio took it instead. "Infighting?"

"Housekeeping. There's word of new leadership; someone's taking control after Marta…"

"So long as that someone's on our side." Or as much on the Crown's side as anyone in the Association could be. During Níkóá's tenure as regent, the Association had grown increasingly chaotic despite everything Asta had done to stifle them. He did not know if it was a situation he had created, but Asta had assured him that if there was any fault to be had, it was on Inness.

If Fen Geli had lived, Asta believed the relationship with the Association would have remained manageable.

"Can't be many left," Zerio said. "They're more cooperative."

"Good."

Taking the scroll from Zerio and tucking it under her arm, the page crinkling against her body, Asta asked, "Any word from the king?"

"Or Kavan?" Zerio added.

Níkóá shook his head and swallowed a sigh. Like Zerio, he had been perturbed by the duke's abrupt departure, with his failure to explain where he was going or why, when he intended to be back, or what he hoped to accomplish. Rhyrdan had said only that it was a matter of war. Níkóá hoped that meant that Kavan had gone to deliver a word, a vision, or some manner of assistance to the king. Maybe he was calling the troops home.

"If anyone's heard anything, it would be Rhyrdan or Ágdhállán; there've been no heralds and I've not spoken with…"

"He's been gone before. He'll be back." Asta remembered some of those extended absences. Thus far, this absence was shorter than any of those. Not yet two weeks. While she was concerned about the timing, she held on to hope that Rhyrdan's words were true, that Kavan sought a way to end the war before blood was spilled. Perhaps he was riding with Lorant and Jerit to provide them hope or some advantage that would hasten their return home alive.

Only two needed to die for their crimes. She would be satisfied to deliver their deaths with her own hands.

"They don't know where he's…?"

Níkóá patted Zerio's arm, hoping to provide a measure of reassurance he did not feel. "We don't have to know where he is. We must trust him."

The lanky man huffed softly. It would be easier to trust Kavan if he had not disappeared without a word. Hopeful for a distraction from the turn his thoughts were taking, realizing he was not the only one clinging to the bard with expectations Kavan could not be expected to fulfill, Zerio motioned to the parchment. "I'll investigate that…get more details. See if anyone can tell us more."

Asta would prefer to do so herself, for the same purpose of distraction, but nodded with a sigh without giving the message back. "We shall go to Madoc together."

"Bring back some good news," Níkóá called after them as the pair left the room. He took their place at the window, stared at the cloudless sky, and groaned. He needed a distraction as well.

Thus far, the day had not produced any.

❮*❯

The force of unnatural power blew the door of his prison open, threw Myreth against the wall, and held him there, toes barely touching the floor, struggling to breathe. He flailed to be free as the crimson-faced woman charged in and clutched at his neck as though to be free of the invisible hand at his throat.

"Where is he?"

Her sharp tone was both a hiss and a scream, a sound that caused the small portion of his brain that could think, that was not fighting for survival, to wonder what Kavan had done. It had to be Kavan. No one else inspired such wrath in the woman glowering in his face. He could not answer her, did not know the answer, and his lack of response infuriated her further so that she cast him aside with a flinging gesture of her arm though she did not touch him. He took a single deep gulp of air before he struck the wall hard enough to cast him into blackness as he landed on the floor like a sack of wet fabric. His curled hand unfolded when it hit the stone, and the ring he always wore on his now limp hand clattered and slipped free of his finger.

Bhás set her booted heel upon it, tempted to destroy it out of spite. Instead, she hesitated, slowly withdrew her foot, and stared at it without touching it. She admired the emerald's glint in the gray light of day though its precious glimmer fueled a flash of jealousy that no one was there to witness. That ring, the ring of her foe, was like a poison, tainting the air, making her recoil every time she was in its proximity. It should not be here. It should not exist. That ring gave Myreth hope, kept him from cooperating with her demands; she should have disposed of it years before. She should be rid of it now, erase another relic and memory of the Heretic-Saint and his bloodline from the world.

But for now, it was useful.

It was Kóráhm's ring, as much as the man wearing it, that would draw the White Bard to her. She would tolerate its saintly venom a little longer if it served its purpose as she hoped it would.

Gingerly, she picked it up, slid it into a dull black pouch of metal chain lined with hairy goat hide, and pulled the drawstring tight to close it. For now, this would hide its power from the traitor's sight. For now, its absence would pull Myreth into a despair that might also draw the bard to him…and thus to her.

Her gaze traveled from Myreth's extended hand, up his arm to his neck where dark bruises were forming where her invisible grasp had choked him. There would be none of his sweet-voiced singing for some time as his voice healed, and that pain, she expected, would also serve as bait…so long as he was alive to make the journey. So long as he emerged from behind the veil that shrouded him, where she could not follow or sense him. When he emerged, he would know.

To be certain he would sense Myreth's pain and come to her, the heel of her foot ground down upon the unconscious man's wrist. The agony of fracturing bone jarred Myreth out of his faint long enough to elicit a scream, then he slid into unconsciousness again.

Bhás sniffed with satisfaction and stalked from the room, slamming the door behind her. That ought to be enough. Myreth's pain ought to be all the bait she needed.

∾*∾

"He is awake…asking for you…"

The strain in Dola's voice, the sad and anxious lines around her weary eyes and drooping lips prompted Kavan to glance at Eridel who nodded and stood up from the table as well. Kavan had seen that expression on too many faces, the grief that came when staring at the inevitable march of mortality.

Urian had held on far beyond the age of most in his condition, waiting for Kavan, waiting to complete the task Orynn had given him.

The legs of his chair screeched on the stone floor as Kavan got to his feet. He wondered if, even then, all those years ago, Orynn had known what lay ahead for them. If all knowledge was passed from mother to daughter, from one k'ílshwythnec to the next, had Earé known this too? Did she know more than what she had told him?

The burden of knowing, he understood from experience, was knowing when such knowledge should be shared and when it must not be. Urian must know that, too.

The three met Sunna outside the bed chamber, a plain wooden box in his hand. Power emanated from its unseen content, dim but detectable enough that the pendants against Kavan's chest hummed and warmed in reaction. Sunna seemed to feel it too, as his expression twisted in pensive discomfort as though he had never touched an item of power before. The dark-skinned man cocked his head toward the door, bidding Kavan to enter first, and then he entered only after the others had done so.

A bundle of bedsheets lay near the door, filling the room with the stench of stale, bitter urine and the too-familiar smells that came with the passing of life. Urian was seated upright as he had been before, his girth adding additional strain on lungs already struggling for air when he laid down. The wheeze in his chest accompanied the erratic flutter and pause of his heart and Kavan, hoping that some miracle would pass through his hands despite not feeling any precursive collection of power that would suggest it, went to the far side of the bed and held the ancient man's hand.

Nothing happened.

No miracle came.

When Kavan faintly groaned, Urian patted his hand with his free one, though the effort to do so made him cough weakly. Dola remained near the door with Eridel's arm around her shoulders, and instead, it was Sunna, after setting the box on the stand near Urian's elbow, who pulled the blind man's arm back to reduce the constriction of his lungs and chest muscles.

"You brought it?" Urian wheezed.

"Yes," replied Sunna.

Not mute at all.

It was the first word he had spoken in Kavan's company.

"Give it to him."

Sunna picked up the box and stretched across Urian's body to offer it to Kavan. Urian placed both of his hands on the box briefly before Kavan hesitantly accepted it, and then seemed to stare at him as Kavan set it on the edge of the mattress, unfastened the claw-hook latch, and opened the box to reveal its contents.

"I never opened it. I don't know what it is…only that she called it máltai sturmyrá…"

Eridel's breath caught. "I've heard of that, an ancient lamp."

Spirit lightbox, or reliquary of holy light, as some called it, a myth told often to Elyri children, a tale Kavan had grown up hearing until he began to read for himself, when Dháná stopped telling him stories or reading ones that she found in printed sources. A box said to emit light for the one holding it, the same way Kavan gathered and created light in the palms of his hands.

What lay within the well-padded, shielded wooden box, however, emitted no trace of light, no hint of what filled the relic with the power it contained. Curious for a closer look after a glance at Urian, Kavan reached into the box, flinched when he touched it, and once he shook off that initial sensation, drew it out so that the others in the room could see it too.

In this underground place, hidden from the world, he felt Bhás' presence for the first time in days. Angry. Bitter. Resentful. Smug and defiant, as though Kavan holding the relic proved some point or laid the foundation for a trap she had waited a long time to spring.

Urian, not sensing any of those things, interrupted Kavan's chain of thoughts. "She said it was crafted by the one called Zythán the Heretic." He could not see the shudder that passed through Kavan. "I don't know why she would want you to have it, but surely it is not a bad thing…"

His weak voice trailed off into coughing. Sunna offered him water, which he refused.

Kavan had to believe that Urian was right, that Orynn would not have steered him to it if it were dangerous or detrimental. Careful that his now trembling hands did not drop the relic to shatter on the floor, he turned it to study every angle, every detail, guessing it to be more than a lamp.

The small glass box, barely the width of his hand, was bound and sealed on all edges and corners with the familiar bright silvery metal Kavan knew to be of Dhóbhaen origin. Contained within, one affixed to the left and right sides, or perhaps the top and bottom, were two tower-shaped octagonal crystals, their flat bases held flush to the glass by metal rods drilled through the glass and through the crystals, rods that allowed the smoky stones, like the fractured one Prince Muir had given to him, to rotate and spin freely. Their points nearly touched in the center, and where there had been darkness in the room before, a small flicker of crackling light, like a miniature bolt of lightning, sizzled between those points.

Fueled by his touch, by his power, Kavan assumed, since there had been no light before he touched it. It might contain the sunlight and moonlight he could harness, hold the glow of a candle or a torch if he held it long enough to funnel that power into it, but he could not fathom how such an item, regardless of the power it contained, could be beneficial against Bhás, in stopping the war. In Bhórdh, such an object would have aided miners, perhaps might have served as some ceremonial centerpiece, but it was not an object of war any more than the Staff of Llyr and the Cup of Drebhoti were.

Hope diminished, he sighed and turned the box to study the clear glass bottom, then the top with a drilled hole rimmed with metal at its center.

Staff and Cup. Llyr and Drebhoti. Zythán. A triumvirate of powerful ancestors and two equal relics. Did this make the third? What if it was meant to work in conjunction with the articles he already possessed? What if it needed to be in the presence of the other two items to fulfill its potential?

What if…?

He set the box on the mattress, barely aware of the others as he untangled the pendants around his neck and pulled the one he wanted over his head. The spindle-like object, resembling a writing nib, appeared to be the same diameter as the hole. Holding his breath, he inserted the nib, like a key into a lock, and slid it into place. The metal point filled the gap between the crystals, and when contact was made between them, the crystals glowed with the same green, blue, and white veins of light and power that the chasm beneath St. Kóráhm's contained. The glow flared within the box, brightening the room with the warmth of a sunny day, and the hum of power within it grew strong enough to flow through the key into Kavan's hand, into his arm, into his core. The power and light brought with them a kaleidoscope of indecipherable images that pounded within his skull like the roar of a stormy sea. The abrupt shock, the pulsing pain behind his eyes, made him yank his hand away, removing the key with it, and though the power began to immediately subside, having not had the opportunity to reach its full strength, the glow of the light took longer to do so.

Kavan blinked and tried to find the words to describe what he felt, what he had seen and heard, but words failed to come. He did not have answers but, after that moment of disappointment, he now felt a flood of hope.

He would have to study this more in-depth.

"A song, my lord? Something to remind me…to remember where we were, our travels together? I never had the privilege of hearing your harp. With your hands restored," Urian clutched his again, wincing from the static pop that passed between them but refusing to release him, "I should like to do so just once."

Urian's voice and the hand clasping his severed Kavan's internal concentration, a relief that eased the pounding of his heart. "I have not brought my…"

"Use mine."

Kavan and Eridel stared at one another. Eridel had never heard the White Bard play, knew only the tales and rumors and ever-growing mythos that surrounded Kavan. He had been driven to his previously presumed death before Kavan's hands were restored, before Kavan had learned the value of his voice as an instrument he had not been comfortable sharing. A gift to them both at the end of this day was the least Kavan could offer in exchange for the relic he had been provided.

Whether the relic would be beneficial against Bhás, whether it could be used to stop a war, it was still a historical item of significance that Kavan would not have found without them both.

All those years ago, both men had been brought to him for a purpose beyond aiding him through the darkest hours of his life. They had fulfilled their parts then; they were fulfilling them now.

Just as Kavan was fulfilling his.

With the sturmyrá in its protective outer box and Eridel's red kestrel harp on his knee, as he perched on the edge of the mattress, Kavan played as he had not played in several weeks. An ode to memory, reflecting the cultures, the heat, of those southern lands, and the anguish of the weeks spent in it. A song interwoven with the tune Eridel had tried to play when Kavan lost his temper and drove him away. An elegy of bravery and resilience, youth and hope, of regret and gratitude and the appreciation he felt for this opportunity to be with them one more time. A hymn offered to make amends for the wrongs he had inflicted upon them.

His fingers moved to the rhythmic thrum of záryph wings when they came, played to the honor and memory of the one who attended with them and took Urian's weak hands in his invisible ones. He played until those sensations, until the power of Kóráhm's aura bled out of the room, absorbing the unsteady beat of Urian's heart and left nothing behind except the unmistakable void of death.

"You have a gift," murmured Sunna, closing Urian's unseeing eyes for the last time and kissing his forehead, his voice low and husky with emotion. "His gratitude was great for the sharing…"

"As is ours," Dola sobbed softly as she dabbed her cheeks. "You gave him what he desired…and he has given you what you need?"

"I…" Handing the harp back to Eridel, his hands feeling empty without it, Kavan closed the latch on the wooden box. "I hope so. I have what I was sent to receive." Time would tell what the purpose and function of the sturmyrá would be. "I am sorry for…"

Dola shook her head. "He suffers no more. He waited…now his wait has ended. I did what I could for him…now it is past. He spoke of you often, your music, your wisdom, and devotion. I am happy his wish was met…happy to have shared it with him."

Cheeks flushed, Kavan bowed his head. "Is there anything I can do?" Unless there was a crypt in the stone caverns or a nearby cave where the body could be interred the way the villagers in Gorbesh disposed of their dead, he assumed Urian would need to be transported down the mountain for burial. He could not preserve the dead from temporary decay as Ártur could, but he could help carry him to his rest. As strong as Sunna appeared to be, it would not be easy for one man to carry such a burden down the steep, rocky path.

"I will wash and wrap him…then we will take him up." Sunna glanced at Eridel as he spoke and then back to Kavan as he eased Urian into to a prone position. "You may accompany us. When he is at rest, we may start down, if that is your wish."

Kavan did not want to rush from these people, this place, from Eridel now that the two men had made peace, nor did he wish to seem hastily ungrateful. But he had been absent from Enesfel for too long. Away from Rhyrdan and his sons. Now that he had the sturmyrá, it was time to return and learn what, if any, effect it would have upon the state of war.

The Sovereignties needed him.

"I would be honored to accompany you and yes…I should return to Rhidam while there is still time."

Sunna nodded.

"Help me take these out and bring fresh water and linen," Eridel murmured, gesturing to the soiled bedding.

Dola backed out of the room and allowed the pair to pass with the stained sheets, remaining as far from them as she could as she followed. In the main room, she turned her attention to the final preparations of the evening meal they had not yet shared.

As they worked, Kavan gathered the items for burning as Sunna directed while Eridel burned them in a worn pit several yards from the hovel's door, the fabric made more flammable by the inclusion of fragrant oils. Eridel explained how in this place, women were the life-givers through birth, tasked with tending the injured, the sick, the dying. But the rituals of death were left on the shoulders of men, those who dealt death through war and the punishment of criminals. He whispered, as they returned to cleanse Urian's room with herb smoke and mountain spring water, his questions about what the glass box was, what it contained, what it did. He expressed his fears that Bhás had led him to Urian, that she knew what the blind man had possessed, that she wanted Kavan to have it so that it might somehow be used against him.

Kavan did not think it was true, but as he followed the men outside with their beloved burden, when he was hit by blazing pain in his wrists and the back of his head so that he stumbled and dropped to his knees, it was Sunna who humbly murmured, "It is her, is it not?"

Shaking, gingerly cradling his wrist as he strove to banish the memory of mutilation that often came with that pain, Kavan shrugged and bobbed his head. This was not rósádhá, not the Sight, but something else, something that brought Myreth's tear-streaked face to mind.

Not dead…but suffering.

Using the mountain's surface to climb to his feet, Kavan turned his face toward the origin of that sensation, but again Sunna spoke. "Do not play her game. Do not heed her. Not until you are ready."

Kavan frowned, wondering what Sunna knew about Bhás, and continued following where the taller man led. If Sunna had experience with her, he wanted to hear it. Now that Sunna had broken his silence, Kavan hoped he could be prompted to reveal more.

They did not climb to the mountain's peak but rather stopped at a plateau barely wide enough for a dozen men to stand on. Sunna gave Urian's shoulders to Kavan to support and then lay a long mat of reeds and grasses woven into intricate multicolored patterns on the stony ground. They placed Urian on the mat, and then Sunna and Eridel peeled back the linen wrappings to expose his pallid nudity to the air. Already, birds of prey circled overhead, respecting the chanted phrases, like ritual prayers, that first Sunna, then Eridel, provided as they worked.

When they stepped back from the corpse, Sunna spoke again. "You share his faith. Will you pray to his gods for him?"

"You do not...?" started Kavan. It was logical that this distant land worshipped different gods, or some different form of k'Ádhá by some different name, but he had not considered it before now.

"The gods have never favored me," Sunna admitted, staring at the dead man's serene face. "I believe in nothing...although for his sake I have tried. After tonight..." His face turned to eye Kavan with a perplexed expression.

Kavan understood. Sunna had felt the záryph. Perhaps he had felt Kóráhm there too. But such experiences might not be enough to sway a man to faith.

"Where do you...where is he to be buried?"

"He wanted the old ways of this place," Eridel replied. "The wind, the rain...the birds and animals...they will take him into themselves so that he will return to the world he was born of."

"He will be left here?" Kavan shuddered. He had seen men left on the battlefield, men killed on the road left to natural decay and the consumption of wild things. Logically speaking, what did it matter if the wild things above the ground would consume him as the worms and bugs of the earth would do below it? But it hardly seemed a fitting end for the gdhededhá.

Eridel shrugged. These were not his customs either, but he had lived among these people long enough to be familiar with their ways. "It's what he wanted. But he did ask..." He removed the dedhá's holy symbol from the pocket of his trousers and put it in Kavan's hand. "Return it, and his writings, to his Order…if you can. They should know he is gone."

Kavan closed his hand around the pendant and his eyes to the grisly images he could envision that would soon become of the man before Kavan made it back to Enesfel. When they would not leave him, when he could not erase them from his thoughts, Kavan sought those comforting Faith presences in the hope that they would come again and perhaps transport Urian's corpse away from this place before he could be desecrated. Then, accepting Sunna's charge, he offered Kóráhm's words back to him in song, offered them to Dhágdhuán, and to k'Ádhá above them.

> *bhelzen k'Ádhá*
> *kunás hwoncáró saeitá phaerás kóh thurás*
> *hábhai ergóthás á dhun*
> *sun hwaerás íth nyl phain res*
> *ed gaeth bhekalomár thráaest*
> *llósté kunás aiónag*
> *kédhé sun dhe*
> *ebh málár ed et aiónag rásár*
> *ásai gaethaelás aetásmá á shwyth thórgae kóh kunás hes*
> *mályhag Dhágdhuán*
> *trodh kunás aehíthé aun aezylag*
> *ít ebh konyses aun k'bhekalomár*
> *sun íth dhózair ithnás phain dhe mál tai*

When the words of prayer faded, when no spiritual entities came to take Urian away, the men stood in silence, listening to the whistle of the wind, to the caws and croaks of the carrion, to the creaks and pops the ancient mountain stone made as it continued its eternal battle against the elements. Eventually, Sunna muttered words Kavan did not understand and started back down the path. Eridel too, murmured a soft "Farewell," and followed.

Kavan stood alone long enough to lift his eyes to the sky, to cast up a farewell prayer without words, and began the three-hundred-yard climb down the mountain to return to the solitary woman in her mountain home.

He wondered what would become of her now.

❧*❦

Steam and smoke billowed around her as the red-hot river flowed over the precipice. She saw him teeter there on the cliff edge, caught in a rushing blast of wind that funneled past, generated by the speed of the molten river as it rushed across ancient blackened stone, a brief horrifying moment in which she reached for his hand.

Tumultuous waves crashed against stone and wood.

Male voices shouting in dismay and alarm, the sound slurred and slowed by the distortion of time as if to offer the hope of redemption.

In the next moment, her hand was empty.

Earé blinked rapidly, her vision shifting from the vivid, shocking imagery to the host camped around her, men marching to fight and die, and the women who traveled with them to offer what support and comfort they could give. She flexed her empty hand upon her lap, trying to erase the despair the act carried with it. It was the first, clearest vision of the future she had Seen since before the armies began their march, the first to fill her with an unwelcome spike of fear. But beneath that fear, there was a sense more powerful still, an unexpected roaring blast of hope.

Though forbidden to interfere in her father's life by tenets older than all the k'ílshwythnec who had gone before her, she could not allow this vision to stand. Hope told her so. There was a chance, however remote and tenuous, that a few words could undo everything about to be done, undercut this impending war, and save countless lives.

Surely that was worth a moment's disobedience. Of what use was her power, her visions, her strengths, if she could not use them for good? If instead of answering petty questions for petty men and women, she could protect the histories of armies, sovereignties, and the innocent lives about to die, was not that worth a lapse in protocol?

Was not this one man's life worth the same risks her mother had taken?

Earé clung to her certainty and closed her eyes again, absently clasping Kaj's hand as she focused her thoughts, her power, to someplace far beyond the reach of any of those around her. Without knowing why, Kaj squeezed her hand, glanced at her serene but fixated expression, and nodded without her seeing it.

She was there, in a room of blood, of hate, of the screaming of tortured bodies and souls, the sounds of men and beasts, a room lit by cobalt and violet flames. Instinctively, she dodged to the side to deflect the unidentified item, or the illusionary sense of one, that was hurled when the woman before her, malevolently dark and vindictively lean, spun toward her in alarm, the unexpected presence of light that appeared without footsteps, beating wings, or blasting wind.

Bhás hissed at the one she recognized, not by face or name or power but by the call of enemy blood that screamed like a siren to her ears. The intruder was a thing of shadow, projected into her space the way she often projected into the space of others. This one was different, however, by a theory she tested with another object thrown at the blonde shadow's head.

The bloody ceremonial blade passed through the woman's chest as though passing through smoke.

She was not here.

Snorting at what she perceived to be the younger woman's weakness, sneering at her inability to manifest materially in Bhás' chamber as no shade would be able to harm her, Bhás growled. "You do not belong here."

"Nor," Earé replied cooly, "do you. Your time is past. You have no future here…"

"You do not frighten me." Bhás waved a dismissive hand. "Mine is the only future…"

"You know who I am. You know the ones who came before me, that see all and know…"

"You know nothing."

There was a twitch on the dark-haired woman's face, a steeling of expression that settled as she pushed away a realization she did not want to make or believe. The corners of Earé's lips twisted with satisfaction, but she did not otherwise move. "You know you cannot win. He will never fall to your vengeance. He has the hosts of Ethenae…"

"He is a man…he will die like the bheturbhae he is. He…and all who share the blood of…"

Standing against the thrust of power as Bhás tested her strengths against Earé, finding herself pushed to retreat further into her body, Earé ignored the threat and said, "End this…or suffer your own wrath. You cannot win this fight. He will not be defeated."

She thrust once with the power to throw Bhás across the room, pulling herself from that reality and the saferoom within her head. Bhás wailed…

…and Earé opened her eyes to find herself slumped against Kaj's shoulder, the man staring absently into the fire. She remained there, silent and troubled by the power she had felt in Bhás, fearing that, in her haste to help her father, she had made things more difficult.

⊱Chapter 38⊰

Leaving Dola in the city marketplace, the woman having accompanied them down the mountain to replenish bedding and other supplies, Kavan passed over the footbridge and entered the courtyard through the door Sunna held open. The power of the Gate was a potent lure and Kavan was satisfied that his creation had succeeded once again. The sun was setting over the sea, a golden and mauve glow that bled the color away from the direction of home.

With this Gate, he might one day return to investigate this unfamiliar land. For now, he was eager to see his sons.

Ominous clouds covered the eastern horizon, rolling toward the sea Kavan had not yet viewed. The wind that drove them was hot and stagnant, heavy with moisture that made Kavan's clothes stick uncomfortably to his skin so that he considered changing out of them after setting down his pack and closing the slatted shutters at Sunna's instruction. The remaining food Dola had packed was spread upon the table as Sunna lit an oil lantern above the hearth and pulled a lever meant to keep the promised rain from dripping through the flue.

"I will go to Enesfel with you," Sunna said as he dragged a three-legged stool to the table to join the others in eating.

"That is not..." began Kavan.

Eridel passed the pitcher he had filled from the well to Kavan. "She will come for you, now that you have the sturmyrá."

Having felt Bhás' presence all the way down the mountain, back along the river, and through the streets of the city, it was precisely why Kavan wanted to place no one else in the path of her vindictive fury.

Sunna broke off chunks of dried meat and gave pieces to each of the men. "She cannot harm me," he said, his voice low and certain. "I am immune to shi cali...immune since birth...and I have sworn an oath. When you face her, I will be there...and she will die."

Unable to countermand an oath taken or argue effectively against the dark man's resolve, Kavan nodded but continued to frown. Whatever the cause of Sunna's oath, whatever fueled his sense of vengeance, if he was somehow immune to Bhás' power, though Kavan did not understand how he could be, then keeping such an ally close was strategically wise, even if he did not want to put anyone else at risk. "And you?" He side-eyed Eridel. "Will you come with us?"

Eridel shook his head. "I will join Dola and return up the mountain. Unlike either of you, I have no defenses against Bhás."

"All the more reason to…"

"I'll be of no use to you. I think I've done all I can. You and I have made peace…" He studied Kavan's face seeking affirmation and, when he found it, smiled softly and nodded. "For now, Dola needs me. Up there, we will be protected. Maybe one day, when this is over…"

"I do not know where I will be when that day comes," Kavan whispered. His future was veiled and uncertain, something he was unable to predict even with the sturmyrá in his care. "If your travels bring you to me, you are welcome…whether that be in Enesfel or Gorbesh. You will always have a place wherever I call home. Your welcome is assured."

"I think I would like to tread that path again, complete the journey you and I started together, see what you saw after we parted. If she finds me again, however…if she comes for me…"

"She won't," Sunna grunted.

Eridel's expression did not change, despite his desire to find assurance in his friend's words. "For now, I think remaining with Dola is the best. I will keep this place tidy and secure," he gestured around them, "and maybe convince her to come down from the mountain now that Urian is…"

Sunna nodded, "You are both welcome to this place."

To Kavan, it sounded like they had discussed this decision before.

Swallowing the contents of his cup, Eridel sighed and began in a softer voice, "Kavan…I ask that you take my harp when you leave here."

Kavan choked and stared at him wide-eyed. "I should not…"

"Your years in this world are greater than mine…and if we do not cross paths again, it will fall into the hands of someone who will not appreciate it as you do. As much as…I have lived so long without it, it does not feel as though it is mine any longer. I can get by, as I always have, and I want you to have it…cherish it…and remember me each time you play. It is a Cliáthan. It belongs with a Cliáth."

Afraid to insult Eridel as he had done long ago, unable to counter his arguments with anything more than feeble demands that Eridel should possess that which had been his when they met, Kavan hung his head, swallowed hard, and tried to think of something to say.

"I will cherish her if you insist…but I beg you to reconsider."

"I have made peace with my decision. I will reconsider…but I will not change my mind."

The first rumble of thunder cracked the air and deposited a barrage of pelting hailstones onto the roof of the home. The white pellets bounced and clattered against the shutters, off the stone courtyard, and against the door.

"When it is over," Sunna continued, "when the house is secure, we will depart when you are ready."

"I am ready now." With the weight of Myreth's pain and Bhás' presence dragging on him and the knowledge that traveling to Rhidam would be moving away from wherever his dark twin was, Kavan knew it was time to go home. There were things he needed to do, people he needed to see, a holy relic he needed to study and understand. He believed Kóráhm would let him know when it was time to face her.

He hoped, when he found Myreth, the man would forgive his delay.

❧*❧

"The shelves are nearly empty." Dhóri could not see their vacancy as he ran his fingers over the lip of one shelf. But he could hear the difference, the echo of his voice and footsteps, the way sound was no longer absorbed by the scrolls, books, and collection of loose parchment, vellum, and paper pages. Projects being copied remained, a host of maps and religious works used for daily study and prayer, as well as some historical tomes that he argued about leaving until last in case his father needed them, were left, but even they were being slowly depleted as Khwílen oversaw their relocation.

If Kavan needed any of them, they could be retrieved from Gorbesh as easily as they could be retrieved from these shelves.

"What shall we do when…?"

St. Kóráhm's k'gdhededhá clucked his tongue as he closed the transport chest and motioned for Bergis to hoist the other end by the handle. "There are crops to tend, preparations to make, people to minister to. There is always prayer and worship…"

"I hope you have not taken everything."

Kavan entered the scriptorium with Sunna trailing behind creating a heavier set of footsteps that made Dhóri cock his head. Or perhaps, the bard mused, it was the object of power he carried in the pack on his back that caught his son's attention.

"Welcome home, my lord," Khwílen said easily, not answering the question since Kavan could see the answer for himself.

"I'm happy you're home." Dhóri set down the smaller chest of ink vials and writing instruments he had picked up to embrace his father in relief. "Have you been to Rhidam yet? Níkóá and Zerio have come nearly every day in search of you."

"I have just returned. I hoped…" He scanned the sparse shelves with a frown.

"Some books remain," Khwílen assured him, tilting his head toward shelves Kavan could not see. "Dhóri would not allow us to move them."

Dhóri grinned. "Instinct. I thought you might need them…"

Or perhaps Kóráhm had guided him. Kavan hoped that was true. "This is Sunna. This is my son Dhóri, Bergis, and k'gdhededhá Khwílen."

Khwílen offered a slight bow, made awkward by the trunk he had not released. "Welcome to St. Kóráhm's. If you will excuse us, my lord; this grows heavy and Valesce is waiting for us. The hour is late."

"Of course, k'dedhá. Dhóri, will you bring Zerio here…and Rhyrdan and Ágdhállán if they are not yet abed?"

"And Sóbhán?"

Kavan opened his mouth but then shook his head. "I will see him soon." He could use Zerio's eidetic memory to seek answers, and perhaps his youngest son could provide insight into the tai sturmyrá in his own way. If he did not invite Rhyrdan's assistance and company after abruptly leaving him on the oratory steps, Kavan would only hurt the younger man.

The assurance of his company might also soothe the power burn he continued to fight as he moved further away from Myreth's shadow.

"I will bring them," Dhóri promised, skirting the tables, benches, and doorways as he hurried after Khwílen to use the same Gate.

Kavan gestured to Sunna to follow. "Do you read?"

"Dola taught me our tongue. Urian tried as much as he could…but Eridel has helped polish my understanding of your Trade tongue. I do not know how much use I may be to you, but I will try. You believe your books will explain the tai sturmyrá?"

"Reference it, perhaps. Provide clues." Given how there were few available details about Zythán and those early days of the Faith and history, Elyri and dhóbhaen…and how few books remained on the shelves when he scanned those Khwílen had directed him to, he did not anticipate finding anything of value here. But he had to try.

By the time he selected several tomes and spread them on the nearest wide table, those he had sent for arrived, each greeting him with the same fervor and relief and each introduced to the stranger that Rhyrdan recognized from the Eagle's Nest two weeks before.

"Eridel?" he growled, secretly hoping the man who had nearly killed him had met his end.

"Remained behind," Kavan assured him, while also, he sensed, disappointing him when he added, "We parted on good terms."

"Remained behind where?" asked Zerio, his eager voice colored by a sheen of dwindling offense about also being left behind.

"That is a tale for another time."

"Did you find what you were looking for? Do you think you can stop the war?" Rhyrdan sat on the end of the bench where Kavan sat, pulled a book from the collection, and opened it to the first page without knowing what he was looking for.

"I found this."

Kavan drew the wooden box from his pack and set it on the table, instantly peaking Ágdhállán's interest so that the boy scooted closer on Kavan's other side to examine the power-humming object. Kavan took the small glass box out of its protective casing and set it on the table, then pulled the pendant key from around his neck.

"I've seen this." Zerio picked up the box as Kavan looked at him with a raised brow. "Not this exactly, but in the details Bhórdh showed me."

Excited by his decision to invite Zerio into his study, Kavan asked, "Do you know what it is? What it does? Why it was made?" Any answers Zerio could give would be a good place to start.

Zerio shook his head as he turned the box several times, studying all its details before handing it back to Kavan. "Claes-Arne might have known…it might be in the Vants library."

"What do you think it is?" asked Rhyrdan who made no effort to touch it but watched as Kavan inserted the white stone key into the hole on the top panel. When the tip slid into its intended gap, the identical crystals again began to glow, the three points sizzling and popping with lightning-like power. The room glowed with a brightness that Dhóri noticed as he leaned his face toward the warmth.

"It is said to hold the light of the spirits…to capture souls," said Sunna, the first detail he had provided.

"Then if one gets close enough," Zerio murmured, low and incredulous, "could we steal Fraen's soul? Without a king in Neth, there'd be no need for war…"

"Or we could steal hers," countered Rhyrdan, meeting Kavan's gaze.

"Hers?"

Kavan shook his head, brushing aside Zerio's query and shuddering in distaste at the thought of entrapping anyone's immortal soul. He had separated soul from body before, set a child free from the torture King Bowen had been about to bestow on everyone that child had known. And he had, he believed, released some part of Coryllien's spirit from this world. But setting a soul free of its body to allow a person, a spirit, peace, was different from trapping it in a reliquary.

Fearing that the glow in the box was somehow created by the torture of trapped souls or even záryph, he began to remove the key, but Ágdhállán's hand upon his prevented him from doing so.

"They're not…it isn't…" The boy struggled to find words to express his limited understanding of what he felt, the same push and pull of power he knew his father felt. "It's like Sóbhán…"

Curious at the comparison, Kavan laid his hand flat, with Ágdhállán's upon it, on top of the box where he could feel the undulating power moving like waves on the shore. How long could he hold the box in his hands, how much power could it, and he, collect, how strong could he become with this in his possession?

Was this the key to overcoming Bhás?

Ágdhállán's smile was serene and enigmatic, but he said nothing, and despite that smile, looked to be afraid, though not afraid enough to pull his hand away from the tai sturmyrá until Kavan did so.

Kavan did not ask what his son was afraid of. That would be a private conversation between them later.

Sliding the box to the center of the table with the key still in place, and pulling one of the books closer, Kavan murmured, "It is said to have been crafted by one called Zythán, a saint or heretic, depending on who you speak with…"

"Like Kóráhm?"

Kavan nodded at Dhóri's question, though his son could not see the gesture. "I believe it is part of a set of relics…old enough to predate any records we have here. But I pray we will be fortunate and find even a single line or paragraph that will help us."

Staring at the remarkable red-haired boy the way the child stared at him, Sunna murmured, "I believe we already are fortunate."

Kavan looked back and forth between them without knowing what the dark man meant.

Hours passed, bringing dawn to St. Kóráhm's and a failure to find any useful details. Ágdhállán slid down to sleep upon the bench with his head on Kavan's lap, and Dhóri, hearing the chimes of Saint Maicel's bells, left the table to bring breakfast back to his companions. Needing a change of position, Kavan slid off the bench to stand, to ease the stiffness in his back, careful not to wake his son.

"There are a few books in the manor still..." Or there had been unless Dhóri had already relocated them to Gorbesh. "Will you stay with Ágdhállán while Rhyrdan and I bring them...?"

"With my life," Sunna nodded.

"Of course," agreed Zerio, not to be outdone by Sunna's agreement of service. He closed the book he had finished perusing and picked up the tai sturmyrá to study it further. He did not appear to feel the power glowing within it. "We'll protect this, too."

Ágdhállán muttered something in his sleep. Sunna, on his other side, put his big hand on the boy's shoulder. His untrained power was enough to ease the child's dreams, and he stilled.

In the manor, Kavan paused in the oratory to offer a short prayer, to hold Rhyrdan's hand to his chest for comfort as he sought Ártur's presence to reassure himself that his cousin, the king, Prince Jerit, and the others with him were well. Then he released Rhyrdan's hand and sent him to his office to collect as many history books as he could carry while Kavan stopped in his room to rub a damp cloth over his skin and change out of the still sticky-feeling clothes he had worn too long. He paused to study the scatter of items displayed above his hearth, remembrances of friends lost, links to decades past he often wished he could revisit. The carving of Wortham was added to the assembly after a brief pressing to his lips and a heavy, heartfelt sigh.

The smooth, radiant, multi-faceted red-orange stone flecked with gold that Audh had given him when he left Dhóbhaen, a tool, the man said, to guide him back whenever he chose to return, caught the fingers of sunlight pushing between the narrowly parted curtains. It reflected a dance of red-amber light on the mirror behind it and out into the room. Kavan picked it up, hoping it would provide a connection to Raebhá, hoping that the additional power absorbed from the tai sturmyrá might provide a stronger, more complete link than he had shared with her in some time.

His head, his heart, his soul, his body ached for her. He longed to behold her face, to absorb the sweetness of her scent, to drown in the gentle sound of her breathing and the tender tones of her voice.

It had been too long.

Instead of Raebhá, however, what he saw was a flash of Earé standing amidst the ruins of Owain's Fiara estate, her voice whispering on the wind, bidding him to come.

To Fiara?

He clenched the sunstone tighter, ignoring the tingle of power in his hand as the bedchamber door opened, Emeria turning the latch and pushing it to allow her brother through.

"I brought what I thought we could use," Rhyrdan chuckled. "From what Dhóri said, I did not think you would have so many still." He seemed not to notice the expression on Kavan's face. "Fortunately, Emeria was there to help."

"Always, brother," she smiled too. "Is there anything I can get you, my lord? He says you are here for books?"

"And a change of clothes," Kavan admitted, looking down at himself with satisfaction. "Now I think I must…"

"I will clean them," Emeria said with a prompt curtsey.

"Will you send these books and give a message to Dhóri? Tell him I have an errand to attend and that he and Zerio and my guest may wait here or in St. Kóráhm's until I return, then we can finish what we started?"

"At once," she easily agreed as her brother frowned and muttered, "Errand? You just returned…"

Hearing her brother's stern tone, not wishing to be involved in any disagreement between him and Kavan, Emeria scooped up the castoff clothes as Rhyrdan deposited the books on the dresser. Kavan returned the sunstone to its place and said, "The king and our forces will be in Fiara, or will arrive shortly. I should meet them there."

"Fiara? In harm's way? With Neth's army…?"

"I will be safe…but you may join me if you wish."

He had not been in Fiara since the retrieval of Owain and Gabrielle's remains so that they could be interred on Káliel away from hands that might want to desecrate their graves or their corpses. Bringing Rhyrdan would serve as both a grounding influence and a deterrence to anyone who might wish to attack him. Rhyrdan would also serve as a buffer between him and

Ártur's anticipated scolding about approaching the war front without adequate protection.

As if Enesfel's army, and every bit of power Kavan could harness, would not be protection enough.

Satisfied with the offer, grunting his approval as if the acceptance of his company was some sort of victory, Rhyrdan nodded. "You know I do. You left me once. You will not do so again."

❧*❧

She detected movement elsewhere in the manor, servants attending daily duties, but her father and brothers were not here. For the best, she mused, passing through the shadows to stand at the hearth where the unusual strength of his presence told her he had been not long before. Something about the power in that place felt off, not in a dangerous way but in a way she had never experienced. She closed her eyes and sought the reason, the source of the difference, but the pull continued to bring her focus back to the shelf above the hearth, to the stone he had recently held, to a stone that would be needed if he were to master prophecy and bring Bhás' schemes to an end. Since facing that woman, Earé had seen this stone, the same flashes of imagery, the same window to the same seemingly unavoidable moment.

She understood what to do…even if she did not want to do it.

Words alone were not going to dissuade or defeat Bhás. In her arrogance, even Earé's warning would not be heeded to prevent the inevitable flow of destiny.

She tucked the stone into her bodice where she would not lose it, where it could absorb her heart's strength in the hope it would enhance its own, and then she left Alberni the way she had come.

She regretted she would not be in Fiara to greet him. If she could not affect the future, however, perhaps others could.

❧*❧

Over the past decade, due to significant aid and trade from Cordash, the damage done to Fiara was being gradually overcome. New buildings replaced those burned or torn down by Neth's troops or that had collapsed during the subsequent earthquake, while those with lesser damage had been repaired with materials already available. With no Lachlan or de Corrmick lord or prince to fill the leadership void and the empty halls, the rebuilding of the once elegant manor had been delayed so that the city could heal first.

Fortunately, the local náós had suffered little damage. Knowing the unsafe conditions of the room in which the manor Gate was located, the náós provided Kavan a safe place to emerge into the city, where he paused to breathe the cooler summer air.

He could hear the echoes of a host of men beyond the city's edge, but from the place where he and Rhyrdan stood, they could not be seen.

So, Lorant had made it to Fiara.

It was not so many more miles before they would leave the forest and enter the threatening reach of Fraen's army.

Kavan hoped that, by coming here, finding Earé, he would be told what he must do, that he would be presented with the means of ending this war before blood was spilled.

She might know how to utilize the tai sturmyrá. Perhaps Zerio was correct. Perhaps if it could draw the soul from a body, confronting Fraen and Bhás with it would be worth his ultimate damnation.

"This way," he said to Rhyrdan, starting in the direction of the manor ruins. Lorant would not be there, nor Jerit or anyone he knew, but it was the place Earé had revealed to him. That was where she bid him to go.

The fallen stone, the collapsed roof, a winter's worth of leaves and weather debris, had been cleared away, leaving the ground level with its rebuilt walls exposed to the open air. One side of the structure showed evidence that the upper floor construction had begun, but the red marble sun, cracked and chipped by the earthquake a decade past, looked otherwise intact. Kavan could feel the power of its Gate through the marble, through his feet as they approached, and he was happy to discover it remained.

This Gate had taken him to Dhóbhaen. From here, he could feel that distant Gate that could take him back to Raebhá. From here, he could unite two worlds.

But the view around him, lacking the clutter of collapsed stone blocks littered with leaves and dust, was not the same as he had seen…and Earé was not here.

"Kavan?"

He and Rhyrdan turned simultaneously toward the voice and smiled to see the young king and his princely companion both healthy and fit, if weary-looking from so many days of travel.

"Why are you here? Is there news from Rhidam? Has something happened? Am I needed there?" Lorant squeezed both of Kavan's hands while Jerit shook Rhyrdan's in greeting.

"No news and nothing has happened. Rhidam is secure." He presumed it must be since neither Zerio nor Rhyrdan had said otherwise, and there had been no premonitions to the contrary. "Did you just arrive in Fiara? How are the others?"

"We've been without incident so far," Jerit replied.

"We arrived last evening, too late for me to come and see…" Lorant's voice trailed off as he looked at the marble floor beneath his feet. "This is the place, isn't it? Where he…?"

Without trying to pinpoint the exact location where Merrek had fallen, not wanting to relive the final moments of Muir's son's life, Kavan replied softly, "This is where Fiara fell."

"There wasn't a need to…" Lorant squatted and splayed his open hand on the red marble. "I'd hoped that by coming here, he'd give me answers…guidance…"

"What answers do you seek?" Kavan crouched next to him, mirroring his actions while blocking the details of conflict from his memory.

Lorant shrugged. "If I'm doing the right thing? If there's some strategy I have not considered, perhaps a parley with Fraen that could prevent what comes next."

"I do not think Fraen is interested in parley," Rhyrdan said.

Jerit nodded, "We do not think so either…but we can hope."

Lorant forced a smile and got to his feet. "Have you changed your mind? Have you come to ride with us?"

Kavan stood as well. "I am here to reassure myself that you have survived your journey thus far…and to offer hope if I can.

"There is little hope here…only the intent to succeed and survive and return home."

"I would call that hope," Jerit lightly chided.

"Come back with me. We are restocking supplies, resting, preparing for the border push. We do not expect our luck to hold once we leave the forest. A few days in your company, a little music, ought to bolster morale."

"Not a few days," Kavan said, his words soft with affection. "I am expected in Alberni. But I can spare a few hours before I must return."

"Come then." Lorant looked at the red sun one more time, hooked his arm around Kavan's, and started back on the path he had followed to reach this place. Rhyrdan followed.

❧ * ❧

"I never thought we'd see land again." With his long red hair tied back from his face and neck with a stained strip of faded cloth, the pale man leaned against a stable dock lamppost and groaned as one of his companions, a man with long blonde hair similarly tied back, helped fasten their vessel to a stanchion with practiced ease. Both men were familiar with the sea, had spent much of their lives aboard this same boat or others like it, but this was the first extended voyage for the redhead and some of the others in their dozen-man crew.

He had believed the odds were against them so many times that he was surprised they had made it to a solid shore.

"Where do you think we are?"

The blonde shrugged. "I do not know its name, but I have been here before." An arid land, devoid of snow, devoid of thick forests or the array of green growing things they knew from home, he had been here long enough to trade the goods he had carried for the supplies he would need to return. He had crude maps drawn from those voyages and some passed on from generations before him, but he could not say exactly where they were.

He knew, however, that they were closer to their destination. They would have to speak to the locals, the tanned, weathered-looking taerén with their unfamiliar language that most on the ship would not understand. He was grateful for the gift that allowed him to do so regardless of what some back home thought of such abilities.

The third man with them, a man with sharp, angular features that made his wide-set blue eyes and cheeks appear sunken, wiped away the trickles of sea spray that clung to his lashes, swept his hand through his short, dusty-blonde hair, and gestured to a lone woman standing at the head of the dock, her white robe, pale yellow hair, and unblemished skin the color of fragrant petals beneath the moonlight. Her paleness stood her apart from those around her, men and women who passed as if she were a stone in the flow of their river of movement, men and women who paused to bow and murmur words to her before going their way after a touch of her hand on their arms, their faces, their heads, or hands. A woman who never looked away from the trio and their foreign ship.

The blonde noted her too, read in her a welcoming aura of kinship, and said over his shoulder to those still securing the boat. "Stock what you can," before striding up the dock toward the stranger.

She was waiting for them. For him. He was certain.

"We're not going to be here long, are we?" asked the redhead.

"We're not here for luxury," the short-haired man reminded him.

"We might already be too late."

That was the blonde's fear, too, that after such a voyage, so long away from home, they would be forced to return to report they had failed to accomplish what they were sent to do. That the one they sought was dead.

But stopping before the woman with the ever more familiar features assured him that hope was not yet lost. He bowed, offering the respect the locals gave, and asked, "You are expecting us?"

He was márbhyndhánis for a reason. He had only ever known one other with power such as this woman wielded. Who she was, how she was related to the White Bard, and thus to him, he did not know, but a beacon of power amidst the taerén was here for a purpose.

Her smile, when it came, was melancholy and serious. "You have come for this." She extended her hand. In her open palm, a sunstone whose cut he recognized very well.

"Is he…?" His voice shook, reaching for the stone but loath to touch it.

"No, but he is in grave danger."

"Where might we find him?" asked the redhead.

"This will take you to him. Take it, read it for yourselves…follow where it guides you."

He was the best person for the task, the one most skilled and practiced with the power on the ship, save for his short-haired companion. The blonde swept his hair back again with his other hand and accepted the sunstone with the hand that had reached for it. The stone gave up its most recently stored memory, the man they had come for standing before an unlit hearth in the pale light of early morning, his mood pensive, his thoughts unfocused as he sought the threads that bound him to his wife. Not dead, but there was a clear sense of threat around him that reflected this woman's claim.

Through the stone he felt a path, not laid by Kavan but by someone else…perhaps this same woman. He felt two simultaneous pulls, one to the north, the other to the west and then north again. He knew north. He knew this coastline, knew the arch of shore that would eventually take him south again without a break in the land to allow him to follow that northerly lure.

He did not know what lay to the west, but he trusted the power of her instruction that matched the premonitions that had brought him to this place.

"Follow it, Audh," she murmured, speaking his name without his having given it to her, trying to hide the concern in her sad eyes. "Do not delay. He will need you…even if he thinks he does not."

Audh bowed, clutching the sunstone, and murmured, "We obey."

She held his face between her hands when he straightened, kissed his forehead tenderly, glanced at the men with him with a nod to each, and then stepped back to be swallowed by the passing throng and vanish from sight as though she had not been there. But he could feel her still, her presence strong enough that he was tempted to follow and ask the sudden rush of questions that erupted in his mind. The sunstone in his hand proved she was real and reminded him, despite that urge, that he had a mission to undertake.

She had fed his flagging hope.

"Do you trust her?" the redhead asked, his voice low and awestruck as he craned his neck to find where she had gone.

"Heed Iólán…we do not know…" began their third companion.

Audh shook his head. "I know what I need to know. We have our path." He held the sunstone up to the sun and studied the path of light it shed upon the ground. "We stock what we can and travel west."

He would not fail this mission. He would not fail Raebhá…nor would he fail the White Bard.

❧*❧

The last time Kavan passed amongst so many men beneath a Lachlan banner, Prince Arlan had been on a quest to return Enesfel's throne to its rightful ruler. Now, another Lachlan was on a quest to return a different throne to a different rightful ruler, and though Kavan believed in both causes, and his participation in both conflicts, he lacked the certainty of success he had carried before. He had Earé's army, her reassurances, but those things did not dispel the sense of impending doom he allowed no one else to see. Ártur's confirmation that Earé had traveled with them from Tarsee should have offered hope, but as he walked with Lorant and Jerit amongst the men, offering what inspiration he had to give, Earé was nowhere to be found.

Like Orynn, he suspected their daughter came and went as her duties as k'ílshwythnec demanded, but not to find her after the vision he had interpreted as a summons was unsettling and worrisome.

Eventually, he returned with the king and prince to the royal tent and the fire built in front of it where the other Elyri healers had gathered and where Rhyrdan and the three military leaders waited to discuss their next course of action as they did every night around their fire. The talk of war, however, waited until the final notes of brass strings bled away and the healers, except for Ártur, drifted away to sleep. His cousin's piercing gaze, a probing expression Kavan was familiar with when the healer sensed something wrong and was looking for answers, reached across the fire but Kavan refused to meet it. He had no answers. Sharing his potentially illogical sense of doom and dread would only create worry where none was needed. These people needed hope and assurance, not more worry and fear.

Kavan listened to the generals' plans, the counter plans, the debates about how to best stand against Fraen's force, having nothing to add as he was no military strategist, and when Lorant stood and beckoned him to follow with his other hand on Jerit's shoulder bidding him to stay, Kavan followed as asked, grateful to be free of Ártur's fears.

He nodded at Rhyrdan to likewise remain at the fire and glean every detail he could. Rhyrdan relented but only because there were many soldiers to keep Kavan safe when he could not.

"This war troubles you."

It was an obvious thing to say, but a statement that Kavan expected would prompt Lorant to speak what was on his mind.

"I'm not too young to understand the gravity of what we're undertaking…though sometimes I think they see me that way. General Declan thinks we are safe here, but I cannot shake this constant sense that I am being watched."

"You are being watched," Kavan agreed.

"Not by the men…by someone out there," he gestured beyond the perimeter of the encampment. "Someone I can't see. I'm sick of riding, sick of tents and this food. I'm sick of sweat and the heat, and having no time for myself…no privacy. Jerit's the only one who listens, who sympathizes without judgment or effort to remind me of duty and honor…without the reminder that every one of these men are suffering as I am. By the stars, most of them have come this far on foot, without a horse to ease their burdens. I should not complain…"

"Some complaints and concerns are natural; they share it with you, as you say, and talk of such things amongst themselves. I am sorry I cannot ease your burden more, but it is good that Jerit is here for you."

"I thought I could do this without him…when I asked him to remain behind…but I'm glad he knew me better than I know myself. Rhyrdan said something about you seeking a means to end this war."

Kavan shook his head, reluctant to shatter the hopeful note in Lorant's voice with his as yet dubious claim to a relic he did not understand. "I have found…something…but I do not yet know how to employ it…what it will do…if it will be enough to change the course of this war. I had hoped Earé would be here, that she could tell me what I have found and how to use it."

"She was here, but I do not know where she has gone. tama Yetek believes she will return before we march, since she did say she would ride with us into battle." Kavan frowned and Lorant continued with a shrug. "tama Yetek speaks highly of her prowess with a sword."

"If she is like her mother, she will be a daunting opponent," Kavan agreed, though the admission was not enough to reassure him. Perhaps that was the root of his uneasiness. "You will see to her safety?"

"As best I can," Lorant promised.

"General Declan says you will leave Fiara in three days?"

Lorant nodded. "That is our plan. I would prefer to remain longer, but there is much talk of Fraen's force taking Ruidoso, ravaging farmland, and pressing men into a war they do not want. Some will remain here to defend Fiara, to protect our back, as there is no military might to defend the city if Fraen's army comes here, but I worry it will not be enough for the task or that it will be too many and will be to the detriment of the rest of our force."

"Fiara will stand." Kavan had no sense that war would touch Owain's city again. Fiara had endured enough.

Lorant side-eyed him, grateful they were far enough beyond the edge of the camp now so that no one could hear their muted voices. "That is something," he admitted. If no harm was to fall to Fiara, then perhaps it meant Neth's army would never reach her walls. Perhaps it meant that he and Enesfel's army and the allies that had joined him would drive Fraen back to the northern shore of Curo, even if they did not ultimately reclaim the de Corrmick throne.

"You will not stay?"

"If I am to learn the nature of what I have found…how it might help you…I must return tonight. I want to keep Enesfel safe as much as I wish it for you. It is late already, and Ágdhállán is expecting me."

"Very well," the king sighed, accepting the answer he had expected without a desire to press his will upon his mentor and friend. Will you wait here while I send Rhyrdan to you, or will you go on ahead to the Gate?"

"I will be here. And tell Ártur…I will see him again soon."

Lorant started down the hillock where they had stopped to overlook the host of men with their dimming campfires that spread like a sea of starlight mirroring the sky above. He turned before he went any further, raced back up the incline, and threw his arms around the bard's neck.

Kavan froze, shocked and blinded by the one thing he had sought to avoid since Lorant had been born, since he had inherited the half-moon pendant from his father.

Metal pressed against metal. Power bloomed. Threads raced through him like liquid needles pulling molten filaments to knot and bind Lachlan king and Elyri bard together through life and death. The abruptness of the binding, the strength and speed with which it occurred, allowed Kavan no time to embrace Lorant in return before the king, embarrassed by the childlike expression of affection, drew back, gazed at Kavan with an adoring smile, and then hurried into the camp with steps as dignified and calm as he could make them.

Kavan waited until he could no longer see Lorant before unlocking his knees and dropping to them, pushing the pendants back beneath his tunic, hands trembling so that he fumbled with them several times before succeeding. If anything happened to Lorant now, Kavan would feel it as surely as he would feel any injury of his own. He did not know how the bond worked in the other direction, if Lorant would also feel Kavan's experiences.

To his knowledge, none of the other kings and one queen who had gone before him had done so.

This was a link between them that Bhás could use against them both if she learned about it. The possibility that she could hurt Lorant and others through that link terrified him. But the wheels of destiny were turning now.

Kavan was helpless to undo it without taking Lorant's life.

Or his own.

&Chapter 39&

"He will be with you shortly." dedhá Hwensen bowed, eager to remain with the bard but unwilling to intrude on the business that brought Kavan to Clarys. Like the whole of the city, the staff and residents of Hes Dhágdhuán were preparing for war despite the resistance of many to believe that a foreign army could breach Elyriá's interior. Such a threat had never existed; Elyriá had always been safe.

As Kavan followed Hwensen through the halls after speaking first with Kluín and Paul, the gaze of every person they passed trailed behind them, some staring in curiosity, some in concern, and some with the lingering distrust and certainty that Kavan was more of a heretic than the living saint some professed him to be. He was only a man. Even Hwensen, however, struggle as he did, sometimes had difficulty making the distinction.

"Is there news about the…?"

"Hwensen." k'gdhededhá Ylár clucked his tongue as he strode into his chamber, the long folds of his Gathering robes swishing around his feet so that he appeared to float above the worn, ancient, stone floor. "There is no need for gossip."

"Not gossip," Hwensen protested. "There is war…or will be a war; people have questions."

"And I will give them answers when I have them. There is no need to pester Lord Cliáth with the same questions over and over."

"It is no trouble," Kavan interjected. While it was true he did not want to repeat himself, he had already answered Kluín and Paul's questions and was about to answer Ylár's. Including Hwensen in their conversation seemed fair. "The King's army was in Fiara. If they departed the city as intended, they should leave the mountains within a few days. Rhidam, Levone, and Alberni have been at rest. We have had no communications from the other sovereignties or Káliel to suggest trouble."

After three peaceful days engrossed in the care and teaching of the children in Rhidam's keep, after perusing every potentially promising book there in the hopes of learning more about the tai sturmyrá, Kavan had come to Clarys in the hope that the Faith's library, or the Kyne's, would offer him valuable details. Phílóá was unavailable but promised him access to any books her staff could locate that contained histories of Bhórdh and its surrounding regions, and Kluín and Paul likewise, after questioning him about some of the finer details of dhóbhaen history they had been asked by those they taught, were rummaging through the vast stores of books the Faith protected for anything that might be useful. They would bring their findings to him by evening, and he had been asked to return to the Kyne to retrieve whatever documents she could provide. He would have permission to take those books to Enesfel long enough to read them, with the condition that they would be returned as soon as he was finished with them.

After his recent time away, he had been reluctant to come to Clarys, but Níkóá's need to deliver a message to the Kyne had given him an excuse. He did not intend to be away from Rhidam any longer than necessary.

"That means they could be…" stammered Hwensen. Like Ylár, he had never been to Neth. What he knew of the landscape came from the study of maps that every gdhededhá in Hes Dhágdhuán was required to undertake to understand the world they served.

Kavan lifted his hand, prompted to clutch the suddenly tingling half-moon pendant against his chest, but he forced himself to lower it and murmured, "I believe I will know when the fighting begins. So far, their journey has been without incident."

"Yes," Ylár agreed, "I believe you will. Hwensen said you wish to speak with me?"

Taking that as his cue to depart, knowing he would be given no further details about the impending war, Hwensen awkwardly bowed and said, "I will aid dedhá Kluín with your request," and backed out of the room.

"Request?" Ylár began the tedious process of removing his layered robes of office, and Kavan, having spent his time serving the Faith as all Elyri children did, set down his pack and began to assist the older man without being asked. Ylár cocked one brow at the unexpected assistance but did not address it.

"I need information about Zythán."

Ylár did not outwardly react. A man of learning and Faith who had been raised in the Zythánite shadow, although few in Elyriá knew it, Ylár was the best hope, Kavan believed, to give answers. The bard had never judged Ylár for his history, had never spoken of it before, but it had only been a matter of time, Ylár supposed, before the questions came.

Kavan continued evenly, setting each item of the regalia aside as he spoke. "I recently acquired two items said to have been created and empowered by him. I seek information about them, their creation, their function and purpose..."

"You think I...?"

"I know of no one else who might know anything, even myth or rumor, that might point me to the answers I seek." If Tíbhyan was still alive, Kavan would have gone to him first. Now, there was no one else he could turn to except the one man he knew with a connection, however distant, to that figure out of Elyriá's past.

When the last piece of the regalia was set aside, Ylár stepped away to wash his face and hands in the water basin set upon an elaborately carved dresser that had been in this room during the reigns of his previous two predecessors. Kavan, meanwhile, removed the wooden box from his pack, removed the tai sturmyrá from within it, jumping, startled, when his fingers touched the glass, and then set it and the white stone stylus from around his neck onto the dresser to the left of the wash basin.

Ylár watched out of the corner of his eye with a perplexed, serious expression, aware of the shifting energy in the room as soon as the sturmyrá was removed from its wooden case.

"Those who gave it to me called it máltai sturmyrá...I am sure you know the folktales. I was told it was intended as a light source..."

His voice trailed off as he touched it again with both hands so that the continual sparking between the paired crystals shot tongues of lightning in every direction within the glass.

He inserted the stone key into the hole. With the connection made between them, the crystals sparked with colored veins of illumination while the contained space around them filled with a swirling mist-like glow. "It absorbs energy...and generates it...but I do not know why."

Ylár passed his hand over the sturmyrá without touching it, marveling at the way the mist shifted as if following his hand. The sizzle of power emanating from it was detectably drawn toward Kavan even though the bard was no longer touching the box and had taken a step away from it.

"There are stories...as you say..." The k'dedhá lowered his hand until it almost touched the glass, felt the power of it stretch up as if to envelope his hand, and then jerked away before it could do so. "He was the Faith's first saint, you know? Only briefly...barely a generation. It was said that he possessed a tool…something infused with dark power that enabled him to perform the acts attributed to him. Something he used to control the weather…to influence people's will, to kill. Those who believed this eventually erased his name from history, turning him into a monster. No one could find this tool or knew what it looked like…what it was. Some said it was buried in the grove, that it corrupted those who believed in him." He looked over his shoulder. "Where did you find this?"

"The key came from Bhórdh. It was given to me by the lómesté. The sturmyrá…it was hidden beyond the desert…"

"Beyond the desert?" Ylár was silent for a moment, then nodded once. "It is said he was a great traveler, a wanderer…but his history, if it was known, was erased, as you are aware. Any record of his travels is lost…just as this was."

Kavan nodded too and removed the key to hang around his neck once more. He cringed at the heat it gave off and adjusted it against his chest. The most he had learned was that the sturmyrá was some a conductor, just as Ágdhállán indicated. Had Zythán made it to gather more power to make the creation of Gates for his travels easier? So that there was no longer the need for multiple people to build one, but so that he could do so alone? Or had it served a function in the sea crossing from Dhóbhaen to their new home in the west? Did it enhance the powers of the staff and cup? And what, he mused, did those three relics combined create?

When the white stone rested against his chest, a searing, sharp bolt of power drove through his sternum and brought with it a strangling thread of unidentified dread. Blood. Smoke. Holy incense and sulfur and the rustling crack of leafy branches. The neighs of panicked horses. The shouts of men caught unaware. A whispered name spoken in hatred and defiance. Horror. Shadows in the shadows at his back, the sense of someone he thought he should know but could not identify. Unable to breathe, Kavan staggered and fell, only avoiding crashing to the floor because of the arms that caught him.

Through the tangle of Enesfel's northern-most mountain forest, or Neth's southern-most mountain forest depending on who one asked, where the overhead branches trapped the heat of St. Bhílycá's Day so that sweat dripped into the eyes of the men leading the procession and down the faces of the men who marched behind, three riders strained their senses seeking the reason the horses were so edgy. Two days out from Fiara, five days from the edge of the heavy gloom this summer day was creating. Those three most experienced in combat, sensitive to their horses' agitation, slowed the pace as they sought the unseen threat amidst the ongoing creak and snap of branches and twigs under the shuffle of hooves, feet, and wagon wheels through the dry leaves lost the winter before.

"A trap?" whispered Garran, passing back a hand signal that would direct the troops to be cautious and watchful.

"Undoubtedly," Bhetá agreed. When a loud cracking sound caused Kaj's horse to startle, she grabbed its reins. Her sideways lean prevented an errant arrow from finding its mark as a host of men armed with clubs, short swords, and the Curna of the Nethite royal guard burst from the trees on both sides of the road. The arrow dug into Kaj's bicep and pitched him from his horse, and shouts and screams and the clatter of combat ripped out from where they were back through the ranks toward the rear of the column.

Only one other arrow was loosed.

Bhetá did not question why as she leaped from her horse and bodily slammed into the armored foe who charged in to take advantage of Kaj's momentary incapacitation.

The healers and dedhá in the wagon dropped to the floorboards when the whir of the second arrow buzzed overhead, bringing with it a burst of fire as the canvas cover above them began to burn.

"Out! Get out!" Ártur shouted. gdhededhá Thrismund, seated closest to the drop-down rear panel, kicked it open and rolled out in front of the swerving supply wagon and the soldiers who dashed forward to surround and protect them. Thrismund pulled the healers from the wagon one by one while, inside it, Hebel and Ybherd did their best to yank the burning canvas down and stomp the fire out before it could set the rest of the wagon alight.

Between the wagons and the three generals, Lorant was the first man off his horse, acting on some gut instinct as he slashed through the first two opponents to reach the caravan. The three men behind that first pair were bigger, broader men, with dirty hands and bearded, grizzled faces, unprotected by helmets and wearing minimal, piecemeal armor. Heedless of the danger of being outnumbered, Lorant charged. At the edge of the footpath, where the ground sloped to allow the spring runoff to rush to a lower elevation, his feet slipped from beneath him as he swung. He rolled to lift his sword defensively against the blows he expected, but the first blow to fall was blocked by Jerit's narrower blade, already bloody from an opponent Lorant had not seen him strike down. Distracted by the new arrival, the other two attackers focused on Jerit instead, allowing Lorant to struggle to his feet to reenter the fray.

His ankle was tender, twisted, barely able to support his weight, but he and Jerit fought side by side until the swarm stopped filtering out of the forest and the day grew still.

Still, that was, except for the groans of injured men that wove from the back of the column.

"Pháraeís, Bhárás, come with me. Ylltán, collect the injured nearest us. Bring them for treatment and see to the king."

It was Ártur's voice, but Lorant could not see him.

"We shouldn't stop here," someone barked. "They'll be back."

"We're not leaving anyone behind," Garran countered.

Clutching his bleeding arm with the broken arrow protruding from it, Kaj reached Ártur's side but spoke to the woman who had begun to pull the enemy dead to the side of the road while others collected any weapon or piece of armor they could find. "They may still be here; perhaps we should pursue them back to their camp."

Bhetá kicked over a dead man and picked up his Curna. "They're undoubtedly out there." They had discussed the possibility of an ambush in the forest, but none of them had expected Neth's army to risk encroaching on Enesfel's border.

Back upon the road now, Lorant leaning on Jerit to keep his weight off his injured ankle, he muttered, "Circle the wagons. Once we're secured, while the healers work, we send scouts ahead."

Ártur pushed others aside to reach Lorant. "You are injured." He did not use Lorant's title, not wanting to draw attention to the king if they were being watched. A lord or king would be a prime target.

"Twisted my ankle." Lorant waved off Ártur's hands. "Take care of the others. You can check on this later."

Ártur nodded and set off toward the back of the column to tend the dead and dying as far back as this enemy force had crossed.

❧*❦

"Kavan."

Ylár's questioning tone gave Kavan something to focus on when the visionary sights and sounds continued to fade from his senses and restore the expected familiarity of the k'gdhededhá's chambers. The older man was concerned and wanted answers and reassurances, but they were not something Kavan felt confident he could provide.

"I…" The sense of Lorant, battle adrenaline, weariness, and throbbing pain washed over him and caused his hands to flex around a sword hilt he could feel, though it was not in his hand. His arm ached from the exertion of combat, and there was blood pounding in his ears as he struggled to breathe calmly. He sat up slowly, finding himself on the k'dedhá's bed, and tested the expected dizziness as he murmured, "War has begun."

Ylár sat beside him, his expression grim. "Have we…?"

"Not here…King Lorant. He is safe…but I do not know how the troops have fared." For a first clash, he could tell that Enesfel had survived from the bloom of relief the young king unknowingly transmitted through the Lachlan-Cliath bond. An ambush by border raiders, it appeared, but the conflict was far from over. One victory meant little when it had been an effort to harass rather than repel them.

What Kavan did glean from the barrage of images that had assailed him was that there was another warning that struck closer to home. He held Ylár's hand, unable to share with him the details he could detect amidst the scattered experiences he had been shown, but he could convey the sense of danger and urgency that came with them.

"You are in danger. I do not know from who…from what…when or how…but please, promise me you will take heed and be cautious."

Ylár scowled, accepting the limitations of the Sight without asking for more details. So, war would strike at the heart of the Faith. Would he live? Would he die? It was best, he decided, that he prepare for the latter while holding on to the faith of the former.

"Thank you for the warning," he said gravely, helping Kavan sit on the edge of the bed and then helping him to his feet when he tried to stand. "You may rest here," he offered. There is no need to hasten your recovery. While you were…Kluín brought these," he gestured to the small bundle of books bound together by leather straps, "and I put the sturmyrá…"

Kavan nodded, dismayed that the collection was not larger but stubbornly hopeful that this was only the start of what else Kluín might find. His pack sat beside the books; he could not see inside, but he trusted that Ylár would not have confiscated the sturmyrá or turned it over to the k'lómesté for evaluation and study.

"I must see Kyne before I return to Rhidam. They must know…"

Again, Ylár nodded. "I will prepare the Faithful, of course…and if I think of anything that might aid in your research, I will send word. Do you think…will the sturmyrá be of use?"

"Perhaps." Ylár, like Kavan, did not believe it a coincidence that such an artifact had fallen into his hands at this moment in history. The will of the divine moved through the White Bard of Bhryell…

…whether Kavan, or anyone else, wished it to.

❧*❦

"We've lost three dozen." Ártur moaned as he sank down at the fire where Lorant rested with his foot propped on Jerit's thigh. His boot had been removed, dropped to one side, so the healer could see in the light of the fire the discoloration the twisting had caused. "Twice as many injured, but few fatally so. We're moving the worst into the wagon to rest." Most of those would be recovered enough to fight again after a decent night's sleep…and after the Elyri healers had rested enough to provide them additional care.

"You're being displaced," muttered Lorant apologetically.

Ártur wrapped his hands gingerly around the king's ankle and nodded when the king winced. "To be expected…and worth the discomfort if it gets those men on their feet…unless you wish to send them back to Fiara." Closer to the city than to the northern treeline, it was an option worth considering if they did not want the injured to slow them down.

Bhetá shook her head when Lorant looked to her for advice. Garran and Kaj were walking among the injured, providing reassurances that the king was unable to give until his injury was tended. Many of Kaj's men had asked for k'ílshwythnec; he could only promise to send her when he found her, rather than disappoint them by revealing that she was not here. Many believed, as he did, that she could fight as well as any man, but thus far she had not proved it.

Not that Kaj had seen.

"We would have to send an escort with them…maybe a physician. Near as they've gotten to Fiara, there's likely to be other ambushes waiting. We need all the men we can keep with us."

Kaj and his scouts had penetrated the forest on both sides of the road, and though they had found the remnant of an encampment, there had been no one there. No one believed Enesfel was lucky enough to destroy the entire ambush party. Survivors had likely retreated elsewhere to prepare for Enesfel's eventual arrival. The scouts would spread on both flanks as they traveled to flush out any ambushes, with the knowledge that such an action might be exactly what Neth hoped they would do, that they would use such an effort to pick off Enesfel's forces one small group at a time.

They could camp until the wounded were ready to travel, send them back to Fiara, or they could be loaded into the healers' wagon so that the army could forge ahead. The generals had already expressed their preferences, and the healers had, it seemed, agreed before the choice was made, and now that Ártur had taken away as much of the pain and damage from his sprained ankle as he could, Lorant, too, saw little need to remain camped as a target.

He looked at Jerit who had not spoken a word since saving Lorant's life. Knowing the time for expressing gratitude would come when others were asleep or when they rode together side by side in the morning, the prince nodded his head. Their expressions were equally strained, equally stricken by the first blood shed by their hands, a memory that there was not enough water in the world to wash away.

Ártur remembered that same look on Arlan's face, on so many young men's faces, when their first drink of war was forced down their tight, aching throats.

It would either get easier for them or harder. Neither, for the healer, was ideal; there was only necessity and the need to survive when the time for bloodshed came again.

"Daybreak then," Lorant muttered, appreciating the healer's unspoken sympathy while wishing it was Kavan seated beside him to offer advice and comfort. "And Ártur...we will find another wagon if we can."

"Aye, My King...if we can."

❧*❧

Kavan listened to the mid-evening silence of the community settling down to bed with Phílóá's promise in his ears, a bittersweet oath wrung out of her despite her reluctance to give it. If anything happened to him, if his efforts to stop Bhás failed, he wanted to be certain the young Kyne would protect Lorant and his heirs for as long as she remained the head of Elyriá's strength. If war did not take her, if illness or childbirth did not take her, it might allow roughly three hundred years of security for the Lachlan dynasty, security that Kavan believed he would not be around to offer.

Until the bond of Faith could be restored between Teren and Elyri, the bond between the Kyne and the Lachlan rulers was the only thing that would unite those sovereignties.

He shifted the pack on his shoulder, ignoring the hum of power he could feel as he took the borrowed books to the scriptorium. More books were gone now, stored safely in Gorbesh, and every book spread open on each writing desk all bore the same text. The story Kavan had written down of the connection between the dhóbhaen, the Elyri, and Dhágdhuán the Intercessor. For as long as scribes remained in St. Kóráhm's, these would be the last words written here. It would have been more fitting, perhaps, for some tale of St. Kóráhm to hold that honor, but for now, there was nothing more of the Saint's life for Kavan to tell.

Some of those secret stories were his words alone, contained below the chellé hábhai, awaiting their turn to be moved to Gorbesh.

He lit a lantern, set it in the study alcove he most often used, and began to pour through the borrowed volumes, one by one, taking advantage of the silence. Rhyrdan would already be irritated that he had not returned to Rhidam for dinner as promised, but Kavan had not foreseen the Sight and the hour or more he had spent stuck in its voice upon Ylár's bed. He had not anticipated the impulse that had demanded he wait for Phílóá to finish her business for the day so that he could speak privately with her. By now, Rhyrdan was either asleep or was sitting in the oratory waiting.

Kavan should go to him.

Tonight, he believed it more important to delve through the books he had borrowed while the opportunity of silence remained.

❧ * ❦

The fortress protecting Rísóri Pass was nestled at the bottom of a sheer gorge between jagged mountain faces dotted with forest wherever the hearty northern pines had found a foothold. It was suspended over a turbulent, narrow river and a steep ancient path cut and worn through the northern Llaethlágárá by centuries of tradesmen with their caravans of sturdy wagons pulled by mules, oxen, and horses. The pines grew denser as the forest spread down the mountains towards the sea, and the river was too rough and littered with discarded boulders to make either a passable, alternative route.

There was only the narrow trade road, made impassible by snow and ice for much of the year, and with the gated Rísóri outpost guarding the path, it was considered by most an impossible place for an invading force to cross. The Nethite fear of Elyri power, the long-held predominant belief that those who lived on the other side of the serrated peaks could obliterate the world with their minds if they chose, had been deterrent enough to prevent anyone from trying.

Now it was midsummer, cool at this altitude and hour of the night, but lacking the hazards of snow and ice. Bhríd stood upon the parapet, staring at the empty road where it rounded the nearest bend and disappeared out of sight. Most men stationed here were asleep, but there were others diligently keeping watch whilst murmuring about the unlikely possibility that Neth would dare come here.

They had an overabundance of weapons, food, and supplies. They had more men than had ever been stationed here. They had a dozen healers from all over Elyriá, and they had gdhededhá Bhílári from Bhryell to serve the spiritual needs of the Faithful, should they face something few Elyri had ever contemplated facing.

War had never come to Elyriá. Those who knew war, like Bhríd, had experienced it elsewhere.

The surprise of Bhílári's presence was only matched by that of the young man at Bhríd's side, peering into the rushing water, listening to the sounds of footsteps and voices that the river made difficult to hear.

"He doesn't know I'm here," Sóbhán said in answer to his kinsman's unspoken question.

"He would tell you to go home." He had been here for a week, coordinating the distribution of supplies and weapons, where to store the excess, where to house the additional men and women who trickled in to support the war effort. He had coordinated scouts to move through the trees, scouts to watch the road, and scouts to position themselves in small groups further down the gorge where word could be swiftly sent back when the first enemy soldiers arrived.

And from those Elyri of power, Bhríd had coordinated other defenses to keep the fortress strong and protected. They were not Kavan, did not have his skills, but whatever they could offer was of use. If Nethite soldiers made it to the head of the gorge, despite Bhríd's best efforts, he wanted to be sure the structure stood.

"You are here. Ártur and Syl are at the battlefront. Though I don't know what he is doing, what he intends to do, k'bhydhá is scared. He anticipates involvement in some way…as if this war is his fault and responsibility. I cannot allow him to shoulder this alone."

Bhríd sighed, unable to refute any of the younger man's claims. "Your father often takes on the responsibilities of others, for others, when he should not." Since the day he and his siblings were recruited to Prince Arlan's cause, Bhríd had often seen how Kavan felt personally responsible for matters he had no control over. This instance was no different.

"He plans to do something," Sóbhán said softly. "Something spectacular, magnificent, horrifying. He will not accept my help, but if Elyriá is in danger, then I should be here. It is my home; I should do my part. Here or Clarys or…anywhere else." He hesitated as he watched a curly-horned mountain ram cross the road to drink from the river and then turn and bound back up the mountain. "You believe they will come here…as he says?"

"I believe him." Again, Bhríd was silent as he gauged the path of the stars in the cloudless sky. "If you insist on being here, you will do exactly as I order…not just as your kin but as your general. He will never forgive me if anything happens to you."

"So long as you don't shelter me from duty, I will obey your leadership," Sóbhán agreed, sounding less certain about his choice than he had moments before.

Bhríd took that as a good sign and hoped those doubts would prompt Sóbhán to go home. Not counting on that, however, he said, "Good. Get some rest…and in the morning, try to keep dedhá Bhílári out of the way. We will secure a space to conduct Gatherings so he may stay there…and then I will find a post for you."

"Wherever I am needed," Sóbhán again agreed. There would be no harp-making here, but he could carve arrows, he could muck stalls, and he could fight. Anywhere Bhríd could use him was good enough.

<h1 style="text-align:center">❧Chapter 40❦</h1>

Four days and two more ambushes brought the loss of more than one hundred men along the secondary trade road they had taken so that by the time Enesfel's army reached the treeline and the revelation of a military camp posted within a thousand yards of the forest's edge that Garran estimated to be five hundred men strong, the king, weary and sick at heart, doubted they would ever make it to Glevum, that they would be able to stand against the might of the Nethite army.

Bhetá assured him that once on flat, open ground, without trees to mask the enemy, where they would see what was ahead and where their force could spread out beyond the three-horse-abreast travel formation the forest road forced them to take, their luck would turn.

Kaj and Garran said the same thing, and Jerit tried to assure him his generals' advice was sound.

Being met by the not-unexpected encampment, likely, Garran said, containing the leadership and serving as the base camp for the forest ambush scouts, Lorant doubted his generals could be right about their chances of success.

"I'll deal with this."

Lorant frowned at Jerit, grabbed his arm, and shook his head. "They'll kill you!"

Grateful he was not wearing a de Corrmick insignia or tabard, thankful that the de Corrmick banner had yet to be raised on his father and nephew's behalf, Jerit shrugged out of his cloak and adjusted his armor. "I'm the best diplomat we have. We don't know who they are…and we can't risk you or the generals." No banners flew over the encampment, no flags or pennants. As far as anyone could see, they could be a collection of displaced peasants or townsfolk trying to avoid Fraen's army. "They won't know who I am. Gather the others, be ready…and I'll do my best to…"

Bhetá said, "Take dedhá Thrismund with you." Until Fraen had stolen the throne, Neth, too, had held four seats on the Teren Faith Council. Inness had ordered one killed on suspicion that he was Vants, and two others had been lost to the plague. The fourth had remained in Ruidoso, as near to Neth as he dared go, and had worked to bolster the Faith's growth there.

He had not been heard from in over a year. Most assumed he was dead.

"That's a risk," Lorant began.

"But a sound one," Thrismund agreed. "They may or may not be soldiers…but they may be men of Faith who will respect me. I may be able to temper their mood, should they take offense at our presence."

Garran motioned to one of the mounted men. "Give him your horse."

There was grumbling, but the soldier did as instructed.

"Two hours," Lorant grunted as Thrismund swung onto the horse with ease. "Two hours and you return to us…or they send their ambassadors. Two hours…then I will come for you."

Not we.

Masking his anxiety with a smile and the suppressed desire to kiss Lorant's pouting lips, Jerit bobbed his head. "I expect nothing less."

Enesfel's recruited soldiers, conscripted men from every duchy across the kingdom, Lachlan guards, and the mercenary host from south of Hatu emerged from the forest behind him, spreading across the open plain, filling in the emptiness as Lorant watched the pair grow smaller as they approached the distant camp. When a small group of men rode forward to meet them, postured as though they expected a fight, Lorant unsheathed the sword Kavan had given him and moved his horse forward, only to be cut off by all three generals who shook their heads and herded him back into the security of his army.

The hum of insects, the chatter of birds in the trees at their backs and in the tall, unfarmed grasses that stretched to the north were a calming mask over a conversation Lorant could not hear. The clatter of his horse's hooves as he paced side to side likewise prevented him from hearing anything, despite how he strained his ears to detect what his eyes could not see. When eventually one of the horses returned to them at a gallop, it took all Bhetá's effort to restrain the king from dashing ahead.

Particularly when it was evident that Thrismund was returning alone.

"Vants, My King," Thrismund said eagerly when Kaj caught his horse's head. "And supporters of King Kjell…awaiting our arrival."

"Out in the open?" Garran asked with a frown. "That doesn't seem…"

"They've had their losses, been picking off scouts and messengers sent from Ruidoso. They say General Waller's out here somewhere, further west on the main road, they believe. They've been posing as mercenaries waiting to catch us, so far, Waller's left them alone.

"How do we know that's not what they are?" asked the man who had given up his horse to Thrismund and who gladly accepted it back now that the dedhá was on the ground.

"I trust the prince's judgment," Thrismund said defiantly. "They welcome us to join their camp and are eager to fight for King Kjell's return if you'll have them, My Liege."

Lorant's countenance darkened. They would fight for Kjell, for Jerit…but would they fight for him? It was logical they should fight on behalf of their homeland, but in a weary pique of frustration, rooted in his concern for Jerit, who had chosen to remain with his people and not come back to him, Lorant contemplated turning his horse, his troops, around and allowing this puny band of mismatched men to fight for themselves.

But this was not just a war for Neth's throne. This was an offensive strike against an army determined to attack everyone around them. Fraen's choices had already proved that it was so. Lorant could not allow that to continue. Nor could he allow Jerit to ride against Glevum for a throne he did not want without Enesfel's strength behind him.

"General?"

"No harm in talking," Garran said. "If they're honest, we'll know soon enough. We could use the men to replace what we've lost."

"We watch for Neth's force. By now they're taking the road we're taking…they'll be on the move to intercept us," Bhetá reminded them.

Kaj cocked his head towards the encampment. "Still half a day to ride if we push on until sunset. We should consider going on…put as much distance as we can between us and our enemies."

The three looked at each other, and at Lorant, before nodding in agreement. A fast messenger was sent ahead as the signal to march was conveyed to all the anxious soldiers with them.

Lorant was not certain it was the wisest choice, but it was, he decided, the best choice they had.

❧*❦

After his late-night return and the restless difficulty he had in falling asleep, his efforts plagued by the queen's revelation of pregnancy and the ongoing pricks of Sight that were too vague and untethered to give him anything specific to hold on to, it was no surprise for Kavan to wake with the afternoon sunlight streaming through his opened windows, or to feel someone else in the room with him. Without clearing his head of the Sight remnants and the heaviness of not enough sleep, he groaned, licked the taste of sea-salt from his lips that supported the images of billowing sails and rolling surf he could recall, rolled over without opening his eyes and murmured, "Have you waited long?" assuming as he spoke that Rhyrdan had been at his side since dawn broke.

"Long enough, átaelás mai."

The familiar voice, heavy with emotion but not Rhyrdan, made Kavan open his eyes and sit to greet his guest properly. The sheet slid from his bare shoulders and pooled around his hips as he rubbed his eyes to clear them.

"I did not know it was…"

"Obviously." The man seated in the desk chair pulled close to the bed tried to grin, but it was a forced expression that made Kavan frown and reach for the saint's hand. Kóráhm pulled his away to brush his hair from his face, and Kavan, unsure if the action was meant to avoid contact that Kóráhm normally accepted, dropped his trembling hand to his lap.

"You have come with a warning." He knew Kóráhm well. After so many years, he could tell if the saint wanted to cheer him, inform him, or answer questions, desired his company, or had something dire to reveal. His dour mien and nervously wandering gaze suggested the latter, and Kavan's breath seized within his chest. "Is it…?"

"I wish I knew." His shaky voice made Kavan's eyes tear. He had never heard Kóráhm sound as melancholy and full of regret. "I have heard her voice as you have…her laughter. She is stronger now, closer, perhaps traveling on the ships that draw near to Káliel and Hatu. They must not be allowed here. They must not come aground. Tell your allies, take warnings…they must be ready."

"If she is…if I go…won't I be…" The Sight had shown him ships. Had revealed the smell of the sea. Had given him the weighted sense of an unidentified threat along with a too familiar laugh and the feeling of hard eyes clawing into his soul from a place he could not see.

Kóráhm faded before his eyes, leaving the question unanswered and the sense of his hand upon Kavan's head.

There was nothing else left.

Bhás. On a boat? Bound for where?

His guess, rooted in everything he had seen over the last decade, was that she was bound for Alberni. Looking for the relics. Looking for Kavan.

Looking to destroy anything connected to the desecration of Coryllien's corpse, his tomb, his legacy.

Hastily dressing, trying to shake off the fear dragging against his hurried steps that made them feel awkward and tentative, he followed the sense of Níkóá through the castle halls until he found both the regent and Rhyrdan engaged in swordplay with Sunna while the boys watched. Zerio entertained Henrik, Hela, and Ida with sleights of hand and intricately folded bits of colored paper while Master Najar read poetry to Queen Seren and the younger girls. When the children saw Kavan, however, they ran to throw their arms around him, and though most of the adults showed more restraint, they too stopped what they were doing to greet him, leaving only Sunna standing a deferential distance away with his head bowed in respect.

"Apologies for not coming sooner; there were delays in Clarys that…"

"You gave the Kyne my message?" asked Níkóá.

"Did k'dedhá Ylár clarify anything?" asked Zerio.

"Are you okay?" The last question was asked simultaneously by both Rhyrdan, who studied him with eyes that sought an explanation for the dark circles of sleeplessness beneath Kavan's eyes, and by Ágdhállán who wrapped his arms around his father's waist and clung to him with his power center open, hoping to absorb the shadows from Kavan's eyes or chase them away with his youthful brightness. Kavan wrapped an arm around his son and held him close.

"I am well." Well did not mean unafraid, but he did not want to voice his fears in front of the children. "I gave your message to the Kyne but did not receive notice from her or the council by the time I departed."

"You need to see what Henrik painted," piped Hella, tugging at Kavan's hand.

"And see our progress," Phaedr and Cáym chimed in. "Lord Sunna has been teaching us how to use his sword…"

"His waji," Ágdhállán corrected.

"Still a sword," grumbled Phaedr.

"We made flower chains for St. Bhílycá," Ónyká said. "Master Najar showed us how. Hella made the prettiest…"

"Kaedís' was much nicer," Hella protested despite her proud grin.

Before the requests could turn into bickering demands for his attention, Kavan nodded to each of them. "Allow me words with Lord McCábhá, then we shall see all in turn. Go inside and prepare for dinner; we will see everything afterward."

"Yes, my lord!" Their exclamations accompanied the sounds of retreating, running footsteps, but Ágdhállán remained where he was, unwilling to relinquish his hold until Rhyrdan gently pried him away. He and the boy would demand time from Kavan later, but this was not the place. Sunna gathered the discarded practice swords and followed Zerio towards the barracks and weapons' house while Níkóá waited where he stood until he and Kavan were alone.

"What is it you can tell me but not them?"

Kavan's eyes remained on his son until the boy was out of sight, and only then answered the question. "You are the only other, besides myself, who knows the Gates..."

"Yóáná and Aunes..."

"They don't know Hatu or Káliel. They're not diplomats."

"You need me to go to Hatu and Káliel?"

"They will be beset with warships soon. They must be prepared."

Níkóá scowled. "That's the sort of thing you typically handle. Isn't that why you went to Clarys? To Fiara?"

"I think it is news they should hear from you, on Lorant's behalf."

"But I do not..."

"Kóráhm...the Sight...warned of warships at their shores, warned them not to allow those ships to dock. I know nothing more detailed than that...and I have been away from the children too much..."

"You have been away from all of us too much," Níkóá agreed. There was something Kavan was not saying, a note of reluctant fear in his voice that made Níkóá believe there was a personal reason Kavan did not want to leave Rhidam or his son. Sullenly, he admitted that sending Kavan to attend to these short-lived diplomatic matters would turn into longer absences if Gamal and Piran requested his attention, his music. But it was the bard's fear that prompted him to sigh and say, "I will do this, but I ask two things of you in return."

"What might I do for you?"

Again, that note of fear. Níkóá clasped his shoulder affectionately and smiled. "Play for us at dinner, please. Your harp has been silent too long, and the halls are empty without your music."

Kavan let out a long breath of relief. "With pleasure," he agreed.

"And then later, when the others sleep, you will tell me what troubles you, what threat looms that you are reluctant to share with anyone else."

Driven as he had been by dutiful absences, sitting with his harp upon his knee would be a welcome distraction and an easy request to fill. Sharing those other secrets would not be so easy.

"I will play for you," he agreed. The discomfiture upon his face was the only response he gave to the second request.

☙*❧

Inness laid the fabric doll the woman named Kes had provided onto the pillow bed she had made for it, wrapping her sheet around it like swaddling and positioning it in the center of the lumpy mattress where the child it represented would not fall onto the floor should he awake and begin to squirm and crawl. Arms tucked around herself, she leaned back on her heels as if leaning into her husband's embrace, her eyes closed as the scent she remembered washed over her.

'You've always kept him safe,' his voice crooned against her ear, his breath caressing her cheek with its gentleness. *'You always do what he needs you to do. You're a good mother. Soon he will be king."*

"He will make you proud, husband…we both will…but he's got a long time before that day. You'll rule for a long time; we both will…"

"I warned you not to trust those closest to you."

Startled by the female voice that interrupted her conversation with Oska, Inness jerked around to find his image, faint and wispy behind her, superimposed upon that of the dark-haired woman with the foreign attire and thick accent she had met only once before. Inness did not remember her name; she did not think she had ever learned it, but she remembered the promise the woman had made, an army that would guarantee her the throne, an army that would be there for her when she needed it.

"Liar," Inness hissed. "You promised an army. You promised success."

Bhás' detached mien did not change. "I warned you about betrayal…"

"That betrayal came from you!" she spat, picking up the fabric doll and hurling it at the woman she had not heard enter the room. As she turned to grab the pillow as well, she failed to notice the doll pass through the image like a horse through the fog rolling in from the sea.

"Your army is here." Bhás gave a cold, non-committal shrug. "And betrayal will come again if you stay in this place."

"Then help me be free! Take me to them! Give me back my throne!"

But the woman, like Oska, was no longer there. Neither would free her. Neither would help her. Neither would ensure that her son would sit upon

Glevum's throne. Only one man had promised to do that, though so far, he, too, had failed.

When Inness screamed into the dark for her husband not to betray her by leaving again, the only reply that came was someone in a nearby building or in the street below shouting for her to be still and let the babies sleep.

Inness dropped to her knees and beat upon the bed with frustrated, impotent fists.

❧*❧

The forced march north to evade the Nethite army they believed was, or would be, in pursuit, detoured west after a collection of Nethite soldiers, lured by the promise of the Lachlan and de Corrmick banners flown to announce their arrival, also joined Enesfel's ranks. Sharing tales of suppression and oppression, the stripping of food, wealth, and usable resources from Ruidoso, it was decided that freeing their allies, restoring the city to its people, and preventing Fraen's forces from maintaining a stronghold at Enesfel's back was the wisest decision. From there, they could march to the southern shore of Lake Curo on the clearest, shortest path toward Glevum.

The larger army passed through villages stripped of goods and men, farms left in the care of women and young children who stared fearfully at yet another army they expected to ravage their lands. At Lorant's order, his men shared what they could with the destitute, clothing, food, and small tools, to prove their goodwill and spread the words of Faith and knowledge that a de Corrmick heir was bound for Glevum's throne.

The news would reach Glevum before they did. Neth's army would intercept them either at Ruidoso or enroute along the lakeshore. Lorant would prefer to choose the time and place of their first true battle, but he had to settle for the time and place of k'Ádhá's choosing and trust that such a choice would be in Enesfel's favor.

❧*❧

The Nethite captain called Roald towered over the other with the puffed-out chest and demeaning sneer, backed him against the wall of the Kelari outpost built by Enesfel but abandoned during the last war and allowed to sit empty during the decade of squabbling that had gone on over the territory south of the lake. Fraen the Elder had claimed the outpost for himself then, and his army claimed it as theirs now, an easily accessible center to fan men out between the lake and the foothills of the Llaethlágárá. Digging in here would keep Enesfel from crossing the Kelari. Digging in here would prevent war from moving into Neth's heartland.

The man known only to Roald as Farzan had pressed him to send more men south in support of General Waller's troops who were already there. But Roald had his orders and refused to budge. If the general wanted more men, he would send for them. Sending more without a request would suggest that Roald considered the general weak. It might cost him his post. Or his life. He had been told to hold the line here, to prevent Enesfel from crossing the river, should the Lachlan army make it this far.

It was more than duty that compelled him to reject Farzan's demands.

"It is impossible. No army can make it up the pass..."

"Impossible...or believed impassible?" Farzan sneered in reply, his use of Trade stilted and thick. He was not afraid of the much larger man crushing him against the building. Roald needed his unit. To keep the mercenaries in place, Roald needed Farzan. Killing him would be the stupidest thing Roald could do.

"I will not send men up the pass. It would be suicide. They're needed here." Roald dropped him with a snort and stepped back, believing his point was made.

Dusting off the knees of his trousers, Farzan snorted as he got to his feet. "You are a coward."

Roald swung. Farzan ducked and bobbed to the side, laughing.

"You're here because the king wants you here," Roald hissed. "You answer to me. Do you understand that? Even your queen..."

"She is not our..."

"...your queen," Roald repeated, "put you at Neth's command. We need every man here if Enesfel comes. You will not go up the pass. You will leave Elyriá alone." As much as he feared Elyri, this war was not about them. This war was about reclaiming what had been stolen from the de Corrmick kings. This was about protecting Glevum from Enesfel's rule.

Even if Farzan could get his men up the Rísóri pass, Elyri could do things. Invaders would be slaughtered.

Farzan huffed with no effort made to disguise the delight in his tone as he strode toward the men who had come into this with him. They outnumbered Fraen's men three to one. Roald thought he could control him, but Farzan would do whatever he wanted...so long as Bhás gave the order.

This time, she had.

Roald's cowardice be damned.

❧ * ❧

They did not see her, but every captain on every galley stationed throughout the foreign eastern oceans heard her voice, heard her command. The time of inaction was over. The time for war had come.

Sails were hoisted to ready. Oars were dropped into their locks on the calm, nearly glassy sea, swords were polished, and men turned their faces toward the horizon where the sun would soon appear, to offer prayers and praise and beseeching pleas for protection.

When it showed its face again, when they had its brightness to guide them, her orders would be obeyed.

The holy war would begin.

❧ * ❧

"Tii madur," Farzan whispered to the corporeal voice that had drawn him and many others together at the eastern edge of the Kelari camp while the Nethites slept. She whom they followed had closed the ears of the sleeping, preventing them from waking so that those she appointed could obey her without interruption. There was no need for bloodshed tonight, no need for conflict or argument over duty and command.

There was only the need for submission so that her blood oath could be upheld.

Honor and blood oaths came before almost everything else.

Only she rose above those things.

Farzan gave the signal and led into the forest, following the instinct, the direction she planted within him, following where she directed without question. The path was steep and unfamiliar, but that did not deter him.

It did not deter any of those behind him either.

"Ca'al duiim."

We will obey.

ᚱChapter 41ᚱ

His limping army, demoralized by mounting losses experienced as they pushed toward Ruidoso, stopped beyond the walled borders of the city, where no arrow or spear could reach them, knowing that if Neth's army came at them from the rear, they would be pinned. They had won those skirmishes, either by demolishing the small forces that came at them like insect swarms or by forcing them to retreat. No one had seen General Waller. No one had seen the woman said to ride at the head of the multitude of darker-skinned mercenaries that looked little different than the host Earé had recruited to fight under the Lachlan banner.

Not even the steady influx of small bands of Association members and Vants, of disillusioned, defecting soldiers, and farmers escaping the conscription of Fraen's army, and of de Corrmick supporters drawn out by the welcomed banners of crimson and amber, green and black, were enough to make up for the dead buried along the way.

If not for Kaj Yetek's stalwart, fearsome men, Lorant doubted they would have made it as far as they had.

General Declan commanded the troops to fan out along Ruidoso's convex face, barricading it on three sides so that the only way in or out of the city was from the side nestled against the Cordashian border of thick conifer forest. A unit under Bhetá's command, men trained with bows and swords, were tasked with guarding that western gate to contain any Nethites stationed inside of the city and prevent reinforcements or supplies from reaching them. At the same time, the debate of dividing Enesfel's number and sending men ahead toward Lake Curo to clear their path continued.

Sheltered from the sweltering heat of the day, lightheaded due to the lack of water now being replenished from the nearby Dagar River where men were building a temporary dam to reduce the city's water supply, the king lay limp upon the cushions Jerit had insisted on procuring while Ártur examined Lorant to be certain that there was nothing wrong beyond

ᚱ463ᚱ

weariness and thirst. Bruised and scraped from previous battles, still troubled by a sprained ankle that had not been given adequate time to properly heal, despite Ártur's efforts, Lorant was thus far unscathed.

What he needed was several days' rest that did not involve sitting on a horse or engaging in combat, and as much water as they could give him. Nodding at Jerit, who squeezed Lorant's shoulder and departed through the open tent flap, the water he would have soon enough.

How much rest depended on how long the siege lasted.

"Would it help…would you like to speak to Kavan?"

Lorant looked at him with exhausted skepticism and a touch of expectation. "Is he here?"

"No," the healer replied. "But there is a way. Prince Arlan used it once, on the eve of entering Rhidam. If he is available, awake…"

It was midday. There were few reasons he could think of why Kavan would not be available. But as the years had passed, the two of them being in frequently close proximity, the need for such communication had become less regular. Kavan was no longer the little boy or unassured young man who had thrived on such contacts. He was still sínréc, but he was also a strong, largely confident man who no longer needed his cousin's advice or reassurance. If he failed to reach him, it might be as much Ártur's lack of practice as any fault or unavailability of Kavan's.

"Give me your hands. Close your eyes. Clear your thoughts."

Less skeptical than Arlan had been, more familiar with the bard's talents and abilities, there was no hesitation in Lorant's obedience. There was only the slowness of his weariness that begged to be eased, followed by the effortlessness of emptying his thoughts that came with the desire to sleep. Ártur reached across the miles to tap against Kavan's mental shields with a silent plea on behalf of the king. When Kavan opened his thoughts, it was as though his cousin was standing in the tent beside them.

His fear of failure was for naught.

Lorant felt him there too, though he knew he would not see him if he opened his eyes. Kavan's presence was a warm embrace, reminding him of so many childhood days when he would throw himself into the bard's arms for affection and reassurance, particularly after his father's death. He tried to form coherent thoughts, wanting to weep but not daring to do so, wanting to ask questions, and beg for a glimpse of the future at the end of this war. But there was only emotion, raw and unrestrained, that Kavan met with the same steadfast calm he had always provided.

There was no revulsion, no pulling away as Kavan had done when Arlan had pressed for similar answers and assurances. What Ártur and Lorant felt was the confidence that they would come home, that their families would be waiting for them, that they would come through these dark times as better men.

Lorant clung to those reassuring threads and bound them around himself as proof that Enesfel would win this war. Ártur, on the other hand, knowing his cousin better, picked at the shards that made him less certain of success and more concerned about the things Kavan was not sharing. When Kavan began to sing, however, soft ethereal notes that flowed through the link and faded as Lorant released his cares and drifted to sleep, the healer let his fears go as well.

Perhaps he had not sensed what he thought he had. Perhaps it was only the melancholy of war that darkened his thoughts and made him fear for the worst. Eyes still closed, he remained with Lorant's hands in his, waiting for Jerit's return with the needed water. When the prince did come, Ártur extracted his hands and stood up with a soft, "Stay with him until he wakes," and then left the tent and the much-needed contact with his cousin behind.

In Rhidam, on a bench sharing a midday respite with the children in the garden around him, Kavan let the impromptu tune fade.

"Another one," begged Princess Hella. "Sing us another."

"I will fetch your harp, k'bhydhá," Ágdhállán declared, already on his feet and racing away.

Kavan swallowed, not realizing the tune for Lorant had been manifested aloud, and nodded. Music would be a good distraction for the children as they awaited the summons for dinner, a good distraction from the vision of the prince and king cornered back-to-back in combat.

The Vants' prophecy would be fulfilled.

It was the unseen, the unknown result, that Kavan feared…if he did not do something soon to stop Bhás.

But there was nothing within him now, nothing from outside, to guide him to her. The sense of Myreth was gone. It seemed she preferred to drag out his torment as she dragged out the war, seemed intent on reminding Kavan that she was in control. Without guidance, there was nothing, as far as he could determine, that he could do.

❧*❦

The rumble of rock, uprooted trees, and scattering dust brought the shouts of men as a pre-dawn rockslide piled against both the front and rear entry and the side wall of the Rísóri Fortress. Some of it tumbled into the Kelari River, some into the courtyard, injuring men on watch and diverting the water's flow as such slides had periodically done for centuries. The courtyard and gates would need to be cleared, but it was decided that, so long as the gates were clear enough to open when necessary, the road blockage, particularly on the western-facing side of the fortress, could be used to their advantage.

Mouth and nose covered to avoid breathing the dust, Bhríd directed the clearing of the interior obstruction by aiding the work, hefting stones small enough to move to build the impasse taller. Sóbhán and others shoveled dirt into the crevices, creating a temporary second wall that any opposing force would have to climb over to reach the fortress gate that currently stood open as the chunks of rock that had fallen inside were moved and the single tree the slide had brought with it was dismembered for kindling, for arrows or other purposes.

With the rising sun at their backs, peeping around the watchtower and the parapets to serve as further detriment to anyone traveling up the pass, most of those toiling at the avalanche site did not expect the abrupt assailing force of arrows that rained out of the tree line, nor the barrage of spears hurled by the soft-stepping host in leather armor that had not been heard over the grunts of exertion and muted conversation of the Elyri workers.

When the first man fell with a scream, followed by others from those at the top of the natural barricade who held no shields and wore little or no armor to impede their labor, Bhríd shouted, "To the walls!"

Men stumbled or tripped as they hastened down the stony barricade toward the shelter of the fortress, losing boots, dropping shovels, picks, and axes, kicking loose debris they had been endeavoring to wedge into a protective shield. From atop the fortress walls, the Elyri archers let loose their return assault to pick off the cinnamon-skinned warriors scaling the stone in the hopes of breaching the open gates.

Not Nethites.

Knocked aside by a falling man with an arrow lodged in his neck, whom he mistakenly tried to catch with his free hand, Sóbhán fell from the midpoint of the collapse with a shout that made Bhríd look away from the enemy clambering up the hill. The younger Elyri lost his hold on the injured man but retained his grip on his shovel, so that when someone leaped at him from above with a long spear, Sóbhán swung the shovel as he rolled, and knocked his assailant into the path of an incoming arrow. Satisfied that Sóbhán was unharmed when he scrambled up and ran to the open gate, satisfied that most of those ill-equipped to fight had retreated, Bhríd focused on the men closing behind him, grateful now that he had worn his sword despite the encumbrance it had caused while moving rocks.

Armed men from inside the fortress raced through the open gate to join him, weaving between the flight paths of retreating men to join their leader atop the avalanche wall. Together, they drove the attackers down the western slope, some continuing to fall beneath the arrows from archers the Elyri could not see, until the ground at the western base was strewn with bodies. Only then did their push to assail the fortress cease. The shuffle of hastily retreating footsteps echoed from around the forested path's bend out of sight, leaving only the groaning of the injured on both sides to pepper the river's gurgling serenade.

"Do we go after them?" someone called, a helmeted man sliding cautiously down the western slope of the mound to drive his sword through opponents who continued to show signs of life.

"No," Bhríd replied, wiping dust from his face. To send men after the withdrawing army was to risk being trapped against the impasse, either forced to retreat uphill at a disadvantage or else unable to do so with the wall at their back. This was not the time for a chase. The narrowness of the trodden path worked in their favor, limiting the number of opponents who could come at them. They, too, would be regrouping and reassessing their strategy as Bhríd would be as soon as he got inside.

"Gather the injured and dead. Man the wall. Be watchful."

He skittered down the hill, scattering stones, helping up those in his path who could stand. Nature had cost them dearly this day, but Sóbhán had survived. Bhríd did not look forward to the duty of reporting differently to the families of those who had not.

"Don't let them reach the cliff!"

Óllbhaer Dínyn swept his wild gray hair peppered with sea spray back from his forehead and scrambled across the deck toward the unmanned crossbow mounted at the prow of the ship while his first mate hurried behind him with an armload of shafts to feed into it. Though primarily a merchant vessel, his crew and the crews of the other ships sailing with him were accustomed to fending off pirates, so such combat was not new. The more agile nature of the three galleys they faced, one having shifted near enough to one of the merchant chasms dug into the sheer face of the more than six-hundred-foot-high cliff, while another ship moved through the surf to drive the defenders back. The last ship positioned itself between the vessel attempting to dock and the Elyri ships defending the quay, firing burning arrows and lobbing short metal-tipped spears at them, forcing the four Elyri ships to keep their distance.

They were not warships, but they had fire arrows too.

Óllbhaer and his captains knew the shifting currents of this stretch of coastline better than anyone. Clarys was their home. They had what they presumed to be the advantage of righteous defense.

The merchant chasm filled with shouts and screams, with the glow of short fire lights and the clash of swords as the invaders engaged with the soldiers stationed to defend the long stairs tunneled up within the basalt stone and compacted earth into the heart of Clarys above. Designed for the loading and unloading of merchant vessels where more traditional docks could not be built, the chasms were not constructed for combat, and when the attacking galley drifted towards another opening that appeared less defended, Óllbhaer aimed at their retreating backs and called over his shoulder, "Again!"

The ram's horn alarm cut the air.

The men and women of Clarys lined the edge of the cliff and the head of the merchant shafts prepared for a day none of them, including the pair watching from the highest spire of the Kyne's palace, had ever expected.

War in Clarys.

Neither Kyne Phílóá nor k'dedhá Ylár knew that, elsewhere along Elyriá's cliffs, other such chasms were likewise under attack.

Unable to reach Enesfel with arrows and sling stones, though unsurprised by General Declan's foresight, General Waller ordered the three catapults to be held out of sight along Ruidoso's eastern wall. Enesfel's army, accompanied by the Lachlan and de Corrmick banners, was a larger force than expected, possibly rivaling Neth's army or outnumbering them, though he could not be sure how many mercenaries were spread out elsewhere under the foreign woman's command. Those captains were supposed to report to him but whatever the cause, few of those reports had come. He did not have enough soldiers within the city to meet the Lachlan force in combat, but he did not need to.

Pigeons were sent.

Soldiers posted elsewhere would get the messages and come to his aid. King Fraen would receive word of Enesfel's numbers and prepare the primary force to pincher them from the rear against Ruidoso's walls. If necessary, Waller had options.

He always kept options open.

When the stillness of the first night fell, when the sounds of construction and the shouts and chatter of men lessened, the catapults were moved into position and began to lob great stones and fiery balls of pitch at the army that had camped well within their range, though not within range of arrows and spears. Waller smirked as the first screams filled the air, as men were crushed and scattered, as tents were set ablaze, and those who were not hit in the first barrage scrambled to move their sieging wall back. The siege tower under construction splintered and threw shards in all directions as it was knocked onto its side and began to burn.

A hastily positioned Lachlan ballista, carefully aimed in the darkness toward the site of one of the catapults, despite the ongoing assault, pierced the soldier manning it so that he was thrown back off the wall, just before another stone demolished the ballista and killed one of the two men using it. Another shot from another ballista killed another man, leaving a single catapult to cast its fiery death.

It provided Enesfel the time to regroup. The remaining ballista and pair of catapults built in Fiara and hastily assembled once they made camp at Ruidoso were moved out of harm's way.

The Ruidoso catapults could not be easily repositioned. There was nowhere else on the city's wall to move them to. After another three strikes from each, once other Nethite soldiers were pressed to man the abandoned weapons, Enesfel's army had successfully retreated too far for the catapults to hit them.

The deaths Neth inflicted, the destruction of the ballista and siege tower, were good enough for Waller. The distance between the army and the city walls allowed him room to consider which option would whittle the Lachlan army down further.

His lost troops were barely considered as townsfolk and foot soldiers collected them for disposal.

His only disappointment, as he studied the movement of torchlight as the siege army continued to regroup, was that the Lachlan and de Corrmick pennants continued to fly.

❧*❧

There were too many dead to offer individual prayers. dedhá Bhílári, his pale face flushed with sickness, disgust, and horror, stopped counting after his first ten prayers and had, instead, offered a single prayer for their collective souls after the last man was brought in from outside the fortress and the gates were closed again. The trio of healers who had come to serve here, along with the one already on permanent station, moved among the bodies, preserving them for transport home after having already tended to the injured. Now, as Bhríd approached, Bhílári squared his shoulders and tried to appear more stalwart than he felt. He dropped the façade when he saw some of his emotions mirrored on the experienced warrior's face.

"Seventy-five," Bhríd murmured without looking the dedhá in the eye. For such a short skirmish, the casualty count was too high. In Enesfel's army, this would not have happened. But Elyri inexperience in war had been compounded by the avalanche and the inadequate preparation of those working at the site of the impasse. Inexperience and nature were not his fault. Permitting men to linger and work outside the walls without weapons and armor was.

"Going to take hours to get them home," Bhílári sighed and wiped the back of his hand over his mouth. "Do you want me to…?"

"We'll deal with that. I need you to go to Clarys…"

"Me?"

"You're the only one with enough speaking experience to plead with the Kyne for more forces." Phílóá had promised more than the two hundred and fifty soldiers he had initially been given. Having just lost nearly one-third of that force and not yet knowing what lay beyond that bend, he did not believe the fortress was equipped for another attack when it came.

Not if.

He knew another assault would come.

So too, he assumed, did Sóbhán, who stood on the parapet, his hands on the wall on either side of him, facing the earthen impasse with its enemy dead on the other side and the road that disappeared beyond it. He had passed the younger man there, heard his quiet mumbling, and assumed he was either praying for strength and success or else trying to manifest his father and bring him here.

Bhríd hoped he succeeded at one or both of those things.

"They'll come again?"

Bhríd nodded. "I'm sure of it. We're protected inside, but we don't know how many are out there. We can't know what awaits us. I would rather have more to face them than not enough."

Shivering, the screams of the dying, the last groans of the dead echoing in his ears, Bhílári shook his head. "I'm no diplomat."

"But you've been there. You know Kluín and Paul…and you've met the Kyne. Seek Bhyrhán Bhíncári; if he is there, he will help you. He will speak for us. She promised more; tell her we need them now."

With a sigh of defeat but also relief for being able to escape the acrid summer stench of the dead who had not yet been preserved, Bhílári asked, "Shall I go now?"

"Yes…while we have the chance to prepare. Before the dead are transported. The sooner the request is met, the sooner those reinforcements can be here. We should not wait."

"Aye…very well. Is there…?" He looked across the sea of corpses and shuddered. "Is there anything else while I am there?"

"Not yet." If there were any other messages to deliver to the Kyne, Bhríd would have to take them himself.

❧*✍

"Lorant?"

Jerit pushed the tent flap open to duck inside where he found the young king, barely a man, a boy only recently deemed old enough to rule but not yet experienced enough to do so easily, let alone lead an army into war, huddled in the rear corner with his knees drawn to his chest. The sun had come up long ago, but after a brief walk amongst those the healers and physicians were steadfastly trying to save, Lorant had retreated here with a sickened expression that had broken Jerit's heart to see. Lorant raised his head only enough to look at the redhead over his knees, but he did not speak and did not move.

The ambushes in the forest had been different. This night, with bodies flattened by rocks, burned by fire, felled by the destroyed siege tower, had given Lorant a different taste of war. His haunted gaze expressed his unreadiness for what he had seen.

No less horrified, having no more experience in war than Lorant, Jerit's only advantage was eight years of maturity and experience with the world. Sitting beside him, adjusting the bedding so it was tucked around them both, Jerit pulled Lorant against his chest and cradled him the way he had sometimes done when Lorant had been much younger, after the death of his father. Despite Jerit's dirty, bloody clothes, despite the grime on his face and the smell of blood, sweat, and offal that wafted off him, accumulated as he helped transport the injured for care, Lorant did not resist.

Those smells seemed to be everywhere.

In Jerit's arms was the place he felt safest.

"We're okay," Jerit murmured. They had lost men. He did not know how many. But their force was still strong. Ruidoso's catapults could no longer reach them. If the commander of the forces defending the city decided to send men out to fight, Enesfel was ready. They would defeat them too. "tama Yetek and Daema Magk are calculating where we could move the catapults and ballista. General Declan is readying a flank of archers to move in at nightfall. The dead will be buried by then, and the injured healed. We're not beaten."

Lorant shuddered but did not argue or agree.

"Come. You need to rest." Slowly, Jerit tried to unfold Lorant's limbs and coaxed him to lie down. But Lorant refused to release him.

"Don't leave," Lorant whispered.

Jerit swallowed the lump in his throat, weighing innumerable silent arguments in his head, before eventually sliding down beside him. Lorant held him tighter and lay his head on Jerit's narrower chest.

"Stay."

He adjusted the blankets. He returned Lorant's embrace. After a glance at the fluttering tent flap and one final internal argument about the opinions of others should they find the king and prince asleep this way, Jerit closed his eyes after a gentle kiss to the top of Lorant's head.

"I'm here. Always."

❧*❧

Again upon the parapet, seeking signs of an enemy he could not see, Bhríd put his hand on Sóbhán's shoulder, startling the younger man who had been in that same spot since the fighting ended and the gates were closed that morning. Sóbhán blinked, opened and closed his mouth a few times as he collected his thoughts and regained a clear-headed realization of where he was and who had touched him, and then he groaned and shook his head mournfully.

"I am sorry, k'bhydhá…I cannot do it."

Expecting him to say he could not fight, willing to accept retreat from Sóbhán because he was Kavan's son, Bhríd said, "It is okay. You do not need to be here."

Sóbhán shook his head. "I am staying. I thought I could…he taught me defenses, protections, but I have not practiced them enough to…I have tried, but my efforts will not be enough to shield us."

Bhríd grunted, a sound both understanding and disappointed, though not in the way Sóbhán interpreted it. It had never occurred to him that some sort of protection through power was possible, or he would have asked Kavan to protect Rísóri.

"You've done enough for today, Sóbhán. You need to rest or you will be useless tomorrow."

"They'll come again."

It was not a question.

"I've sent scouts. We'll see what they tell us. Tonight, there are others on watch." He pointed to people along the wall and a few he had stationed along the lip of the avalanche barricade, archers with bows who could snipe any spies the enemy sent. "dedhá Bhílári has gone for reinforcements. We will see what the morning brings. Tonight, we wait…and sleep."

"I don't think I can." Mentally and physically exhausted, the screams of war and the smell of blood, the taste of dust and sweat on his parched lips, were things he believed likely to prevent him from sleeping ever again.

But Bhríd's words echoed his unfocused thoughts. "Try."

It was all they could do.

Sóbhán nodded. For Bhríd, for the men and women depending on him here, for those he was protecting at home, he would try.

⁊*⁊

The dozen small stone outposts that dotted the sliver of Elyri coast on the east side of the Gorea Fjord were manned by sailors, fishermen, miners, lumbermen, and mountaineers, as well as an assortment of retired Faith guards and some soldiers once employed by Kyne Mórne before her death. They were here to ward off the occasional Nethite pirate ship or anyone foolish enough to attempt to climb a particularly grueling and impassible stretch of the Llaethlágárá which made up Elyriá's western coast. Having seen the galleys sail into Gorea's harbor, word passed between the outposts, resulting in heightened readiness long before official word of potential war reached them.

Their ships were prepared, the supplies stocked and protected, and most of the men and women stationed there had drawn in family and friends to supplement their ranks. But they were still caught unaware when the first ship, not one of the invading galleys but a broad Nethite naval caravel, dared to challenge them in the middle of the night, bombarding them with all manner of projectiles in the hopes of destroying what they perceived to be an Elyri fleet moored there. Outnumbered, unprepared for the Elyri to fight back with such ferocity, the caravel was swiftly surrounded and sunk in the middle of the fjord, its men left to drown in the cold north sea.

The Elyri ships, however, did not return to their moorings. If there had been one ship, there would likely be more. If Neth thought to penetrate Elyriá's borders, despite their historically high fear of those living beyond the Llaethlágárá, the outpost crews and their supporting soldiers, under the leadership of retired Captain Faeárgan Drás, were determined to give Neth a reason to be afraid.

❧*☙

The floorboards creaked.

The comforting presence of the záryph flashed out of existence.

On the oratory floors made of centuries-old stone and not covered by wooden planks, as so many rooms were adorned, the sound was out of place and forced Kavan to look up as the harp fell silent in his hands. Having exchanged study and research for music tonight, feeling deeply in need of something his soul was unable to find as he poured his focus into the care of the children and his studies, he expected his visitor to be Rhyrdan or perhaps Sunna, both of whom had seemed unusually restless today. But in the same instant his thoughts pointed out the absurdity of steps on creaking wooden floors, he laid eyes on the woman at the rear of the oratory bathed in a faint, fiery orange glow.

Startled, his heart thundering in fear of the unexpected, he lurched to his feet, dropping the harp, barely noticing the discordant snapping twang of a breaking brass string, nor the stinging bite it made when it whipped against his bare shin.

How had she gotten here? Not the k'rylag. He would have felt her arrival. She could not have passed through the corridors without notice. He had not heard the door open, and it was closed behind her. There was no surge of power as if from a newly created Gate, although there was a heavy, uncomfortable weight of energy in the room that tried to push down on him, push him back to his knees, back against the marble altar. As often happened with Kóráhm's arrival, she was suddenly there when she had not been, manifest out of the air as the saint often was.

Were their natures the same? Was she ancient, timeless, immortal, and immaterial in the same way Kóráhm was?

Wouldn't Kóráhm have warned him if that was the case?

Wouldn't Kóráhm know?

As though reading his thoughts, she sneered, "What I am, you cannot understand."

"You think you know me. You do not belong here." He pushed those he loved out of his head, hiding their faces, their names, and what they meant to him behind unbreachable walls of power. She might already know those details; she must if she had found her way to him here, but he was not going to risk their exposure if she did not.

There was someone else with them, however, someone with her, also masked but who felt familiar in its barely detectable aura. Ignoring his lingering apprehension, Kavan tried to push his senses past her to draw that other presence into focus.

"The world is mine," she snapped nonchalantly, brushing his effort aside with a wave of her hand as though it were an annoying insect. "As it should have been his. You are a coward, hiding behind the heretic…"

Bhás stepped forward as if to stalk him, the creak of floorboards charging the room again, but then she abruptly stopped, her gaze unfocused, the orange aura flaring and shifting violently around her.

Nothing had changed in the room that he could detect. Reeling from the brushoff that made his head ache outside as if bruised, and inside as he abruptly reabsorbed the power he had spent, he did not turn his head to seek what she was looking at. He did not think anything was there. The incense and candles still burned on the altar, and the power he had meditated on as he composed a new tune thrummed in the air as it had when the záryph were with him. Using words against her felt like a feeble waste of effort.

"And you hide behind your ancestors…"

"Ancestor!" she exclaimed hotly, trying again to take a step toward him. When she could not lift her feet from the floor, she snarled, threw an object that clattered not on wood planks but on the expected stone of the oratory floor, and scoffed, "By the time you come, he will be…"

The oratory door flew open and Bhás, apparently startled by it, evaporated from the room as though no more than spent steam. Sunna, with waji in hand, looked wildly about with the wide-eyed glint of a hunter expecting to have cornered his prey. Seeing nothing, sensing the one who had been here but was no longer, he snarled and strode, still clutching the waji, toward the silent, speechless man on the oratory steps. He paused to pick up the discarded object instead of stepping over it, and put it in Kavan's palm when he reached him.

Kóráhm's ring.

It had been lost more than a decade before. He had never thought to see it again.

More shocking were the vivid, powerful traces of emotion, despair and hope, belief and regret, that had been left on it.

Myreth.

The sense of his dark twin burned brightly enough to open a door in his mind's eye, painting a smoky picture of a small stone room filled with the traces of someone confined there alone within a space devoid of power for too long, waiting for the arrival of someone who failed, with each rising and setting of the sun, to end his captivity.

Kavan could find him. He could reach him now.

Kavan involuntarily took a step toward the Purification Chamber, but Sunna's big hand on his arm prevented him from taking another.

"She wants you to be rash. She wants you to be impulsive. She feeds on such things. She wants you to react on her whim, not your own. Do not give her the satisfaction or power…"

"Myreth needs…"

"He will wait."

"She said…"

"Her words are deceit," he grunted, shoving the waji into his belt. "I have known this all my life. Do not heed her. You will not defeat her if you play by her rules." His lowered gaze as he adjusted his belt made him add, "You are bleeding."

Kavan shuddered and looked at his feet, anticipating the marks of rósádhá there, but instead, there was the short snapping slice left by the brass harp string. The reminder of that broken string pulled his thoughts one step further away from the man who had worn Kóráhm's ring for ten years, and he stared at the discarded instrument with a frustrated sigh.

"You are familiar with her?" he muttered, stooping to pick up the harp with his empty hand.

"I know…of her." His words were odd, vague, and avoidant, but Kavan did not have the chance to press for further details. "She longs for nothing but revenge for a wrong that never touched her. She lives for it…never for herself. I do not know what that wrong was…but she believes that achieving that goal will grant her power over all things and the happiness she has never known. It is implausible, perhaps, but she will continue to wage war against all who slight her, who stood against the ancestor, because it is the only thing she knows. I will not allow her to succeed. Even if…" He dropped his hand from Kavan with a one-shouldered shrug, "I must stop you from going to her now."

"I must stop her."

"Perhaps," Sunna agreed with a nod, "just as I must. But not now. Not on her terms. It must be on yours…when you are ready."

Prevented from fleeing after her, disrupted from going to Myreth by a cooler, wiser sense of caution, and acknowledging his fear of her, his fear for his family and friends, his fear of dying, Kavan did not think he would ever be ready.

If not on her terms, he did not think he would ever have the courage to face a woman whose grasp of power he did not understand.

&Chapter 42&

Though lacking the replacement manpower requested and hoping that dedhá Bhílári's continued absence meant that his entreaty was under consideration, when his night scouts reported approximately two to three hundred soldiers bottlenecked on the road nearly a quarter of a mile around the bend, Bhríd was left with a difficult choice. He could take the risk that his force and theirs were evenly matched, or he could sit idle, waiting for reinforcements, and wait for the enemy to find an upper hand. The Elyri were inexperienced in combat, yes, but they were stronger and faster, and a few of them, including Sóbhán, had abilities that could be used to their advantage.

Or he could wait.

The first risk seemed the most prudent. Waiting might bring him reinforcements, but it might do the same for their adversary. Taking one hundred of the stealthiest people at his command outside the walls left the remaining seventy-five, plus the healers and fortress staff, to hold position until help arrived, no matter what happened to their one hundred comrades.

The palpable fear, like the sound of footsteps and the creak and clatter of armor, was masked by those skilled enough to project a silent shield around them. The scouts from the night before followed their previous path into the trees as the army moved cautiously forward, and a handpicked squad of twenty shapeshifters was selected to fly to the rear of the enemy camp to attack when the signal was given.

Sóbhán, reluctant to stay at the fortress, begged to go with them.

Bhríd kept the younger man at his side and appointed him the leader of those keeping the army undetected until they were in visual range. He would not have Kavan's son fall in a place where Bhríd would be unable to rescue him.

Sóbhán accepted that compromise without argument. He was not on the front line, but he was here. Once the Elyri force was spotted, there would be no need to hide the sound of their approach. His chance to defend Elyriá would come.

The signal to charge, to make themselves known to the sleeping host, came with the rumbling of a dislodged boulder that brought broken trunks and smaller rocks tumbling into the middle of the enemy camp. The mountainside was steep enough that the stones and trees alike, and anything in their path, plunged into the river and swept men, tents, and an array of pack animals into the flow. The shapeshifters darted in, struck down as many unsuspecting soldiers as they could, and then took to the sky again, their wings flapping furiously.

Archers caught two of them before their attention was forced to the chaos at the front of their camp, where combat had been engaged.

The remaining shapeshifters decided in unison to continue their rear-flank assault.

Once the startled soldiers charged into the oncoming mass of Elyri with a ferocity none expected from Nethite rivals, Bhríd could not remain focused on Sóbhán's welfare. He saw him only once, when the young man hurled someone's dropped blade and impaled a man directly behind Bhríd, who had been about to run him through with a short spear. There was no time to express gratitude. The scouts in the trees charged into the fray, cutting a swath through the thinnest part of the enemy ranks, severing the army in two, holding the larger rear unit at bay as Bhríd's force cut through those at the front.

It did not take long for those at the rear to decide to retreat as the narrowness of this portion of the road made forward progress difficult through the Elyri army. They began their evacuation, leaving their comrades to their fate, absorbing the scouts and shapeshifters in their wake and leaving their bodies behind along with those the Elyri had killed on the trampled, blood-soaked road. Rather than pursue, Bhríd held his force back and focused on killing every man the retreating army left behind. By the time the clash of weapons ceased, none were left standing, and Bhríd had his first opportunity to take stock of the survivors, as well as those who had been less fortunate.

He could not get an accurate count as men and women moved about, separating the injured from the dead, but he was unfortunately certain that more littered the road, the edge of the forest, lay scattered at the river's edge, or had, he thought with a frown, been swept west in Kelari's current, than stood around him. He looked again at the enemy force that had moved to the edge of his vision and watched them as they stopped their flight to tend to the wounded.

He did not see his scouts. The shapeshifters had not returned.

"Bring the healers," he shouted to one young woman splattered with blood who had just propped a man against the mountainside and finished tightening her belt around his bleeding arm. He pointed to another dozen, those nearest who were still standing and looked more capable than others, men with bows on their backs and quivers of arrows not used in the closeness of combat, and summoned them to him. "Hold here. Keep watch as we collect the injured. If they move, kill them."

"Aye, sir," they murmured together.

"Bhríd."

He stiffened. He knew the sound of pain from so many past wars. His blood chilled as he left the guards at their station and wove through the dead looking for the source of that pain. He found Sóbhán crumpled and trapped by one twisted leg between the roadside stones, a foot dangling in the river as he tried to pull himself free. Elyri strength was no match for the awkward angle he clung to, so Bhríd slid down the embankment until he reached his side, looking him over carefully as he descended."

"Are you...?"

"Alive. That's good enough," Sóbhán grunted. The blood of the dead was splattered over his face, torso, and arms, but it was the bloody gash at the knee of his free leg spreading crimson up and down his trousers that concerned Bhríd the most.

"Lost a lot of blood. Let me bind this." He wiggled out of his chain shirt and ripped a strip of sweat-soaked fabric free.

"Would rather be free of the rocks..."

"Priorities," Bhríd grunted. He did not take the time to inspect the wound, only to slow the bleeding so that the younger man might live long enough to reach medical attention. "This is going to hurt."

"Already does." He winced and wheezed and gritted his teeth as his leg was bound, and then again when Bhríd pushed the boulder away enough for Sóbhán to free his leg. He lay gasping, his eyes closed, but yelped and dropped into unconsciousness when Bhríd lifted him from the damp earth.

This would not wait for the healers to come. Bhríd would carry Sóbhán back to the fortress, or back to Bhryell if there were not enough healers here to save his life and leg.

❧*❧

"Pigeon's brought word, Your Majesty."

The toothless fellow who smelled like bird dung and sweat, his hands and face stained from a life spent tending the royal coop, offered a tiny clay capsule barely big enough for the rolled bit of paper it contained. Fraen recoiled in disdain, refusing to touch the hand of such an unclean man, and gestured for someone else to take it from him. As there was only the pair of guards who had accompanied the pigeoneer to the room and remained at the door to allow him inside, and Olaric, the younger Fraen forced an exasperated sigh and took the capsule.

Removing the slip of paper gave him the opportunity to read the message without words being filtered through his father's voice.

"de Corrmick banner's reached Ruidoso."

Fraen straightened in his chair. "That's not possible."

"The princes are alive…"

His eyes narrowed, "How do you know…?"

"You told me." The admission had not been direct, but Fraen's words had been clear enough that there had been no other possible interpretation. His father did not need to know that Olaric, too, had spies and sources who had told him the same thing long before he had ever heard the news from the pretend king.

"Henrik's a child," Fraen snorted, crossing his arms over his chest.

"Prince Jerit then. He's old enough…and King Oska was his brother. Would make sense for him to try. Maybe Prince Henrik has a champion…"

"The Lachlans fly the banner to steal our throne."

In an indirect way, if the stories Olaric heard were true, King Lorant had a blood claim to Neth's throne, whether he chose to exercise it or not. Olaric did not think Enesfel's king wanted the de Corrmick throne, but if seizing it and deposing Fraen was what it took to ensure peace in the Sovereignties, perhaps there was no other way.

"Ready our force to…"

Olaric blinked. "You want me to lead…?"

Snorting with laughter, Fraen snatched the message from Olaric's hand and replied, "You weren't much of a soldier before…you're less of one now. Too soft."

Scowling, Olaric refused to retort.

"Bring me the captain and give the order to initiate Inzigaen."

Bristling, the word his father used sending shivers of disgust and dread down his back and bringing bile up in his throat, Olaric protested, "They're nowhere near Glevum…and with the mercenaries still here, Captain Sparding's got more than enough…"

He suspected now that Geiel had missed reporting to King Lorant in Rhidam before Enesfel's army had marched, but he might have left his last report with King Kjell. He did not know how to get word of this latest development to the Lachlan army before they came face to face with the nightmare Fraen suggested, but he had to try. Marta might be his only shot at reaching them, although after discovering that Inness was alive and in Glevum, the Association leader had stopped speaking to him.

He would have to find Sparding and try to reach her through him.

After swallowing the protest he began to make, he muttered, "I'll tell him." He hoped he did not sound as disheartened as he felt.

Fraen's chortle as he strode out of the room past the pigeoneer told Olaric the man did not care about his sensibilities…or anyone else's.

She was no stranger to blood. She was no stranger to the host of wounds people were prone to…lost limbs, punctures, contusions, broken bones. They were part of everyday life as farmers, builders, animal handlers, and others came to her for care. But as the unfamiliar young man who had come to Bhryell to fetch her escorted her through the Rísóri stronghold's courtyard, where dozens of injured men and women lay on low pallets or blankets on the stony ground, it took effort not to disgorge her morning's meal. The smell alone was sickening enough. Though tempted to pause along the way, aid the other healers, physicians, and their assistants in their efforts to treat the fallen, she had not come for that. She had come here for the beloved man who lifted his face as she approached, who frowned with embarrassment, dismay, and regret as their eyes met.

"You shouldn't be here." He cast a sour glance at Bhríd for calling his wife to such a place, a fortress during war, but he was not angry about the choice. Sóbhán had insisted the healers tend to the dying before they treated him, despite Bhríd's scolding and reminder that he had lost too much blood. The tourniquet had lessened the loss, but with it, the circulation to his foot and lower leg as well. His boot had been cut away, his pant leg torn free so that he could see the discoloration already taking place.

Only a healer's effort to block his pain sensors kept him from uttering the same moaning agony as so many others around him did.

"I told you the same thing," Chethá murmured, setting her bag down and kneeling beside him. She tenderly pressed one hand to the side of his face, the other to his swollen, purpling knee, and closed her eyes to see his injury in a way that eyes alone could not assess.

The gash was deep, the bone fractured, the knee shattered into more fragments than she had the skill or experience to treat. The tourniquet had done its job, preventing him from bleeding to death, but it had been in place too long. If her father or mother were here, if Kavan were here, the result might be different.

As it was, her husband had few options.

The tears gathered on the ends of her lashes dripped free when she opened her eyes to look at him. She would not couch the truth. She knew he would not want that.

"I cannot save it," she whispered.

The touch of her hands expressed the words she did not say.

At the foot of the pallet, Bhríd winced at her acknowledgment of the conclusion he had already made.

"You can't take my leg. There must be…"

"It would take more than…I can heal the bleeding but…"

Sóbhán shook his head. "Heal some today, more tomorrow…"

"The tissue is already dying. If I wait, infection will set in, spread, more of your leg could be lost. You could…" she choked on the next whispered word, "die. Think of the girls. Your brothers. Your father. Think of me…"

Sóbhán believed in his wife to the point of having faith that she would be able to reverse the fate he had believed awaited him. He was not ready to die. When he had been conscious, he had stubbornly refused the aid of other healers to avoid anyone else delivering that blow, but he would not avoid his wife.

He was not his brother. He would not be bitter about the fate he was given. Perhaps his stubborn refusal of care for so long had led to this. Perhaps it had been his destiny since choosing to fight for Elyriá. Perhaps it was k'Ádhá's will.

He only hoped his father would forgive him for coming here when he had been warned not to get involved in the fight.

If he had not done so, however, Bhríd might be dead and the Rísóri Pass lost. Sóbhán had done his part. He could live with the rest.

"Give me something for the pain and…"

"We're not barbarians," she scolded, rummaging through her pack for a small bottle of clear liquid and her collection of bandages and salves. She glanced at Bhríd and murmured, "A saw or…"

Both men shuddered, and Bhríd left them alone.

"Drink this."

"I want to see…"

"No," she scolded again, "you don't. I want to do this right; I don't want to hear you scream." She tipped the bottle against his mouth, put it away as he licked the bitter fluid from his lips, then took his head between her hands and pressed her forehead to his. "I am sorry…"

"So am I." His words were already slurring, possibly from the vial's contents, possibly due to an Elyri healer's ability to give their patients a dreamless slumber that would wear off when the trauma to come was over. She tenderly kissed him, sat back, and wrapped her hands around his leg where the tourniquet was tied just above his knee as Bhríd returned.

She grimly met his gaze, thankful that Sóbhán was asleep. "I will stop the bleeding…heal as we go…but you will need to cut…"

Again, Bhríd grimaced but nodded as he took position on Sóbhán's other side. "Kavan, forgive me for this," he whispered as the saw made its first pass through the exposed bone the enemy's blade had already broken.

Both he and Chethá were thankful they could not hear Sóbhán scream.

❧*❧

Having slept in the chair at Ágdhállán's bedside after asking Yóáná to heal the laceration on his leg and replacing the broken harp string, Kavan awoke with a jolt as the same leg kicked out against a searing, cutting sting of unexpected agony. He felt hands wrapped around his knee as he sought the source of the pain, assuming at first that Lorant had been injured in battle, perhaps incapacitated for the rest of the war. But there was no confirmation in that bond, only the faint pulsing throb of power in the long-missed ring he wore once more upon his hand. If not Lorant…Myreth?

No validation came, only another name that made him leap to his feet with a strangled cry.

Ágdhállán was not in his bed. The amber sliver of sunlight through the window suggested late afternoon, his restlessness the night before having caused him to oversleep once slumber did take him, and not even the boy's waking had roused him.

Or perhaps, he thought with growing panic as he took a stumbling step toward the door on a leg that felt both numb and on fire and crashed to the floor when it failed to support him, she had come the way she had come into the oratory, unfelt and silent, and spirited Ágdhállán away to wherever Myreth was held.

"Ágdhi!"

The bedroom door crashed open, and Asta was there, pulling him to his feet, helping him to sit on the edge of the bed as he begged, "Where is Ágdhállán?"

"In the dayroom with Master Najar and the others," she said calmly, impulsively smoothing back his disheveled hair as though he were Henrik or one of the other children. When she realized what she was doing, she stopped, but Kavan clutched her hand and focused his attention there as he traced first his son's presence within the keep to confirm her words, and then forced himself to calm and center and disengage the tight knot of power that had inadvertently formed in his core, waiting to be released in an attack that was not needed.

"Did you See something?"

"Someone's been injured…" he blurted, regretting it at once when the corners of her mouth pulled into a worried frown. He rubbed his throbbing leg with one hand after releasing hers. "I don't know who…what kind of injury except…" He stared at his leg. "I don't know if it has happened…or will happen…or where…"

"Perhaps this is what you've seen?" She took his hand again, allowing him to see what she had now that his attention was no longer consumed by panic. The torso she showed him, bloated and discolored, had been in the Tegid for several days and was missing both its head and limbs. Kavan traced the source of her uneasiness and squeezed her hand.

"I do not believe it is Warde."

"No, but it is his second, the one playing his public persona. I've seen him before. Whatever remnants of chaos remain, they're looking for him."

"He's a Dugan. He'll handle this. He'll be okay."

"Even my father wasn't invincible," Asta reminded him grimly. "I don't want to be the one who brought him here to die…"

"You did not bring him here. You asked him to help. The choice to be in Rhidam, to take the risk for the reward, was his."

"Tell that to Bianca." Asta withdrew her hand, stepped back, and adjusted her tunic. "You saw…"

"Most of the time I'm not certain why I see what I see," he admitted. This time was no different. But he did not think the source of his pain had been a long-dead Association member. This one had been, or would be, someone closer to his heart.

And Bhás was to blame.

❧*❧

"Your Majesty, this is General Rodair."

Nedlin Rodair, a well-known name within Cordash and in military circles outside of it, looked both younger than the general who introduced him and older at the same time. With a knitted cap to cover his bald pate instead of a helm, neatly trimmed white-stubble encircling his mouth, and deep creases at the corners of his eyes resulting from too much time squinting across the sunlit sea, it was evident he had decades of experience in the field, particularly aboard ships. But there was fire in his eyes that General Declan had lost the night King Merrek had died, and a smirking, confident smile that Lorant could not recall seeing on anyone else's face.

He certainly looked more alert than Lorant felt. Dawn was coloring the sky outside of his tent, the camp preparing for whatever the day and those hiding behind Ruidoso's walls would offer. Like those before, this morning was still and thus far uneventful. As with each morning of the last handful of days, by the time Lorant awoke, Jerit was gone.

"Sources told me you were here…redirected my men to join you soon as we could," Rodair interjected with a bow, keeping his eyes respectfully averted as Enesfel's king pulled his tunic on and rose from his pallet bed. Back home, it would have been inappropriate to intrude on the king's privacy this way, but on the battlefield, such intrusions could not be helped.

"How did you get across without being spotted?"

"There's safe places along the Dagar if you know where to look. Been stationed here often enough over the last few years, bringing Ruidoso what we could to sustain them…had our share of run-ins with Fraen's forces too. Waller might not have overpowered her if we'd been here. We've been patrolling the border north of the Dagar, waiting for Waller's men to leave, to take her back. But they've been loitering and you arrived before they could get out. Figure if you're here, there might be a chance, with you and us together, to take the city and catch Waller in the process. Only got a hundred with me, but there's more behind, if we need them."

"He's here then? General Waller?" Bhetá asked hopefully.

"Far as we know. Don't know how many he's got in there, since many went south to the border, and no one's reported him leaving with them."

"Living well while his troops live on scraps," Garran snorted.

Rodair shrugged. "Way of things in Neth. Not the first time, won't be the last."

"Way of things in many places," Kaj agreed with a glance at Lorant, "Your Majesty notwithstanding."

Rodair smiled again, this time at Lorant, and continued, "You're the king, that's different." As far as he was concerned, a king should live in luxury. It was expected. A general should remain nearer to the level of the soldiers beneath him to foster solidarity.

"Nothing's gone in or out while we've been here," Kaj agreed. "We intercepted every merchant, farmer, or herd seller who's tried."

Lorant, now adjusting his boots, huffed, "But they could have a month or more of supplies inside. We don't have that long." He already felt they had remained in one place for too long. Ruidoso was important, but reaching Fraen, taking back Glevum, seemed more so.

"As many soldiers as have been reported…even if they've mostly been assigned elsewhere before you got here, I doubt they have much to live on. But I might…" Rodair scratched his head and adjusted his knitted cap with both hands. "Might be able to get a man or two inside…take a look around…find out the state of things…offer a distraction."

"I'll go with you," Bhetá offered.

Rodair shook his head. "Not going in myself…they'd know me…and you'd stand out. They'll know us as soon as they see us."

"What about one of the dedhá?" suggested Garran. "Hebel?" There was a chance that Thrismund might be recognized, but a novice would not be.

"Boy's got no experience," Bhetá countered.

"I can go." Eyes turned to Kaj, who shrugged and continued. "I might not know a Nethite from anyone else…but I'll know a soldier if I see one. I've gotten out of tight spots before. They'll not know me, and if I don't speak, my accent won't give me away. If I do…who's to say I'm not a merchant caught inside when the siege came?" His traveling gaze held Bhetá's for several moments before ending on the king. "I would endorse k'ílshwythnec, but she is not here. I'm the best option. I can do this."

"And your men? Who'll lead them if something happens to you?"

Kaj nodded at Garran. "They will follow your orders. I've made sure of that. Get me inside, General Rodair, and I'll do whatever is needed."

Silent glances were exchanged, glances that eventually landed on Lorant, who had little to interject in the conversation thus far. The generals were experienced enough to plan a spy mission without his interference, but it was his command they were waiting for, his choice and responsibility to accept, whatever the decision and outcome would be.

"Do we have to wait for nightfall?" Lorant asked, believing he was expected to say something.

Again, Rodair shook his head. "Not unless you prefer it."

Lorant squared his shoulders and pressed his hand against his rumbling stomach as if to quiet the sound in the silent tent. "Do it. See what you can learn…see if you can get access to General Waller and eliminate him. General Rodair, thank you for joining forces with us…for giving us aid."

"Anything to put Frain in his place. I'll get my guy and…tama, is it? You will come with me."

"I will." He bowed his head at Lorant with a slight dropping of his shoulders before following the three generals out of the king's tent. Lorant sank onto the edge of his low bed and watched the flap snap in the morning's rising wind. Soon, Jerit would return with breakfast. Then Lorant would make the camp rounds again and try to get a sense of what the Cordashian soldiers knew and had in mind.

❧*❧

The door closed softly as it had every other time Olaric left her here, the click of the key in the latch and the sliding of the bolt and the wooden brace taking him away from her again.

"He's said it before," she murmured, pulling the unsteady chair to the wall so she could climb upon it to see out of the ventilation grate that was too high for her to reach without it. The desk was even more unsteady, one leg showing signs of past repair, and the bed was too heavy for her to move. Oska never helped, and so Inness was forced to use the chair.

"You could shout to any of them," Oska said offhandedly as she tried to watch the tiny figures move past in the street below. Summer's heat was waning, bringing cooler blasts of wind rolling from the sea and the first morning fog she had seen since arriving here.

Noting that he had ignored her statement, Inness huffed. "They think I am dead. They would think me mad."

"Maybe."

Scowling, Inness was quiet for many moments before continuing, "Out there, I wouldn't do Henrik any good. I am waiting; when he comes…"

"You said…"

"A few weeks; he's said it before," she repeated with frustration as she shifted, rose on her toes, and tried to crane her face toward a commotion down the street in the hopes the noise would be the precursor to whatever unrest Olaric alluded to. The chair rocked, creaking, and when the uneven leg buckled, Inness tumbled to the floor, twisting her ankle and bruising her wrist when she landed. She glowered around her when Oska refused to take her hand and help her up, only to see he had already left.

"A few weeks," she repeated, rubbing her wrist without rising. Olaric had said that before, but she heard the difference in his tone this time. Something had changed. Enesfel's troops were at Ruidoso. He had said so. Not so far from Neth's borders, although Olaric had intimated that it was Neth who held the city and not Enesfel.

If war was in the offing now, it would be war to bring Henrik to her. That could not be done until Fraen was removed from Glevum's throne. Henrik would not be safe until Fraen was dead.

She would wait a few more weeks for that. Anything for her son.

ও•*•ও

The battering ram had not come over the avalanche wall. If it had, those in the towers would have seen it, just as they had seen the opposing army's approach into position behind that mound of earth, just as they had watched them stake claim to its summit as the vantage point from which to conduct another assault. There was barely enough room between it and the western fortress wall to utilize the ram. By the time Elyriá's army was brought to full force on the parapet at dawn, however, the drumming against the front gate of men with a large tree trunk in place of the mechanized ram had begun, and a hail of arrows was loosed from beyond the avalanche walls.

The enemy was near enough to fell the first victims on the wall, but they were also near enough to be met in kind by those stationed there. There were not so many, but they were overpowered by Elyriá's meager force and the protection of the walls, and they knew it. Others scrambled over the loose summit of dirt and rock with a trio of hastily constructed wooden ladders in the hopes of scaling the ramparts and making their way inside.

Not an archer himself, Bhríd shouted orders to those charging up the hewn stairs to join the bulwark defenses while others drew the injured to the eastern side of the fortress and worked to shore up the gate from within with every heavy item they could find.

"I should be…"

Chethá pushed Sóbhán down on his pallet as people around them hoisted the injured to move them out of harm's way. During the night, when he had briefly awakened for water and something to dull the throbbing of an injury he did not attempt to inspect, husband and wife had discussed his return to Bhryell. But Sóbhán resisted the thought of leaving, and no final decision was made before he fell asleep again.

Now dawn had arrived, and it was too late for escape without looking like cowards. Chethá's healing gifts were needed, and Sóbhán did not know if he could make it to the Gate on his own. He would not leave her here.

Chethá did not voice the obvious. Until he learned to move about on one leg, until he was supplied with a crutch or an artificial limb, until the residual pain of amputation subsided, he would be of no use in battle.

"I have to help the others," she murmured, kissing his mouth as she stood. The screams of the injured began anew. The thuds, thumps, and crashing sounds of those propelled off the wall were interspersed with the impact of wood against wood.

She did not believe the gate, as thick as its multiple layers were, would last. She could help the injured and avoid displaying the heart-stopping fear on her face that he could too easily read. He could not protect her.

She would have to protect him.

"Here." From beside the nearest pallet, she grabbed the sword of someone who had died during the night and thrust it into his hand. "If they get through before I return…"

He grabbed her hand, his eyes wide. "Stay away from the gate, the wall. Let someone else collect the injured…and if they break through…"

"Stay here," she repeated before escaping his grip without a promise uttered to follow his instructions.

❧*❦

"Someone else has been here."

The man Kaj followed, introduced only as Evroult, ran his fingers along the wall of the drainage canal carrying rainwater and waste from the lowest levels of Ruidoso's streets, marked with splashes that had not had time to dry. The water was ankle-deep as it had not rained in several weeks, and though here, at the mouth, it was slightly agitated by the movement of the Dagar River, ahead of them the rankness of summer stagnation hovered like a thick fog Kaj could almost taste. It prompted him to tie his pocket cloth around his face to cover his mouth and nose, but it did little to help.

He was not the only one to do so.

"Leaving," Evroult continued. "I'd say not long ago."

"We didn't see…" Kaj began.

"We weren't looking." Evroult glanced at the opposite wall, saw the splash evidence, and grunted. "More than one, but can't say how many."

"We should send word…"

"You gonna do it, or should I? Not enough for an army, I'd say…probably a handful hoping to escape the siege."

Or maybe they were spies sent to infiltrate Enesfel's ranks.

It was a possibility neither man voiced.

Kaj glanced over his shoulder. Someone passing and heading west, away from Enesfel's army, would explain why he and Evroult had not seen them. It made sense that anyone hoping to avoid the Lachlan force would try that route. Maybe they intended to seek assistance from the land to the west, from which Evroult and General Rodair hailed.

Kaj nodded without speaking, agreeing they should continue their mission, and followed Evroult deeper into the putrid darkness.

Thankfully, they did not remain enveloped in it for long. When the last of the gray sunlight behind them faded, Evroult pointed to a grate in the ceiling ahead. It cast its faint squares of light onto the black water and through it, voices and the sounds of the city at midday wafted in faint echoes to be trapped in the passage around them.

"There's more of these, but this'll do. Help me open this, then give me a boost; I'll help you up."

Cautiously, wary of making noise and drawing attention, they eased the grate aside and then, with sword drawn, Kaj waited as Evroult peeped over the edge, assessing the situation, and with a gesture was hoisted into the busy street. People parted for them, some sneering in irritation, others staring with alarm and distrust. A woman yelped in fright but Evroult clasped his hand over her mouth and silenced her with a finger to his.

"They still here?" he croaked.

She stared with wide eyes and did not answer behind his hand.

"Here," said an older man sweeping off a nearby stoop with a straw broom that scraped and scratched against the stone. He seemed to recognize Evroult's accent or something about the pair that made them appear reliable. "But not all of them." He cocked his head toward the still-open grate.

"How many?" asked Kaj as the man pulled him from the tunnel.

"Dunno. Couldn't count 'em…did not get close enough to the barracks to try. Others went out…hope that army's ready for them."

Scowling, Kaj and Evroult glanced at each other, the latter finally letting the woman go. She scurried into the midst of the passersby like a startled rat fleeing a cat, and on the off chance that they were about to be betrayed, Evroult asked, "Where's the barracks?"

The man cocked his head toward the city center and resumed sweeping. One hand came off the broom when Evroult flipped a coin in his direction. He caught it, inspected it, then shoved it into his pocket with a nod.

Cordashian.

Spent the same as anything else.

Maybe those who had gone out had run afoul of some Cordashian scouting party from the west left to protect Ruidoso's forested rear flank that Enesfel had thus far left unguarded.

"Here to get rid of them…with your help," Kaj added as they passed. "Might want to consider joining us."

Perplexed by the dark-haired man's accent, the old man pursed his lips and continued sweeping. Evroult scowled but nodded his agreement. The stranger had been cautiously helpful; maybe he could be trusted. A few helpful insiders might allow them to stir up enough trouble inside the city to make King Lorant's plans on the outside easier to accomplish.

If they had exposed themselves to a traitor, their work here would be a short-lived endeavor.

❧*❧

"Come with me!"

It was a risky plan, but one Bhríd believed in. He could not remain trapped behind the walls, waiting for the ram to break the gate. Dozens of bodies lay in the gap between the walls, dozens more had fallen from the parapet to be collected by the healers. Other than the healers and the injured and those continuing to hold the gate, there was little movement in the courtyard, a warning that those on the wall were all he had left.

He could not wait for reinforcements that might not come, or that might not come in time. He had to be proactive. He had to hope that he and the nine with him, soldiers of strength and experience, could infiltrate behind the avalanche line and deal a harsh blow to however many men remained there that he could not see or count.

Darting between arrows and past a cluster of people who met the flow of enemy soldiers scaling the ladder to tumble into battle on the parapet, Bhríd reached the steep southern edge where the constructed wall of the fort met the mountainside and began to scale up and across its face. A few hundred feet. That was all they needed.

❧*❧

Soldiers in the streets, perhaps three or four dozen, bullying men prone to shoving others out of the way, demanded more than their share from vendors and had their way with any girl that caught their eye. They were easy to track. The barrack Kaj and Evroult eventually located was empty, and the apartment they were directed to by a cluster of hungry boys tempted by the handful of coins Evroult offered, where one said General Waller had roomed, was devoid of personal effects. The bed was unmade, and dry, dusty prints remained around the room, suggesting it had been recently occupied. Now it appeared to have been vacated. Using the privacy of that room, both hoping the former occupant would return for the ambush they were prepared to deliver, they watched the streets through the wide window and discussed the options for what they had been instructed to do, what they had seen, what they could realistically accomplish inside such a large city as two men, until eventually they agreed.

Evroult took to the streets to pass among familiar people to spread the plan to those he deemed most disgruntled with the presence of Nethite soldiers, people who looked to have been city guards once, thugs and malcontents, those harassed by the brutish armored fellows trying to beat submission into, or force goods and services out of, the residents.

Kaj, meanwhile, found his way to one of the watchtowers where the remains of a demolished catapult remained. Stealth gave way to the assassination of two men in unfamiliar armor, men not marked with the green and gray that King Fraen's army wore. The third man, a shabbily dressed fellow without shoes, dropped the scope he was holding and stood quaking with his hands in the air when he and Kaj came face to face.

"You from here?"

The man nodded without speaking.

"Need you to do something." Kaj pulled out a fistful of colored cloths from his vest pocket and tied a green one onto the voulge a fallen soldier had wielded. He thrust the voulge into the man's hands, pointed to the army stationed outside of the city walls, and said, "You want to be free of this," he cocked his head to the dead men, "make sure they see it. Hold this position. Right here. Don't leave this spot until you know they've seen it."

The stranger blinked, bobbed his head, and turned sideways to wave the pendant over the edge of the tower wall.

Kaj sprinted toward the other tower. Soon enough, the enemy would see that flag too. Soon, they would come for the wielder. He had to make certain that did not happen.

❧*❧

Three by three, men and women with swords, a variety of poles, with bows and spike-faced shields, raced from the Rísóri k'rylag into the courtyard as the fortress gate fractured beneath the persistent might of the ram. Those who wielded it dropped it, drew their weapons, and met the line of Elyri soldiers head-on. The delay created by the need to produce swords meant that the Elyri had the advantage and met them at the breach. There were more assailants within the fortress than they expected, more than they had believed could still be alive after the morning's assault. The injured and the dead accumulated in the gateway as they fell, necessitating their removal if the invaders were to get past.

But the Elyri did not relent.

Though the last ladder had fallen, killing men in the gap below, a cluster of those climbing it had gotten over the wall, killing the Elyri who met them at the top. With their attention on reaching the gate, they charged down the stairs to the courtyard. Four raced in the direction from which the Elyri seemed to be spawning, growing their numbers without end. Three followed those transporting the wounded, while the remaining two turned toward the archway where the wounded had previously been collected.

Unnoticed after the first of their number fell to an arrow from a man killed immediately thereafter, Bhríd and his eight on the outside followed the mountain ledge. They could see the eight archers perched on the avalanche wall and another two dozen men behind held back when the fortress gate fell. He did not know if there were more back along the trail, but since no signal had been given to summon reinforcements and the enemy's numbers continued to dwindle, Bhríd hoped it meant there were no reinforcements to be had.

At least none close enough to be of use.

The archers, assessing the rapid depletion of fighting men at the gate as the dead were kicked aside so that others could continue the fight to enter the fortress, having no targets atop the parapet now that every available Elyri had entered the melee in the courtyard, looked at one another with silent nods and began picking off the invaders.

Bhríd could not hear what they said, but the decision to retreat was easily recognized. Hoping to cut off their flight, he hastened his climb and signaled those behind him to do likewise.

❧*❧

The green flag was met with the advance of Enesfel's troops, allowing them to close the gap between them and the city beneath the cloudy, midday sky. On the inside, skirmishes peppered with slurs of fury erupted in a multitude of places Kaj could not see. A mismatched band of people bearing an array of craftsmen tools, picks, small axes, butcher knives, skinning razors, hammers and farm tools, gathered at the city gate, preventing the escape of the first disoriented soldiers and holding it in the expectation of stopping any others as the Nethites realized that their general and a good portion of their force were not coming to their aid. General Waller did not appear. Kaj left the tower to join the people of Ruidoso when the last group of Nethites charged. The residents outnumbered the soldiers, but they lacked the experience and the reaction time to hold their ground.

Kaj lacked neither. He bellowed incoherent words that frightened soldiers and citizens alike, and leaped into the midst from the staircase. City folk at the front, city folk arriving from behind, Kaj swinging at the center, and Evroult pushing in from the fringes where he was hidden by the crowd.

On the outside of the wall, the roar of a ram's horn shook the air.

Enesfel was almost at the gate.

᷿*᷎

Sóbhán forced himself to stand, to wobble and hop to the doorway of the makeshift triage center with the sword used to steady him like a cane until he could lean against the arch. He reached it in time to see the pair bearing down on his position. There were more men in the courtyard than he expected, Elyri in clean, polished armor that suggested dedhá Bhílári's success in Clarys, but from where Sóbhán stood, he could not assess the combat at the gate or on the parapet, nor guess what was happening outside. The only thing he was certain of was that his efforts to ward the fortress as his father could have done had failed. He was also certain that at least the pair heading toward him had gotten past Elyri defenses to kill those inside.

He whistled.

Heads turned in his direction.

One of the enemy soldiers was drawn off to protect his companion as an Elyri whose face was hidden behind a closed helm charged at them. Sóbhán barely parried the blow, but his effort cost his assailant his balance, so that they both landed in a heap on the floor. The sword was knocked from Sóbhán's hand.

Rolling to the side to avoid the hands that tried to close around his throat, feeling the fellow's hot breath that reeked of unfamiliar spices upon his face before he dislodged the man, Sóbhán shrieked when his injured leg smacked against the ground. The pain made him reflexively curl in upon himself, exposing his unshielded back. In the moment he realized he was vulnerable, in the moment he consciously tried to roll again to escape the attack and the pain, a spear drove into the man's ribs, pinning him to the ground. He lost his sword too, one of an unfamiliar curved design, and went rigid in shock and pain.

The helmed Elyri stepped into view and twisted the spear. Ribs cracked, and the man groaned as the metal tip tore through lung and muscle. After a brief struggle to pull the spear free, he lay still as the life bled from his eyes and the ground beneath him grew wet and red.

"Let me get you to safety." The Elyri retrieved the dropped swords and handed them to Sóbhán before helping him up.

"No, get out there and help the others; this won't happen again."

He assumed the infiltrating soldiers were being likewise dealt with, so he did not anticipate others coming for him unless those fighting at the gate fell. Having everyone fit for combat there to protect the fortress's point of entry was more important than his life. "Go."

The individual hesitated, nodded, and muttered, "Aye."

❧*❦

No arrows or catapult stones met Enesfel's late afternoon approach. No rush of soldiers burst from the city to stop them. There was shouting behind the walls, evidence of combat, but the green flag still flew, and their march forward was unimpeded. General Declan held the line steady, watching the distant movement of the Daema's similar progress along the southern wall, until the gate was thrown open and a single man on a horse with a white flag of surrender rode through it.

General Declan lifted a hand. Beside him, Lorant's horse nickered at the abrupt halt and sidestepped away from the general's horse.

"I'll ride forth and…" Garran began.

Waving to the rider between him and Lorant, whose pendant pole sported both Lachlan and de Corrmick flags, Jerit said, "We'll go. If it's surrender they wish, they need a diplomat, not a general."

"If it's a trap?" Lorant muttered, tipping the visor of his helm as he jerked his horse aside to prevent Jerit and the flag bearer from moving.

"Then you'll be behind me with the army to take action."

Their gazes held until Lorant huffed and pulled his horse back. Jerit was right. Lorant was the better soldier, Jerit the better diplomat. With no archers and only a gaggle of mismatched faces visible beyond the open gate, he chose to believe the veracity of the white flag and allowed Jerit to go.

He held his breath, however, when the opposing rider continued moving forward, lowered his flag, and then fell into step beside Jerit when the prince and the flag bearer turned their horses and rode back toward Lorant. With his army stopped behind him, Lorant realized the shouts within Ruidoso had become cheers.

When he recognized Kaj at Jerit's side, when the tama shouted, "Ruidoso is ours," the men behind the king around to cheer as well. A battle had been won without significant bloodshed.

Ruidoso was free.

Lorant led his force to the city gate, hoping to see General Waller's decimated body on display. They might have won Ruidoso, but only if that man were dead would he be able to earnestly celebrate this victory.

Rather than kill the remaining half dozen invaders who, realizing they had no support, attempted to retreat, the captain left in charge of the Rísóri fortress ordered them captured and locked in a room used for the storage of confiscated contraband, while the dead and injured were collected and sorted for treatment, burial, or transport home. Though the loss of life was significant, fewer Elyri had been lost in this encounter than in those previous, and unless there were others hidden beyond the bend, it appeared they had defeated their foe. Using the lumber from the avalanche-felled tree, work began immediately to repair the gaping wound in the splintered gate, and someone from the newly arrived replacement army offered to return to Clarys to hasten the arrival of the rest of the soldiers Bhílári had been promised.

Aided by his wife and one of the younger squires when he insisted on mingling with the troops, the man Sóbhán hoped to see was not there.

"Where's Bhríd?" he begged, shaking the ranking captain's arm to get his attention, his voice colored with distress that his failure to be in this fight might have cost his kinsman's life.

The captain pointed to the mountain face beyond the avalanche wall, where it was difficult to identify anything in the twilight. "Led a squad to pursue the cowards who ran. He'll be back soon as they're dealt with."

"Send another squad to…"

The captain looked at him as though he were an impudent, demanding child who believed his parents had not considered all the details. Gently chiding, he said, "Already have, sir. Long as we're without a gate, we don't want surprises; most of our people are best kept here…just in case. I'll let you know soon as he's back…I'll send him to you."

Swallowing another impetuous question, acknowledging that the captain knew his duties better than Sóbhán did, the younger man grunted his acceptance and muttered, "I appreciate that, Captain."

"Take rest, sir. Nothing you can do. I'll let you know if there's anything you can help with."

The captain returned to his business without seeing the narrow-eyed, penetrating stare at the back of his head. What sounded like a pompous, patronizing promise made Sóbhán growl, but there was no one near enough to hear the sound.

The problem was, thanks to his injury, there was little he could do, and as the rush of battle and near-death adrenaline drained away, he was reminded how tired he was…and how hard it was to remain standing, even with the squire's help.

He should go to his father or send for him. Kavan needed to know his fate, needed to know the truth.

But Sóbhán could not shake the shame of embarrassing his father, of somehow being less than whole. Two sons. He should not have come. Despite a lifetime of experience with the man and his faith, his strong affection and support for those he loved, Sóbhán was afraid that he had disappointed the man who had given him a second life.

When Kavan learned the truth, things he had told neither Bhríd nor Chethá, he feared what his father might do to avenge him.

❧*❧

Beyond the sight of anyone on these foreign shores, the armada of galleys split into four factions, turning oars and sails in the directions the shi cali commanded them to go. Some north, some south, some west, intent on their missions, determined to bring honor to she who led them and the ancestor she spoke for. Soon it would be time for the spilling of blood, for the sacrifice of life and breath, for the claiming of victory over the unclean betrayers of the Way.

❧Chapter 43❧

This time when the encircling pain began to burn just above his knee, a severing sharpness dwindling into a throbbing ache that reminded him how his mangled hands had once felt after the pain of injury, the sensation came with the vague, blurry images of a stark stone room and the comforting yet disquieting nearness of his oldest son. Convinced the things were connected, afraid for Sóbhán's welfare, Kavan tucked his harp case beneath his arm and was on his way to the oratory when Rhyrdan, carrying Ágdhállán on his shoulders, rounded the corridor corner, grinning and laughing until they noted the bard's pensive expression.

He might have been doing no more than going to the oratory to pray and play as he had done more often in recent weeks, but the harp being inside its case said differently.

"Where are you going, k'bhydhá?" the boy asked as Rhyrdan put him down. He wrapped his arms around Kavan's waist, unashamed to express his love to his father or to anyone else.

"You should be heading to bed," Kavan replied cagily, wrapping his empty arm around the boy's shoulders.

Sensing evasion, Rhyrdan adjusted his tunic and tried a different tact, hoping a yes or no question would garner a more direct answer. "Are you going to Alberni for the evening?" The duke had not been to the manor, or to St. Kóráhm's, in several days, and Rhyrdan hoped the cause of his distraction was the need for study or prayer in that holy place rather than a woman who continued to pick at him as though he was a scab on an unhealing wound.

Since the night she had invaded the oratory, Kavan had spent less time there. He considered warding it as he had done St. Kóráhm's, but he was beginning to doubt that his wards were strong enough to protect anyone. Nothing was.

When he sought privacy for prayer and music, he did so in the back garden in front of the wall of Lachlan burial plaques. He had not told anyone about Bhás' appearance in the oratory; he did not know if Sunna had. To most, it appeared he was taking advantage of the gradually cooling evening weather of Eltail's end.

"I am going to Bhryell," he said with a sigh, unable to lie to his son or dearest friend, both of whom would have known he was hiding something. "To see Sóbhán and perhaps Bhen."

Ágdhállán's brow furrowed. "Has something happened?" At this hour, it was late to go calling. His father's stance was uncomfortable, and the boy knew he had been shouldering an unidentified uneasiness since the first experience of leg pain. Kavan had not spoken of the unknown cause, had not mentioned any similar pain or episode of the Sight since, and though it seemed Ágdhállán had not experienced it too, Kavan knew his son sensed something amiss.

"Not that I am aware of. I have duties in the morning and tutoring in the afternoon," Kavan reminded them. "To see either, it must be tonight."

Rhyrdan latched onto the barely perceptible stress in the word 'must', held out his hand to Ágdhállán, and said, "Then we shall go with you."

"There is no…"

"I want to see Sóbhán too…and Maelís." Ágdhállán was less interested in Ydrís, as the girl was just over a year old and thus not an adequate playmate, but Maelís was his junior by only a matter of months.

"She may be asleep…"

"And she may not be. I will stay out of the way," he begged, tugging on his father's arm, "if you take me with you."

"It will be safer if we stay together."

Kavan stared at Rhyrdan's pursed lips, struck by how much he looked like Wortham, and forced the rising sigh to be absorbed into his tense throat. Though he wanted to deny his son's plea, Rhyrdan had a point.

St. Kóráhm's was warded as securely as he could manage. Dhóri was safe if he was there. But Rhidam's keep was more vast, and Kavan had been unable to do anything more than ward single rooms, one or two at a time, in the hopes of protecting those people Bhás was most likely to target.

He could not, however, force people to remain in those warded rooms.

"War may have come to Bhryell; whatever the case, you will do as I instruct and no more. Do you agree?" The question was directed at both, but his gaze was on Rhyrdan.

"To the best of my ability and honor," Rhyrdan agreed with a bobbing bow of his head. Ágdhállán nodded vigorously.

"Come then."

They emerged from the oratory in the Bhryell home of his early adult life into an empty bedroom with an unlit hearth, a room left vacant for Kavan's use but where he had not slept in several years. Kavan paused to listen, to feel the aura of the house, but there was no sign of life there beyond the memories that had seeped into the ancient stone walls and the stale, residual smells of past meals and unwashed laundry. These were not the walls the Sight had shown him, nor was there anywhere in this house that matched both the physical description and the sterile aura he had felt. With the others trailing behind his cautious steps, he went downstairs and then out to the porch to assess the state of the village where he had been born.

Voices behind closed doors, silhouettes cast against backlit windows, the bubbling of the village fountain where his likeness looked over the residents, a monument that made him uneasy every time he saw it. Across the square, in the house that Tíbhyan left to him, a child's laughter and slightly out-of-tune singing voice, and after a glance at Rhyrdan, Kavan led the way across the square.

There were many reasons why Chethá might not be home.

There were fewer reasons why Sóbhán might not be.

Ágdhállán raced ahead, bounded up the porch stairs, and knocked on the door before Kavan could catch or stop him. By the time Bhen opened it, Kavan and Rhyrdan were climbing the steps.

"This is unexpected," Bhen said warmly, clasping Kavan's hand and pulling him inside. Gone were the mountains of books and clutter of a bhydáni's life work. Now the room looked homier, with cushioned chairs around the hearth for guests, a workbench where tools and some of Bhen's projects outside of designing and carving harps were scattered. Nóráh's voice wafted down the stairs, carried on the cries of a discontented Ydrís. Maelís leaped off the sofa where she and Bhen had been engaged in song games and embraced Ágdhállán with a squeal.

"I'm looking for Sóbhán."

In a tone that revealed Bhen knew something the bard might not like, Bhen said, "Maelís, why don't you show Ágdhi the kittens?"

"Yes," she chirped, pulling the boy toward the door that led into the back garden that Bhen had maintained since before the bhydáni's passing.

"Not without me you don't," muttered Rhyrdan, casting Kavan a look that demanded he be told the details later but not waiting for his response.

The door had already bumped shut, starting Ydrís wailing again, so Rhyrdan had to hurry to catch up to the running children.

Poking at the hearth fire to stir its embers so the new log resumed burning to fend off the slight evening chill, Bhen sighed. "She's been particularly fussy today as her teeth come."

"Perhaps it is something more." He did not set the harp down but he did move closer to the fire.

"You think something has happened to Sóbhán."

Kavan frowned. "I think he is not here…that something has happened, wherever he is."

Bhen sighed and rubbed his hands together over the fire. "Rísóri. He's one of about a dozen from Bhryell that followed Bhríd there. I have not heard any news, but a few days ago, Chethá followed. Neither has returned yet. The girls ask about them, but there is nothing to tell.

Rísóri. Kavan shivered. After a glance at the back door and a cocked head that gauged where his youngest son was, Kavan grimly nodded. "Tell Rhyrdan I have gone to them…that I will return as soon as I can."

"You want me to be the bearer of your bad news," Bhen chuckled, his tone somber. Of course Kavan would want to go to his oldest son. No one would fault him for that.

"I want you to be sure Rhyrdan stays with Ágdhállán…with you and the children…until I return." Unable to use the Gates, Rhyrdan would be unable to follow Kavan easily, but it would not prevent him from begging Bhen to take him there if he believed Kavan was putting himself in danger.

"And here I'd hoped you had come to visit me."

"I…" Kavan's voice faltered until Bhen grinned and embraced him, before steering him through the house to the pantry room where Kavan's first attempt to build a Gate had been successful.

"Someday you will learn to recognize teasing, aendhá. You're here, and I see you are well; that is all I need. Right now, if something has happened in Rísóri, to Sóbhán, Chethá, or Bhríd, we need to know.

Flushing and wiping his face with one hand as if to wipe the embarrassment away, Kavan murmured, "Thank you, Bhen," before stepping onto the stone tiles where the power emanated the strongest.

Moments later, before the door opened and closed again, he was gone.

The stench in Rísóri's stronghold, in the room used for Gatherings and meetings among those stationed here, or the merchants traversing the pass, made Kavan clench his jaw and wrinkle his nose in distaste. Blood, death, and dust spoke of recent conflict that he had not Seen or expected. He had known there would be war west of Bhryell, but the location had been uncertain until this moment. Sawing and hammering punctuated the air, interspersed with the voices of men and women in the courtyard and a faint underlayment of the groans and sighs of those injured in combat.

He looked around the empty room, studying the wooden benches, the tables and chairs, and a lectern that, judging by the energy of the room, was also used as an altar by whatever dedhá served here, and then looked at the stone beneath his feet. The pockmarked gray matched what the Sight had revealed. He was in the right place. But Sóbhán was not here.

Not this room.

"Lord Cliáth."

dedhá Bhílári was the last man Kavan expected to find at the center of war. Until his journey to Rhidam to speak in Kavan's defense after the murder of King Hagen, Bhílári had been too timid to travel beyond Bhryell's borders and the immediate farmland. Something, perhaps his own belief in protecting Elyriá from invaders, had brought him here. Seeing his beaming, weary face relieved some of Kavan's initial concerns.

"dedhá. How fares Rísóri? Are Bhríd and…?"

"Lord Cáner is not here." Bhílári met Kavan halfway across the room and offered his hand, as much out of politeness as in the hope of experiencing the touch of the Elyri miracle worker. When Kavan accepted the gesture, he did not attempt to read the other man to learn if he was disappointed that nothing miraculous happened. "We have had three battles…after the most recent, he has led men to pursue those who retreated. He has not yet returned, but we trust he will."

Bhríd was a strong, capable fighter with keen senses and instincts. In war and in tournaments, he had never been bested. Kavan chose to believe that the dedhá's assessment was correct.

Bhílári continued. "We've lost many, but they lost more. Lord Bhíncári is collecting more to station here. Your son…" He sighed and began to walk with a tilt of his head, leading Kavan across the courtyard. "He'll be happy to see you."

The dedhá did not sound confident in his words, but they suggested that Sóbhán was alive. Kavan's shoulders relaxed more.

Those in the yard working to restore the splintered gate, who crafted arrows and sharpened blades beneath the light of torches and lanterns, looked up as Kavan passed, nodding, murmuring welcomes, trying to touch him if they were near enough in the hopes that he would provide some blessing. The dead were being transported to their homes, and the blood on the courtyard stones had been swept over with straw and dust to hide the grizzly reminder, but the memory of death would not be erased. These people had lost friends, family, compatriots. Nothing was going to remove those memories.

They ducked beneath a stone arch into a room littered with injured people murmuring and moaning in their sleep as physicians flitted between them, checking for fevers, for infection, offering water and what relief from pain they could until the healers were rested enough to resume their care. Those with minor injuries or with more severe but not incapacitating injuries that were already healed had returned to the barracks to sleep or had returned to active duty if they were able. Those who remained here were less fortunate.

As Kavan's gaze landed upon Sóbhán's sleeping face, Chethá reached the bard's side and curled her hand around his elbow.

Voice melancholy and exhausted, she murmured, "I told him to go to you…but he won't leave here until I am no longer needed."

"I didn't think you'd…" he whispered, his eyes focused on the sag and fold of the light blanket spread over Sóbhán's body for warmth, the lay of which explaining the obvious without the news being spoken, without his needing to pull the blanket back to see more.

"Bhríd sent for me. Stubborn fool that he is," she continued affectionately, "he was making sure everyone else received care first…that didn't work with me."

"Is he…other than…?"

"Dehydrated from fever, but the fever's gone. Bruised, scraped up, but he will live. You may wake him if you wish."

"I just want to see that he is…"

"If you leave without seeing him, and he learns you were here…"

Kavan nodded. Though not as sensitive as Dhóri, Sóbhán still desired his father's approval and acceptance. Kavan knew how he would feel if those he loved turned away due to a bodily defect. He had lived through that trauma. He had never inflicted that suffering on Dhóri for the loss of his eyesight. He would not inflict it on Sóbhán for the loss of part of his leg.

"I will sit with him until he wakes," he agreed.

Chethá kissed his cheek. "If you can convince him to return to Bhryell, please do so."

"I will try."

If Chethá chose to remain in Rísóri for even a day longer, however, Kavan knew Sóbhán would not go anywhere.

Pulling over one of the squat, three-legged stools that littered the room, one that matched Kavan's vision in every way, he placed his harp case on the floor by his knee and sat next to the bed, cupping Sóbhán's hand between his, hoping for the same miracle that others had hoped for and yet feeling nothing but gratitude that his son was alive and, at least in slumber, at peace. After brushing the dark curls from Sóbhán's forehead, Kavan closed his eyes to pray, thanking k'Ádhá, Dhágdhuán, and Kóráhm for sparing his son, for not taking him away.

He would not probe the young man's mind for details of what had happened. He would allow Sóbhán to share those things on his own.

❧*❧

"We'll stay and see to the city's security," General Rodair repeated his previous proclamation to remind the young king why he and his small squadron would not be joining Enesfel's push toward Lake Curo. Prompted by Evroult and Kaj's encouragement, aided by the unexpected abandonment of the city by the absent General Waller, the people of Ruidoso had reclaimed their city without Enesfel doing anything more than destroying the catapults and sending two men inside to guide them. In gratitude, some of those residents joined the mass of men who had already pulled up their tents and packed their belongings, making up for some of the losses Enesfel had sustained. Most, however, chose to remain in Ruidoso and continue the reclamation and restoration with the help of Rodair's men. Soon, if his words were true, there would be more aid and the protection of the Cordashian reinforcements Rodair had sent for.

"I could leave men to assist you, to secure our back," Lorant began.

"If Waller's ahead of us," Bhetá reminded him, "we will need as many men as we have."

"And more," muttered General Declan, "I doubt there will be many to pick up that he's not already enslaved or slaughtered."

"That's his reputation," Rodair agreed. A rooster crowed, announcing the dawn that had not yet begun to paint the black canvas of the sky. "We will set up a supply line; just send word if there is anything we can provide. If I have men to spare, I will, of course, send them."

"We will." General Declan turned his horse, gestured to his co-generals, and started the easterly march.

❧507❧

Lorant, waiting for Jerit, who had ridden into Ruidoso for something he would not divulge, remained where he had promised he would be when Jerit returned.

Rodair and a handful of men Bhetá had chosen remained with him.

"Is there anything you can tell me about General Waller?" he asked. His generals had experience with the man in battle, but that was from ten years ago. The majority of what they knew now came from gossip and spies.

"He and Fraen are of like temperament…focused on power ahead of all else. I've not fought his command myself. Indeed, beyond any internal matters he has dealt with for Fraen, I don't know how much combat experience he has. But he is ambitious. If he sees a weakness, he will take advantage of it. If he sees an opportunity, he will take it. Be cautious, Your Majesty. Do not let him surprise you."

"I will endeavor to keep your advice, General. Thank you."

"Good luck."

Lorant nodded. He believed Enesfel would need it.

꙰*꙰

"You brought your harp and haven't played it yet."

Kavan opened his eyes, having half dozed mid-prayer on the short, uncomfortable stool, and winced as he raised his head, the shooting ache in his neck and buttocks evidence that his mistake had cost him. Sóbhán smiled sheepishly and squeezed the hand upon his before raising both to kiss the back of his father's hand. Kavan bent over him and kissed Sóbhán's cheek before smoothing his hair.

"Did Chethá send for you?"

"I've been Seeing…I felt…" He absently rubbed his thigh above his knee and sighed before continuing. "It took time to make sense of what I Saw. I was compelled to come…to see…"

"It's just a leg."

The off-handed words were undercut by a flippant pain that cut Kavan to the soul. "It is," he agreed gently, "but that does not make it…does not make you any less than…"

"I know." He released Kavan's hand and rubbed his eyes. "I shouldn't have come; you said so…but I wanted to believe…I should do my part…"

"It was not the Sight that made me beg you to stay away. It was being a father. I didn't know that…"

"Not consciously perhaps…but I think you knew. I didn't listen, thought I could help…and instead…"

"I'm sure you did help." Sóbhán's eyes bore the weight of a man who had taken the lives of others, a soul wound Kavan could not erase. "Every life you took spared someone else. Kept Elyriá safe."

"Did dedhá Bhílári tell you there is fighting in Clarys…ships trying to access the trade caverns. Up and down the coast, there are reports of the same. We have not heard from any of the other passes."

"They'd have to get into Enesfel first."

Sóbhán nodded and used his arms to wiggle up so that he could sit with his back against the wall. He wondered if he should go to Clarys, if he should see if there was some other way he could help from there. But the Kyne had everyone in Clarys at her disposal, men and women who could protect the ruling city, the Kyne, and the whole of the land now that the alleged threat Kavan had foretold had emerged from the darkness of rumor.

With Chethá out of the room, Sóbhán only had his father.

"Can you tell me…?" Kavan glanced at the empty, sagging blanket where his son's lower leg and foot should be, intent on proving that the loss of the limb did not disgust him while simultaneously hoping not to make Sóbhán uncomfortable by dwelling on the injury.

"It was just…war…" He shuddered, not knowing how else to describe the chaotic horror beyond that. "Fighting…shouting. Men, not Nethites but those mercenaries you predicted, I suppose…coming at us along the pass. One came up behind Bhríd, and I shouted to warn him…and then the space between us filled with other people, and I couldn't see him anymore. I don't know how many…how long…it seemed to happen so fast and yet…so slow…Someone swung, cut across my leg…" His gaze flickered down to where his toes should be. "I tried to remain standing as he fell to someone else's blade, but then she was there…"

Kavan shuddered at the emphasis, and Sóbhán continued. "At least…I'm sure it was…she looked as you described her, like you showed me. The only woman among them. She did not fight…she was just there. She stood over me as my leg gave out with such a look…like disdain and triumph and hatred…even fear…and then she lashed out without moving, and I tumbled to the river and got wedged between two boulders before I reached the water. I couldn't get free until Bhríd…by then it was over. By the time he got me, there'd been too much blood loss…too much time…she couldn't save it. It wasn't her fault…she did everything she could."

He did not want his father to blame Chethá, but nor was he ready to accept part of the blame for his choices. Stuck on the word fear, an aspect that for once stood apart from the rest of his knowledge of Bhás, Kavan offered his hand and asked, "May I see her?"

He did not doubt Sóbhán's tale, but in the heat of battle, a man's eyes might not see everything there was to see…and might see things that were not there. He wanted to believe that Bhás had not found and tried to kill his eldest son. But if she had a cause to fear, he needed to know why. And if her actions were meant to lure Kavan here, to her or away from Ágdhállán and Dhóri, he needed to know that too.

"It was her," Sóbhán repeated as he gave Kavan his hand.

In that touch, he did not see the fear as Sóbhán had, only felt his son's fear as he recognized the thin, exotic face of the woman who wanted his father's destruction. But there was something different about her, different in the way her icy stare morphed into something proud and self-assured as she met not Sóbhán's eyes but Kavan's across that battlefield memory that made Kavan jerk his hand away and slam down every mental defense he had opened to read his son.

She had known about Rhyrdan. She had, somehow, learned about Ágdhállán. Until that battle, Kavan had not thought she had been aware of Sóbhán. Until this moment, he had not thought she knew about Dhóri.

She did now.

"k'bhydhá?"

"You must return to Bhryell…or to St. Kóráhm's or Rhidam. You are not safe here."

Sóbhán frowned. "Chethá will never…"

"Then you must convince her. You are not safe here…and if she comes for you again, none of these people will be safe either."

"Do you think the attacks on Rísóri are because I am here?"

Kavan shook his head. "No. They would have come for the pass whether you were here or not." But despite his belief, he could not deny that Sóbhán's presence might have been the lure that kept the enemy coming if Bhás was the one directing them. "I cannot protect you here."

"You can in Bhryell?" He sounded skeptical and rightfully concerned.

"Perhaps not." Not without remaining with him and taking the time to ward every location in Bhryell where Sóbhán was likely to spend time. "St. Kóráhm's is protected" at least the outer walls were, "and many rooms in Rhidam, so long as I am there."

"And the girls? Chethá?"

"She may not know of them, but in time…" If it was a blood debt Bhás wanted to fulfill, then Chethá and her children might be spared because of

Sóbhán's adopted status. But because Kavan considered him his son, and her goal, it seemed, was to torment everyone dear to him and eventually destroy them to get to him, he could not guarantee that Sóbhán's family would remain safe.

"Or go to Gorbesh. You will all be safe there." So long as Earé considered the mountain chellé hábhai to be home, Kavan believed that nothing would ever touch any of those living there.

Perhaps it was time to send Dhóri and Ágdhállán there, too.

"She knows you are…she knows I am…" He stood and picked up his harp. "I must return to Ágdhállán; she mustn't know he is alone and unprotected." Not alone, as Rhyrdan was with him, but the might of a Delamo sword might not be enough to stand between Bhás and Ágdhállán.

"Yes, go. I will talk to Chethá, warn her. I'm…I am sorry, k'bhydhá. For disappointing you…for disobeying…"

Placing the harp on the stool long enough to cup Sóbhán's face between his hands, Kavan kissed his cheeks, his forehead, the top of his head, and his lips. "You are not a child to disobey, kyá, nor am I disappointed. I can love you no less than I ever have…and each day more than yesterday. I want you to be safe. I want you to be happy."

"I will talk to her," Sóbhán promised again, choking on the emotion his father's words elicited. "You will know our choice as soon as we know it…and I will see you soon."

"I look forward to it…as do your brothers. Stay vigilant." It was the best advice Kavan could give.

"I will."

❧*❧

Like the men who had brought their breathless report from the highest tower of the Harcourt castle, King Gamal did not recognize the fleet of galleys that moved across his line of sight. They were too far from shore for land artillery to reach them, and as they appeared to be casually passing by, he could not say if an attack was warranted.

But Kavan's warnings about an assault from the sea, seconded more recently by Regent Níkóá, were ever-present in his mind when he came to this window three times each day, when he requested reports from the harbor patrols, and from the men who stood watch at the docks.

These ships might be merchant vessels of a sort never seen before, but why then would they pass by Hatu's largest port? Most of the ports to the west were smaller and less guarded.

And these galleys had, somehow, gotten past the patrols he had put into place to intercept such a passage.

They would not do so again.

They must be bound for Kilyn, or else for Jardin or Nelori. Should they attempt to retreat, they would find the Bay of Phalla blocked.

But they could not be allowed to reach any of those destinations.

Not a sailor, less of a fighter now than he had been in his youth, Gamal would not take to the sea as he sent a sizable portion of his remaining fleet in pursuit of the swiftly moving galleys while he ordered the readying of his long unused armor and the sharpening of his sword. Pigeons were sent north to Piran, to Enesfel, in the hopes that his warning would reach them in time. If the enemy had come to Hatu, Káliel and Enesfel would be next.

If they were not already under attack.

Should any foreigner set foot on Natrona's soil, Gamal would be waiting for them, sword in hand, prepared to do anything to prevent them from digging deeper into Hatu's heartland.

His racing ships had grown too small to see.

He hoped they were swift enough to prevent the war he suspected had finally come.

∾*∾

Wiping away Ágdhállán's tears, refusing to look at Rhyrdan's expression of fierce disappointment and outrage as he was the only other person who knew the threat behind Sóbhán's injury, Kavan instead continued to look at Dhóri who, though he could not return the gaze, faced him with an expression of heartbreak and tears of his own. Wortham's grave marker felt warm against Kavan's back, like an embrace by his dearest friend that he missed more than anything in moments like this. "He will need you both when he comes…if he comes…as he adjusts to this change. I have asked him to go to Bhryell…or to come here…or Rhidam, so that we can be here for him…but I do not know if he will."

"He's not as stubborn as I was," Dhóri whispered, remembering the long, difficult weeks when his brother had helped him learn to see without eyes, helped him learn to live in ways different than before. Having believed he would never see his father again as punishment for his foolishness, Sóbhán had been the only family Dhóri had. He was determined now to return that devoted favor. "He will come."

"I also recommended that he go to Gorbesh until this war is over…and I think you should both go too."

"I will not leave you," Ágdhállán exclaimed. "It is not time!"

Kavan looked at the boy, but before he could ask what he meant, Dhóri spoke again. "I am sworn to protect St. Kóráhm's if I am able, until there is no hope remaining that she will stand. I will not break that oath. There are still books, materials; there are people to protect."

The residents could have retreated to Gorbesh, but Alberni was their home. The blessed chellé hábhai of St. Kóráhm's was their home. None of those residing here were prepared to give up that home without a fight.

How many would die, Kavan sighed, for refusing to heed his warning? How many of their deaths, how much of what was to come, was preordained despite his cautionary advice?

"Will he walk?" Ágdhállán sniffled, wiping his eyes again.

Kavan nodded. "There are ways, if you will help. It will take time, but he is strong…and so are you." He ruffled the boy's red hair. "You all are."

"That," said Dhóri earnestly, "we get from you."

Kissing the side of Ágdhállán's head with his eyes closed so he would not have to look at anyone with tears on his cheeks, Kavan only wished that proclamation was true. If he were strong, he would have confronted Bhás and defeated her already.

The fear of failure, the fear of never seeing Raebhá again or meeting his youngest son, the fear of exposing his family to Bhás' reach when that failure came, had held him back.

How much longer, he silently asked the man's bones beneath him, could he continue to believe that inaction was best, that remaining at his sons' sides was all that was needed to keep them safe?

*

Thrown from his horse, Lorant scrambled away from the animal's hooves and crawled between the legs of those fighting around him, seeking the last place he had seen Jerit swarmed by men in Nethite armor, men wielding the Nethite Curna, wearing Fraen's chosen colors of gray and green. The de Corrmick pennant had fallen with him, the end, Lorant suspected, was one of the primary goals. Determined that Jerit would live, that he would not lose him here, not like this, Lorant found the dropped pennant and awkwardly hoisted the pole with one hand, ignoring the pain in his knees from the fall, ignoring the wrenching in his shoulder the heavy pole created.

Someone behind him, thinking the same, a boy approximately Lorant's age who had lost his weapon in the initial clash, grabbed the pole with both hands and assisted in raising it above the heads of others so that everyone could see it.

"Here!"

Jerit's voice was barely heard over the din of screaming men and clashing metal. Lorant turned toward Lake Curo's increasingly bloody shore. The boy turned with him, the pennant steady in his hands when Lorant let it go. As Lorant reached for Jerit, the older man barely eight feet away, the boy lurched against his back, his smaller body absorbing the impact of a sword swing that might have been intended for the one who dared to fly the de Corrmick banner or might have been intended for Enesfel's king. The blade scraped along his unprotected ribs, where the leather straps of his breastplate had been severed earlier. The pennant pole fell again. Losing his footing in the bloody dust, trying to recapture the pennant, Lorant stumbled. Jerit jumped to catch him, narrowly avoiding the swing of a Curna intended to decapitate him.

The assailant jumped too. The weight of the pole came down against his helmetless skull with enough force to drive him to his knees at the same instant as the spear Kaj had picked up was driven into the back of his skull.

Blood and brain matter erupted over Lorant's face. Shocked and repulsed, Lorant heaved sideways, losing his midday meal and the bile that came with it onto the corpse at his feet. Jerit's awkward leap from his knees barreled Lorant to the ground while Kaj, forced to release the spear, grabbed the dead man's Curna and parried the blow of the man who had killed the pennant bearer. When the man fell, Kaj took up his sword too and, using his body as a shield, worked Lorant and Jerit toward the lake's edge where the fighting force was thinnest. Jerit wrapped an arm around Lorant's torso, and the pair stumbled together.

By the time they were clear of the thickest fighting, the combat was nearly over, with the remaining Nethites heeding the call to retreat, pulling further east along the shore. A mismatched array of boats formed a line there, blocking the villagers from sailing, preventing supplies from coming ashore. Those on the boats made no effort to come ashore to assist the Nethites they had been sent to aid. Nor did they come to take their place when General Waller ordered the disengagement of his forces.

They did not need to.

Their losses, General Declan later informed Lorant, while the prince futilely tried to clean the blood from his armor, were approximately equal. If not for the Elyri healers, kept apart from combat when Waller's waiting army charged to greet them with ferocious force, Enesfel's losses would be much greater. Those healers gave Enesfel an advantage, but Lorant, staring across the sea of corpses as Jerit cleaned the blood and brains from his face, did not think it would be enough.

Enesfel was a long way from home. Waller had recruited or killed most available people from every solitary homestead and every farming village he had passed through. Crops ready for harvest had been burned to keep them out of Enesfel's hands. Animals raised for winter had been likewise slaughtered or stolen with Neth's passing.

For anyone alive south of Lake Curo, regardless of who eventually claimed ownership of the territory, the winter ahead was going to be brutal.

Lorant, as surely as Fracn, was doing this to them. He did not know if Enesfel would have the chance, the ability, to undo it.

❧*❧

The last time he had knelt with his harp before St. Kóráhm's congregation had been nearly a year ago, when he had shared the first Gathering of St. Kóráhm's Feast Day with them. The benches were fuller today as the citizens of Alberni sensed that something was happening within the chellé without seeing evidence of it.

The Gathering Hall had not changed. The areas accessible to the public had not changed. The residents did their utmost not to reveal the preparations for the potential vacancy that loomed on the horizon.

But perhaps, this afternoon, Kavan thought as the notes from the brass strings beneath his fingers beckoned the congregation to sit when k'gdhededhá Khwílen took his place behind the altar, knowing Enesfel was at war was enough to prompt higher solidarity in Faith. Most likely, the rumor that the White Bard was here and intended to play had brought many to share in the joy of this rarity.

He was Alberni's duke, but for occasions such as this, he was the White Bard of Bhryell. Such occasions for public music were far too rare for their liking. Or for his.

Remaining where he was so as not to distract from the service and the lesson, offering impromptu tunes with each liturgical moment where it seemed fitting to do so, taking his cues from Khwílen, Kavan welcomed the sensation of záryph gathering around him, an occurrence he had not been able to summon in Rhidam's gardens, at Arlan's graveside, or anywhere else he had offered prayerful music. Bhás' presence, or his imagination of it, had stripped away his peace and left a distance between him and the divine that he had not experienced in years.

Only Kóráhm had been there, out of sight, beyond his reach, but always with him as if to hear him play…just as he was today.

When Khwílen bid him to give up a song in place of the expected lesson, Kavan nodded without fear or anxiety and moved to stand in front of the altar. Following a gentle nudge from Kóráhm and the feathery caresses of záryph wings, he set the black kestrel harp on the altar, clasped his hands before him, closed his eyes after catching Kjell's gaze across the room, and began to sing, a sound rarer still in Alberni or anywhere else.

The záryphs' response was immediate, evoking an increasingly brighter glow around Dhágdhuán's empty pyre suspended in the black chasm above and behind him, a beacon in the darkness that he felt warming his back and wrapping its loving tendrils around him. The flock felt it too, their gasps and moans of wonder were absorbed by Kavan's lilting voice and lifted into the highest reaches of the Gathering Hall's arched ceiling. Colored glass rattled with the vibration of power in the walls, the floor, the air, filling the altar so that the harp strings hummed in perfect pitch to his voice and snaked around his feet, his ankles, his legs so that he knew he would be unable to move if he tried.

There was pain, in his knees, in his head, horror in his soul as he watched a man's head erupt behind his closed lids, spattering him with its offal as something sharp cut along his ribs. He knew the hand that reached for him, knew the hand that reached back…

…but it was a pain and horror of a different sort that ripped a piercing note from his throat and made the congregation gape in awe.

He could feel it in his boots, the sticky dampness that came as blood collected around his feet. He could feel it when a gash on the side opposite Lorant's injury opened to stain his white tunic crimson. He felt it in the matching puncture wounds that bit into his wrists and allowed the blood to trickle down his arms when the záryph, or some other invisible force, drew his arms above his head and held them there, mimicking the oft-depicted posture of both the Intercessor and Saint Kóráhm the Heretic.

Power rained over him, heavy and bright, unexpectedly intense enough that the flask of serbháló on the altar behind him burst, spraying its contents across the marble, the harp, and across Kavan's back, stinging where it soaked through to his skin. His mouth moved but he was uncertain if the ethereal music he heard, like a multitude of voices in unison, was coming from his throat or the heights of the hall above. Benches creaked and feet shuffled and he expected that, as in Gorbesh, people would approach to touch or be touched in the expectation of some manner of blood blessing.

Only five pairs of hands touched him. Dhóri and Sunna on one side and Rhyrdan on the other, steadying him as if expecting him to collapse. Ágdhállán sat at his feet with one hand on his boot, softly murmuring words that Kavan could not decipher over the din inside his head. And behind him, where no man should be able to stand, the comfort of Kóráhm's hands lay upon his shoulders, holding him upright, bolstering his flagging spirit when a familiar self-deprecating voice chided him for his unworthiness, his foolishness, for the certainty of rejection he expected was to come.

Only a few outside of Gorbesh knew about the rósádhá.

Soon, he silently groaned, the entire world would know.

Little by little, the otherworldly choir faded, taking with it the gasps of long-held breaths and the scuffing of feet on stone, taking with it the sensation of the blood flowing down his arms and replacing it with the feel of soft fabric against his skin. He tried to open his eyes when Kóráhm withdrew his hands, but after a distant, frustrated, angry shriek split his thoughts, his arms dropped, his knees buckled, and the traces of illuminated power behind his lids gave way to unconscious darkness.

∾Chapter 44∾

"Do you think he's dying?"

Tau lifted his head, perplexed by Kjell's unexpected question, and set aside the stone he was using to sharpen his sword. Thinking the king referred to the son he had bullied into war, the Cíbhóló pursed his lips, shrugged, and asked, "What makes you think…there have been no reports from…"

"Kavan." Kjell had never been as close to the bard as Owain had been, but after a childhood of unsubstantiated rumors, it had been with great honor and respect that Kjell had finally met the White Bard and had those rumors laid to rest. He admired the man's wisdom, his knowledge, and valued his foresight and opinion, even when he did not agree with it or act on it…particularly when it came to matters regarding his son. Seeing so much blood lost on the altar steps from spontaneous wounds that had eventually closed without the aid of a healer, ushered out by a solemn host of dedhá without being allowed to witness the aftermath of what transpired, the reason for it, the cause, what it meant and what would come next was burning in every witness in the Hall. Including him.

Although perhaps, judging by Tau's expressionless face, his Vants protector did not share his curiosity.

"I don't know. I heard tales of rósádhá long ago; it is written in our texts, but I know no more about it than you. I do not see why k'Ádhá might bless a man so only to kill him."

"That was a blessing?" Kjell croaked, interrupted by a rapping on the door before he could say more.

He hoped the visitor had come with news about Kavan.

"Come," called Tau, opening the door as he spoke to allow Raenár to enter the room.

"Your Majesty!" the captain said, barely containing the relieved grin that tugged at the corners of his mouth. "Enesfel has reclaimed Ruidoso!"

Kjell straightened in his chair, the unexpected announcement overshadowing his fears for Kavan. "And Jerit? Is there news?" he blurted before he was able to prevent himself from doing so.

He ignored Tau's smug, knowing expression.

"He was reported well, as is the king. They were pressing north to Lake Curo the day the message was sent. The emissary is resting but will return north at dawn, if you have anything to send with him. I'm taking this news to Regent McCábhá now."

Raenár left the obvious suggestion hanging, but Kjell pretended not to hear it. Asta had not spoken to him since the day of Jerit's departure with Lorant's army. He knew his strong-willed wife too well to think she would ever speak to him again if Jerit failed to come home.

Sending a message to Jerit would receive an equally cold reception.

"Tell her he is well; tell his wife...but tell him..." Kjell shrugged. There was little he could say that Jerit wanted to hear, but he finally added, "Tell him his courage honors our blood. Tell him...he has my respect."

"I will, Sire; I will make sure your messages are sent."

❧*❧

"You have to come!" Dhóri begged, catching his sister's hand as she tried to rise from the Gathering bench beside him. "You didn't see it! So much blood..."

Gently extracting her hand from his with a pained expression, Earé murmured, "You didn't see it either."

He winced as if stung and lowered his hand but his pleading expression did not change. "I could smell it...I could...sense it. They were whispering...rósádhá, they said. I'd heard..."

"But you didn't believe it." Sighing, she stopped at the stone altar, staring at an area on the stone floor still discolored by the blood that had refused to wash away.

Knowing his father was capable of many things, knowing he was special, different, had never made the tales of miracles easier to believe. Dhóri had not doubted Wortham's word, as the man had been one of the most honest Dhóri had known. He had not doubted the saving of child Lorant's life. He had not doubted the miracle that brought his father home as the Yellow Sisters had run its course. But some things were unbelievable without experiencing them.

"He won't wake up. Yóáná has done what she can...Ártur is not there. His breathing is so...his skin...he is so frail." His voice trembled as he whispered, "Ágdhállán says he will be well…but he seems like…he sounds like…he's dying." He choked on the last word and looked away from the gaze he imagined was burning into him.

"You should heed our brother."

Ágdhállán, like Kavan, had the Sight. Dhóri wanted to believe him, but the boy's words conflicted with the evidence of his senses, and Dhóri felt his claim was too far-fetched to be believable.

"You haven't seen him," he mumbled persistently. "Something's changed. He barely sleeps. He enters a room…or leaves it…as if expecting someone to be there. He avoids the oratory…and when he plays it is like his harp is…bleeding. I can tell he is afraid, but he will not say why. We know it is…her…but he will not accept our help…or tell us…"

"There is nothing we can do," Earé mumbled. How well she shared her twin's desire to help their father. How frustrating it was to know that she could do no more than she had done…and what she was destined to do when the time came.

"But you're k'ílshwythnec," he hissed, rising to his feet. "You can do things! You can help him! You can help Sóbhán!"

He knew the stories Kavan and Wortham had told about his mother and had heard from Zelenka the many things it was rumored that She Who Sees was capable of. Having never met the woman nor seen his sister do more than come and go and share what visions of the present and future she chose to share, he could only base his assumptions on things he had heard.

"I'm no healer, but I'll see Sóbhán soon. As for…I can do nothing more than I have. I try to See, but there is a veil beyond which I cannot reach."

"He will face her."

"Yes."

"He will defeat her?"

"I believe so…but it is unclear." That uncertainty continued to eat at her despite her spoken acceptance of being unable to do anything.

"He will…die…"

"I…" She turned to look at him, wishing she could touch him, comfort him, take away his fear, but even that was beyond her. "I do not know. If Ágdhi says…"

"He's a child. He believes what he wants to believe, what makes him feel secure."

"Does it matter why he believes it? He says…and I choose to trust his faith. It is all I can do."

"It's all you will do," Dhóri spat, emphasizing the word will, his scathing glower cast over his shoulder as he marched to the door without running into the benches. He had come to Gorbesh in the hopes of finding her, had been mildly surprised that she was waiting for him, but he was surprised and angry that his twin refused to come to Rhidam to see their father, to try to wake him, help him, soothe his fears, guide him through the thorny path that lay ahead of him.

"If he dies…it will be on you," he whispered as he went out the door. "You'll be the one who abandoned him."

Earé wrapped her arms around herself in frustration and discomfort and groaned. She could not say it, to him, to Kavan, to anyone, but she believed the veil she could not see beyond was her father's death. She believed his fate was upon her shoulders. She wanted to spare her brothers that burden of knowing, just as she spared her father.

❧*❧

Sneaking back to Rhidam to retrieve the sturmyrá from the locked drawer where Kavan had secured it and then tucking it between his father's arm and torso on the bed where he slept had been the easy part. Removing the stylus-like key from around his neck was harder, as it required lifting the man's head from the pillow and untangling the cord from his hair, fearing the entire time that his father would wake and question him while secretly hoping he would.

But Kavan's shallow breathing never changed; his eyes did not flutter. He did not move.

The choice had been made not to take him back to Rhidam, so as not to raise unwanted questions that could only be explained by revealing the miraculous. Instead, he had been settled in one of the chellé's small, empty rooms, where he was bathed of the blood and allowed to rest in seclusion, except for the company of his sons and Rhyrdan, one of whom was always with him while Sunna tirelessly stood guard at the door. In all those hours, as life in the chellé continued as usual, except for an increased number of visitors bringing donations on behalf of their blessed duke, Kavan remained unresponsive to every effort made to rouse him.

The adults were worried. Ágdhállán was the only one who seemed to be at peace, a state that Dhóri attributed to youthful innocence.

Ágdhállán was not afraid. He had faith in his instincts, in the snippets of hope the Sight provided. What Kavan had endured had filled him with an overwhelming amount of power, and so long as there was no outlet for it, no internal balance, he would continue in this unconscious state for as long as it took for the levels to rebalance.

That was where the sturmyrá came in.

Once Dhóri was not here to stop him, having gone to seek aid that the boy did not expect to come, Ágdhállán made it through the Gate to Rhidam alone for the first time, jimmied open the drawer to retrieve the relic the Sight had shown him, and then returned the way he had come with only Sunna noticing.

Man and boy exchanged glances upon Ágdhállán's return. The man nodded. The boy crept silently back into the room.

His father, he thought, would be proud.

Kavan did not understand how the sturmyrá functioned, what it was meant for. Neither did Ágdhállán. He did not know what would happen when he slipped the stone key into the hole at the top. He was unprepared for the arcing burst of power that threw him back so that he tumbled onto the floor with a yelp, crashing into the nightstand as he did so, toppling the clay pitcher so that it shattered and sprayed the water it contained across the floor. He crawled hastily back, his trousers sopping up some of the spilled water as he picked shards of pottery out of his leg and watched the glow within the glass box pulse in time to the flow of power that had filled Kavan since the Gathering.

The once-dim room was as bright as midday despite the feeble gray light of the overcast morning pushing through the window. To Ágdhállán, the rise and fall of his father's chest seemed to normalize. He felt less distant, and the bruising on his ribs and wrists began to fade.

"What has…?" began Rhyrdan, elbowing past Sunna with a meal tray, ignoring the larger man's apologetic expression. Knowing his father's best friend and the man at the door must have heard the breaking pitcher, watching the way they blinked and squinted to shield their eyes from the unnatural brightness, Ágdhállán climbed to his feet to take the tray before it, too, was dropped.

"I knocked the pitcher over," he mumbled. It was the truth but it did not explain everything.

Scowling as he relinquished the tray, Rhyrdan muttered, "I can see that." The air felt as though charged by lightning after a strike, with the same crisp, somewhat burnt smell that such air was prone to during a storm, and when he closed his mouth after speaking, there was a bitter, metallic taste on his tongue. Perhaps such sensory inputs had come in through the window, but the source felt closer, more immediate, centered on the item at Kavan's side that had not been there before.

"Did you…?" he began, but then shook his head as if to retract the question. There were Elyri in St. Kóráhm's who could have taken the boy to Rhidam, and he might have known where Kavan kept this peculiar relic. Why he had brought it here, placed it where it was, was another question.

When Rhyrdan reached for the box after stepping through the pottery debris field, Ágdhállán dashed forward and grabbed his wrist. "Don't. It is helping him."

"What is it doing?" He relinquished his action to Ágdhállán's warning and instead settled his hand on the sleeping man's chest, where he could feel Kavan's heart beating. His breathing, his pulse, felt stronger and, as they had not done before, Kavan's eyes moved behind his lids as though he was dreaming.

"Absorbing power…balancing it. He has too much. He needs help to be steady again." If he had been able to bring Sóbhán to provide a similar sort of aide, he would have tried that too. But his oldest brother had been injured somewhere that Ágdhállán could not go.

He did not admit that the relic box was also feeding that same power back into their father in a slow, steady trickle as though it would allow Kavan to absorb this new level of power slowly, over time, until the increase was Kavan's new normal state. That was something he did not think Sóbhán could do.

He did not think anyone else could hold that much power as a normal thing. He wanted some of that power, but he did not dare touch the box again or interfere with his father's recovery.

"He'll wake up when he's ready…but you won't let Dhóri move the box?" He had been awake most of the night and wanted his turn to sleep now that he believed his father's recovery was secure. But he did not want to leave him until he was certain his efforts were not in vain.

Unable to deny that the glass box, or whatever the boy had done, appeared to be working to Kavan's benefit, though he did not understand how, Rhyrdan nodded. "I will."

❧*☙

Having not spoken since leaving the keep, until they turned down a long, gray street that Asta recognized too well, she was jarred from her thoughts when the man beside her asked, "Lord Magk's news was good?"

Zerio had not been in the keep when Raenár arrived with word about Kavan and Enesfel's army in the north. He had only returned long enough to fetch Asta to a meeting she was not inclined to have. But the distraction was enough to prevent her from dwelling on her son, who was, at the time of the messenger's sending, alive and unharmed. It was enough to prevent her from going to St. Kóráhm's with Raenár and enough to avoid a conflict with Gerna, who had been conspicuously absent most days since her husband had left Rhidam.

Even Ida did not know where her mother spent her time.

Fuming at the thought of it, Asta knew she was not the only one to suspect the woman was having an affair. Not that she could blame her, given the condition of her marriage, but there were matters of appearances, legalities, and necessities that needed to be considered.

If Kjell learned of it, he would first blame her son before turning on Gerna to erase any stain from the de Corrmick name.

"They're making good progress and have secured Ruidoso. I'd say that's encouraging news." The news about Kavan, which Raenár shared with Níkóá alone, Zerio would learn some other way.

"Indeed." He paused and looked around them at the misshapen angular rooftops of wood shingles and pitch, worn and discolored by smoke stains of the great fire so many years ago and exposure to sun and storms, his gaze finally settled on a small shutter that hung precariously by one hinge and bumped against the wall every time a gust of wind pushed behind and lifted it, only to drop it again. Once satisfied with where he was, Zerio walked forward another six feet to an unpainted, unmarked door and knocked once.

The knock was returned, and the door opened. Zerio gestured and Asta ducked inside, careful not to hit her head on the short doorframe. She expected to see one of the familiar Association lieutenants she had come to know over the years.

She did not expect her nephew.

"Don't look so surprised," Warde chuckled, shifting his leg off the arm of the tall-backed chair he sat in and motioning his guests to come closer. There was a scatter of mismatched chairs and tables throughout the room but it was impossible to tell what this place had once been.

Once she and Zerio left, Asta expected that the room would be emptied, leaving no evidence of occupancy.

She grunted. It had been his choice to maintain distance, to prevent anyone within the Association from learning of a link between them. Either the youngster who opened the door was a trusted confidant, or he would be dead by the end of the day. Asta preferred not to know which was true.

"Did your associate tell you…"

"You requested a meeting," she said, avoiding a glance at Zerio. He had been right not to waste time repeating rumors, but if he had known this meeting was to be with Warde, she wished he had said so.

Warde bobbed his head. "There's a woman…" He smirked at Asta's expression and continued, "Not like that. There have been reports, sightings…"

The prickles along her skin made Asta shiver. "Long dark hair?"

"Not Pantel…though she was my first thought too…but someone else. Thought she was a daughter…a spy…stirring up the minions. Thought maybe she was a ghost tale. Haven't found a trace of her before…she's been damn elusive…but I did finally see her."

"Where?"

"Down at the warehouses…the rebuilt ones. Exotic. Looked young. Probably would have ignored her except for the way she stared, like a dog staring at a shank, and the way she spoke to me…in here." He tapped the side of his head with two fingers.

"Elyri?" Zerio frowned, finding that possibility hard to believe. He had never heard of an Elyri being a member of the Association or being prone to sowing distrust within the Sovereignties. Such rumors were common among Nethites, however, though Zerio had never had experience with Elyri to consider the tales to be true.

Kavan was the first Elyri he had met.

Warde shrugged again. "What else? Wasn't so much the how; it's what she said that I thought you should hear. From me, not from a messenger."

He bent forward and beckoned her closer, suggesting that he did not fully trust the youngster at the door, even though he had not been asked to leave. Zerio leaned in too, long enough for an exchange of glances that assured Warde it was safe for Zerio to know this secret.

"She said I look like grandfather. She commented on the coincidence of meeting in that place…said I should stay out of her way unless I want to die as he did." Arms crossed over his chest, Warde sat back with a scowl. "Did some digging, some asking around. Turns out, where we were was where he died. Figure if I could look that up, anyone could, but if she knows who I am…"

Asta scowled too and shifted uncomfortably. "If you want to…"

"Not afraid of her threats." Threats were commonplace in the Association, particularly if one was in a position of power or was trying to be. He had accepted that risk in coming to Rhidam and, so far, he had no cause to regret his decision.

"Think it's her? The same one?" Zerio was familiar now with the account of Caol Dugan's death, gleaned from one drunken evening conversation with Asta. He had also discussed Bhás with Kavan, being one of the few who could recognize and identify her. Though he had not shared her name or many details with his co-inquisitor, at Kavan's insistence, he had mentioned that such a woman had come to Glevum to meet with Inness.

This unnamed woman had cost Asta both her father and may have cost her a son, and Asta wanted her dead even more than she longed for retribution on Inness.

"If she's seen again," Asta grunted without replying to Zerio's question, "I want to know. Where she's seen, the hour, if she's alone. Be cautious, be wary…but if you have a shot, take it." She would prefer to shed this blood herself, and the king would demand a trial as was the duty of a king, but Asta did not want to risk this woman escaping justice.

Warde nodded. So, she agreed with his assessment. "You should be cautious. If she's after me because of…she might be after you."

"I will be," Asta promised, holding out her hand. He stared at it briefly before accepting the gesture and lifting her hand to kiss her knuckles in deference to the queen she was. The gesture did not hide the amused sparkle in his eyes nor the wry twist of his lips. She might be a queen, but he was a Dugan. And she needed him.

☙*❧

The unusual warmth against his ribs and left arm was the first thing Kavan noticed, followed by a throbbing in his head that surged with every beat of his heart. Then came the notice of recent presences in the room, three people who had barely left his side for an unknown number of hours.

He was alone now, however, and so dared to open his eyes to determine where he was and how long he had been there. His stomach growled and his lips and mouth were parched.

Long enough.

Sucking in a surprised breath when he discovered the source of his skin's warmth and the brightness he detected even with is eyes closed, he rolled, picked up the box with one hand, and then sat up without putting it on the bedside table. As before, he felt the ebb and flow of power, a greater well of it within that brought back the memory of rósádhá in front of the whole of St. Kóráhm's and a significant portion of Alberni's population.

The widespread mythology about the miracle-producing White Bard had existed long enough. There would now be more tales to support the stories that haunted him. He groaned, put the box on the bedside table, and hung his head in his hands to rub his face. The separation of contact with the sturmyrá, however, made him feel stretched, unexpectedly heavy inside, and empty at the same time, until he put his hand on the box again.

The sensation subsided.

Whatever the relic had done, it had overcome the influx of too much power the episode of rósádhá brought. Was that the miracle, he wondered, or had there been something else? His hands did not tingle, suggesting the divine power had been spent, but he could not remember when or how.

The power within the box generated an audible crackle.

Kavan stared at it for several thoughtless minutes.

Perhaps Earé could explain this. Perhaps she would know? He had not seen her in weeks and was now overcome with a deep longing and need to speak with her before another day passed. He should go to Gorbesh. Find her. Be certain that everything there was in order.

Yet despite the well of power in his core, he was physically drained, weary, and weak, and so he twisted around to lie down once more and fell quickly to sleep again.

The blaring of a battle horn was answered by the alarm claxon that roused the ships stationed at the Pháne outpost, sending some north around the island, some south, to answer the distress call of the patrol on the east side. The elderly man in regal captain's attire did not wait for confirmation of the nature of the alarm. Instead, he released the pigeons to deliver their messages to the more recently constructed outpost across the channel, people who would have heard the claxon, the battle horn, and begun to respond in kind, to the smaller outlying islands of Jaffe and Mara Qin, where flourishing population centers bustled with the day's business, and to Prime Magistrate Piran in the western ruling city of Káliel.

He had been here the last time an attack had come to the islands, when Prince Muir had given his life to protect home and family and whatever resource on Pháne Prime Magistrate Gabrielle Dilyn had deemed worth protecting. Many doubted, during the peaceful years that followed, that such an assault would come again. But the captain believed.

Thankfully, Prime Magistrate Piran believed too, enough to build the main island outpost across the channel, increase the number of ships in the Káliel fleet, and station them not only in the islands' largest port but in the two outposts on Jaffe and Mara Qin as well.

Káliel would not be caught unprepared again.

The captain called his men to the walls and sent half of his archers to the tiny island's peak. There were no good places for a ship to dock on the seaward side of the island, but anyone foolish enough to try would meet the might Káliel had to offer.

❧*❦

Under the cover of morning fog, the foreign galleys reached the port of Kílyn, pinning most of her ships to her shoreline, assailing them with arrows and wooden spears hurled from a device the people of Hatu had never seen before. The galleys gradually squeezed closer to land, allowing time for balo Ruy, the youngest of Yetek's recruited balo, to rally his unit and meet the enemy on the shore. The ships were met with a similar force, but they ran aground near nightfall, where the land forces were thinnest. Oars were dropped, and men teemed like angry ants over the galleys' sides to thrust at Kilyn's heart.

❧*❦

The men behind him were exhausted by the time they reached the southern shore of the Kelari River, where the retreating force they pursued crossed to join with the larger unit camped there beneath the crossbred Fraen-de Corrmick banner. Not enough men to be a significant match for Lorant's larger army, but after near-daily skirmishes with the dregs of soldiers General Waller left to torment them, each day causing a depletion of manpower that the healers, physicians, and assisting gdhededhá could not stem, the disheartened southern army needed more than a night to rest.

A night was more than they could reasonably expect.

The generals were optimistic they had left no Nethite armies behind to attack Enesfel from the rear as they camped, but that knowledge did little to bolster morale.

Lorant was not the only one to wish Kavan was here to lift their spirits, but in his exhausted melancholy, he was not convinced even the White Bard's music would be enough to encourage the troops to go on.

What Lorant did believe was that they could not remain camped at the Kelari indefinitely, not while Waller's outpost had the opportunity to increase their manpower from within Neth's heartland. Not while the little boats loaded with foreign mercenaries followed Enesfel's movement along Curo's shore and were likely to sail up the river to aid Waller's camp or else, if the river was too shallow for the passage of boats, disembark and march to their aid.

Enesfel had to act while they had the advantage of numbers.

He did not know how to motivate them to do so.

Little by little, through the thickening evergreen forest that flanked the Kelari as it wound its way out of the mountains to the flats that marked the Neth-Elyri border, Bhríd and those with him whittled down the retreating soldiers to less than a dozen. It had been tempting to kill them all and be done with it, but Bhríd resisted, preferring to be led to a larger camp at the mountain base, hoping for information and perhaps a captive or two that he could send back to the outpost and to Clarys where information might be extracted that would be useful in driving the enemy away.

He had lost people too, but those who endured agreed with him.

A distant rumble, the sounds of a large encampment identifiable by the chatter of men, nickering of horses, and the smells of sweat and campfires, did not deter his prey's escape from the lengthening shadows of the evening forest. Not wanting to lose their quarry into an enemy throng, facing the last opportunity to kill them or take them alive, Bhríd gestured for some of his people to skirt one side, some the other, while he and the remaining soldiers raced in from the rear, creating as much noise as they could to suggest that a large group was catching up along the narrow trade road.

All of them, retreating foes and Elyri alike, stopped abruptly when they realized that the force camped on the south side of the Kelari wore Lachlan tabards. Flanked by the river, the forest, and pursuing Elyri, and by an army under a flag they did not recognize, the invading squad chose combat instead of surrender. Some turned to face those in Elyri armor, some charged ahead to meet the men on watch at the edge of the camp, while others turned south as though to skirt Enesfel's army and the pair of Elyri who ran at them from that side.

Hoping they would not be mistaken for the enemy since few outside Elyriá had ever seen Elyri in armor, Bhríd charged at the man, barreling at him, knocked the sword from the enemy's hand with a solid swing, and then tackled him into the fallen needles collected at the edge of the path. It was the only foe he was able to confront, as his force and the Lachlan soldiers on watch took down the others, killing most, fatally wounding others, leaving only the man Bhríd had knocked off his feet as a potential hostage.

"Drop your weapons," someone shouted.

Bhríd rolled his eyes, got to his feet, pulled his captive up by the front of his armor and grunted, "Duke Cáner of Levonne…"

"And I'm a Lachlan prince," the small man making threats strode up to him with his short sword pointed at Bhríd's armored sternum.

"We're Elyri," said a man nursing a bleeding arm but who otherwise appeared uninjured after his fight with the fellow bleeding out at his feet.

"Prove it."

Preferring not to expose Elyri gifts to a gaggle of superstitious peasants and soldiers, Bhríd dropped his sword and gestured with one hand for those around him to do likewise. He did not, however, release his captive. "Bring General Declan. Or the Daema…or anyone you choose. I will prove myself. Bring them. We will wait."

The soldier speaking with bravado glanced at those near him, communicating something Bhríd could not see, until a consensus was reached and someone ran into the camp. The speaker herded the self-professed Elyri into a group and had others gather their weapons while he picked up Bhríd's massive sword and examined its craftsmanship, the greater-than-normal weight of it, and the crest etched into the hilt that made him pause and look at the black-haired man with a shiver of uncertainty.

He did not speak again, nor force Bhríd to let his captive go.

Twenty minutes later, time passage Bhríd marked by the movement of the stars overhead, the cluster of curious Enesfel soldiers parted to allow Daema Magk and Prince Jerit through the line. Both smiled when they saw him; Bhríd returned the greeting with a bow made awkward by his tight-fisted grip on his captive.

"Lord Cáner," called Bhetá as soon as she spotted him. "We did not expect you here."

The man who detained them stepped back, refusing to look chastised or rebuked for doing his duty, so that the Elyri could relax their stances. When Bhetá glowered at him, however, he handed the duke's sword back and gestured for the other weapons to be returned as well.

"Had a bit of trouble…chased them down the pass." Bhríd indicated the prisoner and the dead and wounded men around them. "And you?"

"Bit of trouble," Jerit mimicked his words, "but we made it this far. The king will wish to see you…and your sister, no doubt. Come, dine with us. Rest and…"

"We need to get this one back to the fortress…"

"Eat and rest first. Let us tend to your injured. We'll make sure this one doesn't go anywhere."

Enesfel's generals had decided against taking prisoners. They had no means to manage them. But guarding a single soldier for a few hours would not be a burden.

Bhríd nodded and accepted the offer after a quick study of those with him. Medical attention was, indeed, needed, and a hot meal would be welcome after the last several days of foraging on their way down the pass. "I would like to hear how you fare," he acknowledged.

Men took the captive from his grasp and, after binding him with ropes, dragged him along behind. Sword shoved back into its scabbard, he looked forward to seeing his sister, her husband, and the king. He looked forward to a few hours of rest without the necessity of continued vigilance before returning up the pass.

He believed the fortress stood. It would be a relief to confirm it with his own eyes.

❧*❧

"The shrine! Protect the shrine!"

balo Ruy and his men, fighting as much to protect the unarmed civilian population from looters and scavengers, from rapists, from those who targeted the oldest, the women, the youngest, were pushed to the edge of the city by a horde of like-faced men who were unafraid to die. Shouts and screams continued from the docks and the shore where more galleys had come to moor, and from throughout Kilyn, the flaring of structure fires dotted the landscape and filled the air with smoke, making him pause to cough in the hope that he could catch his breath and continue the fight. Instead, he was knocked off his feet by the running mob screaming in fright and fell onto the bloody street.

He rolled to avoid being trampled, intending to rise, but found himself eye to eye with a gape-mouthed boy of around twelve, a head without a torso, a child without a life. The sight sickened him, not the gruesomeness of death, but the innocence of the victim, and as he retched into a pool of blood, he realized that the enemy, foreign in dress but not so different from himself, raced past without pursuing the townsfolk who fled before them, raced past him without taking the opportunity to strike him down even after a clumsy swing of his sword took one man's legs out from under him.

From this street and those nearby, the destination appeared the same.

But why this shrine?

He did not know this god, this honored person, or the event it was meant to commemorate. In his time here, he had seen that it was more revered by tourists than by the locals who tended it only because of the coin that travelers spent when they came. Why the pirate army would care about this shrine made no sense, but he did not care about the reason.

Holy places should be respected.

He steadied himself after that shout, hand on the nearest wall, and then raced toward the hill where the shrine stood. The pilgrims huddled there, a handful of people without weapons, shrieked and fled down the opposite face of the hillock, away from the raging horde. Town's guards were on their heels, and from the city, another band with a variety of tools charged from another side. Ruy and his men barreled into the attacking gang, cutting the stream of soldiers in two, focusing on keeping the rest back while the townsfolk at the front countered those still racing up the hillock.

Someone got close enough to throw a loop of rope around the top of the shrine. A second rope and a third followed. The ropes, however, fell slack as the town guards and a dozen Harcourt militiamen who had broken free of the dwindling shore engagement, overran them. Raiders skirted the fight to pick up the ropes again, to pull with all their strength until they, too, were cut down.

The dead were collected at the base of the hill and up its face of autumn yellow grass. Horns bellowed off the coast, announcing the arrival of more Hatu military ships, distracting Ruy and others from the fight long enough for another set of hands to pick up the ropes. Ruy, now nearly at the top of the hill, charged. A searing bite in his shoulder threw him backward with enough force that he struck his head when he hit the ground.

The battle around him ended abruptly in darkness.

❧*❧

'You cannot protect him. You cannot protect them all. You cannot protect yourself.'

The scathing voice in his head, distant and disembodied, growling with contempt behind the shroud of power generated by the Zythánite relic at his bedside, ripped Kavan out of bed and sent him fleeing along a path he could not see. Someone raced past him without seeing him, shouting for Healer

Síraelís to come to the dark courtyard where a collection of people gathered around someone on the ground, blocking the individual from view. To one side, with Raenár's hand wrapped tight around his arm, Balint cried, wailing that it was not his fault, that he had not done anything.

As if sensing Kavan's approach, Rhyrdan stood, towering over many around him, and waved the bard through the crowd with a shout and demand for people to move aside.

By the time Kavan reached Rhyrdan, he could hardly breathe, hardly see. He knew without any external sense what he would find.

Bhás had struck his child.

"Don't move him." Rhyrdan pulled Kavan back to prevent him from doing so, but the hindrance made the bard snarl with a feral fury the younger man had never seen. His words and Kavan's response, however, were enough to permit a sliver of rationality to enter Kavan's thoughts, and as he yanked around and dropped to his knees to press a hand against Ágdhállán's face, Healer Síraelís was already breaking through the crowd to join him.

"Move back," ordered Khwílen. "Give them room."

No miracle came from his touch, none of the greater-than-normal well of power within passed through his hand, but the moment of contact before Síraelís brushed him aside was enough to tell Kavan that the boy lived. With blood trickling out of his ears, however, and blood visible on the back of his skull and the stones when Síraelís probed there, there was no guarantee he would survive.

Kavan remembered Gaelán's face after the head injury that had ultimately taken his life. He remembered the trauma the elder Phaedr Cáner had endured, the suffering Prince Henrik continued to endure, as a result of injuries to their heads. Should Ágdhállán survive, there was no guarantee what sort of future his son would have.

Raebhá would never forgive him for allowing harm to come to their oldest child.

Kavan would never forgive himself.

Unable to help his son, Kavan placed one hand on Síraelís' neck, the easiest place for skin-to-skin contact without hindering his hands, and offered as much power as the healer needed to save his son. He held his breath, exhaled and inhaled with explosive gasps and gulps, and repeated the process, building an ache in his chest and a burning of power between his ears and eyes. When at last Síraelís leaned back from his knees to his feet, he nodded, rubbed his wrist over his eyes, and met the bard's gaze.

"He should live." Should, because, as Kavan had silently bemoaned, sometimes one could not tell the results of a head injury until the victim awoke. "He'll have a headache for a few days, and he might have difficulty hearing for a time, but he should live. I've done what I can, but I cannot promise…"

This time when Kavan's breath escaped, it was a long, deadly-sounding hiss that prompted Rhyrdan to clasp the bard's shoulder. On his other side, another hand did likewise. Dhóri…whom Kavan had not realized was there.

Dhóri's loss of vision was not her fault, unless she had somehow generated the plagues that had swept through the Sovereignties as plagues sometimes did. But Bhás had directly caused impairment to two of his sons and would continue to torment them, seek their lives, until the day Kavan put an end to her anger.

As soon as he was certain Ágdhállán would survive, it was time to act. Kavan could not wait any longer.

"I will take him to Rhidam." He did not distrust Síraelís, but he trusted Yóáná more. And the boy's room in Rhidam was warded. It was the only place Kavan believed he might be safe. With Rhidam as his hub, there were things Kavan needed to do.

Kóráhm, forgive me, the thought began.

"This will not happen again…" Raenár started to say, his voice tense, pleading, and apologetic as he twisted Balint's arm in the hopes of prompting an apology from the boy prone to too-rough play without a thought to the consequences.

A psychic shock of a different sort drove through Kavan with such force that the bard did not hear him.

He looked at the sky, his head turned to the southeast, listening to the deafening roar of battle.

He had to get to Kilyn.

❧Chapter 45❧

On the north shore of the Kelari, where Neth's force had felled enough trees to provide an acceptable, if crowded, place to camp, approaching the rear of the inadequate Nethite and mercenary force with the recruits he had gone ahead to collect, General Waller glowered at the joint Lachlan and de Corrmick banners fluttering in the early dawn breeze, wondering who dared raise the de Corrmick crest or if it was a false attempt to win support from any Nethite foolish enough to believe the lie and prone to defect in support of the legal ruling family. Not Prince Henrik, who was too young, and not King Kjell, who had been killed long ago. Prince Jerit was the most likely contender, but even Queen Asta or the long-absent Regent Queen were possibilities. The most dangerous ones, in Waller's opinion, for Inness had been erratic and untrustworthy, while Queen Asta, with her ties to the Lachlans, and, it was said, the Association, had enough strength and cunning to overtake her husband's kingdom and manage it if she chose.

Not cunning enough, he mused with a smirk, to avoid the trap he had set. Funneling Enesfel's army through the most obvious northern path might not appear to be a trap, but those foolish generals did not know the things Waller knew. They did not know what waited for them when they reached Gorea…if he did not rout them here.

His little army, the Inzigaen, would be enough to beat this enemy or any other once they realized who they were fighting.

If Enesfel dared to cross, turning back would come too late.

Having sent his Elyri squad back to the Rísóri fort with their single captive and reassured by having several of tama Yetek's men to block the mouth of the pass to discourage further invaders from pushing into Elyriá, Bhríd chose to remain with Enesfel's army, believing his talents would be more effective in confronting the camped Nethite army to get Enesfel across the river than on escort duty and the restoration of the fortress. He was confident his compatriots could complete their assignment with the southern mercenaries at their back, and promised he would rejoin them at the head of the pass as soon as he was able. His squad left at dawn and now, with the sun's glow barely visible over the peaks of the Llaethlágárá, those men on horseback passed around the charred, collapsing structure that had once been Enesfel's primary border outpost to protect against Nethite raiders and braved the Kelari's weak autumn flow to stand with the longbowmen firing into the horde on the other side.

Neth saw the attack coming. They had time to prepare. Yet the far-reaching arrows did their duty, picking off soldiers throughout their ranks while others, meeting the challenge, fired back. With Enesfel's cavalry pushing ahead under General Declan's command, clearing a slow path toward the north shore, protected by shields and swords, Bhetá and Bhríd led those on foot to slog through the knee-deep flow in the hopes of gaining tentative footing in hostile territory.

The Nethite army had few archers and fewer horses. Here at the Kelari, someone in command had not expected to need them.

"There," shouted Lorant, holding his horse back from the initial charge, reluctantly allowing Kaj and Jerit to lead the second cavalry line. He pointed into the Nethite army as the archery combat turned to melee, to a man at the perimeter of the camp. With his generals and captains, lords and dukes, already engaged, their focus was on the Nethite cavalrymen they could reach, intent on staying alive, no one responded to his voice or looked in the direction he pointed.

Lorant was certain he had locked eyes with General Waller, though he had never seen the man and did not know his crest or armor style. What he did know was the posture of a man in the saddle that spoke of confidence and experience, a man commanding from the rear rather than engaging in the thick of combat. With his face hidden by his visored helm, though he carried no crest, Lorant suspected he believed he would not be recognized.

"With me!" Lorant took advantage of the path the foot soldiers were creating and, with a host of Lachlan Guards trained in the manner of the elite guards of Kaliel, the only giveaway of his identity, charged in the direction of that solitary, too-dignified rider. The last of Enesfel's army, those not selected to protect the healers, dedhá, and abundant camp hangers-on preparing for the inevitable influx of wounded or those chosen to protect the rear of the camp, filled the gap behind him.

So much blood had been spilled between Ruidoso and the Kelari, so many had fallen beneath that man's leadership, that the young king had grown more desensitized to it, so long as it did not spray into his face. Focused on the unmoving rider, it made it easier to forget that those falling to his blade and the weapons of the men with him were people too.

Seeing the king's movement out of the corner of her eye as her horse climbed the muddy riverbank, Bhetá cut through the men trying to prevent her from climbing too. When she finally made her way out of the mud onto dry land, the animal's movement slowed by the sucking of the river's edge, paying little heed to the inconvenience of the dampness of her clothes, her boots, under her armor, she fought to reach his side. Those she struck down were primarily townsfolk and farmers, pressed into unfortunate service without the experience of the mercenaries whom Kaj engaged with an insulted sort of fury that made it difficult for his men to leave the river. Prince Jerit reached Bhríd's position, their horses pounding into earth and flesh while twisting to avoid the gouging weapons aimed at their flanks.

The flat of someone's blade cracked across Bhetá's armored ribs with enough force to hurt but without enough to knock her from the horse. Reflexes made her swing her shield and fling her attacker into the midst of a knotted melee band. He struck someone else's shield, toppled and rolled, and when he stopped beside her again, the subsequent thrust of her sword halted mid-swing.

The face staring at her was no older than her son.

The thought registered, but a host of boots retreating from the surge of Enesfel's army trampled around her and pushed her aside, crushing the boy, blocking him from sight as she was forced to turn in the direction the king had gone.

He had not yet reached his target. She noted the stately rider now, and she, too, guessed that General Waller had engaged them at last instead of fleeing…though he remained at the rear of the conflict and did not draw his sword. It seemed that the distance between Lorant and Waller had grown as Enesfel advanced, until Lorant's soldiers had crossed the river. She swung her horse and began a cumbersome charge in the king's direction.

They fought until the sun crested the mountains, when the Nethites disengaged from combat and retreated into the thin forest. Their mercenary force was disinclined to do the same, but their losses grew, and eventually they, too, followed Waller's command to retreat. With the north bank littered with bodies, knowing how long it would take to sort the injured from the dead, General Declan made the call to stay his force, to pursue with no more than enough men to ensure that the enemy had moved beyond the forest into Neth's flatlands.

Breathless and frustrated that Waller had escaped, more certain of the quarry's identity after the army retreated at his command, Lorant picked his way through the dead until he reached General Declan. The general, having tucked his helm beneath one arm, wiped sweat from his red face with a bloody hand, snorted, and nodded.

"Shouldn't we follow? Send men to…?" Lorant began.

"They'll be off to Gorea, wanting to defend the port. It's where I'd expect you to go…"

"But leaving behind enough to harass us," Bhetá added when she slid off her horse.

"If I was king, I'd have given the order to protect the ports," agreed Jerit, "but I think we should send scouts to confirm it. I can…"

"Yours is the head they want most," Lorant insisted, while knowing his head was at the top of their list. Only after speaking did it occur to him that Jerit might not be volunteering himself.

"There's got to be men among us who know the road, the region, well enough to get around Waller," Bhetá concurred with a nod to Jerit. "We don't want to march to Gorea on a guess and have them outmaneuver us. I'll see it arranged if you can find such men," she said to the prince.

"Good." Sliding off his horse too, thinking the argument sound although he did not expect Waller to be so crafty, General Declan groaned. He kept his hand on the animal's side until his stance was steady and then continued. "We bring everyone across…except the rearguard and those protecting the pass. Get the healers over here and take care of our wounded…bury the dead. We're not camping until it's done. After, we can get most of us out of these damn trees before morning comes again. We don't want to be trapped with our backs to the river."

There were hours of daylight left. Tending the injured and dead would take time, but a forced march would bring most of the army through the forest. Maybe then they would know what they faced next.

Maybe by then, Bhetá mused as she and Jerit set off to find scouts, she would find the courage to tell someone what she had seen.

❧ * ❧

Earon Sparding sat on the edge of the bed, rubbing his eyes, loath to leave despite the distant crowing of one rooster after another that reminded him he was to be on duty soon. He dared not be late. The king demanded strict obedience, and Olaric would be waiting.

The news of Ruidoso's fall into Enesfel's hands, the reports drifting in from villages along Lake Curo about King Lorant's progress toward Kelari, and the flying of the de Corrmick banner, had given rise to the popular possibility that Enesfel might make it to Glevum and birthed a hope for ousting King Fraen. The monarch's fury at the news and at Glevum's growing unrest was not to be trifled with. The streets were rank with the stench of rotting flesh as the king's crackdown on dissidents resulted in so many gruesome displays along the castle walls and at the corners of Glevum's busiest streets that it was difficult to avoid them. So far, the outrage had only inspired a backlash, not subservience.

Coming to this out-of-the-way inn on the southern side of the city as far from the castle as one could get meant that the stench did not reach them here, but Earon knew what he would be met with as soon as he began his trek across the city.

If he were late, his corpse might join the rotting display.

Tender calloused fingers traced slowly down his back, the gentle scratching of neatly trimmed nails making him shiver and look back at the doe-eyed woman smiling softly up at him. The ache in his head was a reminder of the excessive alcohol consumption the night before that resulted in his breaking this promise to himself. But the renewed throbbing in his groin reminded him that he could not blame only the alcohol. That was an excuse. In truth, he knew he had been looking for justification to surrender to her advances for a long time.

Last night had been the night.

When he bent to kiss her mouth one more time and had to resist the lure of the arms that tried to pull him into her amorous embrace, he wondered if he was going to regret that surrender.

"I have to go."

"I know," Marta murmured against his mouth, smoothing his tousled sandy brown hair from his face. "Do I have your word you'll keep our secret…keep your promise?"

He hid his scowl but not his furrowed brow as he nodded and stood to dress. "I always keep my word."

At this moment, however, he could not remember what promises he had made.

"Will I see you tonight?"

Her smile brightened. It was the hook she needed. Marta was tired of waiting for Olaric to act. Earon was her way inside. As soon as she was satisfied that she could trust him, as soon as he devised a way to get her inside, she would have her revenge. She only marginally cared about what the consequences would be for Captain Sparding.

ȣ•*ȣ•

Ágdhállán had not yet awakened, but he was breathing normally, and Kavan could detect nothing unusual within the boy's unprotected thoughts or in the level of his power. The only thing he detected was the moment the boy had fallen from the stone steps that led up along St. Kóráhm's wall, where the guards kept watch from the southern tower. The sensation of shoving hands, like wind against his face, the voice that made him turn on unsteady feet away from the touch. His footing lost, he had fallen about six feet onto the stone courtyard.

Had he climbed higher, fallen further, he would likely be dead.

Balint had been three steps ahead of him, above him. He could not have reached out to push him down without risking a fall. Balint had done nothing to be punished for.

It was that realization that prompted Kavan to set the sturmyrá on the nightstand when Raenár came to him before breakfast to inquire about Ágdhállán's condition and leave his son for the first time under Rhyrdan's attentive watch in a room Kavan had spent the night warding in between worried bouts of fearful weeping.

He needed fresh air. He needed a clear head. He needed a plan.

"Balint did not do this," Kavan murmured as the pair walked side by side through the garden where Níkóá instructed the captain to wait, believing, Kavan suspected, that the bard needed to get out of the keep for a few minutes. The regent was sequestered in the stateroom with his inquisitors and several other advisors while the Great Hall was prepared for the feast that marked the end of the days of fasting in honor of Saint Poul. There were few lords to attend the event, but there were the ladies of the realm to join them, and as the day also marked the pregnant queen's birthday, it seemed fitting that they celebrate this day with her.

She needed a distraction from the pregnancy she had not formally revealed to anyone except Kavan and her father.

The feast might get the women's minds off husbands, suitors, brothers, sons, and fathers far away in a war few of them understood.

"I know he can be…we try to steer him to mercy and fairness…"

"He has the burden of a namesake to live up to, and many who indulge him because of it…despite what you and Bhetá teach to the contrary. It will take time, but he will learn. But this…he did not do this. This was something else…"

"This was an attack?" Raenár did not know much about the reasons or causes behind the prophesied assault on the chellé. He had heard no evidence of combat, had found no arrow or flying slingstone. No one had spoken to him of those things or reacted as though such an attempt had been made. Yet he knew of no reason to doubt the bard's explanation.

"On me…through my sons." Kavan stopped at Arlan's grave and put his hand upon the nameplate. "I must put an end to this…before the chellé is destroyed, before anyone else is hurt…but I am not yet sure how to accomplish it."

"Do you think you can change things? Prevent what you have Seen?"

"I think…" Kavan hung his shaking head and sighed, wondering if the captain could see the tremor in his hand upon the wall. "I believe Gorbesh is the safest place for all of you…all of us. I believe none should remain in Alberni to await the shadow of what is to come. But I understand that I cannot make you do otherwise. I would spare you all death, but your fates are not in my hands. I believe what was must give way to what will be. If it comes…once it is over, I have arranged for the chellé to rest in Lord Kaas' hands. He will welcome you to remain, if you choose…as I am certain the king will welcome you in Rhidam."

"You think…" Raenár frowned. "My pledge is to you, to the dedhá."

"That was before you wed and had a son."

"My oaths come first. Bhetá knows this…she understands." Their oaths to duty had kept one in Rhidam and the other in Alberni since their decision to wed and have a child. Their choices forced their son to live a transient life between two homes, always with one parent or the other but rarely with both. Perhaps Balint's behavior was as much a result of that as it was the accolades his grandfather's name bestowed on him from the day of his birth.

Kavan nodded. Their paths were not his to decide. Whatever Raenár's choice, Kavan would respect it.

The crunch of boots on the gravel path interrupted the discussion before Asta reached them. She bobbed her head at Raenár, then Kavan, and asked, "Is there news?" assuming that news was the reason for Raenár's visit.

"Nothing since the last," Raenár admitted. "I had a matter to discuss with Lord Cliáth." She likely knew what that matter was, but he did not want to discuss it with her. He cast the bard a sideways glance to determine if that matter was concluded. Kavan's almost imperceptible nod was the answer he received. "Now I must return to my duties. Is there any word I should take to the king?"

By king, she knew he meant the husband she refused to see since the army's departure. The longer she went without a reassuring word from Jerit, the less she wanted to speak to Kjell. "There is nothing of note that concerns him. You may tell him Henrik is well, if you wish." Knowing the chosen heir was doing well might not compensate for her avoidance, but it would be news he wanted to hear.

"I will. Good day, my lord…my lady."

Mimicking Kavan as Raenár departed, Asta spread her hand on her father's stone, waiting to speak until the retreating footsteps were no longer heard. The farrier's hammer rang in the distance, and the chatter of children gathering somewhere else in the sweetly fragrant garden began to rise and scatter the songbirds nestled amongst the shrubs that had lost the last of their summer blooms. The children were not near enough to hear her when she spoke. They would not know their favorite tutor was there.

"How is Ágdhállán? Yóáná told me he fell?" Asta had not seen Kavan at the time of his return, but it was little surprise that her daughter had told her what had happened.

"He is sleeping."

"As long as that is all it is." Her soft words were tinged with the bloom of loss and regret, but she quickly stuffed those emotions down. She did not want to think about Gaelán now. "I thought you should know she's here…or was here…the one with Tarmajien…when my father died…"

Kavan winced, locked his knees, and swallowed his breath. "Did you see her?" He did not think she knew what the woman looked like or Bhás' exact connection to Kavan, yet he was grateful she felt compelled to inform him of her presence in Rhidam.

"Warde did. She said things that tipped him to her connection to Father…said there have been reports of someone fitting the description you gave me, stirring people to discontent."

Which was why, Kavan shuddered, he had sensed her so many times since the Festival of St. Matan. She might have been why he had felt Eridel's presence that day, why he felt hunted.

Or it might have been the Sight. He could not say.

"Of course she is," he muttered. "Where did he see her?"

"The new warehouse…on the site where Father…" She wiped dirt from Caol's carved name. "She recognized Warde as his kin…knew his face. I told him he should leave Rhidam if he wished to remain safe."

"But he will not."

"He's a Dugan," she snorted.

"I will go and…"

"I've already been there. There's nothing to see. Nothing to suggest why she was there. All the evidence of the past is gone."

"I might see something you cannot."

Asta began to retort, but then shrugged with a grunt. "Want an escort?"

"It isn't required. If Rhyrdan asks, tell him I will return in an hour."

He did not think Bhás was in Rhidam. He could not feel her, could not hear her. He did not expect danger, and so long as Ágdhállán remained in his room, he expected him to be safe long enough for a brief inspection of the warehouse that might give Kavan the clues he needed to find her.

He toyed with Kóráhm's cross upon his chest as he looked from one grave marker to another, most of the Lachlans he had known and some he had not. Eventually, the oldest markers would be removed to be replaced with newer ones, those markers to be set as paving stones within the royal hall or displayed somewhere else, until all these beloved men and women were erased from this place. He could not fathom remaining in Rhidam as part of the Lachlan House long enough to see that happen.

"I am sure Jerit is well," he eventually said. If anything had happened to the prince, he trusted he would feel it through his bond with Lorant. So far, when he traced that bond along the thread that tied them, he felt primarily exhaustion and an increasing emotional numbness peppered with the aches and pains of war and surges of fear and anxiety…or rarer still a warm sense of joy and stillness that came in the late evening hours when Lorant was able to shed his cares and sleep…always with Jerit at his side.

Asta did not judge her son for that as his father did, but Kavan felt no need to reveal such details. Jerit's welfare was her primary concern.

"Thank you," she whispered. "I hope Ártur and the others are as well…that they will return to us soon."

"Soon."

He could not say how many would return, he could not say when or how. Until he confronted Bhás, soon would not come soon enough.

❧*❦

"I know those passages." Inness' vacant expression changed for the first time since Olaric had entered the room, despite his decision to offer hope that her imprisonment was about to end and assure her that the time for action was near. Her gaze strayed toward the empty pillow beside her and then back to his face. Outrage abruptly brightened her eyes. The blame for someone stealing her child was replaced by the resolution that it had been necessary to allow Henrik the chance to live, a chance she had been certain she no longer had. There had been a brief battle of swords that night, followed by a blackness that resulted in a decade of island captivity.

It made sense that Fraen had done this to take her from the throne so he could sit upon it himself. He would have killed Henrik if he had found him.

It had been to Henrik's benefit that those passages within the castle walls existed.

"Can you find your way?"

She shook her head. "I have never been in them." If she had been, she had been unconscious and did not remember them.

Olaric nodded, relieved. "I can provide a map. I know his routines I know where he should be at certain hours of the day. Once inside, once you find him, it will be up to you to get out…"

Her eyes narrowed. "What if I do not want to get out? What if I stay…and take back what is mine?"

"They think you're dead. They'll kill you if they find out you're not…especially when you kill him. Until Prince Henrik arrives, it will be safer if you remain out of sight."

"I'm tired of hiding."

Olaric's expression was sympathetic. "Aye, I know. I am weary of this game too. But if the rumors are true…if the prince's supporters and King Lorant aren't routed at Gorea…they may yet reach Glevum and give us the hope we need."

"My mother's army must never reach Glevum." The name Lorant meant nothing to her.

Olaric chose not to correct her, to remind her that her mother was dead, and Merrek with her. "It is not up to me. We need them here if we want my father off the throne…and Prince Henrik on it. Enesfel's army…and you…are the ones who can make it happen. If fortune is with us, none of them will stay once the prince is crowned.

"I will not let them stay." Inness continued to scowl, toying with the pillow she held against her stomach, until finally, she grunted, "Bring me your map. Show me where I'll find the imposter."

Olaric nodded. "I'll return with it soon. Have a little more patience, My Queen. You will see your son on Neth's throne. The land will be beholden to you as it never was before."

That possibility, more than any other, made Inness smile.

❧*❦

It took a brief flight with white kestrel wings stretched beneath the early Duar sun to prove to Kavan that if Bhás had been seen in Rhidam, she had been no more than a visual and auditory manifestation, not something tangible that Warde could have killed. It was a skill Bhás had repeatedly exhibited, one Kavan did not possess, one that caused him deep concern over whether, when he did find and confront her, she would be a shade only, something he could therefore not defeat.

He had vanquished Coryllien's ghost, but that man had already been dead. Thinking about Bhás as he completed his third circle around the city, seeking something he thankfully did not find, birthed a list of numerous things he needed to accomplish before he sought to locate her, confront her, and end her threat to his family and Enesfel.

He had an idea, a place to start, but the heaviness of fear continued to burden him with reluctance. Despite the certainty of what he must do, he was afraid to try.

He returned to check on his son before finding Master Najar washing his hands in the back garden fountain while the other children, now in Yóáná and Physician Mauret's care, gathered in the dayroom.

"Lord Cliáth." The stocky man cast him a concerned smile as he vigorously rubbed his wet hands together. "How is Ágdhállán?"

In many ways, the Hatu scholar and natural philosopher brought to Rhidam as a scribe and advisor reminded Kavan of Guthrie McHador, an unexpectedly melancholy realization. They had served well together during Najar's tenure, and Kavan hoped the man intended to stay in the Lachlan employ for many more decades.

"He suffered a fall and is resting." That the boy had not yet awakened concerned Kavan, but he chose not to verbalize his fears lest doing so made them real. "I expect him to return to his studies tomorrow or the day next."

"He is advanced enough in his studies, as you know, that I do not worry about his education. His recovery is all that matters. Shaking his hands to air dry them, he walked beside Kavan. "Will you resume your post as well?"

Kavan shook his head, trying to maintain a neutral expression. "That is what I want to discuss. I know I have been much absent…"

"A duke's responsibilities do not allow for the everyday joy of educating young minds," Najar said with a reassuring smile. Kavan was as much of a scholar as Najar, with several decades more of accumulated knowledge and experience. Kavan's passions were music, history, philosophy, and languages, while Najar's were natural philosophy, astronomy, numbers, and diplomacy. Their varied skills and interests made them an ideal teaching pair. "And war has disrupted us all."

"I wish my duties provided more time…yet I fear they are calling me away again for an indeterminate time. There is a chance I may be able to shorten this war, but I do not know how long doing so will take. Can you manage the children while I am away?"

Though Najar's steps did not falter, Kavan sensed the man's perplexed uneasiness. "I am not the historian or linguist you are, but I believe my knowledge of such things is well-rounded enough to suffice. Bringing an end to the war, if such a thing is possible, bringing the king home…that is an admirable quest. I would be honored to do my part in making it so by tending to the children in your absence."

Like many others, Najar knew the mythos of the White Bard. He did not ask how the duke might end a war when no one else seemed able to accomplish it, but he took Kavan at his word. "Will Ágdhállán…?"

"He will be in his brother's care at St. Kóráhm's for a time…"

"Unless she is attacked?"

Kavan's belief that the abbey might be destroyed, that people would die, was well-known in Rhidam. Najar's question did not surprise him.

He nodded without repeating the words. "Dhóri knows what must be done if that day draws near. I wanted you to be prepared for my absence, however long that might be."

"Aye, I am prepared. The children won't be happy," he smiled again, "but they will forget much of their displeasure when their parents return."

"That is my wish." He wondered if he would be able to spend one more day with the children he loved, be able to impart one more morsel of wisdom or knowledge before he left, but he could not guarantee it.

He was taking the day a minute at a time. It was entirely possible that, should he fail to go to her, find her, she would come to him. That could occur at any time.

When he faced her, he wanted to be as far away from Rhidam, the chellé, and the people he cared about, as he could be.

❧ * ❧

The assault on Pháne came as the sun sank in the west, ships striking the front and rear of the island, men in skiffs or swimming in the petulant current seeking access to the island's interior while the caravels and galleys circled, lobbing projectiles and fire, seeking to ram each other hard enough to send ships to the bottom of the Bay of Phállá. Elsewhere, when other galleys struck the main island, they struck Jaffe and Mara Qin. The naval force that Gabrielle had insisted the island sovereignty would need was only effective against the galleys, however, because of the aid of the additional Hatu ships left at their disposal under the command of balo Seymo Cahryd.

Despite the navy's diligence, invaders made it to shore a handful of times, foreign men with unfamiliar features who sought chaos, plunder, and death, like unruly pirates without a goal beyond pillage.

Docks and fishing boats burned. Crates and barrels awaiting shipment or that had been brought ashore to await distribution were destroyed.

Piran was at the docs to greet them, having left his personal Káliel guards to secure his family inside the villa. He was not a man of war despite his father's training, but he would not allow his people to suffer without trying to stop it. Men did their best to hold the invaders at sea, to hold those who came ashore to the docks, in the hopes that not a single house, a single woman or child, would fall.

❧*❧

A melancholy visit to Tusánt and the dedhá of Hes á Redh brought with it a weight of imagined finality and the assurance that, whatever was to come, Enesfel's first Elyri k'gdhededhá was where he was intended to be, that Hes á Redh would stand and that, in time, the bonds of Faith between Elyri and Teren could be mended. Kavan's city excursion ended with his return to the keep as the Feast of Plenty began in the Great Hall. He was elated to find his somber-faced young son seated between the Cáner boys, Cáym looking unusually fierce when someone he did not recognize got too close to the friend he was determined to protect. Cáym did not move when Kavan entered the Hall to waves and calls of greeting, but Phaedr willingly relinquished his seat, sliding sideways on the bench so Kavan could sit next to his son as the evening's bounty was served.

Ágdhállán looked at his father with a mixed expression of fear and gratitude, confusion and serenity, and put his hand in Kavan's.

"I'm okay," he whispered, feeling his father's concern through the contact. "But I don't know why she…"

Cáym leaned forward to hear their discussion, but his lips drew into a thin, frustrated line when Kavan's reply was made without words.

"It is not you she wants."

The voiceless words passed from hand to hand, and the boy nodded grimly. *"You will stop her?"* The smile Ágdhállán offered Cáym was vague but affectionate, enough to make the other redhead lean back with a huff and a snort before grabbing bread from a passing loaf and dunking it into the bowl of broth he was served.

Kavan nodded. *"If I can."*

"You have to...before she finds Mother and Gaed."

Wincing at that bitter reminder, believing that, for all his ability with the Sight, his son did not know what he asked, Kavan began to eat as well, his first meal of the day, an excuse not to immediately reply though his appetite had evaporated. The first few bites settled like a stone in his stomach and he closed his eyes, before pushing the plate away. Staring into the void of the future he saw there, he did not have the desire to eat.

❧*❧

Under the cover of darkness, the galley came ashore along a rocky, stretch of beach that gave way to fallow fields devoid of their last harvest, The nearby farmers in unlit homes did not notice the host who disembarked and those who remained behind as the vessel and its skeleton crew rowed back out to sea to sit beyond the horizon where no one would easily see it.

Lots had already been drawn, the group split in two before beginning their trek west. The first left before the boat was away. The second waited until the autumn moon climbed higher before taking the same road.

Those within the farmhouses did not hear them pass.

No dogs barked.

No one knew they were there.

Bhás watched them with lids closed, willing the final pieces into place to force the traitor's hand. Her lips curled. Her fists tightened.

She ignored the flicker of streaking stars above her head that spoke of omens she did not deign to decipher.

The traitor would fall.

It was nearly time.

❧*❧

Jemes Osveld watched the fleet of foreign galleys stretch across the horizon, preventing Enesfel's commissioned naval ships in the final throes of preparation and those left in Levonne by tama Yetek from escaping the bay. There should have been a warning, time to launch Hatu's ships and those the king had ordered to meet them, but the guards had not recognized the incoming ships as a threat until too late. The ships were loosed to meet the galleys while the fleet was far enough out to stop them from making shore, but the galleys seemed content to come no closer. They did not attack the vessels facing them. They sat in the bay, silent and still.

Osveld recognized the blockade, the effort to deter Enesfel's largest naval fleet from leaving port or exiting the river. But for what purpose, he mused, as he directed the last arriving foot soldiers and conscripted men to take position on the dock and shore in case any of those galleys broke formation and tried to reach land.

He was not a tactician, but Levone was his to protect so long as Duke Cáner was not here.

Thankfully, the big bald man with the salt and pepper beard who stood with him made up for the battle and tactical knowledge Osveld lacked.

"We send word and we wait…for now," balo Eytor muttered.

Osveld nodded. If the Crown had ships available along the Tegid, even if they were merchant ships that could be enlisted in a fight, he hoped the regent would send them. Ships already bound for Levonne needed to be warned. Even with Eytor and his mercenaries, Osveld was not confident he had a strong enough force to prevent the foreigners from traveling upriver.

He was more confident, however, that Levone would not fall if any of those galleys broke through the line and made it to shore.

❧*❧

Setting camp was delayed by a waiting ambush at the forest's edge, one Enesfel was prepared for, so that the clash was over before most of the second wave of men emerged beneath the starlit sky. Kaj oversaw the dispatch of the three dozen unfortunate souls left to face Enesfel's army when they came, three dozen to fight without a true soldier or mercenary among them. Three dozen men barely older than boys, barely the king's age, were removed for burial before Lorant arrived to inspect the carnage.

The forced march had been exhausting, and there was little of the night in which to rest before they would move again. General Declan did not want to hold their position here longer than necessary. Gorea was not far away. Gorea had a port and could serve as a hub for Nethite reinforcements that

Lorant did not think they could stand against. Enesfel's best hope was to reach the city before those reinforcements could gather and be dispatched.

It meant that their rest tonight would be short-lived.

No tents were erected. No fires were lit to take the edge off the night's chill. Most went without a meal but instead settled for water and warm ale and as much sleep as the king, prince, and generals would allow.

Lorant did not think it would be enough. But he was as determined as his generals to press on. Determined, as Jerit sat beside him, tucked into his bedroll for warmth as he stared across fertile farmland with wonder and disbelief, to give Jerit back what had been taken from him as a child.

Jerit might not be Glevum's heir, but this was his home. A home he had never thought to see again when he and his mother had fled in haste. Lorant wanted to give him that and so much more.

❧*☙

Head covered by the cowl he wore, a pilgrim not by choice who passed unrecognized by those who should have known his name, who would have known him if not for one man who had stripped his dreams and aspirations away, he ignored the creak of the stool next to him and the female voice that asked for the finest spirits the tavern keeper had to offer. Thinking her a whore hoping for his coin, he snorted as the man behind the counter shuffled toward the back room of the establishment to honor her request.

He could almost hear the amused smile on her face without looking at her as she said, "I get what I pay for."

Definitely a whore.

"You'll be lucky to get a bowl of piss in this place. Whatever he gives you, I wouldn't drink it if I were you."

He had been in this dingy, pig farmer town for over a week, hoping for an audience with the dedhá who managed the shrine of Saint Edhriá. He had been forced to accept labor shoveling slop to cover the cost of a single meal a day, a drink or two in this rundown establishment, and a drafty room barely big enough for the lumpy cot in the inn next door. He had spent every night trying to sleep while the whores in the rooms on either side of his plied their trade for more coins than he was making tending hogs, and still, the dedhá did not send for him.

Patron of humility, he snorted again. Humility was not what he needed.

It was not what he wanted.

"Your Faith has not been kind to you," she eventually said after the tavern keeper returned with a bottle sporting a faded, unreadable, hand-stitched label tied around its neck and sealed with a wax pressing. "After all you have given them, you deserve better."

"You don't know me."

"I know you would not be here if not for the Heretic Harper."

He looked at her then, lowering his hood with both hands, exposing a face that, like his hands, was marred by fights he had either instigated or tried to avoid. Most of his straight blonde hair was tied back and tucked into the neck of the cowl, but stray strands hung on either side in front of his sunburned ears. His weary, hardened gaze studied her, but he did not confirm or deny her statement. Instead, he waited for her to continue, waited to hear what other claims about his life she wanted to assert.

Her hair was as black as her eyes, her features angular and striking. Nothing about her appearance suggested she was Elyri except for the aura of power that encircled her, humming like bees seeking flowers. He did not think she was Elyri, but she was not Teren either.

A half-blood, then.

She had his attention.

He sneered and resumed staring into his cup when she did not speak.

The woman put more coins on the counter and gestured when she noted his empty cup. The barkeep pocketed the coins, took the cup out of the other man's hand, and filled it before handing it back.

The guest snorted. No woman could buy his favor like that. No matter how beautiful she was.

"If I told you I can take you there…told you the time was nigh to take back what was taken from you, would you be interested?"

He shook his head, the reluctant movement contradicting his words when he huffed, "I'd never get close enough to get inside. I'd be found before I reached Clarys. I've no interest in death.

"You've plotted a way in a thousand times. You have walked the streets, walked the halls, found their vulnerabilities. They are too proud to see their weaknesses. Clarys cannot spare the time to notice you…I have seen to that. I can get you to the doors without notice…if you wish…"

His cup slowly lowered from his lips. He frowned. Her ability to know his thoughts against his will was offensive and irritating. Clenching his hand around the glass, he hissed, "What's your interest in me? In Clarys?"

Her wry expression was enigmatic, and though she faced him, her gaze seemed to pass through him to something on the other side of the room. He turned to see what was there, but the stool was empty, as was the staircase to the barkeep's living quarters, and the door into the neighboring inn's first floor. She did not say anything until he looked at her again.

"My interests are not your concern. I can get you there…or you can remain here on this fool's errand. Once you're in Clarys, what you make of the opportunity is up to you. Your k'gdhededhá will be unprotected. The city is at war. Your opportunity awaits. My offer will not last. Yes? Or no?"

City at war. He wondered what she meant. Wondered if the k'gdhededhá had pushed the people, the k'lómesté, the dedhá beneath him too far with his blasphemies. He noted that the woman had not opened the bottle but had, instead, tucked it into the flowing layers of her dark robe. She lay more coins on the counter and stood up, hesitating to look at him as though to offer him one more opportunity.

He drank the ale she had paid for and pushed his stool back. Why not take the chance, he thought with a shrug. In his view, his penance had been paid many times over. "Show me."

He followed her into the dark street, where the butchers, tanners, and candlemakers, herb farmers, barrel makers, and tin smiths plied their trade in the daylight hours but now hid behind locked doors to keep out the packs of dogs cleaning up scraps in the street or thieves hoping for a few stolen coins. She offered her hand. Eyes narrowed, expecting a trick or an ambush from the shadows, he hesitantly accepted it.

He blinked and sucked in a startled breath.

She was gone.

There had been no Gate.

For the first time in more than a decade, Lláhy found himself in a quiet street staring up at the spires of Hes Dhágdhuán instead of the grungy street where he had just been. He put his hand on the polished white stone wall in front of him to be certain it was real.

Clarys.

He was home.

❧Chapter 46❧

Sóbhán was not steady on the crutch fashioned for him by those at the Rísóri Pass, but he made it through St. Kóráhm's Gate and then struggled to the Gathering Hall, where he collapsed onto a bench, intending to rest long enough to regain his balance and breath. His wife assured him that in time the phantom pain would diminish, along with the discomfort of the rubbing crutch, but he was not yet willing to believe it. There were metalsmiths in Elyriá who could craft a prosthetic, if he chose to use one. Either way, he could return home unashamed of the loss he had suffered yet he had no desire to do so and endure his family's pity.

Not until he adjusted to the loss himself.

Chethá had not followed him but had instead returned to their children to assure them that their father was well. She would explain his injury to them and respectfully allow him the space he desired while he sought the moral support of his brother. When he was able, when he was ready, he would return to them. For now, he wanted the familiar solace of a náós like the one he had hidden in as a child, wanted the company of his father and brothers. Family and Faith would not judge him. They would not pity him.

"Was told you're here." There were two sets of footsteps; Sóbhán knew before turning that the second belonged to Bergis. The simple man did not make friends easily, but he had latched onto Dhóri on his first day in the chellé and proved himself eager to please and assist the blind Elyri in any way he could. In return, Dhóri had become adept at reading the signs moments before Bergis was struck by the seizures he was prone to and was able to catch him, help him sit or lie down, and ease the worst of the symptoms until they passed. The pair were rarely apart, much the way Kavan had once been rarely separated from Wortham. Sóbhán was happy that his once-troubled brother had found camaraderie in this place.

"Think there's room for me here for a while? I'm..." he sighed when Dhóri sat and lay his hand on his brother's injured leg as though he could see the damage. Sóbhán flinched, expecting pain, but there was only his brother's light touch and reassurance. "I'm not ready to return to Bhryell. I want to be able to walk first. I don't want the girls to see me like this."

He could stay in the manor, but he did not want to be a burden to Emeria and the staff. He wanted the comfort he could find in Faith, with his brother, until he was ready to see his children.

"There are rooms, or you may share mine," Dhóri smiled affectionately. "You don't need to ask." Nor did he need to fear his family's reactions to his loss.

"Father told you then."

"He told me you might be coming."

"Is he here?"

"No. Ágdhállán fell; he took him to Rhidam, to Yóáná. Captain Magk said he has recovered, but they have not returned to Alberni. I suspect," he sighed forlornly, "he has things to do."

Reacting to his brother's dejected tone, Sóbhán asked, "Things?"

Dhóri shrugged. "He's distracted, unsettled, like something's coming."

"The war?" Perhaps concern for Lorant, Jerit, Ártur, and those he cared for on the battlefront was the cause of his mood. More likely, Sóbhán thought, rubbing his leg above his absent knee, their father was afraid of the woman who had tried to kill him. "Or St. Kóráhm's?"

"Nothing here to be afraid of," said Bergis. "Saint Kóráhm protects us."

"He can't protect us from everything." Just as he had been unable to save Dhóri from the loss of his sight, there was no reason to believe that his father's patron was omnipotent.

Bergis brushed off his friend's doubt. "After what happened before…"

"What? What happened?"

With elated excitement in his voice, Bergis replied, "He was blessed with rósádhá…"

A stern look from Dhóri's vacant eyes made Bergis stammer and stop talking. After an unsteady sigh, Dhóri said, "I'll tell you about it later. Everyone here is safe. Very little of import remains to be stolen or destroyed, and Gorbesh is ready for us if we do have to leave, as Father believes. The Groffs have prepared Alberni as much as they can. If Father knows any other details, he has not yet shared them."

It was Sóbhán's turn to nod and sigh. It had always been Kavan's way, to carry burdens alone as long as he could, rarely asking for or accepting assistance or support. "Maybe there is nothing we can do."

"I think he does not want us to worry."

"Like that will stop us." He adjusted the crutch and offered Dhóri his hand. "Chethá will bring some of my things later, but if you could show me to a room, it would be appreciated."

"Let us help you up the stairs."

The impulse to refuse assistance, the way their father would have, was pushed aside. One day, he would not need that assistance. He would grow beyond it. For today, he decided there was no shame in accepting Bergis' strong arms and back for support on stairs he had yet to try to climb.

"If they're too much, we'll set you a room down here," Dhóri promised.

"I'll appreciate that," Sóbhán nodded. "Thank you."

❧*❧

The Feast of Saint Poul ended with music, drawing closed only when Kavan's throat grew scratchy from candle and torch smoke and his fingers on the brass harp strings grew too raw to play comfortably. Little by little, the guests dribbled away until no more than a handful remained, and when Níkóá rose, passed him with a hand brushing his shoulder, and then left the scattered remains of feasting behind for the palace staff to clear, Kavan tucked his harp under one arm and scooped Ágdhállán up with the other.

The boy had not complained of headaches or other effects from the fall. Kavan could trace no signs of trauma except for the occasional cocking of Ágdhállán's head that indicated the rupture in his eardrums had not healed. It appeared his son was safe.

Whatever Bhás' intent, his son's life had been spared this time.

After tucking him into bed and blowing out the bedside candle, Kavan remained in the room with his arms on the sill of the open window and stared across the sleeping city. At Ágdhállán's age, Kavan had not imagined he would spend most of his life in Enesfel, in the palace of the Lachlan kings, a bard, an advisor, a duke.

A father.

A married man.

Rubbing his thumb over the marriage mark to ease the ache of missing Raebhá tonight, feeling secure in this room he had warded so well, he reached within, across the miles that separated them, seeking comfort in the aura of one he had been too remiss in seeking of late. The need to protect her and their second son from Bhás' ever-threatening presence made frequent contact too dangerous.

Tonight, with an unknown fate looming larger, he needed to try. He needed to feel her love, her support, her comfort, and company. One more time, he needed to touch her thoughts, touch the son he believed he would never meet, and verify that his efforts to keep her safe were still successful.

It was easier to reach her this time with the increase of power gained through rósádhá and anchored inside of him by the sturmyrá he now kept near whenever he slept. He believed he could have gated directly to their shared bed if he tried, thought perhaps he could see and be with her this time, feel her touch, not just her thoughts, manifest himself to her the way Bhás had been doing to him.

Knowing he could not go to her, however, lest he be followed, he squeezed his eyes shut as he felt Raebhá's thoughts brush against his.

Every muscle in his body went rigid as a stab of ice pushed through his breast.

His heart felt as if it stopped beating. He could not breathe.

His vision went black.

Elyri ships in a harbor. Earé' with her mother's sword. His daughter pulling someone by a fistful of black hair, pushing him back to his feet. Men screaming through bubbles of viscous crimson. Prince Jerit shouting Lorant's name as the king fell, buried amidst mutilated bodies. Corpses piled around blood-soaked boots, the faces of uncountable children, preventing flight when fire began to rain from the sky and ignite the fabric shield above his head. The rank stench of burning flesh as orange embers shot across his field of vision. Syl calling for Ártur while his cousin sucked in a smoky, ash-laden breath and shrieked.

A wisp of black smoke, like a hand, clawing through him, seeking a hold on the threads of power that bound him to those in Dhóbhaen, fighting to creep along them in search of whatever, whoever, was at the other end that offered Kavan hope and solace.

Gaed's scream merged with Ártur's, becoming one voice.

The blended shout and Ágdhállán's shout of his younger brother's name, the sudden frigid terror of an external power driving into his thoughts, forced Kavan to sever the connection with Raebhá and Gaed at the moment of contact, ripping Kavan out of the vision. He threw his arms around the boy who clung to his side and flung up every bit of shielding power he had and that he could pull from his son around them both as Ágdhállán sobbed, "She wants him," over and over again.

Kavan knew it was true. If not for Ágdhállán, if not for the timing of the Sight and Ártur's scream in it, if not for the increased store of power and that which he absorbed from his son, Bhás might have found access to Raebhá and Gaed.

She would forever come between him and his distant family, would forever be a threat to them.

Never again.

This had to end.

He would reach out to Ártur and warn him…of his peril, of the king's, of a horror in war that Enesfel was not prepared to see, and then he would finish the task of setting his affairs in order.

He would stop Bhás from hurting another soul. Whatever it took.

❧*❧

The front line was met less than a mile from Gorea's outer edge, where homes and businesses met the late-summer crops now trampled beneath the feet of warring men and the horses they brought with them. Nethite cavalry was thicker here, and the darker-faced enemy mercenaries who fought with them seemed to outnumber those wearing the black and gray tabards of their imposter king. Pushing through the line of royal troops so that those who survived the initial assault could proceed to drown in the mass of Enesfel's force, it was the second wave of Nethites that brought the Lachlan army up short long enough for many to fall victim to their hesitation.

"Inzigaen!" shouted Jerit.

Lorant did not know what that word meant. Nor did most of those who heard it. He only knew that the individuals he cut through as the warring forces wedged between him and Jerit, were children.

He lurched to the side and barely had the time to lift his visor before throwing up on the fallen body at his feet. Someone plowed into him and knocked him to the ground. A short pitchfork came down, only to miss its mark when General Declan swung from atop his horse and threw the wielder several feet, clearing a path in the armies that was quickly filled by others as the fighting continued.

Toward the rear flank, where Kaj was swept back by the mass of mercenaries intent on reaching the tents of dedhá, physicians, and Elyri healers who gave Enesfel a significant advantage, bright sparks of flame were loosed across the cloudless azure sky. A few struck men and women who scurried about delivering water, directing the injured who had begun to trickle into their care, or setting up tents in preparation for others who would come later. Some embedded in wooden barrels, and when one struck the side of a wagon, the novices Hebel and Ybherd raced to put the flames out. It was those arrows that struck the canvas of healing tents that were the most dangerous, and when Kaj heard Healer MacLyr's scream, followed by his wife shouting his name, he attempted to hasten his horse's pace, to sail over the collection of men wrestling in the summer-fertile dirt of the fallow field to reach the tents.

The horse's front hooves came down upon a man's leg. The man screeched, though the sound was swallowed by the din of combat, and the horse, unable to attain a steady footing, rolled and pitched forward, throwing Kaj into the band of archers assaulting the camp. Having lost his sword in that fall but not his shield, he used it to roll and protect himself when someone tried to make an opportunistic attack.

The blade shattered against his shield as a hand grabbed his unkempt hair and yanked him to his feet. When he spun, planning to assail a new attacker, the woman ducked to the side, severed a man's bow hand from his arm, and grinned at Kaj with a nod.

"Told you growing your hair was a good thing," Earé shouted, scooping up a dropped flail and thrusting it into Kaj's hand.

Kaj grunted and swung at another archer, wrenching the bow from him. "Wondered when you'd turn up." Her usually lustrous armor, her fair skin, and her white-gold hair were blood-soaked, attesting to how long she had been fighting, though he had not seen her in camp when they had broken, nor when the armies had been unleashed to meet Fraen's force.

"Wouldn't miss this."

The Nethites were thrown off by combat with a woman, but the mercenaries sneered at the pale young thing and decided to focus on her and Kaj rather than the others around them. Even the remaining archers, now that the largest healing tent was ablaze, turned their attention to her…only to be met by a man in the robes of Faith charging towards them with a discarded thresher and a blood-curdling cry that made many falter.

Beneath dedhá Thrismund's assault, that hesitation was their downfall.

The woman, the dedhá, and the soldier stood as one, rallying others around them to push Neth away from the healers.

"de Corrmick!"

Others took up the cry.

Jerit's breath caught when the man riding beside him, bearing the de Corrmick banner as he had promised his father, cast a terrified glance at the prince and began to lower the flag.

"Don't," he hissed, fighting back the child soldiers who seemed determined to pull him from his horse so they could reach him better. Some seemed less certain in their attack as the de Corrmick name spread like a fire, more hesitating or trying to withdraw through the chaos that erupted with each utterance.

There were only those Vants and Association members they had recruited north of Fiara, in Ruidoso, and collected on the way here to fight with him. The southern mercenaries were deployed elsewhere. The Lachlan guard should be protecting their king, although from his position, Jerit could not see Lorant. Nor could he take the time to look for him. Dukes and their retainers, soldiers fighting for lands and lords, those fighting for Enesfel's cause, whether they understood it or not, were scattered so far that Jerit thought Enesfel must surely have reached Gorea by now.

Jerit had to lead and direct those around him and fight on his own.

He kicked his horse's sides and surged into the tight-knit mass of the overwhelmed, frightened Inzigaen.

He wanted to meet Waller in battle. He, more than any other man in King Lorant's army, would be able to take down King Fraen's general, whether their combat was on horseback or foot. It had taken time to spot the dual charging bulls fashioned into the front of Waller's breastplate, but by the time he did, Bhríd spotted something else as well. The king going down. General Declan fighting over him.

Bhetá saw it too.

They glanced at each other before turning their mounts away from the prize both sought.

If Waller fell, Neth's army would scatter, but there was no time.

If Lorant were lost, the same thing would happen to Enesfel.

A renewed surge of men wielding spears and tridents, men more accustomed to sea battles than to land, forced Earé to redirect some of her followers to the east, toward the edge of the city, while Kaj and Thrismund continued to protect the non-combatants. As the battle dragged on, those fighting at the rear gradually returned their attention to the Lachlan troops, drawing them back into the primary battle, and so Kaj disengaged, leaving Thrismund to lead the rearguard as Kaj fought his way in the direction where Earé was last seen. When he reached her, the stocks of bloody corn trampled beneath him so that his ankles twisted and jerked so often he could barely remain on his feet, she was surrounded by a small host of fair-faced men who had not been part of this battle before.

Elyri.

Here?

Kaj did not question it. They had come upon the second wave of soldiers and cut off their retreat, while on the eastern flank, a few dozen daring townsfolk opted for action rather than pacifism. Pinched between the two forces, the men with sea-browned faces did not stand a chance.

General Declan did not want to be here. He felt like an old man, too old for war, too old to be the king's primary protector as they fought side by side without horses to protect or aid them. But Neth's army had humiliated him once, cost him his honor by expelling Enesfel from the Fiara-Ruidoso territories. Worse still, it was Neth's army who had killed King Merrek despite Garran's obligation to protect him. The general had done everything he could to keep the king alive, but in the end, he had failed in his duties to the Crown. He had failed the little boy who had matured into the king who now fought valiantly beside him.

Garran was determined not to fail again.

Yet the mountain of children's bodies gathering around their feet had disheartened Lorant, made him hesitate more than he should, and Garran's sword arm grew weary of trying to force back those among Waller's men who recognized the importance of the general and the one he was trying to defend. Man after man he put down. Man after man, he was forced to retreat with injuries that resulted in death by someone else. But the trio that rushed in to separate him from Lorant were too powerful, too adept, for Garran to defend against alone. He shouted words that were lost among the surrounding screams and shouts and the clash of metal and wood so that, even though Lorant turned to face him after disarming yet another child and hitting him hard enough in the head with his shield to cause the boy to crumple, unconscious, he could not tell what the general had said.

He turned to witness his general whirl to the side as a mace blow knocked his helmet from his head. Garran floundered on the ground, weaponless, disoriented, unable to hear, and before Lorant could parry the incoming second blow, one of the three jammed a spear through a gap in Garran's armor, while another struck his head with a carpenter's mallet.

Two swords swung.

The attack on General Declan was the last thing those three men accomplished.

Bhríd jumped from his horse and shouted, "Stay with me!" The horse stood over the fallen man and did not move, despite the nicks of blades, stones, and arrows that flew past. Bhetá circled them, driving everyone back without heed of their age or intent. For several moments, Lorant could not see, could not hear, could not think.

He could only see Garran's bloody, lifeless body as the battle blazed.

Hemorrhaging troops, concerned that he had lost more lives than he had taken and knowing this could not be his final stand, General Waller pulled his forces out of Gorea, leaving Neth's dead and injured scattered amongst the ruined crops without any thought for the hardship that destruction would create come winter. Having noted the arrival of an untold number of Elyri, a sure indicator that they had come ashore and swept through the city, claiming Gorea as their own, and having no idea how many more of those terrorizing scourges there might be, he thought it best to fall back, regroup, and call upon the reinforcements the king held in Glevum.

Provided the Elyri had not attacked Glevum by sea as well. Provided the royal city was not likewise overrun.

He had not anticipated Elyri involvement. No one could have. But he did not consider this a loss, despite the forced retreat. By his assessment, Enesfel had lost just as many men, making this a win at best, or a stalemate at worst. Gorea could be retaken later. Some of the bodies were injured, not dead, but there was no way an Elyri healer could heal them all.

And they had lost their general.

Waller had seen him go down, though the de Corrmick flag continued to fly. He was reasonably certain that some of his force had defected to unite and fight beneath that banner.

It did not matter. It would not be enough.

If Enesfel were wise, they would lick their wounds and retreat. Or they would gorge on their perceived victory and be easily crushed the next time they met. Regardless of the traitors to the Crown, this was Nethite territory. No Lachlan king had ever conquered Glevum.

He and Fraen would guarantee that it did not happen now.

ᷭChapter 47᷽

With Jerit's hand tightly in his, heedless of any stares the gesture might elicit from others, Lorant watched the squad of eight riders and twenty-four soldiers and the healer Tisá start the journey back to Fiara, the most the king felt he could spare as a royal procession for the late General Declan whom Ártur had preserved the evening before. Once in Fiara, Tisá would take the general to Rhidam, delivering the news of his unfortunate sacrifice and the report of success in Gorea that Lorant did not feel to be accurate.

Enesfel had lost many men. Lorant did not see how a siege against Glevum, where General Waller was likely to collect reinforcements, could succeed even with the addition of several unexpected Elyri fighters. But his fears were not the sort of news he could deliver to his wife and the regent via a dead man's corpse.

tama Kaj was again overseeing the counting and collection of the dead, sifting the children, the Nethite soldiers, and their mercenaries from Enesfel's army as best they could. But men with the armor of the poor were difficult to tell apart, and with the Nethite Vants and Association members, as well as defectors and recruits collected along their journey, the number of potential Enesfel dead became impossible to accurately calculate.

So many children, Lorant thought with another shudder, blinking away tears when General Declan's escort could no longer be seen. Those who had been injured were spared and healed, but what, he wondered, was Enesfel supposed to do with them? He would certainly not allow them to fight for him as they had been forced to do for Fraen.

"Have you reached him?"

Ártur, his hands blood-stained, his hair and clothes singed from the collapse of the burnt tent, shook his head. "I've not had the time to try," he admitted, coughing to clear the dregs of smoke and soot from his lungs. "He didn't respond before…but that may be because I am too weary to…"

"Do you think Lady Earé…?" Lorant hesitated, casting a glance around him in search of the woman who came to him with the collection of Elyri sailors who had come to Enesfel's aid towards the end of the battle. She had been as bloody, as dirty, as every other soldier he saw, her sword covered with the same filth as his, yet she bore none of the haunting evidence of despair and exhaustion that Lorant was certain covered his face and bled into his enflamed eyes. She followed Bhríd and the Elyri to collect the dead and transport them for healing while Ártur, Pháraeís, and Ylltán walked the battlefield to aid those too injured to move or to ease the passing of men and boys who lingered on the cusp of death who were too injured to save.

Tending the general had been an unwanted respite, but the injured were still coming in. Ártur could not linger with the king and it would likely be hours before he was able to try to contact Kavan again.

"Perhaps," Ártur agreed, not eager to admit that she would have a higher chance of reaching Kavan. She was Kavan's daughter. Ártur was only his cousin, sínréc or not.

"Shall I find her?" asked Jerit quietly, feeling the same need to reach out to the Elyri bard, draw him in, beseech him for grounding and reassurance about their efforts and the path ahead.

Lorant tightened his grip on Jerit's hand but shook his head no. They were too weary. Reaching out to Kavan would wait. "Daema?"

The woman on Jerit's other side was stone-faced, her posture statuesque as if she thought she would collapse if she dared to relax. For several moments, she did not respond, her gaze focused on the horizon. When Lorant spoke her title again, she flinched as if startled and cast him an apologetic look.

"I am sorry, My King. I was…"

Lorant bobbed his head sympathetically. "I know. Please, have those who can, make camp. When that is done, bring tama Yetek, Lord Cáner, and Lady Earé to my fire. We need to talk."

She nodded and shuffled away. What, she thought wearily, was there to discuss? The general was dead. What more was there to say?

⇛*⇚

For hours, they sat together on Ágdhállán's bed, caught in a desperate embrace, entangled in a loop of power, Sight, and emotion that neither was able nor willing to break free of. The visions of war…decimated corpses, blood-soaked earth, the bodies of children intermixed with those of armored men scattered across fields of crops no longer fit for harvest. Scattered throughout the images of the war in Neth were the echoes of battle at St. Kóráhm's gate and a coastline Kavan had not visited in too long, the collapse of a hilltop shrine that was, in many ways, central to who Kavan was. Screams, cries, and groans of the injured, shouts of fury and fear, and always the underlying horror that came with knowing she had done this.

Without her prodding Neth into action, without her provision of mercenaries, Neth might never have struck out at Enesfel.

Praise k'Ádhá for Earé and her recruits.

Without the vendetta against Kavan for his defilement of Coryllien's resting place and the crusade to destroy the bloodline of the man who had betrayed her ancestor by chastely loving a woman he had no claim to, none of this would be happening. There would never have been a need.

Kóráhm could not be blamed for his brother's retaliation. The threads of history wove without the meddling of the men and women who lived it.

And now his shrine had fallen. Or was doomed to fall.

Despite what he had felt before, Kavan was not certain which was true.

Ágdhállán was too young to experience these things, but Kavan could not shield him from them. The Sight had no respect for age. Kavan could do his best to absorb the horror, keep his own visions out of his son's head, and comfort the boy through his, all while feeling the occasional tapping of Ártur's thoughts against his.

Kavan could not afford the energy or the split focus to respond. Eventually, Ártur stopped trying. The warmth of day bled into the coolness of night, with Rhyrdan coming multiple times to clasp Kavan's shoulders, touch his face, or embrace father and son as if to rouse or comfort them during the passage of time that carried with it the burden of a dead man he watched echo through his head. Ágdhállán slipped into exhausted sleep at some time during that day or night, his body unable to bear the horrors any longer, but Kavan remained watchful as consciousness returned and pushed the pulse of power back into his regulated well of containment.

The sturmyrá rested on his lap between him and Ágdhállán. He assumed Rhyrdan had put it there. Or realized, as he touched it with one hand without opening his eyes, that Sunna had been the one to bring it. Sunna's was the only aura imprinted on it now.

Kavan frowned, began to pick it up, but stopped when that tapping against his thoughts came again.

Not Ártur.

Earé.

"k'bhydhá?"

Unable to deny her given what he had Seen, he lowered his defenses and welcomed the warmth of her company.

"Are you safe? Are you unharmed?"

She did not ask how he knew. He knew the same way she knew that he and Ágdhállán had suffered with those in war as though they had stood on a hillside and observed it firsthand.

"You know I am," her thoughts murmured affectionately.

"She did this. She has caused…" He choked as if on the words but only felt her nod in return. "This will not end if I do not stop her, will it?"

Her whole body seemed to sigh and Kavan squeezed his eyes tighter. "It will end regardless," she replied, "but not in our favor."

Assuming by 'our' she meant Enesfel's, or the Five Sovereignties', that her words foretold the death of Lorant and the destruction of the Lachlan House, Kavan felt his burden grow heavier. He pushed against the abrupt flare of anger and whispered, "I do not know how to find…"

"You will know when it is time."

As with her mother before her, Earé's words were cryptic enough to imply that his not knowing meant that it was not yet time, that the suffering of those around him would be unavoidable for some time more. Preordained suffering, however, did not make him feel better, but before he could ask for clarification, beg her for what she was not telling him, she continued.

"Lorant seeks comfort. Prince Jerit, aendhá Ártur, and Bhríd too."

"Bhríd is…?"

"Well and fighting with the king, where he should be. Can I tell them…?"

"Tell them…" Ágdhállán shifted in Kavan's arms in a way that prompted Kavan to nestle the boy into his pillows. His arms felt empty without his son there, but the pulsing power of the sturmyrá replaced the sensation with a different warmth as he stood and stared at the sleeping boy.

"Tell them I will end this." He did not know how or when, but it needed to be done. He needed to act before it was too late.

"I will tell them. Tell those in Rhidam…"

"I shall."

"And k'bhydhá…stay strong. I shall see you soon."

Earé broke the connection, and Kavan curled his empty hand at his side. For one short moment, long enough for him to see the image clearly within his mind's eye, St. Kóráhm's shrine fell again.

Kavan knew where he needed to go.

But there were things he needed to do first.

❧*❧

"He sends his prayers," Earé said as she sat at the tavern table in Gorea where the king and his now diminished group of military advisors waited for her arrival. Her face and hands were clean of blood, but her armor had yet to be cleaned, and her braided hair, though tidied and tucked behind her neck, was still streaked with crimson. She had been too busy to do more, and while others had taken their time to make themselves presentable, she was the only one wearing the reminders of war.

The Elyri sailors joined them, pulling chairs to the king's table, and were telling the tale of ongoing coastal harassment by the mercenary galleys when Earé entered the tavern. No attempts were made to breach the shore, to start a conquest of those hard-to-reach outposts, but one Elyri ship and several sailors had been lost, and the outposts had taken significant damage.

With the conquered galleys confiscated by the people of Gorea aided by Enesfel's army, those raids were expected to end. Unless Enesfel routed the Nethite mercenaries, most believed that, sooner or later, the owners of those ships would return for them. Gorea's council, gathered at a table nearby that was moved near enough that they could be part of this conversation while keeping an awkward distance from the Elyri sailors, demanded to know what the King of Enesfel and the de Corrmick prince intended to do to protect them.

Lorant was uncertain that Enesfel could protect their own.

"Is he coming?" asked Lorant.

"It would be good to see him," agreed Bhríd, relieved that Ártur was not part of this conversation to ask a slurry of questions they did not have time for tonight.

"All in Rhidam are well; there has been no unrest. He says," Earé paused to accept the cup a serving girl offered, "he will end this."

"How?" snorted Bhetá, her voice slurred by the uncommon over-indulgence of ale she had been drinking steadily since they sat down. "There's nothing he can…"

"I trust him," interjected Jerit before Bhríd could speak in his kinsman's defense. He had no familial ties to the bard, and he was a de Corrmick prince. He hoped those details counted enough to make his trust in Kavan meaningful.

"How can he…?"

Kaj laid a hand affectionately over Bhetá's. "Whatever his plan, I'm sure he will succeed."

Though she looked at him with gratitude for his kindness, Bhetá pulled her hand away and picked up her empty glass, turning it over this time as she decided not to drink more tonight. "We have lost our general…"

"We have you."

She stared at Kaj with wide, glazed eyes. "I am…"

"Daema. The second general. I have seen you. The troops respect…"

"Do we dare go on?" someone asked, voicing the opposition that so many in the room were thinking and feared. "We have lost so many…"

"What about Gorea?" barked a council member, sounding offended by the possibility of being abandoned.

"So have they, Bhríd countered simultaneously.

"They will have reinforcements when they come," another councilman argued. "Glevum will be defeated."

"With the galleys vacant…" offered one of the Elyri sailors, "our outposts are safe. We can sail the sound, bring others, sail to Glevum to storm the city by sea…"

"And there will be others joining us, now that they know I am here," Jerit reminded them. "Many have already defected, before today and during…more will come. Talk will spread. The closer we get to Glevum…"

"Others will likely come forward," said a third councilman, a ruddy-faced fellow darkened by the blood of those he had killed defending his city. "I've sent messengers…"

Others of the council gawked at him with outrage and offense, which he ignored. "Those loyal to your father will be loyal to you, My Prince. You can count on it."

"That doesn't mean it will be enough." Lorant wanted to be optimistic, but he was too tired for that.

"Would you rather we retreat? Return south of the Kelari?" asked Bhríd in a tone devoid of offense or challenge.

"Or return to Enesfel, surrender when we are so close to accomplishing what we came for?"

Lorant scowled at Jerit, his ego bruised by the word surrender and the lightly goading tone Jerit often used to persuade Lorant to do something he was reluctant to do. "I didn't say surrender…"

"Remaining inactive here," said dedhá Thrismund, speaking for the first time, nursing a cup of steaming cider between his hands, "is not an option. Inactivity will accomplish nothing."

"So, you would leave us to…?"

Kaj shook his head and stared at the offended councilman. "You have citizens to fight for you, and many of the wounded we leave for recovery will be on their feet within days. They can aid in your defense, as will the boys we leave if it comes to that." His expression was grim as he continued, "Men we leave here means men we do not have to confront Fraen."

"And our failure ensures your failure here," Thrismund reminded them. "That is to no one's benefit."

"Kavan says he will…"

Jerit put his hand on Lorant's wrist and spoke over Bhríd's reminder, saying, "Remember what he said, what he told us. I will do this without you if I must."

Having come this far, being this close to Glevum, it was no longer his father's demand that kept Jerit fighting. It was Oska, the people of Neth, and the desire to reclaim what he had lost.

The secession of the southern territory had been one thing.

The loss of the de Corrmick throne to an impostor was another.

Queen-regent Inness might have been a de Corrmick by marriage, but she had held the throne on behalf of her son…Oska's son. A de Corrmick.

Olaric Fraen the Elder was no de Corrmick, regardless of his claims.

"If he is to uphold his part," Earé said in a tone that made many shiver, "we must uphold ours. I did not come…we did not…" she glanced at Kaj, "to surrender or fail. We came for Enesfel, for Elyriá, for the Sovereignties. We came too far to be defeated by despair."

"We fight." k'ílshwythnec's perceived promise of success was all Kaj needed to press on. Her promise would be all his demoralized force, having suffered their share of losses, needed to hear. Fighting for King Lorant or Prince Jerit mattered less than fighting to dethrone Fraen, fighting until She Who Sees said the war was over.

Bhetá met Kaj's gaze, allowing unspoken thoughts to pass between them for several moments as Gorea's council argued, before she looked at Lorant. "We have come this far. The general's sacrifice to keep you alive cannot be meaningless. Give the word and I will lead your army, My Liege. I will finish what he began."

Lorant looked around the room, meeting the gazes of those he could see, internally complaining that the choice to assault Glevum had come down to him. Until now, he had been able to defer, in part, each military decision to General Declan. He no longer had that luxury. He was the king, and this choice was his. Covering Jerit's hand on his wrist with his other hand, Earé was the last person Lorant looked at.

His tutor, his mentor, his friend, could perform miracles. He had repeatedly saved Lorant's life for what? For him to surrender and retreat as a failure? He clung to the belief, when Earé nodded and he met Bhetá's gaze, that Kavan would perform some miracle to save his life this time too.

"At dawn, those who can will march to Glevum. Those who cannot will stay and defend Gorea when they are on their feet. Captain," he looked at the Elyri sailors, "Take what ships you need, retrieve what people you can…some of you defend Gorea, some of you meet us in Glevum." Lastly, he looked at Jerit, struggling with the words that came next. "We will take back your throne, Jerit. We will return it to you."

The three men gathered in the oratory, where Kavan believed them less likely to be overheard by passing servants and less likely to be interrupted by the children practicing weaponry under Zerio and Raenár's tutelage, or learning art and needlework with the queen, her ladies, and Master Najar in the courtyard, looked at one another as the bard rose from his knees where he prayed at the altar. Kavan had spent the morning with the children in the back garden, reading to them, singing to them, leaving them with a lesson that stressed the needs of kindness, generosity, compassion, and the need to always have Faith, even if that Faith was not what everyone else expected it to be. He had laid his hands on each of them, hoping to impress peace upon them, hoping for some glimpse of what their life would become, but he felt only their abiding love for him and left his with them.

He had spoken with Yóáná and Aland on his way into the keep and besought them to remain faithful to the Lachlans with a press of his hands around theirs. Aland detected nothing unusual and agreed wholeheartedly with the duke's silent request, while Yóáná eyed him with her mother's intuitive skepticism and began to question the meaning of his admonitions.

dedhá Charlos' fortuitous passing in the corridor provided Kavan an excuse to leave them both before she could ask questions.

His dialogue with a dedhá he was not overly familiar with lasted only long enough for them to part ways at the corridor's intersection. Charlos was less flexible in his Faith than some, but there was room for growth in the years ahead as he was exposed to daily life in the royal keep. He was a good man at heart and would, Kavan expected, offer Lorant the sort of wise advice Kavan tried to provide.

Alone at the intersection after a short conversation with Zerio, fighting to ease a burst of anxiety that struck him as he considered abandoning the

Lachlans as he had promised Arlan he would never do, Kavan had sought refuge in the oratory in search of peace he did not think he would find.

Despite his experience the last time he had knelt before this altar, he clung to the hope that Bhás was less likely to hear him here, to listen or interfere. A vial of sacred oil, a flask of purified water, and a single candle sat upon the altar, perfuming the air with cleansing spices that spoke of a recent blessing given before the men's arrival.

His normally serene expression was pensive and serious, making each of them wiggle to the edges of the benches where they leaned forward in expectation. He looked as if he wanted to pace, his contained energy making him shift his weight, flex his hands, and roll his head from side to side as if to ease stiffness in his neck.

Each assumed he had silently summoned them, that being here together now was no accident.

"I need each of you to do something for me. I do not ask this lightly…and you are free to refuse if you wish…"

"As though we could refuse you anything," Rhyrdan murmured, the worried rumble in his chest reminding Kavan so much of Wortham that he had to swallow the lump in his throat before continuing.

"You might when you hear…"

Níkóá pulled his feet beneath the bench and leaned further forward. "You won't know unless you ask." It was rare for the bard to request anything other than the daily mundane matters necessary to manage the royal house or his duchy.

"I…" Kavan squared his shoulders, glanced at Sunna who had yet to speak, and continued, "I am going to St. Kóráhm's this evening to visit my sons. Zerio will accompany me and remain until…"

"Is it time?" Rhyrdan asked, his voice rough and anxious.

Kavan's shoulders and mouth twitched, but he did not answer the question or confirm Rhyrdan's fears with his own. "From there, in the morning, I must journey to Kílyn, where I have been led to believe the shrine is under attack…or will be. I do not know if there is anything I can do…but I am compelled to protect it if I can."

"You want us to protect you while you protect the shrine." Rhyrdan exchanged glances with Níkóá. "You know I will follow you anywhere…"

"Is it her?" Sunna asked.

Afraid to speak the name, the words that came with it, Kavan nodded. Sunna nodded in return, the lines of his lips drawn tight, his eyes narrowed as though focused on something only he could see. "Where you go, I go."

"Who?"

Rhyrdan began to reply to the regent's question but Kavan shook his head. He would not have her name spoken in this holy place. He would rather not speak it or hear it at all. Níkóá, less eager to accept the request as he weighed the duties to Enesfel he had been given, said, "Enesfel needs me in the king's stead…"

"Find someone to serve for you," Rhyrdan grunted. "Kavan needs…"

"Enesfel needs…"

Kavan interjected, "I cannot say how long we would be absent…and you are free to deny…"

"It isn't that I wish to deny you, my lord," Níkóá replied. "If the ships in Levonne make land…if they break our defenses and sail up the Tegid…"

"They won't."

Níkóá cast the dark-skinned man an exasperated look that asked how he could be certain of that before continuing, "There has to be someone who can direct…"

"The queen has the authority," Rhyrdan interjected.

Hoping to defend his daughter, Níkóá said, "But not the experience."

Kavan's soft words undercut their argument. "Asta."

Níkóá stared at him.

Asta had the advantage of age and experience over Queen Seren. She had the aptitude and the fortitude of will, gifted to her by her Dugan heritage and a history as queen at Kjell's side where she had aided him in the years of reforms that transformed Neth into a land no longer feared by her neighbors. She had been at the side of multiple kings and a queen and had acquired skills from them and her father that Seren would never have.

Enesfel's queen was wise, kind, and gentle. She was empathetic and intelligent. But Níkóá had not raised her to be a potential ruling monarch. She had not wanted that, and he, during his years as regent for Lorant, had not wanted that for her.

Asta Dugan Cáner de Corrmick was the best choice to temporarily sit upon Enesfel's throne. As fitting a choice as Níkóá was, he admitted. Perhaps better in some ways.

He sighed and bowed his head. "I will talk to her. If she is willing, my sword is yours," he promised.

Kavan accepted the words he did not want to say with another nod.

"Bring only what you require; meet me here at daybreak. Rhyrdan, tell Zerio I am ready when he is." Already knowing about the imminent visit to Alberni, having agreed to alert Asta to his absence, Zerio knew to bring

Ágdhállán to the oratory when it was time, when he was ready. He had not asked why, as if he innately understood.

Seeing so many making the Alberni trip with him would raise questions Kavan hoped he could answer when they came.

❧*❧

"You know the throne isn't for me, that I don't want it." Jerit's statement sounded like a desperate question, but with his head on Lorant's bare chest, his eyes focused on the blonde's long fingers as he absently toyed with them, Lorant could not look into his eyes to confirm it.

"You have a right to it," he replied with a shrug, adjusting the blanket over Jerit's shoulders and shifting his position so they were both covered against the night chill that rolled in from the sea. Lorant had been offered a room in Gorea, but after the suffering his troops had borne on his behalf, he could think of nowhere else he should be than with them here as they faced dawn's impending march. "It was your brothers. It could be yours."

"It belongs to Henrik. Everything I need is in Rhidam." When Lorant stiffened, Jerit propped himself up on his elbow to smile and kiss Lorant's jaw. "You are in Rhidam too, you know…or you will be when this is over."

"Maybe," Lorant mumbled.

It hurt Jerit to see that Lorant had lost so much of his playful, youthful spark, but he did not know how to give it back. When this war was over, only time could reignite that boyish demeanor and make Lorant happy again. The only thing Jerit could do was see him safely home. It was his primary goal when war was met once more.

"Trust Kavan. Trust Lady Earé. If the Sight's rarely wrong…we'll both be home soon. Whatever Kavan plans to do to end this, trust that it will happen. Trust he will succeed."

"I do trust him."

Lorant did not trust himself.

It was the sort of fear he dared not show anyone lest they fail to return Glevum's throne to the de Corrmicks. The sort he dared not even show completely to Jerit, the person he trusted and loved the most in all the world.

❧*❧

Asta let out the long, hissing breath she had been holding only after Níkóá closed the stateroom door. Dinner would be served soon, but she no

❧575❧

longer had the desire to eat it. She did not have the stomach to face those who would be seated there, knowing what she knew.

She did not fault Kavan's choice to go to Kílyn if the Sight compelled him. The bard and his patron saint had saved Enesfel's throne more times than anyone else in the kingdom's history. If Kóráhm bid him go to the shrine, then that is where Kavan must go.

She did not fully understand why he wanted Níkóá to go with him, nor did Níkóá. But for a few days, with Lachlan guards stationed at multiple intervals along the Tegid to prevent invaders from reaching the city, and with the palace guard and sheriff's men on high alert, she did not expect anything significant to occur that she and Madoc could not handle.

She had stood with her father against Halstatt Tarmajien and the Corylliens when little more than a girl. She had stood strong as her first love was lost, and she was left to raise their daughter alone. She had stood strong at Kjell's side as he molded Neth into something better and stayed strong when the throne was taken away from him. She continued to be strong as they plotted and planned ways that Neth's throne could be reclaimed for the de Corrmick House.

She was not afraid of the throne.

Asta only feared the unknowns that Kavan would not speak of and how it was likely entangled with the woman who had killed her father.

♋ * ♋

Kavan's embrace was tighter than usual and lasted longer than it often did. The bearded man with him judged Sóbhán's state with compassion before meeting his gaze over the bard's shoulder. As Sóbhán returned the embrace, thinking at first that his father's reaction was based on his injury or the possibility that his attacker had struck again, he noted Rhyrdan's expression was sterner, more stoic than he was used to seeing. Those details, along with the gaggle of people Kavan had brought with him, raised Sóbhán's suspicions at once.

His father was afraid.

Racing past Sóbhán in the Gathering Hall, Phaedr scurried off in search of Balint as soon as they arrived and dragged Cáym with him despite his brother's reluctance to leave Ágdhállán. Zerio and Raenár followed the boys toward the barracks, speaking in low tones while Níkóá headed out of the Gathering Hall towards the stairs that would take him to Kjell. There was another, a man Sóbhán assumed was Cíbhóló though his complexion was lighter, his hair longer, who followed Kavan into the room but remained a respectable distance away with a look so blank Sóbhán could not guess his thoughts.

"I thought it best to take your advice and stay with Dhóri while I relearn to walk. He provided this," he gestured towards a length of wood on the front bench where he had been seated, a whittling knife, and the beginnings of a pile of wood shavings on the floor that would likely dismay many residents when they saw it.

From the length and shape, Kavan guessed the piece would eventually serve as a replacement for the missing portion of his eldest son's leg.

Noting where Kavan's gaze was as they drew apart, speaking as if to excuse the mess, Sóbhán shrugged. "It is too windy, and here," he gestured around them, "I have the benefit of company and interaction. Dhóri says I shouldn't isolate…that I should not be ashamed of a battle injury."

"Your brother is wise," Kavan admitted, offering support when Sóbhán wavered on his crutch.

"Don't tell him that," chuckled Sóbhán. "You're early." Kavan did not take the bait that comment dangled between them, and so Sóbhán smiled at Ágdhállán instead. "And you, little brother, how go your studies?" He could see that Ágdhállán had either recently been ill or had not been sleeping well, but rather than ask, he chose a less sensitive topic.

"She wants…" Ágdhállán began.

Kavan motioned him closer, cutting him off, and wrapped one arm around him. To Rhyrdan he said, "Emeria will have what is needed…take Sunna with you. Visit the Groffs and inquire if there is anything they need. Take as much time as you need."

Rhyrdan pursed his lips but nodded and walked away, he and Sunna picking up the mostly-empty packs they had brought with them that suggested a trip was planned. Rhyrdan had spent several hours with Madoc the day before, visiting his brother under the pretense of discussing Rhidam's security following the increasing reports of blockade ships in Levonne. Being sent to the manor was his chance to visit his sister, too, in case their efforts to protect the Kílyn shrine, and Kavan, failed.

He left because he knew Kavan wanted to visit his sons privately.

He hesitated halfway down the aisle, looked back, and asked, "Shall we attend the evening Gathering?" He did not expect to return to the chellé in time for the Gathering at noon, nor did he expect that, once they left here, they would set foot in a Gathering Hall for the foreseeable future.

"No." Kavan had no desire to repeat the spectacle from his last visit here. Another episode of rósádhá would incapacitate him and delay his duty. He wanted a peaceful day with his sons, a quiet evening meal with his closest friends in the chellé he had founded, and then a quiet evening in the company of those he had lost.

His gaze traveled again to the sword on Rhyrdan's hip, the waji that once belonged to Wace Elotti, the waji that matched the one Sunna wore. Per Wace's wishes, to leave his death and his legend a mystery to those who whispered his name in awe and fear, the sword had been kept hidden…but no more. Others might believe that Sunna had given it to him. Few would connect the waji to Elotti.

Kavan knew the claim that the waji was the only weapon that could kill shi cali. Sunna had called Bhás that. He had no intention of using it, but Rhyrdan and Sunna, knowing who, or what, they would certainly face, were willing to use the waji against her if necessary.

Ágdhállán withdrew from his father's embrace, accepting the things his father did not want to discuss, and asked, "Shall I find Dhóri?"

Kavan picked up the pack he had set on the bench and the harp Ágdhállán had carried but left behind when he nodded and trudged out of the Gathering Hall. "Is there a place where we can enjoy the sun without the wind troubling us?"

"I know a place. Dhóri will know it too."

The wood and whittling knife were abandoned as Sóbhán accepted Kavan's support to hobble on his crutch through one of the chellé's many doors. There were no clouds, but the wind blew off the sea to the south, bringing with it the smells associated with a heavy storm, and Kavan was grateful that the small garden of now colorless flower bushes, where Ágdhállán and Dhóri joined them on the north side of the building, was tucked away where the wind did not reach.

"This is rare," Dhóri said with a greeting smile as he helped settle Sóbhán on a garden bench. Ágdhállán climbed up beside him and slid as close as he could while Dhóri sat beside Kavan on the other bench. "We don't' sit as a family often anymore."

"There are Gates," Sóbhán teased.

"And there are duties," Dhóri countered affectionately.

Kavan nodded, accepting Dhóri's hand. "Life." His older children had lives of their own, responsibilities that no longer included him. If what he feared awaited him in Kílyn, soon, Ágdhállán's life would not include him either. His expression fell.

"What is it, k'bhydhá?" Dhóri might have felt that wave of worry and melancholy first, but it was Sóbhán, facing him, who saw the shadows fall across their father's face, who noted the exchange of glances between him and Ágdhállán.

The boy wrapped his arm around Sóbhán's and held tight.

"I would spare you…" But it would not be fair to steal away into the dawn as he planned without telling them where he was going…preparing them for what he believed would be the inevitable result of his choices.

"We would rather know the truth," whispered Dhóri. "Is it Bhás?"

Kavan swallowed, toed the pack between his feet, bud did not answer the question. "I have seen Kílyn under attack. I must go…"

"To protect the shrine? Is that why Rhyrdan and…?" Sóbhán began.

"Sunna."

"Sunna. Are they going with you? In case there is trouble?"

Rather than add Níkóá's name to the list, deciding to spare them the worry for Enesfel if he could not spare them worry for himself, Kavan nodded. "There are ships there…or will be. I do not know if she will be there…but the sense of her, her assault on you, on Ágdhállán…I must be prepared to end this before…"

"Before she kills our brother," Ágdhállán interrupted in a strained, squeaking voice.

"Has she…?" asked Sóbhán with concern.

"She has tried…through me. It is not you, not any of you, she wants. She wants me…and she will use all of you to get to me." He believed, however, that killing him might not be enough for Bhás. Sóbhán might be spared, but the blood of his children through Chethá, those who bore Kóráhm's blood, would never be safe so long as Bhás lived. Her need for revenge would extend to each of them, and their children, until the lineage of Kóráhm di Curnydhá was erased.

"And so, you are here to…" Dhóri could not say it. The last time his father had traveled, Dhóri had not said goodbye as he should have. He had stormed off in fury, had nearly died carrying the belief he would never see his father again.

He was not certain this was better.

"Once it is settled," Kavan sighed, "once she is…"

Sóbhán shivered and cut Kavan off. "Can you promise that? That you'll come home?"

"I wish I…k'Ádhá, Kóráhm, and Dhágdhuán willing, we will be together. It is…" He swallowed and stared at his harp case, longing for the instrument in his hands, wishing for the comfort that only prayer and music could provide instead of the harshness of reality. "It is the best I can offer."

Ágdhállán lifted his head and looked from one brother to the next and finally to his father, whose gaze he held for several still moments. "We will be together again."

He sounded so certain that neither his brothers nor his father had the heart to contradict him with their doubts and fears.

*

Lorant's decision to remain in Gorea until the Elyri manned galleys set sail resulted in a longer then intended delay when the early autumn rain brought with it a layer of dense fog that prevented the ships from leaving port until mid-morning. There were few complaints from the troops, as most were not eager to march and face death again so soon, but Jerit's pacing at the head of the dock was irritating enough that the king was thankful when the Elyri captain deemed it safe to sail and the ships drifted out into the bay.

It would not take them long to recruit additional men from the Elyri coastal fortresses. So long as the weather held, no Nethite ships blocked the bay, and the land troops did not meet with significant impediments, both ships and soldiers should reach Glevum at approximately the same time.

Like Bhetá and Kaj, Lorant hoped that would be enough.

"We will go now," he muttered, as he strode past Jerit, irritation bleeding into his voice and quick, marching steps. It was not enough to temper Jerit's mood, however. Only the knowledge of progress toward Glevum could do that.

*

"Lord Cliáth says the king has reached Gorea."

"Kavan is here?"

It was an odd question given the news he had just shared, and Níkóá side-eyed Tau, expecting some clue to explain it. Tau did not see the look as he helped adjust Kjell in his chair at the window and arranged the recently arrived morning meal on the table. Kjell tucked the blanket around his lap and tugged his robe close around his chest to keep the wind's chill from the open window away from his skin.

It had been weeks since Níkóá had visited Kjell. Today, Neth's exiled king did not appear well. The constant dabbing at his nose with a cloth and his thick-sounding, raspy voice confirmed the visual diagnosis. He wondered if he should suggest closing the window, if he should return to Rhidam long enough to give his evaluation to Asta.

Knowing Kjell, neither of those things would be appreciated.

"He is visiting his sons. It is my understanding we will be here to dine later, as there are things we need to do before we depart." He did not specify where their departure would take them, knowing Kjell would assume that departure would take them home to Rhidam. He did not think he should offer unnecessary details to Neth's king.

"If you're here," Kjell muttered, "who's managing Rhidam?"

"Lady Asta and Seren can conduct business until I return." For a day, such an arrangement would not be unusual or unheard of.

He expected Kjell to protest, but instead, the man's expression softened and he said, "She is the most capable woman I know," with a sigh of melancholy longing. "Might have lost both of my sons without her."

"Aye, she is capable," agreed Tau as he sat in the chair across from Kjell and began to eat. "Your heirs owe her their lives."

Kjell huffed without explaining the emotion behind that sound. He might lose his remaining son, by his own prompting. Níkóá, thinking he regretted sending Jerit into war, did not ask him to explain.

"The duke believes," he said instead, "they are soon to march on Glevum, that they have adequate forces to do so." Kavan had not said so, but Níkóá interpreted the things Kavan had said to support that perception of Enesfel's strength.

"Of course they will. But can they take it? Can they hold it?" There were Nethites at Cordash's border, after all, and undoubtedly others stationed along the northern coast and throughout the inland towns, troops likely to be summoned in Glevum's defense if they did not lay down their weapons and take advantage of the attempt to overthrow the imposter king.

Kjell felt that he could no longer adequately judge the actions of the people of Neth.

Some had turned on him, after all. Some had supported Inness, whether by choice or by force, and others now supported Fraen. To Neth, Kjell had died a decade ago. He had convinced Jerit that people would rally to the de Corrmick banner, but he was not certain that was true. With that uncertainty in mind, he had sent his son to war for something he could not guarantee.

"Lord Cliáth believes so. I believe it too," Níkóá' replied.

"The White Bard is rarely wrong about such things," added Tau.

"Stories," Kjell huffed again before waving to the bedside chair and grunting, "Join us. No point standing there; there's enough for all of us. Tell me how Henrik is doing. Tell me about Rhidam."

It was a more positive breakfast conversation than a faraway war that might cost him both his son and his wife.

❧*❧

"Hold!"

Lorant's head snapped up, and his eyes opened as Bhetá's clipped command drove into his sleep-addled brain, and he craned his neck to see what she was looking at. Surprised he had remained on his horse, unsure how long he had dozed since the flat farmland they passed through looked the same with each mile they crossed, he tried to steer to the front of the column, but Jerit, riding in front of him, refused to let him pass. What he could see was a dirty white pennant on a tall lance, a sight that made his heart sour and his breath catch in his suddenly tight chest.

Had Kavan done it? Had Kavan ended the war?

"Let me find out who it is," Jerit said over his shoulder, thinking this more likely to be a ruse, a threat to Lorant, rather than the surrender of Fraen's force. "Stay here." He hesitated long enough for Lorant to bob his head and wipe the back of his hand across his damp chin, and then joined Bhetá and Kaj to ride forward together.

Jerit could not count the approaching force, men in a motley assortment of armor, mostly mounted soldiers of a sort that were less common in Neth than in other Sovereignties.

"How many?" Jerit murmured, glancing at Lorant, who was inching nearer to the front of his force despite the admonition to remain back.

"Maybe two hundred," Bhetá replied, her scowl smoothing into a neutral expression as the strangers drew closer. None had weapons drawn and their approach was cautiously casual, but Kaj, choosing to be vigilant, gestured to the men riding nearest to him, prompting them to be ready in case the innocent approach turned deadly.

The approaching groups stopped beyond the reach of swords and other hand weapons, but near enough to be consciously within the range of Enesfel's archers to further prove they had no ill intent.

"Hail! Daema Magk?"

Bhetá looked at Jerit, the speaker's accent catching them off guard, before nudging her horse forward. There were no markings, no tabards, no pennants, but she recognized the blunt cut of the man's straight hair as she drew close enough to see him clearly.

"You are?"

"Lieutenant Mathias." He could not bow from his horse, but he tipped his head, keeping his relieved expression visible as he held her gaze. "It is our fortune to find you."

"I would say it is ours," said Jerit. Having heard the man's accent, Lorant chose to join Bhetá despite the efforts of others to stop him. Jerit met his gaze with a private, scolding glance that the stranger did not see.

Mathias repeated his head-tipping bow as his gaze swept across the mass of soldiers collecting behind Enesfel's king and Daema. "Indeed, Your Majesty." Enesfel's army was vast, but to his perception, they were weary and disheartened. "If we may be of service…"

"How are you here? Did Govert send you?" Lorant asked.

"Happenstance and fortune. We were separated on the Neth side of the border when the heathen force attacked our outpost. Our captain remained to put them down and bid us sweep the flank…and we've been sweeping ever since. Had a few clashes, gathered some defectors…got word you were at Kelari and hoped to meet you coming north."

"We could have used you at Gorea."

"Or before," added Jerit.

"Indeed. We lost an unfortunate number along the way, conflict slowed us down, but we're here now, if you will have us. Are you bound for Glevum? I could send word back to the captain for more men…"

There was another exchange of glances. It was unlikely that any Cordashian troops could reach them, reach Glevum, before Enesfel engaged in battle again, but as Bhetá expected siege before combat, and a protracted, brutal fight when it came, those reinforcements might still be of use, and thus would be welcome…so long as she and Kaj could keep Enesfel's force in play long enough to utilize them.

"We would welcome any cooperation," Bhetá said after Lorant's nod. "Yours as well as others."

"We are not many, but you shall have us," Mathias agreed with a wave to his men. Lorant managed a grateful smile, but the look and the sentiment did not quite reach his eyes…or his heart.

❧*❦

Zerio yawned and rubbed his eyes when the room finally fell silent. "I shall send for you the next time I have difficulty sleeping."

Unable to sit in his father's lap as the bard entertained the small gathering of guests in the Alberni manor's dining room, Ágdhállán had long ago fallen asleep on Rhyrdan's lap. Cáym and Phaedr had stretched out on the bench on either side of Emeria, each with a head on one of her knees, while Balint likewise slept in his father's arms with his head against his chest. The men and one woman with them had shared light conversation as they dined, some asking questions about Gorbesh over the simple meal or discussing the autumn harvest and how its abundance prepared Alberni, like elsewhere, for the approaching winter. They discussed the upcoming Feast of Saint Edhriá and the community meal the residents of St. Kóráhm's typically prepared for those in Alberni who wished to attend.

Attendance had steadily increased, despite the plagues, so it had become necessary to host the event in the chellé's courtyard and to devise ways to protect the guests from the elements when the winter storms came early. There was time enough to plan, but hoping for the future, for the continuation of normalcy, was better than discussing how, should Kavan's predicted assault come to pass, there might not be a celebration this year.

The feast day would pass regardless of whether anyone remained to celebrate it, regardless of whether St. Kóráhm's continued to stand.

Conversation gave way to music, which, at this late hour, lulled the children to sleep as Kavan intended. As much as he longed to dally in the company of cherished friends and family, this was a night for prayer. If he did not part from these friends now, he might never go.

Or he would go, but his actions would come too late.

"You have but to ask," Kavan murmured, setting the kestrel harp in its case on the table and rubbing his fingers over its black wood. The harp seemed to bleed melancholy so that he, overwhelmed by the sadness, was forced to remove his hand and close the case, hoping his lowered gaze would hide the tears rising in his eyes.

"Let me take Ágdhállán up to bed," murmured Rhyrdan.

"And these two," added Emeria warmly. Unable to lift them both, Níkóá volunteered to help without speaking, picking up the boy nearest him. To Raenár, she said, "Balint is welcome to say."

The captain nodded. "That is generous." He was sure his son would wake on the walk back to the chellé and then be awake for hours, so leaving him with the other boys was a good alternative. Balint would be safe here. Safer, perhaps, than in St. Kóráhm's.

Kavan was right in that. He should consider sending Balint to Rhidam until the war was over and the possibility of an assault on the chellé was negated. With his mother away at war, however, Raenár was reluctant to send him there alone.

To Sóbhán, as Zerio handed him the crutch and helped him to his feet, Kavan said, "You know where I will be."

Níkóá murmured, "We will find you." Looks passed around the room; men nodded. With the midnight Gathering set to begin soon, Khwílen and Dhóri's need to depart serving as the catalyst to bring their evening to an end, most knew what Kavan wanted now. The manor oratory would be too near to too many people who might intrude on his desire for privacy.

What Kavan wanted most, Rhyrdan understood, was to be near to his father one more time. If he believed his father would hear him, Rhyrdan would have elected to visit the man's grave as well. He would have to settle for Kavan reaching Wortham and giving him his youngest son's love.

"We will escort you." Already obligated to escort Kjell to his room, the exiled king having gratefully accepted the invitation that had gotten him out of the chellé for a few hours, Tau assisted him with the cloak Sunna brought. The pair had eyed each other without speaking since their introduction, as though they believed they should know one another, but any recognition was unspoken. Sunna, as was his way, remained silent.

To Tau's statement, however, he nodded in agreement.

The walk through the silent Alberni streets beneath a cloudy, starless sky was joined by a gaggle of townsfolk on their way to attend the Gathering. Their company prevented small talk, prevented Kavan from saying what he wanted to say. Instead, he politely answered the curious questions of his people, nodded at Sheriff Groff as he and his father, the original sheriff, passed on slow patrol from the city center to the docks, and half-listened to his sons' muted dialogue behind him.

He knew they were discussing him. Discussing what came next. Discussing what they might need to tell others, the family in Bhryell, Ártur, when he returned from Neth, when, after the night passed, Kavan left Enesfel to confront the offenses at St. Kóráhm's shrine.

Ártur would take his departure harder than anyone.

Kavan would have to reach out to his cousin when he could safely do so. He did not wish to abandon the healer the way he had once felt that Ártur had abandoned him.

They paused as St. Kóráhm's gates opened to allow the group to enter, and then again once in the courtyard with the gate closing behind them. Raenár left them to begin making his rounds of the chellé's night security. Tau and Sunna escorted the inebriated Kjell into the building, and once the congregants continued past, Khwílen paused to clasp the bard's hands.

"Your soul burdens you," he said heavily. "I wish I could take that from you…but I do not think it is my burden to bear." Any person chosen to endure the rósádhá was one saddled with a holy purpose. As strong in his faith as Khwílen was, he knew he was not that man. He had noted the burden in Kavan's eyes all evening. He wished he had the words to say that could help, words that were not trite platitudes.

"Your burden, as is Raenár's, is to be vigilant and keep these people safe. I know St. Kóráhm's is your home, but it is just buildings. I don't want you to die for a set of buildings."

"St. Kóráhm's is an ideal, a calling, not a collection of buildings," Khwílen replied warmly. "Those are things worth dying for, but…" He cut off Kavan's protest before the words were spoken, "I will pray for you…and I will do my best to get everyone to safety if it is necessary, to keep the ideal alive."

"It will be." Dhóri embraced him to interrupt the melancholic turn of conversation, careful to mask his thoughts so that they would not hinder his father's duty. Kavan returned his son's embrace and said, "Be vigilant as well, átaelás mai…" he looked at Sóbhán over Dhóri's shoulder and added, "Both of you. Be strong for each other…and for your brother."

"We'll see you soon," Dhóri whispered before releasing him.

Sóbhán took his place, his hug made awkward by the crutch. "We'll be waiting to hear about Kílyn…and to know what we must do to restore it."

"Kílyn?" That news appeared to lift some of the weight from Khwílen as his shoulders straightened and the midnight bell tolled. It seemed he missed the comment about restoration as he added, "I must go, but please, tell me about your visit when you return." He had yet to visit St. Kóráhm's shrine despite his years of service and the intention to do so. "Come, Dhóri…Sóbhán…join us in prayer. You are likewise welcome, Lord Kaas."

"Perhaps…I'll consider it." Zerio remained with Kavan, the only one to do so, until they were alone in the courtyard.

"I've been thinking…"

Kavan side-eyed the slender man and then resumed watching his sons until they entered the building, waiting for Zerio to continue.

"Parity delivered of Relzá's hollys' yawn…the key from the mine…Zythán's sturmyrá…"

"You think it is meant to level the field…make us equals?" While Kavan was beginning to understand how the sturmyrá enhanced the strengths of his gifts and the power behind them, it had not occurred to him that it might somehow make him and Bhás equals.

Zerio shrugged. "You speak as if she is your superior…but every strength has a weakness. I do not know if Zythán ever knew her, knew of her, perhaps foresaw her rise…but maybe the sturmyrá was created to counter someone like her…to be used by someone like you."

"I'm not a prophecy…"

Zerio shrugged off the retort because they both understood that, regardless of Kavan's protests, Kavan knew it was true.

Or feared it was.

Having clung to that prophecy for all his years as Vants, meeting the man whom he believed was destined to fulfill at least part of it, Zerio had grown to resent the burden of prophecy in a way he had never expected he would. Whatever lay ahead for the bard, Zerio did not want his friend to suffer for the sake of an ancient prophet's words.

"St. Kóráhm's will remain in good hands; I swear that much to you. I will do everything I can to protect your sons until you return to do so. Is there anything I can do for you now?"

Hearing the emotion behind the question and regretting that he could not give Zerio what he wanted, Kavan clasped the other man's hands. "I am going to pray; you cannot help me. Beseech k'Ádhá to see us all safely through what is to come…and ask Kóráhm, if you will, to stay with me."

Zerio embraced him for the first time, a peculiar display of emotion from a man who most often avoided physical contact with most people, and murmured, "I do not know if he will hear my prayers, but I will do my utmost to be heard."

They walked to the chellé door, where Zerio entered the Gathering Hall without looking back, and Kavan went instead to the cemetery garden alone. He paused at Jermyn's grave, said a prayer for the man's wise guidance and for some of the peace the k'gdhededhá had found in that last moment of torture as he passed out of life. Jermyn's voice was silent in his head, the whispers of it faded by the passage of time, though the memory of his face was as vivid as ever. Not finding what he sought there, he sat once more at Wortham's side, leaning against his stone marker the way he had once leaned into his dearest friend's embrace. There had been many he had loved during the long years of his life, but no one had ever held his heart the way Wortham had.

Only Raebhá…but she was different.

No one had ever replaced what Wortham had been to him.

There were no words, only a torrent of emotion as Kavan closed his eyes and sank into the memory of Wortham's unwavering support.

Coward. Not a man.

Kavan blinked, or thought he did, but the speaker's face would not come into focus where she appeared, looming over him as she once had. Diona's face was different, not young and wrathful but stern and demanding in a different way. Shades surrounded him within the visage of Rhidam's Great Hall, faces fading in and out of shadow, but they were a host he knew well, people whose company he had not shared in a very long time.

Only a coward would risk my grandson's life when he could stop it.

Only a monster would condemn a man to seek death on behalf of someone else. Hasn't he given enough?

Muir's voice did little to ease the sting of his sister's words.

So much, added Owain.

Everything. You have given us everything, Kavan. I would not blame you for putting down your burden and saying no more…but I beseech you…heal Enesfel one more time…if you can.

Arlan.

There was wisdom in Arlan's words, the sort of wisdom that Kavan believed must come to a soul when it passed the bonds of mortality into the eternal, universal energy of always.

Would he gain that same wisdom when his time came?

Arlan's hand brushed over his, but it was the echo of Owain's hiding voice that came back to him next.

You already do.

Few have more, Orryn reminded him in the chastising, affectionate tone she once used to make him see the truth about himself. *You see your path. You know, as you have always known, what must be done.*

For others, he countered bitterly. What about for myself?

His name echoed from far away, a wind-whisper born on the pulse of the sea, a word on repeat that reminded him that his path was not merely for the sake of unnamed others.

It was for his family, and thus, for himself.

He could not shoulder the guilt of inaction. That was not who he was. He had been inactive long enough, and his inability to act had cost his sons too much already. It had nothing to do with the innate willingness to suffer on behalf of others that had long garnered so much praise. This was about knowing what was right.

This was about following a path he had suspected since childhood would be his to follow. He had been blessed with power. He had been blessed with talent and skill. He had been blessed with the drive to know more, to do more, to be more. This was something that only someone of his ability…and his blood connection to Kóráhm, could undertake.

A wrong that only his blood could undo.

"I'm afraid."

The bear-like arms he felt around him made him sob and weep, and he clung to them, desperate that they never let him go. *I know you are,* Wortham said, the first time Kavan had heard his voice since his passing. *Any man would be. I'd do this for you if I could, be with you if I can; it is not fair that I was taken from you too soon, but Rhyrdan will get you through this. He will be what I cannot.*

Kavan could smell him, the musky, earthy scent that was always Wortham's. He could feel the brush of his beard against his skin, his breath, and his heartbeat. "Rhyrdan helps…but he is not you…"

He is what you need. As are the others. Let them help as I would, if I was there.

"Don't…stay with me, Wortham…"

He glanced frantically around the stone-walled room, picking out each person's face. Gabrielle, who had not spoken, but who embraced him with tender affection. Wace and Merrek, Hagan and Donal, men with belief in their eyes that he would do what must be done just as they had. And Bhydáni Tíbhyan, not a physical or visible shape but the sense of him that had supported Kavan in everything he had ever done or tried to do since he had been a little boy learning to master more power than any other Elyri sage had known. The host made an embracing, misty wall of emotive support that slowly reinforced his belief in his own strengths.

Only one person was conspicuously missing.

Kóráhm, it seemed, was unwilling to break into this place of dreams. Or perhaps he was unable to.

So many around him, their company gradually fading once each had spoken their part and accepted his acknowledgment of their presence. He did not want to let them go.

He did not want to be alone. Not tonight.

"All of you…stay…tonight and…"

Tonight and always. Wortham's rumble filled Kavan to his core so that his heart trembled with it. *Always here, Kavan. We will never leave you.*

The words were spoken with such love and devotion, such affection and longing for what had been, that again, Kavan wept.

❧Chapter 48❧

"How dare she!"

It was no surprise to Olaric that his father's fury was not directed at General Waller but rather at the woman who had promised an army, promised success. Being awakened with the news before the sun peeped over the sea's edge did not help lighten the king's mood. The Lachlan army should never have gotten beyond the Kelari River. They should have been held there and slowly strangled until there was none left to cross into Upper Neth. Fraen, believing in the might of his general and his forces, was convinced that, with enough men, Neth should have held at Kelari, but without being on the front line, he had no idea how many men fought on either side, or where his forces had been positioned.

Waller had certainly done his best. Withdrawing to protect Glevum after the blow at Gorea was strategically wise, but the king would have preferred if his general had stayed at Gorea, whittled Enesfel down, kept them from pushing north and taking the heads of the Lachlan king and whoever flew the de Corrmick banner.

Waller must have his reasons. Even the choice to protect Neth's ruling king was, to Fraen, good enough.

"Captain! Get word to the western front…to the north…I want every fighting man brought in…"

"Sire, they'll never get here in time," the captain stammered, a young face Olaric did not recognize, who must have been handed a field promotion after his predecessor was killed in battle.

Fraen lurched from his chair, thrust a pointing finger at the door, and bellowed, "Not if you dally here arguing. And you," he pointed at Captain Sparding, "Put the word out, everyone who can do so is called to arms…"

"The women? The Inzigaen?" Sparding asked with a sickly, squeaking voice, avoiding shifting his gaze toward Olaric to ascertain what the younger Fraen was thinking.

Fraen cinched the belt of his robe tight enough to make him grimace as he snapped, "Them too! The mercenaries. Everyone! Anyone who can hold a weapon is to be sent to the south side of the city. If Lachlan's pitiful force dares to come this far, we shall show them the might of our masses."

The first captain and the handful of soldiers who had entered the throne room with him scurried away like rats fleeing a cat. Sparding followed at a more dignified pace, glad to turn his pallid face away before the king could question his thoughts, while those servants already in attendance to the king stood rigid and silent, awaiting what most assumed would be unpleasant orders. Olaric stood beside the throne, his arms clasped behind him, fists clenched, waiting for the sounds of retreating footsteps to bleed away before asking, "Shall I join them?"

"I want you here," Fraen grunted. "Safest place to be."

Olaric frowned. He needed to speak with Sparding. With Marta. He needed to prepare Inness for what must come next. He could not do so if he was trapped inside the castle when, if, Enesfel's army came. "Should I do my part to secure Glevum?"

"You'll do your part by protecting the throne. Here. With me." He marched down the short steps from the throne platform, fury evident in his posture and steps, and Olaric decided to follow instead of remaining behind.

"I must see to Kes and the girls. They cannot…if Glevum is breached…"

"She won't be. They'll never reach Glevum. Our line will hold."

His string of commands to guards they passed belied that utter confidence. Olaric chose not to debate the obvious folly and the repeated contradictions. "But if she is?"

Guards at the throne room entry pulled the doors open; Fraen stopped when he reached them long enough to look at his son who looked to be having a difficult time keeping up with the king's determined pace.

"Secure your home and bring your wife and children here," he relented as though the concession was an annoyance and distraction from other matters he preferred to think about. Female heirs were better than no heirs, could be married off for royal gain. It made sense to protect them.

"I will return as soon as I can."

He did not say when that would be. His father, marching left down the corridor towards the war room, did not look back or acknowledge his words.

ᕤ*ᕤ

ᕤ592ᕤ

St. Kóráhm's shrine bore the sooty, blackened evidence of attempts to burn the stone structure down, and the air around it was heavy with the stench of smoke, blood, and decaying flesh that Kavan and those with him could smell long before they reached the base of the hillock on the outskirts of Kílyn. At this early hour before the waking of the city, while the moon hung low on the horizon and the sky twinkled with winking stars, there were no sounds of combat as the citizens of the city and the mercenaries defending her had pushed the invaders back to the galleys that remained unmoving off the coast. balo Ruy had chosen not to engage in a naval battle but rather focused on protecting the shore, discouraging the invaders from making landfall again, while the living tended to the injured and the dead. Kavan did not see anyone as he trekked from the náós gate to the shrine, but he knew they were there. Had been there.

He had Seen it.

He could feel it.

After trudging up the hill, through bloody, gouged soil and grass, hoisting the hem of the white robe he had not worn in many years so that it did not become stained, he set his pack at the base of the shrine and placed his hands flat upon the cool stone.

The three men behind him had never seen Kavan adorned in the white robes of his early life. They did not understand what it meant to him to wear it now, nor did they ask. Each assumed the robe had a ritual purpose, and Kavan was satisfied to let them think it.

In some ways, they were right.

St. Kóráhm's monument had not yet fallen. Whatever he had seen and felt before, there was still time to protect it.

"I don't like it here," muttered Rhyrdan, setting his pack beside Kavan's. Sunna and Níkóá, scanning the horizon around them, did likewise. "It doesn't feel right."

"The land is desecrated," Sunna murmured. "It is weeping." He placed both hands on the shrine as if in worship or with the expectation of feeling something. He bowed his head, his lips moved silently, and then he stepped away. His neutral expression did not change.

Hearing nothing but the distant sea and the voices at its edge that drifted inland on the salt breeze, Níkóá grunted, "What would you have us do? Pray with you? Stand watch? Clear away the dead?" Most of the bodies appeared to have been removed, but here and there, a handful remained.

He was not regent here. From the moment the three found the bard spreadeagled on the dew-damp earth at Wortham Delamo's grave before the rising of the sun, when the residents of the chellé slept and his sons were not awake to see them off, Níkóá deferred to Kavan's authority. They waited for him while he changed his clothes and accepted his leadership as they stepped into the Gate and accompanied him to Kílyn.

"Keep watch, if you will. She will come for me…be vigilant, but do not engage when she does." The final instruction was directed specifically at Sunna and Rhyrdan, both eager to end her reign of torment.

"Aye," Sunna said reluctantly.

Rhyrdan did not speak, but he did nod his head.

Kavan knelt at the foot of the shrine, took the sturmyrá from his bag, and inserted the key into it. A burst of light and power lit the hilltop and raced in pulses through his arms and into his core. The half-moon pendant, the crystal shard, St. Kóráhm's cross, and Gaed's crest warmed against his chest as his breath was sucked from his lungs.

His eyes closed. He focused on the power, on the words of every prayer and lamentation he had memorized, penned by Kóráhm's hand. He had not seen the saint in weeks.

If he would ever see him again, it would be in this place.

Kóráhm would tell him what to do. If he knew. Or else he would come to him and commiserate with him one more time over the perceived failings and follies of men.

When Bhás came for him, those with him would surely die if they tried to come between her and her target.

Anyone else approaching St. Kóráhm's shrine with nefarious intent, however, was fair game.

∾*∾

Together with his daughters and Kes, everything of value they possessed, anything that might lead someone to the Vants, was taken into the secret basement that the children had never known existed. The girls had questions, but Olaric did not take the time to answer them as he kept his family focused on the hasty preparations that needed to be complete before Enesfel's army reached Glevum.

Olaric had warned his neighbors and others he passed on the street, wanting them to be prepared, warning them of the king's demand that anyone who could fight was now required to. If he could save even one life with his warning, the effort would be worth it, though he did not feel one life would be enough.

"But Father," whined the youngest, bleary-eyed from having been roused from her sleep and grumpy from having been forced to work so hard when she would rather be in bed, when the last collection of food was stacked beside a warming bowl Kes used to make balms and teas for her patients. "Why don't you stay with us? Why must we…?"

"In battle, men won't care which side people are on," he muttered, lifting the flour sack from his shoulder and giving it to Kes.

"If they come," Kes added, her voice softer in the hope of reducing the children's fears, "it is as likely to be the king's men as anyone else. They may press us to fight. We should stay here, where no one will find us."

With her face cupped between his hands, Olaric kissed the girl's forehead and then did the same to the others while keeping his gaze on Kes. "Once the door is closed, no one except another…like me…will know it is here. You will stay here until I, or one of them, comes for you. As long as you do, you will be safe."

He had given Kes a knife and a sword to defend their family, in case he was wrong, in case someone else did find the Vants' sanctuary that had remained hidden from outsiders for centuries. If it came to it, Kes knew what she would have to do.

Olaric would not leave his daughters with any trace of fear that they might be discovered, however. He wanted them to believe, in their youthful anxiety, that their parents would keep them safe.

"Mother will tell you about this place while I am gone, but you must swear you will never speak of it to another soul if she does." Whether Kes told them the truth about this place and the Vants would be up to her.

"We swear, Father," the oldest said earnestly, her young face solemn and stoic as she tried to appear brave.

Olaric nodded, smiled, and then stepped back to embrace Kes again, pressing kisses to her cheeks and mouth. "Keep them safe," he whispered. "I will return as soon as I can."

It was either security here in the Vants' sanctuary or more dubious safety in the castle.

He believed his family was safer here than under his father's threatening eye.

"Will it be over then?" Kes said against his ear.

"I hope so," he replied before climbing the steps. He looked at each of them, blew kisses and offered smiles, and then masked the hidden door behind him, sealing them in.

By k'Ádhá, he hoped so.

❧*❧

Most of the ships had left their stations on the east side of the island and Pháne, leaving only three to protect the seaward shore and alert Káliel should further threats approach. The remaining four circled north or south to protect the beleaguered ports of Jaffe and Mara Qin from the assaults of galleys content to bombard them without trying to come ashore.

Harried by the island defenses and the ships poking at their flanks, the galleys' supply of arrows and other ranged defenses dwindled, but they refused to move, perhaps out of fear of the barricading ships behind them, perhaps considering another land assault, perhaps awaiting some other purpose or order.

The possibility of ramming them, sinking them, was being discussed. As pacifists, as strangers to war, most of the Káliel sailors were hesitant to act against an enemy that no longer acted like an enemy. Unable to decide a course of action, they waited.

During the night, under the cover of darkness, the galleys began to move again. Not north away from Jaffe or south away from Mara Qin, but towards the main island. Their direction was enough to prompt ships from both ports to follow.

Piran saw them on the horizon, island banners bearing down on the foreign galleys that had, as if in a squeezing manner, begun to push their compatriots and the Káliel ships behind them toward the docks. The ongoing effort to produce additional arrows, to stock the ballista and catapults balo Ruy had requested, gave the soldiers lining the shore hope that the ships would stay far enough out to sea rather than risk being struck…and striking those on land in return.

It would not last. The ships moved closer to be met with ramming speeds by the Hatu ships Ruy commanded. The island ships at sea took the cue and unfurled their sails to allow the wind to enable them to do the same.

Some of the galleys turned to meet those threats, their great oars slapping the water and straining in their riggings and oarlocks. Others continued their path to shore.

Piran could not hold them at bay. They would reach the shore.

It would take every person on Káliel to hold them at the dock.

❧*❧

Having tried each of her usual haunts, unable to find any member of the Association willing to speak to him, willing to divulge her location

❧*596*❧

though promising to take his request to her, it was chance that Olaric crossed paths with the scowling, haggard-looking Captain Sparding directing a large group of men and boys in an assortment of directions despite the wailing of women clinging to them and begging them not to go. It was either the men and boys, Sparding explained, or it was all of them.

The lieutenants beneath him led each group away until only Sparding and the wailing women remained.

No one paid Olaric, called prince by some since his first appearance at the imposter-king's side, though most did not recognize him as anything more than the apothecary's husband, any attention as he pushed to where Sparding stood. They might tolerate him, but his loyalties were suspect.

"It's time."

Sparding glanced at him as he picked up the writ he had dropped. "You think I can…?"

"If Lachlan gets this far, he's going to bar the gates." They had already discussed what needed to be done, what part each would play. Sparding, as Captain of the Guard, would already be inside. "I'll bring her, but you must get her in place, get her secure. Can you do that?"

Sparding nodded.

"You seen Marta?"

He blanched, an odd look that Olaric missed as shouts arose where a woman fought to extract her young son from the line of conscripts, only to be repeatedly struck by one of the escorting soldiers. They were not strong blows, not enough to force her back, as though the soldier was reluctant to harm the frightened woman, but the nearest lieutenant struck her across the face, knocked her to the street, and yanked the boy out of her grasp.

"If you do, tell her I'm keeping my promise. I'm letting her know," Olaric called after him as he marched toward the chaos to reprimand the too-violent lieutenant for the unnecessary use of force.

"I will," Sparding called over his shoulder.

❧*❧

She was nearer now than she had been, nearer in a place he had not believed she would go. It was as if his prayerful beseeching songs of voice and harp drew some of the faithful from their homes to the shrine that had stood centuries longer than any of them had lived, was enough to pique her interest and summon her to where he knelt.

Those braving the dead, the old, the sick, the injured, those who could not fight, who continued to pick at the shore like a scab, took the White

Bard's presence at the shrine as an omen of what was needed to defeat their enemies. It offered them a chance to fight with prayer and supplication in the hopes that the Saint, the Intercessor, and k'Ádhá would save them from another invasion.

Hatu had been at peace since the treaty won by the late Guthrie McHador. The return of war, this time from the sea, was from an enemy most did not know how to fight.

Kavan understood their fear.

If Bhás showed herself, if she emerged from the shadows where he could feel her lurking, he did not know how those around him would fight against her either.

Standing equidistance apart on the north, east, and west sides of the hillock, far enough from Kavan to serve as a barrier if he was attacked by the sea invaders yet near enough to reach him if he needed immediate help, Rhyrdan glanced at both Sunna and Níkóá with a scowling nod, his sword between his hands with its point upon the ground and the waji on his hip. The growing crowd concerned him, as there was no way to screen them for enemy infiltrators. If the fighting at sea moved inland and reached them here, there was no way the three of them could protect against so many.

But they each agreed. If it came to that, they would die trying.

Rhyrdan nodded again once the others acknowledged him and then left his post to pick through the growing throng and kneel at Kavan's side.

"My lord…it is not safe here."

Wondering if he felt Bhás' proximity too, the interruption prompted Kavan to pause his song to rest the red kestrel harp against his thighs and drink from the water skin Rhyrdan provided. He had left the black harp behind to protect it, left it for Ágdhállán, but either the boy or Rhyrdan had seen fit to pack the red kestrel in its place. He feared for the instrument's safety, but he was relieved to have it as he offered music to Ethenae at the foot of his patron's desecrated shrine.

Not destroyed as he had Seen, but that did not mean it would stand.

"Take your son and go to Raebhá; you should be as far from this place as you can. You should not be here when it falls…"

Bhás' presence flared around Kavan, carrying a hint of laughter on the air that it seemed only he could hear, reminding him why, despite the temptation of Rhyrdan's words, he knew he must not seek refuge in Dhóbhaen. "I cannot." He turned his face toward Rhyrdan, keenly aware of the shadow of his father's face that hung over the young man dressed in Wortham's armor and carrying his father's sword. Movement in the crowd startled him before he spoke again, freezing his face in a look of fear. He squeezed Rhyrdan's hand.

"She is here."

Rhyrdan twisted to look in the direction Kavan stared. For a moment, he thought he saw her too, the long black hair, the angular features. He scrambled to his feet, intending to confront the visage, but the bard held him back and by the time he was upright, the woman, if it was indeed Bhás, was no longer visible.

Given the dark bronze and black features of the natives of Hatu, such a figure could have been anyone.

"You think to confront her here." Rhyrdan's expression darkened, and his lips drooped in an unhappy frown. Protecting the shrine was one thing. Confronting the unknowable power that was Bhás was something else.

"It may come to that," Kavan admitted solemnly, adjusting the position of the sturmyrá between his knees, the heat of its glow and the steady ebb and flow of power between it and himself offering a sense of calm he could not capture.

"Then we should send these people away. There is no need for them to be caught in…"

"No. For now…they may stay." Their company was reassuring, their faith in him and their love and adoration bolstering his Faith and fortitude. They were the shield he needed until he was ready. He believed they were the only reason Bhás had not yet come for him.

Unless she was afraid to approach the shrine. Unless she was waiting for something he could not see or sense. Unless she was waiting for his weakness or complacency or some sign he knew nothing about.

He wanted people here. They made him feel safe, even if he was not.

He let go of Rhyrdan's hand. The younger man squeezed his shoulder and rubbed his thumb over the exposed skin of Kavan's neck. "You should eat something at least," he muttered lamely.

"Soon," Kavan agreed as he pressed his cheek against that hand.

Now, he needed to pray. He needed the záryph who had not yet come.

He needed to be with Kóráhm one more time.

❧*❧

The first galley, a gaping hole in her hull letting in water that men were trying desperately to scoop over the side, struck the longest dock with a lurching jolt. Some of the men racing down her length to meet it were thrown off their feet. Others pounded forward to cut off the men streaming from the galley with weapons drawn. The ship drifted, pushed by the current, until it foundered against Káliel's rocky coast. Those men trying to bail the water abandoned their efforts and ship and leaped onto the shore.

Piran and his guardsmen met them there.

Cut down by swords, fishing forks, spears, and the archers positioned on the rise, the galley sailors never made it past the shore or the docks.

There would be more.

Other galleys, pinched to the coast by Káliel ships and some of their own, continued their approach.

❧*❧

"Are you sure that's wise? It's our last chance to turn back…"

Even as he said the words, Lorant knew the answers he would hear from those seated around him whose experienced voices he trusted. Progress slowed by every roadblock General Waller left behind, squads of men and boys posted as sacrifices to be slaughtered or absorbed into Enesfel's ranks, felled trees or other pitfalls to deter them, they remained a half-day's march from Glevum when they had expected to reach the city's outskirts before sunset. Confident that there would be more severe conflict the closer they pressed, the choice was made to camp with the night watch doubled and the remainder of the force ordered to rest.

They were far enough from Glevum that he believed they would know if Neth's army, bolstered by its mercenaries, was approaching. Fraen would know they were here; he would prepare accordingly.

Camping here meant Enesfel lost what little surprise they might have.

"Is there a choice?" muttered Ártur, sitting at the king's fire not as advisor but to tend the strained and bruised wrist Bhetá had suffered when they encountered the largest squad of mismatched, ill-equipped soldiers yet. Having healed as much of the damage as he could before dulling the pain, he finished wrapping it with long strips of cloth to compress the swelling and steady her movement. He did not think either the pain remedies or the wrappings would last when they joined battle the following day.

"Always a choice," Bhetá countered as she flexed her wrist to test its stiffness and the level of pain.

Kaj nodded as he picked through his platter of boiled tubers and stale bread. "Doing nothing…retreating or staying here…are choices."

"Enesfel must have peace."

Lorant stared at Earé long enough to meet the woman's gaze before looking quickly away. Since Gorea, she had been at the forefront of the fight, killing, along with Bhetá, Bhríd, and Kaj, so many that the troops that followed behind met little of those short battle encounters. There had been enough, he thought bitterly, for Enesfel to leave more dead behind them.

She looked as weary as the rest, and more distracted, disconcerted, and perhaps even afraid of what awaited them, and as he had yet to see her afraid of anything, her expression concerned him.

"Is Kavan…?"

"He is doing his part."

Lorant swallowed, the effort painful enough that he choked and coughed on the lump in his throat. He heard the strain in her voice. Ártur heard it too, and stared at her with furrowed brows. She did not see it.

She was afraid for her father.

That made Lorant more anxious than before.

Jerit cleared the stale crumbs from his throat with a long drink of lukewarm ale, and after a few more swallows said, "So long as Fraen's on that throne, Neth's a threat."

"People once said that about the de Corrmicks," someone in the cluster of men seated around them muttered bitterly, his tone subtly inquiring what made Jerit or his nephew different than the de Corrmicks who came before. People's breaths caught, and eyes turned to the prince.

"It is so," Jerit agreed. "Those who came before were not to be trusted or respected. But I believe my father changed the trajectory, proved what a de Corrmick king should be…could be…and that his efforts toward change and peace can continue if given the chance."

"The prince will be a good and fair king," Lorant asserted without specifying if he meant Jerit or Henrik. "But only if Fraen is removed."

"Then we march at dawn?"

Bhetá wanted to hear the king say it. Needed to hear the order that previously would have been spoken by General Declan. Whatever the outcome, whatever the choice, the men who would fight and die in the days ahead needed to be assured their king was with them. They had to believe he had no doubts about whatever command he uttered.

Lorant exchanged a long, searching look with Jerit, whose red hair, having grown longer during these weeks away from Rhidam, shielded his eyes from contact. The king swallowed a resigned sigh. "Dawn," he agreed.

Jerit raised his eyes and nodded.

Lorant nodded back.

Live or die, succeed or fail, the choice was Lorant's alone.

But he continued to hope that, as Earé asserted, whatever Kavan was doing, he would succeed soon.

Maybe by the rise of the sun, there would be no need for battle.

❧ * ❧

The blockade of Levonne's harbor took a twist that Osveld had not expected as he ran up the watchtower steps to get a better view of the warning he had issued. More ships on the horizon, a host that Levonne's substantial city guard could not withstand, was a concern, a problem he was ill-prepared to solve. Rhidam had sent what men they could spare, and men were already collected from nearby farms and villages, but Osveld doubted they would be enough to hold the river, the city, against so many invaders.

Duke Cáner, perhaps, could have done so.

The duke was not here.

Osveld snatched the spyglass from the man on watch and studied the line of approaching ships, holding his breath, expecting the worst.

One moment passed. Two…before his breath hissed out between his teeth. These new ships were not galleys come to the enemy's aid.

They were Hatu caravels sailing beneath the Harcourt pennant.

Unless pirates had overtaken the caravels and were flying the flags as a ruse, unless the enemy had stolen Hatu ships rather than sink them, King Gamal had sent reinforcements.

Levonne might have a chance to hold their shore after all.

ᐯChapter 49ᐯ

The ebb and flow of assault attempts by the galleys at the base of Clarys' cliffs necessitated changes in the routines of Hes Dhágdhuán's services and the movements of the gdhededhá he watched move through the towering náós doors. No longer were those doors open to the public at every hour. No longer did townsfolk enter in a perpetual stream to seek prayer and guidance from the leaders of their Faith except when the doors opened for morning, noon, and evening Gatherings that continued to be performed without interruption. But there were guards at the door, Faith guards, and some from the Kyne's household who inspected those who entered for weapons that might be used to harm either congregants or the dedhá speaking behind the stone altar's protection.

To Lláhy's knowledge, the invaders had not gotten past the trade route guards or the sailors below, but that did not mean that similar attempts were not occurring in other cliffside ports, that invaders had not slipped into Elyriá unnoticed. k'gdhededhá Ylár's precautions were wise, ones Lláhy would have taken in the other man's shoes, where he should be, but those precautions made his infiltration effort a tricky thing to accomplish.

It had taken several days of watching, after slithering through Clarys' streets to judge the current situation, to gather the courage to blend into the daily crowd coming for the Gathering. Disguised behind a hood, with face and hand wrappings worn to cover a feigned disfigurement, suffering through the indignity of inspection for hidden weapons, he made it into the náós that had once been his home for the first time in decades, grateful that those at the door had not attempted to read his thoughts or his purpose. He chose to linger at the back of the crowd, to watch and listen, where his lack of participation would scarcely be noticed and where he could scan the perimeter of the room in the hopes that a plan would come to him.

Elyri did not need weapons to harm one another. If anyone wanted to harm Ylár or someone else, they could accomplish it without bloodying their hands. These invaders, however, were Teren. The Teren were the only threat the guards were looking for.

Lláhy did not believe anyone would suspect him, particularly since no one recognized him as he thought they should. The guards grew more familiar with him as he attended one Gathering after another, but they did not know him.

How dare they forget him.

Had he changed so much?

He knew these benches, these doors, and the halls beyond them. He could not enter through any of the private doors that led into holy chambers, into meeting rooms and residences, into the passages where the leaders of the Faith studied, prayed, and conducted their daily personal affairs. When the time came to act, he would have to enter and exit through the main door.

Getting to Ylár would not be easy.

But with each passing Gathering, he was more certain of the best way to accomplish his goal. He only needed the opportunity.

❧*❧

The harp had fallen silent beneath his fingers, but his song, a shifting, drifting vocalized melody without words, continued to rise and fall, to pull the residents of Kílyn to the shrine for prayer and camaraderie. In the place of prayer and song, behind Kavan's closed lids, he had fallen into a world where Sight and memory intertwined, where the night gave way to morning sun and presented him with images of forgotten wars and long-lost faces, of lazy days beside a lake, of Tíbhyan's probing, thoughtful questions and replies. Tám and Dháná at the dinner table the night Kavan was ejected from his childhood home, eight-year-old Owain clutching his head in agony before fleeing to safety. Gabrielle's lips upon his, the dream of Orynn at this very spot that resulted in the birth of his oldest biological children. Muir dying in his arms. Arlan's hand clutched as he faded. Myreth on the rooftop where they watched the Gorbesh sky together. The tapestry of Kóráhm on the oratory wall…burning, burning as the wall around him burned. The splintering of St. Kóráhm's Gate as two men stood back-to-back in combat, caught before overwhelming odds.

Then came his dark twin's lament through the putrid, acrid smell of sulfur smoke. The sharpness of breaking, crunching glass against the backdrop of roaring surf and laughter, always her laughter, cutting against his skin like a million fire-hot needles.

Heart thundering, his breath coming in short, sharp gulps, Kavan's eyes flew open and he looked abruptly behind him, certain someone had touched him, certain that someone, something, was there. No one was near enough to reach him, as the townsfolk allowed a respectful distance rather than pressing in for miracle touches that so many sought.

He thought it was her. He thought she had come for him. But he was confident, at that moment, that she was not here, that the sense of her that had taunted him since his arrival at the shrine was no longer present.

Bhás was absent, but the Sight-images of the shrine's ruin remained.

If not here, where?

Perhaps she did not intend to take his life at the spot of Kóráhm's martyrdom, giving it more power than she wanted it to have. Perhaps he would be spared death here, as he had feared was his fate.

But the lingering presence of death that replaced her was overwhelming. He might save the shrine, but there was something more to come, something hiding behind a fiery, orange-hot glare of smoke and ash waiting to part the veil and take his soul.

Not Ethenae. Not the place where Tíbhyan had gone. Somewhere darker, more terrifying, a place of torment he could not foresee.

Ágdhállán's thoughts brushed against his as, from somewhere further away, Ártur sought his assurance. Shivering, shuddering, Kavan closed his eyes and wrapped his arms around himself.

It was time to sever those connections so that those he loved would not drown in that place of darkness with him.

It was time to say farewell.

❧*❧

"I love you, sínréc."

Those words lingered in Ártur's mind, giving rise to a stream of tears that spilled down his cheeks despite his efforts to hold them back.

Something was wrong.

Kavan had called him sínréc before, but never, to the healer's recollection, had he professed his love in words.

He felt the depth of it through that brief contact, full and robust, laced with the burden of fear and remorse, regret, and some heavy, unnamed emotion which Kavan tried, but failed, to hide. The words and the sentiments came and went quickly without permitting the opportunity for Ártur to say them in return or question what Kavan was not saying.

He believed he knew what it meant, however.

He was certain he was going to die before he saw his cousin again. He was going to die, and Kavan would be unable to reach him, unable to save him or prevent it from happening as he had done many decades ago.

"kyá?" Syl clutched his hand. "What is it?"

The wagon he rode in halted. Ártur shook his head and craned it toward the front of the column, trying to see why they had stopped.

He could see the peaks of Glevum's tallest buildings in the distance. He knew what awaited them.

"I can't…"

He could not speak what he knew to his wife, to the other healers in the uncovered wagon. They could not share his fear. When the fighting began again, there would be more work to do. He would not allow the fear of death to keep him from his sworn duty. He would die a healer as he had been born and trained to be.

Death would find him, and he would be honored to face it, if afraid, secure in the comfort of knowing his beloved cousin's farewell.

A wall of people barricaded Glevum's southern boundary, where no wall rose to protect her from a force no Nethite king had ever expected to get so close. It had only happened once before when, to avoid destruction, the de Corrmick king had, instead, relinquished Neth's right of ownership of the territory south of Lake Curo.

There would be no parley this time. The land south of the lake had already been reclaimed by Enesfel's might. There was only one thing King Fraen could offer to prevent what was to come next.

Neither Lorant nor Jerit nor any of the men and women riding with them, expected Fraen to surrender the throne.

"How many?"

"Too many," Bhetá replied. Even using the spyglass kept in her saddlebag, she could not judge how thick the lines of people were, could not adequately tell how far east and west the army stretched.

"We could go around?" Jerit offered as a question.

"They're blocked east by the sea…and they'll likely move with us if we shift west." She wondered how thin she could stretch Enesfel's army and if doing so would make any difference.

"They're not approaching," noted Kaj. "Waiting us out?"

"Or reinforcements are coming." From behind, from the west, from the north. Neth still had enough land north and west of Glevum from which to draw soldiers, and any troops being held in reserve out of sight, perhaps on the north side of the city, could be waiting for a signal to trap Enesfel's army against the sea.

"So, we hold here, send out scouts, see what is waiting for us," Lorant decided, more confident in that decision than he was in leading a fight he expected to be more devastating than any thus far. "We stay alert, see what they do, while we decide what should be…"

"I might be able to…" Jerit began.

Lorant shook his head. "No." It did not matter what risk Jerit was about to suggest. They would be risks Lorant did not want to take. He needed Jerit alive. "I need you here."

Jerit nodded without disagreement. Hearing he was needed was enough to temper his rush to action.

❧*❧

There were those he could not reach, men and women of Teren blood whose thoughts were inaccessible at such a great distance without the aid of an Elyri intermediary. dedhá Tusánt would have to share his respect, admiration, and affection with Asta, Madoc, and those in Rhidam's keep he feared he would not see again, and in Alberni, dedhá Khwílen and Raenár would have to share the same with Zerio, Kjell, and Emeria, and everyone else who held to the Faith and the spreading of the truth in St. Kóráhm's or lived and had served his Alberni estate faithfully for all their lives.

Zerio and the Vants' prophecy lingered in Kavan's mind, refusing to be erased. He did not want to be the fulfillment of prophecy…and yet how many times had he already filled that role? For Zerio's sake, for the sake of Enesfel and those he loved, he hoped this time would be enough. For his own sake, he prayed that this time would be the last.

He reached out to his steadfast kinsman as Bhríd stood watch at the front edge of Enesfel's force, the man he charged with protecting Lorant, Jerit, and Henrik to the best of his ability for as long as he could and who, he hoped, could likewise protect Ágdhállán if the boy needed protecting. Forgiving him for the loss of his son's leg that Bhríd had been unable to prevent, he beseeched him to share his love with his sister and be there for Ártur, who would invariably not understand, who would blame himself for whatever past failings he could concoct to be the cause of Kavan's choices. Bhríd would support them all as he could; Kavan hoped that would suffice.

Through the feeble connection to Lorant's Elyri blood and the bond forged by a soul link between bard and Lachlan, as the king paced a twisted path amongst his men, offering encouragement and reassurance to those he led, Kavan swore that his allegiance to Arlan's heir would never waver, no matter what his upcoming path entailed. Lorant stopped on his horse to focus on that faraway voice that spoke to him in colorful, darkly muted bursts of emotion, and when the unexplained tears rushed from his eyes, Lorant hastily turned his horse, hid his face, and wiped his cheeks dry.

Kavan broke the connection with a subconscious clutching of the half-moon pendant against his chest, and wept too.

He could no longer reach Arlan, the reason for all of this, the root that had drawn him out of Elyriá and set his feet upon the path toward destiny. Loving Lorant would have to do.

His unspoken thoughts lingered with Earé, Dhóri, and Sóbhán longer than they should have, offering no instruction, no words of wisdom or admonitions, only sharing the depth of his love that needed no words to express. Of those he loved in Bhryell, he started and stopped with Bhen, leaving it to his younger kinsmen to deliver the messages gleaned from Kavan's thoughts to those there and in Clarys who would need to hear them.

When it came time to reach out to Raebhá, he kept the moment too short, a promise that soon she would be safe, a promise that his love for her and their sons was as eternal as the sun and the moon, an apology for all the ways he might have failed her, before severing the link out of fear that Bhás, whose nearness he had yet to feel again, would try one more time to reach and harm his family.

The others, she already knew about. He could only shield them by confronting her.

Cutting that final message short was also meant to prevent him from changing his mind about what he had to do.

He turned his last thoughts, as he clutched the sturmyrá between his hands and absorbed as much of its power as he could hold to strengthen the bond, was with the little boy he was abandoning to a future without a father.

Ágdhállán would grow to maturity alone, the same as Kavan had, but Kavan did not fear for him. His son had a close-knit community of siblings, extended family, and friends to support him in ways that Kavan had never had. They could give him what Kavan feared he could not. Unlike his father, Ágdhállán already knew and understood the road ahead, what Kavan faced and why, and what the consequences of following that path might be.

The knowing, the acceptance, made their final contact no easier.

Wanting to give Ágdhállán one final gift, hoping that, when the time came, Ágdhállán would share it with others, Kavan trained his eyes on the heart of St. Kóráhm's shrine and began to sing, unwritten, unplanned words pouring forth accompanied by fleeting images he did not take the time to dwell upon.

The dimming sun
draws the whispers of memory
across the death-veil.
From the gray mist, your voice cries,
a luring song
as eternity's tempest devours all.
The brightness we were
the shadow we have become.
The guardian moon collects our tears
until the plains of remembrance shrivel
parched and empty
without the river of your laughter
to give it life.
Fate has dashed us upon black stone shores
as a bottle of priceless wine cast off,
our fragrant innocence
spilled and lost.
Our hours blaze short.
Like the kestrel, we were lifted
until the fires of vengeance burned through us
and the gales of remorse and regret
pulled us into the icy sea.
We sleep assured
that Curnydhá's gates will open.
Our souls will be enfolded into joy
and our hearts will be as one again.

It did not take long for the news of the arrival of the Lachlan army on the outskirts of the city to spread, for the people of Glevum to react in fear and outrage, exaltation and excitement. Many had hidden from the forced conscription in basements and attics, behind barred doors or the reinforced walls of the town hall and the pair of long-unused archer towers that had once marked the western boundary of the city but had since been surrounded by it. Captain Sparding had not taken the time to hunt those people down before he was summoned back to the castle for its protection;

now they were left to fend for themselves. Some approached the rear of the military line to gawk at the equally massive front of men gathered under the joint banners of Lachlan and de Corrmick. As soldiers and messengers dashed through the streets to fortify Glevum against a likely assault, the chaos allowed Olaric to move unnoticed, knocking on some doors, passing by others, whistling a discordant phrase as he traveled through the gloomy, emptying streets before retreating to seek refuge in a recently formed farming commune that had thus far escaped the king's notice.

The recruiting officers had not questioned the presented charter with the king's seal upon it that exempted the community from conscription. They had accepted that the collection of farmers and herdsmen was the primary provider of food to the palace. They did not argue that, should the king be deprived of that food source when so many of the kingdom's farmers had already been pressed into military service, there would be royal retribution that none wanted to face.

No one noticed the ever-growing village of people.

By the time Olaric left it, there was not a single man left to tend the already harvested fields.

It took many cautious hours of avoiding royal patrols to make the roundabout journey, to collect other, smaller groups of men and women from Glevum and a smattering of encampments of seemingly lawless men living outside of Glevum's immediate influence, into a force several hundred strong. Vants, Association, and de Corrmick loyalists, men who had been hiding from King Fraen, existing on the Vants' promise of the return of Neth's rightful king. Olaric had spent a significant amount of time cultivating this small army, and he was pleased that they looked formidable enough to prompt the soldiers on watch at the Lachlan army's western edge to hold them at bay until the men Olaric wanted to speak to arrived.

One man, that was, and a tall, regal-looking woman, with a dozen men behind wearing the mixed tabards of Lachlan and de Corrmick.

Already off his horse, Olaric gave the animal's reins to the nearest soldier to approach the arrivals with as little threat to his demeanor and posture as possible.

"Prince Jerit?"

It had to be. The man before him was too old to be Prince Henrik and, while bearing a resemblance to the late king, he was too young to be Kjell.

Jerit studied the speaker as he, too, dismounted despite Bhetá's disapproving frown. "Do I know you?" He had been a boy the last time he was this close to Glevum. While familiar with many who had come and gone from his father's court, few of them had held the attention of a child who had little expectation of being king and even less interest in doing so.

"Olaric Fraen the Younger." He offered his hand to the hissing schnick of the woman on horseback drawing her sword. "I have no part or interest in my father's intrigues…and none in your throne, My Prince. Indeed, we are here to help you get it back if you will have us."

"I thought there were no heirs," Jerit replied, accepting the handshake with trepidation, hoping that the action would be met with equal trust and would put both Bhetá and the soldiers on both sides at ease.

"He thought me dead until my return to Glevum." Or Olaric assumed he had, since his father had made no effort to find him. "While he hopes to press me into that responsibility, I am no de Corrmick. My place is with my family, not," he snorted, "on the throne. I offer this, if it will help."

From the satchel on his hip, he presented a leather scroll tube etched with the de Corrmick trident. The rolled vellum within bore his father's crest on the green circle of wax that sealed it, a detail that made Jerit cock his head curiously as he eyed the man who had given it to him. The wax circle snapped with a pop as he broke it and quickly read its contents.

de Corrmick loyalists banded together and marching under King Kjell's authority and crest, sworn to protect their king upon his return to Neth. The king…or any agent sent in his place.

Jerit wondered if this was why his father had demanded his presence at the head of Enesfel's army.

"So many…?"

"Not all of us…but as many as I could gather on short notice. We weren't sure, when we got word of your defeat at Gorea…"

"There was no defeat," Bhetá growled.

Olaric chuckled in agreement. "It appears not. We could not be certain you would reach Glevum…but the pigeons have been sent in the hope that, now that you are here…I cannot say what others might arrive before battle is joined, but I offer you and General Declan what Neth can offer if you believe King Lorant will acccpt our assistance."

"I'm certain King Lorant will welcome you. General Declan is not available, but you will be in the capable hands of Daema Magk if you will fight with us."

Olaric smiled at the woman on the horse and bowed. "Daema."

How he would love to see his father's face if, in the end, he was defeated by a woman.

"She will see to your men if you will come with me…"

"I cannot." Olaric shook his head. When Jerit scowled, Olaric hastily continued. "My apologies, My Prince, but I have other errands to aid you from within Glevum; I must be there to see them completed. But this," he motioned to the soldier holding his horse's lead and waited for the other man to come forward, "is Geiel…"

Jerit nodded at the familiar, scar-faced man. "We have met." Not officially, as Jerit had never been told the man's name, but he had seen him in his parents' company, a trusted man who brought messages and left with others. Vants, he believed, as he had noted a camaraderie between this man, Tau, and Zerio on more than one occasion, a trusted man in a world where Kjell trusted very few. His being here, more than the scroll held in his hand, assured Jerit of the legitimacy of the loyalist army.

"Good. Then we can dispense with additional niceties. When we see each other again, I pray it will be at the gates of the keep as I open them and welcome you in." Olaric bowed, using the action to mask the sincerity of his quavering voice and the eagerness he knew shone in his eyes.

A de Corrmick had returned for Neth's throne.

With Inness' help, he felt more confident that they could remove his father from it.

❧*❧

The sensation of hands on his shoulders again, this time those of a much-loved man he had seen too little of in recent months, severed Kavan's concentration on Ágdhállán's comforting presence to exchange it for another. The new comfort lasted no more than a heartbeat before the hands clasped on his lap, wrapped around the sturmyrá, were locked into place by the searing agony of dual punctures through his wrists, before his feet were likewise held in place with an identical shooting pain, and a jolt of it in his side rocked him sideways as though he were shoved by a jostling passerby. He tried to look down, but his face would not turn away from the shrine, although, as his vision turned bloody, he could see no more than shades of yellow, orange, and crimson.

"I am sorry, átaelás mai, that I did not come sooner…"

The mournful tone of the saint's words told Kavan what he needed to know. Kóráhm had not come sooner because he had not wanted to say goodbye. He had come now because there was no other choice but to do so.

If not now, he would never come again.

Around Kavan, men and women began to gasp and loudly proclaim the bloody miracle they could see with their own eyes. Whether they saw Kóráhm there or not did not matter. They saw enough to believe.

With their cries, the blatting of a horn somewhere between Kílyn's docks and the shrine hillock at the city's edge cut the air, the only thing that could have diverted a rapture of adoration that would have been impossible to hold at bay. Shouts and screams and the clamor of weapons clashing spoke of another breach at the docks. Those around Kavan who could do so ran to the base of the hillock in the shrine's defense while Rhyrdan, Níkóá, and Sunna pushed through the shoving, frightened horde toward Kavan.

Eyes that refused to close blinked so that blood tears trickled down his white cheeks. Heart bursting with a lifetime of unwavering love for his patron, despite the occasional strains that had blossomed and withered over the years, Kavan tried to find something to say. The torment of rósádhá, however, worse now than ever before, matched only by the long-ago mutilation of his hands, refused to allow such sounds to pass from his lips.

Words formed within his head, words that only Kóráhm could hear.

You have come one last time…before I die.

'Kavan,' The mournful choking of his name was muted by the press of Kóráhm's lips on the top of the bard's head. '*I have done this…for which I am immeasurably sorry. If I could take this burden…*'

Will you be there when I…will you stay with me at the end…?

'*You will never be alone. We will see each other again, átaelás mai. I swear it to you with all my love.*'

Kóráhm's presence began to fade, bleeding into the sounds of combat that reached the base of the hillock, the invaders again determined to reach the shrine. Remembered images of the past, the assault at the place of Kóráhm's martyrdom, once again bombarded Kavan's mind's eye.

He was certain he would die here.

"We must go, my lord!" shouted Níkóá.

Follow my ring…you have what you need.

Kóráhm's voice was gone, but the sense of him remained, the press of his hands upon the top of Kavan's head.

Kavan shook his head, the action sluggish as if he had little strength in his neck. If he put Kóráhm's ring on his finger, Bhás would find him.

Perhaps that was what Kóráhm wanted.

Perhaps it was what was needed.

It was time.

"Kavan!"

Weapons clashed nearby, the metallic ring slicing through the blood-muted screams of the sick, the aged, the dying, as they pushed back against the invaders with what strength they possessed.

"My bag."

Kavan did not think he spoke aloud despite his efforts to do so, but Rhyrdan dropped down beside him and yanked the bag open, giving no argument against Kavan's request. He was bleeding still, the blood dripping onto the sturmyrá, sizzling with heat that generated a heavy pink-hued smoke. If the rósádhá demanded action, if the hosts of Ethenae asked for obedience from the miracle worker of Bhryell, Rhyrdan would willingly comply with Kavan's commands.

"Kóráhm's ring…put it on my finger…put the box between them."

A swinging sword swept overhead. The wielder had no time to cry out before his head rolled to the base of the shrine.

Sunna's waji dripped with blood.

"Put the box in his hands!" Rhyrdan shouted to Níkóá as he found the ring he had not known Kavan had and slid it onto the bard's bloody finger.

Ropes flew and slapped the stone shrine. Another and another, until one lassoed the top. A second joined it. Men pulled; men fought back.

Inside Kavan's head, Bhás' bitter laughter generated a stab of pain between his eyes.

As the ring moved into place, there was a jolt of power and Sight so bright that it turned Kavan's red vision a brilliant white for the span of a single heartbeat. Such a vivid immersion of sensory input came after, fragrances of stale sweat, hearth fire, old fish…the scent of one man he had not seen in years…joined by the tastes of salt tears and sulfur on his tongue. The man stood at a window, an all too familiar seductive pout on his lips, his black hair unbound and free around his face, and Kavan was certain he could touch Myreth again if he lifted his hand to do so. He Saw flashes that erased Myreth from sight, a small stone room, a mountain spitting fire, blinding rain, and misty smoke that belched into the cold air as fire met the sea so that he could see little else.

He knew where Myreth was.

He had what he needed. He could find him.

He knew she would be there too.

Sunna bent to pick up the red kestrel harp, accidentally dropping the waji onto Kavan's lap as he leaned one hand upon the bard's shoulder to remain steady as Níkóá closed Kavan's bloody hands around the glass sturmyrá. Rhyrdan wrapped his arms around Kavan's torso and tried to pull him to his feet, struggling against the immobilizing force of rósádhá.

Kavan followed the ring's link, followed Myreth's siren call. He screamed against the pain of pulling free of nails and bindings as Kóráhm had once done in this place.

The shrine of St. Kóráhm's fell where he had been sitting.

Kavan and those with him were gone.

Only Kóráhm and the warring forces around them remained.

❧*❧

Dhóri bolted upright.

Across the room, Bergis did likewise.

The raging of the dock klaxon split Alberni's midnight peace. The echoes of the shouts of men followed.

The klaxon fell silent.

The shouts and screams continued to grow.

Dhóri did not need to see to know what was happening.

Alberni was under attack.

❧Chapter 50❦

dedhá Bhídígís opened the door to the largest billeting room and ushered the group of men in, smiling genially to each as they trudged wearily past. Men of Faith making a pilgrimage to the site of Jermyn Tythilius' martyrdom, the oft-frequented náós of the White Bard, the seat of the Teren Faith Council, was an increasingly common thing. As war raged in the north and at sea, or so Bhídígís had heard, pilgrims coming from as far away as Hatu were no surprise. With their style of dress reminiscent of the fashion worn by the foreign soldiers King Lorant employed, they might be additional recruits who had gotten separated during the long march north.

It was too late to summon balo Essem to see to them, so for tonight, k'gdhededhá Tusánt felt obliged by their Faith to take care of their needs.

Even if the shifty gazes of a few gave Bhídígís cause for doubt.

As Tusánt pointed out, however, the man's teary-eyed prayers before the altar having been interrupted by these unexpected arrivals, those from the south of Hatu had never seen anything like the splendor of Hes á Redh. Duke Cliáth had said as much. It was no surprise that the pilgrims felt unsettled and wary in this place.

Tomorrow, they would have a warm meal, would share the Gathering with the dedhá and the people of Rhidam, and then Tusánt and Bhídígís would approach balo Essem for an in-depth discussion with their visitors.

"Thank you," said the smallest of the formidable men, the only one to speak thus far in stilted, broken Trade. "We appreciate the welcome."

"Our Faith is to serve. Take rest and be one with us in the morn."

The small man bowed, looking smaller still, and remained in that posture until Bhídígís backed out of the room. The door closed. Bhídígís looked toward the Gathering Hall, wondering if he should join Tusánt in prayer and offer him comfort in his time of obvious distress. He decided instead to honor the Elyri's wish to be left alone. If the k'dedhá wanted company, he would say so.

❧617❦

Bhídígís felt more inclined to retreat to his room and monitor the comings and goings of the pilgrims across the corridor.

❧*❧

Feet propped on the lip of the rooftop as he sipped ale and watched the unloading of a wagon on the street below, Warde Dugan was the first, perhaps only, person to make note of a dozen or so men creeping through another nearby street horizontal to the Tegid River as though they were afraid to be spotted by nefarious brigands…or the Grand High Sheriff. Not merchants, Warde mused as he dropped his feet, stood, and moved through the shadows to track their progress through Rhidam. They had no wagons, carried minimal personal belongings, and traveled too light, without horses or a wagon, to be merchants.

They might have earlier assaulted and relieved someone of those things, in which case Warde would need to investigate to be certain that this had not been a crime likely to bring the Crown down on the Association's heads. Or they might be in town to make purchases, intending to acquire the horse and wagon they lacked and whatever other commodities they could afford.

Maybe they had simply come into the city from one of the surrounding villages in search of drink and whores.

Either way, they were worth watching.

Warde was alone on his watch, and by the time he made it to the street, the group would be out of sight. But he had their trajectory and decided that following them was a job he should undertake on his own.

The unloaded wagon was clattering away by the time he stepped out of the warehouse. Men looked up as he passed, unmoving as they awaited orders, but then going about the business of organizing the commodities they had procured when he did no more than nod.

Warde turned north. His business was his own, as theirs belong to them. He did not offer, and they did not ask. If this business was something he needed to know about, he would be informed when the time was right.

As would his aunt.

❧*❧

When the alarm sounded during the Gathering earlier in the evening, the gdhededhásur of Hes Dhágdhuán and the armed men standing watch outside rushed many of the congregants out of the náós so they could protect

Clarys from the invaders who were once again attempting to breach the trade passages from the sea. Others fled to their homes, while a handful chose to remain in prayer, begging for peace and success from k'Ádhá behind the náós' locked doors.

Lláhy remaining with them was not seen as a threat.

No one noticed when he took advantage of the disorder to duck into one of the many panel-covered passages used by the dedhá and the serving staff to come and go from the Hall without entering the primary corridors used by whoever was to serve at each Gathering.

From there, there were more doors, more corridors, more rooms than he had ever counted in which he could hide.

Elyri were often creatures of habit. He doubted Ylár's habits had changed significantly in the years he had been gone. Lláhy knew his favorite rooms, or the rooms the man's father had favored, his preferred places to pray, knew what offices he was inclined to conduct business in if not in those reserved for his station.

Lláhy had only to pick one, verify that his memory was accurate, and find the time to strike.

That, he had already decided, would depend on what sort of statement he chose to make to the Faith that had abandoned him to the cruelties of the hostile, secular world.

❧*❧

The need to escape the anarchy at Kóráhm's shrine and the jarring agony of metal spikes ripping free from his wrists and feet created a frenetic swirl of power that broke his hold on where he wanted to be and instead took him to the first recognizable destination his screaming mind was able to identify and connect to. When the four men could breathe again, when the world solidified around them, greeting them with a blast of hot, arid wind, the waji slid from Kavan's lap and clattered onto the black, glassy material at their feet. Having been bent over Kavan at the moment of transport, both Sunna and Níkóá stumbled, one backward as he released the sturmyrá, the other forward so that his weight pitched the bard and Rhyrdan, who still had his arms around Kavan's torso, to the ground as well. Kavan's exclamation of unexpected additional pain prompted Sunna to release the harp and roll away. Rhyrdan rolled in the other direction.

For several minutes they stared, Níkóá and Sunna at the multitude of stars above them, and Rhyrdan at the smooth, hard surface below. He groaned as he sat and looked around at the fruitless fig trees and the eroding remains of whatever temple had once stood here, already knowing where they were. He and Kavan had been here before. Nothing had changed.

The night before Wace Elotti had been killed.

"Shin drua," Sunna groaned as he sat up.

Rhyrdan did not know what the words meant, but from the big man's expression, he guessed Sunna had likewise been here before.

"Help me turn him over."

Kavan's hands and side continued to bleed, staining his white robe red, and Rhyrdan assumed he likewise bled inside of his boots. Blood tears seeped from his eyes, from his nose and mouth, but his hands clutched the undamaged glass box as the power it shared with him illuminated the night.

"There's a well," Níkóá said, pointing at a nearby stone construct.

"No water in it…at least nothing clean," murmured Rhyrdan as he pulled off Kavan's boots. "Won't be of any use until it stops."

Níkóá picked up the dropped harp, examined it for damage, and placed it within Kavan's reach. If the Elyri heard them, knew they were with him, he did not indicate it. "How much can a man bleed before he…?"

Sunna shrugged. "As much as is required." Having positioned Kavan's arms in a more natural pose, leaving the sturmyrá on the bard's abdomen, Sunna retrieved the waji and shoved it through his belt without cleaning it. He strode silently to the grove of wild figs and began searching for any fruit that was good enough to eat.

"It'll kill him."

"I don't think so." It was this place, where rósádhá had happened before, before Kavan's last confrontation with Bhás, that demanded the blood that continued to flow. The memory prompted Rhyrdan to draw Kavan's arms out to his sides so the dripping crimson could quench the earth rather than continue to stain his robe, and then he sat back on his heels, watching Kavan with a pensive frown.

By the time they found Bhás, if that was where Kavan intended them to be, he feared Kavan would be too weak to do anything.

Zythán's box, however, continued to pulse with light as it absorbed power from Kavan, from the air and the ground, and fed it back into the steady rise and fall of his chest.

Trapped with the power in his head, mesmerized by the waves of it that washed over him and drained away like the surf after a storm, Kavan felt the vibration of his companions' words, but he could not hear them with his ears. He did not know what they were saying, but he knew where they were. He recognized the feel of the black glass now supporting his hands, growing slippery with blood as it continued to seep from his wounds. He knew the sensation of Kóráhm's knees supporting his head, invisible hands brushing white hair from his face, the saint's overwhelming grief that could not be assuaged by simple acts of kindness and care.

They had met here before. Kóráhm had warned him then, but Kavan had been unable, unwilling, to heed that warning.

Wace had needed him.

Or so he had believed.

Now those around him needed him too, as did those in Rhidam and Elyriá, and those fighting for stability and peace in Neth. As did those in Alberni, where the violent clanging of the harbor klaxon revealed a threat he had prayed would never come to fruition, despite every instance of the Sight warning him otherwise.

He could not go to his sons to warn or aid them. His leaden limbs would not allow him to rise, to go anywhere until his spirit was prepared. Until he was ready to submit. As his friends gathered, two sitting or kneeling in prayer while the other scanned the horizon for threats or, on a more superstitious note, the rise of the kahi hoi from the desert around them, Kavan wept and hummed within the prison of his mind until the oasis overflowed with the gathered záryph come to provide support and comfort, both to him and his patron with him.

He did not blame Kóráhm for this. He was too weary for blame.

He only wanted the pain, the fear, to end.

❧*❧

Kavan.

He did not speak the name aloud for fear she would hear him, that she would sense his nearing power as he did. He did not think she was here, in the front room where his jailors' snores bled in a muted echo beneath the door of his captivity. He did not think she was outside where the earth rumbled and quaked, not because of the stormy autumn surf but from movement below, as if great fists choked the earth and shook it for some act of treason the stony ground could not defend against.

But he knew she was near. Casting her net, dangling him like a worm or insect upon a lure, the one thing that could draw the white-skinned man and make him vulnerable.

He wanted to warn him away, beg Kavan to leave him here to rot with his prayers and the company of his Faith as his only companions. He also wanted Kavan to come and take him from this place so that he could embrace him, kiss his cheeks, hear him sing.

Unable to submit to either desire, Myreth closed his eyes, pressed his forehead against the window, and prayed forlornly one more time.

Kavan.

❧*☙

Despite Egon Groff's preparations to protect his city, knowing that this war was being fought primarily in Neth, he had misjudged the likelihood of the duke's foretold attack coming to Alberni from the sea. By the time he was roused from his bed and reached the dock, a significant portion of the invading force was pushing through the streets toward St. Kóráhm's, largely ignoring the rest of Alberni in the process. Some men splintered off at the dock from that group, distracted by shops and homes that looked to promise wealth and food better than what their journey had allowed.

He turned the corner, following a pair of men in pursuit of a startled woman, disheveled from her night's work, and ran into his father, nearly knocking the man down.

He grabbed the old man's arm. "Where'd they…?"

The elder Groff pointed to a side street where the clatter of falling debris could be heard. Egon nodded.

"Come on then."

"You go. I've got the docks." The older man would be of little use in a foot chase, but to push the invaders back out to sea with the rising sun, he considered himself strong enough, fit enough, to be of use, limping leg or not. Most of the fighting seemed to be there. He intended that no more would follow the raucous shouts that trailed toward the chellé.

Those protecting St. Kóráhm's would have to hold their own until the sheriff or his father could get there.

Egon did not nod or speak but resumed running, chasing the sounds of a woman's scream.

Kavan's woven Elyri defenses prevented the attackers' initial efforts from breaching the front and rear chellé gates, but they did not prevent arrows and spears from sailing over the walls or assailing the guards in the watchtowers, resulting in injuries and a handful of deaths by the time the sun crested the Llaethlágárá. Eventually, the mercenary army gave up their efforts to break through the wood and iron doors and opted to try to climb over them. With confiscated lumber and tools, men began constructing ladders and a battering ram, endeavors that Raenár and Tau assessed would be complete by midday or soon after, at which time the chellé's residents would be at higher risk. From the watchtower, they could see smoke rising near the docks where the heaviest sound of combat arose. Other pockets of shouting, clattering metal, and the crashing of upended street stalls reverberated throughout the city.

"Need more men," Tau grunted. "Perhaps we should send…"

"Open those gates," countered Raenár as he stepped out of the way of an archer running past toward the tower stairs, "we'll be vulnerable."

"They get those ladders up, we're vulnerable too. There's too many."

Raenár's scowl deepened. He was reluctant to admit that the chellé could be so vulnerable after the work he had done to strengthen her defenses. Without understanding what sort of protections the duke had put into place, he had believed St. Kóráhm's would be more impenetrable than this. Projectiles flying over the wall reminded him otherwise.

If he had been leading that attacking force, he, too, would have made use of the only vulnerability the chellé seemed to possess.

Maybe Kavan had not considered the possibility. He was wise and intelligent, but he was no military man. Overlooking such a weakness made sense…or perhaps what he had done was unable to provide protection there. Raenár glanced around the courtyard where people scurried about bringing arrows and stones to the archers and slingers on the wall, and those residents already pulling the injured and dead into the security of the náós. To the side of the open double doors, four young boys, awakened by the harbor alarm, told to stay inside but choosing not to, stood frozen, watching the disorder of combat, while inside, people collected the last important relics and books to take to Gorbesh with wide-eyed, slack-jawed fear.

The men and women in this place were free to choose their future, to risk their lives to protect their home. But the children should not be here.

If Kjell hoped to be king again one day, he should not be here either.

"King Kjell can take a message to Rhidam…request support…"

Tau snorted and caught a stumbling fellow with a deep purple bruise and blood across his forehead before he fell from the wall. "Never get a horse and rider through," he said as he steadied the man and released him to go his way. "They'd never make it in time…"

"We use the Gates." Asta, they believed, would be more inclined to honor a request for aid from her husband than anyone else.

Tau was less sure that the queen would hear or respect her husband's request, but unless Rhidam was likewise under attack, her fondness for Lord

Cliáth would likely prompt her to send as many men as she could. They could not afford to send any of their fighting men, but Kjell would likely accept such a duty to help if he could not be in the thick of combat. He leaned over the half-wall and whistled to Zerio in the courtyard, where the man was coordinating the placement of a swiveling catapult he had helped design and construct despite k'dedhá Khwílen's protest. When another hail of arrows flew over the walls, wounding another three men, Khwílen nodded his reluctant acceptance of the use of the siege engine as he hastened inside with an armload of sacks from the garden shed.

The catapult let fly a sack of rotting fruit as a test volley as Zerio heard the whistled summons.

Outside the wall, shouts of protest indicated that the shot had struck its target. But those targets would not remain within the range of a straight throw. Each shot was going to be a guess.

"Line up another," Zerio instructed. "I'll be back."

Those operating the catapult worked to tighten the tension for another throw, this time preparing a ball of scrap lumber spiked with nails and bound together by a string for a second test as Zerio raced up the stone stairs to where Tau and Raenár stood.

"Need your eyes up here," Tau shouted, yanking Zerio down to allow an arrow to fly over their heads.

It struck another man on the wall, and he toppled off it.

Raenár, pretending not to hear the heavy thud of the body striking the courtyard, asked, "Think you can do that?"

Without asking why, Zerio popped his head up long enough to cast a glimpse of the men collecting outside the chellé wall. He glanced at the catapult and grinned.

"I've got this." Whatever the reason for their request, being here offered the best vantage point from which to direct the siege engine to maximum effect.

Tau and Raenár ran down the stairs.

Dhóri and Bergis had just come into the courtyard to find the boys standing there in dumbfounded amazement. "You shouldn't be here!" Dhóri shouted, grabbing Ágdhállán's arm. "Go to Rhidam!"

Teary-eyed from the fading contact with his father and the unexpected smells and sounds of fighting that were more vivid than the Sight had shown him, Ágdhállán did not resist but shuffled as if walking in his sleep behind the others Bergis herded indoors.

"We want to help," complained Phaedr.

Balint, sounding much less certain, added, "We should help."

"We promised your parents you'd be safe," Bergis scolded, putting his arms around Cáym and Balint's shoulders when Phaedr sidestepped his reach. He shifted them to the side as the chellé's healers ran by.

"They'll never forgive me if anything happens to you," Dhóri agreed.

He seemed to stare at his brother, but Ágdhállán did not speak as he stopped moving. He looked dazed and pained with a frowning grimace that Dhóri recognized as a side effect of the Sight. Until the expression, the vision, passed, his brother would be unable to follow directions, but there was no time to dally and learn what the boy Saw.

A man at the catapult screamed as he pitched backward with an arrow in his shoulder. Tau, understanding the logistics of the catapult and the only man near enough to assist the launch efforts, shouted, "See to the king."

Raenár did not look back.

He heard Bergis and Dhóri's exchanges with the boys as he reached them and paused long enough to say, "I'm taking King Kjell to Rhidam. Meet me at the Gate. I'll take them."

Bergis quickened the boys' steps and steered them toward the Gate. When the other two did not move, Dhóri took both by the arms and directed them inside as well. Raenár ran up the stairs with the expectation of finding Kjell in his room.

Instead, he found the king nearly to the bottom of the stairs, his breastplate haphazardly fastened at his ribs, his helmet on his head, his sword in hand. He was unsteady, however, and when someone else pushed passed him, clipping his shoulder, he stumbled.

Raenár caught him before he fell.

Kjell growled in annoyance and yanked free from Raenár's hands.

"We need your help."

"Why do you think I'm…?"

"You must not go out there, Sire. It is not…"

"I'm no stranger to…"

"You're too valuable. I've come to take you to Rhidam."

"I will not retreat…"

"Not retreat. We need you to request men from the queen. St. Kóráhm's…Alberni…may fall if we do not have…"

Kjell froze mid-step. "So many?"

"More than enough." With so many eligible fighting men having gone to Neth with King Lorant, Alberni's resources were depleted. "We need help. The queen will heed your…"

Kjell's snort mirrored Tau's earlier one, and his sour expression remained focused on the path that would take him to the courtyard. He could not climb the steps to the watchtowers and would be of little use with a bow if he had one. So long as the gates held, there was little he could do with a sword except stand and wait.

Bringing troops from Rhidam, however, was something he could do. If Asta agreed, the men would need a leader on the race back to Alberni. That was something he could do, too. It was better than helplessly waiting for a breach of the walls.

He stopped at the bottom of the stairs to sheath his sword and pulled his helmet off. "Take me to Rhidam.

"You cannot stay here," Ágdhállán mumbled, the words directed to Dhóri without looking at him as Bergis opened the Purification Chamber curtain and ushered the other three protesting boys inside. Ágdhállán's slipped out of Cáym's reach, but the redhead chose not to pull him away from his conversation with his brother.

He, too, recognized the look on his friend's face.

"I have to take things to Gorbesh," Dhóri replied. He wondered if his brother had Seen something about his future that would happen if he remained in Alberni, but there were responsibilities he needed to attend. One task he knew he was the only one to accomplish. "As soon as it's done, I will join you. I'll take you to Gorbesh."

"I have to…"

"It's what Father wants."

Raenár hastened down the aisle with Kjell behind him, tempering his speed to the pace the elderly king could manage. Their arrival disrupted Dhóri's scolding reminder, and the captain's gentle prodding of the king into the cramped Purification Chamber prevented the other boys from sliding out. One of the residents from across the Gathering Hall desperately called, "Dhóri! Bergis! Help me!"

Bergis released the curtain when Raenár squeezed past. Dhóri kissed his brother's head. "I'll join you as soon as I can." He pushed the boy toward the chamber where Raenár reached for him. Arm appearing heavy, his movement sluggish, Ágdhállán reached back, but instead of taking Raenár's hand, his vision abruptly cleared; he backed away from the captain and ran in a different direction.

Raenár called after him, but the external echoing boom of the catapult's release and the outraged cries from outside the walls swallowed his words and reminded him of the importance of his duty. He pulled Cáym back from his attempt to follow his kinsman, and when everyone's hands completed the circle, he reached for Rhidam and took those with him through the Gate.

He would return for Ágdhállán later.

∞*∞

The charging roar from the host, a portion of those protecting Glevum from invasion, roused those of Lorant's troops who had not slept and those on watch to race into the empty field between the armies and meet them with a thundering wave of force. The glare of the rising sun in their faces hindered their defense, resulting in too many deaths despite Kaj's efforts to shift the battle in their favor. The influx of troops into Enesfel's front line meant the eventual routing of Glevum's preliminary assault when no other men from the shield wall or the city streets came forward to aid them.

Kaj held his line in the center of no man's land, surrounded by the dead they could not afford to bury. Behind him, the Lachlan army readied for the expected en masse movement of Glevum's primary army or another small-scale attack intended to whittle away the sieging force.

"We should attack," growled Bhetá beneath her breath.

"We should wait," countered Earé.

Bhetá met Lorant's gaze, questioning his wishes, expecting him to side with her.

Lorant, through the spyglass, continued to study the opposing force, looking for something he did not see. He did not notice his general's glance.

∞*∞

"We can send ships from Levonne," suggested balo Essem, his chin resting on his fists, propped by his elbows on the table between him and Enesfel's acting regent. Madoc Delamo, serving as the Captain of the Guard in Bhetá's absence, also sat with Asta, Kjell, and Essem, the two men the only ones Asta had called to this emergency meeting when Kjell's arrival was announced. Raenár had remained to report everything he knew about the attack on Alberni, the boats in the harbor, the foreign soldiers unlike any he had seen barreling through the streets intent on gaining entry to the chellé. He could not report on how the rest of Alberni's defenses were holding, but he did confess to St. Kóráhm's great need for an outside force to confront those trying to break through the gates.

By the time Asta sat to discuss strategy without promising troops, Raenár had reluctantly returned to Alberni. The besieged chellé needed every man they could get…even if that man was only him.

Kjell scowled at the closed door. He should have gone back, too, instead of loitering in Rhidam. But it had been a long time since he and Asta had worked together to solve a problem. This reminded both of more pleasant times in Glevum, a time before their world had collapsed.

Madoc doubtingly shook his head. "You'll not get past the blockade."

"We can do it…Balise and I. It is worth a try…"

"And take all of your men from Rhidam?"

"I won't need them. Ships are manned. How many days…?"

"From Levonne to Alberni? Two with a favorable wind," Madoc replied, "if you can get out of the harbor."

"Yóáná can take you to Levonne," Kjell offered, wishing now that Raenár had remained in Rhidam.

Asta frowned. Madoc frowned too. Both would prefer to keep daughter and wife as far from war as possible. With Levonne besieged, the city could be attacked at any time, just as Alberni had been. But a short trip to deliver Essem should not put the younger woman at unnecessary risk.

"Madoc, collect as many men as you can. You'll ride at dusk."

"And leave Rhidam undefended?" he scowled as Kjell offered, "I can ride with them…"

"I'll take care of that." Asta looked from Madoc to her husband's irritated face and added, "I need you here." It would take time to tap into the Association's resources, and she wanted someone in place in the keep to give commands as she did so, in case her efforts exploded in her face.

Kjell stared hard at the woman across from him. It had been a long time since she had professed a need for him. It had been a long time since they had done anything more than discuss the hypotheticals of regaining Neth's throne and argue about their only remaining son and their grandson. He did not know what she had in mind, but her statement was enough to persuade him to stay in Rhidam, where he might continue to be of use.

Not fighting in Alberni, not dying, might also mean he would see Glevum again.

She returned her attention to Madoc once convinced that Kjell would not fight her. "Cavalry, if you can…every horse you can get. The Crown will reimburse horses lost." She would hear complaints about that promise from the chancellor, but it was necessary to get reinforcements to Alberni as quickly as possible. "Take Yóáná; you'll need a healer." Despite her reluctance to send her daughter into harm's way, supplying Enesfel's troops in Alberni with an Elyri healer was the right thing to do. The people there would need Yóáná's assistance. "Get what ships you can out of Levonne's harbor, balo…and pray the wind gets you to Alberni in time to be of use. Kjell…stay. We will prepare."

❧*❧

The sounds of combat at Glevum's edge could be heard throughout the city, creating an ongoing scramble of people seeking shelter, seeking the security of loved ones, and for some, seeking the opportunity to take advantage of empty homes and shops. Some chose to run toward the bedlam of battle without considering that the king would press them into the fight, or, perhaps, with the hopes that they could fight as well. Others fled north in the hopes of getting as far from Glevum as possible in case the city fell.

Olaric could have recruited from both factions, but he had another responsibility before him that he hoped would end the siege before further combat erupted. With the families of the palace guards herded behind the protection of the palace walls, a concession he was surprised his father had allowed, it seemed the best time to sneak Inness inside too. Sparding was on watch at the gate with three Association children waiting in the shadows to pose as Olaric's daughters. With Inness disguised as his wife, both men expected they could sneak her in before the gates closed to give her the opportunity they planned for.

But there were too many people in the streets, too high a risk that someone would recognize the 'late' queen-regent, even after a decade, if they got too close.

Olaric closed the hideout door without going into the building. Inness would have to wait a little longer.

They were going to need another plan.

Olaric could only think of one.

It would be up to Sparding to agree to make it work.

❧*❧

Except for the treasures stored in the catacomb beneath St. Kóráhm's, items safe from invaders so long as the entrance remained hidden, the chellé was empty of everything of value. Only the residents remained; those unskilled with weapons gathered along the náós walls, retrieving the wounded, putting out the fires when flaming arrows struck and ignited what little flammable material remained in the courtyard, while those with any amount of skill took turns manning the walls and watchtowers to ward off the enemy. The constructed ladders had been destroyed with burning oil and torches, but not before a dozen bronze-skinned men made it to the top of the walls. Men on both sides died where they fought or fell to their deaths on either side, while a pair of lightly armored men tried to jump down to confront those manning the catapult. One rolled as he landed and came up on his feet, only to catch an arrow between his shoulder blades and fall face down on the dusty stones. The other landed in a similar fashion, only to be met with a cracking sound that resulted in his leg giving out beneath him when he tried to stand. Men tried to pin him to the ground but were met with his sword blade across their throats before he, too, fell beneath the same archer's shot.

The catapult swiveled to the left under Zerio's instruction.

The bundle of bricks was loosed.

Men outside the chellé screamed.

"We need more!" Tau shouted. There were another six mortar balls and four created from all the slag metal the people of Alberni had been able to provide before St. Kóráhm's gates were closed. As the commotion outside continued to grow, announcing the arrival of more men, neither Tau nor Zerio expected to have enough ammunition to fight off the enemy.

Soon, their store of arrows would be depleted as well.

k'Ádhá help them if reinforcements, be they the citizens of Alberni and her adjacent farms or those requested from Rhidam, failed to arrive in time.

❧ * ❧

The choice of which ships to spare, how many to leave behind, how many to send into combat, was made quickly as Osveld, balo Eytor, and balo Essem watched the silent standoff of ships in Levonne's port. With no easy way to signal the Hatu vessels further out to sea, those that sandwiched the invading galleys between them and those already stationed in the harbor, they could only direct Enesfel's ships and hope the others recognized their play and responded accordingly.

Every man in Levonne who could fight was called to arms, lining up along the docks to the mouth of the Tegid in case the plan failed. A single ship remained at the mouth of the river, another two hung back in the harbor. As two ships sailed east as close to the shore as they could travel, the remaining four began their approach toward the offending fleet.

A single galley, faster moving and more maneuverable than the Hatu caravels, turned toward the eastbound ships while the others pushed toward the conflict it seemed Levonne was seeking. But that single galley found itself cut off by a pair of Hatu ships waiting behind them, while the remaining ships Gamal had sent, their captains recognizing impending combat, pulled anchor and moved closer to the harbor to catch the invaders between the allied forces.

The lone galley, unable to turn as quickly as planned against the outgoing tide, rammed her nose into one of the caravels. Trapped there, the oarsmen struggled to break free, to steer the galley in reverse, but their success came only after a stream of Hatu sailors and soldiers spilled over the damaged caravel's side and onto the galley's deck. The sister caravel slid behind the galley, blocking her easiest path of retreat, and after lashing off to her by well-aimed mooring lines, men from the second caravel swarmed the galley from the rear.

Further to the east, the allied fleets engaged the trapped galleys.

The pair of ships following the coast, pulled along by the retreating tide, slipped past the blockade and sailed east, unimpeded, listening to the cries of men in combat behind them.

They should have stayed. Men were dying on their behalf.

Not theirs, thought Essem with a frown, deferring the steerage to a Levonne captain who knew this sea and coast better than he did. The men they left were dying for Alberni.

They died for k'ílshwythnec. They died for the White Bard.

Soon, he and those with him would engage in a fight of their own.

Those left here would be unable to assist them.

❧*❧

The rósádhá ceased flowing. Hoarse from endless singing during his hours in Kílyn, his throat parched despite the water Níkóá periodically poured into his mouth, Kavan only knew that the flow had stopped when he recognized that Rhyrdan's effort to bathe his skin, wasting what little water they had brought with them, had ceased. Someone, Sunna he deduced from the sound of the man's footsteps on the smooth black glass, without being able to see beyond the crimson sheen over his eyes that blinded him to the world, covered him with a cloak, intending to either keep him warm against the desert's night chill or protect him from the burn of the sun.

Kóráhm's ring on his hand felt heavy, and though he tried to lift it, to reach for Rhyrdan's hand and stay his tender care, he could not. The sense of Myreth strengthened as Kavan's senses returned, and a thread of power stretched north and west like a map he was too weak to follow. On his chest, now covered by that cloak, the heat of the sturmyrá sizzled and snapped like trapped lightning, its burning not yet unpleasant as the warmth converted into power that continued to seep beneath his skin, into the box, and back again, healing the agony of this latest miracle, restoring, albeit too slowly for Kavan's liking, him to full health, strength, and power.

Day or night, he wondered. How much time had passed?

He did not know. What he did know was that he had lost the link with his son that had sustained him…that corporeal sense of both Kóráhm and the záryph were gone, leaving only Kóráhm's spiritual presence in their wake…and that, in Alberni, St. Kóráhm's was under attack.

There was nothing Kavan could do to aid them except pray…

…and cry crimson tears that trickled into the hair at his temples and fed power beneath him with power of his own.

❧Chapter 51☙

Sheriff Groff could not chase every offending invader that rampaged through Alberni's streets, nor did he have men enough to stop them all as they pillaged through one home or storefront after another, taking what they wanted, destroying much of the rest, cutting down many who got in their way, and when met with fierce enough resistance, being cut down by the bravery and determination of the townsfolk. A ring of city residents had collected to protect St. Maicel's, but it had not been enough to prevent the theft, desecration, and destruction of much of its contents nor the death of the gdhededhá who served there. Egon arrived too late to help, and instead of picking through the dead left in the wake of invading chaos, he followed its path in the direction of the duke's manor.

Most of those he and his team followed turned to join their comrades in assaulting St, Kóráhm's. A dozen or so more continued toward the protected manor gates. They banged, they pulled, they tried to scurry over walls much shorter than those of the chellé. They were met with locks they could not break, a puzzle Egon did not take time to consider, and the ferocity of the duke's staff and the farmers who toiled in his fields. By the time Egon and his brigade arrived, a dozen assailants lay in their own blood scattered along the manor wall.

Inside the walls, Laney nodded to the sheriff as he kicked one man's severed hand away from the iron gate where it had caught, and Emeria wiped her bloody hands on her apron. Egon nodded back. He was not surprised to see that she had joined the fight.

She was the daughter of Wortham Delamo after all.

"Help the others," she cried. "We can handle this."

For now, that appeared to be true. But Egon did not doubt that more invaders would come. If Duke Cliath was the target, he and his chellé, eventually his home would again fall under attack.

By then, he hoped one of the duke's famously rumored miracles would burst forth and save them.

He did not believe there were enough men in Alberni for the city to save itself.

ও*ও

Men were pulled onto the beach as they bobbed close enough to be caught in nets or by poles and hands. Men who had fallen into the sea when galleys and caravels alike were dragged to the bottom, burnt, gored, with broken masts and splintered sides. Men from Hatu, natives of Levonne. Men from beyond Hatu's southern borders and the unidentified strangers who had come to wage war on Enesfel. The receding tide had taken many of the dead with it, had taken others who, injured and exhausted, were unable to fight the watery pull. It would take hours to identify and bury them all, but, to Osveld's delight, the ship guarding the Tegid remained untouched and the two bound for Alberni had made it away unscathed.

He had few ships at his disposal now, and few to block the retreat if the remaining invaders chose to flee. Instead, the three remaining galleys, damaged but seaworthy, bobbed silent as the crews of the Hatu ships beyond them tended their wounded and attempted repairs. He sent small skiffs of lumber and tools, food and water, to provide aid to the allied ships they could reach so that they, too, could affect repairs.

One more encounter and Osveld suspected Levonne would be overrun, burnt under the assault, and the harbor would be strewn with sunken relics and the bodies of the dead the sea claimed…unless the messenger sent to Rhidam brought enough reinforcements to hold back the threat.

ও*ও

The movement of a portion of Enesfel's army under the command of Geiel Vagn and one of Lorant's more experienced captains gave the appearance of retreat, but from his third-story chamber in the castle, Fraen the Elder could see the trailing cloud of dust as that brigade moved east and then north as if they would encircle the city. He sent for his son to lead an intercepting force, but Captain Sparding reported no sign of the younger Fraen since having seen him ride into the midst of Glevum's army in search of General Waller.

The news was vaguely heartening, and he was satisfied that Olaric had come around to his side, that he had chosen to fight for Glevum's survival.

But it left him without a reliable officer to lead the counter assault. He wanted Sparding here, in the castle. He wanted Waller, as angry as he was at the man for bringing war to his doorstep, in place to contend with the bulk of the Lachlan army in the south.

He wanted Waller to burn that de Corrmick banner and crush every man wearing the de Corrmick crest. He wanted Prince Jerit's head on a pike. He wanted the world to know that the reign of the de Corrmick dynasty had ended with the might of a Fraen fist.

A messenger was sent to Waller with his orders, and in time, the sounds of war washed in waves over the city from somewhere he could not see. Those cries spurred Waller and the city's defensive wall of men, boys, and some women, forward.

Enesfel's army leaped to meet them.

The de Corrmick banner would fall to the assaulting wave of cavalry.

Fraen smiled with a smug, gratified leer that there was no one to see.

❧*❧

Bhetá expected the other blonde woman to protest the decision to flank the city from the west and north, but Earé said nothing for or against the idea. She had, instead, stared to the west as if looking for something or seeing something that no one else did. Lorant took her silence and her stare as a sign to send troops west around the city while keeping the majority focused on Waller's banner and the increasing number of untrained soldiers filling the Nethite ranks.

Bhetá did not think so many was a good sign, regardless of their inexperience, but at least she could identify a few of the previously encountered child soldiers. Her army was nervous enough. Meeting the Inzigaen again would devastate morale.

The increase in manpower was why she, the king, Prince Jerit, and every other leader with them, believed they would soon meet again.

The war cry from the west brought with it a shout and the charge of Waller's army, but the general remained behind, his flag at the rear of the host flapping in the sea breeze, taller than the outnumbering banners of King Fraen. Surprised by Waller's choice to attack rather than continue to hold his defensive line at the city's edge, Lorant flashed a look at Jerit, then at Earé who nodded once before snapping her helm's visor over her face, and then at Bhetá. She did not nod; she accepted the look as the command it was. With her war cry echoing behind her, she kicked her horse into action and plowed Enesfel's cavalry into the opposing force. Kaj, still holding the line in the middle of no man's land, charged with her, the thundering horses dragging the foot soldiers into battle with them. Earé led those she had recruited to the right, toward the sea, while Jerit led the Nethite defectors, the Vants, and all the de Corrmick loyalists to the west.

Lorant did not move, despite the jostling of men who ran past. His gaze held steady on Waller's banner, confident that Fraen's general, for all his boasting beneath that oversized flag, would not be engaging in the war he had generated. He was watching. Waiting.

Expecting a trap, Lorant thought it wisest to watch and wait too.

❧*❧

The calamity of war on two fronts that erupted near noon and continued long enough that he believed both armies would fall before sunset, presented Olaric with no better opportunity to act. His hurried steps on the wooden stairs, heavy boots shaking the slats and the wooden-paneled walls as he ran, made the woman within the dim chamber shrink back on the bed, her back pressed to the wall when he threw the door of her prison open. She straightened when she saw him, relieved that he was not one of Enesfel's soldiers, and stared with eager expectation.

"He is here? It is time?" Inness recognized the sounds of war from her last night of freedom…and the night she and Oska had robbed her father-in-law of his. War in Glevum meant either an uprising or the arrival of an army intent on taking down the imposter king.

Lachlan most likely. Her kin.

de Corrmick…if Kjell lived, if Prince Jerit had decided to claim the throne, or if someone had raised an army in the name of King Oska's son.

Her son.

Assuming she meant Prince Henrik, Olaric held out a heavy, nondescript brown cloak with a nod. "Put this on…hood up." He glanced at her slippered feet, wondering if he should have brought boots for her. It was too late for that now. Boots would make too much noise where they were going. Once the cloak was around her shoulders, tied in place at her neck after the hood was pulled up to hide her face, Olaric grabbed her hand and pulled her behind him.

Her fingers felt too thin, too frail, in his hand.

He frowned, wondering if she had the strength for what was to come.

"Don't speak. Hurry. We don't have much time."

Most of Glevum's residents who were not fighting were in hiding. Those who had not done so earlier were trying to do so now, now that war was at their border, none of them taking the time to identify the man and woman as anything other than fellow shelter-seekers. They made no notice, asked no questions, when Olaric plopped five coins into the hands of the boy left to watch the rowboat procured earlier that morning. The boy pocketed the fee, grinned, and scampered off to complete the second half of his job.

Olaric helped Innes onto the boat and untied it from its moorings before climbing in beside her and grabbing the oars. She grimaced and gripped the sides when the boat lurched away from the dock, but she did not complain. Questions and fears tumbled through her head, evident in her eyes as the wind caught the hood of her cloak and briefly exposed her face, but she pulled it into place and obeyed the directive she had been given.

Not a sound.

She had not been told how she would get inside the castle, but she trusted that he would get her there. He had told her his basic plan of getting her inside with the families of palace guards and staff, but that plan appeared to have changed as the boat slipped through the current towards the sea side of the keep. Wherever Fraen was, however Olaric got her inside, she would find a way to do what she had longed to do since the night that traitor had robbed her of her son, her freedom, her life. Henrik would be safe. Henrik would be king.

Olaric scanned the shore for signs of his father's soldiers. Many fishing boats had fled to sea, toward Gorea, or the smaller fishing villages in the north, seeking to escape a fight they did not want to participate in. There was no one guarding the inlet that allowed wastewater to flow from the castle into the sea, no guards at the metal-grated gate he had used more than a decade before to spirit this same woman away from Glevum.

Though he had done so intending to use her in his favor someday, he had never thought to take her in the same way he had gotten her out.

There was a single man with a lantern waiting at that place, a man also disguised in an oversized cloak who held down a hand as the rowboat bumped against the slime-covered stone and mortar wall.

"He'll take you inside," Olaric said quietly, standing to hold the boat steady with a hand on the lip of the narrow ledge as he drew Inness up with one hand. "He knows Fraen's routines, knows where he will be. He'll get you into place, give you what you need. The rest will be up to you."

Nose wrinkled in disgust at the stench wafting out of the passage and in the water, Inness studied the stranger on the ledge. She did not recognize the man she could not see, but she recognized the scarred, calloused hands of a soldier. She was reluctant to trust him because of it, as her last experience with soldiers had led to captivity.

Olaric nodded. "You trust me? You want to get to Fraen?"

Inness frowned and reluctantly nodded.

"Then trust that he'll take you there…and he'll get you back here safely. Remember, until Henrik's on the throne, you won't be safe inside, especially once the king is dead, so be careful and return to meet me here."

Henrik.

She offered the stranger her hand, scowling with narrow-eyed determination, and climbed onto the ledge, thankful she did not wear a gown that would have dragged through the muck around her bare feet. Olaric understood her thoughts. He knew her too well.

"Back here after," she muttered. The stranger guided her beyond the normally locked grate, closed it behind them after they were inside, and then led her into the damp darkness with only the light of his lantern to guide them. The rest would soon be up to her.

Before dawn, she expected them all to be dead.

Olaric's boat eased away, turning toward the sea, where he rowed north at the mouth, riding the turbulent wake of another fishing vessel hoping to escape the onset of war.

Minutes later, the grated passage opened…and closed once more.

ᔧ * ᔨ

He had never been here.

Before catching a glimpse of his father's thoughts, as Kavan sang and spilled blood upon black glass so far away that the boy could not fathom the distance, of this unlit earthen tunnel behind a door that was not a door, Ágdhállán had been unaware of its existence. When the contact was abruptly severed, a sensation like having something ripped out of his body, Ágdhállán had seen this same tunnel in Dhóri's thoughts too. Something about treasures bound for Gorbesh that Dhóri had not specified but had been present in his mind when he spoke of having responsibilities in St. Kóráhm's that prevented him from leaving Alberni with his little brother.

He was here now, however, nearing the end of an unlit tunnel, not out of curiosity but because something in his father's thoughts, or perhaps revealed by the saint whom Ágdhállán had felt through his father, had told him he must come here. He did not know why. Wherever the power, wherever Kóráhm, wherever his father led, Ágdhállán was bound to go.

His father needed him. He knew it.

At the end of the tunnel, he produced a flickering tongue of flame in his palm, less brilliant than his father could generate but bright enough to illuminate the cavern. There was a wide chasm that split the room in two, a gaping maw that hid its depths from the glow of the handlight, and beyond that, behind a locked metal gate and a grated panel, were compartmented rows dug into the stone and earth. Some were filled, some appeared empty. He sensed a Gate beyond the chasm, something he could not get to, and with no visible way to cross, he was unsure why he had been led here.

There was power in this place. Power in the alcoves, power in the air, power in the walls. He could feel his father here, a robust enough sensation to reveal that Kavan had either been here recently or visited often enough to leave his imprint. Hoping to glean more information, Ágdhállán pressed his hand to the wall, his fingers splayed as Kavan's often did when reading a large object or distressed animal. Veins of green, blue, and white light seemed to pour from his hand, filling the cracks in the stone with luminescence that spread throughout the room like a web.

He flinched but did not draw his hand away. Though the seemingly natural occurrence was unexpected, the power did not frighten him. Power never had. Nor did the rush of images bombarding his thoughts frighten him as he absorbed what the veins provided and sought to untangle the images from the jumbled mess in which they were delivered.

He smelled smoke. He saw flames illuminating colored glass.

He heard the shouts of frightened, angry people. He saw a prone figure lying face down in front of an altar and another at the foot of the steps, both dressed in the robes of holy office. He could not see their faces, the color of their hair, to identify them, but as the crackle of fire grew louder and the heat of it felt as though it would singe his skin and ignite his hair, Ágdhállán believed two things.

k'gdhededhá Tusánt and those within Hes á Redh were in danger

He had to warn them.

The nearest Gate was out of reach, and the other was a long run back through the tunnel to St. Kóráhm's Purification Chamber. There was no time for that. No time to waste on puzzling out a way across the pitch chasm.

For the first time since his father had begun teaching the skill to him, following the patterns and methods Kavan used to weave power and connect him to someone far away, Ágdhállán took advantage of the power in the illuminated veins and reached toward Rhidam seeking Tusánt's familiar aura. He strained his mind, mimicking that reach with the tip-toed stretching of his leaning body. He touched the k'dedhá's thoughts long enough to implant one image, a face he did not recognize amidst the flames and one word....'danger'... before losing his balance and falling forward.

His free arm broke his fall, the bones above his wrist snapping at the impact of his open palm on stone, and he lay still, head pounding, arm burning in pain, waiting for his tunneled, blacked-out vision and the world around him to become normal again.

The decanter of serbháló Bhídígís had just filled and handed to him slipped out of Tusánt's grasp and shattered when it hit the floor, spraying its fragrant sweetness over the wall beneath the cabinet where the blessed decanters were kept for each Gathering. His sudden rigidity and the breaking of ceramic startled Novice Dhon and prompted Bhídígís to grab Tusánt's arm and steady him with the other hand behind the Elyri's back.

"k'dedhá?" he muttered, trying to pull the man away from the mess. Tusánt's legs would not move until the sensation of pulling, of resistance, broke his daze and made him shake his head.

Gulping air his lungs had been briefly deprived of, he gasped, "Where are our guests?" He wiped his free arm across his nose as if to clear away an unpleasant smell and glanced at the mess he had made.

"The pilgrims? They went to the river to pray," replied Dhon.

"You let them go alone?"

Noting the alarm in the k'gdhededhá's voice, the red-haired novice stammered, "I saw no harm in prayer...didn't think they needed..."

Tusánt dismissed the rest of the reply with a hand wave and shake of his head. "No, of course." balo Essem might have ruled out a connection between Earé's army and the pilgrims before being sent to Levonne, but that had not eased Tusánt's concerns. The balo had not met them; there had not been time or opportunity. Tusánt's distrust was shared by no one else, so he had kept his paranoia to himself as the council offered the pilgrims a tour of the city and the farmlands surrounding it.

"I think..." he shook his head again and withdrew from Bhídígís' hold. "Evening Gathering will be soon. Find them; welcome them to participate and share dinner with us afterward."

Bhídígís scowled but replied, "Aye, we will do that."

Maybe he should not suspect nefarious intent. Maybe they were the ones in danger.

But it was the only time Kavan's son, not Kavan himself, had reached out with a warning from the Sight.

Tusánt would rather have the visitors where he could watch them. He would be a fool not to heed the admonition.

❧*❦

"You didn't tell me you were suspicious of anyone."

Dressed in drab, common clothes, her pale red hair braided and tucked under the shawl over her head and wrapped around her neck and shoulders, she did not think many would recognize her when she plopped down next to the man seated on this grassy stretch of the Tegid's bank, any more than most would recognize him. Those who would wcre clients, associates, or past enemies. As it had taken hours to track her kinsman down, and noting the scrutiny with which he was eyeing a group of men several yards away, she had chosen not to draw him elsewhere for a talk.

Here in the open, with no one near to overhear, was good enough.

"I'm suspicious of a lot of people," he chuckled with a shrug. "Pilgrims have been praying here for a while…it's the other one I've got my eye on." The pilgrims only interested him because he did not understand the language they spoke. Not Cíbhóló, not Cordashian, not Trade or anything else he had ever heard. Their unfamiliar language did not make them suspicious, only interesting. The fellow who disrupted their prayers to speak with the wild gesticulations of someone trying to overcome a language barrier was more curious. A similarly dark-skinned member of the group he had tracked to the warehouse district, where they had bartered an expensive horse, an exotic sword, three kegs of wine, and a pouch containing the largest pearls Warde had ever seen in exchange for the temporary use of a structure to house an incoming delivery, there seemed no reason for the apparent disagreement with the pilgrims.

Maybe he thought they were trespassing. Maybe he thought they were there to steal whatever delivery his companions were waiting for. Whatever the case, Warde mused as he pulled in his fishing line to remove his day's first catch, he thought the altercation was worth watching…as were those who came and went from the warehouse with seemingly no purpose.

"Including me?"

"Not most of the time." As Association, a healthy dose of suspicious caution would keep him alive and free. She was a Dugan, but she was also the High Inquisitor…and the one-time queen of Neth. They were working towards the same goal currently, the restoration of order to Rhidam, but that did not mean their goals would always align.

"You know we sent men to Alberni…"

"Took all our good horses…and some not-so-good ones."

"Necessary for expediency. If Alberni falls, it won't be long before they reach Rhidam." Levone thus far had held the foreigners at bay, preventing ships, war or merchant alike, from reaching Rhidam or leaving the Tegid for the Bay of Phállá, but Asta was under no delusion that war in Rhidam was impossible. It could only be avoided if she protected Alberni and the port cities like her.

Thank Ethenae there had been no other reported attacks in Enesfel.

"With a shortage of manpower…I hope we can rely on you, the network, if it comes to a fight."

"If it comes to a fight, I think all of Rhidam'll be in it." Warde paused as the stranger amid the pilgrims threw his hands up in outrage and stormed away…moments before one of the Hes á Redh novices appeared to collect the pilgrims and usher them to the náós. The warehouse door banged shut, shaking the building and eliciting the annoyed responses of the men inside.

"Gonna pay us soldiers' wages?"

Asta shrugged. "You? Yes. Everyone else…not up to me…and as you say, we'll all be fighting if that time comes…but I'll do what I can." Wars took a toll on the royal treasury. She was not privy to the royal expenses or the cost of this war thus far, nor did she want to be. "Just need you to keep your eyes open."

"Like I'm doing."

She nodded. "Like you're doing…let me know if there's trouble. Help me keep Rhidam safe, and we'll pay those who deserve it when it's over."

Warde nodded and picked up his pail with river water and the fish in it. His replacement on watch should be here soon, someone to sit on this bank and continue fishing as he watched the warehouse occupants until Warde returned from dinner. "Anything we see, you'll know about it as soon as I have something to report."

"Like the one you're watching?" she chuckled as she stood up too.

"Rented a storage with friends. No idea why yet. Might be nothing…"

"And it might be something." Dugan intuition, after all, was the best.

The other man he waited for crossed the Tegid from the opposite shore and took a seat not far from where Warde had been sitting without acknowledging either of them.

Asta did not speak. Nor did Warde. She did not look to see where he was going, nor did he turn back to watch her meander in the direction of the castle and Hes á Redh. She trusted he would do right by her and by Rhidam.

She could not, however, vouch for other members of the Association.

❧*❧

Amazed at the expanse of passages built within the walls of the de Corrmick castle, Inness did her best to memorize the turns, the stairways and rises, the series of panels into unused rooms and leading to another tunnel somewhere else. There were times, in these secret places, when she and her guide were forced to stop to avoid discovery by the servants, advisors, guards, and visiting dignitaries who moved from room to room as they attended the yet unseen king or awaited an audience with him. As dark as the passages were, even with the stranger's lantern to guide them, she had no clear idea how he found his way…unless he was a servant, retainer, or palace guard himself.

Perhaps he was one of those who had stolen her life from her.

As agile as his movements were, she judged him too young for that.

Sometimes she paused to stare into the blackness behind as the muted echo of their steps brought with it the sense that someone else was there, that someone was following. But the sounds stopped when her steps did. There was no rustle of cloth or sound of breathing, and when she waved her arm expecting to feel someone there, there was nothing…not even a light source. It had to be Oska, she decided. Surely, he had known of these passages, though he had never spoken of them. Surely, he was with her now, come to protect their son, here to offer his support the way he had since their earliest childhood days.

"You're here," she mouthed.

Her guide pressed his finger to his lips to silence her. Inness pouted, nodded, and continued to follow.

That was why Oska did not speak. He knew they had to move silently if they did not want to be found.

They reached a closed panel and her guide cocked his head to listen to the rise and fall of voices on the other side. Garbled words, unfamiliar voices. All except one.

"Spends most of his time here," her guide whispered, "or in his chambers where he can see to the south." His voice could not be heard by the bluster of the loudest voice in the room and the apologetic pleadings and questions of the rest. The stranger drew off his glove and rubbed his fingers over the wall in front of them.

"Here…feel this."

He took her hand and placed it lightly against a slightly raised portion of the panel at about chest height. Air moved through a narrow crack that ran from floor to ceiling and brought with it a sliver of yellow light. The voice on the other side barked a command, and footsteps scurried out of the room. Inness looked from the needle of light to her guide.

"This'll open it…but only do it when he's not in the room…or is the only one there. You'll need this…"

"How will I…you're not…?" she stammered with an indignant scowl, thinking he was lying to her though his tone mirrored none of her fears. He seemed disgusted by the demanding voice in the room beyond. She took the sword he offered, and tested its weight in her hand. "You can't…"

"He'll be looking for me. I'll signal you, get you into place if I can get him alone…but if the chance comes before that…"

You know what you need to do.

"Yes, Oska," Inness murmured.

Sparding scowled, but she did not see it.

"I know what I need to do," she assured him.

Sparding nodded. "I'll come back for you."

The lantern's glow receded behind her, taking his footsteps with it. Soon she was alone with her hand on the panel, the thin line of light and push of air that relieved the impulse to panic in this trapping place, with the voice of the traitor burning in her ears.

That focus on the enemy, something she had taught herself long ago, was what prevented her from running after her guide and impaling him with the sword for daring to abandon her.

You're not alone.

She smiled grimly and nodded. She was not alone.

Oska was beside her as he always was.

⧀ * ⧁

The sun sank below the horizon, prompting both armies to limp to their respective camps to nurse their wounds and rethink their strategies for how to proceed. Neth's line failed to break, those desperate to avoid perceived foreign occupation and those afraid of their illegitimate king and the untrusted mercenaries fighting with them as though possessed, while Enesfel's army fought on the principle of the rightful de Corrmick rule and the stubborn faith in peace between all Sovereignties.

Those values and beliefs were no consolation to the injured, the dying, the dead. When Geiel snuck back to camp with the small collection of those who had escaped the clutches of Fraen's army, telling tales of such brutality and their failure to flank to the north or route the western defenses, Lorant sank with a defeated grown inside his tent where no one could see him, uninterested in speaking to anyone as he shouldered this weight alone.

Bhetá and Kaj walked amongst the troops, offering consolation, condolences, encouragement, praise for their ferocity that day, and their mutual certainty that, when they met the opponent again, they would break the line and take the prize they had come for. In the medical tents, the injured were moved in and out as fast as the Elyri and their Teren counterparts could work. Hebel and Ybherd, along with village clergy collected on the journey, walked amongst the weary, suffering soldiers waiting for care while dedhá Thrismund prayed over the dying, blessing them, giving them final rights and easing them from life into the eternal.

It was tempting to go to that tent and ask Thrismund to pray with him, pray for him. It was tempting to seek Ártur, beg him for contact with the man who weighed heavy on Lorant's mind tonight, but interrupting the work of either man would be a selfish thing to do.

Besides, there were few words to say and less desire to say them.

"Something to eat? Drink?" Jerit pushed back the tent flap and peeped inside. In the glow of the lantern he carried, his bruised and swollen lip and jaw and the bandaged gash along his chin looked worse than Lorant remembered seeing when they had crossed paths earlier. Lorant had urged him to go to the healers, to heal what would certainly leave a scar, but thus far, Jerit had not done so.

Lorant shook his head, masking his disappointment that Jerit's perfect face would be forever marred by this day. The knot filling his stomach was too big, too tight, to allow food to settle. He would, he was sure, throw up anything he attempted to force into it.

"Company then?" The prince had already entered, lowered the flap, and placed the lantern on the crate that served as a table for the pieces of armor hanging over it. Though few in the encampment had set up tents, someone had felt it appropriate to erect the king's tent at the rear of the camp where the healers, the female attendants, the gdhededhá, and the wagons and supplies were kept as far out of reach of Fraen's men as possible.

Listening to the stream of groans, moans, screams, and muttering voices from the medical tent was doing nothing for Lorant's frame of mind.

"Not going to be good company," the king muttered.

Jerit sat beside him, clasped his hand, and pressed it to his lips. "We can be not good company together." He hoped that his company would be enough to allow Lorant to sleep…even if he got none himself.

☙*❧

Olaric turned his eyes from the grisly visage of eight men skewered on wood spikes, pretending to be distracted by something from the castle's direction so he could hide his disgust and avoid Waller's bloodthirsty grin of dominance and satisfaction. There had been no alarm raised from the keep so far. He supposed that meant his father was alive.

That knowledge deepened his fleeting scowl.

He had not seen General Waller in months. He would have preferred not to see him now. But every street he tried to use to exit the west side of the city was clogged with arriving mercenaries, while, to the south, the streets were blocked not only with the bedraggled dregs of the king's army but by dying men displayed the same as these eight were.

"Captives?" he inquired nonchalantly, shooing a moth from his face as the creature sought the light of his torch. There were so many other light sources to choose from, hung between the dying and the dead so that others could watch them writhe in the shadow, the moth could have chosen anywhere else to be.

"Defectors. Traitors."

Olaric hissed between his teeth, knowing he sounded disgusted and hoping that Waller, a contemporary who outranked him purely by the whim of the king, would think the notion of men abandoning Neth's army in support of the de Corrmick flag to be an incomprehensible act.

Was it any worse to die as a de Corrmick loyalist than it would be to die on the battlefield for a king not of their choosing?

"Shouldn't we be pressing them into the field instead?"

"And risk them turning against us?" Waller gave a chuckling snort and stared as if to challenge Olaric to disagree.

Instead, Olaric shrugged, side-eyed the nearest man who had ceased squirming, his head lolled to the side, his eyes glazing not with physical torment and pain but with the pallor of death. "Aye…that's a fair point."

Waller's gaze traveled up and down the younger Fraen's form. "You shall join us tomorrow." Olaric's boots and clothes were muddy from his endeavors along the shore, stained from days of usage, and disheveled as he had not had time to pay attention to his appearance. He had not yet seen battle the way Waller thought he should, however.

"You're going into battle too?" As the king's son, Olaric did not have to take orders from the general, but refusing might raise suspicions that Olaric could not afford. It was obvious Waller had not shed blood either, at least not today. Not on the battlefield and, he guessed, not here with the eight traitors. There was no trace of blood on his polished boots except what might have dripped and splattered from the men impaled for display.

There was no indication that Waller had done these deeds himself.

Like their king, it seemed Waller was no longer a man to sully his hand with war when he could force others to do it for him, so long as he could take credit for success at the end.

"We shall rout them, burn that de Corrmick flag, and put each head on a pike, stretching to Fiara and beyond. They're already beaten, though they refuse to concede. They shall know it soon enough."

"By the king's decree?"

"By my own."

His boasting words suggested Waller's interest in the Nethite throne, another imposter determined to spill blood for the sake of power. For Waller, this war was not about loyalty to a king, a throne, or a kingdom. This was about power and how much of it he could take for himself.

Pressing Olaric into combat was intended only to remove the king's son from the line of succession.

"Do you have armor?"

"At home."

Waller motioned to two soldiers, bloody-faced mercenaries who had likely been responsible for these impalements. "Don it then and join us. Come to my tent; we will feast and then we shall fight together. Tomorrow, victory shall be ours."

"I've already eaten." It was the only protest Olaric made before starting toward the apothecary shop. He would not risk being poisoned so near to the fruition of his plans, or the downfall of Glevum or the de Corrmick bloodline, or of Enesfel and the Lachlans.

There was no need to slip the guards he was given. No need to kill them.

Getting inside the royal force had been his plan all day. How else was he to sway men away from Fraen the Elder? How else was he supposed to collect conscripted loyalists and pit them against their own kind?

❧*❦

We will see each other again, átaelás mai.

Kavan did not know how long he was incapacitated by blood loss, how long he slept, but it was night when he opened his eyes and watched the slow parade of stars for several minutes of unexpected peace and calm. He listened to his companions' deep-breathed slumber without feeling any haste or compulsion to move. Eventually, he curled his fingers, proving that the earlier weakness and heaviness of his limbs had passed, as had the pain from martyr wounds in his wrists, feet, and side. The cloak that had covered him had been removed, revealing that the power within Zythán's sturmyrá no longer pulsed, no longer undulated with the intake and outpouring of power. Now the glow held steady, no longer flickering like a candle or torch but shining constant like the silver half-moon above his head.

Protecting the sturmyrá with one hand, fiddling with Kóráhm's ring on the other, he sat, expecting stiffness in his body but finding none, to face the shadow of the Heretic-Saint who stood before him, beyond his reach, intangible, and closed his fist around the half-moon pendant on his chest.

The moon's position and phase this night were not a coincidence.

The power in his center was brighter, more focused, more voluminous than he could remember feeling. It felt as if it would burst free, an irritated prickle that begged for an outlet. He longed for flight, for the release of a handlight. He longed for anything that would ease the roiling tightness.

But he did not give in to those longings as Kóráhm's words echoed in his head. He suspected he would need all the power he could muster before this night was through.

His movement roused Rhyrdan, who shook Níkóá awake. Sunna, lying on his back with his eyes open, also seeming to study the stars, looked at the bard but did not otherwise move.

"We must go." Kavan's words sounded heavy to his own ears, weighed down by meaning he did not need to speak out loud.

Rhyrdan started to protest but the objections about the risks they were to take were cut off when he met Kavan's pleading emerald eyes.

Don't argue, he seemed to say. Don't give me cause to avoid this.

Rhyrdan swallowed hard and nodded.

This would be hard enough. Whatever Kavan expected to do, he needed strength. He needed his friends to be strong, with him, for him.

"Water?" Níkóá asked, offering the skin and one of the figs Sunna had earlier collected.

Though Kavan accepted the water and drank deep, he refused the fig. He placed the sturmyrá into its wooden case and wedged it into his pack, along with the red kestrel harp he had not needed since Kílyn. Imagining the feel of the strings beneath his trembling fingers, he stroked the wooden case and closed his eyes with a heavy sigh.

He missed his black harp, the instrument that had been his since the start of his journey. He should have brought her.

It was best he had not placed his darling at risk.

Níkóá stuffed the water skin into his pack when Kavan returned it to him and buckled it closed.

Sunna's pack was already closed, and his waji lay at his side, within ready reach if there had been trouble. He stretched, curled his hand around the hilt, and was the first to rise.

"She is close."

Kavan nodded. Now that Kóráhm's presence had faded into the shadows at the edges of his periphery, Kavan could feel her too. Impulsively, he reached to draw Kóráhm back in the hopes that the saint's company would drive her away, but that impulse was quashed, and he accepted what was.

Kóráhm could not help him now.

No one could.

Rhyrdan stood, slung his pack over his shoulder, double-checked the security of Wace's waji on one hip and his father's sword on the other, and then helped Kavan to his feet, both hands trembling as they closed around the other. It was an unneeded gesture, but one that cemented their friendship one more time. Tears welled in both men's eyes but Rhyrdan nodded.

The time for protests was past.

Only duty remained. His to Kavan, Kavan's to the world.

How unfair prophecy and fate could be.

Sunna took Rhyrdan's other hand, his feet, like Kavan's, straddling the long crack in the black-glass earth. Níkóá took Sunna's, and then Kavan's, and he nodded too.

"Let's do this," he grunted. He was as ready as he would ever be for whatever the night demanded.

Kavan shifted his pack with a roll of his shoulders and closed his eyes. No one else did. He focused on the power he could draw from two of the other men, on the ring upon his hand, upon the saint who had worn it in life, and upon the man who had given it to him, seeking the threads that bound the three together after a lifetime apart. He remembered his dark twin's amber-sweet voice, the floral-perfumed scent of his hair, the intensity of Myreth's black eyes when he stared with the sort of intense longing that had once made Kavan breathlessly uncomfortable. It was easier to feel him here, in this desert devoid of the distractions of Rhidam or Kílyn. Flight was out of the question if he was to bring the three men with him.

He did not know what parts they were to play, or how they could help. He worried that his selfishness and weakness in wanting them at his side would result in their deaths, but he was certain he needed them, just as they were certain they needed to stand with him.

He could not fly.

He had Gated from this place before, but the effort had not held. He could feel only lingering traces of the power that had been here when Zythán, or someone else, had constructed this place.

He would have to construct a new Gate, properly this time, and hope that, in the resulting days of incapacitated weakness, Bhás would not kill him, kill them all, when he was unable to fight back.

At the end of the silvery thread of memory and power, ignoring the laughter tapping against his focus like a woodpecker, he found Myreth. Kavan encircled him with an embrace of power, squeezed the hands in his, forced all the power from them and within him into the earth, into the ring that burned his hand and the pendants that burned against his chest, and pulled the thread tight.

The pendants seared his skin, making him yelp as the power in his center ignited.

At the other end of the thread, bombarded by the pungent smell of sulfur and pelted by the sting of icy, driving rain, Kavan sagged into Rhyrdan's arms.

❧Chapter 52❧

"**K**avan."

Kavan pitched forward on the uneven ground, grateful that Sunna's broad frame and quick action, and the support of Rhyrdan's arms around him, kept him from falling. He was surprised that, for the first time in his creation of Gates, he did not collapse into blackness as the whole of his power reserve was spent. Power sparked and raced up and down his legs, his spine, into his head as the new Gate wove itself into place beneath his feet. He was weak and unsteady enough, however, that he barely felt it. The sting of the heavy, needle-like rain driven in from the driving surf and the rumbling, shaky earth that produced a plume of molten fire in the distance were distractions that made the newness of the Gate an afterthought as he staggered and tried to regain his footing, clutching Rhyrdan's arms to remain upright.

He had not lost awareness, but he was weaker than he wanted to be.

Thankfully, the sense of Bhás' proximity had not grown stronger. Wherever she was, he did not think she had come for him yet.

Perhaps there was still time.

"There," Sunna said as he pointed. There was a rocky ledge several hundred feet away, not enough to keep them dry but enough to protect them from the worst of the driving wind and rain. He helped Kavan to that place and then settled the Elyri against the backdrop and squatted down so that his back further shielded the bard.

"Where are we?" began Níkóá, wincing when the eruptive fire spewed higher than anything he had ever seen, taller than most trees, taller, he was certain, than the spires of Hes Dhágdhuán in Clarys.

Again, taking water, this time from Rhyrdan, and accepting the younger man's efforts to wipe his silver-white hair from his face, Kavan weakly shrugged. "I don't know." There was nothing familiar about this landscape and no landmarks or traces of energy that might reveal their location. What he did sense, what he did hear, were the reverberations of Sight echoes and the intoxicating nearness of the man he had come to set free. He squinted against the rain and stared beyond Rhyrdan's shoulder.

"There."

He was grateful for the smoky red plume and the rotten-egg smoke it belched into the sky, for the light it produced revealed a manmade structure on a distant plateau. With barely the strength to lift his arm, it sagged into his lap as the three heads turned, but his effort to direct them lasted long enough for them to see what he pointed out.

Rhyrdan opened Kavan's pack, withdrew the sturmyrá from its protective casing, and wrapped Kavan's hands around it. It had provided Kavan regenerative power before; it was, he believed, the thing that kept the bard from collapsing in a faint the moment they reached this forsaken place. He hoped it would help Kavan now, before Bhás arrived.

He was as surprised as Kavan that she was not here to greet them.

"He's there…he must be…" Kavan wanted to go himself, had hoped his Gate would take him directly to Myreth. Instead, it had taken him here. He did not have the energy to ponder why.

"Who?"

"She has been holding him against me…hoping I would…take this…to him…and bring him out."

Kavan slid Kóráhm's ring off his hand and pressed it into Rhyrdan's as his voice trailed off and his head drooped so that his chin was against his chest. After making certain the bard was breathing, Sunna adjusted Kavan against the stone for as much comfort as the slippery earth could offer.

"When we met her before," Rhyrdan murmured, giving the ring to Sunna, "there was someone else…someone from his past…a hostage she took when she escaped. Maybe it's him. We should…"

"Someone needs to remain with him…but none of us should be alone." Níkóá frowned, dropped his pack, and removed a coil of rope Kavan had asked him to bring. It had seemed a peculiar request before, now he was glad he had obeyed it.

"He'll be safe with me." Rhyrdan would die before allowing anything to happen to Kavan while his and friend was too weak to defend himself.

"If she comes, use the waji," Sunna reminded him. Though he considered her to be no more than a woman who shared the White Bard's skills, if she was shi cali, as the stories claimed, it was best they were prepared. It was best that they used what weapons they had that might work against her.

The earth shook as a wave crashed against the shore. The spray of it washed over them but the outcropping protected them from most of the salty sea water. Those who left here would not be so protected.

"I'll go," Níkóá agreed.

"Be careful," murmured Rhyrdan, clasping both men's hands. "k'Ádhá be with you both."

"Dhágdhuán and Kóráhm be with you."

The pair left the outcropping and began to trudge over the rain-slick, pitted stone surface in the direction of the plateau with the fountain of fire to their right and the sea to their left. Rhyrdan squeezed Kavan's wrist with tender affection and watched them go.

"If he's there, we'll find him." Whoever he was. "We'll get him out. We'll all get home safe.

Kavan's lips moved but he uttered no sound.

If he made one, Rhyrdan could not hear it over the crash of another mighty wave.

❧*❧

The pounding of the battering ram against St. Kóráhm's gate ceased again as the heavy wooden frame fractured, sending men tumbling in several directions. It was the fourth battering ram to snap, defeated by the protections Kavan put in place to keep assailants out. Benches and kneelers had been cut into pieces, doused with melted lard and fire, and launched at the attackers, but the chellé would eventually run out of material to throw. Beds would be next. Dressers and desks.

None knew if it would be enough.

Those in the courtyard heard the change in the breaking crash. Those looking believed they saw the great gates shudder as they had not before.

The one who could not see it, though he faced them as everyone else did, felt an imperceptible static pop in the air and a noticeable depletion of the power around him that he had not been consciously aware of before.

Something had happened.

Kavan's defenses were failing.

"Dhóri!"

Sóbhán dropped his crutch and pitched onto the stones as he tried to grab his fleeing brother's arm. Bergis, who had been running burnable materials from inside to the catapult, froze mid-run, his arms full, closer to the fallen man than he was to his friend who was charging toward the gates.

❧653❧

Dropping what he carried, he turned to assist Sóbhán but was shooed away with the man's waving crutch.

"I'm fine. Stop him!"

Khwílen appeared behind them and helped Sóbhán to his feet as Bergis rushed to obey. "Did you feel…?"

"I did."

By the time Bergis reached Dhóri, his hands were splayed across the wood, forcing as much power through his palms as he could muster. His father had shown him how to bind and unbind the threads that guarded the relics in the catacombs. What he felt here was similar but more massive than anything Dhóri had faced, stronger and more complex than he thought he could replicate or repair.

But his father was not here to do so. Dhóri was the only one who stood a chance of success.

When Bergis tried to pull him away, not understanding what his friend was doing, Dhóri was like an immovable tree, roots of power holding him in place so that, even with Bergis' great strength, Dhóri could not be budged. "Sir…" He tried again to push him sideways when pulling did not work, and when that effort failed, he shouted over his shoulder to the men near the door, "I can't move him."

Assuming his brother was trying to save everything Kavan had created to shield St. Kóráhm's, feeling the swirl of power like waves sucking against his skin, Sóbhán hobbled as fast as he could toward his brother. Khwílen followed. They dodged the stones and arrows coming over the wall, and though Khwílen, too, tried to pull Dhóri away, he and Bergis together failed as before. Sóbhán covered Dhóri's hand with his to see, to feel, what Dhóri was experiencing, what he was trying to do.

He blinked. He felt the threads of binding, like steel bands tightened around the chellé, but he did not understand the process Dhóri was trying to use. His brother was capable, but Sóbhán did not think he had the power, or the endurance to succeed. Nor did Sóbhán. Only Kavan did. Sóbhán could not assist with the process, but he was a conduit for power, he could help another way.

"Bergis, bring any Elyri who isn't doing anything…"

"What…?" began Khwílen, not objecting when Sóbhán grabbed his hand, even when he could feel the shifting of power within as it was slowly pulled out of him and channeled into Dhóri.

His aborted question stopped Bergis in his tracks.

"Shoring Father's defenses…Dhóri needs more power."

Unsure he understood but believing that, if anyone could shore up Kavan's failing defenses, it would have to be his children, Khwílen looked at Bergis and barked, "What are you waiting for? Bring them."

Bergis ran.

As before, between the long periods of pounding at the gates, new ladders brought bronze-faced men scrambling upward in the hopes of breaching the wall as three men stood alone at the gates, looking as though they hoped to hold it closed with the strength of their arms. Elyri residents joined them as the climbing men were met again with arrows, hot oil, and buckets of burning material that ignited the ladders and made them weaken and collapse. At the smaller door on the north wall, others began to beat and pound with clubs and axes.

The door held, but without Kavan, it might not continue to do so.

"North gate!" Tau's voice boomed across the courtyard.

People scrambled to obey.

❧*❦

The defenses were failing.

Ágdhállán could feel the rift in energy above his head, as though the binding threads his father had used were rooted in the earth, into this room, drawing energy from there so that the colored veins in the wall began to fade. When the defenses came down, if they came down, those who remained in the chellé would be in grave danger.

As he understood their creation, the battlements could only fail if something happened to his father so that he could no longer sustain them. Instinctively, Ágdhállán knew that, wherever Kavan had gone, he would never be able to reach him, to learn what had happened or bring him home, and not knowing generated a tight ball in his stomach that alternated between fire and ice and made him want to vomit.

Maybe he could fix what his father had built.

He wondered if his brothers were still in the chellé. Did they feel the failing too? Would they vacate St. Kóráhm's when there was nothing to hold the invaders out? What would they do when they did not find him in Rhidam where he was expected to be? If they looked for him in Gorbesh and did not find him, if Captain Magk or Cáym told them that Ágdhállán had not come with them? His brothers would feel compelled to return to St. Kóráhm's; his disobedience would put his brothers, or someone else, in danger. It would be his fault if someone died while looking for him.

He had to get to the Gate. He had to try to help.

Struggling to sit while nursing his broken wrist and generating a handlight in his other hand, trying to pretend that his arm did not hurt so that his father would be unable to feel his pain across the distance that separated them, Ágdhállán froze when the rocks he accidentally kicked skittered and rolled onto the space in front of him without falling into the black chasm. Hesitantly, he scooted closer, nursing his arm, and used his heel to reach out. His foot met resistance, swept side to side to gauge the solid area's width, and then rested there, stretched over the crevasse instead of dangling into it. To his surprise, the area was wide enough to walk on.

Had his father done this, too? Had he created a bridge to allow him to cross from the tunnel to the grated area on the other side?

Hoping that the Gate he sensed would be accessible, a closer option than running back through the unfamiliar tunnels, Ágdhállán swallowed hard and made his choice. Inch by inch with a handlight throbbing in his injured hand, he wiggled across, feeling safer by remaining closer to the surface, as if he might fall over the edge if he tried to stand. Every few feet, he paused to release a gush of breath, replenish it into straining lungs, regenerating the flame in his palm when his fear made the light dim. Only when he reached the other side, where he scampered over the power signature of the Gate on the floor to lean against the metal grating as far from the chasm as he could get, did his shoulders sag and the light in his hand went out.

He struggled to breathe, to slow his pounding heart.

The luminescent veins were dark. If they were the roots that held St. Kóráhm's defenses in place, soon the chellé gates would fall. Soon her attackers would be inside, and there would be nothing to protect those who lived there except the might of Captain Magk and the guards.

Similar threads of power locked the metal gate at his back, but those defenses held strong. Ágdhállán did not ponder why. The pain in his arm and his worry for his brothers occupied all his thoughts.

Go, he silently urged them, not certain if they would hear him, not certain he wanted them to. Do not wait for me. I am safe. The branching, pitch-black tunnels would discourage anyone from looking too far, should they be lucky enough to locate the hidden door. And if anyone made it to this room, odds were, they would fall into the crevasse.

He had only used the Gates alone one other time. He had studied his father's technique every time they traveled together, had listened to his instructions and practiced connecting between points, but he had never asked to try and his father had not offered him the opportunity. There had been no good opportunity to show his father that he could use them as he had not wanted Kavan to worry or warn him about the unnecessary risk of traveling alone. Knowing that danger loomed over his life, a danger Ágdhállán had been aware of since the moment his infant mind began to make memories, he had never felt compelled to wander far from Kavan without his father's knowledge. This was not the ideal time to try, but he had no other choice. This was not the time to explore, not the time to reconsider folly versus bravery. He scooted into the center of the Gate's power and closed his eyes.

Don't.

The whisper of breath and sound brushed past his ear, making him swivel to the side to face its creator, but there was no one there. Not his father's voice, not his brothers', and not k'dedhá Tusánt who lingered within Ágdhállán's head since his contact like some savory dinner morsel in his mouth. Nor was it the voice of the woman who taunted his father's dreams with defiant laughter.

"Who are you?" he asked, forcing unfelt bravado into his voice.

When no reply came, he closed his eyes again and settled his thoughts to focus on those points of light that were again evident within his head.

You are safe. They are safe. Conserve your power. Stay.

The words that time came with warmth and a sense of his father that made Ágdhállán's eyes widen. The light in his palm went out, and he plopped down cross-legged on the Gate's power center, trying instead to reconnect with that voice and the sounds around him.

It was the very first time. He had never thought it would happen to him.

Kóráhm had come.

❧*❧

They could not see where the additional soldiers were coming from, but their presence was made obvious by the bulging Nethite line that expanded in places that had been depleted in each altercation at the city's edge. Each bout of combat sparked by the shifting of fresh Nethite soldiers seeking to take advantage of Enesfel's weariness resulted in the loss of men on both sides. Though the benefit of Elyri healers enabled many of Enesfel's soldiers to return to combat, they could not replace the dead.

No reinforcements were coming for Enesfel, and his army was gradually growing demoralized.

"She isn't here."

Lorant's face lost color when Kaj joined him, his expression grim.

"Isn't…is she…?"

"I've searched the dead, the injured." He shrugged and tried to school his mien to something more casual, less concerned. Expecting the question to come, he shook his head and continued, "She would not allow herself to be captured. k'ílshwythnec is bound by rules…by purposes…no one can comprehend. Wherever she has gone, she will return when she is needed."

"And if she doesn't?" Staring at Jerit while the prince brushed down his weary horse provided a brief distraction, but the smile Jerit gave before being blocked from sight by a unit of fresh soldiers shifting to the front line of the brigade took that distraction away.

"Then she can't." Or won't, but Kaj did not say that. He looked toward a rowdy group of men raising voices in a frustrated argument that dedhá Thrismund happened to be near enough to subvert. The men were tired. This on-again, off-again manner of combat was wearing on all of them. Bhetá was right. The next time they met in combat, Enesfel needed to break the front line. They needed to reach the castle. They needed to flush Frain out, kill General Waller, and slaughter as many of the opposing mercenaries as they could.

While many of those who had traveled north with him would feel more confident of their success if She Who Sees was with them, just as Lorant would, others would take her absence in combat, now that they were used to her being there, as proof of impending failure.

Lorant and his generals knew they needed to get ahead of that sentiment before fighting resumed.

Kaj cleared his throat of the dust inhaled during the last fight and continued. "I have faith. She would not lead us here to die." Even though many who had followed him already had. Such was the nature of war.

"We have men enough. We can do this. Lord Cliáth is…"

Lorant's tone was too weary to sound irritated. "Not here." Just as his daughter was not here. Maybe they were together, accomplishing whatever Kavan intended to do.

Maybe there would not be another battle at Glevum's edge.

Over the heads of the nearby men, Bhetá whistled and waved to Lorant, steering her horse with her knees as she accepted the lance and shield someone offered. Bhríd, riding beside her, carried the same weapons, as did a small group of others. Lorant did not know where the lances had come from, but he guessed his Daema and chamberlain had a plan and that they were prepared to move the army into its ready stance again.

The king sighed. It was impossible to guess if General Waller would perceive that readiness as action and attack or if he would toy with Enesfel's brigade and make them wait.

What Lorant did know was that his army was not ready for a full assault to push into the city.

"Ready your men, tama. Tell them whatever you must to prepare them. One more time…"

Likely, he mused, to be their last.

It was too late to retreat. He had sworn he would finish this.

No matter how frightened of failure he was.

❧*❧

Kavan was here.

Myreth knew it as surely as he knew that the earth had been split with fire that he could see from the window. He had never felt the power of a Gate here before, had never felt power here at all except when Bhás came and went, and though he could see no one in the gray darkness of the storm when he pulled the shutters back and pried the window open to allow a gust of rainy, putrid air to blast into the room, he could feel new power now.

He leaned forward and look down to the ledge beneath his window. Barely wide enough to stand on. Climbing would be too dangerous. Kavan had said once that he could fly in the shape of a bird, so opening the window to the cold wind might give the bard access. Or maybe he would incapacitate the watchers, with means that Myreth had only ever heard about in rumors and myths, and enter through the door.

He did not dare to climb through the window; he had never tried it as he had long ago realized that, on this stormy, rocky island, there was nowhere for him to go. But if Kavan asked it of him now, or if Kavan burst through the door and beckoned him to follow, Myreth was ready.

He hastily pulled on every piece of meager clothing he had been given in his prison, shoved his slippered feet into boots he had not worn since arriving here, and tied his blanket around him like a cloak.

He knew this was a trap. For him, for Kavan. He knew she would come for them rather than permit his escape. But he had faith in Kavan, faith in Kóráhm. If it came to it, he decided as he pressed himself into the corner of the room where he could see both the window and the door, he would rather die trying to escape with his beloved brother than remain in this place alone for another day.

I am here. I am ready.

❧659❧

Hunched against the driving wind and rain as dawn came and the sun climbed higher, unable to hold their cloaks closed as they needed their arms as they climbed over slippery rocks worn and pitted by centuries of weather, Níkóá and Sunna paused at a narrow gulley near the base of the plateau and gazed to the right where the split earth disgorged flame across the black landscape. The wind carried the belching smoke east, away from them, but the stench of sulfur and hot metal and stone was strong enough to make both men stifle their coughs as they watched the distant river of black and orange push closer. A finger of sunlight stretched through a breach in the clouds and created a rainbow that stretched over the eruption like a blanket.

"Think it's a sign?" Níkóá wiped the rain from his eyes and licked the sea salt from his lips as he stared. He had never imagined such a sight.

"Everything is a sign if you know how to read it." Mentally measuring the nearly sheer incline in front of them, Sunna grunted, "Got to do this now." To the left, where the raucous sea met the shore, there appeared to be a path between the structure and a thick pole with a pulley system where a woven rope basket swayed in the storm. A frontal assault through the door would result in bloodshed with the occasionally raised voices he could hear. He would rather avoid bloodshed if he could. But the window above which spilled faint light onto the ledge might provide access so long as it remained open and was large enough for a man to fit through.

Neither knew who they were looking for. They only had a name.

They leaped across the gulley where rain and water from the retreating sea raced away from the earth's flowing core of fire, and then ran the remaining distance to the base of the plateau. Sunna was the first to climb, his nimble steps barely slipping on the wet stone. Níkóá hesitated, rethinking his choices, hesitant to make the same climb, but when the bigger man looked back and held a hand out to him saying, "Come," Níkóá looked toward the bard he could not see, swallowed his apprehension, and accepted the lift to the first steady handhold Sunna guided him to.

Fingers gripping the outcropping, toes finding a purchase that would support his weight, Níkóá gauged the hazards of the climb versus the creeping fire river and nodded as he began his ascent. He did not think they could climb fast enough to accomplish their goal, but the need to do so spurred him on.

"My lord."

Rhyrdan lightly shook Kavan out of his blank-eyed stupor and pointed at the surprising rainbow, interpreting it as a good omen, whether it was one or not. At least he believed Kavan needed to experience one more display of beauty and hope before this new day ended. Kavan stared at the visual spectacle of fire, smoke, and light and held his breath as his senses returned.

He wanted to believe the rainbow was a positive omen as well.

Though he did not sense Bhás nearby, he believed she was there. Watching. Waiting.

Just as he knew his little boy was in pain.

He had not tried to reach Ágdhállán, chose not to expose him to Bhás' imminent threat. His son was safe where he was. He could sense power around the boy, hear the echoes of Kóráhm's reassurance in his head. Kóráhm would protect Ágdhállán.

Kavan could not look back. He could only focus on now.

"How long…are they…?"

"Think it's midday…or nearly so. Hard to tell." That finger of light was gone, swallowed by the storm clouds, so he could not judge where the sun was behind them. "It's a long hike and the ground is treacherous, the wind fierce. I'm sure they will rejoin us soon." He encouraged Kavan to drink and again offered a fig, which Kavan again declined. The water, however, was accepted with a nod of gratitude.

His stomach was too knotted to eat, but his lips and throat were parched. The water would be enough.

Rhyrdan brushed the hair back from Kavan's face after closing the water skin and returning it to his pack. "How do you feel?"

"I…" Kavan's eyes fluttered as he assessed his condition. His core still felt depleted, his limbs shaky and weak, but for being less than a day since the creation of the nearby Gate, he was in a remarkably stable state. Perhaps by the time the others returned, he would have regained enough strength to take all of them away from this island.

Perhaps in doing so, he would be in a better place to demand a confrontation with Bhás at a time and location of his choosing.

"I will be ready," he murmured without specifying what he would be ready for, as he turned his focus onto the active absorption of power from the sturmyrá between his hands. The passive sharing of power was not enough. He needed to actively engage in the process.

When Myreth was at his side, they would go.

He was thankful Rhyrdan did not interrupt.

❧*❦

"It's no use," Khwílen shouted as the gate shuttered beneath Dhóri's hands and pushed back those around them who were attempting to hold it closed, their feet sliding on the courtyard stones. "St. Kóráhm's is lost."

"Longer…" Dhóri gasped, the strain of spent power staining his face red, the flexing of his hands turning his knuckles white. The sun had begun to sink above their heads, its decline toward Rhidam bringing the night once more and an end to the hours of effort Dhóri had thrown into trying to repair what his father had created. The air was filled with angry shouts and anguished screams, with the coppery scent of blood and smoke from fires he could not see. The catapult no longer hurled threats into the enemy encampment and, without arrows, those on the wall were reduced to fending off those trying to scale the walls with whatever weapons they possessed.

He could not fail. His father had taught him how to do this. He could not let his father down.

Sóbhán cut the flow of power he was directing into him from every Elyri willing to help and pulled his brother back, Dhóri's growing weakness having broken his immobile stance, and caught him with one arm as he sagged. "It isn't you," he murmured. "You're not failing him. It is time."

Staggering back, bending forward breathlessly with one hand on his knee, Khwílen gestured to those nearest him. "Get the wounded to Gorbesh. Everyone. Now!" He looked toward the watchtower where Raenár, Tau, and Zerio jointly shoved the last ladder, and everyone on it, away from the wall. More men screamed. There was another sickening thump.

If it was destroyed, it would not take long for another to replace it. If it was not, it would soon be hoisted again.

"Captain!" He waved the three men down to join him. "It's time."

The three cast each other looks of regret, looks of brief defiance, and looks of gratitude for the efforts each put into the protection of the wall, before barking orders at those with them and running down the stairs.

"We can't…" groaned Dhóri, pulling against the arm that tried to steer him toward the náós without knocking his brother off his feet.

"We can't fight," Sóbhán reminded him, bobbing his head gratefully when Bergis took Dhóri's weight and continued guiding him indoors. "There are others who need us if they're to get away. Ágdhállán is waiting." But Dhóri lacked the strength to operate the Gate now. If they were escaping St. Kóráhm's, it was up to Sóbhán to make it happen.

"dedhá?" asked Raenár with a scowl as the chellé gates were rocked with another blow of the battering ram, the shaking more intense now that there was little Elyri power to counteract it.

"Get everyone to Gorbesh."

"I'm not leaving…" began Zerio. "I promised Lord Cliáth…"

Tau snorted, "Vants don't retreat."

"There'll be others…we'd rather die defending our home than giving her up," Raenár agreed.

Khwílen wanted to argue, but felt the same way. He dodged aside to allow a pair of women dragging an injured man to the door, muttered to them "Gorbesh…now," and then to Raenár asked, "What do you suggest?"

Raenár wiped the sweat from his eyes. "Retreat to the doors, hold those while everyone who will, who can, make it away. If we can hold them to the courtyard long enough…"

They met each other's gazes. They each nodded. Khwílen sucked in a breath and said, "Give the order."

The gates shook again and the ram fell silent. There was little protection remaining. Another dozen or fewer strikes and the enemy would be through. Why then, Khwílen wondered, as men and women continued to rush past, had the enemy barrage stopped?

Were they waiting to see what the fleeing soldiers on the bulwark would do?

Were they planning something else?

Two Gates were barely enough. The last of the injured, except for the newest ones, had been evacuated to Gorbesh, and the Elyri who could do so were taking the Teren one by one or in pairs to somewhere that no invading army would reach them. In Gorbesh, Valesce and the residents there, waiting at the Gate on Earé's order, raced through the halls with the influx of refugees they had known would come.

Dhóri, defeated, broken-hearted, sat in St. Kóráhm's on the frontmost bench and waited his turn with his brother. He did not try to wipe away the traitorous tears that wove pink paths down his dusty cheeks.

Everything his father had built, had worked for, would soon be gone. How would he ever forgive Dhóri for that?

❧*❧

"Myreth?"

The dark-haired man with seductive, trembling lips cowered against the wall, trying to make himself smaller, his first impulse at seeing faces at his window being to disappear, to escape at all costs. Having heard the skittering of rocks beneath hands and feet on the cliff under his window, he prayed it was Kavan there to rescue him and yet argued that such a mundane act as climbing the cliff-face was surely beneath the bard's strengths.

Sunna held out his hand. "Come."

Níkóá reached out too. "Kavan is waiting. We'll take you to him."

Myreth glanced at the closed door. If his guardians heard the quiet smoke-gruff voices, they ignored them. As the storm raged throughout the day, bringing periodic lightning and thunder, and the eruption continued to rumble beneath the violent crashing of the sea, perhaps they did not hear the muted voices that beckoned him.

"He is here…he is waiting…"

"I know," Myreth stammered, his voice scratchy and broken from the abuse Bhás had subjected him to before peeling from the corner and stepping cautiously through the rain water gathered on the floor it the window. He peered out, looked down, trying to keep distance between himself and the strangers, and shook his head in first refusal. The pair did not touch him, did not take hold of him to hurl him to his death as he feared. He had no fear of heights, but he was concerned about the slipperiness of the stone, the rain, the gusting wind and the wrapped hand and wrist he clutched to his chest. "I…can't…"

Myreth.

The dark-skinned man, surely from the western lands where Bhás hailed from, pulled something from his pocket and held it forth as the whisper tickled through his head.

Kóráhm's ring.

Trembling, Myreth took the treasure and slid it back onto his finger from whence it had disappeared as the voice came again.

Myreth.

Chairs grated upon the stone floor in the other room. The three men looked toward the sound, expecting the door to open. Instead, the sound came with the opening and closing of the outer door. Sunna gestured, and he and Níkóá pressed as flat to the side of the building as they could on that narrow ledge. A nondescript figure bundled in bland gray clothes to shield him from the rain walked with sliding steps far enough down the path that he could lean to the side and stare at the distant eruption. He did not seem to see the intruders, and when he seemed satisfied that the eruption was no threat to the structure, he retreated and closed the door behind him when he was inside. Muted voices muttered in the other room, chairs slid again, and the evening stillness returned.

Myreth swallowed hard, weighed his options, nodded in surrender and grunted, "Help me down."

This was the best chance for freedom he was going to have.

Kavan was waiting.

❧*❧

Those who served within Hes á Redh, in solidarity with the gdhededhásur in Clarys, had gathered after dinner the night before, barring the public from the náós so the leadership could offer their hearts and souls to k'Ádhá and Dhágdhuán on behalf of the men and women caught in the throes of war. Vocalized prayers and songs from any who felt compelled to utter them, communal, ritualized chants of holy words written centuries before, fasting and tense words lifted into the rafters, praying for the lives of their soldiers and for victory over the sea invaders they had heard were trying to infiltrate Clarys and other cliff cities along Elyriá's coast.

So far, in Enesfel, only Levonne and Alberni were directly touched by war. The Faithful in Hes á Redh prayed for them too.

The heads of the Faith, the brothers and sisters, novices and staff, along with pilgrims and community Faithful who gathered outside the closed doors of the Gathering Hall, came and went as their bodies demanded, some to drink, some to relieve their bodies' needs, a few to nap or indulge themselves when they could fast no longer.

The air was thick with incense and candle smoke. He could still taste the serbháló they had shared. His knees ached from the time spent upon them, and his stomach was beginning to rumble as the hours of fasting crept by. Hearing the muffled sound of movement upon the stone altar steps, a sound that distracted him from the female voices joined in song on the other side of the platform, Tusánt lifted his gaze as the man beside him rose, the spokesman of the pilgrims who had, until now, seemed steadfast in his prayers though he did not sing, did not speak his prayers aloud. Outwardly, there was no evidence that he and his fellow pilgrims were not who they claimed to be. But their silence, compounded by Ágdhállán's premonition, continued to prick at Tusánt's nerves.

Tucked behind the barred doors where no attack could reach them, Tusánt was doing his best to keep everyone safe.

❧*❧

A crack of thunder and a blinding flash of lightning caused Myreth to jerk, lose his awkward grip on the ledge, and fall the remaining six feet to the ground. The bigger man behind him who had already reached the bottom, tried to catch him, an effort that resulted in both tumbling down the incline towards the gulley where the stench and heat of the molten river continued its crawling push toward the sea. By the time Níkóá helped both to their feet and they reached the artery of the glass-crackling lava, the slow-moving flow was less than twenty yards away. Before long, it would reach its destination and push into the sea.

"Can't chance it," Sunna grunted, shaking off a prickle that made his skin crawl and forced him to study the roiling ocean with concern.

Supporting Myreth's weight, the man breathless and unsteady from exertion, his hand and wrist in obvious pain, Níkóá looked to see what Sunna was staring at but instead of seeing a ship on the sea or the men from the building, he noted only a narrower part of the gully about a dozen feet from them, nearer the water's edge. "Think we can make that?" he asked.

He trusted Sunna could leap the gap. He was less certain Myreth could.

Clutching his injured hand close, holding the green stone of Kóráhm's ring inside his fist, Myreth nodded stubbornly. Taking his first breaths of freedom, even though they tasted more like sulfur and salt then they had inside his room, made him more determined to reach the sense of Kavan that felt nearer now.

Bhás had not yet come. Perhaps she did not know Kavan was here.

"I will," Myreth replied stubbornly.

Facing the onshore wind, blinded by the pelting rain, they plowed toward the place Níkóá had indicated, where Sunna stopped, planted his feet, and continued his unyielding stare toward the undulating sea.

"Go."

"What…?" began Níkóá.

One shoulder hitched. Sunna could not explain what he felt. Whatever it was, the lava funneling into the chasm, the darkening clouds of evening that spat forks of light at the sea and earth, or the suffocating heaviness of the air, as if the storm meant to suck away their breath, he did not like it.

One of them had to go first. Níkóá decided not to debate the command and jumped, tripping on a large stone on the opposite side so that he fell to his knees with a pained yelp. Myreth's steps slipped when he followed so that his jump came up short and left him clinging to the lip of the gulley with one hand. It was not a far drop to the bottom, but as the earth spat up a higher fountain than before and a new rush of orange-red stone began to rush over the blackening lava that paved the way before it with the sounds of rumbling, roaring, and glass crunching beneath heavy boots, pulling Myreth up from the bottom would create an unwanted, desperate delay.

"Give me your hand."

Myreth shook his head and tried to scramble for a foothold away from the heat. Níkóá grabbed his wrapped wrist. He did not have the footing to gain sufficient leverage to pull. Only when Sunna jumped across and reached to assist him were they able to drag Myreth onto the gulley's edge.

Someone behind them shouted. Unable to tell if they were spotted, if Myreth's absence was noted or if the raised alarm was in response to the volcano's increased output, there was no choice but to run, to reach Kavan and make it through the safety of the Gate before they were caught.

❧*❧

There were no choir voices in the apse for this special gathering of clergy, making the raised chamber with its wooden lattice front the ideal place for Lláhy to observe those in the náós below. His plan to use a Gate to sneak into Ylár's chamber had been thwarted by the announcement of the Feast of Prayer and Penance declared on behalf of those at war.

He glowered at the back of the man's scarred, bald head as the chorus of voices carried their entreaties to Ethenae, filling the Gathering Hall with the echoes of their Faith. It was the first time he had been so close to the perfume of incense in all the years he had been away. It was no surprise Ylár had not changed. Lláhy could not say the same about himself. His years of exile had scarred him too, darkened his skin, and etched lines on his face that should not be there.

It did not matter if Ylár was not responsible for the exile, for the selection of the one who had come between. He was not responsible for his own later nomination, only for accepting it. He had taken what should have been his after his father's death, and Lláhy intended to rectify that wrong.

Even if it had to be done in front of every gdhededhá in Clarys.

❧*❧

The rush of something cold, colder than the rain that splashed against the ground and sprayed into his face, colder than the wind that swirled around the outcropping that protected him and Rhyrdan from the worst of the weather yet tugged at the edges of their damp hair, made Kavan shiver and clutch his hand around the pendants against his chest. A thick veil clouded his internal vision, preventing him from Seeing anything, from reading the atmosphere, from judging what threat was waiting beyond his senses. He could not identify it, but he knew it by name without that proof.

He shuddered again and studied the fiery fountain. If he reached the Gate, he could leave now and avoid what lay before him. But that would mean leaving three men behind. He had come for Myreth, and his friends relied on him. He could not abandon them to her. If Bhás was coming for him here, if he could no longer avoid her, so be it. His sons behind St. Kóráhm's fallen defenses were safe for now.

He had to make certain they stayed that way.

He shoved the sturmyrá into his pack without taking time to protect it, handed the pack to Rhyrdan, and got to his feet. He did not yet feel strong enough for what was to come, but he had to act now if he was to act at all.

"We can't stay here. We need to move."

The wind shifted, gusting the sulfurous smoke to the west so that they choked and coughed. From the direction of Kavan's resolute steps, Rhyrdan assumed they were avoiding being trapped behind the embankment by the acrid billows or else they were returning to the Gate to meet the others there, though he could not see or hear them through the roar of the volcano and the storm. He shoved the waji through his belt, scooped up every pack without noticing the awkward burden, and hurried to catch up to Kavan.

Surrounded by the Inzigaen, a fact that made him shudder beneath the burden of the deepening sick pit in his stomach, Olaric found himself in the front of the charge, under Waller's suspicious gaze, when the general ordered the entire might of Neth's army into battle. Waller would lose sight of him once combat was met, but for now, Olaric had to look as though he belonged there, as though his hatred for the Lachlan and de Corrmick flags was as deep as Wallers.

He saw no benefit in a full engagement at night, when it was more difficult to tell enemy from ally, but the choice was not his.

Olaric hoped he could turn that choice in his favor.

The setting sun erased the enemy from view, leaving only shadows and spots of light that likewise lunged forward to meet them.

On the other side of the battle lines, King Lorant squared his shoulders, gave a shout, and led his army once more into battle.

❧Chapter 53❦

The trio of galleys emerged from the fog, from the dark, two cutting off the Elyri ships from their efforts to protect the trade passages so that the third ship was able to dock and disgorge its crew. So many men spilled over the galley's side that they overwhelmed the soldiers protecting the bottom of the passage. They began to climb. Two by two in a steady stream, their numbers so immense that those guarding the passage at the top could not suppress them. Invaders spilled into the streets of Clarys for the first time in history and dispersed in haphazard directions, with no other apparent goal than to spread chaos and kill anyone who opposed them.

There were barely enough trained soldiers in Clarys to confront them as most were deployed elsewhere. The remaining galleys fought to keep the Elyri ships from reaching the dock, pushing them further out to sea, sinking one. Efforts were made to rescue as many men as they could while Captain Dínyn continued to push to reach the trade passage. Despite his efforts, he was unable to send men up to aid in dispersing the land attack.

He could only listen to the screams.

Centuries of non-violence doctrine made most of his people reluctant or unable to fight. Those willing to do so were forced to protect those who barricaded themselves and their families behind locked doors and latched shutters or who ran screaming into dead-end alleys or gathered in squares around fountains and prayed they found safety in numbers. Sometimes the invaders passed those clusters without a glance.

Sometimes, emboldened by the lack of resistance, they charged into those small crowds with swings that felled the mass one by one. There were few to stop them.

The doors of Hes Dhágdhuán rattled. The voices inside fell silent as men and women fell to their knees or prostrated themselves in the aisles, holding their breaths as they turned eyes and ears to the rear of the Gathering Hall, expecting the tall ornate doors to splinter and the enemy to burst inside to slaughter them. Ylár stood in front of the altar, the single man to remain on his feet, to dare to defy death to its face. He continued to pray aloud, his booming voice filling the vast room.

In the apse, Lláhy pressed his face to the lattice and prepared his shot.

He would have no better opportunity. He would only have one.

"Stay here, Kyne," Bhyrhán barked, pulling Phílóá from the window to the center of the room. The tower room she preferred to use was too high, too shielded by the breadth of the gardens, walls, and smaller structures within the palace for any archer to touch her, but even she acknowledged that they had underestimated the nature of the invaders Kavan had warned against. She wanted to watch, to monitor, to help her people, but the best way she could do so was to remain level-headed and safe.

"Send for the k'lómesté, the bhydáni," she ordered as Bhyrhán reached the door and yanked it open. There were things the k'lómesté and those bhydáni who served her could do together, though she guessed some would be reluctant to try. She was not above demanding their obedience. It was why she had been chosen as Kyne over other candidates in her bloodline.

"Aye."

He did not know if she heard him as the chamber door banged closed. His training with sword and bow had come too late in life for him to consider himself proficient with either, but he chose, after delivering the summons to one of the many servants in the halls, to join the host gathering atop the Kyne's walls and in the watchtowers.

They could not see the invaders. They could only hear the cries of the frightened, the injured, the dying, as the enemy moved throughout the city, gradually pushing further away from the trade passage.

In their united memory, Elyriá had never known the horror of invasion.

Bhyrhán, saddened to have lived to see this day, intended to do his part to ensure it never happened again.

❦*❧

Neth's mercenary army pummeled the walls of every outpost fortress built upon the Neth-Cordash border from the sea to the banks of the Poldris River, with the Cordashians unaware that their sister outposts were suffering the same.

Unprepared, Captain Rodair and his ragtag collection of scouts managed to close the gates, but not before a few dozen mercenaries made it inside. While he continued to man the wall defenses in the hopes of keeping the disorganized exterior assault at bay, he left Evroult in charge of enough men to hunt and kill those who had dared infiltrate Ruidoso.

From the wall, Rodair could see towering flames and billows of smoke as far across the horizon as he could see, each bonfire marking the location of a farmstead, a village, one settlement after another. He imagined it was the same across the land, from Lake Curo to the forest, from the Cordash border to the Llaethlágárá, not a single farm left intact. How many were dead? How would survivors, if there were any, live through the winter?

He should send men to aid them, as many as he could collect. But he was trapped behind Ruidoso's gates, precisely where, he thought with a bitter frown, the mercenaries wanted him to be.

Evroult's war cry rose out of the darkness, a bellow louder than all but the nearest frightened townsfolk. Evroult had gotten inside before. Perhaps, Rodair mused as soon as the invaders were dealt with, he would send Evroult out the way he had come in, send him and men east and south to save as many farmers and peasants, kill as many mercenaries, as they could before the land was bereft of its future.

From the western side of the island of Mara Qin, where attacking mercenaries had not sailed, a single galley emerged from the Káliel shipyards and approached the blockade from the rear, slipping through the fog like a wraith. No one was certain where the vessel had come from, as it had been found adrift, unmanned, many decades before; it had been towed into the Mara Qin shipyard for study and, perhaps, eventual replication. The Council had been unable to agree on the need for a ship with so little room for trade cargo, and requiring an abundance of men to sail, and so she had been held at dock, maintained to remain sea-worthy but nothing more, in the hopes of the shipwrights that there might come a day when she would be needed.

That day, at Magistrate Piran's order, had come.

Determined to reach the shore, intending to deposit another murderous host to replenish the force Káliel's people had captured or killed, the men in the nearest enemy galley were unaware that the sounds of oars slicing through the sea in the fog did not belong to one of their own. Outfitted at the prow with a metal-tipped snout, when the ship caught some of its oars on the prow of the enemy galley, others flailed for a purchase in the water they could not get. Men were thrown into the sea, caught between their abruptly upended vessel and the one nearest to it when the movement of Káliel's confiscated galley pushed them together.

Men shouted and were silenced as the island's deadly currents dragged them under. Enemy galleys turned away from the blockade toward the new threat, and as most retreated to pursue Káliel's galley, they were, in turn, pursued by the majority of the island's fleet. One ship remained behind, the only one to prevent the last remaining galley from docking.

Piran waited, sword ready, for the last wave of soldiers to come ashore.

❧＊❧

The shrine of St. Kóráhm had fallen.

King Gamal knew this from the Kílyn messengers who had crossed paths with the additional troops he had sent there. When the reports began to arrive that the galleys were returning from the west, fewer now than had sailed past Natrona's port weeks before, he assumed that destroying the shrine had been the invaders' primary objective, although it made no sense.

He did not know if Kílyn stood. No messengers had arrived in days to bring him any news.

With their objective seemingly met, Gamal and his generals could not guess whether the retreating galleys meant to sail into the open sea toward wherever they had come from, or if they would turn their focus on Natrona.

Gamal was prepared for both possibilities. Every man of fighting age clogged the docks and the streets nearest to the sea, daring the galleys to come ashore. Every ship at Hatu's disposal, naval, merchant, and fishing vessel alike, was instructed to form a barricade across the mouth of the bay and sink any ship trying to leave it. Ships recruited from Nelori and Jardin, sailing on behalf of King Lorant, pursued the galleys from the west, arriving at Kílyn as the galleys departed. Through his spyglass, Gamal shifted his attention between the ships that stopped beyond Natrona's coast as if reconsidering a land assault, and the ones he could see approaching the nearest blockade ships on the horizon.

Those ships were determined to pass.

Hatu's navy was determined to prevent it.

Just as the soldiers on the dock, supplemented by the brigade tama Yetek had left behind, were determined to protect the royal city.

The galleys tried to retreat.

Before long, they would meet the cordon. With the ships from Jardin and Nelori behind, Gamal expected they would meet their ends there.

For now, the soldiers were held along the sea's edge in case the galleys decided to return.

❧*❧

Squeezed between the Hatu ships and the few remaining to protect Levonne's harbor and the mouth of the Tegid, the captains of the galleys saw no other choice. They were unlikely to make it to sea alive and their orders, their customs, were clear.

Orders were meant to be followed. When they could not be, death was preferable to retreat. Until a new order was given, they fought, and died, where they were.

Those on the galleys who could, who were not heaving oars with enough force to push the boats ashore, fought viciously with the crews of the caravels. Some climbed aboard the caravels, where men were pulled down and thrown into the sea. When first one galley and then another forced their way onto the sand, the living spilled out, running with bellows and drawn weapons toward the men lining the shore waiting for them.

Osveld was among them. There were others left to protect the Dubuais-Cáner estate and vineyards, under the direction of the Bodils. It was Osveld's duty to ensure that such protection was unneeded…to ensure that no enemy soldier made it off the beach, the dock, or out of the sea.

❧*❧

The stone and wood bridge constructed across the Tegid River had existed in various forms for as long as Rhidam had stood, allowing horse, wagon, and foot traffic to enter the city while also serving as a marker to prevent merchant barges from Levonne from running aground in the increasingly more shallow and wider waterway that continued towards Dorshur. There had been discussions by more than one king about the need to build a more permanent structure, a bridge that did not require the periodic replacement of rotted, failing timbers. But the consensus had been that the bridge needed to remain accessible, rather than be closed for any significant amount of time to undertake permanent reconstruction, and, since King Innis' death, there had been an unending string of projects and problems to drain the royal coffers and prevent attention turning to the matter of the Tegid bridge.

With the mouth of the river in Levonne closed to prevent ships from sailing to Rhidam, no merchant vessels or barges had sailed here in weeks.

Small boats, however, ferrying goods between downriver villages and farms, Rhidam and Dorshur, had continued without interruption.

Warde and his spies thought little of those insignificant boats. The Association's focus was elsewhere, primarily on its own business, offering spy services to the Crown's inquisitor and monitoring the comings and goings from a warehouse Warde was certain was a front for something nefarious that did not involve members of the Association.

He knew underhanded actions when he saw them. He did not want external competition in Rhidam.

There were always people there, preventing him from getting inside, and he was not prepared to take a hostage for interrogation. He did not want to tip his hand that he was there.

The smell of hot castle-black rising from within today had been enough for Warde to collect two dozen men to investigate. By his count, there should be six men inside. It was the best chance he would have to see inside for himself. But before his men could converge on the warehouse and demand entry, the wide doors opened, and a pair of shaggy, gray-faced oxen were guided out pulling a cart containing eight large barrels of the steaming, putrid liquid. The last six men followed, two heading deeper into town, one riding a horse who crossed the bridge and rode north, passing a mule-drawn cart with its hunched drivers huddled against the night's cool temperatures. The remaining pair closed the doors and then tugged the oxen into motion, steering them at a plodding pace across the bridge.

Warde frowned. Castle-black was often used to seal boats, to harden the wood and prevent leaks. There was a boatwright to the south across the river who could utilize such a quantity of the product. But transporting so much in a smoking, steaming, stinking state was not practical, was normally only done if some major building enterprise was underway nearby, and so Warde rose from his hiding place, pointed, and shouted, "You there! Stop!"

The pitch wagon was at the center of the bridge. The mule wagon passed on its other side. In the same instant as his shout, tongues of flames arched from rooftops and warehouses around him and out of the darkness on the other side of the river. Splashes hit the water as the arrows struck the barrels in both wagons, igniting their wooden shells until the pitch in one reacted with the flame and oily substance in the others, creating a ball of fire that shot high enough into the air that much of Rhidam could see it. The rest could hear the repercussive blast that rattled the air, shook the doors, and broke windows in several of the nearest structures.

The thunderous sound, like the moon falling into the heart of Rhidam, lurched those in Hes á Redh up from their prone, kneeling, or seated posts in alarm, many into the waiting arms of the pilgrims they had given succor. Several found knives against their throats or in their ribs, knives that cut deep and left men and women bleeding on the altar steps. Bhídígís was thrown to the side, out of harm's way, as he was rising to his knees when the blast shook the náós. Tusánt, spared because the man nearest to him had left the Gathering Hall minutes before, reached for the pilgrim who held Novice Dhon in his grasp. They were beyond his reach. dedhá Charlos, come from the keep to share with his brothers in prayer, tried to pull away from the man who held him. The blade cut deep. Blood spurted across the back of Dhon's head as both Dhon and his captor were thrown back.

The candelabra behind them fell against the altar. The prayer cloth over the marble ignited, as did the pilgrim's robes and soon, Dhon and Charlos' robes too. Bhídígís yanked Dhon free of the pile and began patting out flaming clothes and hair with his bare hands. The pilgrim who had left the Hall returned with a small keg of what Tusánt expected to be water, which he splashed onto the two burning men and the floor around them. Charlos flopped and flailed as his nervous system reacted to the burst of flame created by the oil added to it but the blood streaming from his neck spared him the worst of that burning agony. The pilgrim, however, thrashed and screamed and tried to stand, to avoid the flames that were consuming him.

People scrambled to apprehend the assailants, all of whom, except for the burning man, raced toward the main door of the náós. Embers from burning fabric and splattered oil sparked in all directions, igniting anything flammable the fire could reach. Unaware that the doors were barred to keep the public out, the men hoped for escape.

Tusánt had thought he was keeping the threat out. He had never imagined he had sealed the danger inside with them. The pilgrims reached the doors but could not open them, and in their initial haste, they were not level-headed enough to lift the bar that kept the doors closed. Bhídígís remained with Dhon, dragging him to one side where the fire had not yet spread and trying to stem the bleeding.

Reacting on an impulse he was not aware he had, Tusánt caught the arm of the man who carried the oil keg and yanked him aside. The dregs of oil splashed in all directions as both men, unsteady in that action, tumbled down the altar stairs and landed against the frontmost bench. Something fell, or was thrown, striking Tusánt in the back of the head so that the last thing he saw was the pilgrim's bulge-eyed expression of shock.

"What was…?"

The cloud of fire and smoke that mushroomed from the Tegid was visible to Asta, Kjell, and Chancellor Dahl from the courtyard where they quietly discussed how much funds were in the treasury and how many additional men they might secure to send more aid to Alberni and Levonne.

The chancellor leaped up, pointing elsewhere. "The náós!"

"Get that fire out," Asta barked, already running toward the gates of the keep. Rhidam could not afford another great fire.

"Asta!"

She was too far away to be stopped and he was too infirm to catch either her or the chancellor as both ran from the keep, followed by every soldier, servant, groundskeeper, and stableman that could be spared.

Instead, Kjell limped inside to gather the children and servants into what he believed was the most protected part of the castle.

He knew Asta had gone to the Tegid, in the direction where the last great fire had started. She had spoken of the damage that fire had caused…the fire that had contributed to her father's death.

She would not allow that to happen to her husband and grandson. Kjell trusted her to do her duty. She had to trust that he would do his.

❧*❧

There were too many.

Bhríd led the charge through the center of the Nethite line, his horse was lost but not his resolve to reach the street end where he had seen General Waller's banner flying over the heads of Neth's troops.

Too many, he scowled behind his helmet as he cut through three men, threw his shield arm into the face of someone else to push them into the path of someone's mace, and low-kicked another so that he pitched face first to the ground to be trodden by the dance of soldier boots that sought forward progress in the bloody autumn dust. Torches dotted the landscape, but most had gone out now, dropped and trampled, leaving only the light of the moon and stars and the glow of Glevum's windows to see by.

The folly of night combat. Enesfel had no choice but to engage. He wondered what advantage Fraen thought this tactic offered.

It was not an advantage Neth needed, however.

Compared to Enesfel's numbers, there were too many. What Lorant's army needed was a miracle.

Chapter 54

Kavan's chest ached, the effort of holding his breath against the burning sulfur stench and the anxious waiting for the arrival of one he had twice thought to never see again making him nauseous and unsteady so that he leaned against Rhyrdan for support. It was also an effort, no matter how foolish, to remain still, to avoid being detected by the woman he had come to thwart. With each step closer the three men took, boots sliding on stone, bringing the crunching glass sound with them, she drew closer too, a boulder of dread Kavan could not escape.

Desperately, he scrambled to remove Zythán's sturmyrá from his pack. He clasped one hand around it without pulling it free, clutched the pendants around his neck with the other, and squeezed his eyes closed, aware now of the expanding ball of power knotting tighter within his core.

If the three hurried, he had the strength to build another Gate where he stood if they could not reach the other before she reached him. He might be able to get them to safety.

He did not want to die.

But Kóráhm's last words that continued to echo in his head and his stifling fears told him he would.

He wanted to get his friends away before a lifetime of inevitable fate came for him, crashed over him, and swept him up in its wake.

"Kavan!"

Not 'my lord'. Not any other honorific or endearment that croaking amber-honey voice could have uttered. Only his name, alive with adoration and jointly colored with delight, dread, disbelief, forced Kavan to turn to the sound so that it washed over and through him. It was not enough to ease his fear, but it was enough to allow him to stand up straight away from Rhyrdan's shoulder and place the glass box in his companion's hands.

She was near…they both were. What power he had stored now would have to be enough.

Expecting Myreth to throw himself at his feet, Kavan was caught off guard by the man's desperate embrace. Eyes closed, forcing tears of joy to escape at the corners, noting his wrapped wrist and the dark, fading bruises around his neck, Kavan returned the embrace only long enough to prove to himself that Myreth was alive.

"We must go," he rasped, willing the others to lay their hands on him in frantic hope as Myreth choked, "I knew you would come…"

Another voice, cutting and cold as the stone on which they stood, countered Myreth's with an arrogant, scornful retort. "bhedhuaethag."

Kavan forced his eyes open against his better judgment, aware of the final unraveling of distant power threads within him and the overwhelming loss of family, of Kóráhm, of hope.

Bhás.

❧*❧

The iron gates of the duke's manor were flung open, throwing back the servants, staff, and farmhands who tried to keep the foreign horde at bay. There were not so many, as the majority were congregated at St. Kóráhm's gates, but there were enough to break the locks and barrel inside once the duke's invisible defenses failed. Egon Groff and the men who had followed him through town, picking off the siege-makers from the back, were too far away to prevent the opening, too far away to prevent the surge into the manor's courtyard, but he ran after them, continuing to swing, taking advantage of the barricade made by the duke's staff to kill a few more in the hopes that not a single one would defile the manor, that not a single one of the duke's staff would fall to the enemy's blades.

It was too late for that.

The gates of St. Kóráhm's, too, splintered. Another strike, perhaps two, and the invaders would be inside.

"Last chance," growled Tau, his fluid stance, weaving to the mutable sounds of imminent invasion, preparing himself for combat when it came.

"I…" Khwílen began, his resolution wavering now that the inevitable was at hand.

Zerio squared his shoulders and swept his tail of chestnut hair back over his shoulder, muttering, "No shame in retreat."

Khwílen was no soldier. He had never trained as one.

But he was St. Kóráhm's leader. This was his fight.

❧678❧

His grip tightened on the metal-wrapped staff that someone had dropped, and shook his head, refusing to speak, refusing to leave.

The ram met resistance again. Splinters of wood erupted in all directions and yet the gate held.

Khwílen's lips pursed. He squinted. Those on either side of him braced for the tide that would engulf them when the next strike came.

Tau and Zerio nodded at one another. "For Vants?"

Tau nodded. "For Vants."

"For Kóráhm," hissed Khwílen.

The impact came.

"For Kóráhm!" The cry rang out, a cry echoed by the distant blatting of a war horn not heard before.

A third of his force was directed toward the manor. Another third was pointed through the center of Alberni toward the enemy ships in her harbor. The remainder followed on Madoc's heels toward the heart of the conflict as he knew it.

He wished then he had kept Yóáná away as she leaned low to her horse's neck and raced along beside her husband.

It was too late for wishes now.

❧*❧

Child soldiers were cast aside as Enesfel's ranks preferred not to kill them if they could avoid doing so, but as Kaj and his brigade pushed nearer to Glevum's houses and barricaded streets, many of the dead they trampled and tripped over were the small bodies of the Inzigaen, pressed into an adult war too young. Nose broken from the impact of someone's elbow, blood dripping down his lip as his head pounded and his ears rang, he swung and charged, wove out of danger and back into it, led by the instinct to survive. When someone grabbed his arm, he spun with his blade low, thankful at the last minute that the familiar face across from him belonged to a man armored heavily enough to prevent the blow from being fatal.

"Look at this!" The man whom Kaj believed to be the son of Neth's current ruler, a man he had seen in Lorant's company before, banged on the front of his shield. It was painted with the now familiar Fraen crest, but it had a thick black sash painted across the image from left to right."

"Pass it on. They're with the prince." Olaric was sucked into the throes of combat, and, as if to make his point, he ran through the nearest fellow who swung at Kaj with a sword too big for his small stature, possibly a child; it was too difficult to tell. What Kaj did make note of, as he swiveled and pressed his back to Olaric's to fight together, was that the fallen soldier's shield did not bear the black sash.

Prince. Not king.

de Corrmick supporters.

However many there might be, as he noted more such shields within the field of nighttime's vision, perhaps this day would not be lost.

⤶*⤷

Though the last great fire was a distant memory for some, there were enough people in Rhidam who had lived through it and remembered the horror that had destroyed so much of the city. They scrambled like frantic ants to isolate and contain the flames eating Hes á Redh from the inside, working to save those within who they relied upon as the cornerstones of their Faith. There was no White Bard to extinguish the fire this time, to brave the flames and bring out those trapped inside.

The citizens of Rhidam, and the Association with them, were forced to save the náós themselves.

At the Tegid, men fought fire too, though there was little they could do except douse the city perimeter of the bridge fire with sand and soil and race to contain each small island of flame that dropped from the bridge and floated ashore on the downriver current. Men lined the river to the south, and others, having pulled flat timbers and small boats into the Tegid, were paddling hastily across to fight the uncontained spread on the other side.

The Association aided the efforts there as well, but it was the apprehension of the archers from nearby rooftops, the pulling out of the river those men who had driven the weaponized wagons, that Warde made their primary objective. He ordered others to comb the panicked city streets for the faces seen at the warehouse over the past several days, but he was found at the river, shoveling clods of dirt onto pockets of shore fires, when Asta and the Lachlan Guards who had followed her arrived.

He looked at her. She looked at him.

Asta threw off her cloak and jumped down the embankment beside him to begin digging too.

⤶*⤷

Without considering his actions or their consequences, Kavan tried to shove Myreth behind him as Myreth, in turn, tried to step between the woman and the one his captivity had been used to lure to this deserted place. In his breast, in the center of his power, Kavan felt a spark, fed by the pulsating sturmyrá in the pack slung over his shoulder, that began to tighten into a familiar knot. Rhyrdan, the man closest to him, yanked the waji from his belt and darted toward the offending woman with an outraged roar, but a casual flick of her hand threw him several hundred feet into the path of a dozen men racing toward them from Myreth's distant prison. His father's sword slipped from its scabbard and clattered across the ground.

Myreth protested the effort to protect him as he stumbled on the slippery stones and fell, the sturmyrá now in his hands.

The earth shook. The air split with a cracking roar, and the distant flaming mountain spewed a plume of fire higher than before. The flow of molten rock spread faster down its flanks, pushing the head of the lava river along faster, covering over it, and, in some places, filling it so that the lava overflowed the gulley and fanned out upon the land.

Bhás seemed to chuckle without making a sound.

Hearing the thunderous din of their battle cries, Níkóá turned back the way they had come to pull Rhyrdan to his feet while Sunna, with the hood of his cloak raised to shield his face, drew his waji and followed with a low growl. Charging the shi cali was pointless when she was focused and prepared for conflict. He would bide his time and strike when her guard was down. For now, the men coming from their rear were more important.

She did not look at him, did not appear to notice or care that a fiery doom awaited them. She wanted only the one she had sworn to bestow her ancient vengeance upon.

Beneath the walls of St. Kóráhm's, Ágdhállán felt his father's fear. He saw her within his mind, heard her laughter. He smelled noxious, acidic smoke and grimaced at the explosive roar that shook the air, shook his father's focus, shook along the threads of power that bound them. Wincing at the pain in his wrist as he braced himself, Ágdhállán struggled to his feet and pressed his hand against the closest wall. Sparks of light raced like veins through the stone. The power within the room intensified and began to converge beneath his flat palm. He sucked the power into himself and fought to reach the point of power within that was his father. He could not make the connection until the sensation of hands on his shoulders caused the power to arc, flash, and speed through the ether to supplement his father's strengths.

Kavan's eyes narrowed. There were too many men, dressed in thick, gray padding against the cold, possibly wearing armor beneath the layers, for his companions to easily fight. If he turned his attention from Bhás to aid them, she would strike him down. He reached into the pulsing well of static power, intending to throw an invisible fist at her, only to be met with a shock as he sensed Ágdhállán inside his head.

Again, Bhás laughed and the hooked needles of power she sought to sink into his psyche made note of the boy. To Kavan's horror, she focused on Ágdhállán instead of him. Expending only as much power as he thought necessary, he slammed the connection closed between himself and his son, knocking the boy off his feet…

…but not before Bhás' power slammed against a wall more ancient than either of them. She bellowed in outrage and threw the whole of her power into a piercing, buzzing screech inside Kavan's mind. He fell face-first onto the ground and clutched his head between his hands with a scream.

Ágdhállán dropped over the edge of the chasm.

❧*❧

The arrival of two vessels would normally not have been enough to frighten the handful of men assigned to duty on the galley as their companions tore through the city the defiler called home. But there was only a handful of them, not enough to row, to steer the ship into the attack, not enough to prevent one of the two ships from sailing near enough to the shore to deposit its host of men bearing the banner of the Lachlan kings.

The second ship, balo Essem's ship, maneuvered alongside the galley, breaking unmanned oars as they broadsided her. Mooring ropes with clawed hooks were flung across, some finding purchase in the damp wood, others missing the mark and reeled back to be thrown again. Soldiers and barefoot sailors slid across the ropes and dropped onto the galley's deck to quickly subdue those who resisted and claim the galley as their own.

Men on the Hatu caravel shouted victory.

Essem turned the ship to the dock so that his men, too, could set to purging the poison infecting Alberni, as those already ashore raced into the streets towards the sounds of terror and death.

❧*❧

In the streets of Clarys, Elyri screamed. Elyri died.

❧682❧

At the gates of the Kyne's palace, a dozen or more dark-skinned soldiers in peculiar armor bearing blades and weapons no Elyri had ever seen, fought their way inside while avoiding the barrage of stones and arrows cast down on them from the parapet above.

The clamor at the doors of Hes Dhágdhuán grew louder.

Kluín turned his head towards the altar, hearing movement there. He was met with Ylár's rebellious stance, his defiant, narrow-eyed stare. Feeling as though he was slogging through cold honey, Kluín forced himself to his knees, to his feet, and turned to face the door too.

Hwensen followed suit, as did Paul and a handful of others willing to match their k'gdhededhá and stand insolent in the face of death.

The doors rattled, shook, and cracked again.

In the apse, Lláhy shifted his footing and readied his weapon as Ylár moved to stand in front of the altar.

❧*❧

Hands caught Ágdhállán's uninjured wrist, solid hands belonging to a man he could not see as his feet flailed, seeking purchase on anything solid that might keep him from falling to his death. He screamed, mentally anguished by the abruptly severed connection, the shock of being thrown back from the wall, the fear of dying, and the surprise of the hands that caught him, all culminating in a stream of violent sound that did not stop until he was deposited on the floor on the opposite side of the chasm, away from the Gate, away from the relics, away, he felt, from any chance to help his father.

Perhaps he could not, but the one with him could.

"Go to him," Ágdhállán begged.

The words were barely spoken; the presence of Saint Kóráhm the Heretic was gone.

Ágdhállán was alone when his father needed him most.

❧*❧

Tucking the sturmyrá under one arm, unaware of its import, Myreth struggled to his feet, scooped up Wortham's sword, and shouted, "They're not all flesh!" as he stumbled toward those joining against the horde Bhás had summoned. At most, he had four men watching over him. There was only one way there could be so many men against them now.

He had seen this before, shadows summoned from the earth to fight battles when she did not wish to fight herself and did not have command of enough people to fight. They were shades…but they could still kill.

Sunna looked back in response to Myreth's cry. Three or four against a dozen would never stand.

Kavan would have to face Bhás alone long enough for Sunna to address this other threat.

Beyond them, the lava that overflowed the banks of the gulley began a relentless push toward the shadow soldiers and his companions. Sunna ran faster to join them.

Not pushing, Kavan sensed as Bhás' power dragged him across stone that tore at fabric and skin, as his fingers and feet sought purchase on the damp ground to enable him to struggle up while trying to claw free of the drilling sound of power in his head. The earth's blood was being pulled toward them, a river powerful enough to sweep them over the cliff and smash them against the craggy peaks below. Unable to even the odds, to summon shadows of his own to fight beside his friends, or to hold the lava at bay if the screeching within continued unabated, Kavan took the first risk that came to mind.

Now on his hands and knees, a song, a prayer, tones high and pure enough to rattle glass, cutting through the sound of the surf and the belching thunder of the eruption, was cast into the sky as he tipped his head back like a baying wolf and focused his eyes on the ribbons of green, white, and purple in the storm clouds he had not noticed before. A prayer of Kóráhm, the first he had learned, the first he had set to music, prompted by the fleeting sense of his patron he had felt through the contact with Ágdhállán.

Kóráhm was with his son. Ágdhállán was safe.

Bhás' violent recoil away from Kóráhm gave Kavan hope. The saint's words, whether she recognized them as his or not, made her recoil as well.

The scream of vibrating power in his head ceased.

He cast ropes of power around her in the hopes of holding her as he stood at last. This time her shriek was audible, covering over the first clatter of steel against steel and Rhyrdan's furious battle cry.

❧ * ❦

The stream of voices and footsteps finally stopped moving in and out of the room. For several minutes, Inness stood in the darkness alone, trying to keep her sight focused on the sliver of light that entered the passage as she strained her ears for an indication of additional threats. The light faded and brightened as her eyes played tricks on her, driven by the hammering of her heart and her increasingly erratic breathing. Not even Oska's soothing murmurs, a voice whispering out of the darkness where her guide had long ago disappeared, could calm her.

Only when she depressed the stone with her violently trembling hand, only when the passage door groaned open so that the glow and aroma of scented tallow candles and a blast of cool air from the nearby open window swirled toward her, did she breathe easy. She crept cautiously out of the passage after taking a hasty but thorough glance around the room to be sure she was alone, without thinking about closing the passage.

It would not have mattered if she wanted to. Her guide had not shown or told her how to close it…and she would need that route of escape until it was safe for her to return to her rightful place.

Not until Henrik was secure on Glevum's throne.

The Black Room.

She remembered it well.

Footsteps came and went in the corridor, but she was alone to circle the room, to run her fingers over familiar surfaces as if collecting the memories found there. Conversations and faces, Oska at the fire, warming his hands. Oska and Kjell bent over this same table discussing matters of rule that she had wanted to hear but had been discouraged from sharing. She could hear sounds like a tournament beyond the open window, fighting in Glevum's streets, fighting that she assumed, with a soaring heart, would bring Henrik to her. She turned toward the sound, wanting to see for herself, but she took only one step before the floor creaked behind her.

The door opened. She spun, sword ready.

For the span of a half dozen heartbeats, the queen-regent locked eyes with the imposter king, the man who had betrayed her. His shock at finding her there, older but still much the same, a woman he believed dead having emerged from a gaping black hole in the wall where there should have been a solid panel, robbed Fraen the Elder of his voice and ability to react. When she charged, sword poised like a jouster's lance, screaming, "For Henrik!" he did not have the presence of mind to draw his sword to counter her.

Her blade pierced through his breast, driving him backward against the frame of the door, pinning him there as the blade bit into the wood.

Fraen's expression, as she pressed against him, staring into his eyes with fire and fury and a snarl of revenge-filled hate, was one of slow dawning realization that the throne he had stolen had been reclaimed. Not by the Lachlan army at Glevum's border, not by one of the exiled de Corrmick princes, but by the de Corrmick he had stolen it from.

He sneered. "You'll never hold it…"

She sneered back, his blood running down the blade onto her hands, dripping onto the floor at their feet.

"I don't have to."

The light faded from his eyes.

❧*❧

There was no time for words, no need to expend energy on speech that would not be heard over the din of combat. The Nethite line had given out, allowing Lorant's army to fight their way into the heart of Glevum until he and Jerit, fighting side by side in their quest to corner General Waller, found themselves alone.

Sever the head, the body would fall.

Shouts arose around them, out of the dark, from the city's edge on the west and south, from the east where Glevum met the sea, but Lorant could not tell who had the upper hand as each street peeled back layers of soldiers, dividing the Lachlan force, spreading them thin. There was no way to tell the state of Enesfel's army or if the breaking line had been a trap laid down to suck Enesfel into the maze of unfamiliar streets.

He could only tell the state of the soldiers, Lachlan Guards, and recruited de Corrmick loyalists, who fought around him. The streets were littered with the dead so that now, with the castle gates in sight, he had less than three dozen men to rally as he pulled Jerit onto a scaffold stained with the blood of those Fraen had recently executed.

Nethite soldiers, reinforced by their foreign mercenaries, poured into the square from every direction.

Back-to-back, as the first wave reached the lip of the scaffold, Lorant and Jerit fought as one.

❧*❧

The threads of power that bound her were easily shrugged off and used in turn to pull Kavan towards her. His heels ached from the effort to keep his footing on the wet rock and his head felt as if it would split as he tried to cut the threads he had created. The words of the songs fell away, leaving only the notes that bolstered his morale, his sense of purpose, more than they did the building bubble of power that undulated and popped around them like a thin, gelatinous skin. He no longer heard the sounds of combat; he could only hear the crinkling sound of breaking glass that heralded the rapidly approaching lava. The air was hot, the searing stench made him cough, and the occasional splash of mountainous waves against the shore that shot its spray across the land felt as if it sizzled against his skin, filling the air with a steamy mist that made it difficult to see.

He did not need to see her.

Unable to break the lines of power now turned against him, he reached into the core of the sturmyrá, which Myreth continued to protect, and through it, with an unvoiced cry for the guidance of k'Ádhá, Dhágdhuán, and Kóráhm, he summoned as much power from the air as he could. There was a vast sucking sensation as the bubble burst and power rushed into him from the sky, from the sea, from the earth beneath his feet. Silver threads wrapped around the still-growing leaden ball of power inside, but the rest, gold and green, white and blue, began to weave into a shield as he continued to fight against her pull.

Perhaps he could release that frightening ball of power as he had once unknowingly done to Owain.

Once the shield was in place, once her grasp on the threads between them weakened, he believed he would have enough to begin his assault without her counter-influence undermining his efforts, but his companions on the outside of the shield, men fighting for their lives against foes real and projected, would be vulnerable to anything she chose to do.

Kavan prayed he could end this before any of those he loved fell prey to her strikes.

Why, his thoughts cried as she fought to steal the energy he gathered. We could be allies. We need not be enemies.

bheturbhae. bhesómá. bhedhuaethag. bhemethán.

Words he had heard at Dawid Coryllien's tomb.

Words directed at Kóráhm as much as at himself.

She was as much a puppet of ancient history as Kavan, a path of vengeance she had been lured into, chosen for, and committed to before he had been born. A path she had waited a lifetime to fulfill against a man who had been given no choice by the accident of his birth.

The shield was nearly complete.

She fought harder to undermine the power he collected, to take it and use it for herself.

I am not Kóráhm.

A shriek of power, as audible as it was internal, cut through his shield at the mention of that name. As the shield began to disintegrate, he recoiled at what he Saw.

Raebhá. On her knees. Cradling a small form bound in blood-soaked wrappings. Waves rising. Crashing over the sands of Gálínphel. Receding.

Until nothing remained of the city, or the people in it.

Until Raebhá and Gaed were gone.

Convinced of the reality of what he was shown, Kavan fell to his knees with a wail of despair.

The shield he had woven collapsed around him.

❬*❭

"We're safe, Oska. You are king now."

There was no one else the soft footsteps behind her could belong to. She knew those steps. She knew the smell of him, the warmth of his presence in the room, the only human warmth, other than her father's, she had ever succumbed to. Releasing the sword hilt, the blade remaining stuck in the doorframe, keeping Fraen upright, Inness took a step back and turned, expecting his embrace, expecting to see his beloved face beaming with pride at her success. She had the strength to be queen. She had proven that to her mother once again.

Inness was instead met by the wild-eyed fanatical gaze of a woman she did not recognize and the piercing pinch of a blade that slid through her unarmored skin, between her ribs, into her lung, and twisted just enough to tear a deeper gash there.

She opened her mouth, confused about where Oska had gone, confused by this stranger, and surprised by the startling stab of anguish. Blood bubbled over her lips, rising in her throat, making her cough, cutting off words her mind refused to string together.

Marta pulled the narrow knife free and dispassionately watched the woman fall to the floor, still trying to voice her confusion and surprise but unable to do so.

Marta did not speak. Inness Lachlan de Corrmick, royalty though she might be, did not deserve the honor of an explanation.

The words did not need to be spoken.

She had retribution.

Fen was at peace.

Marta knew however, as she slipped back into the passage from whence she had emerged and closed it behind her, leaving the dead and dying to their fates, that she would never have that same peace.

There was only the fulfillment of revenge promised and achieved.

❧*❦

With blood spreading down his arm, Jerit accepted the sword Lorant offered despite the knowledge that taking it, the sword Kavan had bestowed on Lorant the day of his coronation, meant that Lorant was unarmed.

Jerit was the better swordsman. If they had any chance to survive the swarm that continued to assail the scaffold, it would be with the sword in Jerit's hands. To Lorant's left, Bhríd joined Earé on scaffold and struggled to push the assailants back while Enesfel's army, fighting beneath both the Lachlan and de Corrmick flags, fought into the square, preventing Neth's soldiers from escaping.

Lorant ducked out of the way of a thrown spear.

On his right, Bhetá knocked the projectile aside with her crimson-stained shield. Someone amidst the mass of men around the scaffold screamed as it struck a different target than intended.

Ours or theirs, Lorant wondered.

He thought once he saw the banner of Cordashian kings at the western edge of the square. Distracted by Earé's shout as she leaped off the platform, the woman having not been present when the battle began and now landed in the middle of those trying to reach Enesfel's king and Neth's prince, by the time Lorant looked again, the banner he expected was gone.

He was abruptly forced off his feet when Bhetá crashed into him, knocked off balance by the arrow now embedded beneath her collarbone where her armor had been earlier compromised. An axe came down but met the resistance of the Daema's shield, its metal surface and her body weight the only things that prevented the blade from sinking into Lorant's skull.

"My King." Bhetá, her face bloody from the impact of her bleeding shield arm twisting painfully as she fought to her feet, thrust her sword into Lorant's hands, and drew her shorter one from her hip. Jerit drew Lorant up with one hand, his shield lost into the crowd. Lorant barely made it upright when he fell again with a scream as a blade cut across his thigh.

Bhríd loomed over him, shielding him from the rain of blows that followed. Bhetá moved into position at Jerit's back.

The only faces around them were men determined to kill them. Earé had been absorbed into their mass and could no longer be seen. None of

Enesfel's soldiers were close enough to fight for their king except the three with him on the scaffold.

None of them believed it would be enough.

Enesfel would fall here.

੬*੭

The flash of Sight, the vivid image of Inness lying in a spreading pool of her own blood, superimposed on the horrific proof of the danger Bhás presented to those he loved, was not enough to undercut the too-real sensation of a blade slashing across his thigh, the feeling of falling, the stifling press of boots and blades, fear-sweat and the heavy scent of death, and the frightened cry of a young king Kavan should have been there to protect. A young king he had vowed to protect by putting an end to Bhás and the stranglehold of terrorism she had inflicted upon the Sovereignties.

He should unleash the power within. Unable to breach her mind the way she could his, despite a lifetime's practice at blocking out the thoughts and power of others, sídysá might not be enough to defeat her, but if he could entrap her long enough, he believed he could squeeze the life out of her the way he could squeeze stone to dust.

Or that the release of power, bolstered by the strength of Zythán and all of Kavan's ancestors behind him, might be enough to explode her brain inside of her skull and end this.

It might also kill the men whose hand-to-hand struggle drew ever closer, driven by the spread of the lava.

He shuddered. He did not want to kill anyone.

If she had killed his wife and child as he believed, however, there was no choice but to destroy her.

Better they all die here than Bhás be allowed to continue her war against those she believed had besmirched her ancestor. Better they all die here than allow those they loved, brothers and sisters, parents, friends, children, and spouses, to suffer and die as well.

Kavan believed those with him would agree.

He did not resist as Bhás dragged him closer. Instead, he focused his power into the ground, constricting stone like a giant snake, enduring image after image of Raebhá's death, each one just different enough that he began to realize none of them were real.

She and Gaed were not beyond saving.

Bhás caught his shoulders, lifted him off his feet with unnatural strength so that he dangled like a cloth doll who refused to resist except to clutch at the invisible hand that began to constrict around his neck, cutting off the flow of air.

Blood began to gush from his wrists, his side, from his feet within his boots. Recoiling from the sacred power of rósádhá, Bhás dropped to her knees, screeching as if burned, and flung Kavan away as the lava reached the cliff and spilled into the sea. Belching plumes of smoke, ash, and steam filled the air.

With one hand behind him, using enough strength to prevent him from being dashed to the ground, Kavan forced out every bit of power he could pull from within and from the world around him, from Bhás and every other Elyri mind he had ever touched.

Sunna turned. He could see it. He could sense it. She was vulnerable. This was his time.

The woman who had disgorged him into the world and discarded him was destined to die at her child's hand.

The waji flew.

The cliff crumbled into the sea as if carved away by the fast-flowing lava as sídysá was released.

Kavan felt the power explode within the screaming woman upon impact, felt the shockwave pulse outward from where he stood in the short moment before her release of blinding power erupted around him too…and the ground beneath his feet gave way.

❧692❧

❧Chapter 55❦

Fleeing with the injured and those tending them as Neth's army bore down on the camp, covered with the blood of the wounded and the dead, Ártur stumbled and fell, pushed into the mud by something he could not see. Not the hands of gdhededhá Thrismund who propelled others along in front of him as he swung a discarded sword with the other. Not the hands of Healer Ylltán who had given up healing for wielding a cleaver and shield to ward off the assailants directly behind Ártur, who likewise stumbled with a shriek and then stood momentarily frozen in place.

Rather, the hands were a shockwave of unfathomable power that blasted over and through him and stripped him of his own as it held him face down against the ground.

His thoughts burned with the belief that he would die as he had feared.

His lips, however, gave testimony to the certainty in his soul.

"sínréc…no…"

Kept awake by thoughts and feelings he could not describe, unable to explain them to Nóráh and unwilling to disturb her sleep as he tried to determine the origin of his melancholy, Bhen paced the ground level of what had once been bhydáni Tíbhyan's home, seeking a remedy for the sick, unsettled churning in his stomach that tea had not soothed. A noise, like a cry on the wind, an echo of a distant, suffering voice, brought him to the stairs to go up again, believing his wife had summoned him. Instead, when the sucking of power and the great backlash in its wake came, he was flung down the stairs to land in a heap at the bottom, crumpled, twisted, his eyes wide and unseeing.

Their brother wasn't there.

No one had seen him since the final evacuation of St. Kóráhm's began. They knew Ágdhállán was not in Rhidam; Cáym had said as much.

He had said Ágdhállán had remained in the chellé when Raenár took the other boys to Rhidam.

Neither Dhóri nor Sóbhán wanted to believe it.

Now, there was no other option except to believe.

"We go back," Sóbhán agreed, pushing into the oratory Gate.

They did not know what they would find, if the chellé had fallen, if it was overrun. If Zerio, Tau, and Khwílen were dead.

Neither could fight an invading army. For their young brother, however, and for their father's sake, they were determined to try.

Dhóri put his hands on Sóbhán's. The power of the Gate was abruptly sucked away beneath their feet, taking the familiar weight of energy out of both, only to replace it with an eruption of power a heartbeat later that surged through the floor, into them, and the world beyond the Chamber.

The brothers slumped in each other's arms and slid to the floor.

She felt him within her, terrified, alone, a bright burning pinpoint of power hotter than anything she had ever experienced or imagined that felt as if it was sucking away all the power Dhóbhaen held.

"Gaed!" she cried, seeing, too, the one Kavan called threat, even though Raebhá had no inkling how she could be. The boy was already running across the sand toward her, wide-eyed as though pursued by a menace they could not see. When that pinpoint burst inside of her, that power was released, powerful enough to flatten the smaller trees, powerful enough to throw Gaed off his feet as the incoming waves of a distant storm washed over him, powerful enough to steal her sight, breath, and consciousness.

Ágdhállán remained where Kóráhm had dropped him, robbed of sight when the power veins went dark, robbed of the power to produce a handlight, robbed of everything except the urgent, consuming knowledge that the Saint had gone to his father…but had gone too late.

Protected from the worst of the power eruption that rocked the room, knocked items loose from the alcoves that contained them, and rattled the metal gate and the breath within his chest, Ágdhállán reached out for a power he could not feel, fell face first to the floor, and screamed.

A hand reached for hers as the world's power was sucked away.

No.

She clenched the offered hand, fighting the racking sense in her breast.

It had to be now.

One moment Earé was on her feet, her hand in Kaj's.
The next moment she saw nothing but the void.

☙695☙

✦Chapter 56✦

After hours spent working the lattice loose, masking the sounds behind the chanted prayers and songs of those gathered in Hes Dhágdhuán and the rattling bangs at the threshold, Lláhy saw his chance. The arrogant man in front of the altar and those beside him, pretending they did not fear the wolves at the door, pretending they believed k'Ádhá would protect them when they dared turn on one of their own and expel him from the fold was the last straw. Knife in hand, he was prepared to kick the lattice free, to leap as close to Ylár as he could get, and jam the blade into his flesh. Blaming the k'gdhededhá for that too, certain the older man knew he was there, that he was being punished again, when the great sucking of power began, Lláhy kicked…

…just as a wave of power stronger than he had ever felt threw him through the lattice and out of the apse. People screamed, frightened by a surge they did not understand that knocked many off their feet and was immediately blamed on the enemy outside, by the fracturing of the náós doors upon their hinges, and by the unexpected emergence of the man who flew through the splintered lattice, struck the edge of the marble altar with a bone-snapping crack, and rolled over it to land at Ylár's side, where the k'gdhededhá had fallen, the knife still clutched in his hand. Ylár stared at the older, yet familiar face with a scowl of disbelief, understanding what the man had intended, knowing that, whatever the cause of the absence of power in the world, it had been done at the hands of the White Bard who had exposed this would-be assassin. He looked at the collection of armored men in the doorway and held his breath, quaking in shock and amazement, afraid of the emptiness within, afraid of the emptiness without, certain that Kavan had saved his life from one form of death.

Now he was exposed to another.

As one, the mercenary soldiers stopped moving.

Ylár was certain, as he genuflected where he sprawled in front of the altar and opened his mouth to utter a final prayer and praise of gratitude, that whatever the bard had done, he had saved Ylár's life…and the lives of everyone else…in that moment too.

Surrounded by his father's Inzigaen army, children who tried, as soon as Enesfel's army pushed them back, to escape combat by seeking refuge in any unlocked building they came across, Olaric was separated from the dark-haired man called Kaj long enough to have doubts about his survival. The man seemed to be a good soldier, seemed capable and strong, and had his own men fighting beside him, but in the unfamiliar narrow streets, such advantages did not guarantee survival. Nothing did.

Olaric had lost most of the squad of loyalists he had been fighting with, and only continued to survive because Nethite after Nethite recognized the black sash painted on his shield and chose to fight with him rather than against him. The uproar from the palace square announced the arrival of Lachlan troops at the castle gate, and it was there Olaric was trying to reach.

If he was not there already, General Waller would be there soon.

As he barreled out of a side street to merge into a host of men in Nethite armor, a great upheaval like an earthquake, like the wind forced into motion at the moment of an explosion, caused someone to crash headlong into Olaric as he parried the arc of someone's sword and knocked that person to the ground. Unprepared for the collision, interpreting it as an attack as he too was jarred off his feet, Olaric turned and drove the Curna he had picked up along the way into the exposed side of his assailant before recognizing the man's face.

"General!"

Olaric's surprise was genuine enough that Waller believed the blow to be an error as he slid to the ground. He reached for Olaric's hand, silently asking for assistance to his feet, but Olaric, pushed along by the bumping combat around him, forced to continue to fight, was moved further away.

He was sure he left the general breathing, but he was also sure the man was being trampled. If someone did not stop to help him, he would lay bleeding into the street until the fighting was over. Maybe he would live. Or maybe, by the time the day was done, by the time it mattered, someone would find his body and the war would end.

There was no one to lead except Olaric, who had no desire to do so.

If he led anyone, it would be against the man locked in Glevum's castle.

❧*❧

Kaj's men were pursued by the foreign host as far as the shores of the sea, separated from the collection of defecting Nethites led by Fraen the Younger when the street they followed dead ended at an east-west intersection. The lure of combat on the sea, the hope of reinforcements, brought Kaj to where the Elyri-manned galley confiscated in Gorea and several Elyri ships had routed the barely manned foreign ships harbored there. The Elyri sailors, seeing the Enesfel banner the brigade had managed not to lose, charged the dock, catching the enemy force in the middle.

It was then Kaj saw her, as armies squeezed the enemy into a narrow strip of beach. Her beautiful face was spattered with the blood of her opponents, her pale hair worked loose from the cord and the braid that bound it so that bloody tendrils framed her determined face. Choosing to fight with her, Kaj cut his way towards her, but he arrived too late. He saw her stiffen as the ground heaved beneath their feet, saw her fall when the force of the air rocked the ships in the harbor and pushed the waves of the sea away from the shore. Roaring with disbelief and frightened fury, Kaj doubled his efforts until he was able to find her, bend over her, and drag her out from amongst the boots around her. As he pulled her with one hand toward the shelter of an open door, backing away from the fight to fend anyone who followed with his now dented and damaged sword, he noticed something no one else seemed to.

The enemy mercenaries had ceased fighting. Confused, they were slaughtered with few attempting to fight back.

Kaj lay Earé on a low wooden bench and felt her neck for signs of life. Her heart was beating. She was breathing. He could tell nothing else.

❧*❧

At the door of the duke's manor, Madoc and his brigade drove the intruders aside as those living there fought like cornered bears to keep them out. Some charged the buildings where the harvests were stored, slaughtering animals when they could, determined to force anyone in Alberni who remained alive to suffer and starve. Others charged the manor door, seeking to destroy the home of the defiler as their patron demanded.

Four pushed past Emeria, knocking her down, knocking her out when her head hit the wall, leaving her for dead as they surged inside.

The earth and air shook. Madoc, following with sword in hand to the doorway, stumbled when the world underfoot bucked and threw him against the jamb. He braced himself, prepared to run, only to find that the four he pursued had been knocked off their feet too and, to his surprise, sat shaking their heads, staring at one another and the room around them as though they had no recollection of where they were or how they had come to be there.

It did not stop Madoc from hastily apprehending them while, protected by a small group of men outside the manor walls, Yóáná doubled over, clutching her head with a sharp cry.

The gates of St. Kóráhm's shattered. The horde pushed and clambered over one another in their haste to get inside as Zerio, Raenár, Tau, and a handful of others left the shielding barricade of bodies at the chellé door and rushed the attackers in a desperate attempt to buy the non-militant among them time to flee if they chose. They could hear combat at the rear of the enemy line outside the walls without knowing who had come to fight on the chellé's behalf. Another arrow fired over the wall caught Zerio in the shoulder, pitching him to the ground…which trembled violently beneath him as he landed. Met with a force of air like a winter storm at sea, Raenár and Tau were pitched forward into combat before they were ready, and tumbled with the enemy onto the bloodstained stones. Raenár's shield arm twisted and snapped when he landed, aware as he did so that where there had once been the comfort of power within, there was now an empty pit. Tau's head struck someone else's with a stunning force.

But none of those events, mystical or otherwise, explained why the invaders stopped running or remained where they fell, blinking in confusion, at the unfamiliar landscape and the pre-dawn sky.

❧*❦

The galleys in Káliel's harbor ceased their forward push and, once the violent thrust of waves settled back into an autumn day's tranquil sea, drifted slowly with the current away from the island. Sailors took advantage of the lull in combat, not questioning what it meant, to repair damage, to prevent water from penetrating the hull, and prepare for the next round of engagement. The invaders who had made it ashore stopped mid-swing to either fall where they stood when Piran and his men struck, or else avoided death by laying down their weapons and stepping beyond the reach of Kaliel's men. The pulsing gush of air that washed over the island had shattered windows, torn vines from trellises, knocked over unmanned vendor carts, and dashed smaller boats against the docks with enough force to crack their wooden skins.

Piran hesitated, one fist raised above his head, commanding those closest to him to pause their attack. When the invaders refused to charge, the men gave a shout of victory that echoed from every voice on the island. The enemy dropped to their knees and waited in obvious confusion for whatever these pale-skinned people would do.

Káliel, led by the son of Gabrielle Dilyn and Owain Lachlan, had won the only war she had ever known. Piran did not quite believe it was anything he had done.

❧*❧

Stripped of the Elyri power he was accustomed to feeling, stunned by the quaking earth and the blast that shattered the windows of colored glass, forced the fires to go out, and tore the suspended figure of Dhágdhuán's pyre from the chains that held it so that it crashed against the altar, shattered, and dropped pieces into the still smoking pool of oil in front of it, Tusánt threw open the náós doors to allow the Lachlan Guards inside. Some apprehended the pilgrims náós residents had cornered, others removed the injured from the dangers of falling chunks of charred debris. It was too late to save dedhá Charlos and novice Dhon, perhaps too late Bhídígís unless he could get immediate medical attention for the burns he had suffered in trying to save Dhon, but the others, he was confident, would live. As before, Hes á Redh could be repaired. Lost lives could not.

The miracle that stayed the hand of the attackers, put out the fire, saved the náós and many lives, would be an enduring legend to be talked about for centuries to come. Whether Tusánt spoke his beliefs aloud, spoke of the sense of the only man capable of such feats, the rumors, the tales of miracles at the hands of the White Bard would grow and spread, whether people could prove their claims or not.

The earth trembled. A shockwave from a different, distant explosion, something too far away to see or hear, pushed through Rhidam and the countryside around it. With the wooden portions of the bridge burned beyond use, when the forces of air and earth collided with the flaming structure, the bridge collapsed into the river. The violent surge of air and power none of them could feel snuffed out all but the smallest tongues of bobbing flame that had already drifted down river.

Perhaps, mused Asta as she stomped on a piece of debris fished ashore, her anger seeking an outlet upon what had previously been a flaming chunk of wood, those flames had gone out too. She could not see them to know.

Without the bridge, trade would be limited. Without the bridge, they might never apprehend the three instrumental in destroying it.

Others, however, a marksman on a nearby roof and a fellow who had remained inside the warehouse, were already in Warde's custody. Dawn was not far off. She would have to deal with those two men and any others the Association brought later.

She nodded at Warde, giving consent without drawing attention to it, for him to continue overseeing matters at the river's edge and apprehend anyone involved. She had to see to the náós' condition. She had to speak with Kjell, the royal advisors, and make a plan.

She had to reassure the royal children, and the people of the city, that Rhidam was safe…once she was certain it was.

She wanted first to speak to Kavan, to hear his interpretation of the night's events.

For now, exhausted from the exertion of putting out the fire, Asta wanted nothing more than sleep.

ȣ*ȣ

Jerit did not know if it was the quaking earth, the blasting force that slammed into his chest and robbed him of breath or the clawing that grabbed his ankles that knocked him off his feet and threw him from the scaffold when he tried to pull Lorant up. Lorant and Bhetá were also tossed into the dust while Bhríd was thrown against one of the posts sometimes used as gallows, shoved hard enough to crack the post and produce a searing pain in his skull that had little to do with the impact against the post.

What Jerit did know, as he scrambled to take shelter beneath the platform to crawl to the other side where Lorant had been dumped, was that the abundant mercenaries fighting on behalf of Fraen in the city square had stopped moving, stopped fighting, at nearly the same moment.

Noting the same peculiarity, Lorant struggled up, barely able to stand on a leg that soaked his sweaty, muddy trousers with red, and leaned against the lip of the scaffold before glancing at Bhríd, at Bhetá, and then into Jerit's eyes as the prince took his hand and wiggled out beside him.

Throughout Glevum, beneath the fingers of orange and mauve dawn that traced streaks through the clouds across the sky, the air grew calm. No more shouting or weapons clatter, except near the sea and at the far western edge of the city. At that moment, where movement and sound ceased, it was impossible to tell if perhaps Enesfel was not as outnumbered as the young king had feared, if the desperation of their predicament had seemed more frightening, because here, at the scaffold in front of the palace gates, there were few soldiers to fight for their king.

One last twang of a bow string. One clinking strike as Bhríd deflected the arrow with the flat of his broadsword, his face dark with a grimace of pain that revealed an injury Lorant could not see.

He was certain of two things as men in the square laid down their weapons.

He and Jerit had survived.

And wherever he was, whatever he had done, Kavan had kept his word.

The war for the throne of Neth and the peace of the Sovereignties was, as far as he could tell in that first breathless moment, over.

∿Chapter 57∿

óráhm's cry echoed on the wind, a fading note of despair that Rhyrdan tried to shake off as his brain fought to recognize the reality before him in the instant that Kavan fell.

The volcano spat another flare so high that the molten debris splattered on the stones around Rhyrdan's feet, but none of them struck him.

His vision tunneled to the place where Kavan had last stood so that he did not see if the others with him were likewise spared.

Unlike them, the explosive blast did not knock Rhyrdan off his feet. It generated a throbbing pain in his head, in his chest, that made him squint and wince, and he wobbled on the unsteady ground, but he did not fall. His feet felt rooted in place by spikes of disbelieving despair. He could not breathe, although the stink and burn of the steam created as the lava hit the sea made him choke and cough, a panicking sensation that he thought should rob him of consciousness if only he could collapse to succumb to it.

Four bodies lay around them. The rest they had fought were gone.

The waji fell from his hand and clattered upon the stone. He did not hear it, only felt the vibration of it through his soaked leather boots and the thump of the hilt striking his toes.

He could not say it hurt.

In the sky above, the ribbons of green and purple had exploded into a vaporous mist, leaving the sparkle of stars in the west and the herald colors of dawn in the east, neither of which he could see.

A new day.

He saw only the absence of Kavan.

His father would never forgive him for this.

"Help me!"

Rhyrdan heard the cry, one that sounded distant and faint through the pounding of blood and horror in his ears, the deafening ringing that explosion of power had left in its wake, but he could only move his eyes towards the sound. Níkóá lay flat on the cliff, one arm stretched over the edge with only the Elyri blood in his veins giving him the strength to keep Kavan from falling into the hot, churning sea. Sunna, being closest, was the first to reach him, and with Myreth pulling at Níkóá's ankles, the sturmyrá set safely aside, the bigger man was able to bring Kavan onto solid ground. He shot a glance at the still-spreading lava, coughing as the fumes of the steam grew thicker, and grunted, "Need to move him away from here."

He picked up the bard's limp, unresponsive body and retreated from the island's newly crumbled edge and the lava's wrath, seeking a high position away from the lava where its flow and the smoke and ash it generated would be less likely to reach them. Myreth helped Níkóá to his feet, picked up the sturmyrá, and followed stumblingly behind.

Rhyrdan could not move. Only his bloodshot eyes tracked Kavan's passing, noting the red, blistered swelling on his face and neck, on one exposed arm where the heat of the steam and the blast of Elyri power had torn, or burned, the fabric away. White hair singed black at the ends. Blood on both hands and his side, evidence of rósádhá still wet as it flowed, blood seeping from his ears, the corners of his mouth, the corners of his eyes. Blistered palms where the power had burned from the inside out…and a faded vacancy in wide-opened eyes that seemed unable to see anything.

Rhyrdan knew the meaning of such vacancy. Only death left that emptiness in its wake.

Tears spilled down his cheeks. He could not stop them.

He did not try.

"Rhyrdan." His head tipped at last to make note of Níkóá's empty hand on his arm, a hand that prompted him to move, though his shuffling steps felt as though they dragged an anchor behind him.

They made it to the overhang where they had found shelter before, stopping long enough to retrieve the dropped packs, and then trudged another hundred feet inland to higher ground. There was no outcropping here to protect them from the wind but the lava river produced enough heat to remove the worst of the chill. Níkóá sank out of Myreth's grasp to the ground with an uncomfortable wheezing groan. Like Kavan, the side of his face, the arm and hand he had used to keep the bard from falling, was blistered by the toxic steam. He accepted the sturmyrá from Myreth who, with his hands now free, pulled Kavan's pack from his back, surprised that it had not fallen into the sea, and then helped Sunna lay him down on the flattest surface they could find, the pain in his wrist forgotten.

"What about the Gate?" asked Sunna, shedding his wet cloak to form a pillowing bundle upon which to rest Kavan's head.

Níkóá shook his head. They had passed over the place upon which Kavan's Gate had been generated but Níkóá had been unable to sense it. He was afraid to admit he could feel no power at all, that he could only feel anguish and anxious despair beneath the physical trauma.

Compared to the heartbreak, the pain of burned flesh seemed inconsequential.

"Maybe if I rest…"

"He might not have…" began Sunna.

Rhyrdan's eyes widened in skeptical disbelief. "He is…?"

"Breathing," the big man said as he removed his tunic and poured water onto it to begin the cautious task of tending the bard's wounds.

Breath meant life. Rhyrdan dropped down on Kavan's other side with a gasp and took the sturmyrá from Myreth. Its glass was cracked in several places, the key no longer in place as though it had been forcefully half ejected from its setting. He was surprised it had not fallen out. Having witnessed the power the box contained and its effects on Kavan, he set the box on the bard's sunken chest and wiggled the key back into place.

But the cracked casing meant that the crystals were no longer aligned. The stone key could not bridge the gap. A faint white streak of power sparked and popped and then fizzled out as if it was water dripped onto a hot iron pan.

If it had any effect on Kavan, Rhyrdan could not see it.

"We need bandages…ointments…" rasped Níkóá.

"There might be some," Myreth offered, pointing at the building from which he had been rescued. As long as he had been held in that place, as many caretakers that had come and gone, there must have been a need for medical supplies kept on hand for emergencies caused by sea, fire, or the clumsiness of man. "This is my fault…I can…"

Sunna shook his head. "I'll go." He could not guess if the lava flow would be passable, if there was a way to cross it and reach the plateau. But Níkóá was in no state to try and Myreth, having been kept prisoner there for more than a decade, was not likely to be in any condition to either cross the lava or climb the plateau again. And though the landscape was dotted with the four men they had killed, the shades having evaporated when their master went over the cliff or had been consumed by lava, he might be the only one to fight off others, if there were any there.

Rhyrdan, meanwhile, rummaged through his pack for the medical supplies he thought to bring in the hopes that they would not need them. "Will this do?" he asked as Sunna shoved Elotti's waji into his belt. His own was gone.

"Do what you can for him," Sunna agreed with a nod., looking at the unresponsive bard, wondering what Bhás had done in those final moments of non-physical combat. "Don't let him die."

Rhyrdan nodded solemnly. Closing Kavan's eyes so that he could not witness their gradually fading light, he did not think there was much he could do to keep his friend alive. He would trade his life for Kavan's if Kóráhm, k'Ádhá, or the host of Ethenae would accept the trade, but for the first time in his life, he lacked the faith to believe it was so.

None of them had protected Kavan from this. None of them had done anything.

Including Rhyrdan.

∾*∾

She could not heal the wounded as she had done for most of her life, robbed of power as she was, but she could care for them as any Teren physician did, and so Yóáná did her best, along with the similarly stripped healers in St. Kóráhm's, to treat them in the chellé's courtyard while Alberni's physicians and those with a modicum of skill combed the city for people needing help.

Yóáná did not know if power had gone out of the world, had been taken from all Elyri, or if they could not feel it for some reason, but instead of panicking, after that initial moment of pain and alarm, she set to work.

Madoc, Tau, and Sheriff Groff led the effort to capture and detain every enemy soldier they could find, uncertain what they should do with so many. Alberni lacked the capacity to hold them and none of the three felt they had the right to condemn so many to a mass execution. In times past, enemy soldiers, most often the peasants and those of lesser means from the opposing kingdom, would be returned to their homes as part of a treaty pact, while lords and nobles might require some ransom to be paid by the opposing king for their release.

But no one spoke the language of these befuddled foreigners, and no one knew where they could be released to.

When the rain began to fall, it was decided to house them in their galleys under balo Essem's watch.

Mass graves again dotted the outskirts of Alberni so that the unidentifiable dead, or those without means or family to claim them could be buried, while in St. Kóráhm's, the living who remained gave their lost brothers and sisters respectable burials alongside Wortham, Zelenka, k'gdhededhá Tythilius and those who had passed before.

Khwílen wept until he felt there were no more tears to shed. The process would take days, and with no dedhá in the defiled St. Maicel's to assist, he and the handful of dedhá who remained shouldered the responsibility for prayer and services for the dead.

He could not call anyone from Gorbesh to assist them. The power feeding the Gates was no longer perceptible. Those remaining in Alberni were on their own.

Once their wounds were tended, Raenár focused on the damage done to the chellé walls, gates, and towers, while Zerio, nursing his shoulder without grumbling about the pain, walked with the town elders through the streets assessing the damage, determining the priorities for repair and reconstruction that would be necessary as the autumn months turned to winter. The rain and cold and snow would be a detriment to the living if there was not enough shelter for them.

Fortunately, there were structures still standing empty and unused after the plague a decade before. Some could be repurposed, some dismantled, some given to those without homes to return to, or used as temporary residences for those who needed homes repaired.

Alberni had survived before, through famine, drought, and plague. The people of Duke Cliáth's city were determined they would survive again. With the aid of the contingent of soldiers who had come from Rhidam and those come on a pair of Hatu ships from Levonne, they had defeated the invaders from the sea…although none of them could explain why the enemy chose to lay down their arms and cease to fight.

St. Kóráhm, some said.

The White Bard and his miracles, said others.

Zerio guessed Kavan's mythos would birth an amalgamation of both.

❧*❧

Asta circled the charred bodies fished from the Tegid, dead from the explosion or else badly injured enough to have drowned in its swift-moving current. There were pilgrims from Hes á Redh detained in the castle dungeon, men bearing similar features to those mercenaries Kavan's daughter had brought, but not, it turned out, the same language. They and the pair the Association had captured for her earlier were awaiting trial, but for now, Asta believed that responsibility should rest on the shoulders of the king, or the regent he had appointed, neither of whom she was certain would come home.

The sun had reached its zenith behind dull gray clouds, promising rain that had not yet come. She hoped it did.

Rhidam needed a purging rain to wash away what the fires left behind.

"I wanted them alive," she groused to the man at her side who rocked on his heels as though anxious for the ransom payment the crown had promised. There were appearances to be kept after all, between the inquisitor and the Association.

Warde chortled softly, unaware of how his stance and behavior reminded Asta of her father. "Don't think I could have saved them if I'd wanted to."

"And the others?" she tipped her head toward the corpses in the back of a mule-drawn flat cart, men with the sort of wounds that indicated they had not been apprehended without a fight.

"If I'd wanted to," he repeated with a shrug. "Does it matter?"

Asta started to protest; Warde had done an admirable job in bringing the Association to heal with several strategic assassinations; such deaths were his style. Reprisal against enemies of the Crown was not his, or the Association's, charge. In this instance, however, she agreed that the men's deaths did not matter. The fires were out; the dead were dead. The rest...

"I want anyone else you find brought to me alive. Alive. Understood?"

Warde nodded, gestured for the people with him to take the dead away for disposition, and accepted the pouch of coin Asta placed in his palm.

Some of the coins would pay those who had brought the dead to justice. The rest would be donated to the náós for its eventual reconstruction. Warde did not want the money. He had his means.

"I'll do my best."

◈*◈

Unable to find a way to the plateau structure without walking on the too-hot lava, Sunna stood at the place where his mother had fallen and looked into the waves, half expecting to see her body, or the waji, on the rocks below. By now, both had been swallowed by the see.

Mother by birth only. They had known each other for only a few hours after his birth; there had never been a bond between them. For most of his life, he had not been aware of her.

There was no remorse for her death.

He could not even say with certainty that he had been the one to kill her. But his soul was certain she was dead.

He had inspected the dead men too, looking for anything they carried that they could use, particularly clothing for bandages and the weapons they had dropped. He could not blame them for the fight. Under the spell of shi cali, they had not, he knew, been aware of their plight. Maybe they had gone to her willingly at first, as he had entered the service of Lord Cliáth, but the choice to remain in her sway had not been theirs.

Sunna almost felt sorry for killing them.

Almost.

If he could find a way to the sea, find a safe place to do so, he could fish for sustenance until the lava cooled and he could find a way across it…unless they could find a way off the island by then. The rain, if it was consistent, might provide enough water to keep them alive, and in time, if they had to, they could bring Kavan' to the only shelter the island offered.

He had seen men burned before.

He did not expect, despite clinging to hope, that the valiant bard would live that long.

If no boats came, if the Gate failed to work so that Níkóá could return them to Rhidam, they might make their home in the now-empty building, until the food and water ran out and they starved to death. But Kavan would not survive.

❧*❧

Lorant did not care about propriety. When the mercenaries laid down their weapons, the Nethite soldiers who had not defected to the Lachlan-de Corrmick side realized they were outnumbered by the combined forces of Enesfel, Cordash, Elyriá, men they assumed were from Hatu, as well as men from their own side; they likewise, surrendered the fight. The realization that they had won all but the taking of Glevum's keep…and perhaps other brigades scattered to the west toward Cordash's border, had prompted Lorant to fall into Jerit's embrace and remain there longer than he should.

He did not care.

Barring those possible Nethite units across the land who might come to support the imposter king, he considered Glevum to be taken. He considered Neth to be defeated. The worst of the war, in Lorant's eyes, was behind them. His certainty that he would die had been thwarted.

Someone had gone to fetch a healer, and though Healer Pháraeís was brought to tend to the king, his arrival came with the news that the Elyri healers could no longer heal. Not in the Elyri fashion, at least.

Bhríd did not seem surprised at the news, but the weary duke only shrugged and returned to the task of directing arrests, collecting the wounded, collecting the dead. A perimeter was established around Glevum so they would not be surprised by an ambush while the city disposed of the dead and collected the criminals.

Lorant's leg was stitched and bound to staunch the bleeding. Bhetá's fractured leg was splinted and, once she was helped onto a horse, she too, helped instruct the troops without remaining confined to the scaffold. As they left the king, assigning men to guard them at the scaffold, it left the forlorn-faced Kaj to circle the square, to separate the foreigners from his people, and scan the crowd for someone he did not see.

Jerit caught Lorant's face between his hands and raised it to look into his eyes. Both were muddy and bloody, bearing dark circles beneath their eyes, cuts and bruises across exposed flesh, and many more, he knew, beneath their armor. "I thought you were dead…"

"Likewise," Lorant snuffled and pressed his forehead to Jerit's.

"Here; you should have this back." Jerit drew far enough from Lorant's embrace to return the sword the king had given him. Lorant shook his head.

"Keep it…for now. We might still…" He glanced around the square and down at his throbbing thigh and grimaced. Without an Elyri healer, such an injury might mean he would never run again, at least not as easily or swiftly as he once had. Today, that hardly seemed to matter.

The ineffectuality of the healers, however, did.

"Your Majesties!"

The voice calling through the crowd was unfamiliar, but the face of the man who parted them, hunched as he dragged a corpse by the armor it wore, was recognized by both.

"You're gonna want this one." With a heaving pull that took the last of Olaric's strength, he hoisted the body and dropped it on the platform. Finding the man's corpse in the battle zone had not been easy, but knowing where he had last seen him had helped. Any resisting Nethite soldiers were going to need proof of their general's demise if they were going to surrender.

What they needed most, however, was inside the castle.

He grinned wearily as he stretched his back and shoulders, satisfied with the expressions of the two younger men on the platform. "And you're going to want what's in there."

Jerit toed General Waller as if verifying he was dead. "He's not going to let us in…" he mumbled.

"No…but I can." If not through the front gates, there was another way Olaric could get men inside. He would prefer not to expose those passages to Enesfel's troops if it could be avoided, but showing the way to Prince Jerit and a handful of trusted Vants, might be necessary. Olaric could take them inside that way too.

"He's going to know he's beaten eventually," Lorant snorted, stifling the urge to kick the dead man like a petulant child. "He'll have to hear it."

The cessation of combat. The shouts and cries of celebration and relief that continued to fill the air in random pockets across Glevum.

Lorant nodded. "Thank you, Lord Fraen." He did not know if Olaric had killed the general or had found his body. He did not care. Wondering how easy it would be for Olaric to give up his father, he continued, "We'll give him until sundown." The hour was early, morning having given way to midday, and there was work to be done to secure Glevum and collect as many fighting men at the castle gates as they could to break down that last barrier. "You will offer our demands; we'll see what he says."

Though potentially a response to the now obvious victory of the Lachlan army and the fear that would inspire, the wailing heard inside the castle walls, Olaric hoped, meant something much different, something that meant they would not need to wait until sunset for this war to end. Nor did he intend to wait that long. Lorant Lachlan was not his king. Prince Jerit ruled here, at least until the chosen heir was crowned, and so it was to him Olaric owed his fealty.

He wanted this over.

He wanted to be certain that Kes and his girls were safe.

❧*❧

The Gates would not work.

More accurately, as Sóbhán kept watch at the busy castle gate, the world felt flat and empty, devoid of the living spark that normally filled it, devoid of the single most important thing that set Elyri apart from Teren. He could not feel it. Dhóri could not feel it. Sóbhán believed there was no Elyri in the world who could feel it. They had either been cut off from feeling it or there was no more power to feel.

Only one man, if it had been a man, could have robbed the world of power, could have controlled it, could have destroyed it. Surely the use of that much power at once would be enough to kill anyone.

Their father was the strongest ágdháni who had ever lived. If anyone could have done such a thing and survived, it was their father.

Neither he nor Dhóri wanted to dwell on the other possibility.

The only thing the brothers could do was find Ágdhállán. The only way to verify that he was not in St. Kóráhm's was to ride to Alberni. Sóbhán had not yet tried to ride after the loss of his leg, but Dhóri and Bergis, sharing a horse, could travel to Alberni and back so long as the people responsible for the destruction of the Tegid bridge and the fire in the náós were all caught and there were no foreign soldiers marauding across Enesfel.

No one knew if war still raged. No one knew what the pair would find when they reached Alberni.

Directing the borrowed horse, Bergis stopped next to Sóbhán at the gate, waiting for Dhóri to come up behind him. Before doing so, the blind man clutched his brother's hand, wishing Sóbhán was coming with him.

"Be careful," Sóbhán murmured, missing the power that should exist in that physical contact. To Bergis he said, "Keep him safe."

Bergis patted his sword. "I will."

Dhóri embraced him with a sighing quaver in his voice, "If he's there, I'll bring him home." Home for Dhóri, as for the other residents of St. Kóráhm's would now be Gorbesh until Kavan decided otherwise. Sóbhán did not ask if he meant that distant chellé or if he meant Rhidam or even the Alberni estate.

Maybe he meant Bhryell, where Sóbhán's wife, daughters, and the rest of the family were certainly experiencing the same absence of Elyri power.

He helped Dhóri onto the horse, and watched as the pair rode through the gate unhindered, perhaps recognized by the soldiers directing people in and out as the whole of Rhidam hunted for arsonists, terrorists, and the soldiers sent to aid Alberni.

He wondered what a world without Elyri power would become…what it would mean for healers, for travelers…

…what it would mean for his father most of all.

❮*❯

"We don't know." Kluín looked at the man who had once been part of the Faith's innermost circle of leadership until the greed for power and a rigidness of doctrine had compelled him to kill his father, the highest head of the Elyri Faith. His chest rose and fell, suggesting he was alive, but he had not awakened since his fall from the apse and not a single healer, not one of those called bhydáni, could treat him or touch his thoughts to discover whether the blow to his spine and skull had robbed him of a life outside of his damaged shell.

No one could say whether he would walk, move, or talk again. Without Elyri power, what sort of life would such a man have?

"He tried to kill you," Hwensen reminded the man he served, wiping his hands on the front of his robe as if to clean them of some contaminant they might have contracted from touching Lláhy's unmoving form.

"He might have," agreed Ylár absently, "if not for Lord Cliáth."

Paul's lips pursed. "You believe he…?"

Realizing he had said too much, Ylár shrugged as though the idea was a speculative one. "Who else could rob the world of power except k'Ádhá…and why would k'Ádhá do that? Who else could make armies cease fighting?" He could think of no reason for either to do so, but those were the only options he could think of. Reports already came from throughout Clarys, along with the tales of failed Elyri power, about how the invaders had surrendered as one man, dropping weapons, stopping mid-actions, capitulating to the Elyri, and accepting arrest without resistance.

Kyne Phílóá would have her hands full deciding what to do with them. They could not be read to determine guilt or motive, no one could communicate with them without Elyri power, and the death penalty did not exist in Elyri except under the most rare and dire situations. The debate about whether these were such circumstances could last for decades…long past the time when the invaders were likely to succumb to old age.

Kluín sank onto the nearby bench and rubbed his temples. "There will be those who disagree…"

"There will be more who will believe it to be true, even if it is not." Hwensen was certain of that.

Again, Kluín sighed. "He'll hate it."

Ylár nodded, his expression melancholy as he ran his fingers over Lláhy's face, relieved that the men with him had not taken his words as proof of his private belief. "He will hate it…but who are we to question the will of k'Ádhá? We will do our best to protect him from unnecessary rumors…but he cannot deny it if it is true."

The bard who had shunned the epithets of miracle worker and saint in favor of being no more than a man would, once again, be faced with a choice he could not make.

That choice would fall into the hands of the adherents of the Faith, and into the hands of every person throughout the Sovereignties who would come to the Faith for answers.

How could Ylár, or anyone, else purport otherwise?

৵*৵

"If I had waited in Gorbesh…waited for him…"

"You didn't do this." Níkóá's throat and lungs burned from the smoke and steam, making speech difficult, but he felt compelled to reassure the dark-haired man who sat at Kavan's head and toyed with his silver-white locks. Rhyrdan had closed the bard's eyes, unable to bear their vacancy, and though Kavan did not move, did not respond, he continued to take short, shallow, wheezing breaths at intervals too sporadic to sustain life.

His lungs must have burned. Unable to cough, there would be fluid and ash collecting there. Eventually, he would choke and drown.

They needed a healer they did not have. They needed to return to Rhidam or Alberni.

"I know," Myreth whispered, "but she couldn't have gotten to him without me."

Rhyrdan shook his head without looking from Kavan's face. "This started before any of us…before you or…she wanted him dead." He choked on the final word and looked as if he would throw up.

"She would have found a way."

Myreth looked towards the sound of boots on stone as the speaker approached, and Níkóá rolled his eyes to observe Sunna's return without moving his head. He set the bundle of clothing and weapons on the ground he had collected from the four dead men and then knelt next to Níkóá."

"Can't reach the building…not until the earth cools…but this ought to work for bandaging," Sunna explained.

Heads nodded. They had expected as much. The food in their packs would have to suffice.

Using his uninjured hand, Níkóá brushed Sunna's away. "He needs it more than I do."

"He isn't going to…"

Níkóá adamantly shook his head. "Anything left, I'll take. Help him."

One unseen hand in the catacombs beneath the chellé that bore his name, cradling the boy sheltered there, reached across the miles between them, unhindered by the absence of power. Pressing a hand on Kavan's barely rising chest, Kóráhm did the only thing he could to right the wrongs he had wrought.

If anyone was to blame for any of this, it was Kóráhm.

Trying to keep Kavan alive with what little power his son could spare, while offering beseeching prayers for one more miracle that most around Kavan had given up on, was the most Kóráhm could offer.

If a miracle were to be granted, it would be Rhyrdan's faith in Kavan that allowed it and made it so.

❧Chapter 58❦

Jerit was reluctant to leave Lorant's side and Lorant was reluctant to let him go, but both agreed it was the right thing to do. Taking Glevum's castle was the de Corrmick prince's right and Lorant, his leg still oozing blood and hurting too much to walk on, could not join him.

They had waited long enough. The siege was in place; it was time to demand capitulation from Fraen the Elder.

Jerit would not go alone. With Olaric leading the way and eighteen of the best soldiers from the Lachlan Guard, the Vants, and de Corrmick loyalists, Bhríd promised Lorant that no harm would come to Jerit and accompanied him to the still-barred gates. It was not yet evening, as Lorant had intended, but the commotion within the walls, yelling, wailing, shouted orders and the thunder of armored steps in and out of the keep was disturbing enough to demand answers.

King and prince wanted the truth; they would not have it by remaining outside. It was time to see if Fraen the Younger was as good as his word.

The guards in the tower hastened to open the gates when Olaric announced himself, and though reluctant to allow Enesfel inside, the men behind him, flying the de Corrmick banner, were a welcome relief. Jerit did not yet reveal himself. He had been a boy when he was last here. He did not think he looked enough like his father to be recognizable.

"My lord!" Captain Sparding rushed across the courtyard from the palace door when he saw them, one arm outstretched in greeting but the expression on his face was one of shock and dismay. "It is good you have come. The…your father…he is…"

Heads around the courtyard turned, the soldiers' collective breath held expectantly for verbal confirmation and explanation of the commotion that bled through open windows. Sparding grabbed Olaric's arm in a more familiar manner than two friendly soldiers warranted and tugged him inside. "Come…see for yourself."

Jerit and Bhríd looked at one another and followed.

Sparding did not speak again until they turned down a corridor where light spilled through an open door at the end. Though he had been too young to be permitted in that room, Jerit recognized where they were, where they were heading. The Black Room was a favorite of de Corrmick kings for strategizing with advisors over public policy and war. He held his breath as they drew closer.

"We don't know what…how it happened," he stammered, the anxiety in his voice sounding more earnest than Olaric expected from a man who had played his part. "We don't know how she…we thought she was dead."

"Who?" started Jerit, before further words were ripped from his lips as they reached the open door.

The man pinned to the door frame by the sword run through him was older and yet near enough to his memories for Jerit to identify him, despite the inappropriate royal robes he wore. He did not need the twitching at the corners of Olaric's mouth and eyes to confirm that this was his father, the imposter king. But Jerit's gaze did not linger there. Instead, it fell to the woman on the floor a step or two away, a woman who had fallen awkwardly and lay in a pool of blood that spread out on both sides. He removed his helmet to see her better.

She, also, was older, grayer. But Jerit knew her too.

A Lachlan princess. His brother's wife. Henrik's mother.

"What happened?" Jerit's voice sounded like a squeak to his ears as he stepped forward, avoiding the spattered blood on the floor. Bhríd caught his arm to hold him back, but Jerit pulled away and squawked, "She is my brother's wife! We were told she was dead!"

"Brother's…" chirped Sparding as his face lost what color remained.

Simultaneously, Olaric muttered, "Apparently not, but how…?" He had planned an elaborate explanation that would have given credence to his father holding the missing queen-regent in the castle as a secret wife, a tale that would have been difficult for anyone except a handful of servants to refute. He was prepared to pay those servants heartily for their silence.

Sparding coughed and tried to reclaim some of his dignity. "No one knows, my lord. There's no way in…"

"What about…?" began Jerit, kneeling now beside Inness, turning her onto her back to reveal the puncture low through her ribs. He glanced at Fraen, then at Olaric, and scowled.

Olaric met his gaze, the man's expression peculiar, and to Jerit, confusingly unreadable, enough so that he closed his mouth. Memories of hidden passages used the night his mother had whisked him to safety seemed a secret best kept. If Asta had known of those passages, it was likely Kjell had too…and possible that Oska and his bride had shared the knowledge that Jerit had been too young to know.

Jerit looked at Bhríd. "Did he…?" There was no other blade visible except for the blade that had run him through. The windows were open, but they were too high from the ground for any except experienced Association assassins to utilize. Whoever had been here would have to have taken the second murder weapon with them and left the room through this same door.

That meant they might still be in the castle. They must be found at once. "Can you read her?"

Bhríd shook his head, his eyes heavy with remorse and yet gratitude that Queen Diona was not alive to hear of her daughter's end. "Not until…and I do not think she will keep that long."

Jerit smoothed his red curls, likewise relieved that Oska was not here to see this. He knew of the speculation that she had killed her husband…his brother…but Jerit continued to believe she had loved him, even if that love had been expressed in ways that had not always made sense to him.

"We should bury her with my brother," he whispered, kissing his fingertips and then pressing them to her lips. "Henrik will want that."

Oska would want that too.

"And him?" asked Olaric in a low voice, averting his eyes from both bodies now that they had been discovered, hoping the act made him look sick and disgusted by their grizzly ends rather than suggesting he knew anything about how they had come to pass.

"What do you want done with him?" Jerit asked.

He grunted, his anger bleeding through at last. Father by blood, but no father. "He is a traitor. If he kept her here all this time…he is a kidnapper and a monster, too. All those children…the Inzigaen" He shuddered. "He deserves…"

A traitor's death, but he was dead already. At Inness' hand, it appeared, but ultimately at his own. Whatever the reason the Elyri could not read the dead, Olaric was grateful for it. An Elyri was the only one who could reveal the truth. He had not expected one to be here when the deed was done, but perhaps he should have.

Jerit was not the king; he did not think it should be his decision to make. But he was the only de Corrmick present, the only one who could make a legal decision on behalf of his father's crown. He considered what his father would do, what his mother would do, if they were here. He considered what Oska might have done and what Inness, too, would have considered.

She had done her part. She had executed a traitor. As much as the answer sickened him, it was a Nethite custom and law he had to uphold. It was what the people of Glevum, of Neth, expected.

"Install a gibbet at the gate, let all of Glevum see…and not a word of this…" He pointed at Inness.

"People will talk. They will want to know…" Sparding stammered.

"They believe she is dead. There is no need to resurrect her for this. For Prince Henrik's sake, keep her name out of it." Or they made public the rumor that the woman Fraen had held hostage for a decade, had forced to marry him so that he could rule, had taken his life when the Lachlan and de Corrmick banners were finally at her door. Jerit squared his shoulders. "If they need someone to blame, let them blame me."

A de Corrmick reclaiming the throne was better than placing blame on another who might be forced to face execution for the killing of a king, rightful ruler or not.

"We must send word to Rhidam," Bhríd said. "They should come."

It would be a many-week journey for a courier and the de Corrmicks in Rhidam, to make without a usable Gate. It would force Jerit to act as interim king, a position he hoped to avoid.

At least until he was well enough to travel, Lorant would be here to aid and advise him.

"Send word that Fraen the Elder is dead. Send word that Neth is to lay aside her arms and make peace. Let them know…" Jerit hesitated to look at Inness one more time as he got to his feet, "that a de Corrmick once more sits upon the throne."

For a few days, he could rule as he thought Oska would have ruled, had he lived long enough to do so. Then he would relinquish the throne to his father or his nephew, whoever was to rule.

Jerit's only intention was to follow wherever Lorant went…which meant his return to Rhidam.

∾*∾

Though the volcano continued to burp and growl and belch smoke into the air, new lava ceased to spill onto the landscape, and as the day turned to evening, the orange veins and red pockets lost their glow, though beneath its black surface, the heat still burned. The rain stopped falling, the sea calmed to a glassy black, capped with white lines of the moving surf. But without trees to shelter them, without a fire to warm them, the evening wind brought a deeper chill to their damp bones. The cloaks of the dead and some of the protective clothing they had worn allowed for barely adequate warmth but he dared not put any of it on the bard. Fabric against the fire blisters across his skin would be agony.

Kavan did not stir. He did not make a sound. Even when Myreth bent low to sing into his ear, a haunting holy song he hoped Kavan would remember, a song he hoped would transport his pale twin to the days of their earliest meetings, he did not respond.

His pulse never quickened; his breathing never changed. Blood still oozed from the rósádhá wounds and pinkish fluid dribbled from blisters that burst whenever Rhyrdan tried to clean the man's wounds. They were treating the burns with what supplies he had brought, but it would not be enough. If Kavan lived, without a miracle he would be forever scarred as Kóráhm had been scarred.

Rhyrdan wondered if Kavan clung to life only because he would not let the bard go. But he could not.

He was not ready for Kavan to die.

❧*❦

"It is over."

The strained murmur of the saint's voice made Ágdhállán lift his weary head as if to see him in the total darkness of the chamber.

He could not.

"He's not..." the boy protested, trying to reach through the link Kóráhm maintained to his father but unable to do so.

"The war." The war between sovereignties, the war between himself and his half-brother that never should have been. "You must take word to Rhidam...to Glevum..."

"But I've never...and I'm so...tired." He felt a gentle kiss on the top of his head.

"You were protected here, kyá. You can access your power. It can only be you. Come...I will help you."

Wrist still aching, the bruises of breakage invisible in the dark, Ágdhállán made it to his feet and trudged back across the chasm, this time without thinking about the path and barely caring if he fell, and stopped upon the dull, faint signature of the Gate that had been stronger when he had last stood upon it. The embrace of unseen arms held him up, gave him enough strength to find the familiar point of his father's Rhidam oratory, and after a brief struggle through the undulating mist, stumbled through the Purification Chamber curtain into a room occupied by children he had thought he might never see again.

"Ágdhi," exclaimed Cáym, leaving the tutor gaping in surprise as he scooped up his cousin. Ágdhállán' winced and yelped when the other boy grabbed his wrist, a sign of pain that brought Physician Mauret to him.

"I need…" started Ágdhállán.

"Allow me to tend your…"

"I need," he met Henrik's gaze, "your grandparents. Bring them here."

"I know where they are," Hella offered, tugging Henrik by one hand so they could run from the room together.

"Bring them to my room," Aland called after them.

"Master Ágdhállán," Najar scolded from his place on the altar steps where Phaedr, Balint, Ida, Onyka, and Kaedís were also gathered, "your brothers have been looking for you."

"I was…"

"Sóbhán is here. Should I let him know?" asked Cáym.

Ágdhállán shook his head. "No. Stay here. I'll find them when…as soon as I'm ready."

Though Cáym frowned at being told to stay behind, he obeyed his friend's request. A physician's care, while often necessary, was less pleasant than the care of an Elyri healer. Cáym assumed Ágdhállán did not want others to see him cry in pain when his arm was treated.

Maybe he thought he was being taken to Yóáná. He could not know that she was not in Rhidam.

By the time Aland splinted the fracture, wrapped it with long strips of linen, and reluctantly followed him back to the oratory, Henrik was pulling Asta, and Hella was pulling Kjell, through the door of the physician's room. Asta rushed to the boy, took his hand, and turned his wrapped arm back and forth to examine it.

"What happened? Where have you been?"

"I fell." He did not answer the second question. Like his father, Ágdhállán could be frustratingly elusive when he wanted to be.

Unable to see the bruising except on his exposed fingers, she assumed he had fallen during the earthquake.

"Hella says you…"

"King Fraen is dead. Glevum is won." Instead of letting the adults question his knowledge, he added, "Kóráhm told me."

Kóráhm had told him, shown him, many things. Most of them, Ágdhállán did not want to share.

Asta and Kjell looked at each other. It was known that the boy, like his father, often saw things before, or when, they were occurring. Distant things he should not know. They were unaware, however, that he might commune with the saint the way it was said that Kavan did.

"He says…I can take you there…you should be there…"

"If the war is won," grunted Kjell, clinging to his stubbornness rather than daring to hope that the news was true, "someone should have…"

"They cannot. Their power is…" He shrugged. Depleted or erased, muted or rendered useless, he could not say. For reasons he did not understand, he had retained his access to it, or at least carried enough, thanks to Kóráhm, that he could do as the saint asked until that power was depleted. "I can take you. You'll be safe."

Kjell and Asta stared at each other for several moments. She had been burdened with the care of Enesfel in Lorant and Níkóá's stead. He did not have Tau at his side. But if Ágdhállán's words were true, both the exiled king and the anointed heir needed to be in Glevum.

"It could be a trap," Kjell muttered.

"I trust St. Kóráhm." And she trusted Kavan's son. "If it is time…go. When I can, I will join you. Tau will join you."

"I want to go, for Henrik," Hella chimed in.

"Yes," the young prince agreed, his trembling voice and pale cheeks proving that he understood what was being suggested. If the war was over, if Lorant and Jerit had won, then it was time for him to go to Glevum…to be king. He did not want to do either without Hella.

"No, not yet. Not now." Asta wrapped her arm around the princess' shoulders. "There are things that must be done first. When we're sure it is…the armies will be very busy. Henrik will be very busy. When it is time…we will take you to Glevum."

Glevum would one day be Hella's home. It was right she should see it. Henrik would fare better if Hella was there to help him cope through the transition from prince to king. But the center of a war zone, even if that war was said to be over, was no place for a young princess.

It was barely the place for a prince Henrik's age. She trusted he would be safe with his grandfather because she had to believe it. She had to believe it for all of them.

"I will be with you," Kjell said to Henrik as he nodded, accepting his wife's unspoken words, conceding the risk to himself and the boy and promising to protect him without saying so. His reassurance did not appear to help either of them. "Your grandmother will come."

"I will, as soon as the king returns to Rhidam."

Henrik sighed, looked at the adults, at Hella, and finally at Ágdhállán. "Let's go to Glevum," he whispered. The hour was late, but the demands of duty circumvented the need for sleep. He accepted Kjell's hand, though he shivered at the unwanted contact, and added, "Let's go home."

He had no memory of being there, but a part of him understood that the city where he had been born was home in a way Rhidam was not.

❧*❧

"I'm not going back to Rhidam until Neth is secure," Lorant huffed. "Not like an invalid. There're men who need leadership."

"You think I lack leadership?"

Despite his desire to keep Lorant in Glevum, the irritation in Jerit's voice was not masked by the affection with which he spoke. He sat on the platform steps rather than on Neth's throne while Syl, again, refreshed the stitches and bandaging on Lorant's leg. There were more severely wounded men to treat, but it would not do for Enesfel's king to die of an infection in an untreated wound just because he was too stubborn to accept help. Now that access to the keep had been gained, now that it was officially won and Lorant had the opportunity to sleep in a bed for the first time in weeks, Jerit had stipulated that bed rest was to be part of Lorant's treatment.

There were soldiers at watch around Glevum, soldiers combing the streets and surrounding farms to round up every mercenary soldier they could find. The king and prince were as safe as they could be.

Yet Lorant was here, with him, rather than accepting an empty bed in a solitary room.

"I think they're still Enesfel's men…for the most part…and Daema is injured too. They need a king…" Lorant muttered.

"They have one…"

"Not if I return to Rhidam…"

They paid little heed to the footsteps outside of the hall as servants and soldiers bustled about despite the late hour. The familiar voice they heard was the last one they expected tonight.

"Ágdhi!"

Nor did they expect the boy who hurried into Syl's arms as quickly as his weariness allowed and collapsed there, trembling with his face buried against her neck as Jerit rose to greet them.

Lorant remained seated, the evidence of new blood against his freshly sewn red skin preventing him from rising and serving as an understandable excuse for not doing so.

Jerit steeled his expression and swallowed his emotions. "Father."

"Ágdhállán says you did it." Kjell choked with emotion as he offered his hand to Lorant, blaming the avoidance of his son's greeting on the embrace that Henrik threw around his uncle's waist. Kjell's gaze, however, roamed a room he had not seen in over a decade, passing frequently over Jerit's still-bloody clothes and armor. Only his face and hands were clean. The rest, Jerit intended to deal with when his responsibilities allowed time.

"We had help," Lorant admitted. Enesfel alone would never have survived to see this day. "Our victory is as much Jerit's as mine."

"The best successes are often joint ones." This time, Kjell offered his hand to his son. Reluctantly, Jerit accepted it. "How did you…?"

"Not in front of the children," Syl scolded as she smoothed Ágdhállán's red hair. He had to be the one responsible for bringing Kjell and Henrik to Glevum though she did not know how he could access the Gates when she, Ártur, and the other Elyri could not.

"I'm not a baby," protested Henrik.

Ágdhállán did not speak. His haunted expression spoke of horrors, of knowing things his eyes had not seen. As a child with Sight, she suspected he had witnessed more than many who had survived the battlefield.

"No, you are not," Jerit assured Henrik. There would be time for tales of battle later. "Now…there is something Henrik must see."

Trying not to scowl, Kjell replied, "Yes, I will take him to…"

Lorant caught Kjell's hand to hold him back, a bold gesture the exiled king did not expect. "If you will assist me, I will take you to Daema Magk; she and Lord Cáner can speak of the state of Glevum."

He knew what Jerit intended to do. Such responsibility should be shouldered by one with the compassion to soften the blow. Kjell's anger at the woman who had imprisoned him made him ill-suited to the task. It was better he not be there when Henrik was told the truth.

"Is there a room where Ágdhállán can sleep," asked Syl. She could take him to Ártur, but she felt no need to escort the boy through the streets, the soldiers, townsfolk and the dead, nor to expose him to the barrage of questions Ártur was likely to heap upon his young, exhausted shoulders. There would be time for that reunion and accompanying questions later too.

"Yes," Jerit replied before his father could do so, as though the order was his to give. He motioned to one of the wide-eyed pages in the shadows around the fringe of the lantern-lit room. "There's a chamber with blue curtains, is there not? One that overlooks the sea? Is it empty? Is it free?"

"It is, Your Majesty," one of the boys stammered.

It had been Jerit's room once. Perhaps it would be again. Tonight, if he could not share it with Lorant, he wanted the boys to use it. With his father here, it would likely be several more hours before most of them enjoyed the luxury of sleep after battle.

"Take Healer MacLyr and Ágdhállán. Henrik will join him later."

"Guarded at all times," Lorant added, leaning on Kjell for support as he struggled to his feet.

"Yes, Your Majesty." Boys scurried in different directions, some to find the requested guards, some to lead Syl and Ágdhállán away.

Jerit waited until the throne room was empty before putting a hand on Henrik's back to steer him in the direction of the stateroom, minimizing touch as much as he could.

Henrik's movements were stiff until Jerit's hand fell away. "Where are we going?" began the prince, the words muffled by a yawn he tried to hide.

"Before you hear it from others…you need to hear this from me. You need to know…" He paused with his hand on the unlatched door, nodding at Sparding who had been selected to stand watch over the contents behind it. "Your mother is here. She is…"

"My mother?" Henrik took a step as though he would barrel into the room but he stopped short of doing so. "I thought she was…"

Jerit nodded and pushed the door open. "She is."

He led the way inside so as not to force Henrik to go first, offered his hand, and waited for the boy to take it if he would. Rather than doing so, Henrik inched his way inside where a woman's body lay on the long table where affairs of the kingdom were often discussed. By now she had been changed into a clean gown, all traces of blood washed away so that it was not obvious how she had died. The two servants who tended her and the soldiers who had moved her here were sworn to secrecy.

The less the public knew about her involvement, the better.

With tongue-clicking noises in his throat that Henrik sometimes made in moments of stress, he whispered, "How did she get here?"

Henrik circled the table, both hands flapping anxiously, the clicking noise growing faster.

"We don't know…and what we do know should be up to you to make public, or keep secret, if you wish."

"Me?" The prince stopped walking so abruptly that he almost pitched forward to the floor. Only a hand on the nearest chair prevented it.

"You're the heir…the king. My father…your grandfather, will want one thing. My mother, your grandmother, may want another. But it is not up to them, or me. You have the right to know, to decide how she is to be buried. She assassinated Fraen the Elder…freed the throne for the return of the de Corrmicks. She did it for you."

That much Jerit was certain of. Inness would have done anything for Oska's only son.

"We can take her to Rhidam, to bury her with her parents and brothers, if you wish, or we can bury her with your father."

"Grandfather will never allow…"

"The choice is not up to him. Whatever you want, whatever you choose, I will see it is done."

The clicking sound was replaced with a soft, discordant hum.

"Those who know….it is being said that I killed Fraen…and that Fraen killed her. I am sure that is the story my father will hear. But I want you to know the truth…as much of it as we know."

He could not say for certain who had killed her; blaming Fraen was the best story they had. No one wanted to dig deeper. Where she had been for the last decade, how she had come to be in that room to kill the imposter, were things no one would ever know without an Elyri to read the scene. To Jerit, it was a blessing that none were currently capable of doing so. It was in Neth's best interest to allow the past to die with Inness.

He refused to ask Ágdhállán to do what the adults could not.

"I think…" His hands stopped moving before Henrik spoke, started again after, and then the prince tucked his flapping hands beneath his armpits. "She'd like to be with my father." Lord Cliáth had spoken often enough of his parents' love for each other and hers for their son that Henrik believed it was true. He stopped his slow circles of the table when he reached Jerit and lowered his hands. They were no longer flapping. "Can we do that? In the morning?"

Jerit nodded. "I will make arrangements to have it done. Dedhá Thrismund will be happy to lay her to rest and give her peace…and you should rest too." Jerit expected that, come the rising of the sun, the new day would be very busy for all of them. Henrik needed to rest while he had the opportunity, since it was already past his bed time.

"Yes…in the morning."

Offering a soothing smile, Jerit added, "You've been brave, Henrik. I'm proud of you. She…and your father…would be proud of you too."

Henrik shook his head, his eyes never leaving his mother's face, and awkwardly took Jerit's hand. "Not as brave as you."

Jerit chuckled and gently squeezed the smaller hand.

❧*❧

Seren embraced Asta tightly, soaking her shoulder with tears of joy she had not thought she would cry. So far tonight, they were the only two in Rhidam, other than Physician Mauret and the household's children, to know the truth, to know that the war was over. Until she saw proof of it with her own eyes, until Lorant and Jerit stood in front of her so that she could both welcome them home and scold them for leaving her to worry, she was reticent to speak openly about the news to anyone else. She did not want the city to celebrate too soon. She did not want anyone to get their hopes up the way hers were now.

For tonight, as the moon's arc crept toward the coming of dawn, sharing the secret with Asta was enough.

The king would return to Rhidam.

Her child's father was coming home.

❧*❧

The movement of troops beyond the castle wall and the eternal pulse of the sea had not changed between the moment Syl tucked him into the biggest bed he had ever seen, one he was told had, and might again, belonged to Prince Jerit, and the moment a faint flicker of power made him wake. There was no light in the sky peeping through the gaps around the shutters, and yet the aura's glow was enough to allow him to identify the one standing at the end of the bed.

"taesne" he mumbled, using the High Elyri form of the language the way their father normally did.

Earé pressed her fingers to her lips and beckoned him to follow. Henrik, placed on the bed sometime after Ágdhállán had fallen asleep, moaned, mumbled indecipherable words, and rolled over. He did not wake as Ágdhállán slid off the bed, adjusted his borrowed nightshirt, and picked up the still-burning tallow candle from the bedside table. The guards at the door were also asleep and did not stir when he followed his sister into the corridor and closed the door.

"I need your help."

"Anything," he replied without hesitation. His sister, rivaled in power only by his father it was said, was mortal as he was. If she needed something from her much younger brother, it must be of supreme importance.

"He needs me. I must go to him."

Ágdhállán's face grew sad. "He…is he…?"

Earé gave a soft sound, a sighing, squeaking hiss of breath, and took his hand. "Not yet. But he may if I cannot…" A distance filled her eyes, like a shadow of memory or a veil between what was and what might be, before she continued. "He is spent. He has no strength. He has absorbed the power of the world…spent it, and cannot…"

"He needs my strength." Ágdhállán looked at his empty hand sadly. "I tried to…Kóráhm and I tried to…but it wasn't enough." Raising his head, he asked, "If I go to him, can I…?"

"You must not. You must see to our brothers. They must know. I can reach him, follow him…do my best to see he survives…"

"You believe he will die." His lips quivered, and his shoulders began to sag while he assessed Earé's weak flicker of power. Strong enough to bring her to him, strong enough to wake him, but perhaps not strong enough to bring them both to their father, even if Ágdhállán gave her all he had.

They reached the castle's only Gate, where he took her hands without her asking and opened a bond of power between them so that she could take whatever Kavan needed. If she took it all, he would find some other way to reach his brothers, even if it meant stealing a horse and traveling alone or waiting to travel south with Ártur, Syl, and Enesfel's army.

"Will I," he choked when she released him. "Will we see him again?" His sense of his father was faint enough that he continued to fear Kavan was dying, a prospect he had known might come due when the time came to oppose Bhás. He had faith in his father, he had hope, but the grief in Earé's eyes eroded both. Her reply, when it came, a whisper that filled the space where she had stood, devoured the majority of what he had left.

Earé knew things. Earé's connection to the Sight was unlike anything Ágdhállán could hope to have.

"I don't know," were the darkest, heaviest words she could utter.

"I hope so," Ágdhállán whispered into the emptiness, not knowing if she would hear him. Swallowing his fear, squaring his shoulders, he added with a rush sudden unsubstantiated certainty. "I will."

He had faith.

It was time to offer the same to his brother.

He had just enough power, he believed, to return to Enesfel.

Whether he had enough after to accomplish anything else might not matter if his father never came home.

❧*❧

A handful of people gathered in the mausoleum beneath Glevum's castle, where centuries of de Corrmicks were buried, most of whom had been exhumed so that their bones could be interred in a vast ossuary to make room for the more recently deceased. Kjell had emptied the room of most of them when he had become king, wanting no ghosts of Neth's violent, bloody past to haunt his reign. Only Oska remained.

He had never seen this room. He had not wanted to see it. But now, as they gathered at Henrik's insistence to bury his mother with her husband, Kjell was met with that single stone sarcophagus carved in the likeness of the son who had turned against him.

He continued to wonder if he had somehow betrayed Oska, if he had deserved the fate he had been dealt.

He refused to believe that Oska, whatever his deeds, had deserved the manipulation and madness of the too-short reign he had endured.

That, too, he blamed on Inness. Inness was the root of all of it.

But Jerit was right. He had chosen to bestow the reins of Neth's leadership into Henrik's untried hands. He would serve as his grandson's regent until the boy was of age, but this burial was Henrik's choice to make.

His very first as Neth's king.

Those gathered as the lid of Inness' sarcophagus was slid into place by tama Kaj and three of his men…meant to limit Nethite participation and the spread of rumor, as dedhá Thrismund completed the ritual burial prayers, was primarily those who had known her. The MacLyrs, both of whom were beside themselves with worry for the boy they could not find, Lorant, Bhetá, Bhríd, Olaric the Younger, Jerit, and Henrik, neither of whom spoke, not even when Thrismund performed the ritualistic responsories.

Henrik loathed public speaking…and today had not been the day to pressure him into it.

Jerit had not known what to say.

And there was Kjell.

His hands curled. Asta should be with him.

But there was no one to take word, for reasons Kjell did not understand.

Maybe it was better that she had not been here.

Afterward, an equally limited coronation ceremony was performed, hastily arranged and quickly concluded, with the same attendees in the secrecy of the burial vault. Performed for the sake of legitimacy, to fill the void in the monarchy in case someone else stepped forward to attempt to seize the throne as Fraen the Elder had done, it was a necessary act, important for Neth, important for Henrik.

The fact that doing so was yet another layer peeled away that further distanced Kjell from the throne he had lost, was a bitter, heavy burden he had little choice but to bear.

He felt certain, when the rite was over and Henrik stood, flanked by soldiers, upon the castle gate tower to be announced as king of Neth to every citizen of Glevum within hearing range, that his beloved Owain must have felt the same way when he relinquished the throne to Arlan Lachlan.

A necessity of right, perhaps, but a bitter tincture to swallow.

❧*❧

The damage done to St. Maicel's was visible as they rode past, destruction Bergis described to Dhóri rather than describing the stains of blood on doorsteps, on stones in the streets, a reminder of the bedlam they had been emersed in days before. Though the sounds of combat could no longer be heard, the stench of death hung thick, permeating the air as the dead continued to be collected and buried. Birds sang in the branches of unburned trees and the eaves of the rooftops they trudged past. Dogs barked. Men and women, cleaning their stoops, covering broken windows with planks of scavenged wood, trading with neighbors for necessities that had been looted and dropped elsewhere, called out to the two on horseback, offering Dhóri hope that Alberni had survived its private war.

The people were weary and heavy-hearted, frustrated and mournful, but they were also resilient. Thanks to the years of warning their duke had provided, his planning that had allowed them some opportunity to prepare, Alberni had survived as it always had.

Dhóri hung his head as the last turn of the horse told him they were approaching St. Kóráhm's. What would they do, he wondered, when those who had lived their learned about his father's involvement and fate?

They passed without a word through the swath of land where the mercenary army had laid siege to the chellé. Dhóri could smell the stale aroma of extinguished campfires, sweat and blood and a peculiar scent he attributed to the burning of flesh and more created by the variety of objects Zerio's catapult had hurled over the wall. There was no army here now. He wondered where they had gone, where they had been taken if captured, where they had been buried if killed. He wondered if his father had a hand in the last moments of battle that had brought such an abrupt end to the war.

It had to be abrupt. He had not been gone that long.

"Master Dhóri."

"Tau."

The Vants soldier caught the horse's head as it passed through the splintered chellé gates and brought it to a halt. Dhóri recognized his voice but was surprised that he, or anyone else, had survived when the gates fell.

"Why have you…?"

"Think I'd stay away?" He did not mention his brother's name, afraid of any news Tau might have. "How are…did we…?"

"Other than damage to the façade, the walls and gates, the chellé's intact. Few made it into the courtyard and no one made it to the door."

"Praise be!" exclaimed Bergis as he assisted Dhóri off the horse.

"The others?"

Bergis took up the dropped reins and patted the horse's neck as Tau stood ready to steady the blind man if he needed it after the long ride. "Many dead, as you know. But not as many as there could be. Has there been word from the north? Any word from either king?"

"Kjell is safe in Rhidam. The Gates will not…" Dhóri shook his head. "There was no word from the north before I left. If it is there as it is here…" he turned his head to listen to the people moving around him, working to clear debris from the courtyard, "we can pray that the war has ended and Enesfel is victorious."

"We can hope," Tau agreed. "dedhá Khwílen is in the náós, preparing for the next round of burials, and Lord Kaas is likely still assessing the city damage with Sheriff Groff…if you wish to assist…"

Dhóri patted Bergis' arm. "See to the horse, then do what you can to help. I will find Khwílen…"

"What about…?" started Bergis, knowing the reason they had traveled so far without stopping for rest.

"I will find him." More than helping his brothers and sisters in Faith, more than ensuring that his father's friends were alive and well, Dhóri was here for Ágdhállán. He knew the places his brother was likely to be. He hoped to find the boy in one of those places, hidden from battle, and reassured by Tau's words that, if the interior of the chellé had not been breached, then his brother had to be safe.

He did not want to speak of it to Tau.

Bergis nodded. Dhóri would be of less help in the repairs and cleanup when he could not see the work to be done, but there were other ways he could help. With the conflict over, Bergis trusted that his friend would be safe here. He would find his brother, converse with the dedhá, and when it was time, the three would return to Rhidam.

Tau did not ask what they meant. He was already moving away, resuming the heavy work of lifting broken blocks of stone from where they had landed in the center of the yard.

❧*❧

Seeing King Kjell before him, the man older, frail from the abuses the years had heaped upon him, made every action he had taken, every sacrifice he had made, worth the risks and costs. If he were to be found out now as Inness Lachlan's abductor, as the mastermind of his father's manipulated death, Olaric would still die a satisfied man, regretting nothing except abandoning his wife and daughters.

But Kes was a survivor. The city needed her skills. She would continue without him if she had to.

The important thing was, the de Corrmick line was restored.

With luck, if King Henrik proved to be the king his grandfather had been, Neth would know peace and prosperity.

Marta had played her part too, though in a manner against his wishes, but the past had been laid to rest at last. Those the queen-regent had murdered were avenged. Maybe he would find Marta later, learn how it was done. Maybe he would never see her again.

He did not think it mattered now.

But opening the Vants chamber and rushing into the arms of his wife and daughters, beholding their smiling, weeping faces, hearing their relieved, tearful voices, knowing they were safe and knowing Neth would survive, was the greatest reward Olaric could hope for.

The Vants would rise again, prophecy fulfilled, and his children would grow, prosper, and know peace.

There was nothing more any man could ask for.

❧Chapter 59❧

"Neither's doing well," Myreth muttered as he closed the water flask and adjusted Níkóá's head on the bundle of clothing that supported it.

"I can hear you," the redhead mumbled, his lips swollen and cracked from the onset of dehydration. Until now, he had rejected water, rejected treatment, so that Kavan could receive the bulk of what they had, but this time the water trickled over his lips was impulsively swallowed before he was fully awake and his hand, when he tried to push any more of the offering away, had been too weak to succeed. His suppurated and burned skin stung with an ache that felt tighter and deeper as blisters burst and the fluid they contained dried upon his skin.

He could only imagine how Kavan must feel behind lids that refused to open. If Níkóá had a choice, he would have chosen endless sleep as well, but he believed Kavan needed him, needed all of them, to be vigilant on his behalf. Death was not an option until they had the bard away from this place…and they prayed not even then.

Power dripped into Níkóá's soul little by little, but it was not enough to manipulate the Gate and take Kavan home. The others did not say it, but Níkóá believed it was true, believed it was his fault.

They were running out of time.

Through barely open lids, trying to conserve what energy he could, he watched Myreth refill the flask from a puddle of rainwater that had collected in the rocks. He heard Sunna prying lichen from the stones, which he collected throughout the day to add to another brief coal fire for warmth when the night fell again. He had found a path to the sea and returned with mussels and a bundle of sea plants they hoped would burn, but as damp as it was, as damp as the lichen was, neither burned well.

The sun crept above the horizon in the dull gray cloudless sky. Everything was gray. The ground, the lichen, the fish. The sky and the endlessly stretching sea that rolled and churned but had not brought rain or biting wind again.

The unmoving lava from the quiet volcano was the darkest gray of all.

Kavan's normally white skin was gray too.

Even the steam damage on his body looked gray to Rhyrdan, and he was sure the bard's eyes would likewise be gray if he opened them. His breath continued to rattle, eased by Sunna's resolve to periodically turn Kavan onto his uninjured side so he could expel pink-gray foam and fluid from his lungs.

The last time they had tried, there had been blood.

Rhyrdan was certain that the next time they tried to help him breathe would be the last. His prayers for a miracle were for naught. There was nothing his father, or Kóráhm it seemed, could do, and if k'Ádhá or Dhágdhuán were able, they chose not to intervene.

In his heart, Rhyrdan's bitterness towards them grew.

Why must Kavan make this sacrifice? What had he done to justify this?

When Myreth abruptly scrambled up, Rhyrdan looked toward the approaching footsteps, expecting to see Sunna returning with whatever his foraging efforts had procured this time. Instead, what he saw brought Rhyrdan to his feet; he left Kavan's side for the first time, releasing his uninjured hand so that it flopped onto his chest as Rhyrdan embraced an unexpected but welcome visitor.

"He's dying!" he choked on the words to stifle the threatening wail, and then hastily pulled the woman along with him. "You must help him!"

Weariness was etched onto Earé's bloody face. Her clothes were spattered and smeared with the evidence of war, and she moved as though each step was agony. When she gently pushed past Rhyrdan and reached her father, it was with the foreknowledge of what she expected to find.

Seeing the strong, brave man so frail, listening to the tail of life squeak and hiss out of him each time he exhaled, was so much worse than her expectations.

She sank to her knees, lay one hand over his chest, and brushed his hair from his face with the other. The external damage was bad, but in time, perhaps, it would heal…so long as he lived long enough. It was the absence of everything within him, however, an absence where there should have been long-honed mental barriers to keep her out of empty thoughts and only the smallest ember of power that sputtered and popped in response to her contact but refused to respond to what little power she could feed into it. If he lost that ember, he would never recover.

If the sturmyrá held any power, if it offered any hope as it rose and fell upon his shallow chest movements, she could not feel it.

She had seen this moment long ago. The certainty of what it meant continued to strangle her.

Why? Why is this sacrifice required of him?

Why couldn't the power of Ethenae take her, take anyone else, instead?

Her effort to anchor him to Ágdhállán, so it might give him a reason to fight for survival, faltered; she could barely reach her brother.

"Take him back." Níkóá's eyes had begun to close before but had reopened when Rhyrdan had gotten to his feet. They burned now with purpose as he tried to reach Earé's arm to get her attention.

"Like you, I do not have enough power to…"

"We will remain here," Myreth offered with encouraging desperation. "You need only take him to his cousin, the healer…"

Sunna dropped the collection of lichen and pieces of driftwood he had been lucky to find with a nod. He had not met this woman before but he recognized her kinship to Kavan. "It will hurt to move him…but he must go. We will survive until your return." Without Kavan to care for, he believed he could get the others safely to the structure on the plateau where there was food, possibly medical supplies, and shelter from the elements.

"It isn't…the world has been stripped bare. I had enough strength to bring me here…to him…" In time, she might have enough to take them all to Rhidam. But that was time her father did not have.

There was only one way. One hope. She had seen that possibility too, had done her best to facilitate its outcome, but the veil of final knowing refused to allow her to see beyond it. Not knowing if her efforts had been enough, she could only continue to hope.

But it was hope she was afraid to cling to.

She did not know if Kavan could survive that long.

"I tried to…" rasped Níkóá.

"We all did," Rhyrdan whispered, choking on emotion that was growing more difficult to control.

Myreth, unsure who the woman was but accepting that the others knew her, hung his head so that his dark hair, stringy and matted from the salty sea air, hid his face.

"He should not have come for me."

"This was not done solely for you, Myreth. This is not your fault."

He lifted his head to stare at her, surprised she knew his name.

"This is for all of us. Fate has not been kind to my father..." But still, there was a chance.

Father. Myreth choked and his eyes went wide. Yes...he could see that similarity in her now.

He had known there was a son...but not a daughter, too.

So much had changed since he had met the White Bard. Now he would lose him wholly, and the world would change again.

Praying that her hands on her father would be enough to save him, the men fell silent and gathered around them, except for Sunna who, unable to remain still, focused on the necessities of survival. He did not share their Faith. He did not think Kavan would respond to his touch and company as he might to theirs. And so, he chose his own path of assistance.

As the sun rose higher, its glow remained obscured behind the misty veil of fog, volcanic steam, and sea spray. The sporadic call of sea birds rose from somewhere to the east and wove overhead, hidden with the sun, and the cooling lava continued to crackle and hiss as it expanded, contracted, and cooled a little more as a rising breeze caressed over its coarse surface. Eventually, Sunna returned and sat long enough to fillet the fish he had caught, build a small fire, and expose its inner flesh to the flame so they could eat.

There was another life to provide for now, one Kavan needed. But when it came time to eat, she refused what was offered.

Food was not what she needed.

She needed the strength, the knowledge, of her mother's kin. She wanted answers. She wanted her father to live.

A few hours more, when the fish was consumed and the fire extinguished, when an eastern wind brought a reversing swirl in the mist, the brightness behind her closed eyes made Earé stand at last.

"They are here."

Believing she meant the záryph had come for Kavan's soul, expecting her to ask something of them, Sunna and Myreth stood with her.

Rhyrdan could not let go of Kavan's hand.

The others saw it too.

To the west, between the horizon and the narrow stretch of stony coast where Sunna had been gathering burnables and food, a small ship unlike any they had ever seen bobbed against the current as though tethered in place. A smaller craft took advantage of the incoming tide to drift closer, propelled by oars wielded by one of the three figures they could see.

Sunna cocked his head, glanced at the woman, and then hurried to the shore to meet them. Earé followed more cautiously, the soles of her battle-worn boots unsteady on the slippery rocks.

Myreth refused to move. Níkóá could not. Rhyrdan would not.

"Men," Myreth murmured. "A ship."

Rhyrdan drew Wortham's sword without releasing Kavan's hand.

Sunna caught the bow of the boat and heaved it as far as he could onto the sand to anchor it. There was nothing but stone to tie the boat to. High tide would end soon and the sea would begin its retreat. Whatever the three had come for, they would have to be gone again quickly if they wanted not to be stranded here for a day.

"I was afraid you would not come," Earé said in a shaky voice as the first stepped out of the boat, a man with sharp features and piercing blue eyes. Behind him, the man who rowed the boat pulled the oars up into the hull while the third swept his loose blonde hair from his shoulders with one hand and accepted Sunna's with the other so that he, too, could get out of the boat and stare with amazement. Once on the beach, he held the sunstone to her in his open palm as the last settled the oars and likewise disembarked.

Sunna chose not to react to their curious looks.

"The storm delayed us, but we persevered. Is he here? Has he…?"

Eare did not need the brush of her fingers against his hand to feel his undiminished power. She could feel it in each of them. Something, the sea or the storm, had protected these men from the depletion of power that Kavan had inflicted upon the rest of the world.

Or perhaps k'Ádhá, Dhágdhuán, or even Kóráhm had seen fit to provide one final miracle after all. Perhaps this was something they had offered in return for the sacrifice of pain he had made.

Earé swallowed hard. She was k'ílshwythnec. She was supposed to voice the future, express what she knew of what was and what would be, with the neutrality of one outside of the world. Like her mother before her, however, she instead spoke of Kavan as one in the world, an attachment she accepted without shame.

He was her father, something few like her had ever known. How could she not feel this moment with her entire soul?

"He is fading." The words were difficult to say.

The man with the piercing blue eyes took a satchel from the boat, slung it over his shoulder, and said, "Take me to him."

Sunna nodded. "Come."

He could hear their voices, and it appeared to Rhyrdan that the strangers knew Kavan's daughter. It was not enough to allow him to loosen his grip on the sword's hilt as he watched them approach, but it was enough to prompt him to move in between the strangers and the injured man on the ground behind him.

One man with long red hair, tied behind his neck in the hopes of preventing the wind from whipping all but a few stray tendrils against his face. Another, whose blonde hair fell around his shoulders, and a third with shorter hair of a paler shade of red, short at the sides with tousled curls on top. There was little else distinctive about them, but Rhyrdan was confident of one thing.

All three strangers were Elyri. The sharp-featured one, coming first, following hard on Sunna's heels, carrying a weather-beaten leather satchel, paused and looked between the two suffering men then knelt at the bard's side without speaking, his expression sad.

"Don't touch him," hissed Myreth, shoving the man's hand away.

Rhyrdan, however did not move. There was something…

"We are here to help."

The blonde scowled and began to push Myreth's hand away but Earé calmed them both with her hands on each wrist. "Dáhmán is the finest healer in Gálínphel. He would never hurt…"

"Gálínphel." The word was a squeak. Rhyrdan looked from the healer, to the long-haired blonde, and finally to the redhead. "You're dhóbhaen. You're…"

Hair the same color as Raebhá's.

"He spoke of us then," said the redhead, gesturing first to his long-haired companion and then to himself. "This is Audh. I am Iólán."

"Raebhá's brother." The sword dropped from Rhyrdan's hand with a clattering thud. "Can you save him?"

"I…" began Dáhmán.

Audh, meanwhile, knelt and pressed his hands against the sides of Kavan's face, careful to avoid the blistered skin. "He is…" he choked. What the pale Seeress said was true. Kavan was fading.

For all the power he contained as márbhyndhánis, for all the training he and Dáhmán shared between them, he did not know if there was anything to be done.

He took Dáhmán's hand so that what he saw, what he felt, could pass between them since Myreth had yet to release his grip on the healer's wrist.

Dáhmán's eyes closed.

"The burns…that is an easy thing…" Though the pale man had suffered for days, he thought he could repair his outer shell easily enough, but he did not know if he could undo the internal trauma his lungs had endured. Without being able to breathe properly, he would not live long. "That which sustains him…it is too far-faded. It is beyond…"

"But you can do it." Níkóá forced himself to sit, grimacing and gasping, forcing the words out of his equally damaged lungs. Kavan, he believed, would endure physical torments as long as he could sing and play his harp again…so long as he lived.

He had to live.

"I don't…it could take weeks to undo what has been done. It could take months or even years…"

"Or," groaned Iólán, resting his hand on Kavan's uninjured shoulder, "he will be lost before we…"

"He will come with us." Audh dropped both hands, and, now that others had touched Kavan too without the bard's reaction and with no obvious intent to harm, Myreth released Dáhmán with a panicked, croaking noise.

"Take him with you?"

Audh sighed, "If he is to…he will need all of the márbhyndhánis to…"

"You said you cannot help him," Myreth spat with frustration.

Audh began again, but Earé cut him off. "She is waiting."

"She?" So many foreign words, so many hints at an already perceived irreversible loss. Myreth was not ready to bear any of it.

"His wife," whispered Rhyrdan, speaking for the first time as he wiped his eyes on the back of his wrist. He understood what the three men had come for, what they intended to do. As much as he did not want to be parted from Kavan, he wanted him to live even more.

He wanted Kavan with him. He wanted to bury him beside Wortham if he was to die. He wanted him close enough that there would always be some part of the bard with him. But deep inside, he knew that was not what Kavan would want. Kavan had promised Raebhá he would return to her.

Whether he survived what would be an arduous sea journey, whether this healer and those with him could keep him alive long enough for him to see his wife and unmet son, if Kavan was to be buried, he would want to be near the mother of his children.

If he were to die, he would be with Wortham, regardless of where his body was put to rest.

"I will go with him," he murmured.

"As will I," Myreth hastily added, refusing to be separated again from the man who had suffered so much to rescue him.

"There is no room on our ship," Iólán began sadly.

Earé touched the back of Rhyrdan's head. "The children need you. Ártur needs you…everyone else…they will need you both. You made a promise, Rhyrdan…and where he is going…you may not go."

Rhyrdan clenched his fists, knowing her words were true.

Kavan would die.

His heart tore in two.

He had known this would be his fate, to persevere on Kavan's behalf, do what Kavan could no longer do, before they had come to this place.

But he did not want to endure it.

Dáhmán stepped around the others to kneel beside Níkóá. "Allow me to…"

"Save your strength for him," Níkóá hissed adamantly. He would sooner be scarred for life than to have even a shred of power that might save Kavan's life spent on him. "We'll get home…I'll find a healer."

If not, he thought stoically, if not in time, so be it.

"You'll hurt him if you move him," Myreth huffed.

Audh nodded and sighed. "Where he is now…he will not feel it."

Glances were exchanged and settled at last on Rhyrdan, as though he had to be the one to make the choice, to decide a future that was already decided. He snorted, a sound less angry than frustrated and hurt, and then spread the blanket from his pack upon the ground. Earé picked up the sturmyrá so it would not fall while the others worked together to jostle the seemingly lifeless body onto it. With Sunna and Rhyrdan at the corners near his head and Iólán at his feet, they carefully lifted him and began the cautious trek to the rowboat.

Earé helped Níkóá to his feet. It was only right that he be there too, that he had the opportunity to speak his farewells.

Myreth picked up Kavan's pack, feeling the dead weight of the harp within it, assuming it was the black kestrel he had heard so much about, and trudged at the rear of the column, the dragging of his feet cutting against the still air and the sea's steady pulse.

With the cold tide lapping at their feet, seeping in over the tops of their boots, Iólán fought to keep the boat steady so that the others could maneuver Kavan into it. Myreth reluctantly yielded Kavan's bag to Rhyrdan, who, with flooding tears he no longer tried to hold back, handed it to Audh, upon whose lap Kavan's feet rested. Earé waded deeper into the water at the edge of the boat and one by one removed the pendants from around Kavan's neck. All except one.

For as long as he drew breath, he was bound to the Lachlan House.

Perhaps, she mused, that would be enough to keep him alive.

She leaned closer, tipping the boat, and kissed her father's cheek as she slid Kóráhm's ring off his finger too.

She whispered something no one else could hear.

Audh caught her wrist and they exchanged a long look. When he released her, she bowed her head and dried her eyes. She could do it now. He had given her the strength to take the others home.

What came after that, she could not say.

Sunna touched the pale man's thigh from where he stood, not endeavoring to get closer. Earé pressed the sunstone into his hand and closed his fist around it. "As they are to you, so shall they be to me," he promised without looking at what he had been given. Bhás was no longer a threat to Kavan's family, but the world was full of others. For as long as he drew breath, he would protect those Kavan had fought to save. It was a fitting exchange, his life and honor for the White Bard's sacrifice.

Níkóá had no words to say, only kissed Kavan's hand and shared his private thoughts, his love, his unspoken promises in a way that Kavan might know. Wherever the bard's soul was, he might not hear spoken words, but he would feel Níkóá's intent. He would carry those thoughts with him for as long as this healer and those with him kept him alive.

Myreth impulsively nudged Níkóá aside, reached over the boat with both arms, and did his best to embrace Kavan without causing further injury or pain. "I failed you," he wept into the man's white hair. "If I had waited…but I will wait for you now. Kóráhm grant me his strength to sing for you until our spirits are one. I will make this up to you. I swear it."

Earé gently pried him back. The tide's retreat had begun. Sunna and Iólán's effort to hold the boat against the pull grew harder.

And there was still one more farewell to be said.

"My heart goes with you, Kavan," Rhyrdan whispered, clutching the bard's arm, stroking his hair, kissing his cheek, his forehead, his mouth. His tears flowed over the man's gray skin, but Rhyrdan did not try to dry them. His tears were the last gift he could offer. "They will not forget what you have done for them. None of them. Take my love with you…take it to my father if you see him…and know that I am here as he was. I will keep your children safe until we meet again."

Choking on emotion, as Iólán climbed into the boat, he let Kavan go, stumbling back against Sunna when the big man released it to the sea. Iólán held the oars steady as Dáhmán pressed his hands to both sides of Kavan's face. The three nodded at those on the beach and the boat bobbed away.

It grew smaller until it reached the ship. Rhyrdan held his breath as long as he could, taking quick gulps when necessary, until Kavan was lifted onto the deck and out of sight. Eventually, that too faded, diminishing into the setting sun.

On the higher ground behind them, Kóráhm watched too, his own expression broken and morose.

We will see each other again, átaelás mai.

His words were no more than a soft moaning into the wind.

❧Chapter 60❧

Sóbhán did not ask how his youngest brother had done it, how he had come through the Gate alone when Sóbhán barely had the power to manipulate the pale white handlight he had been using for meditation in the hours spent in the oratory since Dhóri's departure from Rhidam. The boy had been there waiting for him, perhaps for minutes, perhaps for hours, when he opened his eyes from slumber on the altar steps, staring at him with an expression that tore Sóbhán's heart in two when Ágdhállán held out his hand.

When he took the small hand in his, bracing for the horror he presumed had befallen their brother in Alberni, he did not ask how the boy could take them both through the Gate to St. Kóráhm's. His unsteady leg nearly buckled as Ágdhállán led him out of the k'rylag, and Zerio and Yóáná, who happened to be passing, rushed to steady Kavan's injured eldest son.

"Come." Ágdhállán's strained, almost ethereal whisper demanded compliance from each of them.

Through corridors filled with the wounded, through the unending flow of people engaged in the recovery efforts the city demanded, into the gardens where the dead of St. Kóráhm's were being buried, past the place where the first of them, Jermyn Tythilius, lay, to the place where Wortham rested. Dhóri waited there, slump-shouldered and weary, leaning against Bergis whose eyes darted quick and restless as he tried to think of some way to comfort his friend.

Bergis did not need to announce their arrival. Dhóri knew the footsteps of each. As if sensing them with what little power he had remaining, particularly the presence of the one who carried more power than Dhóri thought he should, he turned and cried, "Where have you been?" with both consternation and relief.

His question went unanswered. The air shimmered as though filled with swirling mist…and then others, more unexpected, stood with them.

Earé. Sunna. Rhyrdan. The badly scalded Níkóá collapsed with a groan, only to be caught by Zerio before he landed with a yelp of pain. And a dark-haired man none of those gathered knew.

But Kavan was not among them.

"Where is he?" squawked Sóbhán, hobbling hastily forward. His crutch stuck in the soft earth and twisted under him so that he fell too, directly into Bergis' arms.

Yóáná's first thought was to hold up Níkóá with a look of concern. Rhyrdan looked as if he would crumble, but he locked his knees and remained standing, unable to make eye contact with anyone.

Ágdhállán remained where he was, distant from them, meeting only his sister's gaze as tears rolled down his cheeks. "They have…they came? He has gone…with them?" he whispered. The birds and insects grew still. The sounds in the courtyard on the other side of the náós ceased.

To those gathered here, it felt, at that moment, that the world had ended without anyone knowing it yet.

Dhóri choked, feeling his siblings' upset without being able to see it. It hung in the air with a smothering weight, drowning all but the emotion in their voices, their breathing, and the scent of Ágdhállán's tears. "With…the záryph…? He is…?"

He slid from the top edge of Wortham's grave marker and sagged against it. Earé joined him and wrapped him in her embrace; he returned the comforting gesture. Despite her pleading gaze, neither Sóbhán nor Ágdhállán moved.

"He will be with Raebhá soon." Soon could be months, could be years, depending on the cooperation of the sea and wind and Audh and Iólán's sailing prowess. Soon might never come, should everything Dáhmán and Audh could do in that time fail to be enough.

It was the best Earé could offer. This time, She Who Sees could not see enough.

"He's…dying…" groaned Níkóá.

"But the threat is past," Sunna reassured them in a tone heavy with grief. "Bhás is no more."

"The war is over," Earé sighed, lifting her face from Dhóri's shoulder.

"Over?" Zerio and Yóáná helped Níkóá to the ground.

She nodded and wiped her cheek on her shoulder. "Glevum has fallen. Neth is won." She reached for Yóáná's wrist and forced most of her remaining power to allow this one last duty on Kavan's behalf. Yóáná jerked at the influx of power, blinked, and sucked in a quick breath, and then without a verbal expression of gratitude allowed the power to pass through her to heal the scalding burns on the side of Níkóá's face and as much of his lungs as she could. The rest, his arm, side, and the remainder of internal damage, would have to wait.

Or they might never be healed.

But Yóáná expected he would live. She was not certain, from the words being spoken around her, if Kavan would too.

Arms empty, Zerio brushed his fingers through the tears on Rhyrdan's face and in a voice thick with grief and awe, murmured, "The prophecy is fulfilled…he has saved us all."

But why had it needed to come to this?

"He'll come back, won't he?" Dhóri begged.

Myreth, feeling out of place amongst his white twin's children, forlornly shook his head. He wanted to believe it was possible. Right now, he felt no hope.

There was no honest answer to be given. Spoken words and Myreth's headshake stood on their own.

Kavan was dying.

Perhaps, thought Sóbhán, as the pit in his belly tightened into a sick, dismayed knot, he was dead already.

If there was hope for a different fate, it was not reflected on Earé's face.

Whatever was behind Ágdhállán's downcast stare could not be interpreted, but Sóbhán believed his slumped posture said enough.

Their father was never coming back.

❧*❦

"You will send Asta and Tau when you reach home?" Kjell asked Lorant, his too-stern expression stoically in place as it had been since Jerit's earlier rebuff when Enesfel's entourage prepared for the journey south. The request that Jerit remain in Glevum until his mother arrived, that he remain in support of Henrik's newborn reign, had appeared to be accepted until Lorant announced that, despite his injury, he was returning to Rhidam.

Lorant had accomplished what he had come to Neth to do. There were enough de Corrmick loyalists and converted Nethite troops to hold Glevum and retake any villages or cities that resisted the regime change. tama Kaj and his men agreed to remain in Glevum until Neth was settled into peace again, until the last of Bhás' mercenaries were collected and dealt with in whatever way Henrik and Kjell deemed appropriate. In the hopes of finding the still missing Earé, Kaj was determined not to leave Glevum until she was found safe…or dead.

There was no need for Enesfel's soldiers to remain. Lorant's choice to depart prompted Jerit to choose to do likewise.

After Jerit's efforts and success in reclaiming Glevum without any measure of gratitude, his father's bitterness about that choice did nothing to prompt Jerit to change his mind.

Others, likewise, chose to remain in Glevum on the child-king's behalf. dedhá Thrismund, along with Novice Hebel, remained in the hopes of founding the first naós in Glevum to have stood in centuries. Healer Tyrnás, a man familiar with medical conditions of the mind, after a discussion with the MacLyrs and then Kjell, chose to remain in the Glevum court on King Henrik's behalf. Syl chose to remain with the other healers until the need to care for so many injured soldiers was no longer required. Ylltán also planned to stay indefinitely when the other Elyri recruits sailed for home.

With Ágdhállán still missing, she and Ártur agreed that one of them needed to remain until the boy was found. Henrik's promise that Ágdhállán had gone home allowed Ártur to dare to depart to care for the king and prince, in the hopes that the boy-king's claim was true. By the time he reached Rhidam, perhaps the Gates would work. Perhaps healers would once more be able to heal.

Either he or his wife would find Kavan's young son and let the other know. Beneath the growing shadow of deep, nameless despair, Ártur hoped he would find an answer in Rhidam that would take all that building grief away. The emptiness in his soul needed an answer. He needed to see Kavan to fill that void and right the world again.

Nearby, Bhríd, largely silent since the fall of Glevum when he was not giving orders, waited upon his nervous horse as he and Bhetá counted the passing troops, waiting for the king to join them, waiting for Jerit to take his horse's reins to begin the journey before the sun climbed much higher. The day promised rain and they were not the only two to hope to outrun the storm and make it to Gorea before nightfall.

Lorant, like Kjell, looked from Bhríd's unsettled expression and back to one another. Thanks in part to the Elyri duke's prowess, Neth was won. With the belief that the Sovereignties would remain at peace at the top of every noble, every soldier, every common man's mind, Lorant, like Kjell, did not think Levonne's duke would go to war for Enesfel ever again.

"I will give them your request," Lorant promised as he adjusted the hood of his cloak against the wind, his gaze tracking Jerit's movement as the prince walked in quiet conversation with Olaric, their heads bent together sharing some secret Lorant did not believe he would hear about later. Something to do with the Vants, he suspected, some missive to pass on to both Mr. Kaas and Tau when Lorant saw them.

He was sure Tau would join Kjell as soon as he was able. If the Elyri Gates functioned by then, Tau's arrival in Glevum would come within a matter of weeks rather than a month or more. Kjell would be more at ease when his aide was back at his side. But neither he nor Lorant had control over Asta's choice. Perhaps she would remain as the Lachlan Inquisitor, remain with her son, daughter, and other two grandchildren in Rhidam. Or perhaps she would choose to join the grandson she had raised to support his new reign. Lorant would leave the choice to her.

He did not want to think that far into the future. He wanted to focus on the next few weeks of riding with Jerit, without war weighing on their shoulders, and return to Seren in Rhidam before winter fully set in.

He wanted only to understand why the half-moon pendant upon his chest felt so leaden against his skin. He had considered taking it off. In the end, he could not convince himself to do it.

Kjell offered his hand. "You sheltered and gave me hope when I had neither, despite my failure to your father. You supported me and my family and made this day possible. The House of de Corrmick shall be forever in your debt. I pray we remain allies and kin and maintain the peace."

"We shall," Lorant agreed, accepting the older man's hand. Matters of an Enesfel-Neth alliance were already under preliminary discussion. Who would control the territory south of Lake Curo would be decided in the spring when the storms ended and the de Corrmicks had Neth's security in hand. Until then, both Sovereignties together would do everything they could to aid the people ravaged and displaced by Fraen's war. "I will bring Lord Cliáth when I come again. He will want to see how we have fared. I think he will be proud of our accomplishments."

"He has no reason to stay away so long. If he chooses to come sooner, he, like you, are welcome here."

Kjell believed it too. What others had claimed must be true. Without Duke Cliáth, success would not have been possible. Kjell was determined to offer the bard his gratitude in person as soon as he was able.

"It is time, Your Majesty." Bhríd had given the reins of Jerit's horse to the prince while Bhetá turned her horse and offered the king the reins of his. The healer wagon, now containing only Ártur, Novice Ybherd, and a smattering of physicians eager to return to homes along the long road back to Rhidam, had lurched into motion. The Lachlan Guard awaited their king's command to march.

"We will see each other soon," Lorant promised. "I will keep Jerit safe. I swear it."

Kjell began to retort, but instead bobbed his head. He had kept Henrik from being here so the boy would not make a scene at his uncle's departure.

It would not do for Kjell to do so in his place.

His son, silhouetted by the rising sun, had survived and carried the de Corrmick banner with pride and honor. He had reclaimed Neth's throne.

For Kjell, that would have to be enough.

❧*❦

Feeling castoff, uncertain, and out of place as the siblings huddled together at Captain Delamo's grave, a man Myreth had heard much about but had never met, he aided the lady healer in assisting Níkóá through the chellé halls and into the first empty prayer alcove she located. The holy air of the place reminded Myreth of Gorbesh, which in turn reminded him of the day he first met the bard and his ultimate folly in pursuing Kavan from that place across a vast, unfamiliar world he had been ill-prepared to meet.

He stopped and Níkóá was pulled from his grasp and made comfortable as the remorse and grief swept over Myreth where he stood, adrift again now that he had no purpose. The hands of a gentle-featured blonde man, záryph-like in manner and face despite the blood on his hands and clothes, caught his shoulders as he swept around Myreth with long, hasty steps.

"My lord." Khwílen dropped down to his knees at Níkóá's side. "What happened?" He recognized the fire damage to his flesh, to the clothes along the right side of Níkóá's body; to his knowledge, the regent had last been in Kavan's company, set off to attend to some duty that the bard had claimed would end the war. "Where is…?"

"He is not here," whispered Myreth, unable to stop himself. "He will never be…" He fell silent with a sob and pursed his lips together to avoid saying more. Khwílen looked at Yóáná who shrugged as she removed the damaged fabric of the regent's tunic to get a better look at his blistered skin.

She had heard the conversation in the cemetery but it had made little sense to her. She would have the truth later, but for now, there were people who needed her medical skills, Níkóá among them. "I must fetch my kit…"

"Of course," began Khwílen. Someone near the náós door shouted his name. "A moment," he called as Yóáná started away. He took a step, turned long enough to clutch Myreth's hands as though to acknowledge a level of grief he did not understand. "You are welcome here, sir. Stay with Regent McCábhá. I will return to hear more of the tale you have to tell."

Myreth interpreted the words as a command and sank onto the bench opposite Níkóá.

There was so much to learn. So much to know.

So much to reveal.

If he had entered St. Kóráhm's comforting halls sooner, Kavan might have shared this place with him. He might have found peace here. Kavan might not have died.

Now he would need to learn such things alone if he could make peace with himself and the ghost that was sure to haunt him…or else flee Alberni again, never to return.

❧*❦

Despite sharing the grief that Kavan's children shared, Zerio felt duty-bound to share Eare's news with everyone in St. Kóráhm's. Someone else should be doing this. He was the only one who could. The only one here, other than the Cliáths, to know.

"It is over!" he exclaimed, his words ringing over the heads of the soldiers streaming back into St. Kóráhm's after a day collecting the mercenary army, collecting the dead. Madoc lifted his head towards the cry, as did Raenár and Tau as the three coordinated the next day's agenda while the weary soldiers sought a hot meal and a place to rest. Burying the dead, finding others they had missed, would continue through the night as Sheriff Groff and his brigade took over the responsibilities. The three watched the slender man elbow through the sweaty, bloody crowd, dragging a disheartened Rhyrdan with him because he did not think it wise to leave the man standing at his father's grave alone.

"Neth's fallen," he crowed. "Glevum's ours!" By ours, he did not mean Enesfel's, only that the joint forces had succeeded at the mission they had set out to accomplish.

"How have you…?" began Madoc, his concern for his silent, rigid, heartbroken brother evident on his face.

"Lord Cliáth's daughter brought word…"

They looked at one another again. Tau and Madoc did not know the woman, though they had met her and had heard the claims that she, too, had the Sight. While Raenár had only spoken to her in passing a handful of times, he knew those claims to be true. They took Rhyrdan's expression to mean that the Elyri duke had somehow had a hand in Enesfel's success…and had paid dearly for it.

"I must take this news to Rhidam, to the king," Tau grunted, believing Kjell to still be with his wife in the royal keep. He motioned to a passing soldier and said, "Bring me my horse."

"I must…go with you…" They were the first words Rhyrdan had spoken. His voice was tight and slurred with emotions he was trying to strangle and avoid feeling.

Reaching for his brother's arm, Madoc snorted, "You are in no condition to go anywhere."

Rhyrdan shrugged his brother's hand away.

"There are things there I must do." People to face. Responsibilities on Kavan's behalf to address. As many reminders of the bard as Rhidam would contain, being there was far better than remaining here in St. Kóráhm's suffocating presence or returning to the empty Alberni manor. He should see to its condition, to Emeria and the staff, but he lacked the courage for those things.

There was too much of Kavan in those places, too.

He had no desire or intention to forget, but for now, he did not want to remember.

"I will…"

Rhyrdan shook his head at his brother. "You'll finish what you've started here." He had overheard the talk of others, his brother's agreement to continue the restoration of Alberni's peace while Raenár, despite his injury, continued to oversee the cleanup of the chellé and participate in the burial of the dead. Tau's primary responsibility was to King Kjell.

And Zerio would, he knew, see to the needs of Kavan's children until Rhyrdan joined them again.

As if reading his thoughts when Rhyrdan's eyes passed, Zerio nodded.

"We can ride faster if we share a horse." A single animal, particularly in Rhyrdan's unwell condition, would suffice.

"Tell k'dedhá Tusánt about St. Maicel's…tell them St. Kóráhm's stands," said Raenár as Tau swung onto his horse.

Tau reached for Rhyrdan's hand; Zerio and Madoc helped him up together. "We shall celebrate victory and rebuild, Tau promised. If Zerio's words were true, if prophecy had been fulfilled, soon the entire world would celebrate what the Lachlans and de Corrmicks had done together.

All, perhaps, except Rhyrdan.

ᕗ*ᕘ

The early autumn glow of mauve and amber colored the sky before the siblings left their place of grieving at Wortham's grave, each one wearing the piece of their father that Earé had saved for them. The shattered crystal Prince Muir had given Kavan hung around Sóbhán's neck. Gaed's pendant, adopted as the Cliáthan crest, hung around Dhóri's, and, as it was too large for his finger, St. Kóráhm's ring hung on a cord around Ágdhállán's neck. Kóráhm's cross was saved for Myreth but had not yet been given to him.

"What about you?" Sóbhán asked. "What about Rhyrdan?"

"We have our remembrances," Earé replied with a melancholy sigh and a kiss into his dark curls. What those were, she did not share. Perhaps, he mused when they joined hands in a circle at that place, and then separated to arrive without fanfare in the sitting room of his home in Bhryell, the home that had been Kavan's security as a discarded child, Earé wanted no reminders of the pain she carried at having witnessed their father's death.

He did not believe Rhyrdan would feel the same.

Chethá met them there and threw herself into her husband's arms, but her relief at having him home for the first time since he had lost his leg, her fear over the loss of her healing gifts, were overcome by the remorse of those gathered with her. Young Maelís, happy to have her father home, did not immediately detect the mood of the room and gladly skipped off to bring Bhen to the house at her father's request. By the time she returned with him, the others had sunk into chairs around the room, rejecting the offer of the meal that none had the stomach to eat.

Kavan's chair remained empty.

"What's happened?" Bhen begged. He had been told about the loss of Sóbhán's leg but he could tell that what he was called to hear was more serious. Some deep loss had brought Kavan's children together this day.

Bhen could only think of one thing that could cause such despair.

He shook his head, his face losing color as Dhóri took his hand and Sóbhán took Chethá's.

"No."

He yanked his hand away in disbelief and avoided Ágdhállán's touch when the boy tried to catch it instead.

"He is not. He cannot be."

"When we…unless k'Ádhá sees fit to bless him with one of his own miracles…" began Earé in a quavering voice.

"He cannot be…"

Tears slipped free, and he slid to the floor, elbows on his knees, his face in his hands. Maelís, understanding then that something had happened to her beloved Kavan, threw her arms around her father's waist and buried her face against his stomach, weeping too as Chethá did against Sóbhán's neck.

Ágdhállán placed his hands on Bhen's shoulders. Slowly, trance-like, Bhen lifted his face to stare into the boy's eyes.

Gradually, feeding off Ágdhállán's unspoken hope, Bhen felt hope too. Ágdhállán believed in that miracle.

Regardless of what anyone said, what anyone else believed, Bhen chose to believe too. Kavan was the bastion of faith. His son had the Sight.

His head bowed as if accepting a holy duty from the child. He would spread the news. He, like Ágdhállán and others, would spread hope. How could he do otherwise in the face of such defiant surety?

How could anyone believe the White Bard of Bhryell was dead?

❧Chapter 61❧

"This is your home now."

Grateful that Zerio had remained as a buffer between him and his wife as long as he had, while they conducted a tour of the Alberni manor, Jerit watched Ida run off with Emeria's children with the promise of playing with the lambs collected in one of the nearby fields. He had hoped the man would stay longer, but some matter of repairs to St. Kóráhm's had taken him away and left Jerit in the library where his wife had dutifully awaited him.

Gerna's eyes were wide but her expression remained skeptical. They had barely spoken since his return from Neth, and there were times he was sure that she would rather he had been killed in battle. She had not been told the purpose of this trip to Alberni and had behaved aloof and bitter during the carriage ride. He suspected she thought his words some sort of trap.

"Yours and Ida's. It remains Lord Cliáth's estate…"

"The duke is dead," she huffed.

Shivering at her callous tone, not wanting to debate with her, he continued, "At his insistence, and with the Crown's permission, I have assumed the title of Duke of Alberni." For now. "The rights of the lands, its wealth…the responsibilities that come with it, belong to us, so long as nothing is sold, nothing destroyed or removed. The staff is to remain in perpetuity. You will not fire or replace any of them without my knowledge and permission if they do not wish to go. You will otherwise have free rein when I am not here."

Something changed in her eyes that made him sigh and look away, confirming a suspicion he had carried since his return. How could he blame her, however, when he was as guilty as she was? How could he accuse her of infidelity or hold her to a standard he could not keep?

"Gerna…" He paused, turned toward the window to collect his thoughts, and then began again without looking at her. "I cannot give you what you want, beyond a home and title and the wealth that comes with those things. I will respect you, support you, provide for you and Ida…and ask only that you publicly return those duties to me. In all functions, we are Lord and Lady of Alberni. I will not object to the taking of lovers if that is your wish, so long as you bear no other man's child. Should you do so, I will not raise or support such children as my own. You will lose your privileges as duchess…but you are entitled to affections I cannot give you."

Surprised at his words and that he had called her by name which he rarely did, she snorted and began, "Ida…"

"Ida is my own. When I die, if Lord Cliáth has not reclaimed what is his…if his children do not…Ida will inherit all of this and the title that comes with it." He gestured around them, agreeing to Kavan's terms, to Lorant's terms, though he did so with a heavy heart. "Upon her death, without exception, Alberni will revert to Crown property." Only a future king, Lorant or one of his heirs, could change that, but Jerit was content with the decision. No one beyond Jerit or his adopted daughter would lay claim to Alberni until both were gone.

Unless, perhaps, he, Ida, or the Crown chose to annex the estate to St. Kóráhm's. It was a possibility Jerit had considered from the moment Chamberlain Cáner expressed Kavan's wishes for the estate.

Jerit was not the only one to conclude that the duke had left Enesfel to face the one called Bhás with the knowledge, that he would not return.

Why else would he have given St. Kóráhm's into Zerio's care, with enough funds to facilitate the necessary repairs, upgrades, and a budget, drawn from the duchy's earnings to continue increasing the library that once resided there? St. Maicel's would be rebuilt, would remain the center of Faith in Alberni, while St. Kóráhm's would become the largest library in the Sovereignties, and, Jerit believed, the unofficial, or perhaps official, home of the Vants in Enesfel.

He eagerly looked forward to making both things happen.

For several minutes as she circled the room, rubbing fingers on dustless surfaces, over the spines of a small collection of books Ida was eager to read, over the sills of the windows that brought her back to Jerit's side, Gerna did not speak. Undoubtedly, she was weighing the pros and cons of the life he offered. A life of wealth and entitlement. A life away from Rhidam where she did not have to feel humiliated by her husband's preference for King Lorant's company. A life where she did not have to hide her dalliances, whoever they were with, from the eyes of the royal court, where they might present a scandal that would hurt all three of them.

In Alberni, she could live as she pleased. With him remaining in Rhidam much of the time, there would be no need for the constant friction between them. It was not the life she had envisioned when she had agreed to marry the de Corrmick prince, but it was a better life than she had come to believe she would have.

The only potentially better option would be to travel to Glevum and reside in King Henrik's court. Ida's desire to remain near her adopted father, however, and Gerna's ties to those she knew, would, for now, keep them both in Enesfel.

"Agreed, my lord," she finally said in a coolly neutral tone.

There was no need to say anything further.

❧*❧

Asta turned her horse toward the man riding next to her, watching Henrik and Kjell set chase of a fox across the field with a host of retainers, nobles, and palace guards. It was Henrik's first hunt, and while she worried about how he would behave once an actual kill was made, particularly if the animal fell to his clumsy archery shots, it was an activity that Kjell insisted the king must participate in at least once. The hunt was a well-honored pastime of Nethite kings.

Henrik had, at least, seemed eager to impress his grandfather.

"You will protect him at all costs?"

Tau's attentive stare did not change. He chose to trust the king and his father out of his sight this once, but that trust did not keep him from following the sounds of the hunt. "You know I will. Your Majesty." He had already sworn an oath of protection for the boy-king to the ex-king whose life he had helped save. "Are you planning to leave us?"

As soon as word had come of victory in Glevum, as soon as Jerit and King Lorant returned to Enesfel with news that Henrik had been crowned, Asta traveled immediately to Glevum without giving Lorant time to replace her as inquisitor. While she did not doubt Kjell's motives as regent, she knew her husband's desire to return to Neth's throne had burned in him since the day of his capture. It would be easy for a man of his intensity to overpower a boy like Henrik, and without understanding Henrik's peculiarities, it would be too easy, she feared, for Kjell to decide that the boy was incapable of serving as king and perhaps finding some way to be rid of him, Oska's son or not.

Once Kjell had sworn never to kill a king simply to gain the throne for himself. Asta was no longer certain he held to those beliefs. His time of imprisonment, his time in exile, had changed him.

Henrik needed her if he was to remain the king he was destined to be.

"I'm not going anywhere," she grunted.

"You worry for your husband then."

Asta side-eyed him. "I want Henrik to be safe. I lost a son to this throne. I thought I lost a husband. I will not risk a grandson too."

Tau's nod was barely perceptible. "I have a duty to the regent…but he swore my first allegiance to the king upon his public coronation. I am Vants. My oath is my blood and my bond."

"Good." She did not think he was lying and considered, for the first time, that Kjell too, might have planned for the possibility of his failings. Perhaps more of her husband remained behind the bitterness of the past years than she had believed there to be. Perhaps, in time, they could find their way back to what they had once shared.

King Lorant and Enesfel would have to see to their future without her. She would see Yóáná and her grandchildren again, but with Warde at the helm of the Association, she was not needed there. She had few doubts that her father's legacy would endure and the Association would not be a problem for the Crown for years to come. Another Inquisitor would be appointed. Asta had done enough.

᚛*᚜

Winter had come. Winter had gone. The first flowers of spring bloomed again.

The Gates were working at last and the healers, once more, could perform the duties they had dedicated their lives to.

Months had passed since his return to Rhidam, months without the ability to heal, months without the ability to search for his beloved sínréc that so many proclaimed dead…or refused to believe to be so. During those first days, the Gates had worked only a handful of times. Once to bring home those who had seen Kavan last. Once to allow Ágdhállán to take Kjell and Henrik to Glevum before collecting his brothers and joining their sister in Bhryell where the word of the White Bard's fate spread like a fire throughout the town and eventually throughout all Elyriá. Once to bring the siblings and those with them back to Rhidam.

It was said, when Bhyrhán returned to Rhidam, appointed now as the Kyne's permanent ambassador in the Lachlan court, that many in Clarys talked of bestowing sainthood upon the one who had saved k'gdhededhá Ylár's life and ended the war. Nothing except the White Bard's great miracles could have stripped the world of power. Nothing else could have exposed the intended killer and stopped him from accomplishing the great sin that would have generated as much chaos in Clarys as the invasion of enemy forces had created.

Kavan. A saint.

How he would grieve for that fate.

There was already talk of it in Bhryell, where news of the Clarys invasion had finally spread, where the news of Kavan's death had spread like a spider's web by the time Ártur was able to make his first visit home since before the war. Reverence had fully replaced the disregard with which Bhryell had once held Kavan, as if so many who had known the boy had forgotten what had once been. With that reverence came a renewed interest in the harps that was his family's legacy, bringing an increase of bounty for the family, but it was not enough to keep some of them there.

Unlike those few, however, Bhen and Nóráh, Sóbhán and Chethá and their children, Dháná could not escape the past. She would remain in Bhryell with the rest of the family, a version of herself diminished by rumor, memory, regret, and grief.

dedhá Bhílári, Sámel, and Llucás promised to see to her welfare, and Ártur promised to visit as often as he could, but Bhryell held so many reminders of the life that had gone before that Ártur was uncertain if he would ever actually return to it.

The far-off cry of an infant made Ártur cock his head to listen, but there was no need to hasten to see to the prince's care. Yóáná would see to Seren and her son, the Lachlan heir to the throne, the first, Ártur sighed, to grow up without Kavan's tutelage and guidance since Arlan had claimed the throne. The prince would have Physician Mauret and Lady Aunes to care for him, would have Master Najar to teach him, but to Ártur, none of that seemed right.

Nothing seemed right any longer.

He paused to peer into the courtyard where Aunes was overseeing Kaedís, the Cáner children, Princess Hella, and others as they chased a ball around the courtyard with Balint at the head of the game. Since learning of Kavan's death, since learning his father would not be coming back, the boy had become a much different, more cooperative child. Like Bhetá's mother, Raenár's longevity and his decision to ultimately follow k'dedhá Khwílen and the rest of St. Kóráhm's residents to Gorbesh, had prompted a tale of his being missing in battle, a story that would be explained more fully when Bhetá believed her son was old enough, strong enough, to accept the truth.

Perhaps replacing the glory of war with the grim reality of death was what Balint needed. What the result would be when the truth came out was something Ártur was grateful he would not be here to see.

Until the day Princess Hella officially became King Henrik's wife, Aunes would remain as her chambermaid in Rhidam. She was too afraid to travel to Glevum, despite the changes the new king and his regent father were restoring to Neth, so when that day came, Aunes would focus her service on Queen Seren and the newborn prince. She could have returned to Bhryell; she could have chosen Gorbesh, as so many others were doing.

She decided to do neither and remain where she was.

Ártur likewise tried to convince Tusánt to make the exodus to Gorbesh, but Enesfel's k'gdhededhá politely refused. Kavan's legacy, k'gdhededhá Tythilius' legacy, were best served, he believed, if he remained in Rhidam at the post Kavan had helped him attain. There was the damaged náós to repair, so many dedhá and novices to replace, and with a burgeoning potential of an improved relationship with the Faithful in Clarys to nurse into full bloom, there was much for Tusánt to do. There were still sticking points between the joint Faith Councils, but the one thing both sides were inclined to agree upon was that the miracle-working White Bard had ended the war with miraculous feats that grew more fanciful with every retelling.

Lorant's royal decree, coinciding with those made by the Faith in Clarys and the council in Rhidam, had generated the appointment of a yearly feast in Kavan's honor, to be held in conjunction with St. Kóráhm's festival. The centers of those celebrations would be in Alberni, Bhryell, Rhidam, and Clarys, and maybe one day at St. Kóráhm's shrine in Kílyn. Tusánt wanted to be present at each location to tell the tale, not of a saint but of a man…the only thing Kavan had ever wanted to be.

Ártur doubted Tusánt's efforts, and those of Hwensen, Kluín, and a handful of others, would be enough to stem the tide of impending sainthood.

The last time Ártur had spoken to Rhyrdan, before his pilgrimage with Níkóá, Sunna, and Earé to assess the Kílyn shrine and determine what was required to restore it, Wortham's son had assured him that none of those tales were true. The events of Kavan's final days had been both a simpler and more fantastic story than men could tell. One day, Rhyrdan promised, when his pilgrimage to the shrine, to the birthplace of St. Kóráhm, and then to follow the road his father had once traveled with Kavan into the lands of the south, Rhyrdan would tell him the story.

When the three had ridden out of the Rhidam castle's gate, it had been a tale too painfully fresh to tell.

Myreth, the mysterious stranger who had come to Enesfel with them and who had answers of his own, had sequestered himself in St. Kóráhm's with dedhá Khwílen, assuming a vow of silence he would not break…until the day he returned to the place where his journey with Kavan had begun.

Ágdhállán assured his uncle that, when that day came, Myreth would reveal as much of the story as he knew.

Ártur had to trust that Kavan's son spoke the truth.

In the courtyard, Cáym stopped in his chase to adjust the buckle of his boot, using his body to block Phaedr's effort to coax Ágdhállán into the game. Near the gate, Bhríd called to his children to join him as he broke away from the conversation he had been having with the tama, the Daema, and a collection of newly promoted captains. Now that tama Kaj had returned to Rhidam with those who had come to Enesfel to serve with him, days had been spent in negotiations with the king as to what his future would entail. He accepted the role of general in Garran's place, a position Bhetá turned down. She was content with Captain of the Guard as it kept her near to her son. And Bhríd, in talks with Bhyrhán, Kyne Phílóá, and King Lorant, had made his own choices.

Unlike most who had come to Rhidam with Prince Arlan, Bhríd would remain awhile longer. Until the day Phaedr was old enough to assume responsibility for the Dubuais-Cáner vineyards and the duchy of Levonne, a promise that had been made to Madeline a lifetime ago, Bhríd would stay as King Lorant's chamberlain. When the day of endings came, he had given his word to Elyriá's kyne to accept residency in Clarys and take up the role of Elyria's first general.

War in Clarys was over, but the damage to their security had been done. The once non-violent sovereignty of Elyriá would never again be caught unprepared for war.

Cáym had begged to go wherever Ágdhállán went. Now that the Gates could be used again, there was no reason for Bhríd not to consider the option. He, like Ártur, was confident Kavan would have wanted Cáym at Ágdhállán's side. Phaedr would remain in Levonne in the care of Jemes Osveld and, until she was old enough to make her own decision, Ónyká would remain in Rhidam with Princess Hella and Aunes. Bhríd would visit each of his children often, but once he went to Clarys, they would each be without the others.

On that day when Bhríd stepped down, Prince Jerit would accept the role of Lorant's primary advisor. Perhaps not chamberlain, but something equally important. With the restorations of the Gates, it was understood that Zerio would remain as the inquisitor but would be able to travel often to both Gorbesh and Alberni, to make use of the library and acquire books for the one he was restoring while training his apprentice to assume his position with the Association.

With the need for a new chamberlain and new inquisitor, so many changes loomed ahead that to Ártur, it felt less like home. Once Bhyrhán's arrival from Clarys confirmed the working Gates, resulting in a flurry of activity in the weeks that came after, as people were transported or fetched on King Lorant's behalf or at the request of others, the choice Ártur and others faced had inevitably been made.

In many ways, Rhidam would always be his home. He had spent most of his adult life in these halls with the Lachlan House. Without Kavan, however, there was no desire to remain any longer. The choice was made to follow where Ágdhállán led…to the place where others had already gone. To the place the boy swore they would see Kavan again.

Ártur clung to the boy's belief despite despairing, plaguing thoughts. Hope was all any of them had.

Syl's arm slid around his waist, and her head rested between his shoulder blades, the first awareness he had of her entering the room. "One more dinner with the king?" she murmured before shifting her head, kissing his shoulder, and then settling into place again.

He caught his breath. Held it.

"One more dinner," he whispered.

There would be no reason to keep them away, so long as there were Gates. No reason they could not come back to Rhidam any time they chose.

But once they followed Ágdhállán through the Gate to Gorbesh at evening's end, Ártur had a sinking feeling he would not see Rhidam again.

❧*❦

Rhyrdan ran his hand over the fractured, fallen marble, the last few pieces that remained of a shrine that had stood upon this hillock for centuries. He did not know where the rest of it had gone, whether the people of Kílyn had repurposed the material to repair the damage done elsewhere in the wounded city, or whether opportunistic thieves had stolen it with the intent of selling chunks as holy relics to those who could afford it.

They had known the shrine was destroyed; they had been here at the time of assault, and Kavan had foreseen what was to come. They had already procured an agreement with Prime Magistrate Piran to transport stone from the island of Pháne to rebuild it as seemed fitting given the island's connection to the saint and to Kavan.

But they had hoped more of the original material had remained.

King Gamal permitted them to erect temporary shelters at the base of the hill to serve them for as long as the reconstruction lasted. Stonemasons were hired and the base of the shrine was already under repair. When the work was complete, hopefully by Kavan's birth day, by St. Kóráhm's Feast Day, the three men and Earé would join them here, celebrate with them, and then travel together into the lands of the south, the way her mother and Rhyrdan's father had once traveled with Kavan. Together they would tell everyone they met that the White Bard of Bhryell was alive…even if they sometimes had doubts, without physical proof, that their tale was true.

Ágdhállán had sent them on this quest. Had said this was what Kóráhm wanted, a path that Rhyrdan was ardently determined to complete. In time, they would reach the doors of Gorbesh and rejoin friends and family there.

They did not know how long that would take. None of them asked Earé. They did not want to be discouraged.

Rebuilding the shrine was taking long enough.

But it did not matter.

The time spent at the site of Kóráhm's martyrdom allowed Rhyrdan to come to terms, in his way, with Kavan's absence and the emptiness the bard left in his wake. He was grateful that Sunna and Níkóá had come with him, but he would have made this pilgrimage alone if necessary.

Hands on his shoulders. He turned his head, expecting Níkóá and his now-healed burns to be behind him. He was not. He and Sunna had gone back down the hill to light their fire anew, to share a meal with the smattering of pilgrims who had come to the shrine earlier in the day, and to share their purpose here as well.

Not alone. Not Kavan's hands, but not alone.

He was confident and relieved that Kóráhm was with them.

For the first time in months, Rhyrdan almost smiled.

❧*❧

The air was hot and heavy with the red dust the day's wind stirred when the four gathered on the rooftop for the first time, listening to the chirp of unfamiliar insects and birds, to the murmurs of a handful of people in the courtyard who, like them, were unable to sleep on this night. Some had come from sharing one last dinner with King Lorant, friends, and families in Rhidam's keep. Some had come from Bhryell, some had already taken shelter here in the weeks before war had come to St. Kóráhm's. Each snippet of overheard conversation brought morsels of memory to life for those gathered high above the valley floor, sparking pain and melancholy longing they doubted would ever be shed.

"I stood here with him once," Myreth murmured. "It was my favorite place when I wished for solitude…shared with no one but him." He shook his head and closed his hand around the cross of St. Kóráhm that hung around his neck. "I should never have left. I should have waited."

"We all have parts to play," soothed Dhóri, unable to see the vista of starlight and the silver moon that cast glittering fingers on the coarse sand. As dearly as he missed his father, the choice for self-loathing and self-doubt was no longer practical. His father wanted a community built in this arid place, a place where Kóráhm had once sought and received shelter, a place where the bard's blood had been spilled in blessing on the chapel floor.

No one had told Dhóri that tale.

He had found it in the chapel, breathed it in the air, felt it in the stones beneath his bare feet the first time he entered there. The stones had spoken their story to him more clearly than any voice could have.

Kavan had loved this place. Dhóri hoped that, in time, those united here under Kavan and Kóráhm's names would grow to love it too.

Having struggled to the rooftop, relying on Myreth and his brothers to reach the top, Sóbhán wrapped an arm around Ágdhállán's shoulders without looking at him. Sometimes when he did so, Kavan was all he could see. Sometimes when the boy laughed, Kavan's voice was all he could hear. Such things filled him with longing, joy, and melancholy all at once.

This was not the forested beauty of Bhryell, but it was home now. Sóbhán did not regret his choice.

"When do you think he will…?" he began.

Ágdhállán's shoulders twitched beneath his embrace. "I don't know." He had not Seen anything to offer specifics, and so far, Earé had likewise offered no proof or hope to support his claim. But still, Ágdhállán believed.

"But he will?" asked Myreth with a begging note of desperation.

A cock crowed in the courtyard and the voices there slowly drifted into the mountainside chellé hábhai.

Ágdhállán nodded.

He had nothing to offer but faith.

It was enough to give them hope.

❧*❧

With her son's hand in hers, she watched the long-absent ship part the spring mist, her breath held for so long that it burned within her chest until her nostrils flared and her vision began to blur. Others gathered with her, their breaths also baited, let them out together in a single gush of sound when the wooden hull thumped against the dock, and the men aboard her hurried to tie her to the stanchions as she pulled against her dropped anchor.

She waited. She watched.

The boy's teeth chattered in the cold, but his pale green eyes were alight with expectation and a degree of belief she was afraid to cling to.

It had been so long.

What if they had failed?

Finally, she spotted her brother's red hair when he climbed onto the dock and directed the actions of men behind him. The next familiar men guided the gentle lowering of a pallet into her brother's care.

The boy released her hand and ran across the sand, onto the dock, his light steps echoing against the backdrop of the morning tide.

"Gaed!"

He did not respond to her plea to come back to her.

She continued to wait. Her feet, her legs, fearfully refused to move. It was too late. Every fiber of her being feared it was so.

The men stopped before her, the pallet between them, upon which the beloved snow-skinned man lay as if in deep repose. Gaed reached for the stranger's hand and clutched it tightly, his young face tight with disquiet.

Blinking back tears, thinking him dead, Raebhá bent over the husband she had not seen in more than a decade, cupped his face in her hands, and pressed her lips against his. In the chill of the morning, his skin was cold. He did not stir.

Tears she had fought during the long months of her brother's absence, waiting for the ship's return, spilled free, unable to be contained any longer.

"Welcome home, aislé," she whispered against his cheek so that only he and their son would hear her if they were capable.

To her brother, to Audh, to the healer Dáhmán with them, without meeting their gazes as she straightened and squeezed Gaed's hand, she murmured, "Let us take him inside."

❧Epilogue❧

íth phail kait
zagn íth aecállae phain aetásmá
llagn íth aedhyagnaghk
sun íth zaene tuó dhe bhán dhíthé
et aelás bhesylag aebhánys
ubé aedhózair uaem thurgag endástás
íth llóstén ebh im
íth duis ebh góst
íth bhezugdhu kaiim cónys kunás aedhíthé
yó íth hórges phain aetásmá cron
aelás chune et aelás háyl
ainau íth hyl phain dhe aetaeá
sun zened ith aiónag
aión ydhenár keh móz ghrysá hyd
ubé et dryn phain edhená serbháló ullísár
kunás phry aelás curá
truár et raedár
kunás tó thórgae thur
ubé íth káyná ebh phunár
yó íth taithé phain medhárós thórgae állís ebh
et íth uaem phain aehíthé et aellórd
zagnes ebh kóh íth aisyag hyln
ebh ghlaebh hásurag
it Curnydhá's rylagthé pháses
kunás saeitá sóures kóh ithnás
et kunás hes cónyses phrae

It was the same song every year.

The last song father had shared with son before the link between them fell silent.

Looking up from the journal open before him on the unadorned wooden pedestal, its spine well-creased from extended use, Ártur ran a hand through his pale red hair as he caressed the final page with the other and gazed out the window into the starlit sky.

At least the stars never changed.

He hated reading the words he had set down years before. There were too many memories contained there, and always new details he learned or remembered upon rereading that prompted him to revise the book again so that nothing would be forgotten in the decades, the centuries, to come.

He hated it…but he read it, and rewrote it, each year, ending the saga on this same night. It was torture. Some had tried, at first, to stop him from subjecting himself to this pain. Now they no longer did. He was the Keeper of the Saga after all, his own accounts and those Kavan had spent so many hours recording himself. The oldest to know of the events written here, gleaned from those around him, both living and dead. It was his right, perhaps even his duty, to keep this ritual alive, to improve upon it, for as long as he could, for as long as it took…just as it was the duty of others to keep that song alive.

He marked every passing day, counting them religiously, and would continue counting until the course of his life forced him to stop.

Soft footsteps on stone passed in the corridor outside of his room. Brothers and sisters, family and friends, the gdhededhá from St. Kóráhm's who now called Gorbesh home. Ártur tilted his head to listen, to identify the individuals with a flash of expectation.

They were not him.

They would never be him.

He wondered why he was still here, why he continued to live in a place amongst people who reminded him too much of what he had lost. He wondered why he had not returned to Bhryell, to Rhidam, or to the halls of St. Kóráhm's in Alberni where he went once a year to deliver Zerio Kaas to and from the halls of education he curated and pay his respects to the dead buried in her gardens. Was it memory? Was it fear? Was it family? Or was it the admitted realization that those places carried their own memories, and the knowledge that, wherever he went, those memories would be carried with him, regardless of how he tried to outrun them.

He did not think he would ever know.

In truth, he did not want to forget.

There was only the certainty that, for now, Gorbesh was where he belonged. Maybe someday he would move on, take his family, and put the past behind him.

For now, the thought of leaving so many beloved souls hurt too much.

It had been too long. There was little hope left any longer, little hope in the eyes of others who shared this place with him.

sínréc was gone.

He could not get back any part of that man, the white-skinned infant he had welcomed into the world. The boy who had grown to adulthood despite Ártur's failings. The cornerstone who had saved his life, saved countless lives, all while asking so little in return. The bard who had grown into a legend larger than life throughout the whole of the Sovereignties and beyond, while attempting to live the simple life of any other man.

There were only the memories,

How could Ártur endure when the underpinning of his life was gone?

All he had left were the words he lovingly, painstakingly gathered from the private journals, from books of prayer and song, from the mouths of those who had known Kavan best. Collections of musings and life events the healer would continue to compile as they came to him, that the dedhá meticulously copied so that those who cared to know the truth could find it.

But few seeking that truth traveled this far south. Few asked, preferring myth and legend and religious fervor to reality. To Ártur, it was as if the White Bard of Bhryell had never lived beyond the confines of the stories that had sprung up around him.

Here, in Gorbesh, there were only these words, the combined memories of those who had shared Kavan's life, and the silent black kestrel harp encased in glass in the main chapel.

There was nothing else.

Kavan was not coming back to him this time.

"Are you joining us, k'aendáthé?"

The healer turned. The eyes of the young man in the doorway, one sand gold, the other emerald green, flickered with expectation. Though his skin was not snow-white as Kavan's, nor his copper hair the same silver-white, Ágdhállán looked so much like Kavan that Ártur could not suppress the shiver up and down his spine. There was no new music, no wise words uttered from the White Bard's lips, but this young man remained.

The dark-haired záryph of a man behind him looked sad but resolute.

Ártur sighed. What was the point? Kavan would not be there.

He opened his mouth to speak but was unable to release the words that stuck in his throat. Ágdhállán moved to allow Myreth to enter the room, his bare feet not making a sound on the stones as he crossed, knelt beside the chair, ant put a hand on Ártur's arm. His dark eyes met the healer's briefly, then quickly lowered as he blinked away tears and shook his head.

It was the same every year. The same question. The same emotion. And every year, the same tears.

Ártur was sure Myreth's sorrow mirrored his own.

"Perhaps not," Myreth said to Ártur's silent response, "but we do not do this for him. We do it for ourselves. We need this more than he does. We need to remember. To hope. To wait. It is all we have." His voice cracked.

Ágdhállán entered and wound his hand in Myreth's dark, chocolate hair in a comforting manner, a gesture more intimate than any his father might have displayed. He pressed his other hand to Ártur's cheek and bent to kiss the healer's forehead tenderly.

"Have faith, k'aendáthé. It will come to pass. We will see him again."

His hands dropped, he smiled warmly at each of them, and then withdrew from the room, moving on silent bare feet with a grace that reminded them both of the man of whom Ágdhállán spoke. Both held their breath until he was out of the room. Both released it as soon as he was gone.

It was easy to think the loss of his father had driven him mad.

"He continues to believe," began Myreth, his voice trailing off to meld with the songs of night birds and insects that wafted in through the open window.

"I know." Ágdhállán, like his father, had the Sight. He had Seen many things since their arrival in Gorbesh, events that had come to pass, disasters that had been avoided because of his warnings. He was much sought after by the people of the village and surrounding lands, nearly as much as his sister was. Perhaps he had Seen Kavan's return.

How could any of them doubt the Sight's veracity?

Maybe the son simply refused to give up on reuniting with the father he had lost too soon.

"You must join us, ílMairós. You must come. We need you. You are part of the circle…and I think you need us too. Restore your optimism, your faith. Begin the cycle again with renewed hope. If not for your own peace, do it for his children."

With those words echoing in his ears, Ártur did not speak as Myreth departed. When he was alone again, he turned his focus to the half-moon that shimmered in the sky beyond his window, his fingers again caressing the final page of the book. Eventually, convinced by the echoes of memory that flitted through his head like feathers on a breeze, he stood up and left the desk, leaving the manuscript open to the last page he had read.

Myreth was right. Ártur needed this. Particularly tonight. Do it for Kavan's children. Myreth's seductive-voiced words caught like barbs in his heart and spread their roots there, sifting into the shadowed places of the healer's soul. For the children, indeed. If Ágdhállán, if Dhóri, if Sóbhán, if Earé wanted him there, Ártur would go. He would do anything those children asked.

The ritual would be repeated. Ártur's faith would be restored, and the cycle would commence for another year.

After all, Ágdhállán had the Sight. He believed in his father's return. Ártur wanted desperately to believe that the younger man was not as mad as some secretly thought.

Ágdhállán believed it. Ártur wanted to believe it too.

The final page of Volume Eight of the Life of Kavan Kóráhm Cliáth fluttered in the breeze that followed Ártur out of the room.

In the year following the loss of the White Bard, the cycle began. Each year, on the night of his taking, when war ended and the terror that plagued the world was defeated, those who love him gather at the spot where his ivory feet last touched the soil of the known lands, where his flesh was burned and his blood was spilled so that all would know peace. They gather from wherever their lives have taken them, bound by memory and the need never to forget.

They do not mourn. Grief does not touch them there.

For the oldest among them, the healer who did not witness the taking, the ones who had become his brothers, and the children left behind, believe this is not the end. They believe in the chance. Through their faith, others continue to believe as well. Word Spreads. Hope blossoms. They continue to believe because the youngest among them has spoken it and his word is Prophecy.

When they gather, it is said that the Holy Saint gathers with them, giving credence to their hope, giving breath to the Prophecy.

Time passes. They gather still, away from the eyes of the world. In that place they pray and sing, then come together to eat and drink and remember with communion in the sacred halls blessed

with his blood. They read his words, sing his hymns, and share the Last Song so it will not be forgotten.
They Remember.
They await the return of the White Bard of Gálínphel. The White Bard of Bhryell. The Duke of Alberni. The Beloved of the Saint. They remember Kavan Cliáth.

The End

Character Index Book 8

Aendrás--a bhydáni in Bhryell

Ágdhállán Kóráhm Cliáth--son of Kavan and Raebhá, born in Curnydhá

Aland Mauret--Teren physician who trained under Rouvyn for six years before assuming the post of Court Physician at Rouvyn's death.

Aleski MacLyr--son of Sámel MacLyr, nephew of Ártur, cousin of-Kavan; he is a harp maker in Bhryell.

Alyná Dubuais Cáner Dilyn--daughter of Bhríd Cáner and Madalyn Dubuais-Cáner. Youngest twin. Marries Prime Magistrate Piran Dilyn

Annet--daughter of Bianca and Wilred Dugan

Arlan Trebor Lachlan--The youngest son of King Innis of Enesfel. He was the 25th king of Enesfel, responsible for peaceful relations with Hatu, increasing Enesfel's size via the war with Neth, and opening a dialogue with the islands of Káliel.

Ártur MacLyr--Elyri healer, employed by each Lachlan monarch since King Innis. Married to Syl Cáner, father of Llucás, Chethá, and Kaedís, and is cousin to Kavan Cliáth.

Asta Deidre Dugan de Corrmick--The daughter of Princess Deidre Lachlan and Lord High Inquisitor Caol Dugan, she is married to King Kjell of Neth. Mother of Yóáná, Oska, Rika, and Jerit, grandmother of Prince Henrik

Audh di Cliáth, márbhyndhánis--cousin of Ombhrís and best friend of Iólán di Curnydhá; a márbhyndhánis who serves Raebhá and a very distant relative of Kavan's.

Augustus Bodil--teenage nephew of Leon, the only surviving Bodils, he is learning to be a vintner from his uncle and serves the Dubuais-Cáner estate.

Aunes--wet nurse taken on to care for Ágdhállán

Balint Gabersdon, Sir--Once the youngest knight in Enesfel, he is the Duke of Nelori and father of Bhetá.

Balint Magk--son of Bhetá Gabersdon and Raenár Magk, named after his grandfather, heir to the duchy of Nelori.

Bergis--an orphan in Rhidam who was sent to St. Kóráhm's in Alberni after a fire in the orphan house; he befriended Dhóri and assists in the care of Ágdhállán as well as with other tasks in St. Kóráhm's.

Bertram Earl Lachlan--The eldest son of Arlan Lachlan and twin of Diona Lachlan, he was killed at the age of nine by a Coryllien dagger in a skirmish between Caol Dugan and Halstatt Tarmajien.

Bhárás Mulóy--an Elyri healer recruited to aid Enesfel in battle, betrothed to Syróá Dunne.

Bhás--a descendent of Dhábhiyhá Coryllien.

Bhendhámyn (Bhen) MacLyr--The youngest son of Sámel MacLyr, nephew of Ártur MacLyr. He is a harp maker in the Cliáth tradition.

Bhetá Gabersdon-Magk, Daema--daughter of Duke Balint Gabersdon and the Elyri woman; she has become the only Daema currently serving in Enesfel. Serves as Captain of the Guard in Rhidam. Married to Raenár Magk and shares one son, Balint, with him.

Bhídígís Bhól, dedhá—served the Faith in Clarys since the age of eleven; was introduced to Tusánt by Kluín during one of Tusánt's visits to Clarys and came to serve in Hes á Redh after the plagues ended.

Bhílári, gdhededhá-- gdhededhá in Hes Índári Náós, Bhryell.

Bhílycá, málneag--A female Elyri healer who was canonized for her extreme piety and her generous care of the sick. She is particularly known for her work with those suffering from the Great Plague, which she contracted. It ultimately caused her death though she continued to care for the sick and dying up until she could no longer able to. She became the patron of healers (particularly Elyri healers) and the terminally ill. After several childless women reported having conceived children after visiting her shrine, Bhílycá has also become the patron of women wanting children.

Bhríd Cáner, Lord--A distant cousin of the MacLyrs, Duke of Levonne. He is known as the best swordsman in the Five Sovereignties, and was the Queen's Champion.

Bhyrhán Bhíncári--One of many grandsons of Kyne Mórne Bhíncári, the previous High Mother. He chose the life of a minstrel, and plays the shawm, served Queen Diona until her death, and then returned to Clarys as an emissary to the Kyne. He is distantly related to Kavan Cliáth, whose mother's maiden name was Bhíncári.

Bianca MacLyr Dugan--An orphaned Teren, adopted by Ártur and Syl MacLyr, she was married to Wilred Dugan and lives with her family in Durham.

Brulyn Geli--son of Fen Geli and Marta, part of the Association

Caol Dugan--Originally the son of a member of the Association, and part of the Lachlan court and family, since he married Princess Deidre Lachlan, King Arlan's sister. He performed the duties of Lord High Inquisitor until his death during the 2nd Elyri Persecution.

Cáym Cáner--son of Bhríd and Editt, twin of Phaedr.

Charlos Rion--novice, orphaned during the plagues. He had some military training as a boy before entering the Faith. His cheery disposition earns him the position of dedhá within the Lachlan castle.

Chethá MacLyr Cliáth--The daughter of Ártur and Syl MacLyr. Healer serving in Bhryell; married to Sóbhán Cliáth. Mother of Maelís and Ydrís.

Claes-Arne Vissaer--Grand Master of the Vants, lives in Glevum.

Dáhmán--a healer from Curnydhá.

Dawid Coryllien--A figure once thought of as mythical, whose name is connected to the death of many Elyri and many Teren during the historical period known as the Persecution. His name was given to the daggers connected with those murders. Very little is known about him in the Five Sovereignties.

Dervis, Lord—fleet management for King Gamal of Hatu

Dewel Dary--the oldest of Emeria and Laney's adopted children.

Dhábhiyhá Coryllien--The true birth name of the man who came to be known as Dawid Coryllien to the people in the Five Sovereignties.

Dhágdhuán--The founder of the Elyri Faith, believed to have been Elyri by birth and semi-divine during his life. The Faith has no documents recording his origins or place of birth. Elyri stories only concern his teachings and his death upon a pyre, presumably at the hand of the Teren. According to dhóbhaen teachings, he was a fisherman from the land of the taeré to the island, and there taught his doctrines to the dhóbhaen who soon killed him for inciting heresy and treason. This suggests that he could be Teren, or possibly phae, but there is no proof to support any of the theories of his origins.

Dháná MacLyr--mother of Ártur. Raised Kavan as a little boy.

Dhon Sáróes--novice, entered the Faith as a little boy. Came to Hes á Redh in the years when Paul served as a liaison between the Rhidam and Elyri Faith establishments. Came from a family of healers.

Dhóri Kóráhm Cliáth--Kavan's son with Orynn, twin of Earé

Diona Cordelia Lachlan--The only daughter of King Arlan Lachlan; Queen of Enesfel. Grandmother of Lorant.

Dola--a physician from west of the Cíbhóló

Drebhoti —one of those banished from Dhóbhaen who came to settle in the west with Llyr and Zythán.

Earé--Kavan's daughter with Orynn, twin of Dhóri, now carries the title of k'ílshwythnec.

Earon Sparding, Captain--a Nethite captain serving under King Fraen who serves as Captain of the Guard in Glevum

Egon Groff--inherited the position of sheriff of Alberni from his father.

Emeria Dary--Only daughter of Wortham and Zelenka, she marries Laney Dary and remains in the Alberni estate in service to Kavan's household.

Emil Waller, General--a Nethite soldier promoted to General under King Fraen.

Eridel--a harper Kavan met in Hatu after his hands were mangled. Presumed dead but later returned to try to kill him. Escaped incarceration in St. Kóráhm's

Essem Rahal, balo--balo left to serve in Rhidam

Evroult Lul--Cordashian scout and spy

Eytor Balise, balo--balo selected to remain with the southern mercenary force stationed in Levonne.

Faeárgan Drás--Elyri sailor stationed in the outposts along the Gorea Fjord.

Farrell Lachlan, King--father of Níkóá McCábhá

Farzan--one of the mercenaries recruited by Bhás to fight with Neth

Fendel Geli--Inquisitor after Asta Dugan marries King Kjell

Gabrielle Dilyn Lachlan--was the Prime Magistrate of Káliel and mother of Clianthe and Piran. She was also the wife of Owain Lachlan. Retired to Fiara to care for Owain during his long decline in health.

Gaed di Cliáth--a dhóbhaen master-builder of both instruments and ships, shipwrecked with Dhedec di Curnydhá in the lands west of the Hínesur; both were saved by a Dhágdhuán and returned to the land of the dhóbhaen with them. Adopting his teaching and that which welcomed training in the use of power, he was among those banished to the distant west where he served as one of the founders of the Elyri people.

Gaed Cliáth--the youngest son of Kavan and Raebhá, named after his ancestor. Born in Curnydhá, he has never met his father or his siblings.

Gaelán Ágdhrán Cáner--The youngest son of Bhríd Cáner and Madalyn Dubuais who has shown that he possesses the Elyri talent to heal despite being half-Teren. Killed by his brother after fathering Yóáná with Asta Dugan. Married to Asta in a secret ceremony to legitimize their child.

Gamal Lachlan-Harcourt, King--Eldest son of Queen Diona Lachlan and Prince Espen Harcourt of Hatu. Twin to Liahm, the elder by thirteen minutes, he is anointed King of Hatu when Espen's brother fails to produce a male heir.

Jemes Osveld--household chamberlain in the Cáner estate in Levonne. Hired after the plague. Has some military training and knows the business of the vineyard.

Jerit de Corrmick, Prince--Youngest child of Asta Dugan and King Kjell de Corrmick of Neth.

Jermyn Tythilius, k'gdhededhá--A former brother in the Order of málneag Kóráhm in Clarys, Elyriá, he was ordained as the k'gdhededhá of Rhidam and is later murdered in the outbreak of violence. He is buried in St. Kóráhm's in Alberni.

Kaedís MacLyr--youngest child of Ártur and Syl, training to be a healer.

Kaj Yetek, tama--the leader of the army recruited from the southern lands. Has spent his life as a mercenary soldier serving k'ílshwythnec and amassing an army for her. Aids Enesfel in the war against Neth.

Kavan Kóráhm Cliáth--Only child of Rístyrd and Llyárá, cousin of Ártur MacLyr. He is an admired harper, possessor of the Sight, and holder of great psionic capabilities. Known as the White Bard of Bhryell for his tremendous musical talent and unique physical appearance, he was employed by Arlan as his court bard until his flight from Rhidam to the lands south of Hatu. He is also the Duke of Alberni and the founder of Saint Kóráhm's chellé hábhai.

Kes--had been an apothecary apprentice working with Claes-Arne in Glevum. She married Olaric the Younger after he helped her escape Glevum and has three daughters with him.

Khwílen Kesábhá, gdhededhá--Abbot of Saint Kóráhm's chellé hábhai in Alberni due to his gifts of oratory, learning, and painting.

Kjell de Corrmick--The youngest son of Loris of Neth, he is the brother of King Merkar de Corrmick. Nethite king who has been living in exile in Enesfel. Father of Prince Jerit, grandfather of Prince Henrik.

Kluín, gdhededhá--a member of the Order of Saint Kóráhm, has twice been a candidate for the post of k'gdhededhá in Clarys. Instrumental in clearing Kavan of excommunication.

Kólmárá Tyrnás--an Elyri healer recruited to aid Enesfel in battle. Chosen to serve Henrik de Corrmick as court healer in Glevum after Henrik is crowned.

Kóráhm di Curnydhá, Saint--Elyri saint for whom Kavan was named, also known as Kóráhm the Rón by many in Elyriá because of some controversial writings he made before the time of his martyrdom. Few of his books are available and he is not commonly discussed.

Laney Dary--husband of Emeria, son of Martin Dary, takes his father's place as master of the Alberni estate for the duke.

Leon Bodil--Bhríd's primary vintner in Levonne since the loss of his family in the plague. Came to Levonne from Nelori.

Lláhy--once a gdhededhá in Clarys, he was excommunicated and banished for murdering his father, k'gdhededhá Dórímyr.

Llyr di Bhíncári--brother of Zythán, a healer from a family whose craft was cups, platters, eating utensils, and ceremonial tools. As a healer, he was trained in the use of power, and with Drebhoti, trained others in secret to use the power as well. Was included among those to be banished to the west.

Lorant Lachlan, King--eldest child of Prince Merrek and Princess Arlana, the heir to the Lachlan throne.

Llucás MacLyr--son of Ártur and Syl, lives in Bhryell and works as part of the Cliáthan harp-making tradition.

Madoc Delamo, Lord High Justice--Eldest child of Wortham Delamo and Zelenka. He served as Sheriff in Alberni for a few years, and after an act of valor on the Crown's behalf was elevated to Lord High Justice in the Queen's court in Rhidam. Married to Yóáná, father of Peigen and Nya.

Mádhu, gdhededhá--serves with Bhílári in Bhryell

Maelís Cliáth--eldest daughter of Sóbhán and Chethá.

Maicel, málneag--One of the Elyri saints, sometimes seen as the patron of merchants and tradesmen.

Márllís--a resident of Bhórdh who serves as Kavan's guide up the mountain

Marta--An Association member used as a contact by Asta Dugan, mother of Fen Geli's children. Left Rhidam and went to Glevum after Fen's murder, leaving the Association in Rhidam without leadership.

Mátán, málneag--An Elyri saint, popular for advocating wise and judicious use of Elyri abilities. He was a scholar and a teacher who was in Enesfel when the first Lachlan became King. Though he denied involvement, and Teren chronicles do not mention his name, many believe that Mátán was at least partially responsible for the Lachlans gaining the throne. He is the patron of scholars, students, and those seeking political change.

Mathias, Lieutenant--Cordashian soldier leading troops sent to help Lorant & Jerit.

Maxan Tablyn, General--Cordash's top cavalry general

Merrek Lachlan, King--Only child of Prince Muir Lachlan and Clianthe Dilyn, he was raised by Kavan when his mother proved unfit and later took her own life after Muir's death. A Lachlan by name though not by blood, Queen Diona names him heir to the Lachlan throne after Prince Liahm's death. Died in Fiara fighting Neth.

Morne--previous Kyne in Clarys.

Muir Innis Lachlan--The bastard son of Owain Lachlan and Brenna Weylin Lachlan, he was raised as Arlan Lachlan's son. Upon reaching adulthood he gave his land and title as Duke of Alberni to Kavan Cliáth and relocated to Fiara with his father. Died in combat on the island of Pháne. Father King Merrek, grandfather of Lorant.

Myreth--A singer of extraordinary talent, of unknown mixed heritage, raised in the cloister of Gorbesh and held hostage by Bhás for decades.

Nedlin Rodair--Cordash's second general, whose men excel at stealth and guerilla tactics. Has family in Ruidoso and has been tasked for the last ten years with smuggling goods into that city since its fall to Fraen's troops at the end of Queen-Regent Inness' reign.

Níkóá McCábhá--half-Elyri illegitimate son of King Farrell Lachlan, Queen Diona appointed him Chamberlain as part of a ruse to stop the anti-Elyri violence, and retains him in that post afterward. Appointed regent to Prince Lorant until he comes of age.

Nóráh MacLyr--wife of Bhen. seamstress

Nya Delamo--daughter of Yóáná and Madoc.

Olaric Fraen the Elder, King--was a Nethite Captain during Inness Lachlan's time as Queen-Regent in Glevum, named after his father who sided with King Merkar after the death of General Glucke and was thrown into the bear pit for treason. After Inness' disappearance, he appointed himself as king of Neth.

Olaric Fraen the Younger--Nethite soldier, only living child of Fraen the Elder, the third Fraen to bear that name. Moved north to Pravek after his father claimed the throne and lived there with his new family for many years. Has been appointed Grand Master of the Vants and is working to revive the order. Called Lari by his wife.

Óllbhaer Dínyn--an experienced Elyri merchant ship captain whose crew is adept at infiltrating pirate ships.

Onea Pantel--The former head of the Fiara branch of the Association, now head of the Association in Glevum. She maintained contact with Asta since the death of Asta's father. Had ties to Claes-Arne Vissaer of the

Vants. Burned at the stake, along with Fen Geli, by Queen-Regent Inness.

Ónyká Cáner--youngest child and only daughter of Bhríd Cáner and Editt. Sister of Phaedr and Cáym.

Orynn--A member of all three known races (k'kairá, Elyri, and Teren) she was chosen by Kóráhm and her own people to contact Kavan and assist in his quest for healing, redemption, and the items needed to cleanse the thur thol below the Rhidam keep. She is known among the people in the barbarian territories as k'ílshwythnec, "she who sees," because of her tremendous knowledge of the past, present, and future. Through the use of power, she is the mother of Dhóri and Earé.

Oska de Corrmick, Prince--Eldest child of King Kjell de Corrmick and Asta Dugan de-Corrmick. Served briefly as Neth's king.

Owain Ustes Lachlan--He was believed to be the 5th child of Innis, son of Ula de Corrmick of Neth; he was the 24th king of Enesfel. He was the only child of Guthrie McHador. He relinquished the throne to Arlan Lachlan and lived in the Neth city of Fiara since then. He assumed the title of Duke of Fiara when the area of Neth south of Lake Curo seceded and became part of Enesfel. He was the father of Muir Innis and, later, after marriage to Gabrielle Dilyn of Káliel, fathered Piran Guthrie Lachlan.

Paul, gdhededhá--Teren gdhededhá from Rhidam who serves as an emissary in Clarys between them and the Faith outside of Elyriá

Peigen Delamo--son of Yóáná and Madoc.

Peter Dahl--former page of Queen Diona and eventually elevated to the position of Chancellor.

Pháraeís Dunne--Elyri healer who agrees to aid Enesfel in battle. Father of Syróá and Tisá.

Phaedr Cáner--son of Bhríd and Editt, twin of Cáym, named after his deceased uncle. He is the heir to the Dubuais-Cáner vineyards & the duchy of Levonne.

Phílóá Bhíncári-- niece of Bhyrhán Bhíncári, one of the High Mother's granddaughters chosen to replace her as Kyne upon her death.

Piran Guthrie Lachlan--The son of Owain Lachlan and Gabrielle Dilyn-Lachlan; he assumed the position of Prime Magistrate upon his mother's retirement.

Poul, Saint--Teren saint; patron of patience

Pras Najar, Master--the secondary royal tutor serving the Lachlan House. Originally came to St. Kóráhm's from Hatu. Recruited to teach numbers, sciences, and world knowledge, as well as Hatuish

Qol--A member of the race known as the phae k'kairá who served as k'gdhededhá in the cloister of Gorbesh.

Raebhá di Curnydhá--kymyhé of the ghísaer of Curnydhá, married to Kavan, she is the mother of Ágdhállán and Gaed.

Raenár Magk, Captain--had been the captain of the ecclesiastical guard in Clarys, now lives in Saint Kóráhm's and serves as captain of the guard. Married to Daema Bhetá Gabersdon and shares one son, Balint, with her.

Rankin, gdhededhá--Highest-ranking Teren gdhededhá in Hes á Redh, Rhidam.

Rhyrdan Delamo--the youngest son of Wortham Delamo and Zelenka; he serves Kavan in whatever capacity is needed.

Rika Valdis, Queen--Second child of King Kjell de Corrmick and Asta Dugan de Corrmick and only daughter; despite poor vision and hearing, she marries King Govert of Cordash.

Roald, Captain--a Nethite Captain serving beneath General Waller.

Rouvyn Talis--A Teren physician and native of Rhidam, he has been serving as the Lachlans' Teren court healer.

Ruy Gaddo, balo--balo selected to serve King Gamal. Has no captaining experience but has worked as a sailor most of his life before his recruitment into Earé's military force.

Sámel MacLyr--brother of Ártur, head of Cliáthan harp making after the death of Tám. Father of Bhendhámyn and Aleski.

Seren McCábhá-Lachlan--only living child of Níkóá McCábhá, marries Lorant to become Queen of Enesfel.

Seymo Cahryd, balo--one of tama Yetek's balo; originally a pirate, he is elected to lead the Hatu fleet of ships stationed at Káliel.

Síraelís--a healer residing in St. K6ráhm's.

Sóbhán Cliáth--Kavan's adopted son, he has taken the Cliáth name and become a harp maker in Bhryell, assumes training in the Faith choir, and marries Chethá MacLyr.

Sunna Satva--a man of unknown background from beyond the Cíbhóló desert.

Syl Cáner MacLyr--The wife of Ártur MacLyr, she is also a healer and sister of Bhríd Cáner. She is the mother of Llucás, Chethá, and Kaedís. Serves in Rhidam as court healer.

Ydrís Cliáth--youngest daughter of Sóbhán and Chethá.

Ylár, gdhededhá--k'gdhededhá of Clarys

Ylltán Phrás--an Elyri healer recruited to aid Enesfel in battle. Trained with weapons despite being a healer; often criticized for his belief that healing should not preclude taking a life if necessary.

Yóáná Delamo--The daughter of Asta Dugan and Gaelán Cáner, she is a healer. Was raised by Kavan alongside the Delamo children, and later married the eldest, Madoc Delamo. Mother of Peigen and Nya.

Zelenka--A young woman from Gorbesh marries Wortham. They have three children, Madoc, Emeria, and Rhyrdan. She died during the plague and is buried next to Wortham in St. Kóráhm's cemetery.

Zerio Kaas--spy hired into the de Corrmick household, member of the Order of the Vants who comes to Rhidam as secondary inquisitor.

Zythán--said by some to be a heretic or a saint, he came west with Llyr and Drebhoti but left them to travel north.

Elyri Phonetics

á--ä (as in m**o**p)
a--ă (as in c**a**t)
ae--ā (as in **a**ce)
ag--ä (as in m**o**p) (HE**)
ai--ī (as in **i**ce)
au--aù (as in **ou**t)
é--ŭ (as in b**u**t)
e--ĕ (as in b**e**t

i--ē (as in b**e**)
í--ĭ (as in s**i**t)
ó--ō (as in g**o**)
o--ŏ (as in m**o**p)
u--ū (as in bl**ue**)
y--ē (as in b**e**)
yh--y (as in **y**es)

b--b
bh--v
c--k
ch--ch
d--d
dh--j
gae--gwā
gdh--zh (as in vi**si**on)
gh--g (as in go)
gk--k̲ as in loch (HE)
h--h
hw--w (breathy, as in whale)
k'--k
k--k

l--l
Ll--l
m--m
mh--m (slightly breathy)
n--n
ne--nyä
p--p
ph--f
r--r
s--sh
t--t
th--th (as in thistle)
z--z

· **C** is always pronounced **K** but the letter **K** is most often used to designate this sound. **C** mainly appears at the beginning of some proper surnames and place names and occasionally in the center or at the end of a word. This is believed to be a carryover from the earliest days of the Elyri language, or to have been influenced by the Teren languages, but Elyri linguists and scholars have not yet determined its significance. However, in keeping with this unspoken, unexplained rule, no Elyri have first names, or middle names, starting with **C**.

•   The combination **gk** (pronounced as in the German ich) occurs only at the end of words, unless there is a verb suffix or plural suffix behind it, and only in those words of High Elyri and Old Elyri origin.

•   The letter combination **ag** occurs at the end of words of High Elyri/Old Elyri origin. If the combination appears elsewhere in a word, it will either be as a product of two words having been combined or will be the result of a suffix having been added. Though some Standard Elyri words have retained their **ag** ending, most words carried into the standard will have the **ag** combination replaced with **á** when written, though they sound alike when spoken.

•   The **H** sound only appears in High Elyri/Old Elyri words and in some names carried over from ancient sources; Standard Elyri derivatives will normally drop the **h** from the original word but there are exceptions to the rule.

•   Double **L**'s are found at the beginning of words, single **l**'s in the body or at the end. When words do have the double **L** in a location other than the beginning, it is always the result of two words being combined into one.

•   In the High Elyri/Old Elyri there were no naturally occurring **B, P,** or **AU** (as in cow) sounds. These did not get introduced until Elyri acquired their current religious faith. Even then, the sounds were not commonly used until the standard Teren tongue influenced everyday life. These sounds mainly appear in proper names or religious settings.

•   The combination of the letters **ne** occurs almost exclusively at the end of a word, and is always pronounced **nya**, regardless of where it occurs.

•   In Standard and High Elyri the **ee** sound at the beginning or end of a word is always represented with an **I**. In the center of words, it is represented with a **Y**. When the **ee** sound is represented in the center of a word by the letter **I,** it is a result of two words being combined into one. In some cases, as with the name Cliáth, the original words may no longer be known.

•   In Old Elyri, the prefix **YII** that changes a verb to one of its two noun forms is also pronounced **ee**. The few exceptions where Standard or High Elyri words begin with a Y for the ee sound are believed to have originated as intentional misspellings.

•   There is no **S** sound in the Elyri language. S's are always pronounced **sh**.

•   The letter **Z** appears only in the High Elyri/Old Elyri, in words derived from the High Elyri/Old Elyri, or originated as misspellings in one of the Teren languages and were absorbed back into Elyri in the aberrant form.

Elyri Grammar

In most Elyri words, the stress falls on the second to last. Words where the stress falls on the final syllable (or on the first syllable in words with more than two syllables) are either names, the result of an Elyri translation of a Teren word, caused by the addition of a prefix or suffix, or the result of a word being truncated, having dropped the last syllable over time.

The **k'** at the beginning of a word signifies importance or singularity. It is applied to a word that can have a common meaning and a special meaning: k'tyne would be a favorite niece or female cousin, whereas tyne is simply a niece or female cousin. In the case of the phae k'kairá, when the Terens translated the term into "the Others" it is the **k'** that indicates the O to be capitalized; not just any others but the Others. In Old Elyri, the **k** is attached directly to the word without the '.

The Elyri written language does not have additional characters for capitalization. The first letters words may carry a dot beneath them to signify that the word is a proper name, a place, or a title, but first letters of sentences are not capitalized.

Sentence breaks are characterized by either a new line of text or by a symbol that looks similar to an s. This has resulted in many mistranslations from Elyri into other languages.

Nouns

Noun forms of verbs do not have gender. When these nouns are made plural they take the plural inclusive suffix sur.

The prefix **íl** added to a verb makes it into a noun; the word then means "one who" as in "íldaeni"-one who instructs, i.e.: teacher.

Some nouns are formed by adding the prefix **ai** to a verb; the verb dhesá means touch, aidhesá also means touch but is a noun. Not all verbs can accept the **ai** prefix.

-thé: the standard plural suffix

-té: the standard plural suffix in Old Elyri. Some words, however, such as márbhyndhánis, are both singular and plural without the suffix, depending on the context of the sentence

Nouns ending in **I** are both singular and plural and do not take the -**thé** ending.

Elyri monetary denominations are both singular and plural.

There are other exceptions to the singular/plural rule, most being words carried over from the High Elyri. High Elyri/Old Elyri contains very few words that are NOT both plural and singular. Any exceptions to the rule are noted.

Some words have gender. A word ending in **ne** is feminine and a word ending in **dhá** is masculine. Both are made plural in the same way (with the **thé** ending). Some gender-neutral words that have been altered from their original form may have either ending.

Some words in Standard, those referring to a group that includes both male and female individuals, require the -**sur** ending, creating the plural inclusive form of the word. The same ending exists in High Elyri.

Adjectives

There are few adjectives in the Elyri language. Instead of saying someone is beautiful, or wise, an Elyri would say they possess beauty or they possess wisdom.

To modify such qualities, an Elyri speaker would say:

Bhykólé aelá shwyth --She possesses wisdom.--Teren: She is wise.

Ochbhykóle aelá shwyth --She possesses more wisdom.--Teren: She is wiser.

Utbhykólé aelá shwyth --She possesses the most wisdom.--Teren: She is wisest.

Naimbhykólé aelá shwyth --She possesses no wisdom.--Teren: She is not wise; or She is a fool.

The few adjectives that do exist come through the High Elyri and are believed by most linguists to have their origins in some language other than the Elyri.

Verbs

When **ibh** modifies a verb (i.e.: is singing, is looking) it is attached as a suffix to the verb. In all other instances, it is a separate word (bhydáni ibh gaeth.--He is bhydáni.)

When **im** modifies a verb (i.e.: was singing, was looking) it is attached as a suffix to the verb. In all other instances, it is a separate word (ílDaeni im gaeth.--He was a teacher)

There is no "be" in the Elyri language. Whereas a Teren would say, "He will be singing" the Elyri would say "He will sing." Instead of "I will be there" it would be "I will come" or I will go"; instead of "I will be here" it would be "I will stay", "I will attend," or "I am here."

Rather than using verbs such as "strengthened" or "beautified", in Elyri they would say "given strength" or "given beauty"

Verb Tenses (Standard Elyri)

(present) do, does	(past) (ár) did, have done	(present) (ibh) am, are, is doing	(past) (im) was, is, were doing	(future) (ád) will do, to do, be done
aelá	aelár	aelibh	aelim	aelád
ándás	ándásár	ándásibh	ándásim	ándásád
árá	árár	áráibh	áráim	árád
bhaeá	bhaeár	bhaeibh	bhaeim	bhaeád
bheken	bhekár	bhekibh	bhenim	bhekád
bhair	bhairár	bhairibh	bhairim	bhairád
bhólon	bhólár	bhólibh	bhólim	bhólád
chóne	chóneár	chóníbh	chónim	chónád
daeni	daenár	daenibh	daenim	daenád
dhesá	dhesár	dhesibh	dhesim	dhesád
dhys	dhysár	dhysibh	dhysim	dhysád
donai	donár	donaiibh	donim	donád
ghlaiph	ghlaiphár	ghlaiphibh	ghlaiphim	ghlaiphád
ghytae	ghytár	ghytibh	ghytim	ghytád
kelém	kelémár	kelémibh	kelémim	kelémád
mairós	mairár	mairibh	mairim	mairád
naeth	naethár	naethibh	naethim	naethád
yháth	yháthár	yháthibh	yháthim	yháthád
zene	zenár	zenibh	zenim	zenád
zólágk	zólágkár	zólágkibh	zólágkim	zólágkád

Verb/Noun Tenses

	noun form 1(íl)	**noun 2(ai)**
aelá	ílAelá (one who owns)	
ándás	ílAndás (one who honors)	aiándás
bhaeá	ílBhaeá (one who asks)	
bheken	ílBheken	
bhair	ílBhair (one who accepts)	aibhair (acceptance)
bhólon	ílBhólon (one who purifies)	
chóne	ílChóne (one who brings)	
daeni	ílDaeni (one who instructs)	
dhesá	ílDhesá (one who touches)	aidhesá
donai	ílDonai (one who endures)	aidonai
ghlaiph	ílGhlaiph (one who sleeps)	aiglaiph
ghytae	ílGhytae (one who threatens)	aighytae (threat)
kelém	ílKelém (one who passes)	
mairós	ílMairós (one who heals)	aimairós
naeth	ílNaeth (one who finds)	
zene	ílZene (one who gives)	
zólágk	ílZólágk (one who reveals)	

Verb Tenses (High Elyri)

(present)	**(past)(-ár)**	**(future)(-es)**
phaerás	phaerásár	phaeres
hábhai	hábhaiár	hábhaies
hwaerás	hwaerár	hwaeres
ásai	ásár	ásáres
dhózair	dhózaiár	dhózaires
híthé	híthár	híthes
kalom	kalomár	kalomes
kédhé	kédhár	kédhes
konys	konysár	konyses
elzen	elzenár	elzenes
llósté	llóstár	llóstes
málár	málár	máles
phaerás	phaerár	phaeres
rásé	rásár	ráses
tásmá	tásmár	tásmáes
thórgae	thórgár	thórges
trodh	trodhár	trodhes
zylag	zylagár	zylages

Verb/Noun Tenses (High Elyri)

(noun 1) (bhe-)	**(noun 2) (ae-)**
bhephaerás (one who kneels)	
bhehábhai (one who seeks)	aehábhai (monk/student)
bhehwaerás (one who bears)	
bheásai (one who might/can)	
bhedhózair (one who is eternal)	aedhózair (eternity)
bhehíthé (one who grieves)	
bhekalom (one who goes)	
bhckédhé (one who leads, instructs	aekédhé (teacher)
bhekonys (one who unites)	aekonys (ambassador)
bhelzen (one who gives)	aeelzen (gift)
bhellósté (one who lights)	aellósté (lamplighter)
bhemálár (one who blesses)	
bhepharás (one who bows)	
bherásé (one who shares)	
bhetásmá (one who remembers)	
bhethórgae (one who burns)	
bhetrodh (one who eases)	aetrodh (assistant/servant)
bhezylag (one who hopes)	

Verb Tenses (Old Elyri)

(present)	**(past)(-aer)**	**(future)(- íst)**
turphálós	turphálósaer	turphálósíst
ky	kyaer	kyíst
már	máraer	márist
bhyn	bhynaer	bhyníst

Verb/Noun Tenses (Old Elyri)

(noun 1)(phe-)	**(noun2)(yll-)**
pheturbhálós (one who betrays)	yllturphálós (betrayal)
pheky (one who loves)	yllky (love)
phemár (one who blesses)	yllmár (blessing)
phebhyn (one who teaches)	yllbhyn (teaching)

Foreign Phrase Index

ELYRI WORDS

HE: High Elyri   SE: Standard Elyri   OE: Old Elyri
n--noun   v--verb   adj—adjective
adv--adverb   prn--pronoun   prp--preposition
pl--plural   sng--singular   psv—possessive
pl in--plural inclusive

á (ä) (prp)--HE/SE; and, also, together with, together

Ádhá (Ä-jä) (n)--HE/SE; god; k'Ádhá-supreme deity in the Elyri
    monotheistic religion

aebhánys (ā-vä-NĒSH) (n) (sng and pl)--HE; song, performance, piece of
        music

aecállae (ā-kä-LĀ) (n)--HE; whisper

aedhíthé-(ā-JĬTH-ŭ) (v)--HE; tears

aedhózair (ā-jō-ZĪR) (n) (sng and pl)--HE; eternity

aedhyagn (Ā-jē-än) (v)--HE; death

aedhyagnaghk (Ā-jē-än-ägk) (v)--HE; death veil, the expression of the
    dead

aehíthé (ā-hĭth ŭ) (n)--HE; grief, mourning

aehíthé-(ā-HĬTH-ŭ) (n)--HE; grief, mourning, sadness

aekédhé (ā-kŭj-ŭ) (n) (pl: aekédhéthé)--HE; instructor/teacher

aelás (Ā-läsh) (v)--HE; Have (has), possess, own

aellórd (Ā-lōrd) (n)--HE; regret

aellósté (ā-LŌSH-tŭ) (n)--HE; light

aendhá (ĀN-jä) (n) (pl: aendáthé)--SE; A father's male relatives,
    including his father, grandfathers, uncles, brothers, and cousins.

aesómá (ā-SHŌ-mä) (v)--HE; thief.

aetaeá (ā-TĀ-ä) (v)--HE; laughter

aetásmá (ā-TÄSH-mä) (n)--HE; memory, remembrance

aezylag (ā-ZĒ-lä) (n)--HE; hope, anticipation

ágdh (äzh) (n) (sng and pl)--OE; the soul or spirit, what remains of an
    individual separate from the physical body

ágdhá (Ä-zhä) (n) (sng)--OE; a single member of the ágdháthé, one of the
    gods

ágdháni (ä-ZHÄ-nē) (n) (sng and pl)--HE; the title for any Elyri trained in
    the use of nature's energy. Humans have no word that can be used,
    though they often translate it as sorcerer, wizard, or some other
    similar term. In common science fiction parlance, it can be translated

as psionist. In sources predating the earliest known High Elyri
documents, this word would be translated the same as dhesádhá.

aghk (ägk) (n)--HE; veil, curtain, covering

ainau (Ī-now) (prep)--HE; without

aión (ī-ōn) (n)--HE; fate, destiny

aiónag (ī-Ō-nä) (n) (pl: aiónagthé)--HE; path, destiny, life

aislé (ĪSH-lŭ) (n)--OE; Loved one, beloved, lover. This word carries
   almost sacred connotations and is rarely used outside of some
   intensely passionate, spiritual, emotional relationship. It is believed
   that in a person's life, while one could have several lovers, they can
   have only one aeslag, thus many hesitate to use the term at all and
   may only apply it to someone in their past when they are old and
   nearing death.

aisyag (ī-SHĒ-ä) (adj)--HE; cold, icy, frigid, frozen

állís (Ä-lĭsh) (prp)--HE; through

ásai (ä-SHĪ) (v)--HE; may, might, can

átaelás (ä-TĀ-läsh) (prn psv)--HE; mine, my

áti (Ä-tē) (prn)--HE; I, me, myself

aun (aủn) (prp)--HE; with

bhán (vän) (n)--HE; voice

bhedhuaethag (vĕ-jū-Ā-thä) (n) (sng and pl)--HE; defiler

bhekalomár (bhe-kăl-ŏ-MÄR) (n)--HE; one who has gone

bhekédhé (bhe-KŬJ-ŭ) (n)--HE; one who leads, one who guides

bhelzen (vĕl-ZĔN) (n) (sng and pl)--HE; one who gives; giver; one who is
giving; one who brings

bhemethán (vĕ-mĕ- THÄN) (n) (sng and pl)--HE; murderer, executioner
bhesómá

bhesylag (ā-SHĒ-lä) (adj)--HE; alluring, seductive, tempting; one who
   possesses allure

bheturbhae (vĕ-TŪR-vā)(n) (sng and pl)--HE; traitor

bhezugdhu (vĕ-ZŪ zhū) (n) (pl: bhezugdhuthé)--HE; one who protects

bhir (vēr) (adj)--OE; white

bhydáni (vē-DÄN-ē) (n) (sng and pl)--HE; This is both a title and a social
   standing. It can be translated as teacher, master, sage, or wise one,
   though it actually encompasses all of these meanings. The title is
   given to those who, through their exceptional psionic capabilities,
   wisdom, and intelligence, have demonstrated their worth. Psionic
   ability is the key to the title, though great ability without wisdom and
   intelligence will not gain the title. With the title comes the privilege of
   teaching their knowledge to the children, particularly their psionic

knowledge. Each city, town, or village will have at least one bhydáni. Either the bhydáni will ask another into their ranks, or, in the event that a location has no functioning bhydáni, the inhabitants will select someone to fill the position. In extremely rare cases, someone can become bhydáni by accident; they accept the mentorship of someone and others begin to ask for the privilege of learning from them as well. By becoming an unofficial teacher, the individual has become bhydáni. A little less than 2/3 of all bhydáni are female.

bhydhá (VĒ-jä) (n) (pl: bhydháthé)--SE; Father.

bhyne (VĒ-nyä) (n) (pl: bhynethé)--HE/SE; Mother.

cállae (kä-LĀ) (v)--HE; whisper

chellé (CHĔL-ŭ) (n) (sng and pl)--HE; home, house, dwelling, residence; also frequently used as the shortened form of chellé hábhai, or Seeking House, the residences of various religious orders.

chellé hábhai (CHĔL-ŭ hä-VĪ) (n) (sng and pl)--HE/SE; Seeking House, an abbey or place of religious instruction

chune (CHŪ-nyä) (adj)--HE; dryness, devoid of moisture, without water

cónys (kō-NĒSH) (v) (v)--HE: join, meet, gather

cónyses (kō-NĒSH-ĕsh) (v)--HE: be joined, meet, gather

cron (krŏn) (v)--HE; shrivel, shrink, make smaller

curá (kū-rä) (n)--HE; fragrance

dedhá (DĚ-jä) (n) (sng and pl)--SE; priest or monk; the term makes no distinction between the two. The shortened form came into use after the Teren came into the lands and adopted the Faith as their own.

Dhágdhuán (JÄ-zhū-än) (n)--HE/OE; the Intercessor, considered to be the founder of the Faith because his death is said to make it possible for mortals to reach the divine,

dhe (jĕ) (pn) (pl: dhethé)--HE; You; occasionally interchanged with the Standard form dhi

dhíthé (JĬTH-ŭ) (v)--HE; cry, weep

dhóbhaen (jō-VĀN) (n)--OE; The Kindred; to those banished to the west the word came to mean The Forgiven (by k'Ádhá) and eventually morphed into the Elyri word for forgive

dhózair (jō-ZĪR) (v)--HE; last, endure, enduring, lasting, eternal, to be unending, to be forever

dhun (jūn) (n) --(HE); courage

dhyagn (JĒ-än) (v)--HE; die

dryn (drēn) (n)--HE; bottle, jug

duis (DŪ-ĭsh) (n)--HE; shadow, darkness, shade

ebh (ĕv) (pn)--HE/SE; we, us

ed (ĕd) (conj)--HE; for

edhená (ĕ-JĔN-Ä) (adj)--HE; priceless, expensive, valuable,

elyry (ĕ-LĒR-ē) (adj)--OE; defiant, disobedient

elyryhánag (ĕl-ēr-ē-ÄN-ä) (n) (sng and pl)--OE; defiant of the natural
  order; used to refer to those dhóbhaen who learned to use the power
  without permission of the márbhyndhánis; the banished group took on
  the name elyryhánag as a badge of distinction; is the root for the name
  Elyri

elzen (ĕl-ZĔN) (v)--HE; give, bring

endástás (ĕn-DÄSH-täsh) (sng) (n)--HE, all, everything

ergothás(ĕr-GÄ-thäsh) (n) (sng and pl)--HE; strength, fortitude

et (ĕt) (prp)--HE; a

Ethenae (ĕ-THĔN-ā) (n)--HE/SE; the peaceful afterworld where the
  blessed and holy reside after death.

gaeth (gwāth) (prn)--HE/SE; he, him, himself

gaethaelás (gwāth-Ā-läsh) (prn psv)--HE; his

gdhededhá (zhĕ-DĔ-jä) (n) (sng and pl)--SE; priest or faith teacher or
  disciple; the term makes no distinction between them.

ghlaebh (glāv) (v)--HE: sleep

ghlághylá (glä GĒ lä) (n)--HE/SE; a rare white stone, either translucent or
  opaque, originating only from two mines in the Llaethlágárá
  Mountains near the town of Bhryell. Prized for its sharpness and
  rarity.

ghrysá (grē-shä) (n)--HE; stone

ghynag (GĒ-nä) (n)--HE; walk, saunter, move slowly

góst (gōsht) (v)--HE; become/is becoming/has become; góstár-became,
  did become, has become; góstes-will become

hábhai (HÄ-vī) (v)--HE; look, search; seek, seeking, seeks

hánag (HÄN-ä) (n) (sng and pl)--OE; natural order of the universe, life,
  the world

hásurag (hă-SHŪR-ä) (v)--HE; assure, assured

háyl (hä-ĒL) (n) emptiness

hes (hĕsh) (n) (sng and pl)--HE; heart

hithé (hĭth-ŭ) (v) grieve, mourn

hórges (hōr-GĔSH) (n)--HE; plain, desert, field (not farming)

hwaerás (hwā-räsh) (v)--HE; bear, deliver, take, carry

hwoncáró (hwän-KÄR-ō) (adj)--HE; sad, bereft, heartbroken

hyd (hēd) (n)--HE; coast, shore, beach, sometimes dock

hyl (hēl) (n̄)--HE; river

hylá (HĒL-ä) (n)--HE; water

hyln (hēln) (n)--HE; sea, big water

ibh (ēv) (v)--HE/SE; Is, are, am; its translation is dependent upon the rest
of the sentence.

ílMairós (ĭl-MĪ-rōsh) (n) (sng and pl)--SE; healer, physician.

im (ēm) (v)--HE/SE; Was, were; its translation is dependent upon the rest
of the sentence.

it (ēt) (prn)--HE/SE; this/that. The rest of the sentence implies its
translation.

íth (ĭth) (prp)--HE/SE; the

ithnás (ĒTH-näsh) (n)--HE; bliss, joy, happiness

k'bhekalomár (k-vĕ-KÄ-lŏm-är) (n)--HE: those who have gone before;
ancestors, the deceased

k'gdhededhá (k zhĕ-DĔ-jä) (n) (sng and pl)--HE/SE; The Elyri
designation for the male individual who is elected as the head of the
Faith.

k'kairá (also **phae k'kairá**) (fä k KĪ-rä) (n) (sng and pl)--HE; The name
given to the race of beings who inhabited the territory of the Five
Sovereignties before the Elyri arrived. By the time the Elyri came, all
that remained of the k'kairá (as they are sometimes called) were
crumbling stone circles, mounds, and huts, some of which bore
written symbols upon them. Unlike most High Elyri words which end
with the ah sound, this one does not end with the letter combination
ag.

kaiim (kī-ĒM) (n)--HE; moon

kait (kī-ĒT) (n)--HE; sun

kalom (kă-LŎM) (v)--HE; pass, progress, proceed, go

káyná (kā- Ē-nä) (n)--HE; kestrel

kédhé (KŬJ-ŭ) (v)--HE; lead, guide, direct, instruct

keh (kĕh) (prp)--HE; on, upon

kóh (kō) (prep)--HE/SE; in, within, inside

konys (KŎ-nēsh) (v)--HE; unite, bring together

konyses (kŏ-NĒSH-ĕsh) (v)--HE; will unite, will be united

k'phóredhet (k phō-RĔJ-ĕt) (n)--SE; ecclesiastical tribunal of the Faith in
Clarys; when the k'gdhededhá is indisposed or has passed, the
Tribunal rules in his place. Often used for trials of a religious nature
and used to discuss matters of Faith with the k'gdhededhá

krá (krä) (av) –SE; here, there; in, at, or to this or that place or position

kunás (kū-NÄSH) (prn)--HE; our/ours

ky (kē) (prp)--HE; beside

Kyne (KĒ-nyä) (n) (sng and pl)--HE/SE; The High Mother, the Matriarchal ruler of Elyriá. It includes the translation "Mother ruler", "Mother protector", and "exalted mother". Since nearly all Elyri families can trace some familial link to the Bhíncári, the Kyne is both a figurative, and near literal, mother of all Elyri. This position is both hereditary and elected, chosen from among all of the women in the Bhíncári family.

llagn (län) (prep)--HE; across/in front of/past

llánec (LÄ-nyäk) (n)--HE; the occasional Elyri "ability" of being given insight into the future. Unlike other Elyri abilities, this one cannot be learned or controlled; an individual must be born with it. One who possesses it endures periodic "blackouts" as events are revealed to them but they cannot summon visions. Generally, the things they "see" are vague in nature, and rarely involve the seer. It is often translated into the Trade language as "the Sight." Literally translated as "bitter sight"

llórd (lōrd) (v)--HE; regret (v)

llósté (LŌSH-tŭ) (v)--HE; light, lighting, illuminate, illuminating

llóstén (lō-SHTĔN) (n)--HE; brightness

lómesté (lō-MĔSH-tŭ) (n) (pl: lómestéthé)--HE/SE; translated in the Trade tongue as council, it is a unit of 5 to 9 elders and bhydáni that govern a single town or region; k'lómesté is the Elyri High Council in Clarys. All bhydáni in the region will be a member of the lómesté, but the lómesté need not consist solely of bhydáni.

mai (MĪ) (n) (pl: maithé)—HE/SE; child; used in the Standard as a term of endearment

mál (mäl) (adj)--HE/SE; sacred, holy, blessed, divine

málár (mäl-ÄR) (v)--HE; are blessed,

máltai (mäl-TĪ) (n)--HE; divine light

mályhag (MÄL-yä) (adj)--HE; sacred, holy, blessed. This is one of the few adjectives in the High Elyri and it (as well as all other such adjectives) is believed by some linguists to have its origins in some language other than Elyri though in this case there does appear to be a common root with the term saint which is believed to be a true High Elyri term.

márbhyndhánis (mär-vēn-JÄN-ēsh) (n) (sng and pl)--OE; literally 'blessed teacher' the title of those dhóbhaen who are the keepers of knowledge. They are the only ones, other than healers, allowed to be trained in the use of power. Also responsible to educate children and 'recondition' those who break the law.

medhárós (mĕ-JÄR-ōsh) (n)--HE; revenge, vengeance, retaliation

móz (mōz) (adj)--HE/SE; black

náós (nä-ŌSH) (n) (sng and pl)--HE/SE; a place of worship, temple; also occasionally used to refer to the altar.

nyl (nēl) (n)--(HE) burden, hardship

phael (fãl) (v)--HE; brighten

phaerás (FÄ-räsh) (v)--(HE) bend, kneel, bow; a gesture of respect or pleading.

phail (fĩl) (v)--HE; dim, is dimming, dimming, dims

phain (fĩn) (prp)--HE/SE; of

phás (fäsh) (v)--HE; open

pháses (fäsh-ĔSH) (v)--HE; will open

Phekóntudhurág (fĕh kōn tū jū rä) (n)--OE; he who brings the rain

phrae (frä) (adv)--HE;-again

phry (frē) (n)--HE; innocence

phun (fūn) (v)--HE; lift, raise

phunar (fū-NÄR) (v)--HE; were lifted, were raised

raedá (RÄ-dä) (v)--HE; lose

raedár (rä-DÄR) (v)--HE; lost

rásár (rä-SHÄR) (v)--HE; have shared, did share

rásé (RÄ-shŭ) (v)--HE; share

redh (rĕj) (n) (sng and pl)--HE grace, sometimes used as forgiveness in a religious sense

Relzá (rĕl-zä) (n/name)--SE/HE;-the river that runs from the Llaethlágárá through Bhórdh

res (rĕsh) (n)--HE; loss

rósádhá (rō-SHÄ-jä) (n)--HE; Literally translated as the Wounds of the God, it refers to the manifestation of the death wounds of Dhágdhuán which afflicted many saints and holy individuals. These include punctures in both wrists from where the founder was hung by his wrists, sometimes accompanied by the burn of a rope on the left wrist, punctures in both ankles where his feet were secured to the pyre post, possibly the scars of ropes on the ankles as well, and, very rarely, the marks of burning flesh on the lower body.

rylag (RĒ-lä) (n) (pl: rylagthé)--HE; gate, doorway

saeitá (shä-Ē-chä) (n)--HE: ghost or spirit or soul

said (shīd) (interjective question)--HE; may they, can they

sain (shīn) (interjective question)--HE; may we; can we

scenyhur (shkĕn-YŪR) (v)--HE; call, name, refer to

serbháló (shĕr-VÄ-lō) (n)--SE; A form of Elyri wine with almost no alcohol content, used only for religious ceremonies.

shwyth (shwhēth) (n)--HE; wisdom

sínréc (shĭn-RŬK) (n) (sng and pl)--HE; This word has no direct translation. Blood kin with a special bond, is about the closest it can be described. Any blood kin can be sínréc, but saying "he is my cousin," is different from saying "he is my sínréc" (or "he is sínréc."). It is sometimes used for non-relatives who are extremely close.

sómá (SHŌ-mä) (v)--HE; steal, rob, unlawfully take.

sóurá (shō-Ū-rä) (v)--HE; embrace

sóures (shō-Ū-rĕsh) (v)--HE; will be embraced

sturmyrá (shtūr_mē rä) (n)--HE; box, container, reliquary

sun (shūn) (prp)--HE/SE; to/from

sylag (SHĒ-lä) (v)--HE; seduce, tempt, lure

taeá (TĀ-ä) (v)--HE; laugh

tai (tī) (n)--HE; light, most often with an unknown source, not a torch, a lantern, fire, the sun, or moon

taithé (tīth-ŭ) (n)--HE; fires, flames

tásmá (TÄSH-mä) (v)--HE; remember

thórgae (thōr-GWĀ) (v)--HE; burn, be burned, am burning, is burning

thráaest (thrä-ĀSHT) (adv)--HE; before, ahead of, in front of

thur (thūr) (adj)--HE; little, small, tiny

thurás (THŪ-räsh) (n)--HE; prayer; supplication

thurgag (thūr-GÄ) (v)--HE; eat, consume, devour, eating

tó (tō) (n)--HE; time

trodh (trŏj) (v)--HE; ease, lessen, lighten, reduce

tru (trū) (v)--HE; spill

truár-(trū-ÄR) (v)--HE; spilled

tuó (TŪ ō) (n)--HE; mist, fog (sometimes clouds)

tyreth (TĒR-ĕth) (v)--HE; know, knows

tyrethár (TĒR-ĕth-är) (v)--HE; did know, knew, has known

uaem (ū-ĀM) (n)--HE; storm, tempest, bad weather

ubé (ū-BŬ) (prep)--HE: while, as, meanwhile, in the meantime, during

ullís (ū-lĭsh) (v)--HE; discard

ullísár (ū-lĭsh-ÄR) (v)--HE; discarded

ydhen (ē-JĔN) (v)--HE; throw, dash, hurl

ydhenár (ē-jĕn-ÄR) (v)--HE; threw, dashed, hurled

yhánách (yän-äch) (n)--HE; well, hole, pit, mine

yne (Ē-nyĕ) (n)--SE; mother's female relatives
yó (Ē-ō) (conj/prp)--HE; until
zaene (ZĀ-nyä) (adj)--HE; gray
zagn (zän) (v)--HE; pull/pulls, draw, tug, drag
zagnes (zän-ĕsh) (v)--HE; will pull/pulls, draw, tug, drag
záryph (zä-RĒF) (n) (sng and pl)--HE/SE; winged beings connected to
    the realm of the holy; angels
zened (zĕ-NED) (v)--HE; give, gives
zylag (ZĒ-lä) (v)--HE; hope, anticipated

Translations

'áti ibh krá.'-I am here
"Ca'al duiim."-We will obey
Tii madur-My honor

máltai sturmyrá-spirit light box; reliquary of holy light

bhelzen k'Ádhá (*Gracious k'Ádhá*)
kunás hwoncáró saeitá phaerás kóh thurás (*our bereaved spirit bends in
    supplication*)
hábhai ergóthás á dhun (*seeking strength and courage*)
sun hwaerás íth nyl phain res (*to bear the burden of loss*)
ed gaeth bhekalomár thráaest (*of he who has gone before*)
lllósté kunás aiónag (*lighting our path*)
kédhé sun dhe (*leading to you*)
ebh málár ed et aiónag rásár (*blessed are we for a life shared*)
ásai gaethaelás aetásmá á shwyth thórgae kóh kunás hes (*may his memory
    and wisdom be bound in our heart*)
mályhag Dhágdhuán (*blessed Dhágdhuán*)
trodh kunás aehíthé aun aezylag (*ease our grief with hope*)
ít ebh konyses aun k'bhekalomár (*that we will be united with those who
    have gone before*)
sun íth dhózair ithnás phain dhe mál tai (*to the eternal bliss of your divine
    light*)

Inzigaen-the infrequently used Nethite child army, consisting of children
    as young as seven years old.

Shin drua-the name in Sunna's language for the black stone/glass oasis in
    the Cíbhóló desert)

Kavan's Final Song

íth phail kait
zagn íth aecállae phain aetásmá
llagn íth aedhyagnaghk
sun íth zaene tuó dhe bhán dhíthé
et aelás bhesylag aebhánys
ubé aedhózair uaem thurgag endástás
íth llóstén ebh im
íth duis ebh góst
íth bhezugdhu kaiim cónys kunás
      aedhíthé
yó íth hórges phain aetásmá cron

aelás chune et aelás háyl
ainau íth hyl phain dhe aetaeá
sun zened ith aiónag
aión ydhenár keh móz ghrysá hyd

ubé et dryn phain edhená serbháló
      ullísár
kunás phry aelás curá
truár et raedár
kunás tó thórgae thur
ubé íth káyná ebh phunár
yó íth taithé phain medhárós thórgae
      állís ebh
et íth uaem phain aehíthé et aellórd
zagnes ebh kóh íth aisyag hyln
ebh ghlaebh hásurag
it Curnydhá's rylagthé pháses
kunás saeitá sóures kóh ithnás
et kunás hes cónyses phrae

The dimming sun
draws the whispers of memory
across the death-veil.
From the gray mist your voice cries
a luring song
as eternity's tempest devours all.
The brightness we were;
the shadow we have become.
The guardian moon collects our
tears,
until the plains of remembrance
shrivel,
parched and empty
without the river of your laughter
to give it life.
Fate has dashed us upon black
stone shores
as a bottle of priceless wine cast
off;
our fragrant innocence
spilled and lost.
Our hours blaze short.
Like the kestrel we were lifted
until the fires of vengeance
burned thru us,
and the gales of remorse and regret
pulled us into the icy sea.
We sleep assured
that Curnydhá's gates will open,
our souls will be enfolded into joy,
and our hearts will be as one again.

Pronunciation of Elyri Names

Aendrás (ĀN-dräsh)

Ágdhállán (ÄZH-äl-än)

Aleski (ä-LĔSH-kē)

Alyná (ä-LĒ-nä)

Ártur (är-TŪR)

Audh (ouj)

Aunes (ou-NĔSH)

Bharás Muɫóy (VÄR-äsh mū LŌ-ē)

Bhás-(väsh)

Bhendhámyn (VĔN-jä-mēn)

Bhetá-(VĔ-tä)

Bhídígís Bhól (VĬD-ĭ-gĭsh VŌL)

Bhílári (vĭ-LÄR-ē)

Bhílycá (VĬL-lē-kä)

Bhíncári (vĭn-CÄ-rē)

Bhórdh-(vōrj)

Bhríd (vrĭd)

Bhryell (vrē-ĔL)

Bhyrhán (VĒR hän)

Cáner (KÄ-nyär)

Cáym (kä-ĒM)

Chethá (CHĔ-thä)

Cíbhóló (kĭ-VŌ-lō)

Clarys (klär-ĒSH)

Cliáth (klē-ÄTH)

Curnydhá-(kūr-NĒ-jä)

Dáhmán (DÄ män)

Dhábhiyhá (jä-VĒ-yä)

Dhágdhuán_(JÄ-zhū-än)

Dháná (JÄ-nä)

dhóbhaen-(jō-VÄN)

Dhon-(jän)

Dhóri (JŌR-ē)

Drebhoti (drĕ-VÄ-tē)

Earé (ĒR-ä)

Elyri (ĕ-LĒR-ē)

Elyri (ĕ-LĒR-ē)

Elyriá (ĕ-LĒR-ē-ä)

Faeárgan Drás (fä-ÄR-găn DRĀSH)

Gaed (gwäd)

Gaelán (GWĀ län)

Hwensen (HWĔN-shĕn)

Iólún-(ē -Ō-län)

Kaedís (KĀ dĭsh)

Káliel (kä-LĒ-ĕl)

Kavan (KĂ-văn) (in Elyri his name is spelt Kabhan)

Khwílen Kesábhá_(KHWĬL-ĕn kĕsh-ä-vä)

Kílyn (kĭ-LĒN)

Kluín (KLŪ-ĭn)

Kólmárá Tyrnás (kōl-MÄR-ä TĒR-näsh)

Kóráhm di Curnydhá (KŌR-äm DĒ kūr-NĒ-jä)

Lláhy (LÄ-hē)

Llucás (LŪ käsh)

Llyr (lēr)

MacLyr (mäk-LĒR)

Mádhu (MÄ-jū)

Maelís (MĀ-lĭsh)

Márllís (mär-LĬSH)

Mátán (mä-TÄN)

Mórne (MŌR-nyä)

Níkóá McCábhá (nĭ-KŌ-ä mc-KÄ-vä)

Nóráh (NŌ-rä)

Óllbhaer Dínyn (ŌL-vär dĭn-ĒN)

Ónyká (Ō-nē-kä)

Pháraeís Dunne (fä-RĀ-ĭsh dū-NYÄ)

Phaedr (FĀ-der)
Pháne (FÄN-yä)
Phílóá (fĭ-LŌ-ä)
Raebhá (RĀ-vä)
Raenár Magk (RĀ-när mä<u>k</u>)
Sámel (shä-MĔL)
Seren (shĕr-ĕn)
Síraelís (shĭ-RĀ-lĭsh)
Sóbhán (shō-VÄN)
Syl (shēl)
Sylyhá (shē-LĒ-hä)
Syróá Dunne (shē-RŌ-ä)

Tám (täm)
Tíbhyan (TĬ-vē-ăn)
Tisá (TĒ shä)
Tusánt (tū-SHÄNT)
Whíllá (WĬL-ä)
Ybherd (Ē-vĕrd)
Ydrís (Ē-drĭsh)
Ylár (Ē-lär)
Ylltán Phrás (ĒL-tän)
Yóáná- (ē-ō-Ä-nä)
Zythán (ZĒ-thän)

The Five Sovereignties - City Legend

Enesfel

1-*Rhidam
2-Alberni
3-Bryn
4-Chantel
5-Dorshur
6-Durham
7-Erleta
8-Jardin
9-Kamin
10-Kilmacud
11-Levonne
12-Nelori
13-Seres
14-Talladegah
15-Tarsee
16-Theron
17-Wexel

Cordash

1-*Aralt
2-Anzet
3-Ediug
4-Eleva
5-Jassett
6-Kakkoris
7-Korr
8-Liatti
9-Lindumn
10-Matina
11-Pesek
12-Sebring
13-Trallan
14-Verbier
15-Vioe
16-Vron
17-Wynett

Elyriá

1-Clarys
2- Ánásair
3-Bhástyán
4-Bhórdh
5-Bhryell
6-Cármycá
7-Cylleá
8-Dhánthes
9-Ibhórys
10-Káská
11-Khwíncanon
12-Rísóri
13-Sábhóne
14-Sídhári
15-Turyn

Hatu

1-*Natrona
2-Avarrou
3-Cran Ufa
4-Drisoge
5-Enda
6-Fa Ruqi
7-Furr Katio
8-Kílyn
9-Palil
10-Wasilla
11-Yd Haszafni

Neth

1-*Glevum
2-Fiara
3-Gorea
4-Mawr
5-Nogero
6-Pravek
7-Ruidoso
8-Venago

Káliel

1-*Káliel
2-Jaffe
3-Mara Qin
4-Pháne
5-Shola

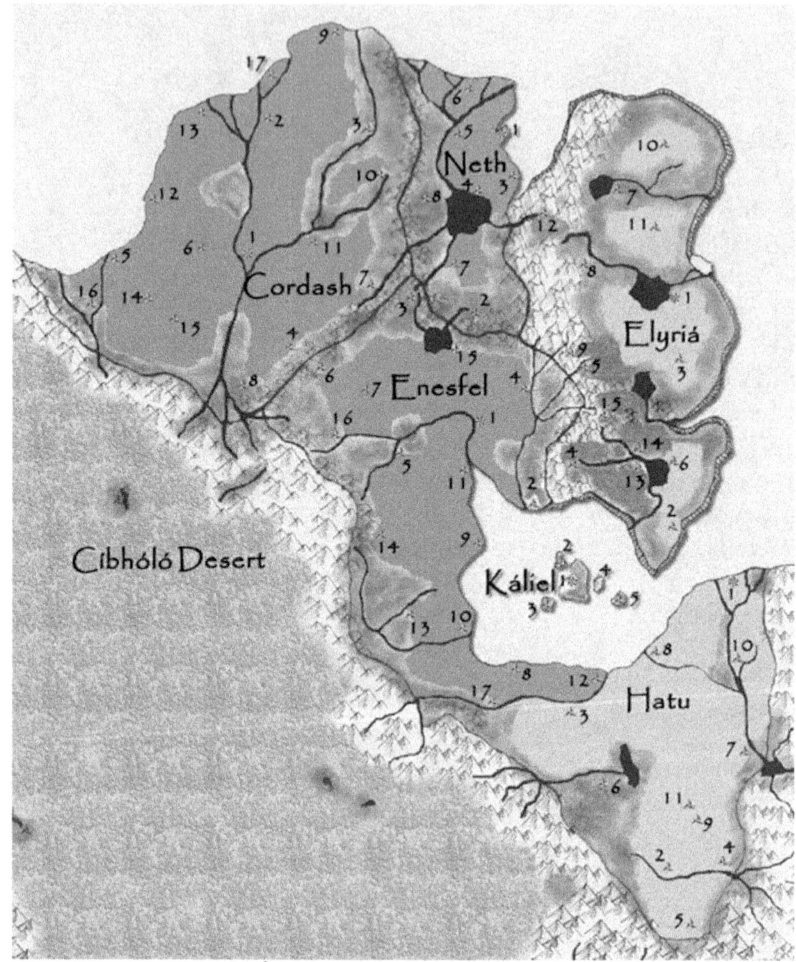

The Five Sovereignties

About the Author

Unsatisfied with 'how the story ends' as a young reader, Tamara took on the challenge of crafting endings to the tales of others to better suit her vision of the world. That desire to mold reality into how she imagined it should be, gave birth to a lifelong fascination with the written word, and its capacity, particularly through realms of fantasy and science fiction, to foster an understanding of the people, events, thoughts, and emotions that make us who we are.

Kavan's story, the Kestrel Harper Saga, is a lifelong labor of love.

A long-time resident of Clearlake, California, after a life that took her back and forth across the country, Tamara is owned by a pack of papillions, a pride of cats, and an eclectic arsenal of films she enjoys in her off-moments.